of love & life

ISBN 978-0-276-44277-3

www.readersdigest.co.uk

The Reader's Digest Association Limited, 11 Westferry Circus, Canary Wharf, London E14 4HE

of **love** *&* **life**

Three novels selected and condensed
by **Reader's Digest**

The Reader's Digest Association Limited, London

CONTENTS

Sophie Kinsella

Remember Me?

Lexi Smart is having a bad day. Her boyfriend has stood her up, she didn't get a bonus from her dead-end job, and now she's standing in the rain, trying to flag down a taxi—and it's her dad's funeral tomorrow.

Everything seems hopeless, but in a matter of seconds life can change in the most extraordinary of ways . . .

Prologue

OF ALL THE CRAP, crap, crappy nights I've ever had in the whole of my crap life. On a scale of one to ten we're talking . . . a minus six. And it's not as if I even have very high standards.

Rain spatters down my collar as I shift from one blistered foot to another. I just want to find a taxi, get home, and kick off these stupid boots. But there's no sign of a cab.

My toes are *agony*. I'm never buying shoes from Cut-Price Fashion again. I bought these boots last week in the sale (flat black patent, I only ever wear flats). They were half a size too small but the girl said they would stretch, and I believed her. I'm the world's biggest sucker.

We're all standing on the corner of some street in southwest London with music pounding faintly from the club below our feet. Carolyn got us discounted entry, so that's why we schlepped here. Only now we have to get home, and I'm the only one even *looking* for a cab.

Fi has commandeered the only nearby doorway and has her tongue down the throat of the guy she chatted up earlier on at the bar. A few feet away Carolyn and Debs are sheltering underneath a newspaper, arm in arm, caterwauling 'It's Raining Men'. 'Lexi!' yells Debs, extending an arm for me to join in.

'It isn't bloody raining men!' I call back morosely. 'It's just raining!'

I normally love karaoke, too. But I'm not in a singing mood tonight. I feel all sore inside. If only Loser Dave had turned up like he promised. Loser Dave works in car telesales and has been my boyfriend since we got together at Carolyn's friend's barbecue last summer. I don't call him

Loser Dave to insult him—it's just his nickname, the way I'm Snaggletooth. I've been called that since I was eleven. And sometimes Snagglehair. To be fair, my hair is pretty frizzy. And my teeth are kind of crooked. But I always say they give my face character.

(Actually, that's a lie. It's Fi who says they give my face character. Personally, I'm planning to fix them, as soon as I've got the cash.)

A taxi comes into sight and I stick out my hand—but some people ahead flag it down. Great. I shove my hands in my pockets miserably.

It's not just Loser Dave standing me up, it's the bonuses. Today was the end of the financial year at work. Everyone was given paper slips saying how much they'd got and started jumping about with excitement. Carolyn started planning a holiday to New York with her boyfriend Matt. Debs booked highlights at Nicky Clarke. Fi called Harvey Nichols and reserved herself a new cool bag.

And then there was me, with nada, because to get a bonus you have to have worked for the company for a year, and I missed qualifying by a week. One *week*. It's so penny-pinching. I'm telling you, if they asked me what I thought about it . . . as if Simon Johnson would ever ask the opinion of an Associate Junior Sales Manager (Flooring).

'Hey, Lexi.' I look up to see that Fi has unsuckered herself from the cute guy. She comes over and gets out a lipstick.

'Hi,' I say, blinking rainwater off my lashes. 'Where's lover boy gone?'

'To tell the girl he came with that he's leaving.'

'Fi!'

'What?' Fi looks unrepentant. 'They're not an item. Or much of one.' She carefully redoes her mouth in pillar-box red. 'I'm getting a whole new load of make-up,' she says. 'I can afford it now!'

'You should!' I nod, trying to sound enthusiastic.

'Oh bollocks. Sorry, Lexi. You should have got a bonus. It's not fair.'

'It's fine.' I try to smile. 'Next year.'

'You OK?' Fi eyes me narrowly. 'You want to go for a drink?'

'No, I need to get to bed. I've got an early start in the morning.'

'*Jesus*. I forgot all about that, too. What with the bonuses and everything . . . Lexi, I'm sorry. This is a really shit time for you.'

'It's fine!' I say at once. 'It's . . . I'm trying not to make it a huge deal.'

No one likes a whinger. So somehow I make myself smile brightly, just to show I'm fine with being the snaggly-toothed, stood-up, no-bonus girl whose dad just died.

'Things'll turn around for you,' Fi says.

'You think?'

'Uh-huh.' She nods, with more energy. 'You just have to believe it.

Come on.' She squeezes me. 'What are you, woman or walrus?' Fi's been using that expression since we were both fifteen, and every time, it makes me smile. 'And you know what?' she adds. 'I think your dad would have *wanted* you to turn up to his funeral hung over.'

She met my dad a couple of times. She's probably right.

'Hey, Lexi.' Fi's voice is softer, and I brace myself. If she says something nice about my dad, I might cry. I didn't know him that well, but you only get one dad . . . 'Do you have a spare condom?'

Right. So I probably didn't need to worry about the sympathy overload. I root inside my green Accessorize bag and produce a Durex which I discreetly hand to her.

'Thanks, babe.' She kisses me on the cheek. 'Hey, there's a taxi!'

I hurry to the edge of the pavement as the cab pulls up and beckon to Debs and Carolyn, who are now screeching out 'Dancing Queen'. Carolyn's glasses are spattered with raindrops and she's about five notes ahead of Debs. 'Hi there!' I lean through the window. 'Could you possibly take us to—'

'Sorry, love, no karaoke.' The taxi driver cuts me off, with a baleful glance at Debs and Carolyn.

I stare at him, confused, but before I can reply, he puts the taxi into gear and roars away down the road.

'You can't have a "no karaoke" rule!' I shout after the cab in outrage. 'It's . . . discrimination! It's against the law! It's . . .'

I trail off helplessly and look around. We'll be stuck out here in the rain all night. Those banana cocktails were noxious, I should have stopped after four. I have my dad's funeral tomorrow. Loser Dave's probably in bed with some other girl right this second. 'Taxi!' I instinctively scream the word, almost before I've registered the distant yellow light. I have to get this cab. I *have* to. I run along the pavement, skidding slightly, yelling till I'm hoarse. The pavement is crowded with people and I skirt round them and up the steps to some grand municipal building. There's a balustraded platform with steps going right and left. I'll hail the taxi from up here, then run down and jump in. 'TAXI! TAAA-XEE!'

Yes! It's pulling up. Thank God! 'Here!' I call out. 'Just coming . . .'

To my consternation I notice a guy on the pavement below heading towards the taxi. 'It's ours!' I roar, and start pelting down the opposite steps. 'Don't you even dare—Argh! *Aaaaargh!*' My foot skids on the wet step. I've slipped on my stupid, cheap, shiny-soled boots. I'm tumbling right over, down the steps. Oh shit. The ground's coming straight towards me, there's nothing I can do, this is really, *really* going to hurt . . .

One

HOW LONG HAVE I been awake? Five minutes? Half an hour, maybe? Is it morning yet? I feel so rough. What happened last night? God, my head hurts. I feel so woozy. What day is it?

For a moment I just lie still. My head is pounding. I'm dry-throated and aching all over. My skin feels like sandpaper.

Where was I last night? What's wrong with my brain? It's like a fog has descended over everything. I'm never drinking again. I must have alcohol poisoning or something. I'm trying to remember last night but all that's coming into my head is images from the past, flashing by in random order.

Sunflowers waving against a blue sky . . .

Amy as a newborn baby, looking like a little pink sausage . . .

The sack race at school sports day. Oh God, *not* this memory again . . . I'm seven years old and winning by miles, but it feels so uncomfortable to be out front that I stop and wait for all my friends. They catch me up—then in the melee I trip over and come last. I can still feel the humiliation, hear the laughter, feel the dust in my throat, the taste of bananas . . . Hang on. I force my brain to hold steady for a moment.

Bananas.

Through the fog another memory is glimmering . . . Yes. Got it. Banana cocktails. We were drinking cocktails.

I can't even open my eyes. They feel heavy and stuck down. Cautiously, I move a hand up to my chest and hear a rustle of sheets. They don't sound like the ones at home. And I'm wearing some soft cottony T-shirt thing I don't recognise. Where am I? What on earth—

I didn't pull, did I? Am I wearing some hot guy's oversized T-shirt that I borrowed to sleep in after we had passionate sex all night—

No, I've never been unfaithful in my life. I must just have stayed overnight with one of the girls or something.

With a huge effort I wrench my eyes open and incline myself up a few inches. *Shit.* What the hell?

I'm lying in a dim room, in a metal bed. There's a panel of buttons to my right. There's a bunch of flowers on the bedside cabinet. With an inward gulp I see a drip in my left arm, attached to a bag of fluid.

This is unreal. I'm in hospital. What's going on? What *happened*?

I mentally prod my brain, but it's a big, stupid empty balloon. I'm holding on to my one fragment of memory like it's an island in the ocean. Banana cocktails . . . Yes! I was out with the girls from work. At that dodgy club with the pink neon ceiling in . . . somewhere. I can remember nursing my cocktail, totally miserable.

Why was I so down? What had happened?

Bonuses. Of course. And Loser Dave never showed up. Double whammy. But none of that explains why I'm in hospital.

This is weird. I'll text Fi and ask her what happened.

Where's my phone? Where's all my stuff? Wincing, I swivel my head from side to side—but I can't see any clothes or anything. Now I come to think of it, where are all the doctors and nurses?

It occurs to me to press a button on the little panel. I select the one that looks like a person—and a few moments later the door opens. It worked! A grey-haired nurse in dark blue uniform enters and smiles at me.

'Hello, Lexi!' she says. 'Feeling all right?'

'Um, OK, thanks. Thirsty. And my head hurts.'

'I'll fetch you a painkiller.' She brings me over a plastic cup of water.

'Thanks,' I say after gulping the water. 'So . . . I'm guessing I'm in hospital? Or, like, a really high-tech spa?'

The nurse smiles. 'Sorry. Hospital. But you don't remember how you got here?'

'No.' I shake my head. 'I'm a bit hazy, to be honest.'

'That's because you had quite a bump on the head. Do you remember anything about your accident?'

Accident . . . accident . . . And suddenly, in a rush, it all comes back. Of *course*. Running for the taxi, slipping on my stupid cheap boots . . . Jeez Louise. I must have really bashed my head.

'Yeah. I think so.' I nod. 'Kind of. So . . . what's the time?'

'It's eight o'clock at night.'

Eight o'clock? Wow. I've been out of it for a whole *day*?

'I'm Maureen.' She takes the cup from me. 'You were only transferred to this room a few hours ago. Is there anything else I can get you?'

'I'd love some orange juice, if there is any? And I can't see my phone anywhere, or my bag.'

'All your valuables will have been put somewhere safe. I'll check.' She heads out and I look around the silent room. I still don't know which hospital I'm in . . . how I got here . . . has anyone told my family? And there's something else nagging at me like an undertow . . .

I was anxious to get home. Yes. That's right. Because—Oh *fuck*. My dad's funeral. It was the next day, eleven o'clock. I've missed it. It's not as if I really knew my dad well. He was never around that much, in fact he felt more like an uncle. The kind of jokey, roguish uncle who brings you sweets at Christmas and smells of drink and cigarettes.

Nor was it a massive shock him dying. He was having some big heart-bypass operation, and everyone knew there was a fifty-fifty risk. But still, I should have been there today, along with Mum and Amy. I mean, Amy's only twelve, and a timid little twelve at that.

I suddenly feel a tear rolling down my face. It's the day of my dad's funeral, and here I am in hospital and no one's come to visit me. Where're all my anxious friends and family, sitting round the bed and holding my hand?

Well. I suppose Mum's been at the funeral with Amy. And Loser Dave can sod off. But Fi and the others. Where are they?

Another fat tear trickles down my face, just as the door opens and Maureen comes in again. She's holding a tray and a carrier bag with 'Lexi Smart' written on it in marker.

'Oh dear!' she says as she sees me wiping my eyes. 'Are you in pain?' She hands me a tablet and a little cup of water. 'This should help.'

'Thanks very much.' I gulp down the pill. 'But it's not that. It's my life.' I spread my hands hopelessly. 'It's total rubbish, from start to finish. My so-called career is going nowhere, and my boyfriend stood me up last night, and my dad just died.'

There's silence. Maureen looks flummoxed. 'Well, that does all sound rather . . . tricky,' she says at last. She gives me a sympathetic smile and holds out her hand for the cup.

I pass it back—and as I do so, I suddenly notice my nails. Bloody hell. What on earth—My nails have always been bitten-down stumps, but these look amazing. All neat and varnished pale pink . . . and long. I blink at them in astonishment, trying to work out what's happened. Did we go for a late-night manicure last night or something and I've forgotten? Did I get acrylics?

'Your handbag's in here, by the way,' Maureen adds, putting the carrier bag on my bed. 'I'll just go and get you some juice.'

'Thanks,' I say. As Maureen leaves, I reach into the carrier—and pull out a smart Louis Vuitton tote with calfskin handles, all glossy and expensive-looking.

Oh, *great*. This isn't my bag. They've got me mixed up with someone else. As if I, Lexi Smart, would possess a Louis Vuitton bag. Then, I drop it down onto the floor, flop back on my pillows and close my eyes.

I wake up to find morning light edging underneath the drawn curtains. Maureen is bustling about in the corner of the room. The drip has magically disappeared out of my arm, and I feel a lot more normal.

'Hi, Maureen,' I say, my voice scratchy. 'What time is it?'

She turns round, her eyebrows raised. 'You remember me?'

'Of course,' I say in surprise. 'We met last night. We talked.'

'Excellent! That shows you've come out of post-traumatic amnesia. Don't look alarmed!' she adds, smiling. 'It's a normal stage of confusion after a head injury.'

Instinctively I put my hand up to my head and feel a dressing. Wow. I must really have whacked it on those steps.

There's a knock at the door, then it opens and a tall, slim woman in her fifties comes in. She has blue eyes, high cheekbones and wavy greying-blonde hair. She's wearing a red quilted waistcoat over a long printed dress, and an amber necklace, and holding a paper bag.

It's Mum. I mean, I'm ninety-nine per cent certain it is. I don't know why I'm even hesitating. 'The *heating* in this place!' she exclaims in her familiar, thin, little-girl voice. OK, it's definitely Mum.

'I feel quite faint!' She fans herself. She glances towards the bed almost as an afterthought, and says to Maureen, 'How is she?'

Maureen smiles. 'Lexi's much better today. Far less confused.'

'Thank goodness for that!' Mum lowers her voice a fraction. 'It was like talking to a lunatic yesterday, or some . . . *retarded* person.'

'Lexi isn't a lunatic,' says Maureen evenly, heading to the door. 'She can understand everything you say.'

The truth is, I'm barely listening. I can't help staring at Mum. What's *wrong* with her? She looks different. Thinner. And kind of . . . older.

'Here you are, darling,' she says, in over-loud, clear tones. 'It's me. Your mother.' She hands me the paper bag, which contains a bottle of shampoo, and drops a kiss on my cheek.

'Hi, Mum.' I reach to hug her—but my arms hit thin air. She's already turned away and is consulting her tiny gold watch.

'I can't stay more than a minute, I'm afraid,' she says. 'I'm due to see a specialist about Roly.'

'Roly?'

'From Smoky's latest litter, darling.' Mum shoots me a glance of reproach. 'You remember little Roly.'

I don't know how Mum expects me to keep track of all her dogs' names. There's at least twenty of them and they're all whippets.

'The traffic was terrible,' Mum says. 'People in London are so aggressive. I had a *very* unpleasant altercation with a man in a van.'

'What happened?' I say, already knowing that Mum will shake her head.

'Let's not talk about it, darling.' Mum finds a lot of things too painful to talk about.

'I've got a card for you,' she says, rooting in her bag. 'Where is it, now? From Andrew and Sylvia.'

I stare at her, bemused. 'Who?'

'Andrew and Sylvia next door!' she says, as though it's obvious.

Our next-door neighbours are called Philip and Maggie. 'Mum—'

'Anyway, they send their love,' she interrupts. 'And Andrew wants to ask your advice on skiing.'

Skiing? I don't know how to ski. 'Mum . . .' I put a hand to my head, forgetting about my injury, and wince. 'What are you *talking* about?'

Maureen comes back into the room. 'Dr Harman's just coming along to check you over.'

'I must go, darling.' Mum gets to her feet. 'I left the car on some extortionate parking meter. And the congestion charge! Eight pounds!'

That's not right either. I'm *sure* the congestion charge is only five quid, not that I ever use a car. Oh my God, Mum's going senile.

'I'll be back later with Amy and Eric,' she says, heading out of the door. *Eric?* She calls her dogs some really odd names.

I feel a bit shaken up. That was crazy. What if Mum has to go into a home? What will I do with all the dogs? My thoughts are interrupted by a knock at the door and a youngish doctor with dark hair enters.

'Hello there, Lexi,' he says in a pleasant, brisk manner. 'I'm Dr Harman, resident neurologist. How are you feeling?'

'Fine! Except my left hand feels a bit weird,' I admit. 'Like I've been sleeping on it and it isn't working properly?'

'Right.' The doctor nods. 'We'll take a look at that; you may need some physio. But first I'm going to ask you a few questions. Bear with me if some of them seem blindingly obvious.' He flashes a professional smile. 'Can you tell me your name?'

'My name's Lexi Smart,' I reply promptly. Dr Harman nods and makes a note in his folder.

'And when you were born?'

'Nineteen seventy-nine.'

'Very good.' He makes another note. 'Now, Lexi, when you crashed your car, you bumped your head against the windscreen. There was a small amount of swelling to your brain, but it looks as though you've been very lucky. I do still need to do some checks though . . .'

Doctors don't let you get a word in, do they? 'Excuse me! I'm afraid you've mixed me up with someone else. I didn't crash any car.'

Dr Harman frowns and flips back two pages in his folder. 'It says the patient was involved in a road traffic accident.'

'Well, they must have written it down wrong,' I say firmly. 'I was out clubbing with my friends and we were running for a taxi and I fell.'

Dr Harman and Maureen are exchanging puzzled looks.

'It was definitely a road traffic accident,' murmurs Maureen. 'Two vehicles, side-on. I was down in A&E and I saw her come in.'

'I couldn't have been in a car crash.' I try to keep my patience. 'For a start, I don't have a car. I don't even know how to drive!'

'You haven't got a . . .' Dr Harman flips over a page and squints at the writing. 'A Mercedes convertible?'

'A *Mercedes*?' I snort with laughter. 'I'll tell you how much twenty-five-year-old sales associates at Deller Carpets earn, OK? And you tell me if I can afford a Mercedes convertible.'

Now Dr Harman is gazing at me with a grave expression. My stomach starts flip-flapping. I've seen *ER*, I know what that expression means. 'Is something really wrong with me?' I say almost aggressively.

'Lexi, I want to ask you another question.' Dr Harman's voice is gentler. 'Can you tell me what year it is?'

'What *year* it is?' I stare back, thrown.

'Don't be alarmed,' he says reassuringly. 'It's a standard check.'

I look from face to face. 'It's 2004,' I say at last.

There's a weird stillness in the room, as if no one wants to breathe.

'OK.' Dr Harman sits down on the bed. 'Lexi, today is May the 6th, 2007.' His face is serious.

'But . . . that's the *future*,' I say.

'Lexi, this is bound to be a shock,' says Maureen, putting a kindly hand on my shoulder. 'But it's true. It's May 2007.'

I feel as if the two sides of my brain aren't connecting or something.

'It can't be 2007,' I say, trying not to give away how rattled I am. 'It's 2004. I'm not *stupid*—'

'Don't get upset,' says Dr Harman. 'Let's take this slowly. Why don't you tell us what you last remember?'

'OK, well . . .' I rub my face. 'The last thing I remember is going out with some friends from work. We were trying to get a taxi in the rain and I slipped on the steps and fell. And I woke up in hospital. That was February 20, 2004.' My voice is trembling. 'I know the date exactly, because it was my dad's funeral the next day!'

'Lexi, all of that happened more than three years ago,' Maureen says.

Panic is rising inside me as I look at their faces.

'What else do you remember?' asks Dr Harman.

'I don't know,' I say defensively. 'Being at work . . . moving into my flat . . . everything!'

'Is your memory foggy at all?'

'A bit,' I admit reluctantly. That's why nothing made sense. It's not Mum who's confused—it's me. 'So I've been lying here in a coma . . .' I swallow, '. . . for three years?'

I can't believe it. I've been Coma Girl. My family and friends have probably made me tapes, kept vigils, sung songs and everything . . .

But Dr Harman is shaking his head. 'No, that's not it. Lexi, you were only admitted five days ago.'

What? 'I don't understand! Am I hallucinating? Have I gone *crazy*?'

'No!' says Dr Harman. 'Lexi, I think you're suffering from what we call retrograde amnesia. It's a condition that normally arises following head injuries. You've forgotten a chunk of your life, Lexi. That's all.'

I want to cry. My head's whirling with confusion—

And then suddenly I freeze. I've just spotted a small, distinctive V-shaped scar near my elbow. A scar I've never seen before. A scar I don't recognise. It's not new, either. It must be months old.

'Lexi, are you all right?' asks Dr Harman.

Heart thumping, I slowly move my gaze down to my hands. These nails aren't acrylics. Acrylics aren't that good. These are my real nails. And there's no way they could have grown this long in five days.

'You're saying . . .' I clear my hoarse throat. 'I've lost three years of my memory.'

'That's what it looks like at the moment.' Dr Harman nods.

It really is the year 2007. Which means I must be . . . Oh my God. I'm twenty-eight. I'm *old*.

They've made me a nice strong cup of tea. Because that cures amnesia, doesn't it, a cup of tea? No, stop it. Don't be so sarky. I'm grateful for the tea. At least it's something to hold on to. As Dr Harman talks about neurological exams and CT scans, I'm nodding calmly, but inside I'm freaking. The truth keeps hitting me in the guts.

When at last he has to leave, I feel a huge sense of relief. I can't be talked at any more. I'm not following any of what he says, anyway. I take a gulp of tea and flop back on my pillows.

Maureen has gone off duty and a blonde nurse, Nicole, is in the room, scribbling on my chart.

'When people get amnesia,' I venture, 'do the missing memories ever come back?'

'Usually.' She gives a reassuring nod.

'So, tell me about 2007. Who's Prime Minister now? And President of America?'

'That would be Tony Blair,' replies Nicole. 'And President Bush.'

'Oh. Same.' I cast around. 'So . . . have they solved global warming?' Nicole shrugs. 'Not yet.'

You'd think a bit more would have happened in three years.

'Would you like a magazine?' adds Nicole. She hands me a copy of *Hello!* I run my eyes down the coverlines—and feel a jolt of shock.

'"Jennifer Aniston and Her New Man,"' I read aloud. 'What new man?'

'Oh yes. You know she split up from Brad Pitt?'

'Jennifer and Brad *split*?' I stare up at her, aghast. 'You can't be serious! They can't have done!'

'They're divorced now. He went off with Angelina Jolie.'

Jennifer and Brad are divorced. The world is a different place.

'Everyone's pretty much got used to it.' Nicole pats my shoulder soothingly. 'I'll get you some breakfast. Would you like full English, continental, or fruit basket? Or all three?'

'Um . . . continental, please. Thanks very much.' I open the magazine, then put it down again. 'Hang on. Fruit basket? Did the NHS suddenly get a load of money or something?'

'This isn't NHS.' She smiles. 'You're in the private wing.'

Private? I can't afford to go private. 'I can't afford all this,' I say in an embarrassed rush. 'I'm sorry, I don't know why I'm in this posh room. I should have been taken to an NHS hospital. I'm happy to move . . .'

'It's all covered by your private health insurance,' she says, surprised.

'Oh,' I say, taken aback. 'Oh, right.' I took out private health insurance? Well, of course I did. I'm twenty-eight now. I'm sensible. *I'm twenty-eight.*

I'm a different person. I'm not me any more.

I mean, obviously I'm still *me*. But I'm twenty-eight-year-old me. Someone who can afford private health insurance, obviously, and gets a really good manicure, and . . . Wait a minute. Slowly I turn my head and focus again on the glossy Louis Vuitton.

'Nicole? D'you think . . . Is that bag . . . *mine*?'

'Should be.' Nicole nods. 'I'll just check for you . . .' She opens the bag, pulls out a matching Louis Vuitton wallet and snaps it open. 'Yes, it's yours.' She turns the wallet round to display a platinum Amex card with 'Lexi Smart' printed across it.

My head is short-circuiting as I stare at the embossed letters. That's my platinum credit card. This is my bag. Where did I *get* it? Am I earning loads of money or something?

'So, I was really in a car crash?' I look up, suddenly wanting to know everything about myself, all at once. 'I was really driving? A *Mercedes*?'

'Apparently.' She takes in my expression of disbelief. 'Didn't you have a Mercedes in 2004, then?'

'Are you joking? I can't even drive!'

'Look in your bag,' suggests Nicole. 'Maybe the things inside will jog your memory.'

'Good idea.' I reach in—and the first thing I pull out is a tiny, gold-plated Estée Lauder compact. At once I flip it open to have a look.

'You've had some cuts to the face, Lexi,' puts in Nicole quickly. 'Don't be alarmed, they'll heal.'

As I meet my own eye in the tiny mirror, I feel a sudden relief. It's still me, even if there's a huge graze on my eyelid. I move the mirror about, trying to get a good view; flinching as I see the bandage on my head. I tilt it further down: there are my lips, looking weirdly full and pink, as if I was snogging all last night, and—

Oh my God. Those aren't my teeth. They're all white. They're all gleamy. I'm looking at a stranger's mouth.

'Are you OK?' Nicole interrupts my daze. 'Lexi?'

'I'd like a proper mirror, please,' I manage at last.

'There's one in the bathroom.' She comes forward. 'In fact, it's a good idea for you to get moving. I'll help you . . .'

I manage to totter into the adjoining bathroom. Nicole swings the door shut, to reveal a full-length mirror on the back of it.

Is that . . . *me*? I can't speak. My legs have turned to jelly.

'I know your injuries look bad.' Nicole has a strong arm round me. 'But believe me, they're just surface wounds.'

I'm not even looking at the cuts. Or the bandage or the staple on my forehead. It's what's underneath.

'That's not . . .' I gesture at my reflection. 'That's not what I look like.'

I close my eyes and visualise my old self, just to make sure I'm not going crazy. Mouse-coloured frizzy hair, blue eyes, slightly fatter than I'd like to be. Niceish face but nothing special. Black eyeliner and bright-pink Tesco lipstick. The standard Lexi Smart look.

Then I open my eyes again. A different girl is staring back at me. Some of my hair has been messed up by the crash, but the rest is a bright, unfamiliar shade of chestnut, all straight and sleek with not one bit of frizz. My toenails are perfectly pink and polished. My legs are tanned golden-brown, and thinner than before. And more muscly.

'What's changed?' Nicole is looking at my reflection curiously.

'Everything!' I manage. 'I look all . . . sheeny. My hair, my legs, my *teeth* . . .' I can't take my eyes off those immaculate pearly whites. They must have cost a bloody fortune.

'They're nice!' She nods politely.

'No. No, no.' I'm shaking my head vigorously. 'You don't understand. I have the worst teeth in the world. My nickname is Snaggletooth.'

'Shouldn't think it is any more.' Nicole raises an amused eyebrow.

'And I've lost loads of weight . . . and my face is different.' My lips seem fuller somehow . . . I peer more closely in suspicion. Have I had something *done*? Have I turned into someone *who has work done*?

I tear myself away from the mirror, my head spinning.

'Take it easy,' Nicole warns, hurrying after me. 'You've had a shock.'

Ignoring her, I grab the Louis Vuitton bag and start yanking things out of it. God, just *look* at this stuff. A Tiffany key fob, a pair of Prada sunglasses, a lip gloss: Lancôme, not Tesco.

And here's a small, pale green Smythson diary. I open it and a small pile of business cards falls out. I pick one up, glance down at the name—and freeze.

It's a card from the company I work at, Deller Carpets—although it's been given a new trendy logo. And the name is printed in clear charcoal grey: *Lexi Smart, Director, Flooring*.

I feel as though the ground has fallen away from me.

'Lexi?' Nicole is regarding me in concern. 'You've gone very pale.'

'Look at this.' I hold the card out. '"Director." That's like, boss of the whole department. How could I possibly be the boss?' My voice rises more shrilly than I intended. 'I've only been at the company a year.'

Hands trembling, I reach into the bag again. I have to find my phone, call my friends, my family, *someone* who knows what's going on . . .

Got it. It's a sleek new model that I don't recognise, but still pretty simple to work out. I haven't got any voice messages, although there's a new, unread text. I select it and peer at the tiny screen:

Running late, I'll call when I can. E

Who's E? I rack my brains but I can't think of a single person I know whose name begins with E. Someone new at work? I go to my stored texts—and the first one is from E, too:

I don't think so. E

Is E my new best friend, or something?

I'll trawl through my messages later. Right now, I have to talk to someone who knows me, who can tell me exactly what's been going on in my life these last three years . . . I speed-dial Fi's number.

'Hi, you've reached Fiona Roper, please leave a message . . .'

'Hey, Fi,' I say as soon as the bleep sounds. 'It's me, Lexi! Listen, I know this'll sound weird, but I've had an accident. I'm in hospital and I just . . . I need to talk to you. It's quite important. Can you give me a call? Bye!' As I close the phone up, Nicole puts a reproving hand on it.

'You're not supposed to use these in here,' she says. 'You can use a land line, though. I'll set you up with a receiver.'

'OK.' I nod. 'Thanks.' I'm about to start scrolling through all my old texts when there's a knock on the door and another nurse comes in.

'I've got your clothes here . . .' She puts a carrier bag down on my bed. I reach in, pull out a pair of dark jeans, and stare at them. What are these? The waist is too high and they're *way* too narrow, almost like tights. How are you supposed to get a pair of boots on under those?

'Seven For All Mankind,' says Nicole, raising her eyebrows. 'Very nice. About two hundred quid a pop, aren't they?'

Seven for what? Two hundred pounds? For *jeans*?

'And here's your jewellery,' adds the other nurse, holding out a transparent polythene bag. 'It had to come off for the scans.'

Still stunned by the jeans, I take the bag. There's an expensive-looking bracelet made of hammered gold, and a matching necklace, plus a watch. 'Wow. This is nice.' Caught up among the knotted strands of gold is a ring, and after a bit of careful unweaving I manage to untangle it. There's a general intake of breath.

I'm holding a huge, shiny, diamond solitaire ring.

'Hey!' Nicole suddenly exclaims. 'There's something else. Hold out your hand, Lexi . . .' She tips up the bag and taps the corner. There's a moment's stillness—then out onto my palm falls a plain gold band.

There's a kind of rushing in my ears as I stare down at it.

'You must be married!' says Nicole brightly.

No. No way. Surely I'd *know* if I was married?

'She is.' The second nurse nods. 'You are. Don't you remember, love?'

I shake my head dumbly.

'You don't remember your wedding?' Nicole looks agog.

'No.' I look up in sudden horror. 'I didn't marry Loser Dave, did I?'

'I don't know!' Nicole gives a giggle and claps her hand over her mouth. 'I'm sorry. You just looked so appalled. Do you know what his name is?' She looks at the other nurse, who shakes her head.

'Look, the ring's engraved!' exclaims Nicole, taking it from me. '"A.S. and E.G., June 3, 2005."' She hands it back. 'Is that you?'

I'm breathing fast. It's true. It's carved here in solid gold.

'I'm A.S.,' I say at last. 'A for Alexia. But I have no idea who E.G. is.'

The 'E' from my phone, I suddenly realise. My husband. Texting me.

I'm twenty-eight, I have perfect white teeth, a Louis Vuitton bag, a card saying 'Director' and a husband.

How the hell did all *that* happen?

Edward. Ethan. Errol.

It's an hour later and I'm still in a state of shock. I keep looking in disbelief at my wedding ring, resting on the bedside cabinet.

Elliott. Eamonn. Egbert.

Please God, not Egbert.

I've ransacked the Louis Vuitton bag. I've looked all the way through the diary. I've skimmed through all my stored mobile numbers. But I still haven't found out what 'E' stands for.

When the door opens, I stiffen, almost expecting it to be him. But it's Mum again, looking pink and harassed.

'Those traffic wardens have no *hearts*. I was only twenty minutes—'

'Mum, I've got amnesia.' I cut her off in a rush. 'I've lost my memory. I've lost a whole chunk of my life. I'm really . . . freaked out.'

'Oh. Yes, the nurse mentioned it.' Her gaze meets mine briefly, then flicks away again. Mum's not the greatest at eye contact.

Now she's sitting down and peeling off her waistcoat. 'I know *exactly* how you feel,' she begins. 'My memory gets worse every day.'

'Mum . . .' I inhale deeply, trying to stay calm. 'You don't know how I feel. I've lost three years of my life! I don't look the same, none of my things are the same, and I found these rings . . .' My voice is jumping about with apprehension. 'Mum . . . am I really *married*?'

'Of course you're married!' Mum appears surprised that I need to ask. 'Eric will be here any minute. I told you that earlier.'

'Eric's my husband?' I stare at her. 'I thought Eric was a dog.'

'A *dog*? Goodness, darling! You did get a bump on the head!'

Eric. I'm rolling the name experimentally around my head. *My husband, Eric.* It means nothing to me.

'He had a very important meeting this morning. But otherwise, he's been here with you night and day.'

'Right.' I digest this. 'So . . . so what's he like?'

'He's *very* nice,' says Mum, as though she's talking about a sponge cake.

'Is he . . .' I stop. I can't ask if he's good-looking. That would be really shallow. And what if she avoids the question and says he has a wonderful sense of humour?

We lapse into silence. We've never been into cosy mother–daughter chats. I once tried to confide in her, when I split up with my first boyfriend. Big mistake. She didn't sympathise, or hug me, or even really listen. So I gave up and called Fi instead.

'Did you manage to order those sofa covers for me, Lexi?' Mum interrupts my thoughts. 'Off the Internet,' she adds at my blank look. 'You were going to do it last week.'

Has she listened to *anything* I've said? 'Mum, I don't know,' I say, slowly and clearly. 'I don't remember anything about the last three years.'

'Sorry, darling.' Mum is nodding, a distant look in her eyes, as though she's processing my words. 'The thing is, I don't remember the name of the website. So if you *do* happen to recall . . .'

'I'll let you know, OK?' I can't help snapping. 'If my memory returns, the first thing I'll do is call you about your sofa covers. Jesus!'

OK. So in 2007 Mum still officially drives me up the wall. Surely I'm supposed to have grown out of being irritated by my mother?

'So, what does Eric do?' I return to the subject of my so-called husband. I still can't really believe he's real.

'He sells property,' says Mum. 'He's rather good at it, actually.'

I've married an estate agent called Eric. How? *Why?*

'Do we live in my flat?'

Mum looks bemused. 'Darling, you have a marital home now!'

I feel a pang. I love my flat. It's in Balham and is tiny but cosy, with blue-painted window frames that I did myself, and a lovely squashy sofa, and piles of colourful cushions everywhere, and fairy lights round the mirror. But now I live in a marital home. With my marital husband.

For the millionth time I look at the wedding ring and diamond solitaire. Then I shoot an automatic glance at Mum's hand. She still wears Dad's ring, despite the way he's behaved towards her over the years—

Dad. Dad's funeral.

'Mum,' I venture cautiously. 'I'm really sorry I missed Dad's funeral.'

'You didn't miss it, darling.' She peers at me as though I'm crazy.

'Oh.' I stare at her, confused. 'Right. Of course. I just don't remember anything about it.' Heaving a massive sigh, I lean back on my pillows. 'So, how was it?'

'Oh, it all went off as well as these things ever do . . .' Mum's looking twitchy, the way she always is when the subject of Dad comes up.

'Were many people there?'

'Let's not *dwell* on it, darling. It was years ago, now.' She gets up, as though to remove herself from my questioning. 'Have you had any lunch? I'll go and find something for us both. And make sure you eat properly, Lexi,' she adds. 'None of this no-carbs obsession. A potato won't kill you.'

No carbs? Is that how I got this shape? I glance down at my legs. It has to be said, they look as if they don't know what a potato *is*.

'I won't be long.' Mum picks up her embroidered shoulder bag. 'And Amy should be here any moment.'

'Amy's here?' My spirits lift as I visualise my little sister, in her pink fleecy jerkin and flower-embroidered jeans.

'She was just buying some chocolate downstairs.' Mum opens the door. 'She loves those mint KitKats.'

The door closes behind her and I stare at it. They've invented mint *KitKats*? 2007 really is a different world.

Amy's my full sister—not my half-sister like most people presume—but there's twelve years between us and my mum and dad had split up before she was born.

Maybe 'split up' is too strong. I'm not sure what went on exactly—all I know is, my dad was never around much when I was growing up. The official reason was that his business was based abroad. The *real* reason was that he was a feckless chancer. I was only eight when I heard him described like that by one of my aunts at a Christmas party.

The first time he left home, I was seven. Mum said he'd gone on a business trip to America, so when Melanie at school said she'd seen him in the Co-op with a woman in red jeans, I told her she was a fat liar.

A couple of years later he disappeared again, for a few months this time. Then he started up a property business in Spain which went bust. Then he got involved in some dodgy pyramid scheme. Somewhere along the line he became an alcoholic . . . then he moved in for a bit with some Spanish woman . . . but Mum kept taking him back. Then at last, about three years ago, he moved to Portugal for good, apparently to get away from the tax man. Mum had various other 'gentlemen friends' over the years, but she and Dad never divorced; never really let go of each other at all. And evidently, on one of his jovial Christmas visits back, she and he must have . . .

Well. I don't exactly want to picture it. We got Amy, that's the point. And she's the most adorable little thing.

There's a faint knocking at the door and I look up. 'Hello? Come in!'

'Hi, Lexi?' An unfamiliar girl of about sixteen has edged into the room. She's tall and skinny, with jeans falling off her midriff, a pierced navel, and spiky blue-streaked hair. I have no idea who she is.

As she sees me, she grimaces. 'Your face still looks all fucked up.'

'Oh,' I say, taken aback.

The girl's eyes narrow as she surveys me. 'Lexi . . . it's me. You do know it's me, don't you?'

'Right!' I make an apologetic face. 'Look, I'm really sorry, but I've had this accident and I'm having some problems with my memory.'

'Lexi?' She sounds incredulous; almost hurt. 'It's me! It's *Amy*.'

I'm speechless. I'm beyond speechless. This cannot be my baby sister. But it is. Amy's turned into a tall, sassy teenager. Practically an adult. I'm mesmerised by the height of her. The *confidence* of her.

'Is there any food here? I'm starving.' She has the same sweet, husky voice she always did—but modulated. Cooler and more streetwise.

'Mum's getting me some lunch. You can share if you like.'

'Great.' She sits down in a chair and swings her long legs over the arm. 'So you don't remember anything? That's so cool.'

'It's not cool,' I retort. 'It's horrible. I remember up to the day before Dad's funeral . . . and then it just goes fuzzy. All I remember is you being twelve. With your ponytail and braces. And those cute hair-slides you used to wear.'

'Don't remind me.' Amy mimes puking. 'So . . . let me get this straight. The whole of the last three years is a total blank.'

'Like a big black hole. And even before that it's a bit foggy. Apparently I'm *married*?' I laugh nervously. 'I had no idea!'

'Yeah,' she says distractedly. 'Hey, Lexi, I don't want to bring this up when you're feeling so ill and everything, but . . .' She twists a strand of hair, looking awkward.

'What?' I look at her in surprise. 'Tell me.'

'Well, it's just that you owe me seventy quid.' She shrugs apologetically. 'You borrowed it last week when your cash card wasn't working and you said you'd pay me back. I don't suppose you'll remember . . .'

'Oh,' I say, taken aback. 'Of course. Just help yourself.' I gesture at the Louis Vuitton bag. 'I don't know if there's any cash in there.'

'There will be,' says Amy, swiftly unzipping it with a tiny smile. 'Thanks!' She pockets the notes and then looks up, suddenly alert. 'Wait a minute. Do you know about—' She stops herself.

'What?'

She surveys me with narrowed, disbelieving eyes. 'No one's told you, have they? *Jesus*. I suppose they're trying to break things to you gradually, but, I mean . . .' She shakes her head, nibbling her nails. 'Personally, I think you should know sooner rather than later.'

'Know what?' I feel a beat of alarm. 'What, Amy? Tell me!'

'Wait here.' She disappears out of the room for a few moments. Then the door opens again and she appears, clutching an Asian-looking baby of about a year old. 'This is Lennon,' she says, her expression softening. 'This is your son.'

I stare at them both, frozen in terror. What's she talking about?

'I guess you don't remember?' Amy strokes his hair fondly. 'You adopted him from Vietnam six months ago. Say hello to your child!' She carts him over to the bed. 'He calls you "Moo-mah", by the way.'

'Hi, Lennon,' I say at last, my voice stiff with self-consciousness. 'It's . . . it's Moo-mah!' I try to adopt a motherly, cooing voice.

I look up to see Amy's lips trembling strangely. Suddenly she gives a snort of laughter and claps a hand over her mouth. 'Sorry!'

'Amy, what's going on?' I stare at her, suspicion dawning. 'Is this really my baby?'

'I saw him in the corridor before,' she splutters. 'I couldn't resist it. Your face!' She's in paroxysms of laughter. '"It's Moo-mah!"'

I can hear muffled cries and shouts coming from outside the door.

'That must be his parents!' I hiss in consternation. 'You bloody little . . . Put him *back*!' I collapse onto my pillows in relief, my heart pounding. Thank goodness. I don't have a child.

And I cannot get over Amy. She used to be so sweet and innocent. What's *happened* to her?

'I nearly had a heart attack,' I say reproachfully as she comes back in, holding a can of Diet Coke. 'If I died, it would be your fault.'

'Well, you need to get savvy,' she retorts with an unrepentant grin. 'People could feed you all kinds of bullshit.'

Amy's right. People could take total advantage of me. I have so much to learn and I don't even know where to start.

Well. I could start with the obvious.

'So.' I try to sound casual. 'What's my husband like? Mum said he was nice?' I try to hide my apprehension.

'He is lovely.' She nods seriously. 'He has a real sense of humour. And they're going to operate on his hump.'

'Yeah. Nice try, Amy.' I roll my eyes.

'Lexi! He'd be really hurt if he heard that!' Amy looks taken aback. 'It's not *his* fault his back was damaged when he was a baby.'

Now I'm hot with shame. Maybe my husband does have a hump. I shouldn't be hump-ist. 'Can he walk?' I ask nervously.

'He walked for the first time at your wedding,' says Amy. 'He got up out of his wheelchair to say his vows. Everyone was in tears. The vicar could hardly speak . . .' Her mouth is twitching again.

'You little cow!' I exclaim. 'He doesn't have a hump, does he?'

'I'm sorry.' She starts giggling. 'But this is *such* a good game.'

'It's not a game!' I clutch at my hair. 'It's my life. I have no idea who my husband is, or how I met him, or anything . . .'

'OK.' She appears to relent. 'You met him on a TV show.'

'Try again.' I lift my eyes to heaven.

'It's true! I'm not bullshitting now. You were on that reality show, *Ambition*. Where people want to get to the top in business. He was one of the judges and you were a contestant. You didn't get very far on the show, but you met Eric, and you hit it off.'

There's silence. I'm waiting for her to crack up laughing and produce some punch line, but she just swigs from the can of Diet Coke.

'I was on a reality show?' I say sceptically.

'Yeah. It was really cool. You should have won!'

I eye her closely but her face is totally serious. Is she telling the truth?

'Why on earth did I go on a show like that?'

'To be the boss?' Amy shrugs. 'To get ahead. That's when you had your teeth and hair done, too, to look good on TV.'

'But I'm not ambitious. I mean, I'm not *that* ambitious . . .'

'Are you kidding?' Amy opens her eyes wide. 'You're like, the most ambitious person in the world! As soon as your boss resigned you went for his job. All the bigwigs at your company had seen you on telly and they were really impressed. So they gave it to you.'

My mind flashes back to those business cards in my diary.

'You're the youngest director they've ever had in the company,' Amy adds. 'You don't remember *any* of this?'

'No! Nothing!'

The door opens and Mum appears, holding a tray bearing a covered plate, a pot of chocolate mousse and a glass of water.

'Here we are,' she says. 'I've brought you some lasagne. And guess what? Eric's here!'

'*Here?*' The blood drains from my face.

Mum nods. 'He's on his way up right now to see you!'

'Mum, I'm not sure I can do this,' I say in panic. 'I mean . . . I don't feel up to meeting him yet. Maybe I should see him tomorrow.'

'Lexi, darling!' remonstrates Mum. 'You can't turn your husband away. He's rushed here from his business especially to see you!'

'But I don't know him! I won't know what to say or what to do . . .'

'He might trigger your memory,' chimes in Amy, who has helped herself to the chocolate mousse pot and is ripping the top off. 'You might see him and go "Eric! My love! It all comes back to me!"'

'Shut up,' I snap. 'And that's *my* chocolate mousse.'

'You don't eat carbs,' she retorts. 'Have you forgotten that too?'

'Nice try, Amy,' I say, rolling my eyes. 'There's no way I would ever have given up chocolate.'

'You *never* eat chocolate any more. Does she, Mum?'

She has to be bullshitting me. I'm about to tell her to piss off and hand over the mousse, when there's a knock at the door.

'Oh my God.' I look wildly from face to face. 'Is that him? Already?' My stomach is churning in dread. I can't meet some total stranger who's apparently my husband. It's just too freaky.

'Mum. Please. It's too soon. Tell him to come back later.'

'Don't be silly, darling!' Mum laughs. How can she *laugh*?

As Mum heads towards the door I'm gripping the sheets so hard the blood is squashed out of my fingertips. 'What if I hate him?'

'Really, Lexi,' says Mum, 'there's nothing to worry about. He's nice.'

'As long as you don't mention his toupee,' puts in Amy.

'Amy!' Mum clicks her tongue. 'Eric! Come in.'

There's an unbearably long pause—then the door opens. And into the room, carrying an enormous bouquet of flowers, walks the most drop-dead gorgeous man I've ever seen.

Two

I CAN'T SPEAK. All I can do is gaze up at him, a bubble of disbelief rising inside me. This man is seriously, achingly good-looking. Like, Armani-model good-looking. He has mid-brown curly hair, cropped short. He has blue eyes, broad shoulders and an expensive-looking suit. He has a square jaw, impeccably shaved. How did I land this guy? *How?*

'Hi,' he says, and his voice is all deep and rounded like an actor's.

'Hi!' I manage breathlessly.

'My darling.' He strides to the bed in a rustle of expensive flowers. 'You look so much better than yesterday. And this room is nicer than the one before. How are you feeling?'

'I feel fine. Um . . . thanks very much.' I take the bouquet from him. It's the most amazing, trendy, designer-looking bouquet I've ever seen.

'So . . . you're Eric?' I add, just to be one hundred per cent sure.

I can see the shock reverberate through his face, but he manages a smile. 'Yes. That's right. I'm Eric. You still don't know me?'

'Not really. In fact . . . not at all.'

'I told you,' chips in Mum, shaking her head. 'I'm *so* sorry, Eric. But I'm sure she'll remember soon, if she makes a real effort.'

'I'm *trying* to remember, OK?' I say indignantly.

'We'll take it slowly,' says Eric. He sits down on the bed. 'Let's see if we can trigger some memories. May I?' He nods at my hand.

'Um . . . yes. OK.' I nod, and he takes it in his.

'Lexi, it's me,' he says in firm, resonant tones. 'It's Eric. Your husband. We've been married for nearly two years.'

I'm too mesmerised to reply. He's even better looking up close. His skin is really smooth and tanned, and his teeth are a perfect gleaming white . . . *Oh my God, I've had sex with this man.*

I wonder what he's like in bed. Surreptitiously, I run my eyes over his body. Well, I married him. He must be pretty good, surely . . .

'Is something on your mind?' Eric has noticed my wandering gaze.

'Nothing!' I flush. 'Nothing. Sorry. Carry on.'

'We met nearly three years ago,' Eric continues, 'at a reception at Pyramid TV. They make *Ambition*, the reality show we were both involved in. We were attracted instantly. We were married the following June and honeymooned in Paris. We had a suite at the George V. It was wonderful . . .' He breaks off. 'Do you recall any of this?'

'Not really,' I say, feeling guilty. 'Sorry.'

Maybe Mum's right. I should try harder to remember. Come on. Paris. The Mona Lisa. Men with stripy shirts. *Think*. I cast my mind back, desperately trying to trigger some memory . . . To my slight relief, there's a knock at the door and I call out, 'Come in!'

Nicole enters, holding a clipboard. 'Just need to do a quick blood-pressure check—' she begins, then breaks off as she sees Eric holding my hand. 'Oh, I'm sorry. I didn't mean to interrupt.'

'Don't worry!' I say. 'This is Nicole, one of the nurses who's looking after me.' I gesture round the room. 'This is my mum, and sister . . . and my husband, who's called—' I meet her eyes significantly, 'Eric.'

'*Eric!*' Nicole's eyes light up. 'Very nice to meet you, Eric.'

'It's a pleasure. I'm eternally grateful to you for looking after my wife.'

Wife. My stomach flips over at the word. I'm his wife. This is all so grown-up. I bet we have a mortgage, too. And a burglar alarm.

'My pleasure.' Nicole gives him a professional smile. 'Lexi's a great patient.' She wraps the blood-pressure cuff round my arm and turns to face me. 'I'll just pump this up . . . *He's gorgeous!*' she mouths, and I can't help beaming back. 'Lexi, that all looks fine.' Nicole writes something on my notes. 'I'm going to ask everyone not to stay *too* much longer.' She turns to Mum and Amy. 'Lexi's still fragile. She needs to take it easy.'

Mum and Amy start to gather their things—but Eric stays put. 'I'd like a few moments, just the two of us. If that's OK, Lexi?'

'Oh,' I say with a dart of apprehension. 'Er . . . fine!'

Then the door closes behind Mum and Amy and I'm left alone with Eric, in still, strange silence.

'So,' says Eric at last. 'Have the doctors said whether you'll ever retrieve your memories?'

'They think I will. But they don't know when.'

Eric gets up and strides to the window. 'So it's a waiting game,' he says at last. 'Is there anything I can do to speed the process?'

'I don't know,' I say helplessly. 'Maybe you could tell me some more about us and our relationship? Where do we live?'

'We live in Kensington in a loft-style apartment.' He proclaims the words as though they're capitalised. 'That's my business. Loft-style living.' As he says the phrase 'loft-style living' he makes a parallel-hands gesture, as though he's moving bricks along a conveyor belt.

Wow. We live in Kensington!

'What sort of things do we do together?' I say eventually.

'We eat fine food, we watch movies . . . We went to see the ballet last week. Had dinner at the Ivy afterwards.'

'The Ivy?' I can't help gasping. I've been to dinner at the Ivy?

Why can't I remember any of this? I shut my eyes tightly, trying to mentally kick-start my brain into action. But . . . nothing.

At last I open my eyes again, feeling a bit dizzy, to see Eric has noticed the rings on the cabinet. 'That's your wedding ring, isn't it?'

'They took it off for the scans,' I explain.

'Shall I?' He picks up the ring and takes hold of my left hand.

'I . . . um . . . no . . .' Before I can stop myself I yank my hand away and Eric flinches. 'I'm sorry,' I say, after an awkward pause. 'I'm really sorry. I just . . . you're a stranger.'

'Of course.' Eric has turned away. 'Of course. Stupid of me.'

'I'm sorry, Eric.' I bite my lip. 'You must be a wonderful person or I wouldn't have married you. And you look really good,' I add encouragingly. 'I wasn't expecting anyone nearly so handsome. I mean, my last boyfriend wasn't a *patch* on you.'

I look up to see Eric staring at me.

'It's strange,' he says at last. 'You're not yourself. The doctors warned me, but I didn't realise it would be so extreme.' For a moment he looks almost overcome—then his shoulders straighten. 'Anyway. We'll get you right again.' He takes my hand. 'And just so you know, Lexi . . . I love you.'

'*Really?*' I give a delighted beam before I can stop myself. 'I mean . . . fab. Thanks very much!'

'Eat your lunch and take a rest.' He pats my shoulder. 'I'll leave you in peace.' He lets himself out quietly. I sit still in the silence for a moment. My head's starting to throb again and I'm a bit dazed. It's all too much. Amy has blue hair and Brad Pitt's with Angelina Jolie and I have a gorgeous husband. I'm half expecting to go to sleep and wake up back in 2004, hung over on Carolyn's floor, to find this was all a dream.

But it was no dream. I wake up the next morning and it's still 2007. I'm just eating my third piece of toast when the door opens and Nicole appears, wheeling a trolley laden with flowers. I gape at it.

'So . . . is one of these mine?' I can't help asking.

'All of them. They were left in your old room. You're a popular girl! We've run out of vases!' She hands me a stack of little cards. 'Here are your messages.'

'Wow.' I take the first card and read it.

Lexi—darling girl. Look after yourself, get well, see you very soon, all my love Rosalie.

Rosalie? I don't know anyone called Rosalie.

Lexi, get well soon! You'll soon be back to three hundred reps! From all your friends at the gym.

Three hundred reps? Me?

Well, I guess that would account for the muscly legs. I reach for the next card—and at last, it's from people I actually know.

Get well soon, Lexi. All best wishes from Fi, Debs, Carolyn, and everyone in Flooring.

As I read the familiar names, I feel a warm glow inside. It's stupid, but I almost thought my friends had forgotten all about me.

'So your husband's quite a stunner!' Nicole interrupts my thoughts.

'D'you think so?' I try to appear nonchalant.

'He's amazing! And you know, he came round the ward yesterday, thanking us all again for looking after you. Not many people do that.'

There's a knock on the door and Nicole calls, 'Come in!'

It opens and in come Mum and Amy, lugging between them about six carrier bags stuffed with photograph albums and envelopes.

'Lexi, darling, we've brought some pictures to show you. Maybe they'll trigger your memory.'

Ten minutes later, I haven't seen a single photo, because Mum and Amy keep arguing about where to start.

'We don't want to *overwhelm* her,' Mum keeps saying, as they both root through the bags of pictures. 'Now, here we are.' She picks up a photo in a cardboard frame.

'No *way*.' Amy grabs it from her. 'I've got a zit on my chin.'

'Amy, it's a tiny pimple. You can hardly see it.'

'Yes you can. And this one is even grosser!' She starts ripping both photographs into shreds.

Here I am, waiting to learn all about my long-lost life, and Amy's destroying the evidence? 'I won't look at your zits!' I call over. 'Just show me a picture! Anything!'

'All right.' Mum advances towards the bed, holding an unframed print. 'I'll hold it up, Lexi. See if the image jogs anything. Ready?' Mum turns the print round. It's a picture of a dog dressed up as Santa Claus.

I try to control my frustration. 'Why are you showing me a dog?'

'Darling, it's Tosca!' Mum appears wounded. 'And here's Raphael with Amy last week, both looking lovely . . .'

'I look *hideous*.' Amy snatches the picture and rips it up.

'Stop ripping up the pictures!' I yell. 'Mum, did you bring photographs of anything else? Like, people?'

'Hey, Lexi, do you remember this?' Amy comes forward, holding up a distinctive necklace with a rose made out of jade. I squint at it, trying desperately to dredge some memory up.

'No,' I say at last. 'It doesn't jog anything at all.'

'Cool. Can I have it then?'

'Amy!' says Mum. She riffles through the pictures in her hand in dissatisfaction. 'Maybe we should just wait for Eric to come with the wedding DVD. If that doesn't trigger your memory, nothing will.'

The wedding DVD. *My wedding.*

Every time I think about this, my stomach curls up with a kind of excited, nervous anticipation. 'He seems nice,' I say. 'Eric, I mean.'

'He's super.' Mum nods absently, still leafing through pictures of dogs. 'He does a lot for charity, you know. Or the company does, I should say. But it's his own company, so it's all the same.'

'He has his own company? I thought he was an estate agent.'

'It's a company that *sells properties*, darling. Big loft developments all over London. They sold off a large part of it last year, but he still retains a controlling interest.'

'He made ten million quid,' says Amy.

'He *what*?' I stare at her.

'He's stinking rich.' She looks up. 'Don't say you hadn't guessed that?'

I can't quite speak. In fact, I'm feeling a bit faint. Ten million quid?

There's a knock at the door. 'Lexi? May I come in?'

The door swings open—and there he is, manhandling two carrier bags, another bunch of flowers and a gift basket full of fruit.

'Hi, darling.' He kisses me on the cheek. 'How are you doing?'

'Much better, thanks.' I smile up at him.

'But she still doesn't know who you are,' puts in Amy.

Eric doesn't look fazed. Maybe he's used to Amy being bolshy.

'Well, we're going to tackle that today.' He hefts up the bags, sounding energised. 'I've brought along photos, DVDs, souvenirs . . . let's reintroduce you to your life. Barbara, why don't you put on the wedding DVD?' He hands a shiny disc to Mum. 'And to get you started, our wedding album.' He heaves an expensive-looking album onto the bed.

I open it and my stomach seems to drop a mile. I'm staring at a black and white photograph of me as a bride. I'm wearing a long white sheath dress, my hair's in a sleek knot and I'm holding a minimalist bouquet of lilies. Soundlessly I turn to the next page. There's Eric standing next to me, dressed in black tie. We look so *glossy*.

From the TV screen suddenly comes the mingled sound of people laughing and chattering. I look up and feel a fresh shock. Up there on the telly, Eric and I are posing in our wedding outfits. We're standing next to a huge white cake, holding a knife together, laughing at someone off the screen. I can't take my eyes off myself.

The camera swings round, catching the faces of people I don't recognise. I spot Mum, in a navy suit, and Amy, wearing a purple strappy dress. We're in some huge, modern-looking space with glass walls and trendy chairs and floral arrangements everywhere.

'Where's this place?' I ask.

'Sweetheart . . .' Eric gives a disconcerted laugh. 'This is our home.'

'Our *home*? But it's massive! It's like a football pitch. And who's that?' I point at a pretty girl in a strapless dress.

'That's Rosalie. Your best friend.'

My *best friend*? I've never seen this woman before in my life. She's skinny and tanned, with huge blue eyes, a massive bracelet on her wrist and sunglasses pushed up on her blonde, California-girl hair.

She sent me flowers, I suddenly remember. *Darling girl. All my love Rosalie.*

'Now, this is us on holiday in Mauritius last year . . .' Eric has fast-forwarded the DVD and I stare disbelievingly at the screen. Is that girl walking along the sand *me*? My hair's braided and I'm tanned and thin and wearing a red string bikini.

'And this is us at a charity ball . . .' Eric's fast-forwarded and there we are again. I'm wearing a slinky blue evening dress, dancing with Eric.

'Eric is a *very* generous benefactor,' says Mum, but I don't respond. I'm riveted by a handsome, dark-haired guy standing near the dance floor. Wait a moment. Don't I know him from somewhere?

'Lexi?' Eric has noticed my expression. 'Is this jolting your memory?'

'Yes!' I can't help a joyful smile. 'I remember that guy on the left.' I point at the screen. 'I'm not sure who he is exactly, but I *know* him. Really well! He's warm, and funny, and I think maybe he's a doctor . . .'

'Lexi . . .' Eric gently cuts me off. 'That's George Clooney, the actor. He was a fellow guest at the ball.'

'Oh.' I rub my nose, discomfited. 'Oh right.'

When I think of all the hideous, mortifying things I *can* remember. Having to eat semolina at school when I was seven and nearly vomiting. Wearing a white swimsuit when I was fifteen and getting out of the pool and it was transparent and all the boys laughed. I remember that humiliation as if it were yesterday. But I can't remember walking along a beach in Mauritius. I can't remember dancing with my husband at some grand ball. Hello, brain? Do you have *any* priorities?

'I was reading up about amnesia last night,' says Amy from her cross-legged position on the floor. 'You know which sense triggers memory the best? Smell. What you two should do is have sex. You need the pungent smell of each other's bodily—'

'Amy!' Mum cuts her off. 'Darling!'

Maybe Amy's right. Maybe we should have sex. I glance at Eric—and I'm convinced he's thinking the same thing.

'It's still early days.' Eric smiles as he closes the wedding album.

'What if I never remember?' I look around the room. 'What if all those memories are lost for good and I can never get them back? *Ever?*'

That afternoon I see a neuropsychologist. He's a friendly guy in jeans called Neil and I sit at a table with him, doing tests.

'You're functioning extremely well, Lexi,' says Neil after he fills in the last check box. 'Your executive skills are there, your short-term memory is pretty good, considering, you have no major cognitive problems . . . but you're suffering from a severe focal retrograde amnesia.'

'But *why?*'

'Well, it's all to do with the way you hit your head. When you hit the windscreen, your brain was thrown around in your skull, and a small area of your brain was, shall we say, tweaked. It could be you've done damage to your warehouse of memories . . . or it could be that you've done damage to your *ability* to retrieve memories.'

'Can't you hit me over the head or something?' I say in frustration.

'I'm afraid not.' He looks amused. 'Contrary to popular belief, hitting an amnesiac over the head is not going to bring their memory back. So don't try that at home. Let me walk you to your room.'

We arrive back at my room to find Mum and Amy still watching the home DVD while Eric talks on his mobile phone. Immediately he finishes his conversation and claps his phone shut. 'How did you get on?'

'What did you remember, darling?' chimes in Mum.

'Nothing,' I admit.

'Once Lexi gets back to familiar surroundings, she'll probably find her memory returns quite naturally,' says Neil reassuringly. 'Although it may take time.'

'Right.' Eric nods earnestly. 'So what next?'

'Well.' Neil flips through my notes. 'You're in good shape physically, Lexi. I would say you'll be discharged tomorrow. I'll make an appointment for you in a month's time as an outpatient. Until then, the best place for you is home.' He looks at Eric and Mum. 'You can help by giving Lexi as much information as possible about her life. Write things down. Take her back to places she's been. Any problems, just call me.'

The door closes behind Neil. Mum and Eric exchange looks.

'Sweetheart, your mother and I were talking earlier about how we would . . .' Eric hesitates. 'Tackle your release.'

Tackle my release. As if I'm a dangerous, psychotic prisoner.

'We're in a pretty strange situation here,' he continues. 'Obviously, I would love it if you wanted to come home and resume your life again. But I appreciate you may find that uncomfortable.'

'I said to Eric, you're very welcome to come and stay with me for a bit,' puts in Mum. 'Obviously, it will be a *little* disruptive, and you'll have to share with Jake and Florian, but they're good dogs . . .'

'That room smells,' says Amy.

'It does not *smell*, Amy.' Mum seems affronted. 'That builder chap said it was simply a question of dry . . . something-or-other.'

'Rot,' says Amy. 'And it does smell.'

Mum is blinking hard in annoyance. Meanwhile, Eric has come over, his face concerned. 'Lexi, please don't think I'll be offended. I'm a stranger to you. Why on earth would you want to come home with me?'

I know it's my cue to answer—but I've suddenly been distracted by an image on the TV screen. It's of me and Eric on a speedboat. We're both wearing sunglasses and we look totally glamorous, like something out of a James Bond movie.

I want this life, rushes through my brain. *It belongs to me. I earned it. I'm not going to let it slip through my fingers.*

OK. Let's just get my options absolutely clear here:

1. A rotting room in Kent that I have to share with two whippets.

2. A palatial loft in Kensington with Eric my good-looking husband who can drive a speedboat.

'You know what, Eric?' I say carefully, measuring out my words. 'I think I *should* come and live with you.'

'Are you serious?' His face lights up. 'But you don't know me.'

'I'll get to know you again!' I say with growing enthusiasm. 'Surely the best chance I have of remembering my life is to live it. You can tell me about yourself, and me, and our marriage . . . I can learn it all again!'

'It would be wonderful to have you back.' Eric still looks troubled. 'Obviously you won't want to . . . I mean . . . I'll take the guest suite.'

'I would appreciate that,' I say. 'Thank you, Eric.'

'Well, if you're sure about this . . .' His whole face has brightened. 'Let's do this properly, shall we?' He glances questioningly at the rings, still lying on the cabinet, and I follow his gaze.

'Yes, let's!' I nod, suddenly excited.

He picks up the rings and self-consciously I hold out my left hand. I watch, transfixed, as Eric slips the rings onto my finger. There's a hush in the room as I gaze down at my beringed hand.

Fuck, that diamond's huge.

It has to be karma. I must have been amazingly noble in a previous existence: rescued children from a burning building or given up my life to help lepers. It's the only explanation I can think of for how I've landed the dream life. Here I am, zooming along the Embankment, with my handsome husband, *in his open-top Mercedes*.

I keep glancing down at myself in wonder. I'm wearing a pair of cropped jeans, *two sizes* smaller than I used to wear. And a top by Miu Miu, which is one of those names I only used to know about from magazines. On the back seat are all the bouquets and presents from my hospital room, including a massive basket of tropical fruit from Deller Carpets. There was a letter attached from someone called Clare, who said she would send me the minutes of the latest board meeting, signed, 'Clare Abrahams, Assistant to Lexi Smart'.

Assistant to Lexi Smart. I have my own personal assistant. Me!

My cuts and bruises are a lot better and the plastic staple has been taken out of my head. My hair is freshly washed and glossy and my teeth are as movie-star perfect as ever. I'm Cinderella. No, I'm *better* than Cinderella, because she only got the prince, didn't she? I'm Cinderella with fab teeth and a shit-hot job.

Eric signals left. 'Well, here we are . . .' He pulls off the road into a grand pillared entrance, past a porter in a glass box, into a car space and turns off the engine. 'Come and see your home.'

You know how some hyped-up things are a total letdown when you actually get to them? Like, you save up for ages to go to an expensive restaurant and the waiters are snooty and the table is too small.

Well, my new home is exactly the opposite of that. It's way *better* than I imagined. As I walk around, I'm awe-struck. It's massive. It's light. It has views over the river. There's a vast, L-shaped cream sofa and the coolest black-granite cocktail bar.

'Do you remember any of this?' Eric is watching me intently.

'No. But it's absolutely stunning!'

We must have some cool parties here. I can just *see* Fi, Carolyn and Debs perched at the cocktail bar, tequila shooters going, music blaring over the sound system. I pause by the sofa and run my hand along the plushy fabric. 'This is an amazing sofa!' I look up at Eric. 'It must have cost a packet.'

'Ten thousand pounds.' Eric nods.

Shit. I draw my hand back. How can a sofa cost that much? What's it stuffed with, *caviar*? I edge away, thanking God I didn't sit down on it.

'I really love this . . . er . . . light fitting.' I gesture to a freestanding, undulating piece of metal.

'That's a radiator.' Eric smiles.

'Oh, right,' I say, confused. 'I thought *that* was a radiator.' I point to an old-fashioned iron radiator fitted halfway up the opposite wall.

'That's a piece of art,' Eric corrects me. 'It's by Hector James-John. *Disintegration Falls.*'

Disintegration Falls. Black radiator. Nope, no idea.

I turn away from the radiator-art thing and focus on a giant screen, which almost fills the opposite wall. There's a second screen across the room, too, by the dining table, and I noticed one in the bedroom. Eric clearly likes the telly.

'What would you like?' He notices me looking. 'Try this.' He picks up a remote control and flicks it at the screen. The next minute I'm looking at a massive blazing, crackling fire.

'Wow!' I stare at it in surprise.

'Or this.' The picture changes to brightly coloured tropical fish weaving through fronds of seaweed. 'It's the latest in home-screen-system technology,' he says proudly. 'It's art, it's entertainment, it's communication. You can email on these things, you can listen to music, read books . . . You can even have a virtual pet.'

'A pet?' I'm still gazing at the screen, dazzled.

'We each have one.' Eric smiles. 'This is mine, Titan.' He flicks his control and on the screen appears an image of a massive stripy spider.

'Oh my *God*!' I back away, feeling sick. I've never been great with spiders. 'Could you possibly switch that off, please?'

'What's wrong?' Eric looks surprised. 'I showed Titan to you on your first visit here. You said you thought he was adorable.'

Great. It was our first date, I said I liked the spider to be polite, and now I'm stuck with it. 'So I have a pet too?' I say quickly, to distract him.

'Here you go.' He zaps at the screen. 'Here's Arthur.' A fluffy white kitten appears on the screen and I cry out in delight.

'He's so *cute*!' I watch him playing with a ball of string, batting it and tumbling over. 'Does he grow up into a cat?'

'No.' Eric smiles. 'He stays as a kitten indefinitely. All your life, if you want. They have a life capacity of one hundred thousand years.'

'Oh, right,' I say after a pause. Actually, that's freakish.

Eric's phone beeps. 'Sweetheart, my driver's here. As I said, I'm going to have to go out briefly to the office. But Rosalie is on her way, to keep you company. Until then, if anything bothers you, just call me at once—or you can email me through the system.' He hands me a rectangular white gadget with a screen. 'Here's your remote control. It controls heating, ventilation, lighting . . . everything here is intelligent. But you shouldn't need to use it. All the settings are in place.'

'We have a remote-control *house*?' I want to laugh.

'It's all part of loft-style living!' He makes the parallel-hands gesture again, and I nod, trying not to give away how overwhelmed I am.

'So . . . how exactly does Rosalie fit in?'

'She's the wife of my partner, Clive.'

'Does she hang out with me and the other girls from the office?' I ask. 'Like Fi and Carolyn? Do we all go out together?'

'Who?' Eric looks blank. Maybe he's one of those guys who doesn't keep up with his wife's social life.

'Never mind,' I say quickly. 'I'll work it all out.'

'Gianna will be back later, too. Our housekeeper. Any problems, she'll help you.' He comes over, hesitates, then takes my hand. His skin is smooth and immaculate. 'Welcome back, darling,' he says, a little gruffly. Then he disengages his hand and heads towards the door.

I'm alone. Alone in my marital home. As I look around the huge space again, I realise I can't see that many signs of *me*. There are no brightly coloured pottery jugs or fairy lights or piles of paperbacks.

Still. Eric and I probably wanted to start again, choosing things together. I pull out my phone and start texting Fi. I *have* to talk to her about all of this:

Hi! Back home—give me a call! Can't wait to c u!!! Lxxxx

I send the same text to Carolyn and Debs. Then I put my phone away and swivel round on the shiny wooden floor. A sudden laugh bubbles to my lips. I mean, it's crazy. Me. In this place! I swivel again on the floor, then start twirling, my arms out, laughing madly. I, Lexi Smart, live here in this state-of-the-art, remote-controlled palace!

Sorry, Lexi Gardiner.

Crash. The sound of breaking glass interrupts my thoughts. I stop twirling in horror. Somehow I accidentally caught my hand on a glass leopard that was leaping through the air on a display shelf. Now it's lying on the floor in two pieces. *Shit.* I'm hot with panic. What am I going to do? What if it was worth ten thousand quid like the sofa? What if it's some family heirloom of Eric's?

Gingerly, I pick up the first piece, and then the second—

An electronic bleep interrupts me and my head jerks up. The giant screen opposite has turned bright blue, with a message in green capitals. 'HI LEXI—HOW ARE YOU DOING?'

Fuck! He's watching me. It's Big Brother! In terror I shove the two pieces of glass under a cushion on the sofa.

'Hi,' I say to the blue screen, my heart pounding. 'I didn't mean to do that, it was an accident . . .' Silence. The screen isn't reacting in any way.

'Eric?' I try again. There's no reply.

OK, maybe he can't see me after all. He must be typing this from the car. Cautiously I venture over to the screen and notice a wall-mounted keyboard plus tiny silver mouse, discreetly tucked away to the side. I click on 'Reply' and slowly type 'FINE THANKS!'

I could leave it there. I could find a way to fix the leopard . . . No. Come on. Own up. 'HAVE BROKEN GLASS LEOPARD BY MISTAKE,' I type in. 'REALLY SORRY. HOPE IT'S NOT IRREPLACEABLE?'

I press 'Send' and pace about as I wait for the reply, telling myself not to worry. I mean, I don't know for certain that it's a priceless ornament, do I? Maybe we won it in a raffle. Maybe it's mine and Eric's always hated it. How am I supposed to know? I sink down onto a chair, suddenly overwhelmed by how little I know about my own life.

There's a bleep from the screen. I catch my breath and look up. 'OF COURSE IT'S NOT IRREPLACEABLE! DON'T WORRY.'

I feel a huge whoosh of relief. It's all right.

'THANKS!' I type in, smiling. 'WON'T BREAK ANYTHING ELSE, PROMISE!'

I can't believe I overreacted like that. I can't believe I hid the pieces.

What am I, five years old? I lift up the cushion to retrieve the pieces—
and freeze. *Shit*. The bloody glass has ripped the bloody sofa. The ten-
thousand-pound sofa. I can't tell Eric I've ruined the sofa too. I *can't*.

Flustered, I rearrange the cushions so the rip isn't visible. There. I
grab the bits of glass leopard and head into the kitchen, which is all
glossy grey-lacquer cupboards and rubber floor. I manage to track
down the bin behind a door, and chuck the bits in.

A buzzer sounds through the apartment and I look up, my spirits
lifting. This must be Rosalie, my new best friend.

Rosalie turns out to be even skinnier than she looked on the wedding
DVD. She's dressed in black capri pants, and a pink cashmere
V-neck. As I open the door she gives a small shriek and drops the Jo
Malone gift bag she's holding. '*Oh* my God, Lexi. Look at your poor face.'

'It's fine!' I say reassuringly. 'Honestly, you should have seen me six
days ago. I had a plastic staple in my head.'

'You poor thing. What a *night*mare.' She retrieves her gift bag, then
kisses me on each cheek. 'I would have come round earlier, only you
know how long I waited to get that slot at Cheriton Spa.'

'Come in.' I gesture to the kitchen. 'Would you like a cup of coffee?'

'Sweetie . . .' She looks puzzled. 'I don't drink coffee. Dr André
banned me. You know that.'

'Oh.' I pause. 'The thing is . . . I don't remember. I have amnesia.'

Rosalie is gazing at me, politely blank. Doesn't she know?

'I don't remember anything about the last three years,' I try again. 'I
hit my head and it's all been wiped from my memory.'

'*Oh* my God.' Rosalie's hand goes to her mouth. 'Eric kept saying
things about amnesia. I thought he was joking!'

I want to giggle at her horrified expression. 'No, he wasn't joking. To
me you're . . . a stranger.'

There's a short silence during which I can see Rosalie processing this
information. Her eyes widen and her cheeks puff out and she chews
her lip. '*Oh* my God,' she says at last. '*Night*mare.'

'I don't know this place.' I spread my arms around. 'I don't know
what my life is like. If you could tell me a few things . . .'

'Absolutely! Let's sit down.' She leads the way into the kitchen area.
She dumps the Jo Malone bag on the counter and sits down at the
trendy steel breakfast table—and I follow suit.

'What do you want to know?' She leans forward expectantly.

'Well . . .' I think for a moment. 'How did we two meet?'

'It was about two years ago.' Rosalie nods firmly. 'At a drinks party at
Trudy Swinson's? You know, who used to be an air hostess, but she met

Adrian on a flight to New York, and everyone says she zeroed in on him as soon as she spotted his black Amex . . .' She trails off, as if the enormity of the situation is hitting her for the first time. 'So you don't remember any *gossip*?'

'Well . . . no.'

'*Oh* my God.' She blows out sharply. 'I have so much to fill you in on. Where shall I start? OK, so there's me.' She pulls a pen out of her bag and starts writing. 'And my husband, Clive, and his evil-bitch ex—'

'Do we ever hang out with my friends from work?' I interrupt. 'Like Fi and Carolyn? Or Debs? Do you know them?'

Rosalie looks blank. 'Sweetie, to be honest, I've never heard you mention them. As far as I know, you never socialise with colleagues from work.'

'What? But it's our thing! We go clubbing and have cocktails . . .'

Rosalie laughs. 'Lexi, I've never even *seen* you with a cocktail! You and Eric are both so serious about wine.'

Wine? All I know about wine is it comes from Oddbins.

'You look confused,' says Rosalie anxiously. 'I'm bombarding you with too much information. What would you like to do?'

'Maybe we could just do whatever we normally do together?'

'Absolutely! We should go to the gym.'

'The gym,' I echo, trying to sound enthused. 'Of course. So . . . I go to the gym a lot?'

'Sweetie, you're addicted! You run for an hour every other morning.'

Running? I never run. It's painful and it makes your boobs bounce around. I once did a fun run with Fi and Carolyn, and I nearly died. Although at least I was better than Fi, who walked, smoking a cigarette, and was banned from any future Cancer Research fundraisers.

'But don't worry, we'll do something lovely and restful today,' says Rosalie reassuringly. 'A massage, or a nice gentle stretch class. Just grab your exercise clothes and we'll go!'

'OK!' I hesitate. 'Actually, this is a bit embarrassing . . . but I don't know where my clothes are. The cupboards in our bedroom are all full of Eric's suits. I can't find any of mine.'

Rosalie looks utterly poleaxed. 'You don't know where your *clothes* are?' Tears suddenly spring to her huge blue eyes and she fans her face. 'I'm sorry,' she gulps. 'But it's just come home to me how horrific and scary this must be for you. To have forgotten your entire wardrobe. Come with me, sweetie. I'll show you.'

OK. So the reason I couldn't find my clothes is they're not in a wardrobe, they're in a whole other room, behind a concealed door that looks like a mirror. And the reason they need a whole other room is because there's *so bloody many of them*. I feel faint. I've never seen so many clothes, not outside a shop. Crisp white shirts, tailored black trousers, suits in shades of mushroom and taupe. Chiffony evening wear. Tights rolled up in their own special drawer. Folded silky knickers with La Perla labels. I can't see anything that doesn't look brand-new and immaculate. There are no baggy jeans, no sloppy jumpers, no comfy old PJs.

I leaf through a row of jackets, all pretty much identical apart from the buttons. I can't believe I've spent so much money on beige clothes.

'What do you think?' Rosalie is watching me, her eyes sparkling.

'Amazing!'

'Ann has a great eye.' She nods sagely. 'Ann, your personal shopper.'

'I have a personal shopper?'

'Just for the main pieces each season.' Rosalie pulls out a dark blue dress with spaghetti straps and the tiniest ruffle round the hem. 'Look, this is the dress you wore when we first met . . . don't you remember?'

'Not really.'

'What about this Catherine Walker? You *must* remember that . . . or your Roland Mouret . . .' Rosalie is whipping out dress after dress, none of which looks remotely familiar. Then her face lights up. 'Try the shoes. You *have* to remember your shoes.' She heads to the other side of the room and flings open a cupboard door. And I stare in disbelief. I've never seen so many shoes. All in neat rows, most of them high-heeled. What am I doing with high-heeled shoes?

'This is unbelievable.' I turn to Rosalie. 'I can't even *walk* in heels.'

'Yes, you can.' Rosalie looks puzzled. 'Of course you can.'

'No.' I shake my head. 'I've never been able to do heels. I fall over.'

'Sweetie.' Rosalie's eyes are wide. 'You *live* in heels. You were wearing these last time we had lunch.' She pulls out a pair of black pumps with four-inch, skinny stiletto heels. 'Put them on!' she says.

Cautiously I slip off my loafers and step into the pointy heels. Almost at once I topple over and grab on to Rosalie. 'You see? I can't balance.'

'Lexi, you can walk in these,' says Rosalie firmly. 'I've seen you do it.'

I try another step, but my ankle bends like Plasticine. 'It's no good.' I exhale in frustration. 'I wasn't meant to do this.'

'Yes, you were. Try again! Find the zone!' Rosalie sounds like she's coaching me for the Olympics. 'You can do it, Lexi.'

I totter to the other side of the room and cling on to the curtain. 'I'll never crack this,' I say despairingly.

'Of course you will. Just don't think about it. I know! We'll sing a song! Land of hope and glor-eeee . . . Come on, Lexi, *sing*!'

Reluctantly I join in. 'Land of hope and glor-eeee . . .' Trying to keep my mind focused on the song, I take a step forward. Then another. Then another. Oh my God. I'm doing it. I'm walking in high heels!

'You see?' crows Rosalie in triumph. 'I told you! You *are* a heels girl.' She opens a drawer, scoops up some gym clothes and pops them into an oversized tote. 'Come on, let's go.'

We drive to the gym in Rosalie's car. It's a sumptuous Range Rover with designer carrier bags strewn all over the back seat.

'So, what do you do?' I say.

'I do a lot of voluntary work.' She nods earnestly.

'Wow.' I feel a bit shamefaced. Rosalie didn't strike me as the voluntary-work type, which shows how prejudiced I am. 'What kind?'

'Event planning, mainly.'

'For a particular charity?'

'No, mostly for friends. You know, if they need a helping hand with the flowers or party favours or whatever . . . I do the odd bits for the company, too,' she adds. 'Eric's such a sweetie, he always gets me involved in launches, that kind of thing.'

'So you like Eric?' I'm dying to hear what she thinks of him.

'Oh, he's the perfect husband. Absolutely perfect. Here we are!' She drives into a tiny car park and pulls up next to a Porsche.

'Now, don't worry,' she says as she pushes her way into a smart reception area. 'I'll do all the talking . . . Hi there!'

'Hi, ladies.' The receptionist's face falls as she sees me. 'Lexi! You poor thing! We heard about the accident. Are you all right?'

'I'm fine, thanks.' I venture a smile. 'Thanks for the flowers.'

'Poor Lexi has amnesia,' says Rosalie impressively. 'She doesn't remember this place. She doesn't remember *anything*.'

'Goodness!'

'Come on!' Rosalie takes hold of my arm firmly. 'We'll get changed.'

The changing rooms are the most palatial ones I've ever seen. I disappear into a cubicle and pull on a pair of leggings. Then I pull on the leotard bit. It's got a thong, I realise to my horror. Reluctantly I pull it on, then edge out of the cubicle, hands over my eyes. This could be really gross. I count to five—then force myself to take a peek in the mirror.

Actually, I don't look too bad. I remove my hands completely and stare at myself. I look all long and lean and . . . different. Experimentally I flex my arm—and a biceps muscle I've never seen before pops up. I stare at it in astonishment.

Rosalie ushers me into a large, airy exercise studio, where rows of extremely well-groomed women are already in position on yoga mats.

'Sorry we're late,' she says momentously. 'But Lexi has got amnesia. She doesn't remember *anything*. About *any* of you.'

I get the feeling Rosalie is enjoying this. 'Hi.' I do a shy wave.

'I heard about your accident, Lexi.' The exercise teacher is coming over with a sympathetic smile. 'Please take it easy today.'

'OK. Thanks.'

'We're trying to trigger her memory,' Rosalie chimes in. 'So everyone just *act normal*.'

I nervously take a mat and sit down. Gym has never exactly been my strong point. I stretch my legs out in front of me and reach for my toes, although there's no way I'll ever be able to—

Bloody hell. I can touch my toes. What's *happened* to me?

In disbelief I follow the next manoeuvre—and I can do that one too!

'And now, the advanced dancer position . . .' the teacher is saying.

Cautiously I start tugging on my ankle—and it obeys me! I'm pulling my leg right above my head! I feel like yelling, 'Look at me, everyone!'

'Don't overdo it, Lexi.' The teacher looks alarmed. 'Maybe take it easy now. I'd leave out the splits this week.'

No way. I can do the *splits*?

Afterwards in the changing room I'm exhilarated. 'I can't get over it,' I keep saying to Rosalie. 'I was always so crap at exercise!'

'Sweetie, you're a natural!'

I survey my reflection. For the millionth time, my gaze is drawn to my gleaming white teeth—and my full pink lips.

'Rosalie.' I lower my voice. 'Did I ever have anything done? To my face? Like Botox? Or . . .' I lower my voice still further, '*surgery*?'

'Sweetie! Sssh! Of course we haven't had anything done!' She winks.

What does that wink mean?

'Rosalie, you *have* to tell me what I've had done . . .' I trail off suddenly, distracted by my reflection in the mirror. Without noticing what I've been doing, I've been taking hairpins from the pot in front of me and putting my hair up on autopilot. In about thirty seconds I've constructed the most perfect chignon. *How the fuck did I do that?*

As I survey my own hands I can feel slight hysteria rising inside me. What else can I do? Assassinate someone with one blow of my hand?

'What is it?' Rosalie catches my gaze.

'I just put my hair up. I've never done that before in my life.'

'Yes, you have.' She looks puzzled. 'You wear it like that for work.'

'But I don't *remember*. It's like . . . it's like Superwoman's taken over my body or something. It's not *me*.'

'Sweetie, it *is* you.' Rosalie squeezes my arm. 'Get used to it!'

We have lunch in the juice bar and then Rosalie drives me home. As we travel up in the lift I'm suddenly exhausted. 'I feel pretty wiped out,' I say. 'Do you mind if I go and have a rest?'

'Of course not!' She pats my arm. 'I'll wait out here for you.'

'Don't be silly.' I smile. 'I'll be fine until Eric comes home, really. And . . . thanks, Rosalie. You've been so kind.'

'Darling girl.' She gives me a hug and picks up her bag. 'I'll give you a call.' She's halfway out of the door when something occurs to me.

'Rosalie!' I call. 'What should I make Eric for dinner tonight?'

She turns and blinks several times. 'Sweetie, *you* don't make the dinner. Gianna makes the dinner. Your housekeeper?'

'Oh, right. Of course!' Bloody hell. I've never even had a *cleaner* before.

'Well, I guess I'll go to bed then,' I say. 'Bye.'

Rosalie blows me a kiss and closes the door behind her, and I head into the bedroom, which is all cream and luxurious dark wood. Eric has insisted I take the main bedroom, which is very kind and noble of him. I kick off my heels, climb underneath the duvet and feel myself instantly relax. I'll just close my eyes and have a tiny kip . . .

I wake to a dim light and the sound of chinking crockery.

'Darling?' comes a voice from outside the door. 'Are you awake?' The door opens and in comes Eric, holding a tray and a carrier bag.

'You've been asleep for hours. I've brought you some supper.' He switches on the bedside light. 'It's Thai chicken soup.'

'I love Thai chicken soup!' I say in delight. 'Thanks!'

Eric smiles and hands me a spoon. 'Rosalie told me you two girls went to the gym today?'

'Yes. It was great.' I take a spoonful of soup and it's absolutely delicious. God, I'm ravenous. 'Eric, you couldn't get me a piece of bread, could you?' I raise my head. 'Just to mop this up?'

'Bread?' Eric frowns, looking puzzled. 'Darling, we don't keep bread in the house. We're both low-carb.'

Oh, right. I'd forgotten about the low-carb thing.

'Which brings me to my little gift,' says Eric. 'Or, in fact, two gifts. This is the first one . . .' He reaches into the carrier bag and produces a laminated ring-bound booklet, which he hands to me with a flourish. The front cover reads: *Eric and Lexi Gardiner: Marriage Manual.*

'You remember the doctor suggested writing down all the details of our life together?' Eric looks proud. 'Well, I've compiled this booklet for you. Any question you have about our marriage and life together, the answer should be in there.'

I flip through the booklet. I can see sections on holidays, family, laundry, weekends . . .

'I've organised the entries in alphabetical order,' Eric explains. 'And indexed them. It should be fairly simple to use.'

I flip to the index and run my eyes down the page at random.

Tomatoes—pp. 5, 23

Tongs—see 'Barbecue'

Tongues—p. 24

Tongues? Immediately I start flipping to page 24.

'Don't try and read it now. You need to eat and sleep.'

I'll look up 'Tongues' later. When he's gone.

I finish the rest of the soup and lean back with a contented sigh. 'Thank you so much, Eric. That was perfect.'

'It's no trouble, my darling.' Eric removes the tray and puts it on the dressing table. As he does so, he notices my shoes on the floor. 'Lexi.' He flashes me a smile. 'Shoes go in your dressing room.'

'Oh,' I say. 'Sorry.'

'No problem. There's a lot to learn.' Eric comes back over to the bed and reaches into his pocket. 'And this is my other gift . . .' He produces a little jewellery box, made of leather. 'I'd like you to have something you actually *remember* me giving you,' he says with a rueful smile.

I prise it open—and find a single diamond strung on a gold chain.

'It's . . . it's amazing!' I stammer. 'I love it! Thank you so much!'

Eric reaches over and strokes my hair. 'It's good to have you home.'

'It's good to *be* home,' I reply with fervour.

Which is almost true. I can't honestly say this place feels like home yet. But it feels like a really swish five-star hotel, which is even *better*.

'Eric,' I say, a bit shyly. 'When we two first met, what did you see in me? Why did you fall in love with me?'

A reminiscent smile flickers across his face. 'I fell in love with you, Lexi,' he says, 'because you're dynamic. You're hungry for success, like me. People call us hard, but we're not. We're just intensely competitive.'

'Right,' I say after a slight pause.

'And I fell in love with your beautiful mouth.' Eric touches my top lip gently. 'And your long legs. And the way you swing your briefcase.' *He called me beautiful.* 'I'll leave you now. Sleep well. See you in the morning.'

He closes the door and I'm left alone with my necklace and my marriage manual and my glow of euphoria. I have the dream husband. He brought me Thai chicken soup and gave me a diamond and fell in love with the way I swing my briefcase.

I must have been Gandhi.

Three

I'VE BEEN FLICKING through the marriage manual ever since I woke up this morning—and it's totally, utterly riveting. I feel as if I'm spying on my own life. Not to mention Eric's. I know everything, from where he buys his cuff links to the fact that he checks his scrotum for lumps every month. (Which is a bit more than I bargained for.)

It's breakfast time, and we're both sitting in the kitchen. Eric's reading the *FT* and I'm consulting the index to see what I normally eat. But *Foreplay* looks a whole lot more interesting than *Food*.

Oh my God. He has written three paragraphs on foreplay! Under 'general routine': '. . . *sweeping, regular motion . . . normally clockwise direction . . . gentle stimulation of the inner thighs . . .*'

I splutter into my coffee and Eric looks up.

'All right, darling?' He smiles. 'Is the manual helpful?'

'Yes!' I flick to another section, feeling like a kid looking up rude words in the dictionary. 'Just finding out what I have for breakfast.'

'Gianna's left some scrambled egg and bacon in the oven,' says Eric. 'And you usually have some green juice.' He gestures at a jug of what looks like sludgy marsh-water on the counter. 'It's a vitamin drink.'

I suppress a shudder. 'I think I'll give that a miss today.' I take some egg and bacon and try to quell my longing for toast to go with it.

'Your new car should be delivered later on. Although I'm guessing you won't want to drive in a hurry. You can't yet, anyway, until you've retaken your driving test.' He wipes his mouth with a linen napkin and gets up. 'There's another thing, Lexi. If you don't mind, I'd like to schedule in a small dinner party for next week. Just a few old friends.'

'A dinner party?' I echo, apprehensive.

'Gianna will do the catering, but if you're not up to it . . .'

'Of course I'm up to it!' I say quickly. 'I'm tired of everyone treating me like I'm an invalid. I feel great!'

'Well. In which case, that brings me to another subject. Work.' Eric is shrugging on his jacket. 'Obviously you're not up to returning full-time just yet, but Simon was wondering if you'd like to go into the office for a visit. Simon Johnson,' he clarifies. 'Do you remember him?'

'Simon Johnson? The managing director?'

'Uh-huh.' Eric nods. 'He called here last night. We had a good chat.'

'I didn't think he'd even *heard* of me!' I say in disbelief.

'Lexi, you're an important member of the senior-management team,' says Eric patiently. 'Of course he's heard of you.'

'Oh, right. Of course.' Simon Johnson knows who I am!

'We agreed it would be helpful for you to visit the office,' Eric is continuing. 'It might help bring back your memory—as well as giving reassurance to your department.'

'I think it's a great idea,' I say with enthusiasm. 'I could get to know my new job, see all the girls, we could have lunch . . .'

'Your deputy is standing in for you at the moment,' says Eric. 'Byron Foster. Just till you return, obviously.'

'Byron's my deputy?' I say incredulously. 'Byron used to be my boss!'

Eric taps something into his BlackBerry, then puts it away and picks up his briefcase. 'Have a good day, darling.'

'You too . . . er . . . darling!' I stand up as he turns to face me—and there's a sudden frisson between us. 'Would I normally . . . kiss you goodbye at this point?'

'You normally would, yes.' Eric sounds stiff.

'Right.' I nod. 'So . . . um . . .' I reach out for his waist, trying to appear natural. 'Like this? Tell me if it's not the way I normally do it . . .'

'Probably just one hand,' says Eric after a moment's thought.

'OK!' I shift one hand up to his shoulder.

Eric leans forward and his mouth brushes briefly against mine, and I feel . . . nothing. I was hoping our first kiss would trigger all sorts of sensations, but as he draws away I feel totally, one hundred per cent blank. I can see the anticipation in Eric's face and quickly search for something encouraging to say. 'That was lovely! Very . . .' I trail off, unable to think of a single word other than 'quick', which I'm not sure hits the right note.

'It didn't bring back any memories?' Eric is studying my face.

'Well . . . no,' I say apologetically. 'But, I mean, that doesn't mean it wasn't really . . . I mean it was . . . I feel quite turned on!'

'Really?' Eric lights up and he puts his briefcase down.

Oh no. No no no. Nooo. I cannot possibly have sex with Eric yet. One, I don't even know him, hardly. Two, I haven't read what happens after gentle stimulation of the inner thighs.

'Not *that* turned on,' I amend hastily. 'I mean, just enough to know . . . obviously we have a great . . . when it comes to the bedroom . . . um . . . arena . . .' *Stop. Talking. Lexi. Now.* 'Have a great day.'

'You too.' Eric touches my cheek gently, then turns and strides off. That was a bit close. I reach for the marriage manual and quickly flick to the 'F' section. I need to read up on Foreplay. Not to mention Fellatio, I suddenly notice. And Frequency (sexual).

This could take me a while.

Two hours and three cups of coffee later, I've read the manual cover to cover. I've learned that Eric and I often spend weekends away at 'luxury boutique hotels'. We enjoy watching business documentaries and *The West Wing*. Eric and I share a love of wine from the Bordeaux region. I'm 'driven' and 'focused' and 'work 24-7 to get the job done'. I 'don't suffer fools gladly', 'despise time-wasters' and am 'someone who appreciates the finer things in life'.

Which is kind of news to me.

The more I learn about twenty-eight-year-old Lexi, the more I feel like she's a different person from me. She doesn't just look different. She *is* different. She's a boss. She wears designer clothes. She knows about wine. She never eats bread. She's a grown-up.

How on earth did I get from me . . . to her?

On sudden impulse I get up and head into the clothes room. There have to be some clues somewhere. I sit down at my minimalist dressing table, and regard it. I mean, look at this, for a start. My old dressing table was painted pink and a total mess—all scarves, necklaces and pots of make-up everywhere. But this is immaculate. Silver pots in rows, a single dish containing one pair of earrings.

I open a drawer at random and find a pile of neatly folded scarves, on top of which is a shiny DVD marked *Ambition: EP1* in felt-tip. It's that programme Amy was talking about. This is me on the telly!

Oh my God, I *have* to see this. I hurry into the living room, eventually manage to locate the DVD player behind a translucent panel, and slot it in. I fast-forward until my face appears on screen—then press Play.

I'm all prepared to cringe with embarrassment but actually, I don't look that bad! My teeth have already been capped—although my mouth looks much thinner than it does now. (I have *definitely* had collagen implants.) I'm wearing a black suit and an aquamarine shirt and I look totally businesslike.

'I need to win this,' I'm saying to an off-camera interviewer.

Blimey. I look so *serious*. I don't understand it. Why did I suddenly want to win a reality business show?

'Good morning, Lexi!' A voice makes me jump out of my skin. I jab at Stop on the remote and turn round to see a woman in a flowery overall holding a plastic bucket full of cleaning things. 'You're up!' she says. 'How you feeling? Any better today?'

'Are you Gianna?' I say cautiously.

'Oh my Lord in heaven.' She crosses herself. 'Eric warned me. You're not right in the head, poor girl. Well, I am Gianna.' She hits her chest.

'Great! Er, thanks.' I move aside as Gianna starts flicking over the surface of the coffee table with a duster. I twist my fingers awkwardly. How can I just *stand* here, watching another woman clean my house?

'What would you like me to cook for dinner tonight?' she says.

'Oh,' I say, looking up in horror. 'Nothing! Really!'

I can't ask someone else to cook my supper. It's obscene.

'Nothing?' She pauses. 'Are you going out?'

'No! I just thought . . . maybe I'd do the cooking myself tonight.'

'Oh, I see,' she says, her face set. 'Well, it's up to you.'

Oh God. I've offended her. 'Actually, on second thoughts . . . maybe you could make a little something. Whatever *you* enjoy cooking!'

How am I ever going to get used to all this?

'Aiee! The sofa has been damaged! Ripped!' Gianna looks at me defensively. 'I tell you. Yesterday I left it in good condition, no rips . . .'

'That . . . that was me,' I stammer. 'It was a mistake. Please don't tell Eric. He doesn't know. I put the cushion over the rip. To hide it.'

Gianna stares at me for a few disbelieving moments, then her severe face creases into a laugh. She pats me on the arm. 'I'll sew it. Little tiny stitches. He'll never know.'

'Really?' I feel a wash of relief. 'Oh, thank God. I'd be so grateful.'

Gianna is surveying me with a perplexed frown, her broad arms folded across her chest. 'You're sure nothing happened when you bumped your head?' she says at last. 'Like . . . personality transplant?'

'What?' I give an uncertain laugh. 'I don't think so . . .' The door buzzer goes. 'Oh. I'd better get this.' I lift the entryphone. 'Hello?'

'Hello?' comes a guttural voice. 'Car delivery for Gardiner.'

'Sign here . . . and here . . .' The car-delivery man is holding out a clipboard. I scribble on the paper. 'Here's your keys, tax disc, all your paperwork. Cheers, love.' The guy heads out of the gates, leaving me alone with a silver Mercedes convertible. I dangle the shiny car keys in my fingers, feeling a frisson of excitement. Maybe I'll just check it over inside. In an instinctive gesture I hold out the key fob and press the little button—then jump as the car bleeps and all the lights flash on.

Well. I've obviously done that before. I open the door, slide into the driver's seat and inhale deeply. Wow. Now, *this* is a car. It has the most wonderful scent of new leather. The seats are wide and comfortable. Cautiously I place my hands on the steering wheel. The thing is . . . I *can* drive. At some stage I must have passed my test.

And this is such a cool car. It would be a shame not to have a go. Experimentally I push the key into the slot beside the steering wheel—and it fits! I rotate it forward cautiously, and a few lights pop on around the dashboard.

Now what? I survey the controls hopefully for inspiration—but none comes. But the point is . . . I *have* done it. It's like walking in heels, it's a skill that is locked away inside me. If I can just distract myself enough then maybe I'll find myself driving automatically.

Maybe I should sing a song, that worked before. 'Land of hope and glor-eee,' I begin tunelessly, 'mother of the freeee . . .' *Oh God.* It's working. My hands and feet are moving in sync, I don't dare register what they're doing. All I know is I've switched on the engine and pushed down one of the pedals and there's a kind of rumbling and . . . I did it!

Right. Collect yourself, Lexi. Handbrake. I know what that is. And the gearstick. Cautiously I release both—and at once the car moves forward. Hastily I press my foot down on one of the pedals, to stop it, and the car bucks, with an ominous grinding noise. Shit. That didn't sound good. I release my foot—and the car creeps forward again. I'm not sure I want it doing that. Trying to stay calm I press my foot down again, hard. But this time it doesn't even stop, just keeps going inexorably forward, heading towards an expensive-looking sports car parked opposite. In desperation I thrust both feet down again, hitting two pedals at once with a shrieking engine-breaking sound. Oh God, oh God . . .

Suddenly I notice a dark-haired man in jeans coming through the gates. He sees me gliding forward towards the sports car and his whole face jolts. 'Stop!' he yells, his voice faint through the window.

'I can't stop!' I yell back desperately.

'Steer!' He mimes turning the steering wheel.

The *steering wheel.* Of course. I'm a moron. I wrench it round to the right, and now I'm heading straight towards a brick wall.

'Brake!' The guy is running alongside me. 'Brake, Lexi!'

The handbrake, I suddenly remember. Quick. I yank it back with both hands and the car stops with a judder. My breaths are coming fast and hoarse; I'm never driving again. Never.

'Are you OK?' The guy is at my window. I jab randomly at the buttons on the door until the window winds down. 'What *happened*?'

'I . . . panicked. I can't actually drive a car. I thought I'd remember how to, but I've had amnesia, you see . . .'

I see the guy is just staring at me as if I'm talking a foreign language. He's got a pretty striking face, now I come to notice it. High cheekbones, dark grey eyes and slanted eyebrows gathered in a frown, with dark brown untidy hair. He's a bit older than me, maybe early thirties.

He also seems totally dumbfounded. Which I guess is not surprising.

'I was in a car crash, a few days ago,' I explain hurriedly.

'I know you were in a car crash,' he says at last. He has a very distinctive voice, dry and kind of intense.

'Wait a minute!' I click my tongue, suddenly realising. 'You called out my name. Do we know each other?'

A jolt of shock passes over the guy's face. 'You don't remember me?' he says at last.

'Um, no,' I say with an apologetic shrug. 'I'm sorry, I'm not being rude, I don't remember anyone I've met in the last three years. My friends . . . my husband, even.' I smile—but the guy doesn't smile back or express sympathy. In fact, his expression almost makes me nervous.

'Do you want me to park that for you?' he says abruptly.

'Oh. Yes, please. This is my brand-new car. If I'd crashed it, I can't even *think* . . .' I wince at the idea. 'My husband got it for me, to replace the other one. Do you know him? Eric Gardiner?'

'Yes,' he says after a pause. 'I know him.'

He signals to me to get out of the way and gets into the car. The next moment he's expertly reversed the car safely back into its parking spot.

'Thanks,' I say fervently as he gets out. 'I really appreciate it.'

'What did they say about the amnesia?' he says, suddenly. 'Have your memories gone for ever?'

'They might come back any time,' I explain. 'Or they might not. No one knows. I'm just trying to learn about my life again. Eric's being really helpful. He's the most perfect husband!' I smile again, attempting to lighten the atmosphere. 'So . . . where do you fit into the picture?'

There's no response at all from the dark-haired guy. He's shoved his hands in his pockets and his face is all screwed up, as though he's in pain. 'I have to go,' he says. 'Bye, Lexi.' He turns on his heel.

'Bye . . .' What a weird guy. He never even told me his name.

I'm going into work today. I stare at myself in the huge mirror in my dressing room. 2004-Lexi used to pitch up at the office in a pair of black trousers from Next. Not any more. I'm wearing a black suit with a pencil skirt and a nipped-in waist. My hair is blow-dried and twisted up into my signature chignon. I look like an illustration from a child's picture book. Boss Lady.

Eric comes into the room. 'All set?'

'I guess!' I pick up my black Bottega Veneta tote bag.

I tried asking Eric about Fi yesterday, but he barely seemed to know who she was, even though she's my oldest friend—we met at the age of six. It's so weird that she hasn't been in touch. I've texted her several more times since I got out of hospital. I've sent a few jokey emails and even written thanking her for the flowers. But I haven't heard a word back. Anyway, I'll see her today, and there'll be some explanation. I expect we'll all go out for a drink at lunchtime and have a catch-up.

Deller Carpets is the company everyone remembers from the TV ads back in the eighties. The first one showed a woman lying on some blue-swirling-patterned carpet in a shop, pretending it was so soft and luxurious she immediately had to have sex on it with the nerdy sales assistant. Then there was the follow-up ad where she married the nerdy assistant and had the whole aisle carpeted in flowery Deller Carpet. And then they had twins, who couldn't sleep unless they had blue and pink Deller Carpet in their cots. They were pretty tacky ads, but they did make Deller Carpets a household name. Which is part of its trouble. The company tried to change its name a few years ago, to just Deller. There was a new logo and mission statement and everything. But nobody takes any notice of that. You say you work at Deller and they frown, and then say 'You mean, Deller Carpets?'

It's even more ironic because carpets is only a fraction of the company these days. They expanded into all sorts of cleaning products and gadgets, and now the mail-order business is huge. So are soft furnishings and fabrics. But poor old carpets have fallen by the wayside. Trouble is, they're not cool these days, carpets. It's all slate and laminate wood flooring. We do sell laminate flooring—but hardly anyone realises we do, because they think we're still called Deller Carpets. It's like one big vicious circle that always leads back to shagpile.

I know carpets aren't cool. And I know patterned carpets are even less cool. But secretly, I really love them. Especially all the old retro designs from the seventies. I've got an old pattern book on my desk and once I found a whole box of old samples at the warehouse. No one wanted them, so I took them back to the office and pinned them up on the wall next to my desk.

That's to say, my old desk. I guess I've been upgraded now. As I head towards the familiar building on Victoria Palace Road, I feel a fizz of anticipation in my stomach. I push open the glass doors to reception— and stop in surprise. The foyer is different. It looks really cool!

'Lexi!' A plump woman in a pink shirt and tapered black trousers is bustling towards me. I know her . . . head of human resources . . .

'Dana.' I gasp the name in relief. 'Hi.'

'Lexi.' She holds out a hand to shake mine. 'Welcome back! You poor thing! Come this way . . . I thought we could have a short chat in my office, pop in on the budget meeting, and then see your department!'

'Great! Good idea.' *My department.* I used to just have a desk.

We travel up in the lift, get out at the second floor and Dana ushers me into her office. 'Take a seat.' She pulls out a plushy chair and sits down at her desk. 'So now, obviously, we need to talk about your . . . *condition.*' She lowers her voice discreetly as though I have some embarrassing ailment. 'Is this amnesia permanent or temporary?'

'The doctors said I might start remembering things at any time.'

'Marvellous!' Her face brightens. 'Obviously, from *our* point of view it would be great if you could remember everything by the 21st Sales conference!' she adds, giving me an expectant look.

'Right,' I say after a pause. 'I'll do my best.'

'You can't do better than that!' She trills with laughter and pushes back her chair. 'Now, let's go and say hello to Simon and the others. You remember Simon Johnson, the MD?'

'Of course!' How could I not remember the boss of the whole company? Trying to conceal my nerves, I follow Dana up in the lift again to the eighth floor. She leads me briskly to the boardroom, knocks on the heavy door and pushes it open.

'Sorry to interrupt! Only Lexi's popped in for a visit.'

'Lexi! Our superstar!' Simon Johnson comes over, clasps my hand as if we're old friends and kisses my cheek. 'How are you feeling?'

The MD of the whole company just *kissed* me.

'Er . . . fine thanks!' I try to keep my composure. 'Much better.'

I glance around the room, taking in a whole bunch of other high-powered company people in suits. Byron, who used to be my direct boss, is sitting on the other side of the conference table. He's pale and lanky with dark hair. He gives me a pinched smile and I grin back, relieved to recognise someone.

'You had quite a knock to the head, we understand,' Simon Johnson is saying in his mellifluous, public-school voice.

'That's right.'

'Well, hurry back!' he exclaims with mock urgency. 'Byron here is standing in for you very well.' He gestures at Byron. 'But whether you can trust him to safeguard your departmental budget . . .'

'I don't know.' I raise my eyebrows. '*Should* I be worried?'

There's an appreciative laugh around the table, and I notice Byron shooting me daggers. Honestly. I was only making a joke.

'Seriously, though, Lexi. I need to talk to you about our recent . . . discussions.' Simon Johnson gives me a meaningful nod. 'We'll have lunch when you get back properly.'

'Absolutely.' I match his confidential tone, even though I have no idea what he's talking about.

'Simon.' Dana steps forward discreetly. 'Lexi may have some problems with memory . . .'

'Lexi, I have every confidence in you,' says Simon Johnson firmly. He turns to a red-haired guy sitting nearby. 'Daniel, you two haven't met yet, have you? Daniel is our new finance controller. Daniel, you might have seen Lexi on television? This young woman has had the most meteoric rise through this company. From junior sales associate to director of her department within eighteen months. She's a natural leader. She's inspirational. She has some exciting strategic visions for the future . . . This is a very, *very* talented member of the company.' As he finishes, Simon is beaming at me.

I'm in a state of total shock. My face is puce; my legs are wobbling. No one's ever spoken about me like that. Ever, in my whole life.

'Well . . . thanks!' I stutter at last.

'Can we tempt you to stay for the budget meeting?'

'Er . . .' I glance at Dana for help.

'She's not staying long today, Simon,' says Dana. 'We're popping down to Flooring now.'

'Of course.' Simon Johnson nods. 'Well, you're missing a treat. Everyone loves a budget meeting.' His eyes crinkle with humour.

'Don't you realise I *did* this to avoid the budget meeting?' I gesture at the last remaining graze on my head and there's another huge laugh.

As Dana and I leave the boardroom I'm light-headed with exhilaration. I bantered with Simon Johnson. I have strategic visions for the future!

I just hope I wrote them down somewhere.

'So, you remember where the Flooring department is?' Dana says as we descend again in the lift. 'I know everyone's eager to see you.' Her phone gives a little chirrup. 'Oh dear!' she says as she glances at it. 'I should take this. Do you want to pop along to your office and I'll see you in there.'

I stride down the corridor. The Flooring department is just along to the left. And to the right is Gavin's office. I mean, *my* office. As I reach for the door handle, I see a girl of about twenty darting out of the main office. Her hands go to her mouth.

'Oh!' she says. 'Lexi! You're back!'

'Yes.' I peer uncertainly at her. 'You'll have to forgive me, I've had this accident, my memory's gone . . .'

'Yeah, they said.' She looks nervous. 'I'm Clare. Your assistant?'

'Oh hi! Nice to meet you! So I'm in here?' I jerk my head towards Gavin's door.

'That's right. Can I bring you a cup of coffee?'

'Yes, please!' I try to hide my delight. 'That would be great.'

I have an assistant who brings me cups of coffee. I have really, really made it. I step into the office. *Wow*. I'd forgotten how big this room was. It has a sweeping desk and a plant and a sofa . . . and everything. I'm the boss! I can't help laughing in euphoria as I swing round and jump onto the sofa. I bounce up and down a few times—then stop abruptly as there's a knocking on the door.

Shit. Catching my breath, I hurry over to the desk. 'Come in!'

'Lexi!' Dana bustles in. 'Clare told me you didn't even recognise her! This is going to be tricky. I hadn't quite appreciated . . .' She shakes her head, her brow creased. 'So you don't remember *anything*?'

'Well . . . no,' I admit. 'But I'm sure it'll all come back to me.'

'Let's hope you're right!' She still looks anxious. 'Now, let's go through to the department, reacquaint yourself with everybody . . .'

We head out—and I suddenly see Fi coming out of the Flooring office. She looks different from the way I remember her, with a new red streak in her hair and a thinner face, somehow. But it's her.

'Fi!' I exclaim in excitement. 'Oh my God! Hi! I'm back!'

Fi visibly starts. She turns, and for a few seconds just gapes at me as if I'm a lunatic. I suppose I did sound a bit overexcited.

'Hi, Lexi,' she says at last, eyeing my face. 'How're you doing?'

'I'm fine!' I say, my words tumbling out eagerly. 'How are you? You look great! I love your new hair!'

Everyone's staring at me now.

'Anyway.' I force myself to sound more composed. 'Maybe we can catch up properly later? With the others?'

'Uh—yeah.' Fi nods, without looking me in the eye.

Why is she being so off? What's wrong? Coldness clenches me round the chest. Maybe that's why she never replied to any of my messages. We've had some huge row and I just don't remember . . .

'After you, Lexi!' Dana ushers me into the main open-plan office. I can see Carolyn, and Debs, and Melanie and several others I know. They all look familiar . . . but three years on. Their hair and clothes all look different. Debs has super-toned arms and is tanned, as though she's just got back from some exotic holiday; Carolyn's wearing new rimless glasses and her hair's cropped even shorter than before . . .

'You all know that Lexi has been ill following her accident,' Dana is announcing to the room. 'We're delighted that she's back with us today for a visit. She's suffered a few side effects from her injuries, in particular amnesia. But I'm sure you'll all help her to remember her way around and give her a big welcome back.' She turns to me. 'Lexi, do you want to say a few motivational words to the department?' Her phone chirrups again. 'I'm sorry. Excuse me!' She hurries out to the corridor and I'm left alone, facing my department.

Come on. Simon Johnson says I'm a natural leader. I can do this.

'Hi, everyone!' I give a small wave around the office, which no one returns. 'I just wanted to say that I'll be back soon, and . . .' I flounder for something motivational. 'Who's the best department in the company? We are!' I give the air a little punch, like a cheerleader. 'F! L! O! R!—'

'It should be another O,' interrupts a girl I don't recognise.

'Sorry?' I stop, breathless.

'There's a double O in Flooring.' She rolls her eyes. Two girls next to her are giggling, while Carolyn and Debs are just gaping at me.

'Right,' I say, flustered. 'Anyway . . . well done, everybody . . .'

'So are you back now, Lexi?' demands a girl in red.

'Not exactly—'

'Only I need my expenses form signed, urgently.'

'Have you spoken to Simon about our targets?' Melanie is coming forward, frowning. 'Only they're totally unworkable as they are—'

'Have we sorted the Thorne Group order?'

Suddenly everyone in the room seems to be swarming towards me, asking questions. 'I don't know!' I'm saying desperately. 'I'm sorry, I can't remember . . . I'll see you later!' Breathing hard, I back out across the corridor and into my own office and slam the door.

Shit. What was all that about?

There's a knock at the door. 'Hello?' I call out, my voice strangled.

'Hi!' says Clare, coming in under a vast pile of letters and documents. 'While you're here, could you just have a quick run-through of these? You need to get back to Tony Dukes from Biltons and authorise the payment to Sixpack and some guy called Jeremy Northpool has rung several times, says he hopes you can resume discussions . . .'

'I can't authorise anything,' I say in panic. 'I can't sign anything. I've never heard of Tony Dukes. I don't remember any of this stuff!'

'Oh. Well . . . who's going to run the department?'

'I don't know. I mean . . . me. Look, leave all that with me.' I try to pull myself together. 'I'll have a read-through. Maybe it'll come back to me.'

'OK,' says Clare, clearly relieved. 'I'll just bring your coffee through.'

My head spinning, I sit down at the desk and pick up the first letter. It's about some complaint. 'Expect your immediate response . . .'

I turn to the next document. It's a monthly budget forecast for all the departments in the company. There are six graphs and a Post-it on which someone has scribbled, 'Could I get your views, Lexi?'

'Your coffee.' Clare taps on the door.

'Ah, yes,' I say, summoning a boss-like tone. 'Thank you, Clare.'

The minute she's gone I drop my head down on the desk in despair. How on earth do I do it? How do I know what to say and what decisions to make? There's another knocking at the door and I hastily sit up.

'Everything all right, Lexi?' It's Byron, holding a bottle of water and a sheaf of papers. Truth be told, I never got on with Byron.

'Fine! Great! I thought you were in the budget meeting.'

'We've broken for lunch.' His eye is running over the pile of papers on my desk. 'Have you decided what to do about Tony Dukes? Because Accounts were onto me yesterday.'

'Well.' I hesitate. 'Actually, I don't quite . . . I'm not . . .' I swallow, feeling colour sweep through my face. 'The thing is, I've had amnesia since my accident, and . . .' I trail off, twisting my fingers into knots.

Byron's face suddenly snaps in comprehension. 'Jesus,' he says. 'You don't know who Tony Dukes *is*, do you?'

Tony Dukes. Tony Dukes. I rack my brain frantically—but nothing.

'I . . . um . . . well . . . no. But if you could just remind me?'

Byron ignores me. He comes further into the room. 'Let me get this straight,' he says slowly. 'You remember absolutely nothing?'

All my instincts are prickling. He's like a cat prodding a mouse, working out exactly how weak its prey is. *He wants my job.*

'I don't remember *nothing*!' I exclaim quickly, as if the very idea's ridiculous. 'Just . . . the last three years is a bit of a blank.'

'The last three years?' Byron laughs incredulously. 'I'm sorry, Lexi, but in this business three years is a lifetime!'

'Well, I'll soon pick it all up again,' I say, trying to sound robust. 'And the doctors said I might remember everything at any time.'

'Or presumably you might not.' He adopts a concerned, sympathetic expression. 'That must be a great worry for you, Lexi. That your head will be blank for ever.'

I meet his gaze with as much steel as I can muster. *Nice try.* 'I'm sure I'll be back to normal very soon,' I say briskly.

'So what do you want to do about Tony Dukes?'

Fuck. He's outmanoeuvred me. There's nothing I can say about Tony Dukes and he knows it. I shuffle the papers on my desk. 'Maybe . . . you could make a decision on that?' I say at last.

'I'd be happy to.' He gives me a patronising smile. 'I'll take care of everything. You just look after yourself. Don't worry about a thing!'

'So!' Dana appears at the door. 'Are you two having a nice chat? Super!' She glances at her watch. 'Now Lexi, I have to shoot off to lunch, but I can see you out if we leave now . . .'

'Don't worry, Dana,' I say quickly. 'I'll stay on and read through some paperwork.' I'm not leaving this building without talking to Fi.

'Okey-doke.' She beams. 'Well, lovely to see you, Lexi, and let's talk on the phone about when you want to return properly.'

The two of them walk away, and I hear Byron saying, 'Dana, with the greatest respect to Lexi, she's *clearly* not fit to lead this department . . .'

Bastard. He didn't even bother waiting until he was out of earshot. I lift a paper at random from the heap in front of me and stare at it. It's something about insurance premiums. How do I *know* all this stuff, anyway? When did I learn it? I feel as if I've woken up clinging to the top of Mount Everest and I don't even know what a crampon is.

Heaving a huge sigh, I put the sheet down. I need to talk to someone. Fi. I lift the phone receiver and dial 352.

'Flooring department, Fiona Roper speaking.'

'Fi, it's me!' I say. 'Lexi. Listen, can we talk?'

'Of course,' says Fi in formal tones. 'Do you want me to come in now?'

My heart sinks. She sounds so . . . remote.

'I just meant we could have a chat! Unless you're busy . . .'

'Actually, I was about to go to lunch.'

'Well, I'll come too!' I say eagerly. 'Like old times!'

'Lexi . . .'

'Fi, I really need to talk to you, OK? I . . . I don't remember anything. And it's freaking me out a bit. Just hang on, I'll be out in a moment . . .'

I thrust down the receiver and grab a piece of paper. I scrawl, 'Please action all these, Byron. Many thanks, Lexi.' I know I'm playing into his hands. But right now all I care about is seeing my friends. I hurry out of my office and into the main Flooring department.

'Hi, Lexi,' says a nearby girl. 'Did you want something?'

'No, it's OK, thanks, I'm just meeting Fi for lunch . . .' I trail off. I can't see Fi anywhere in the office. Or Carolyn. Or Debs.

The girl looks surprised. 'I think they've already gone to lunch.'

'Oh, right.' I try to hide my discomposure. 'Thanks. I expect they meant to meet in the lobby.' I swivel on my heel, then walk as fast as

I can in my spiky shoes along the corridor—just in time to see Debs disappearing into a lift. 'Wait!' I cry out, breaking into a run. 'I'm here! Debs!' But the lift doors are already closing.

She heard me. I know she did.

I shove open the door to the stairs and clatter down. Are they avoiding me? What the fuck has gone on, these last three years?

I arrive at the ground floor and almost tumble into the foyer. I see Carolyn and Debs heading out of the main glass doors, with Fi just in front of them. 'Wait!' I pelt towards the glass doors and at last catch up with them on the front steps of the building. 'I thought we were going to have lunch together!' I say, panting.

There's silence. No one is meeting my eyes.

'What's going on? Fi, why didn't you return any of my messages?' None of them speaks. 'You guys.' I attempt a smile. 'Please. You have to help me out. I've had amnesia. Did we have a . . . a row or something?'

'No.' Fi shrugs.

'Well, I don't understand it.' I look around the faces entreatingly. 'Last I remember, we were best mates! Going out on a Friday night. We had banana cocktails, Loser Dave stood me up, we did karaoke . . . remember?'

'Look.' Fi sighs. 'That was a *long* time ago. Let's just leave it. You've had this accident, you're ill, we don't want to upset you . . .'

'Don't *patronise* me!' My voice is sharper than I meant. 'I need you to tell me the truth.' I look around the group in desperation. 'If we didn't have a row, what's wrong? What happened?'

'Lexi, nothing happened.' Fi sounds awkward. 'It's just . . . we don't really hang out with you any more. We're not mates.'

'But why not? Is this because I'm the boss now?'

'It's not because you're the *boss*—' Fi breaks off. 'If I'm honest, it's because you're a bit of a . . . snotty cow.'

'Total bitch-boss-from-hell, more like,' mutters Carolyn.

The air seems to freeze solid in my lungs. Bitch-boss-from-hell? Me?

'I . . . I don't understand,' I stammer at last. 'Aren't I a good boss?'

'Oh, you're great.' Carolyn's voice drips with sarcasm. 'You penalise us if we're late. You time our lunch hours, you do spot checks on our expenses . . . oh, it's a bundle of fun in Flooring!'

My cheeks are throbbing as though she's hit me. 'I can't be a bitch,' I manage at last, my voice trembling. 'I can't be. I'm your friend! We have fun together, we go out dancing together, we get pissed . . .' Tears are pricking my eyes. 'I'm me! Lexi. Snaggletooth. Remember *me*?'

Fi and Carolyn exchange looks. 'Lexi,' says Fi, almost gently. 'You're our boss. We do what you say. But we don't have lunch. And we don't go out.' She sighs again. 'Look, come along today if you want to . . .'

'No,' I say, stung. 'It's OK, thanks.' And I turn and walk away.

I'm numb with shock.

All the way home from the office, I sat in my taxi in a kind of trance. Somehow I managed to talk to Gianna about the dinner-party arrangements and now it's early evening and I'm in the bath. But all the time my thoughts have been circulating, round and round. *I'm a bitch-boss-from-hell. My friends all hate me.* Have I really turned into a bitch over the last three years? But how? *Why?*

The water is growing tepid and at last I heave myself out. It's already six, and in an hour I have to host a dinner party.

I wrap a towel around myself and pad into the bedroom—then double back into the dressing room for my clothes. Jeez Louise. I know why rich people are so thin: it's from trekking round their humungous houses.

I pick out a little black dress and some black satin shoes. As I trail back into the bedroom I let my towel drop onto the floor.

'Hi, Lexi!'

'*Aargh!*' I jump in fright. The big screen at the base of the bed has lit up with a huge image of Eric's face. I clap my hands over my chest and duck behind a chair. 'Eric, can you see me?' I say in a high-pitched voice.

'Not right now.' He laughs. 'Put the setting to "Camera".'

'Oh! OK!' I say in relief. 'Just give me a sec . . .'

I sling on a dressing gown, then quickly start gathering the clothes I've dropped about the room. Eric doesn't like things lying around. Or basically any kind of mess at all. I shove them all under the duvet.

'Ready!' I head to the screen and swivel the dial to 'Camera'.

'Move back,' instructs Eric. 'Now I can see you! I've got one more meeting, then I'll be on my way home. Is everything set up for dinner?'

'I think so!'

'Excellent.' His huge pixellated mouth spreads in a jerky beam. 'And how was work?'

'It was great!' Somehow I manage a cheerful tone. 'I saw Simon Johnson and all my department, and my friends . . .' I trail off. Can I even describe them as friends any more?

'Marvellous. I'll see you later, darling.'

'Wait,' I say on impulse. This is my husband. I may barely know him—but he knows me. If anyone can reassure me, it's him. 'Today, Fi said . . .' I can hardly bring myself to say the words. 'She said I was a bitch. Is that true?'

'Of course you're not a bitch.'

'Really?' I feel a pang of hope. Eric sounds so sure, I relax in relief.

'I'd say you were . . . tough,' he adds. 'You're focused. You're driven. You drive your department hard.' He smiles. 'Now, I must go.'

The screen goes dark and I stare at it, more alarmed than ever. Isn't 'tough' just another way of saying 'bitch-boss-from-hell'?

It's an hour later, and my spirits have risen a little. I've put on my new diamond necklace and I've had a sneaky little glass of wine, which has made everything look a lot better. So maybe I've fallen out with my friends; maybe Byron is after my job; maybe I don't have a clue who Tony Dukes is. But I can put it all right. And I'm still the luckiest girl in the world. I have a gorgeous husband, a wonderful marriage and a stunning apartment. Tonight the place looks even more jaw-dropping than ever. There are arrangements of lilies and roses everywhere. The dining table has been extended right out and laid for dinner with gleaming silverware and crystal and a centrepiece like at weddings.

I carefully apply my Lancôme lipstick and blot it. When I've finished I step back and automatically the lights change from the mirror spot-light to more of an ambient glow. The 'intelligent lighting' in this room is like magic: it works out where you are from heat sensors and then adjusts accordingly. I quite like trying to catch it out by running round the room and shouting 'Ha! Not so intelligent *now*, are you?' When Eric's out, obviously.

'Darling!' I jump, and turn to see him standing at the door, in his business suit. 'You look wonderful,' he declares.

'Thanks!' I glow with pleasure, and pat my hair.

'One tiny thing. Briefcase in the hall. Good idea?' His smile doesn't waver, but I can hear the annoyance in his voice.

Shit. 'I'll move it,' I say hastily. 'Sorry.'

'Good.' He nods. 'But first, taste this.' He hands me a glass of ruby-red wine. 'It's the Château Branaire-Ducru. I'd like your opinion.'

'Right.' I try to sound confident. 'Absolutely.'

Cautiously I take a mouthful, racking my brain for all the wine-buff words I can think of. OK, I'll say it's a full-bodied vintage with hints of strawberries. I swallow the mouthful and nod knowledgeably at Eric.

'You know, I think this is a div—'

'It's shocking, isn't it?' Eric cuts me off. 'Corked. Totally off.'

Off? 'Oh! Er . . . yes!' I regain my composure. 'Urggh.' I make a face.

That was a close shave. I put the glass down on a side table and the intelligent lighting adjusts again.

'Eric,' I say, trying not to give away my exasperation. 'Can we have a lighting mix which just stays the same all night? I don't know if that's possible—'

'*Anything* is possible.' Eric sounds a bit offended. 'We have infinite choice. That's what loft-style living is all about.' He passes me a remote control. 'Here. You can override the system with this. Pick a mood.'

I head into the sitting room, find 'Lighting' on the remote and start experimenting with moods. 'Daylight' is too bright. 'Cinema' is too dark. I scroll much further down. 'Disco' . . . Hey. We have disco lights? I press the remote—and laugh out loud as the room is suddenly filled with pulsating, multicoloured light beams. Now let's try 'Strobe'. A moment later the room is flashing black and white and I gleefully start robotic dancing round the coffee table. This is like a club!

'Jesus Christ, Lexi, what are you *doing*!' Eric's voice pierces the flashing room. 'You put the whole fucking apartment on strobe light! Gianna nearly chopped her arm off!'

'Oh no! Sorry.' Guiltily I jab the remote until we're back on disco. 'You never told me we had disco and strobe lights! This is fantastic!'

'We never use them.' Eric's face is a multicoloured whirl. 'Now find something sensible, for God's sake.' He turns and disappears.

How can we have disco lights and never use them? What a waste! I *have* to have Fi and the others round for a party. And then my heart constricts as I remember. That won't be happening any time soon.

My plan for the dinner party was to memorise each guest's face and name using visualisation techniques. But this scheme disintegrates almost at once when three golfing buddies of Eric's arrive together in identical suits, with identical faces and even more identical wives. I sip my drink and smile a lot, and then about ten more guests arrive at once and I have no idea who anyone is except Rosalie.

After a bit my ears are ringing and I feel dizzy. Gianna is serving drinks and her niece is handing out canapés and everything seems under control. So I murmur an excuse and head out to the terrace.

I take a few lungfuls of clean air, my head still spinning.

'Darling! There you are!' I turn to see Eric pushing the sliding doors open. 'Let me introduce Jon, my architect.' Eric ushers out a dark-haired man in black jeans and a charcoal linen jacket.

'Hey!' I exclaim. 'You're the guy from the car.'

An odd expression flickers across the man's face. Almost like disappointment. Then he nods. 'That's right. I'm the guy from the car.'

'Jon's our creative spirit,' says Eric, slapping him on the back. 'He's the talent. I may have the financial sense, but this is the man who *brings* the world . . .' he pauses momentously, 'loft-style living.' As he says the words, he does the parallel-hands-sweeping-bricks gesture again.

'Great!' I try to sound enthused. I know it's Eric's business and everything, but that phrase 'loft-style living' is really starting to bug me.

Jon takes a sip of his drink. 'So, you still don't remember anything?'

'Nothing.' I shake my head.

'That must be strange for you.'

'It is . . . but I'm getting used to it. And Eric's really helpful. He's made me this book to help me remember. It's like a marriage manual.'

'A manual?' echoes Jon and his nose starts twitching. 'You're serious?'

'Ah, there's Graham. I must just have a word, excuse me . . .' Eric heads off inside, leaving me and Jon the architect guy alone.

'What's wrong with a marriage manual?' I hear myself demanding.

'Nothing.' He shakes his head gravely. 'It's very sensible. Otherwise you might not know when you were supposed to kiss each other.'

'Exactly! Eric's put in a whole section on—' I break off. Jon's mouth is crinkled up as if he's trying not to laugh. Does he think this is *funny*? 'The manual covers all sorts of areas,' I say rather stonily. 'And it's been very helpful for both of us. You know, it's difficult for Eric, too, having a wife who doesn't remember the first thing about him! Or perhaps you hadn't appreciated that?'

There's silence. All the humour has melted out of his face. 'Believe me,' he says at last, 'I appreciate it.'

Then the sliding doors open and Rosalie comes tottering over. 'Eric says dinner's about to begin.'

'Oh, we'd better go in. D'you two know each other?'

'Jon and I are *old* friends,' says Rosalie sweetly. 'Aren't we, darling?'

'See you.' Jon disappears through the glass doors.

'Awful man.' Rosalie makes a face at his departing back.

'Awful?' I echo in surprise. 'Eric seems to like him.'

'Oh, Eric likes him,' she says disdainfully. 'And Clive thinks he's the bee's knees. He's visionary and wins prizes, blah blah blah.' She tosses her head. 'But he's the rudest man I ever met. When I asked him to donate to my charity last year, he refused. In fact, he laughed.'

'He *laughed*?' I say, shocked. 'That's terrible! What was the charity?'

'It was called An Apple a Day,' she says proudly. 'I thought the whole idea up myself. The idea was, once a year we'd give an apple to every schoolchild in an inner-city borough. Full of lovely nutrients!'

'Er . . . great idea,' I say cautiously. 'So, did it work out?'

'Well, it started off well,' Rosalie says, rather crossly. 'We gave out *thousands* of apples and we had a van with an apple logo to drive about in. It was such fun! Until the council started sending us stupid letters about fruit being abandoned in the street and causing vermin.'

'Oh dear.' I bite my lip. The truth is, now *I* want to laugh.

As I find my place at the long glass dining table, nodding and smiling as people greet me, I feel like I'm in some weird dream. These people all know me. And I've never even *seen* them before.

'Ladies and gentlemen.' Eric is standing up at the other end of the table, and the chatter dies to a hush as everyone sits down. 'Welcome to our home. As you know, Lexi is suffering the aftereffects of her recent accident, which means her memory's not too hot.' Eric gives a rueful smile. 'So what I propose is that each of you reintroduces yourself to Lexi. Stand up, give your name, and maybe some memorable event that links you.'

'I'll start!' says Rosalie, leaping to her feet. 'Lexi, I'm your best friend Rosalie, which you already know. And *our* memorable incident was that time we both got waxed, and the girl got a bit carried away . . .' She breaks into a giggle, beams around the table then sits down.

'Right,' says Eric, sounding a bit taken aback. 'Who's next. Charlie?'

'I'm Charlie Mancroft.' A gruff man next to Rosalie stands up and nods at me. 'I suppose our memorable incident would be the time we were all at Wentworth for that corporate do. Montgomerie made a birdie on the eighteenth. Stunning play.' He looks at me expectantly.

'Of course!' I have no idea what he's talking about. Golf? Or snooker, maybe. 'Er . . . thanks.'

'Well done, Charlie!' Eric chimes in heartily. 'Jon? Your turn.'

Across the table from me, Jon gets to his feet. 'Hi,' he says in his dry voice. 'I'm Jon. We met earlier.' He lapses into silence.

'What's your memorable event involving Lexi?' prompts Eric.

Jon surveys me for a moment with those dark, intense eyes. At last he spreads his hands. 'Nothing comes to mind.'

'Nothing?' I'm slightly stung, despite myself.

'Anything at all!' says Eric encouragingly. 'Just some special moment the two of you shared . . .'

'I don't recall anything,' he says at last. 'Nothing I could describe.'

'Well, all right,' says Eric, sounding a bit impatient. 'Let's move on.'

By the time everyone round the table has stood up and recounted their anecdote, I've forgotten who the first people were. But it's a start, I suppose. Gianna and her niece serve dinner, and I talk to someone called Ralph about his divorce settlement. And then the plates are cleared, and Gianna is taking coffee orders.

'I'll make the coffee,' I say, jumping up. I've grown increasingly uncomfortable seeing her scurrying round the table with heavy plates. No one even looked at her as they took their food. And that awful man Charlie barked at her when he wanted some more water. It's so *rude*.

'Lexi!' says Eric with a laugh. 'That's hardly necessary.'

'I want to,' I say stubbornly. 'Gianna, sit down.'

Gianna looks perplexed. 'I'll go and turn down your bed,' she says.

I smile around the table. 'Now, who would like coffee? Hands up . . .' I start counting the hands. 'And anyone for mint tea?'

'I'll help,' says Jon suddenly, pushing his chair back.

'Oh,' I say, taken aback. 'Well . . . OK. Thanks.'

I head into the kitchen, fill the kettle and switch it on. Then I start looking in cupboards for cups. Meanwhile Jon is just pacing around the kitchen in some distant daydream, not helping at all.

'Are you OK?' I say at last, with a flash of irritation. 'I don't suppose you know where the coffee cups are, do you?'

Jon doesn't even seem to hear the question. He stops pacing and regards me, an even stranger expression on his face. 'You really don't remember? This isn't some kind of game you're playing with me?'

'Remember *what*?' I say, totally bewildered.

'OK. OK.' He turns and resumes pacing. At last he turns to face me again. 'Here's the thing. I love you.'

'What?' I look at him in confusion.

'And you love me,' he continues. 'We're lovers.'

'Sweetie!' The door bursts open and Rosalie's face appears. 'Two more orders for mint tea and a decaff for Clive.'

'Coming up!' I say, my voice strangled.

Rosalie disappears and the kitchen door swings shut. There's silence between us, the most prickling silence I've ever known.

'I . . . don't understand,' I say, trying to summon some composure. 'You're trying to tell me we've been having an *affair*?'

'We've been seeing each other for eight months.' His dark gaze is fixed on mine. 'You're planning to leave Eric for me.'

I can't stop a gurgle of laughter.

'You were about to tell Eric you couldn't be with him any more,' he says, speaking faster. 'You were about to leave him, we'd made plans— Then you had the accident.' His face is deadly serious.

'But that's ludicrous! I'm not the unfaithful type. Plus, I have a great marriage, a fantastic husband, I'm happy—'

'You're not happy with Eric.' Jon interrupts me. 'Believe me.'

'Of course I'm happy with Eric! I have the dream life!'

'The dream life? That's what you think?'

'Of course!' I swing my arms around the kitchen. 'Look at this place! Look at Eric! It's all fantastic! Why would I throw it all away—'

I break off abruptly as the kitchen door swings open.

'Sweetheart.' Eric beams at me from the doorway. 'How are those coffees going?'

'They're on their way,' I say, flustered. 'Sorry, darling.' I turn away to hide the blood pumping through my cheeks, and start spooning coffee messily into the cafetière. I just want this man to *leave*.

'Eric, I'm afraid I have to go,' says Jon behind me, as though reading my mind. 'Thanks for a great evening. Goodbye, Lexi. Nice to make your acquaintance again.'

'Goodbye, Jon.' Somehow I force myself to turn and present a hostessy smile. He bends forward and kisses me lightly on the cheek.

'You don't know anything about your life,' he murmurs in my ear, then strides out of the kitchen without looking back.

Four

IT CAN'T BE TRUE.

Morning light is creeping in around the blinds and I've been awake for a while, but I haven't got out of bed. Every time I replay the events of yesterday I feel giddy. I thought I was getting to grips with this new life of mine but now it's like everything is slipping and sliding away. Fi says I'm a bitch-boss-from-hell. Some guy says I'm his secret lover. What next? I discover I'm an FBI agent?

It cannot be true. End of story. Why would I ever cheat on Eric? He's good-looking and caring and a multimillionaire and knows how to drive a speedboat. Whereas Jon is scruffy. And kind of . . . spiky.

This Jon guy is probably a psycho. There's no evidence we're having an affair. None. I haven't seen any mention of him, no scribbled notes, no photos, no mementos.

But then . . . I'd hardly leave them around for Eric to find, would I? says a tiny voice at the back of my brain.

I lie perfectly still for a moment, letting my thoughts swill around.

Then inspiration hits me. Underwear drawer. If I was going to hide anything, it would be there. I get up and head into my clothes room. I open the wardrobe and pull open my knicker drawer. I reach down among the La Perla—but I can't feel anything. Nor in my bra drawer . . .

'Looking for something?' Eric's voice makes me jump. I turn my head to see him standing at the door, watching me search, and at once my cheeks stain pink. He knows.

No he doesn't. Don't be stupid. There's nothing *to* know.

'Hi, Eric! I just thought I'd look for . . . some bras!'

OK, this is the main reason why I can't be having an affair. I'm the most crap liar in the world. Why would I need 'some bras'? Do I suddenly have six boobs?

'Actually, I was wondering,' I continue hastily. 'Is there any more of my stuff anywhere? Letters, diaries, that kind of thing?'

'There's your desk in the office. That's where you keep all your files.'

'Of course.' I thought the office was more Eric's domain than mine.

'It was a marvellous evening last night, I thought.' Eric comes into the room. 'Bravo, darling. You weren't too overwhelmed?'

'A little.' I shoot him a bright smile. 'There's still so much to learn.'

'Well, you know you can ask me anything about your life. That's what I'm here for.' Eric spreads his hands. 'Is anything on your mind?'

I stare back at him speechlessly for a moment. *Have I been shagging your architect, do you happen to know?* 'Well.' I clear my throat. 'Since you ask, I was just wondering. We are happy together, aren't we? We do have a happy . . . faithful . . . marriage?' I'm thinking I dropped in 'faithful' quite subtly there, but Eric's keen ears pick it up straight away.

'Faithful?' He frowns. 'Lexi, I would never *think* of being unfaithful to you. I can't even imagine how such an idea came to you.' He looks quite shocked. 'Has someone been saying otherwise?'

'No! I just . . . thought I'd ask. Just out of interest.'

I shut the bra drawer and open another at random. I should move away from this whole subject area. But I can't help it, I have to probe.

'So, um, that guy . . .' I wrinkle my brow artificially. 'The architect. He seems like a pretty good guy.' I shrug, trying to appear casual.

'Jon? Oh, one of the best,' says Eric firmly. 'He's been a massive part of our success. That guy has more imagination than anyone I know.'

'Imagination?' I seize on this. 'Like . . . a bit of a fantasist?'

'No.' Eric seems puzzled. 'Not at all. You'd trust Jon with your life.'

To my relief, the phone suddenly gives a shrill ring, before he can ask why I'm so interested in Jon. He disappears into the bedroom to answer and I shut the drawer. I'm about to give up on searching in my wardrobe when suddenly I see a concealed drawer at the base of the unit, with a tiny keypad located to the right.

My heart starts to thump. Slowly I reach down and punch in the pin number I've always used—4591. There's a tiny click, and the drawer opens. I gingerly stretch out my hand and clasp something hard . . .

It's a whip.

I'm too gobsmacked to move. Am I now a fetishist who goes to S&M bars? Suddenly I can feel eyes on me and turn to see Eric in the doorway. His gaze falls on the whip and he raises his eyebrows quizzically.

'Oh!' I say, starting in panic. 'I just found that! I didn't know . . .'

'You'd better not leave that around for Gianna to find.'

I stare back, my befuddled brain working overtime. Eric knows about the whip. He's smiling. That therefore would mean . . .

No. Way. No way no way no way.

'This wasn't in the manual, Eric!' My voice is shrill.

'Not everything's in the manual.' His eyes twinkle.

OK, this is changing the rules. I thought *everything* was supposed to be in the manual. I glance at the whip nervously. So . . . what happens? Do I whip him? Or does he—No. I can't think about it any more. I shove it back in the drawer and bang it shut, my hands sweaty.

'That's right.' Eric gives me a tiny wink. 'Keep it safe. See you later.' He heads out and a few moments later I hear the front door bang.

I think I might need a small vodka.

In the end I settle for a cup of coffee and two biscuits that Gianna gives me from her private stash. God, I've missed biscuits. Mum's coming over to visit at eleven, but I have nothing to do till then. On impulse I head into the office. There's my desk, all spick and span with the chair pushed under tidily. I sit down and open the first drawer. It's full of letters, tidily clipped together in plastic files. The second is full of bank statements, threaded onto a piece of blue office string.

Jeez Louise. Since when did I become so *anal*?

I pull out the bank statements and flick through them, my eyes widening as I clock my monthly salary. Most of my money seems to be going out of my single account into the joint account I hold with Eric, except one big sum every month, going to something called 'Unito Acc'. I'll have to find out what that is.

I put the bank statements away and reach into the bottom drawer. It's empty apart from two scraps of paper. One is covered in my own handwriting, but is so abbreviated I can't make anything out. The other has three words in pencil scrawled across it: *I just wish*

I stare at it, riveted. What? What did I wish?

Mum has brought three of the dogs along with her. Three huge, energetic whippets. To an immaculate apartment full of immaculate things.

'The poor things looked so lonely as I was leaving.' She embraces one of them. 'Agnes is feeling rather *vulnerable* at the moment.'

'Right,' I say, trying to sound sympathetic. 'Poor old Agnes. Could she maybe go in the car?'

'I can't just abandon her!' Mum raises her eyes with a martyred air. 'You know, it wasn't easy organising this trip to London as it is.'

Oh, for God's sake. I knew she didn't really want to come today.

To my horror I notice one of the dogs is on the sofa grabbing a cushion in its jaws. Jesus. 'Mum, could you get that dog off the sofa?'

'Raphael won't do any harm!' says Mum, looking hurt. She lets go of Agnes, who bounces over to join Raphael and whatever the other one is called. There are now three whippets romping joyfully on Eric's sofa.

'Have you got any Diet Coke?' Amy has sauntered in behind Mum.

'In the kitchen I think,' I say distractedly. 'Here dogs! Off the sofa!'

All three dogs ignore me.

'Come here, darlings!' Mum produces some dog biscuits out of her cardigan pockets, and the dogs magically stop chewing the upholstery. One sits at her feet and the other two snuggle up beside her, resting their heads on her faded skirt. 'There,' says Mum. 'No harm done.'

I look at the mangled cushion. It's really not worth saying anything.

'There's no Diet Coke.' Amy reappears from the kitchen.

I look at her, suddenly distracted. 'Shouldn't you be at school?'

'I've been suspended.' With a swagger, Amy heads over to a chair, sits down and puts her feet up on the coffee table.

'*Suspended?* Why?' I look from her to Mum. There's silence. Mum doesn't appear to have heard me. 'Mum, *why?*'

'I'm afraid Amy's been up to her old tricks again,' says Mum.

'Old tricks? What did you do, Ame?'

'It was nothing! They so *totally* overreacted.' Amy sighs with exaggerated patience. 'All I did was bring this psychic into school. I charged ten quid each and she told all the girls they'd meet a boy tomorrow. Everyone was happy. Until some teacher found out.'

'Ten quid?' I stare at her in disbelief. 'No wonder you got in trouble!'

'I'm on my final warning,' she says proudly.

'Why? Amy, what else have you done?'

'Nothing much! Just . . . in the holidays I collected money for this maths teacher, Mrs Winters, who was in hospital.' Amy shrugs. 'I said she was on the way out and everyone gave loads.'

'Darling, it's extorting money under false pretences,' says Mum.

I'm trying to find something to say but I'm too gobsmacked. How did my sister turn from cute, innocent little Amy into . . . *this*?

'I need some lipsalve,' Amy adds, swinging her legs down off the sofa. 'Can I get some off your dressing table?'

'Um, sure.' As soon as she's out of the room I turn to Mum. 'What's going on? How long has Amy been getting into trouble?'

'Oh . . . for the last couple of years.' Mum doesn't look at me but addresses the dog on her lap. 'She's a good, sweet girl really, *isn't* she, Agnes? She just gets led astray. Some older girls encouraged her into the stealing, that really wasn't her fault . . .'

'Stealing?' I echo in horror.

'Yes. Well. She took a jacket from a fellow pupil and sewed her own name-tape into the back. But she really was very repentant.'

'But . . . *why*?'

'Darling, nobody knows. She took her father's death quite badly. That reminds me. I've got something for you.' Mum reaches into her bag and produces a DVD. 'This is the last message from your father. He did a farewell recording before the operation, just in case. It was played at the funeral. If you don't remember it, you should probably see it.'

I take the DVD and stare at it. 'It'll be like seeing him again. How amazing that he did a recording.'

'Well. You know your father. Always had to be the centre of attention.'

'It's fair enough to be the centre of attention at your own *funeral*.'

Again, Mum appears not to have heard. That's always her trick whenever anyone starts talking about a topic she doesn't like. She just blanks the whole conversation and changes the subject. Sure enough, a moment later she says, 'Maybe *you* could help Amy, darling. You were going to find her a work-experience placement at your office.'

'Work experience?' I frown doubtfully. 'I'm not sure about that.' My work situation is complicated enough right now without Amy flouncing around the place.

'Just for a week or two. You've done so well in your career.'

'Mum, I was wondering about that,' I say. '*Why* did I go on that TV show? Why did I become all hard and ambitious overnight? I don't get it.'

'I have no idea.' She seems preoccupied. 'Natural career advancement.'

'But it *wasn't* natural.' I lean forward, trying to get her attention. 'I was never a high-powered career woman, you know I wasn't.'

'Darling, it was all so long ago, I really can't remember . . . *Aren't* you a good girl? *Aren't* you the most beautiful girl in the world?'

She's addressing one of the dogs, I suddenly realise. She isn't even listening to me. Typical. I look up to see Amy approaching us.

'Amy, Lexi was just talking about you doing some work experience at her office!' says Mum brightly. 'Would you like that?'

'Maybe,' I put in quickly. 'There'd have to be some ground rules. You can't rip off my colleagues. Or steal from them.'

'I don't steal!' Amy looks stung. 'It was one jacket. *Jesus.*'

'Sweetheart, it wasn't just the jacket, was it?' says Mum, after a pause.

'Everyone thinks the worst of me. Every time anything goes missing, I'm the scapegoat.' Amy's eyes are glittering in her pale face. Suddenly I feel bad. I've judged her without even knowing the facts. 'I'm sorry,' I say awkwardly. 'I'm sure you don't steal. Come here.' I hold my arms out for a hug.

'Leave me alone,' she says, almost savagely. She backs away urgently.

'But you're my little sister!' I lean forward and give her a tight hug—then draw back almost immediately, rubbing my ribs. 'Ow! What the hell—You're all lumpy!'

'No, I'm not,' says Amy after a fraction of a beat.

'Yes, you are! What on earth have you got in your pockets?'

'Tins of food,' says Amy seamlessly. 'Tuna and sweetcorn.'

'Not again.' Mum shuts her eyes. 'Amy, what have you taken?'

'Give me a break! I haven't taken anything!' Amy yells. She throws her hand up in a defensive motion and two Chanel lipsticks fly out of the sleeve of her jacket. We all stare at them.

'Are those mine?' I say at last.

'Like you'd even *notice.*' She shrugs sulkily. 'You've got thousands.'

'Oh, Amy,' says Mum sorrowfully. 'Turn out your pockets.'

Shooting Mum a murderous glance, Amy starts unpacking her pockets. Two unopened moisturisers. A Jo Malone candle. A load of make-up. I watch her in silence, goggling at her haul.

'Now take off your T-shirt,' orders Mum.

'This is *so* unfair,' mutters Amy. She struggles out of the T-shirt and my jaw drops. Underneath, she's wearing an Armani slip dress that I recognise from my wardrobe, all scrunched up under her jeans, and about five La Perla bras round her middle.

'You took a *dress*?' I suppress a giggle. 'And *bras*?'

'You want your dress back. *Fine.*' She catches the expression on my face. 'It's not *my* fault. Mum won't give me any money for clothes.'

'Amy, that's nonsense!' exclaims Mum. 'You have plenty of clothes!'

'They're all out of date!' she yells instantly back.

I'm flummoxed by all of this. 'Amy, maybe we should have a little talk. Mum, why don't you go and make some coffee or something?'

When she's gone I sit down on the floor, across from where Amy has plonked herself. 'Amy, listen,' I say, in my best understanding-grown-up-sister-but-still-pretty-cool voice. 'You can't steal, OK? You can't extort money from people.'

'Fuck off,' says Amy, without raising her head.

'You'll get in trouble. You'll get chucked out of school!'

'Fuck,' says Amy conversationally. 'Off. Fuck off, fuck off, fuck off.'

'Look!' I say, trying to keep my patience. 'If you've ever got any problems, I'm here for you. Just call me, or text me, any time. We could go out for a . . .'

Amy's texting with one hand. With the other she has slowly moved her thumb and index finger into the 'Loser' sign.

'Oh, fuck off yourself!' I exclaim furiously, hugging my knees.

We sit there in grouchy silence for a bit. Then I reach for the DVD of Dad's funeral message and plug it into the machine. The huge screen opposite lights up and after a few moments my father's face appears. Dad's sitting in an armchair, wearing a red plushy dressing gown. His face is gaunt, the way I remember it after he got ill. But his green eyes are twinkling and there's a cigar in his hand.

'Hello,' he says, his voice hoarse. 'It's me. We all know this operation has a fifty-fifty chance. My own fault for buggering up my body. So I thought I'd do a little message to you, my family, just in case.'

He pauses. Suddenly there's a hard lump in my throat. I glance over at Amy. She's let her phone drop down and is watching, too, transfixed.

'Live a good life,' Dad is saying to the camera. 'Be kind to one another. Barbara, stop living your life through those dogs. They're never going to love you or go to bed with you. Unless you're *very* desperate.'

I clap my hand over my mouth. 'He *didn't* say that!'

'He did.' Amy gives a little snort of laughter. 'Mum walked out.'

'You only get one life, loves. Don't waste it. I know I've fucked up here and there. I haven't been the best family man. But I did my best. Cheers, m'dears. See you on the other side.' He raises a glass to the camera and drinks. Then the screen goes blank.

As I gaze at the blank screen I feel even more marooned than before. My dad's dead. I can never talk to him again. I can never ask him for advice. Not that you'd ask Dad for advice on anything except where to buy sexy underwear for a mistress—but still.

'That was a really nice message,' I say. 'Dad came good.'

'Yeah.' Amy nods. 'He did.'

The frostiness between us seems to have melted. I know things haven't gone that well between us today—but maybe in the past she's been my friend. My confidante, even.

'Hey, Amy,' I say in a low, cautious voice. 'Did we talk much before the accident? The two of us, I mean. About . . . stuff.'

'A bit.' She shrugs. 'What stuff?'

'I was just wondering, did I ever mention anyone called . . . Jon?'

'Jon?' Amy pauses. 'You mean the one you had sex with?'

'*What?*' My voice shoots out like a rocket. 'Are you sure?'

'Yeah. You told me at New Year's Eve. You were quite pissed.'

'What else did I tell you?' My heart is thumping wildly.

'All the gory details. It was your first time ever, and he lost the condom, and you were freezing to death on the school pitch . . .'

'School pitch . . .?' I stare at Amy. 'Are you talking about *James*?'

'Oh yeah!' She clicks her tongue in realisation. 'That's who I meant. James. Why, who are you talking about? Who's Jon?'

'He's no one,' I say hastily. 'Just . . . some guy. He's nothing.'

You see. There's no evidence. If I was really having an affair I would have left a trail. And the point is, I'm happily married to Eric.

It's much later that evening. Mum and Amy left a while ago, and now I'm in the car with Eric, zipping along the Embankment. He's having a meeting with Ava, his interior designer, and suggested I come along and see the show flat of his latest development, 'Blue 42'. All Eric's buildings are called 'Blue' and some number. It's the company's brand.

'Hey, Eric,' I say as we drive along. 'I was looking at my bank statement today. I seem to pay all this regular money to something called Unito. I rang up the bank, and they said it's an offshore account. Do you know anything about it?'

'No.' He shrugs. 'Not a bad idea, though, putting some of your money offshore. I just need to get some petrol.' Eric swings off the road into a BP station. 'I won't be a moment . . .'

'Hey,' I say as he opens the door. 'Could you get me some crisps in the shop? Salt 'n' vinegar if they have them.'

'Crisps?' He stares at me as though I've asked for some heroin. 'Darling, you don't eat crisps. It was all in the manual. Our nutritionist recommended a low-carb, high-protein diet.'

'I know. But everyone's allowed a treat once in a while, aren't they?'

For a moment Eric seems lost for an answer. 'Sweetheart.' He adopts a loving tone. 'I know how hard you've worked at reducing those two dress sizes. If you want to throw it away on a bag of crisps, then that's your choice. Do you still want the crisps?'

'Yes,' I say, a bit more defiantly than I meant to.

I see a flash of annoyance pass over Eric's face, which he manages to convert into a smile. 'No problem.' A few minutes later I see him walking back from the garage, holding a packet of crisps. 'Here you are.'

'Thank you!' As he drives off, I try to open the packet—but my left hand is still clumsy after the accident and I can't get a proper grip on the foil. At last I put the packet between my teeth, yank as hard as I can with my right hand—and the entire packet explodes.

Shit. There are crisps everywhere. All over the seats, all over the gearstick and all over Eric.

'Jesus! Are those in my *hair*?'

'Sorry,' I gasp, brushing at his jacket. 'I'm really, really sorry . . .'

The reek of salt 'n' vinegar has filled the car. Mmm.

'I'll have to have the car valeted.' Eric's nose is wrinkled in distaste. 'And my jacket will be covered in grease.'

'I'm sorry, Eric,' I say again, humbly, brushing the last crumbs off his shoulder. 'I'll pay for the dry-cleaning.'

We drive on a while in silence. Surreptitiously I eat a few crisps, which landed on my lap, trying to crunch them quietly.

'It's not your fault,' says Eric, staring ahead at the road. 'You had a bump on the head. I can't expect normality yet.'

I stiffen. OK, I may not be totally recovered. But I do know that eating one packet of crisps doesn't make you mentally ill. I'm about to tell that to Eric, when he signals and turns through a pair of electric gates that has opened for us.

'Here we are.' I can hear the pride crackling in his voice.

I stare up, totally overcome, forgetting all about crisps. In front of us is a brand-new white building. It has curved balconies and black granite steps up to a pair of grand silver-framed doors. A uniformed porter opens the door for us. The foyer is all palest marble and white pillars. This place is a *palace*. 'It's amazing. It's so glamorous!'

'The penthouse has its own lift.' With a nod to the porter, Eric ushers me to the rear of the lobby and into a beautiful marquetry-lined lift. 'There's a pool in the basement, a gym and a residents' cinema. Although of course most apartments have their own private gyms and cinemas as well,' he adds.

I look up sharply to see if he's joking—but I don't think he is.

'And here we are . . .'

I'm looking at the most massive room. No, *space*. It has floor-to-ceiling windows, a walk-in fireplace on one wall, and on another, a gigantic steel sheet down which are cascading endless streams of water.

'Is that real water?' I say stupidly. 'Inside a house?'

Eric laughs. 'Our customers like a statement. It's fun, huh? Ava?' He raises his voice and a moment later, a skinny blonde-haired woman in rimless glasses, grey trousers and a white shirt appears.

'Hi there!' she says in a mid-Atlantic accent. 'Lexi! You're up and about!' She grasps my hand with both of hers. 'You poor thing.'

'I'm fine, really.' I smile. 'This place is amazing! All that water . . .'

'Water is the theme of the show apartment,' says Eric. 'We've followed feng shui principles pretty closely, haven't we, Ava? Very important for some of our ultra-high-net-worths.'

'Ultra-what?' I say, confused.

'The very rich,' Eric translates. 'Our target market. Feng shui is vital for ultra-highs.'

Ava nods earnestly. 'Eric, I've just taken delivery of the fish for the master suite. They're stunning! Each fish is worth three hundred pounds,' she adds to me. 'We hired them.'

Ultra-high-whatevers. Fish for hire. It's a different world.

'Here you are.' Ava hands me an intricate scale model made out of paper and wooden sticks. 'This is the building. You'll notice I've mirrored the curved balconies in the scalloped edges of the scatter pillows.'

'Er . . . excellent! So, how did you think of it all?' I gesture at the water feature, which is now bathed in orange light.

'Oh, that wasn't me.' Ava shakes her head. 'My area is soft furnishings, sensual details. The big concept stuff was all down to Jon.'

I feel a tiny lurch inside. 'Jon?' I tilt my head, adopting the vaguest expression I can muster.

'Jon Blythe,' Eric prompts helpfully. 'The architect.'

'Jon, there you are!' Ava calls out. 'We were just talking about you!'

He's *here*? My hands clench involuntarily round the model. I don't want to see him. I don't want him to see me. I have to leave—

But too late. 'Hi Eric, Lexi.' He nods politely as he approaches—then stares at my hands. I look down and feel a jerk of dismay. The model's totally crushed.

'*Lexi!*' Eric has just noticed it. 'How on earth did that happen?'

'Jon.' Ava's brow crumples in distress. 'Your model!'

'I'm really sorry!' I say, flustered. 'I don't know how it happened . . .'

'Don't worry.' Jon shrugs. 'It only took me a month to make.'

'A *month*?' I echo, aghast. 'Look, if you give me some Sellotape I'll fix it.' I'm patting at the roof, desperately trying to prod it back into shape.

'Maybe not quite a month,' Jon says, watching me. 'Maybe a couple of hours.'

'Oh.' I stop patting. 'Well, anyway, I'm sorry.'

Jon shoots me a brief glance. 'You can make it up to me.'

Make it up to him? What does that mean?

'The apartment's very impressive, Jon.' I adopt a bland, corporate-wife-type manner, sweeping an arm around the space. 'Congratulations.'

'Thank you, I'm pleased with it,' he replies in equally bland tones. 'How's the memory doing?'

'Pretty much the same as before.'

'You haven't remembered anything new?'

'No. Nothing.'

I'm trying to stay natural—but there's an electric atmosphere growing between us as we face each other. I glance up at Eric. Can't he feel it? Can't he *see* it?

'Eric, we need to talk about the Bayswater project—,' says Ava.

'Lexi, why don't you look around the apartment while Ava and I talk?' Eric cuts her off. 'Jon will show you.'

'Oh.' I stiffen. 'No, don't worry.'

'Darling, Jon designed the whole building,' says Eric reprovingly. 'It's a great opportunity for you to find out about the company's vision.'

'Come this way and I'll explain the initial concept.' Jon gestures at the other side of the room.

Fine. If he wants to talk, I'll talk. I follow Jon across the room and we pause next to the tumbling streams of the water feature. How could anyone live with water thundering down the wall like this?

'So,' I say politely. 'How do you think of all these ideas?'

Jon frowns thoughtfully and my heart sinks. I hope he's not going to come up with a load of pretentious stuff about his artistic genius.

'I just ask myself, what would a wanker like?' he says at last.

I half laugh with shock. 'Well, if I were a wanker I'd love this.'

'There you go.' He takes a step nearer and lowers his voice beneath the sound of the water. 'So you really haven't remembered anything?'

'No. Nothing at all.'

'OK.' He exhales sharply. 'We have to meet. We have to talk. You'll notice the high ceilings, Lexi,' he adds in a much louder voice. 'They're a trademark feature of all our developments.'

'Are you crazy?' I hiss, glancing over to make sure Eric can't hear. 'I'm not meeting you! For your information, I haven't found a single piece of evidence that you and I are having an affair. Not one.'

'Lexi. It was a secret affair. *An affair which you keep secret.*'

'So you have no proof. I knew it.' I turn on my heel and stride away towards the fireplace, Jon following closely behind.

'You want proof?' I can hear him muttering in low, incredulous tones. 'What, like . . . you have a strawberry mark on your left buttock?'

'I *don't*—' I swivel round in triumph, then stop abruptly as Eric glances across the room at us. I wave at Eric, who waves back.

'I *know* you don't have a birthmark on your buttock.' Jon rolls his eyes. 'You don't have any birthmarks at all. Just a mole on your arm.'

I'm briefly silenced. He's right. But so what?

'That could be a lucky guess.' I fold my arms.

'I know. But it's not. Lexi, I'm not making it up. We're having an affair. We love each other. Deeply and passionately.'

'Look.' I thrust my hands through my hair. 'This is just mad! I wouldn't have an affair. Not with you or anyone. I've never been unfaithful to anybody in my life—'

'We had sex on that floor four weeks ago,' he cuts me off.

'Stop it!' I wheel round and stride away towards the far end of the space, where a trendy Perspex staircase rises to a mezzanine level.

'Let's take a look at the wet-room complex,' Jon says loudly, as he follows me up. 'I think you'll like it . . .'

We both reach the top of the staircase and turn to look over the steel balustrade. Beside me, Jon is sniffing the air. 'Hey,' he says. 'Have you been eating salt and vinegar crisps?'

'Maybe.' I give him a suspicious look.

'I'm impressed. How did you sneak those past the food fascist?'

'He's not a food fascist,' I say, feeling an immediate need to defend Eric. 'He just . . . cares about nutrition.'

'He's Hitler. If he could round up every loaf of bread and put it in a camp, he would. He'd gas them all. Finger rolls first. Then croissants.'

'*Stop* it.' My mouth twists with an urge to giggle and I turn away. This guy is funnier than I thought at first. And he's kind of sexy.

'What do you want?' At last I turn to face Jon, helpless.

'What do I want? I want you to tell your husband you don't love him and come home with me so we can start a new life together.'

'You're a total psycho.' I shake my head.

'I'm not a psycho,' he says patiently. 'I love you. You love me. Really. You have to take my word for that.'

'I don't have to take your word for anything!' I suddenly resent his confidence. 'I'm *married*, OK? I have a husband whom I love.'

'You love him? Right deep down here?' Jon thumps his chest.

I want to snap, 'Yes, I'm desperately in love with Eric' and shut him up for good. But for some reason I can't quite bring myself to lie.

'Eric's a fantastic guy, everything's wonderful between us . . .' I say.

'Uh-huh.' Jon nods politely. 'You haven't had sex since the accident, have you?' To my surprise he reaches for one of my hands. Then, very slowly, he starts tracing over the skin with his thumb. My skin is fizzing; his thumb is leaving a trail of delicious sensation wherever it goes.

'So what do you think?' Eric's booming voice heralds from below and I jump a mile, whipping my hand away. What am I *thinking*?

'It's great, darling!' I trill back over the balustrade. I draw back, out of sight of the floor below. 'Look, I've had enough,' I say in a swift under-tone. 'Leave me alone. I don't know you. I don't love you. I just want to get on with my life, with my husband. OK?'

'No! Not OK!' Jon grabs hold of my arm. 'Lexi, you don't know the whole picture. You're unhappy with Eric. He doesn't *understand* you—you can't throw us away.' He's scanning my face desperately. 'It's in there. It's all in there somewhere, I know it is.'

'You're wrong!' I wrench my arm out of his grasp. 'It's not!' I clatter down the stairs without looking back, straight into Eric's arms.

In the days since we got back from the show apartment, I've done noth-ing but immerse myself in the last three years. I've looked through photo albums, watched movies, listened to songs . . . But nothing's worked.

Yesterday I went to see that neuropsychologist, Neil. He said maybe it would help to write out a timeline, and I could go and see a therapist if I liked. But I don't need therapy. I need my *memory*.

'Lexi? I'm off.' Eric comes into the bedroom holding a DVD, out of its box. 'Darling, you left this on the rug. Sensible location for a DVD?'

'I'm sorry, Eric.' I take the disc from him. It's the *Ambition* DVD.

'Your taxi will be here at ten,' says Eric. 'I'm off now.'

I'm going back into work today, full-time. Not to take over the department—obviously I'm not ready to do that. But to start relearning my job; catching up on what I've missed. I head into the sitting room and slot the *Ambition* DVD into the player. I never did watch the rest of this. Maybe it'll help me get back into office mode.

'. . . Lexi and her teammates won't be taking it easy tonight,' a male voice-over is saying. The camera focuses in on me.

'We're going to win this task!' I'm saying in a sharp voice to the guys. 'If we have to work round the clock, we're going to win. No excuses.'

My jaw drops slightly. I've never spoken like that in my *life*.

'As ever, Lexi is taking her team to task,' says the voice-over. 'But has the Cobra gone too far this time?'

I don't understand what he's talking about. What cobra?

The picture now flashes to one of the guys. 'She isn't human,' he's muttering. 'There's only so many fucking hours in the day. We're all doing our best, you know, but does she fucking care?'

Now the picture cuts to a full, stand-up row between me and the same guy. He's trying to defend himself, but I'm not letting him get a word in. 'You're sacked!' I snap at last, my voice so scathing that I wince. 'You're sacked from my team!'

'And the Cobra has struck!' the jaunty voice-over adds. 'Let's see that moment again!'

Hang on a minute. Is he saying—*I'm* the Cobra?

To menacing music, a slow-motion replay has begun on screen, zooming right into my face. 'You're sssssacked!' I'm hissing.

I stare, light-headed with horror. What have they done? They've manipulated my voice. It sounds like I'm a snake.

'And Lexi's on top venomous form this week!' says the voice-over.

A different group of people in suits appears on the screen and starts arguing about a price negotiation. But I'm too shell-shocked to move.

Why didn't anyone tell me? Why didn't anyone *warn* me about this?

I'm a snake. No wonder everyone hates me.

As my taxi wends its way towards Victoria Palace Road, I sit rigid on the back seat, clutching three glossy gift bags—I've bought presents for Fi, Debs and Carolyn—giving myself a pep talk. Everyone knows the TV skews things. No one really thinks I'm a snake. Everyone's probably forgotten about that TV show—

Oh God. The trouble with giving yourself a pep talk is, deep down you know it's all bullshit.

The taxi deposits me outside the building and I make my way up to the third floor. As I step out of the lift the first thing I see is Fi, Carolyn and Debs, standing by the coffee machine.

'Hi, you guys!' I smile. 'I'm back again!'

'Hi, Lexi.' There's a general muted reply.

'You look really nice, Fi! That top's great.' I gesture at her cream shirt and she follows my gaze in surprise. 'And Debs, you look fab too. And Carolyn! Your hair looks so cool, all cropped like that, and . . .'

I'm gabbling with nerves. No wonder they all seem nonplussed. 'So, anyway.' I force myself to slow down a bit. 'I got you all a little something. Fi, this is for you, and Debs . . .'

'What's this for?' says Debs blankly.

'Well, you know! Just to . . . ' I falter slightly. 'Go on. Open them!'

Giving each other uncertain looks, all three start ripping at their wrapping paper.

'*Gucci?*' Fi says in disbelief as she pulls out a green jewellery box. 'Lexi, I can't accept—'

'Yes, you can! Please. Just open it, you'll see . . .'

Silently, Fi snaps it open to reveal a gold bangle watch.

'D'you remember?' I say eagerly. 'We always used to look at them in the shop windows. Every weekend. And now you've actually got one!'

'Actually . . .' Fi sighs. 'Lexi, I got it two years ago.' She lifts up her sleeve and she's wearing exactly the same watch.

'Oh,' I say, my heart sinking. 'Well, I can exchange it . . .'

'Lexi, I can't use this,' Carolyn chimes in, and hands back the perfume gift set I bought her. 'That smell makes me gag.'

'But it's your favourite,' I say in bewilderment.

'*Was*,' she corrects me. 'Before I fell pregnant.'

'You're *pregnant*?' I stare at her, overwhelmed. 'Carolyn, congratulations! I'm *so* happy for you. Matt will be the best dad ever—'

'It's not Matt's baby.' She cuts me off flat.

'It's not?' I say stupidly. 'But what . . . Did you two break *up*?'

They can't have broken up. It's impossible. Everyone assumed Carolyn and Matt would be together for ever.

'I don't want to talk about it, OK?' Carolyn says, almost in a whisper. To my horror I see her eyes have turned pink behind her glasses and she's breathing hard. 'See you.' She turns and strides off.

'Great, Lexi,' says Fi sarcastically. 'Just when we thought she'd finally got over Matt.'

'I didn't know!' I say, aghast. 'I had no idea. I'm so sorry . . .' I rub my face, feeling hot and flustered. 'Debs, open your present.' I've bought Debs a cross, studded with tiny diamonds. She *has* to love it.

In silence, Debs pulls off the wrapping. 'This is a cross!' Debs thrusts the box back at me, her nose wrinkled as though it smells of something rancid. 'I can't wear this! I'm Jewish.'

'You're *Jewish*?' My mouth hangs open. 'Since when?'

'Since I've been engaged to Jacob,' she says. 'I've converted.'

'Wow!' I say joyfully. 'You're *engaged*?' And of course now I can't miss the diamond ring on her left hand. Debs wears so many rings, I hadn't noticed it. 'When's the wedding?' My words spill out in excitement.

'Next month.' She looks away.

'Next *month*! Oh my God, Debs! But I haven't got—' I break off abruptly into a thudding silence. I was about to say 'But I haven't got an invitation.' I haven't got an invitation because I haven't been invited. 'I mean . . . um . . . congratulations!' Somehow I keep a bright smile plastered on my face. 'I hope it all goes brilliantly. And don't worry, I can easily return the cross . . . and the watch . . . and the perfume . . .'

'Yeah,' says Fi in an awkward voice. 'Well, see you, Lexi.'

They both walk off and I watch them go, my chin stiff from wanting to cry. Great work, Lexi. You didn't win your friends back, you just fucked up everything even more.

'A present for me?' Byron's sarcastic voice hits the back of my head and I turn to see him loping along the corridor, coffee in hand.

God, he gives me the creeps. *He's* the snake.

'Hi, Byron,' I say as briskly as I can. 'Good to see you.'

'It's very brave of you to come back, Lexi,' Byron says. 'Any questions, you know where I am. Although today I'll be with James Garrison most of the day. You remember James Garrison?'

Bloody bloody bloody. *Why* does he pick the people I've never heard of? 'Remind me,' I say reluctantly.

'He's head of our distributor, Southeys? They distribute stock around the country? They drive it around in lorries?'

'I remember Southeys,' I say cuttingly. 'Why are you seeing them?'

'Well,' says Byron after a pause. 'They've lost their way. If they can't improve their systems, we're going to have to look elsewhere.'

'Right.' I nod in as boss-like a way as I can. 'Well, keep me posted.' We've reached my office and I open the door. 'See you later, Byron.'

I close the door, dump my gift bags on the sofa, open the filing cabinet and take out an entire drawer's worth of files. Trying not to feel daunted, I sit down at the desk and open the first one.

Twenty minutes later, my brain is already aching. I've started a sheet of paper: *Questions to ask* and already I'm onto the second side.

'How are you doing?' The door has opened silently and Byron is looking in. Doesn't he *knock*?

'Fine,' I say defensively. 'I just have a couple of tiny questions . . .'

'Fire away.' He leans against the doorjamb.

'OK. First, what's QAS?'

'Our accounting system software. Everyone's been trained in it.'

'Well, I can get trained too,' I say briskly. 'And who's Services.Com?'

'Our online customer-service provider.'

'But what about the customer-services department?'

'All made redundant years ago,' says Byron, sounding bored. 'The company was restructured, loads of departments were contracted out.'

'Right.' I nod. 'So what about BD Brooks? What's that?'

'They're our ad agency,' says Byron with exaggerated patience. 'Jesus, Lexi, you're never going to pick all this up again.' Byron is surveying me pityingly. 'Lexi, face it. You're mentally ill. You shouldn't be putting your head under this kind of strain—'

'I'm not *mentally ill*!' I exclaim furiously, and get to my feet. I push roughly past Byron out of the door, and Clare looks up in alarm.

'Hi, Lexi. Did you want something? A cup of coffee?'

She looks terrified, as if I'm about to bite her head off. OK, now is my chance to show her I'm not a bitch-boss-from-hell. I'm *me*.

'Hi, Clare!' I say in my most friendly, warm manner. 'I just wondered if you'd like me to get you a coffee?'

'You?' She stares as though suspecting a trick. 'Get *me* a coffee?'

'Yes! Why not?' I beam, and she flinches.

'It's . . . it's OK.' She slides out of her chair, her eyes fixed on me as though she thinks I really *am* a cobra. 'I'll get one.'

'Wait!' I say, almost desperately. 'You know, Clare, I'd like to get to know you better. Maybe one day we could have lunch together . . .'

Clare looks even more poleaxed than before.

'Um . . . yeah. OK, Lexi,' she mumbles, and scuttles down the corridor. I turn to see Byron still in the doorway, cracking up.

'What?' I snap.

'You really are a different person, aren't you?'

'Maybe I just want to be friendly with my staff and treat them with respect,' I say defiantly. 'Anything wrong with that?'

'No!' Byron lifts his hands. 'That reminds me. There's one thing I left for you to deal with as director of the department. I thought it only right.'

At last. He's treating me like the boss. 'Oh yes?' I lift my chin. 'What?'

'We've had this email from on high about people abusing lunch hours.' He reaches into his pocket and produces a piece of paper. 'SJ wants all directors to give their teams a bollocking. Today, preferably.' Byron raises his eyebrows innocently. 'Can I leave that one to you?'

Bastard. *Bastard.*

I'm pacing about my office, sipping my coffee. I've never told anyone off before. Let alone a whole department.

I look yet again at the printed-out email from Natasha, Simon Johnson's PA.

Colleagues. It has come to Simon's attention that members of staff are regularly pushing the limit of lunchtime well beyond the standard hour. This is unacceptable. He would be grateful if you could make this plain to your teams asap, and enforce a stricter policy of checks. Thanks. Natasha

OK. The point is, it doesn't actually *say* 'give your department a bollocking'. I don't need to be aggressive or anything. I can make the point while still being pleasant. Maybe I can be all jokey.

Yes. That sounds good. Taking a deep breath, I head out of my office, into the main open-plan Flooring office.

'Hi, everyone!' I say, my face prickling. 'How's it going?'

No one replies, or even acknowledges that I've spoken. They're all just staring up with the same mute, get-on-with-it expression.

'Anyway! I just wanted to say . . . Are your lunch hours long enough?' And I roll my eyes to show I'm being ironic.

The girl at my desk looks blank. 'Are we allowed longer ones?'

'No!' I say hurriedly. 'I mean . . . they're *too* long.'

'I think they're fine.' She shrugs. 'An hour's just right.'

'Yeah,' agrees another girl. 'You can just make it to the King's Road.'

OK, I am really not getting my point across here. 'Listen, everyone! I have to tell you something. About lunch hours. Some people in the company . . . um . . . I mean, not necessarily any of *you* . . .'

'Lexi,' says Carolyn clearly. 'What the fuck are you talking about?'

'Look, guys.' I try to keep my composure. 'This is serious.'

'Seriousssss,' someone echoes.

'Very funny!' I try to smile. 'But listen, seriously—'

'Sssseriousssly.'

Now almost everyone in the room seems to be hissing or laughing or both. All the faces are alive; everyone's enjoying the joke, except me.

'OK, well, look, just don't take too long over lunch, OK?' I say desperately. No one's listening. All of a sudden a paper aeroplane hits me on the nose, followed by a rubber. In spite of myself, tears spring to my eyes. I turn and stumble out of the office. That was the single most humiliating experience of my life.

There's only one way to go. And that's to get really, really, *really* drunk. An hour later and I'm slumped at the bar at the Bathgate Hotel, round the corner from work, finishing my third mojito. Already the world has turned a little blurry—but that's fine by me.

'Hi.' I lift my hand to the barman. 'I'd like another one, please.'

The barman raises his eyebrows, then says, 'Of course.'

He puts the cocktail on a coaster and adds a bowl of peanuts, which I push aside scornfully. I don't want anything soaking up the alcohol.

'Do I look like a bitch to you?' I say. 'Honestly?'

'No.' The barman smiles.

'Well, I am, apparently.' I take another slug of mojito. 'That's what all my friends say. I have a car crash . . . and boom! I wake up and I'm trapped in the body of a bitch. You know, I'm not drinking to forget,' I add conversationally to the barman. 'I already forgot everything.' This suddenly strikes me as being so funny, I start giggling uncontrollably.

'I had one bang on the head and I forgot everything.' I'm clutching my stomach; tears are edging out of my eyes. 'I even forgot I had a husband. But I do!'

'Uh-huh.' The barman is exchanging glances with a guy sitting at the end of the bar.

'I'd get her a strong black coffee,' I can hear the guy saying in an undertone. Bloody nerve. I don't *want* a coffee. I'm about to tell him this when my phone beeps. After a small struggle with the zip of my bag I get my phone out—and it's a text from Eric:

Hi, on my way home. E

'That's from my husband,' I inform the barman as I put away my phone. 'You know, he can drive a speedboat.'

'Great,' says the barman politely.

'Yeah. It is.' I nod emphatically, about seven times. 'It's the perfect marriage . . .' I consider for a moment. 'Except we haven't had sex.'

'You haven't had sex?' the guy at the bar echoes in astonishment.

'We have *had* sex.' I take a slug of mojito and lean towards him confidentially. 'I just don't remember it.'

'That good, huh?' He starts to laugh. 'Blew your mind, huh?'

Blew my mind. His words land in my brain like a big neon light.

'You know what?' I say slowly. 'You may not realise it, but that's very sig . . . sigficant . . . significant.' If I have sex, maybe it'll blow my mind. Maybe that's just what I need! Maybe Amy was right all along.

I put my glass down. 'I'm going to have sex with my husband!'

'You go girl!' says the barman, laughing too. 'Have fun.'

As I ride home in a taxi I'm quite excited. As soon as I get back, I'll jump him. The only tiny snag I can think of is I don't have the marriage manual on me. And I can't *totally* remember the order of foreplay.

I close my eyes, trying to recall exactly what Eric wrote. OK. I think I have it. Buttocks first, then inner thighs, *then* scrotum . . .

'Sorry?' says the taxi driver.

Oops. I didn't realise I was speaking aloud. Anyway, it doesn't matter. What I can't remember I'll make up. I mean, it can't be that we do it *exactly the same way* each time, can it?

I let myself into the apartment and call 'Eric!'

There's no answer, so I head towards the office. I am quite pissed, to tell the truth. We'd better not try and do it standing up.

I arrive at the door of the office and look for a few moments at Eric, who's working at his computer. On the screen I can see the brochure for Blue 42, his new building. The launch party is in a few days.

OK, what he should do now is sense the charged sexual vibe in the room, and turn round. But he doesn't. 'Eric,' I say in my most husky, sensual voice, but still he doesn't move. Suddenly I realise he's wearing earphones. 'Eric!' I yell, and at last he turns round. 'Eric . . . take me.' I push a hand through my hair. 'Let's do it.'

He peers at me. 'Sweetheart, have you been drinking?'

'I may have had a couple of cocktails. Or three.' I nod, then hold on to the door frame for balance. 'The point is, they made me realise what I want. What I *need*. Sex.'

'Oooo-kay.' Eric raises his eyebrows. 'Maybe you should sober up.'

What's wrong with him? I was expecting him to leap on me. 'Come on.' I lift my chin in a challenging way. 'I'm your wife.'

I can see Eric's mind working as he stares at me. 'Well . . . OK!' He shuts down the document, turns off the computer, then walks over, puts his arms around me, and starts kissing me. And it's . . . nice.

It is. It's . . . pleasant. His mouth is quite soft. I noticed that before. It's a bit weird for a man. I mean, it's not exactly *unsexy*, but—

'Are you comfortable, Lexi?' Eric's breathy voice comes in my ear. 'Shall we move to the bedroom?'

'OK!' I whisper back.

In the bedroom, we resume kissing. Eric seems really into it. Now he's pulling me down onto the bed. I have to reciprocate. But with what? I'm going to go with . . . chest. Unbutton the shirt. Sweeping strokes. Clockwise.

'Are you comfortable with me touching your breasts?' he murmurs.

'I guess so,' I murmur back. Why is he squeezing me? It's like he's buying fruit. He's going to give me a bruise in a minute.

Anyway. Stop being picky. This is all great.

Ouch. That was my *nipple*.

'I'm sorry,' whispers Eric. 'Listen, sweetheart, are you comfortable with me touching your abdomen?'

'Er . . . I guess!' Why did he ask that? Why would I be comfortable with the breasts and not the abdomen? That doesn't make sense.

Eric's breath is hot on my neck. I think it's time for me to do something else. Buttocks, maybe, or—Oh, right. From the way Eric's hands are moving, looks like we're jumping straight to inner thighs. I'm about three steps behind on the whole foreplay thing. But Eric doesn't even seem to have noticed.

'Lexi, sweetheart?' he murmurs breathily, right in my ear.

'Yes?' I whisper back, wondering if he's about to say 'I love you'.

'Are you comfortable with me putting my penis into your—'

Uurk! Before I can stop myself, I push him off me and roll away.

Oops. I didn't mean to shove quite so hard.

'What's wrong?' Eric sits up in alarm. 'Lexi! What happened? Why weren't you comfortable? Was it some traumatic memory resurfacing?'

Oh God. He looks so earnest. I have to lie.

No. I can't lie. Marriages only work if you're totally honest.

'It wasn't because of a traumatic memory,' I say at last, carefully looking past him at the duvet. 'It was because you said "penis".'

'"Penis"?' Eric looks utterly stumped. 'What's wrong with "penis"?'

'It's just . . . you know. Not very sexy. As words go.'

Eric's brow knits in a frown. 'I find "penis" sexy,' he says at last.

'Anyway, it wasn't just that.' I hastily change the subject. 'It was the way you kept asking me if I was comfortable every two seconds. It made things a bit . . . over-formal. Don't you think?'

'I'm just trying to be considerate,' says Eric stiffly. 'This is a pretty strange situation for both of us.' Without meeting my eye he gets up. 'I think I'll take a shower.'

'OK.' Left alone, I slump back on the pillows. Great. I didn't have sex. I didn't remember anything. My mission totally failed.

I find 'penis' sexy. I give a sudden gurgle and clap my hand over my mouth in case he can hear me. Beside the bed the phone starts ringing.

'Hello?'

'Hi,' comes a dry, familiar voice. 'It's Jon.'

'Are you crazy?' I hiss in lowered, furious tones. 'What are you ringing here for? It's so risky! What if Eric picked up?'

'I was expecting Eric to pick up.' Jon sounds a bit baffled. 'I need to speak with him.'

'Oh.' I halt in sudden realisation. I'm so *stupid*. 'Oh . . . right.'

'But I need to speak with you more. We have to talk.'

'We can't! You have to stop this. This whole . . . talking thing. On the phone. And also not on the phone.'

'Lexi, are you pissed?' says Jon.

'No.' I survey my bloodshot reflection. 'OK . . . maybe a tad.'

There's a snuffling sound at the end of the phone. Is he *laughing*?

'I love you,' he says.

'You love the Cobra?' I retort sharply. 'You love the bitch from hell?'

'You're not a bitch from hell.' He's definitely laughing at me. 'You were unhappy. And you made some pretty big mistakes. But you weren't a bitch.'

Beneath my drunken haze, I'm absorbing every word. It's like he's rubbing salve on some raw part of me. I want to hear more. 'What . . .' I swallow. 'What kind of mistakes?'

'I'll tell you when we meet. Lexi, I've missed you so much . . .'

Suddenly his intimate, familiar tone is making me uneasy. What am I getting into here? 'Stop. Just stop!' I cut across him. 'I need to think.'

We could meet, and just talk . . . No. *No.*

'Eric and I just had sex!' I say defiantly.

I'm not even quite sure why I said that. There's silence down the line and I wonder whether Jon is so offended he's gone.

'Your point would be?' His voice comes down the line.

'You know. That changes things, surely.'

'I'm not following. You think I won't be in love with you any more because you had sex with Eric? Or you think having sex with him somehow proves you love him?' His voice is relentless.

'I don't know!' I say, rattled. 'I thought it might trigger my memories. I just keep thinking, maybe my memory's all there, all locked up, and if only I could get to it . . . It's so *frustrating* . . .'

'Tell me about it,' says Jon wryly, and I suddenly imagine him standing in his grey T-shirt and jeans, scrunching his face up in that way he does. The image is so vivid that I blink.

'Look, I have to go,' I say in a rush. 'I'll get Eric for you.'

Five

I'VE TRIED. I really have tried. I've done everything I can think of to show the department that I'm not a bitch.

I've put up a poster asking for ideas for a fun department outing— but no one's filled any in. I've put flowers on the windowsills, but no one's even mentioned them. Today I brought in a massive basket of muffins, together with a sign saying 'From Lexi—Help Yourself!!' and not a single one has been taken.

I turn a page in the file I've been reading, then click on the onscreen document. I'm working through paper files and computer files at the same time, trying to cross-reference everything. I'm tired. I mean, I'm *knackered.* I've been coming in every morning at 7 a.m., just to get through some more of this mountain of paperwork.

I nearly didn't come back here at all. The day after Eric and I kind of had sex, I woke up with the most crashing headache. I staggered into the kitchen, sat down and wrote out on a sheet of paper:

OPTIONS

1. Give up

2. Don't give up.

I stared at it for ages. Then at last I put a line through Give up. The thing with giving up is then you never know whether you could have done the job. And I'm sick of not knowing about my life. So here I am reading a debate on carpet-fibre cost trends, dating from 2005.

No. Come on. It can't be important. I close the file, tiptoe to my door and open it a crack. I can just glimpse the basket in the main office through the window. It's still intact.

I sit back down at my desk and open a recent financial report. After a few moments I lean back. These figures are just confirming what I already know: the department performance is terrible. We're going to be in real trouble if we don't turn things around. I mentioned it to Byron the other day, and he didn't even seem bothered. I make a note on a Post-it— 'Discuss sales with Byron'.

Why don't they want my muffins?

A tiny, sensible voice in my head is telling me to forget about it. But I can't. They must totally hate me. I mean, you'd have to loathe someone to refuse a muffin, wouldn't you? On impulse I leap to my feet again, and head into the main office.

'So!' I try to sound relaxed. 'Nobody want a muffin?'

'Muffin?' says Fi at last, her brow wrinkled. 'I can't see any muffins.'

Everyone shrugs, as though equally baffled.

'They do muffins at Starbucks. I could send out if you like,' says Debs, barely hiding her giggles.

Ha ha. Really funny. 'Fine! Just forget it.' Breathing hard, I stalk out again. I can hear the sniggers behind me, but I try to block my ears. I mustn't rise, I mustn't react . . .

Oh God. I can't help it. How can they be so mean?

'Actually, it's not fine.' I march back into the office, my face burning. 'Look, I went to a lot of trouble to get these muffins, and now you're pretending you can't even *see* them . . .'

'I'm sorry, Lexi.' Fi appears blank and apologetic. 'I honestly don't know what you're talking about.'

Carolyn snorts with laughter—and something inside me snaps.

'*I'm talking about this!*' I grab a chocolate-chip muffin. 'It's a muffin! Well, if you're not going to eat it then I will!' I stuff the muffin into my mouth and start chewing it furiously. Huge crumbs are falling all over the floor. 'In fact, I'll eat all of them!' I grab an iced blueberry muffin and cram that in my mouth, too. 'Mmm, yum!'

'Lexi?' I turn and my insides shrivel up. Simon Johnson and Byron are standing at the door.

Byron looks as if he's about to burst with delight. Simon's regarding me as though I'm a crazy gorilla throwing its food around at the zoo.

'Simon!' I splutter muffin crumbs in horror. 'Um . . . hi!'

'A quick word, if you're not busy?' Simon raises his eyebrows.

'Of course!' I smooth my hair down, desperately trying to swallow my claggy mouthful. 'Come through to my office.'

'So, Lexi,' says Simon as I close the door. 'I just had a good meeting with Byron about June 07. I'm sure he's been filling you in on developments.'

'Sure.' I nod, trying to look as if I know what he's referring to. But 'June 07' means absolutely nothing to me.

'I'm scheduling in a final decision meeting for Monday. I won't say any more just now, obviously discretion is crucial . . . I know you've had reservations, Lexi. We all have. But really, there are no more options.'

What's he talking about? *What?*

'Well, Simon, I'm sure we can work it out,' I bluff.

'Good girl, Lexi. Knew you'd come round.' He raises his voice again, sounding more cheerful. 'Now, I'm seeing James Garrison later on, the new guy at Southeys. What do you make of him?'

Thank God. At last, something I've heard of.

'Ah yes,' I say briskly. 'Well unfortunately I gather Southeys aren't up to scratch, Simon. We'll have to look elsewhere for a distributor.'

'I beg to differ, Lexi!' Byron cuts in with a laugh. 'Southeys have just offered us an improved package.' He turns to Simon. 'I was with them all day last week. James Garrison has turned the place around.'

'Lexi, don't you agree with Byron?' Simon turns to me in surprise.

I swallow. 'I'm . . . I'm sure you're right, Byron.' *Bastard*. He has completely shafted me. On purpose. There's a horrible pause. I can see Simon regarding me with puzzled disappointment. 'Right,' he says at last. 'Well, I must be off. Good to see you, Lexi.'

'Bye, Simon.' I usher him out of my office.

'Hey, Lexi,' says Byron suddenly, gesturing at my bum. 'There's something on your skirt.' I grope behind, and find myself peeling off a Post-it. Someone's printed, in pink felt-tip: *I fancy Simon Johnson.*

I can't look at Simon Johnson. Byron snorts with laughter. 'Just the staff having a bit of . . . fun . . .' I crumple up the Post-it desperately.

Simon Johnson doesn't look amused. 'Right. Well, I'll see you, Lexi.'

He turns on his heel and heads away down the corridor with Byron.

After a moment I hear Byron saying, 'Simon, *now* do you see . . .?'

I stand, watching them go, still quivering in shock. That's it. My career's ruined. I walk back into my office, and sink into my chair. I can't do this job. I'm knackered. Byron's shafted me. No one wants my muffins. I bury my face in my arms and soon I'm convulsing with sobs.

'Hi.'

I raise my head to see Fi standing just inside the doorway. 'Oh. Hi.' I wipe my eyes roughly.

'Sorry about the Post-it,' she says awkwardly. 'We never thought Simon would come down. What did he say?'

'He wasn't impressed.' I sigh. 'But he's not impressed with me anyway, so what's the difference?' I tear off a bit of chocolate muffin, stuff it in my mouth and feel better. For about a nanosecond.

Fi is just staring at me. 'I thought you didn't eat carbs any more.'

'Yeah, right. Like I could live without chocolate.' I take another massive bite of muffin. 'Women need chocolate. It's a scientific fact.'

There's silence, and I look up to see Fi still gazing at me uncertainly. 'It's so strange,' she says. 'You sound like the old Lexi.'

'I *am* the old Lexi. Fi . . . imagine you woke up tomorrow and it was suddenly 2010. And you had to slot into some new life and be some new person. Well, that's what this is like for me. I don't recognise the new person. I don't know why she is like she is. And it's . . . it's hard.'

There's a long silence. 'Lexi, I'm sorry.' Fi's voice is so quiet, I barely hear it. 'We didn't realise. I mean . . . you don't *look* any different . . .'

'I know.' I give her a rueful smile. 'I look like a brunette Barbie.'

'Look . . .' She's chewing her lip. 'Why don't you have lunch with us?'

'That'd be nice.' I give her a grateful smile. 'But I can't today. I'm seeing Loser Dave for lunch.'

'Loser *Dave*? Why? Lexi, you're not thinking of—'

'No! I'm just trying to work out what's happened in my life during the last three years. Fi, do you know how it ended with me and Loser Dave?'

'No idea.' Fi shrugs. 'You never told us. You shut us all out. It was like all you cared about was your career. So in the end we stopped trying.'

'I'm sorry, Fi,' I say awkwardly. 'I didn't mean to shut you out. At least, I don't *think* I did. I'd better go.' I get to my feet.

'Hey, Lexi,' says Fi, looking embarrassed. 'You missed one.' I pull off another Post-it. It reads: *Simon Johnson: I would.*

'I so *wouldn't*,' I say, crumpling it.

'Wouldn't you?' Fi grins wickedly. 'I would.'

'No, you wouldn't!' I catch her eye and suddenly we're both laughing helplessly, like in the old days.

'God, I've missed you,' says Fi at last, still gulping.

'I've missed you too.' I take a deep breath, trying to collect my thoughts. 'Fi, really. I'm sorry for whatever I was like . . .'

'Don't be a sap.' Fi cuts me off. 'Go and see Loser Dave.'

Loser Dave's done really well for himself, it turns out. I mean, *really* well. He now works for Auto Repair Workshop in some senior sales role. As he emerges from the lift, he's all dapper in a pinstripe suit. I can't help exclaiming, 'Loser Dave! Look at *you*!'

Immediately he winces, and looks warily around the lobby. 'I'm David, OK?' he snaps in a low voice.

'Oh, right. Sorry . . . er . . . David.'

His paunch has disappeared too, I notice. He must be working out properly these days, as opposed to his old routine, which was five heaves of a dumbbell, followed by cracking open a beer and turning on the soccer. Now I look back, I can't believe I put up with him.

We head out of the office towards what Loser Dave calls a 'good local eaterie', and all the while he's on his phone, talking loudly about 'deals' and 'mill', his eyes constantly sliding towards me.

'Wow,' I say as he puts his phone away. 'You're really senior now.'

'Got a Ford Focus.' He casually shoots his cuffs. 'Company Amex.'

'That's great!' We've reached the restaurant, which is a small Italian place. We sit down and I lean forward. 'David,' I begin. 'I don't know if you got the message about why I wanted to meet up?'

'My secretary told me you wanted to talk over old times?'

'Yeah. The thing is, I had this car accident. And I'm trying to piece together my life, work out what happened, talk about our breakup . . .'

Loser Dave sighs. 'Sweetheart, is this really a good idea, dredging all that up again? We both had our say at the time . . .'

'But I have no idea what happened! I have amnesia. Didn't your secretary explain? I don't remember anything.'

Loser Dave stares at me, as though suspecting a joke. 'Fuck me.' He shakes his head as a waiter comes over, then goes through the rigmarole of tasting and pouring the wine. 'So you don't remember anything?'

'The last thing I remember is the night before my dad's funeral. I was in this nightclub, and I was really pissed off with you because you didn't turn up . . . and then I fell down some steps in the rain . . .'

'Yeah.' He's nodding thoughtfully. 'I remember that night. That's why we split up. You chucked me the next morning because I never turned up.' He takes a gulp of wine, visibly relaxing.

'*Really?*' I say, astonished. 'So, did we have a big row?'

'Not so much a row,' says Loser Dave after a moment's consideration. 'More like a mature discussion. We agreed it was right to end things. I offered to come along to your dad's funeral, show support, but you turned me down.' He takes another gulp of wine. 'I didn't bear you a grudge, though. I said, "Lexi, I will always care for you." I gave you a single rose and a final kiss. Then I walked away. It was beautiful.'

I put my glass down and survey him. His gaze is as open and blameless as it used to be when he conned customers into taking extra premium total-scam insurance on their cars.

'Loser Dave . . . is that *really* what happened?'

'Of course,' he says, injured. 'And stop calling me Loser Dave.'

'Sorry.' I sigh. Maybe he's telling the truth. Maybe I did chuck him. I was certainly pissed off with him.

'So, did anything else happen back then? Is there anything you can remember? Like, why did I suddenly get so career-oriented?'

'Search me.' Loser Dave is perusing the specials menu.

'It's all just so confusing.' I rub my brow. 'I feel like I've been plonked in the middle of a map, with one of those big arrows pointing, "You Are Here". And what I want to know is, how did I *get* here?'

'What you want is satnav,' Loser Dave says, like the Dalai Lama making a pronouncement on top of a mountain.

'That's it! Exactly!' I nod eagerly. 'I feel lost . . .'

Loser Dave is nodding wisely. 'I can do you a deal.'

'What?' I say, not understanding.

'I can do you a deal on satnav.' He taps his nose. 'We're branching out at Auto Repair.'

For a moment I think I might explode with frustration. 'I don't literally need satnav!' I almost yell. 'It's a metaphor! Me-ta-phor!'

'Right, right. Yeah, of course.' Loser Dave nods, his brow furrowed. 'Is that an in-built system?'

I don't believe it. Did I actually go out with this guy? 'Yeah, that's right,' I say finally. 'Honda make it. Let's have the garlic bread.'

As I arrive home later, I'm planning to ask Eric what he knows about my breakup with Loser Dave. But when I walk into the loft, I sense straight away that this isn't the moment. He's looking stressed. 'Come on, Lexi. We'll be late.'

'For what?'

'For *what*?' echoes Eric. 'For the launch!'

Shit. It's the Blue 42 launch party tonight. I did know that, it just slipped my mind. 'Of course,' I say hurriedly. 'I'll just go and get ready.'

In a total fluster, I change into a black silk tailored suit, put on my highest black pumps, and quickly shove my hair up into its chignon. I accessorise with diamonds, then turn to survey myself.

Aargh. I look so boring. Don't I have any brooches any more? Or any silk flowers or scarves or sparkly hair clips? Anything *fun*? I root around for a bit in my drawers, but can't find anything.

'Ready?' Eric strides in. 'Let's go.' I've never seen him so tense before.

'I'm sure it'll go really well,' I say encouragingly.

'It has to. This is our big sales push. Lots of ultra-highs. Lots of press. This is where we make Blue 42 into the talk of the city.'

As we turn into the entrance gates I can't help gasping. Burning torches lead the way to the front doors. Lasers sweep the sky. There's a red carpet for guests to walk down and even a couple of photographers waiting. It looks like a film premiere. 'Eric, this is amazing.' Impulsively I squeeze his hand. 'It's going to be a triumph.'

'Let's hope.' Eric gives me a quick, tight smile. 'Oh, Lexi, before I forget. I've been meaning to give you this.' He hands me a piece of paper.

'What's this?' I smile as I unfold it. Then my smile kind of melts away. It's an invoice. *Large Blown Leopard: quantity 1. To pay: £3,200.*

'I ordered a replacement,' Eric is saying. 'You can settle up any time. Cheque is fine, or just put a transfer into my bank account . . .'

He's *invoicing* me?

'You want me to pay for the leopard?' I force a little laugh.

'Well, you broke it.' Eric sounds surprised. 'Is there a problem?'

'No! That's . . . that's fine.' I swallow. 'I'll write you a cheque.'

It's fine, I tell myself firmly. It's fair for him to invoice me. *That's not how a marriage should work.* No. Stop it. It's fine. It's lovely.

I stuff the paper into my bag and follow Eric along the red carpet.

Bloody hell. This is a real, serious, glitzy party. The whole building is alive with light and thudding music. The penthouse loft looks even more spectacular than before, with flowers everywhere, and waiters in cool black outfits holding trays of champagne. Ava and Jon and a few other people I don't recognise are gathered by the window, and Eric strides straight over to them.

'People,' he says. 'Have we done the run-down on the guests? Sarah, you've got the press list? All under control? Let's sell this building.'

The next moment a couple in expensive-looking coats enter, and Eric springs into full charm-offensive, taking them over to see the view. More people are arriving, and soon there's a small crowd, chattering and leafing through the brochure and eyeing up the water feature.

Jon is about ten yards away, to my left, wearing a dark suit. All I'm aware of in this entire roomful of people is him. Where he is, what he's doing, who he's talking to. I dart a glance at him and he meets my eye. Cheeks flaming, I swivel right away so he's out of my sightline. Eric appears beside me.

'Lexi, darling, come with me.' Before I can stop him, he's leading me firmly over to Jon, who's talking to another rich-looking couple. 'Let me introduce my wife, Lexi.' Eric beams at them. 'One of the greatest fans of . . .' He pauses, and I tense up, waiting for it. 'Loft-style living!' If I hear that phrase one more time I'm going to *shoot* myself.

'Hi, Lexi.' Jon meets my eye briefly as Eric heads off. 'How are you?'

'I'm fine, thanks, Jon.' I try to sound calm. 'So . . . how do you like the loft?' I turn to the woman.

The couple exchange doubtful glances. 'We have one concern,' says the man, in a European accent. 'The space. Whether it is *big* enough.'

I'm stumped. This place is like a bloody aircraft hangar.

'You could knock two or even three units together if you need a larger space,' says Jon.

'Our other problem is the design,' says the man. 'At our home we have touches of gold. Gold paintings. Gold lamps. Gold . . .' He seems to run out of steam.

'Carpets,' the woman puts in, rolling the 'rrr' heavily.

The man jabs at the brochure. 'Here I see a lot of silver. Chrome.'

'I see.' Jon nods, deadpan. 'Well, obviously the loft can be customised. We could, for example, have the fireplace gold-plated.'

'A gold-plated fireplace?' says the woman uncertainly. 'Would that be . . . too much?'

'Is there such a thing as too much gold?' Jon replies pleasantly. 'And Lexi could help you with the gold carpet. Couldn't you, Lexi?'

'Of course.' I nod, praying desperately I don't suddenly snort with laughter.

'Yes. Well, we will think about it.' The couple move off.

Jon knocks back his drink. 'Not big enough. Jesus Christ. *Ten* of our units at Ridgeway would fit into this space.'

'What's Ridgeway?'

'Our affordable-housing project.' He sees my blank look. 'We only get planning for a place like this if we put up some affordable units.'

'Oh, right,' I say in surprise. 'Eric's never mentioned it.'

'I'd say his heart isn't totally in that aspect of the job,' Jon says, as Eric steps up onto a small podium in front of the mantelpiece.

'Welcome!' he says, his voice ringing out around the space. 'Welcome to Blue 42, the latest in the Blue series of projects, dedicated to . . .'

I hold my breath. Please don't say it, please don't say it . . .

'Loft-style living!' His hands sweep along.

Jon glances at me, and takes a step back, away from the crowd. After a moment I move back too, my eyes fixed firmly ahead. My whole body is crackling with apprehension. And . . . excitement.

Behind Eric, a massive screen is lighting up with images of lofts from all angles. Punchy music fills the air and the room becomes even darker. I have to hand it to Eric, this is a fantastic presentation.

'You know, we first met each other at a loft launch like this one.' Jon's voice is so low, I can barely hear it above the music. 'The minute you spoke I knew I liked you.'

Curiosity prickles at me. 'What did I say?' I whisper back.

'You said, "If I hear that phrase 'loft-style living' again, I'm going to shoot myself."'

'*No.*' I stare at him, then splutter with laughter.

For a few moments we watch Eric in a hard hat on screen, striding over a building site.

'You make no sense,' I say quietly. 'If you think lofts are for rich wankers, why do you design them?'

'That's a good question. I should move on. But I like Eric. He gave me my first chance, he runs a great company . . .'

'You *like* Eric?' I shake my head in disbelief. 'Of course you do. That's why you keep telling me to leave him.'

'I do. He's a great guy. He's honest, he's loyal . . . I don't *want* to fuck Eric's life up,' he says finally. 'It wasn't in the plan.'

'So why . . .'

'He doesn't understand you.' Jon looks directly at me.

'And you do, I suppose?' I retort, just as the lights come up and applause breaks out around the room. Instinctively I take a step away from Jon, and we both watch as Eric mounts the podium again.

'So, have you encountered Mont Blanc yet?' says Jon, clapping.

'What's Mont Blanc?' I give him a suspicious glance.

'You'll find out.'

'Jon! There you are. Emergency!' Ava appears behind us. 'The ornamental rocks for the master bedroom fish tank have only just arrived from Italy. But I've got to see to the kitchen place settings, so can you do it?' She shoves a hessian sack into Jon's arms. 'Just arrange the rocks in the tank before the presentation finishes.'

'No problem. Lexi, want to come with me and help?'

This is a challenge. I have to say no. 'Um . . . yes.' I swallow. 'Sure.'

We head into the main bedroom and Jon closes the door. 'So,' he says.

'Look.' My voice is sharp with nerves. 'I can't carry on like this! All this whispering, creeping around . . . I'm happy with Eric!'

'No.' He shakes his head. 'You won't be with him in a year. You'll try your best, you'll try to mould yourself . . . but your spirit's too free for him. In the end you won't be able to stand it any more.'

'Thanks for the warning,' I snap. 'We should do the rocks.' I jerk my head towards the sack, but Jon ignores me. He comes towards me, his eyes intense and questioning.

'All the time we spent together . . . there has to be *something* to trigger your memory. Do sunflowers mean anything to you?'

In spite of myself I rack my brain. Sunflowers. Didn't I once . . . No, it's gone. 'Nothing,' I say at last. 'I mean, I *like* sunflowers, but . . .'

He's so close I can feel his gentle breath on my skin. 'Does this mean anything to you?' He leans down and brushes a kiss against my neck.

'Stop it,' I say feebly, but I can barely get the words out. I want to kiss him. I want to kiss him in a way I didn't want to kiss Eric.

And then it's happening, his mouth is on mine and my entire body's telling me this is the right thing to do. He smells right. He tastes right. My eyes are closed, I'm losing myself, this is so right . . .

'Jon?' Ava's voice comes through the door.

I fly away from Jon, cursing under my breath, 'Fuck!'

'Sssh!' He looks thrown, too. 'Stay cool. Hi, Ava. What's up?'

Rocks. I grab the sack and start chucking rocks into the fish tank.

'Everything OK?' Ava puts her head round the door. 'I'm about to lead a party of guests up here for the tour . . .'

'No problem,' Jon says reassuringly. 'Nearly done.'

As soon as Ava disappears, he comes back to me. 'Lexi.' He grasps my face. 'If you only knew, this has been *torture* . . .'

'Stop it!' I draw away. 'I'm married! We can't—' I gasp. 'Oh shit!' I'm not looking at Jon any more. I'm looking at the fish tank.

'What?' Jon follows my gaze. 'Oh. Oops.'

All the tropical fish are swimming peacefully among the marble rocks. Except one blue stripy one, which is floating on top. 'I've killed a fish!' I let out a horrified giggle. 'I've brained it with one of the rocks.'

'So you have,' says Jon, going over to survey the tank. 'Nice aim.'

'What am I going to do? The guests will be in here any moment!'

Jon grins. 'OK, I'll go and delay Ava. You flush it away.' He holds my hand a moment. 'We haven't finished.' He heads out of the room, leaving me to reach into the warm water, wincing, and pick up the fish.

I hurry into the high-tech bathroom. I drop the fish in the loo and look for the flush. There isn't one. This must be an intelligent loo.

'Flush,' I say aloud, waving my arms to set off the sensors. 'Flush!'

Nothing happens.

This cannot be happening. If anything is going to put a customer off a high-end, luxury apartment, it's a dead fish in the loo. I pull out my phone from my pocket and scroll down the Contacts until I find J. That must be him. I press speed-dial and a moment later, he answers.

'The fish is in the loo!' I hiss. 'But I can't flush it!'

'The sensors should set it off automatically.'

'I know! But they're not. What am I going to do?'

'Go to the panel next to the bed. You can override it and flush it from there. Hey, Eric! How are you doing?' The phone cuts off. I hurry over to the bed and locate a panel in the wall. A scary digital display blinks at me and I can't help a moan. How can anyone live in a house more complicated than NASA? Why does a house have to be intelligent, anyway? Why can't it be nice and stupid?

My fingers fumbling, I press 'Menu', then 'Override' and 'Options'. I scan down the list. 'Temperature' . . . 'Lighting' . . . Where's 'Bathroom'?

Suddenly I notice another panel on the other side of the bed. Maybe that's it. I rush to it and start jabbing at random.

A sound draws me up short. It's a wail. A kind of distant siren. What on earth . . . I look more carefully at the panel I've been hitting. It's flashing at me in red: *Panic Alert—Secure Space*. I look up to see a metal grille descending steadily over the window.

What the— Frantically I jab again at the panel, but it flashes back at me *Unauthorised*, then returns to *Panic Alert—Secure Space*.

Oh my God. I dart to the door of the bedroom and look down to the space below. It's mayhem. The siren is even louder out here. Metal grilles are descending everywhere, over the windows, the paintings, the water feature. All the rich guests are clinging to each other like hostages.

'Is it a robbery?' a woman in a white trouser-suit is exclaiming hysterically, wrenching at her hands. 'George, swallow my rings!'

'It's coming from the master bedroom!' shouts one of Eric's staff. 'Someone's set off the panic alarm. The police are on their way.'

I've ruined the party. Eric will kill me, he'll *kill* me . . .

And then, with no warning, the noise stops. 'Ladies and gentlemen.' A voice comes from the stairs. It's Jon. He's holding a remote control. 'We hope you enjoyed our security demonstration. Rest assured, we are not under attack from robbers.'

He pauses, and a few people laugh nervously. Around the room the grilles have already started retracting. 'However,' Jon continues, 'as all of you know, in London today, security is of prime consideration. This system is MI5 quality—and it's here for your protection.'

He's saved my life. As he continues talking, I totter back into the bedroom suite and find the blue fish still floating in the loo. I plunge my hand in, grab the fish and, with a shudder, stuff it in my bag. I wash my hands, wait a few minutes, then unobtrusively slip down the stairs. I grab a glass of champagne from a passing waiter and take a deep swig.

'Sweetie!' Rosalie's voice makes me jump. '*Oh my God.* Wasn't that genius? That'll make a few diary pieces tomorrow. You know it cost three hundred grand? Just for the security system!'

Three hundred grand, and the loo doesn't even flush. 'Great!' I say.

'Lexi.' Rosalie is giving me a thoughtful look. 'Sweetie . . . can I have a little word? About Jon. I saw you talking to him earlier. I know you had your bump on the head and everything.' She leans forward. 'But do you *remember* anything about Jon? From your past?'

'Um . . . not really.'

Rosalie pulls me still nearer. 'Sweetie, I'm going to give you a bit of a shock,' she says in a low, breathy voice. 'A while ago you told me something in confidence. Girlfriend to girlfriend.'

I'm transfixed. Does Rosalie *know?*

Rosalie hustles closer. 'Jon kept pestering you. I just thought I should warn you in case he tried it on again.'

Pestering me? 'What do you mean?' I stammer at last.

'What do you think? He's tried it on with all of us.' She rolls her eyes. 'He told me Clive doesn't understand me. Which is true,' she says after a moment's thought, 'but that doesn't mean I'm going to rush off and be a notch on his bedpost, does it? And he went after Margo, too,' she adds, waving merrily at a woman across the room. '*Such* a nerve. He said he knew her better than her own husband and she deserved more.' She clicks her tongue dismissively. 'Margo's theory is he targets married women and tells them whatever they want to hear. He was quite persistent with you.' She peers at me. 'Don't you remember any of this?'

'No,' I say at last. 'I don't remember any of it. So . . . what did I do?'

'You kept telling him to leave you alone. You were very dignified, sweetie.' She suddenly focuses over my shoulder. 'Darling, I must just dash and have a word with Clive about our dinner arrangements. Are you OK? I just thought I should warn you . . .'

'No.' I come to. 'I'm glad you did.'

Rosalie trips away into the party, but my feet are rooted to the ground. I've never felt so humiliated in my life, so gullible, so *vain.*

I believed it all. I fell for his blarney. *We've been having a secret affair . . .*

I know you better than Eric does . . . It's all bullshit. He took advantage of my memory loss. And all he wanted was to get me into bed like a . . . a trophy. I feel hot with mortification. I *knew* I would never have an affair! I have a decent husband who loves me. And I allowed my head to be swayed. I nearly ruined everything.

Well, not any more. I take a few deep gulps of champagne. Then I lift my head high and walk forward through the crowd until I find Eric. 'Darling, the party's going wonderfully. You're brilliant.'

'I think we've pulled it off. Narrow escape with that alarm. Trust Jon to save the day. Hey, there he is! Jon!'

I clutch Eric's arm even more tightly as Jon walks towards us. Eric hands him a glass of champagne from a nearby tray. 'Here's to you,' he exclaims. 'Here's to Jon.'

'To Jon,' I echo tightly. I'm just going to pretend he doesn't exist.

A bleep from my bag disturbs my thoughts, and I pull out my phone to see a new message. From Jon. I do not *believe* this. He's texting me in front of Eric:

Old Canal House in Islington, any evening from 6. We have so much to talk about. I love you. J. PS Delete this message. PPS What did you do with the fish??

My face is burning with fury. Rosalie's words ring in my head.

'It's a text from Amy!' I say to Eric, my voice shrill. 'I might just quickly reply . . .' Without looking at Jon, I start texting:

Yeah. Right. I suppose you thought it was a laugh, taking advantage of the girl who lost her memory. Well, I know your stupid game, OK? I'm a married woman. Leave me alone.

I send the text and put my phone away. A moment later, Jon frowns at his watch and says, 'Is that the right time? I think I'm fast.' He takes his mobile phone out and squints at the display as though checking, but I can see him read the message and his face jerks with shock.

Ha. Got him.

After a few moments, he seems to recover. 'I'm six minutes out,' he says, tapping at the phone. 'I'll just change the clock . . .' I don't know why he's bothering with an excuse. Eric's not even paying attention.

Three seconds later my phone beeps again and I pull it out.

'Another text from Amy,' I say disparagingly. 'She's such a pain.' I dart a glance at Jon as I put my finger on 'Delete', and his eyes widen with apparent consternation. Huh.

'Is that a good idea?' he says quickly. 'Deleting a message without even reading it?'

'I'm really not interested.' I shoot him a sweet smile, press 'Delete', switch off my phone and drop it into my bag.

'So!' Eric turns back to us, glowing and ebullient. 'The Clarksons want a repeat viewing tomorrow. I think we have another sale.'

'Well done, my darling, I'm so proud of you!' I exclaim, putting an arm round him in an extravagant gesture. 'I love you even more now than I did on our wedding day.'

I'm still a bit shaken the next morning, as I go into the kitchen for breakfast and take the jug of green juice out of the fridge. I must have been crazy last night. Why would I kiss some guy in the back bedroom, whatever his story was?

I pour a little green juice into a glass and swirl it around to look like dregs, which is what I do every morning. (I can't drink that pond-weed stuff.) Then I take a boiled egg from the pan. I'm really getting into this low-carb start to the day. I have a boiled egg every morning without fail. And then sometimes a bagel on the way to work.

As I sit down, the kitchen seems tranquil. But I'm still jittery. I could have wrecked everything. I've only had this marriage for a few weeks and already I'm risking it. I need to *cherish* it. Like a yucca plant.

'Morning!' Eric breezes into the kitchen. 'Sleep well?'

'Great, thanks!'

We're not sharing a bedroom yet, nor have we tried sex again. But if I'm going to cherish my marriage, maybe we should be getting more physical. I stand up to get the pepper and run my hand down his jaw-line. Eric's eyes meet mine questioningly, and he puts a hand up to meet mine. I glance quickly at the clock. There isn't time, thank God. No. I didn't think that. I need to be *positive*. Sex with Eric is going to be great. Maybe we just need to do it in the dark. And not talk to each other.

I put on my jacket. 'Bye, darling.'

'Bye, sweetheart.' Eric comes over and we kiss each other goodbye. I am at the door when something hits me.

'Hey, Eric,' I say as casually as possible. 'What's Mont Blanc?'

'Mont Blanc?' Eric turns, his face searching mine in disbelief. 'You're kidding. Do you remember Mont Blanc?'

OK. I really fell into this one. I can't say 'No, Jon told me.' 'I don't *remember*, exactly,' I improvise. 'But the name "Mont Blanc" came back to me. Does it mean something . . . special?'

'You'll find out, darling.' I can see the suppressed pleasure in Eric's face. 'I won't say any more for now. This has to be a good sign!'

'Maybe!' I try to match his excitement. 'Well, see you later!' *Mont Blanc*. Skiing? Those posh fountain pens? A great big snowy mountain?

I have absolutely no idea.

I get off the tube at Victoria, buy a bagel and nibble it as I walk along. But as I get near the office, I'm suddenly not hungry any more. I have a nasty churning in my stomach. Fi might be my friend again, but no one else is. And I messed up in front of Simon Johnson, and I still don't feel on top of anything . . .

I head straight up to my office, sit down and pull my pile of papers towards me, when there's a knock at the door.

'Hi, Lexi.' Debs edges her way into the room, holding an envelope. 'How are you?' She sounds awkward.

'I'm . . . fine.' The door widens to reveal Fi and Carolyn, both looking ill at ease, too. 'Hi!' I exclaim in surprise. 'Is everything OK?'

'I told them what you told me,' says Fi.

'We didn't realise,' says Debs, looking worried. 'We didn't give you a chance. We just assumed you were still . . .' She casts around.

'A power-crazed nightmare,' supplies Carolyn, deadpan.

'We feel bad.' Debs bites her lip as she looks at the others. 'Don't we? So, I just wanted to give you this.' Debs hands me the envelope. I rip it open and pull out a stiff white engraved card. A wedding invitation.

'Hope you can come.' Debs has shoved her hands into her pockets. 'You and Eric.'

I feel a rush of humiliation. Her body language is obvious. The last thing she wants is us at her wedding. 'Look, Debs, you don't have to ask me. It's really kind of you . . . but I know you don't really—'

'Yes, I do.' She puts her hand on mine, stopping me, and I look up. 'You were one of my best friends, Lexi. You should be there.'

'Well . . . thanks,' I mumble. 'I'd love to come.' I turn the invitation over, running a finger over the engraving. 'How did you get your mother to agree to such a late guest? Did she threaten to stop your allowance?'

'*Yes!*' exclaims Debs and we all break into giggles. Debs's mum has been threatening to stop her allowance ever since I've known her— even though she stopped giving Debs an allowance years ago.

'We've bought some muffins too,' says Fi. 'To say sorry for yester- day—' She stops as there's a tapping at the door. Simon Johnson is standing in the doorway.

'We'll go,' says Fi hurriedly, and hustles the others out. 'Thanks for that . . . er . . . information, Lexi. Very useful.'

'I won't take up your time,' says Simon, shutting the door as they leave. 'Just wanted to give you the final run-down for Monday's meet- ing. Obviously keep it close to your chest. Within this department, only you and Byron have this information.' He holds out a folder.

As I take the folder from him, I see 'June 07' typed discreetly in the top right-hand corner and feel a twinge of foreboding. I still have no idea what June 07 means. I've found nothing in my files.

'Looking forward to it!' I pat the folder, hoping I look convincing.

'Good. It's Monday, twelve noon sharp in the boardroom.'

The minute Simon has left, I whip open the folder. The first page is entitled 'Summary': *June 07 . . . major restructuring . . .*

After a few seconds I sink down into my chair, feeling overwhelmed. No wonder this is a big secret. The whole company's being changed around. We're acquiring a home technology company . . . we're amalgamating several departments . . . I flick my eyes further down.

. . . context of its current sales performance . . . plans to disband . . .

What? I read the words again. And again.

With a surge of adrenaline, I leap to my feet, hurtle to the door and out, down the corridor. There's Simon, by the lifts, talking to Byron.

'Simon!' I'm gulping air in my panic. 'Could I have a quick word?' I look around, checking there's no one nearby to overhear. 'I just wanted to . . . to . . . clarify a couple of things. These plans to disband the Flooring section.' I tap the folder. 'You can't really mean . . .'

'She's finally twigged.' Byron folds his arms, shaking his head with such amusement I want to punch him. He *knew* about this?

Simon sighs. 'Lexi, we've been through this many times, as you know. You've done marvels with your sales force, we all appreciate that. But the department is unsustainable.'

'But you can't get rid of Flooring! Deller Carpets is all about Flooring!'

'Keep your voice down!' Simon snaps sotto voce. 'You and Byron will both have new roles in senior management. It's all been worked out. I don't have time for this.' The lift arrives and he steps into it.

'But, Simon,' I say desperately, 'you can't just *fire* the whole department . . .' It's too late. The lift doors have closed.

'It's not called firing,' Byron's sardonic voice comes from behind me. 'It's called making redundant. Get your terms right.'

I wheel round, incensed. 'How come I didn't know about this?'

'Oh, didn't I tell you?' Byron clicks his tongue in mock self-reproach.

'Where are the files? Why didn't I see this before?'

'I may have borrowed them.' He heads towards his office.

'No! Wait!' I push my way in behind him and close the door. 'I don't understand. Why are they axing the department?'

'Have you *looked* at our sales recently?' Byron rolls his eyes. 'Lexi, carpet is old news. We've failed to penetrate the other flooring markets. We've only got a couple of contracts to see out. The party's over.'

'But those original carpet designs are classics! What about rugs?'

Byron stares at me incredulously for a moment, then bursts into laughter. 'You do know you're repeating yourself? You said all this at the first crisis meeting. "We could make the carpets into rugs!" Give up.'

'But they'll all be out of a job! The whole team!'

'Yeah. Shame.' He sits at his desk and motions towards the door.

'You're a *bastard*,' I say, my voice shaking. I stride out of his office.

'Lexi!' My head jerks up and instinctively I clasp the folder closer to my chest. Fi is standing at the door of the main Flooring office, beckoning me. 'Come in! Have a muffin.'

I can't refuse. I have to appear normal.

I follow Fi into the main office. A banner has been strung up between two window latches, reading 'WELCOME BACK, LEXI!!!' A plate of fresh muffins is on the filing cabinet, along with an Aveda gift basket.

'We never gave you a proper welcome back,' says Fi, her face slightly pink. 'And we just wanted to say we're glad you're OK.' She addresses the room. 'To those of you who didn't know Lexi way back when, I just want to say that I think this accident has changed things. I know she's going to be the most fantastic boss. Here's to you, Lexi.'

She lifts her coffee mug and the whole room breaks into applause.

'Thanks, everyone,' I manage, my face puce. 'You're . . . all great.'

They're all about to lose their jobs. They have no idea. And they've bought me muffins and a gift basket.

Somehow I raise a sick smile. I'm in a bad dream.

As I finally leave work at six thirty, the nightmare hasn't lifted. I have the weekend to put together a defence of the Flooring department somehow. As I'm jabbing the ground-floor button in the lift, Byron slips in, wearing his overcoat. 'Working at home?' He raises his eyebrows as he sees my stuffed bag.

'I have to save the department,' I say shortly.

'You have to be kidding.' Byron shakes his head incredulously. 'Lexi, haven't you read the proposal? This is going to be *better* for you and me.'

'That's not the point!' I cry in a blaze of fury. 'What about all our friends who won't have anything?'

'Sob sob,' Byron drawls. 'They'll find jobs. You know, you weren't bothered before you had that car crash. You were all for getting rid of Flooring. Once you saw your package. More power for us, more money . . . what's not to love?'

A coldness creeps over me. 'I don't believe you.' My voice is jerky. 'I don't believe you. I would *never* have sold out my friends.'

Byron just looks at me pityingly. 'Yeah, you would. You're not a saint.'

I arrive at Langridge's department store, and travel up to the personal-shopping department as though in a daze. I have an appointment at six o'clock with my shopper, Ann. 'Lexi! How *are* you?' A voice greets me as I approach the reception area. Ann is very petite, with a distinct perfume that turns my stomach instantly.

'I'm fine, thanks. All recovered now.' I attempt a smile.

'Good! Now, I have some *fabulous* pieces for you to see.' Ann ushers me into a cubicle and presents a rail of clothes to me with a flourish. 'You'll see some new shapes and styles here . . .'

What is she talking about, new shapes and styles? They're all suits in neutral colours. I have a cupboard full of these already.

Ann is showing me jacket after jacket, talking about pockets and lengths, but I can't hear a word. Something is buzzing in my head like a trapped insect; it's getting louder and louder . . . 'Do you have anything different?' I cut her off abruptly. 'Anything . . . *alive*?'

'Alive?' Ann echoes uncertainly.

I stride out of the cubicle onto the shop floor. Blood is rushing through my ears. I feel a bit deranged, to be honest. 'This.' I seize a purple minidress with bright splodges on it. 'This is great. I could go clubbing in this.'

Ann looks as if she wants to pass out. 'Lexi,' she says at last. 'That's . . . not what I would call your style.'

'Well, I would.' I pluck a beige sleeveless dress out of her arms and hold it up. 'I'm not this person, I'm just not. I need fun. I need colour.'

'You've existed perfectly well for several years in beige and black.' Ann's face has tightened. 'This.' She comes up with another beige suit, with tiny pleats. '*This* is you.'

'It's not me! It's not! I'm not this person! I won't be her!' Tears are stinging my eyes. I start tugging pins out of my chignon, suddenly desperate to get rid of it. 'I'm not the kind of person who wears beige suits! I'm not the kind of person who wears her hair in a bun every day. I'm not the kind of person who . . . who sells out her friends . . .'

I'm gulping with sobs by now. I wipe my eyes with the back of my hand, and, in horror, Ann whips the beige dress away.

'Don't get tears on the Armani!' she snaps.

'Here.' I shove the sleeveless dress back to her. 'You're welcome to it.'

I head to the café on the ground floor, order a hot chocolate and a doughnut. After a while, all the carbs have settled in my stomach like a warm, comforting cushion, and I feel better. I'll work all weekend, I'll find the solution, I'll save the department . . .

A beep from my pocket interrupts my thoughts. I pull out my phone and see it's a text from Eric: How are you doing? Working late?

As I stare at the words I'm touched. Eric cares about me: On my way home now, I type back. I missed you today!!

It's not exactly true, but it has the right sound to it.

I missed you too! comes back instantly.

I knew there was a point to marriage. And this is it. Someone to care about you when everything's crap. The phone beeps once more. Fancy a Mont Blanc?? :) :)

Again with the Mont Blanc. What *is* this? A cocktail, maybe?

Well, it's obviously really special to Eric. And there's only one way I'll find out. Great! I text back. Can't wait!

It only takes about twenty minutes to get home, during which time I stare out of the taxi window, my mind working overtime. I *know* there's still value in the Deller Carpets brand . . .

'Love?' The taxi driver breaks my reverie. 'We're here.'

'Oh, right. Thanks.' I'm fumbling for my purse when my phone beeps yet again. I'm ready!

Ready? This gets more and more mysterious.

As I let myself into the flat, the lights are dim, on a setting that I recognise as 'Seduction'. 'Hi!' I call out cautiously, hanging up my coat.

'Hi!' Eric's distant voice seems to be coming from my bedroom.

Well. I guess, officially, our bedroom.

I head through to the bedroom and push the door open. And at the sight before me I nearly scream out loud.

This is Mont Blanc? *This* is Mont Blanc?

Eric is lying on the bed. Totally naked. Except for the most massive mound of whipped cream on his genital region. 'Hi, darling.' He raises his eyebrows with a knowing twinkle, then glances downwards. 'Dive in!'

In? Dive? Dive *in*? I'm paralysed with horror as I survey the creamy, whippy mountain. Every cell in my body is telling me that I do not want to dive in. But I can't just turn and run away, can I? This is my husband. This is obviously . . . what we do. Oh God, oh God . . .

Gingerly I edge forward towards the creamy edifice. Barely knowing what I'm doing, I extend a finger and take a tiny scoop from the top of the mound, then put it in my mouth. 'It's . . . it's sweetened!'

'Low calorie.' Eric beams back at me.

No. No. I'm sorry. I have to come up with an excuse . . .

'I feel dizzy!' The words come out of nowhere. I clap a hand to my eyes and back away from the bed. 'Oh my God. I'm having a flashback.'

'A *flashback?*' Eric sits up, alert.

'Yes! I had a sudden image of . . . the wedding,' I improvise.

'Sit down, darling!' Eric is frowning anxiously. 'Take it easy. Maybe some more memories will come back.'

'I might just go and lie down quietly in the other room, if you don't mind. I'm sorry, Eric . . .'

Before he can say anything, I hurry out and flop down on the big cream sofa. My head is spinning, whether from the Mont Blanc shocker or the whole day . . . I don't know. All I know is, I can't cope with this life of mine. Any of it.

Six

I CAN'T LOOK AT ERIC without seeing whipped cream. Thankfully we've barely seen each other this weekend. Eric's been doing corporate entertaining and I've been trying desperately to come up with a plan to save Flooring. I've read through all the paperwork. To be honest, it's a crap situation. Not only are orders too low, no one even seems *interested* in Flooring any more. We have a fraction of the advertising and marketing budget that other departments do.

But all that will change, if I have anything to do with it. Over the weekend I've devised a total relaunch. It'll need a bit of money and faith and cost-trimming—but I'm positive we can kick-start sales. I can't let all my friends lose their jobs.

Oh God. My stomach heaves yet again with nerves. I'm sitting in the taxi on the way to work, my hair firmly up, my presentation folder in my lap. The meeting is in an hour. All the other directors are expecting to vote to disband Flooring. I'm going to have to argue my socks off.

My phone rings, and I nearly jump off the seat, I'm so on edge.

'Hello?'

'Lexi?' comes a small voice. 'It's Amy. I'm in trouble. You have to come. Please.'

'What kind of trouble?' I say, alarmed. She sounds desperate.

'Please come.' Her voice is quivering. 'I'm in Notting Hill, on the corner of Ladbroke Grove and Kensington Park Gardens.'

'Amy . . .' I clutch my head. 'I can't come now! I have a meeting, it's really important. Can't you phone Mum?'

'No!' Amy's voice rockets in panic. 'Lexi, you said I could ring whenever I wanted, that you were my big sister, that you'd be there for me.'

'But I have this presentation . . . Look, any other time . . .'

'Fine.' Her voice is suddenly tiny. 'Go to your meeting. Don't worry.'

Guilt drenches me. I stare blindly out of the window. There are forty-five minutes until the meeting. I don't have time, I just don't.

I might do, if I went right now. It's only ten minutes to Notting Hill. But I can't risk being late for the meeting, I just *can't*.

And then suddenly, against the crackly background of the phone line, I can hear a man's voice shouting. I can't leave my little sister in trouble. What if she's about to be beaten up?

'Amy, hold on,' I say abruptly. 'I'm coming.'

As the taxi heads up Ladbroke Grove, I'm leaning forward, trying to glimpse Amy . . . And then suddenly I see a police car. On the corner of Kensington Park Gardens. I'm too late. She's been shot. She's been knifed.

Weak with terror, I thrust some cash at the driver and get out of the cab. There's a throng of people in front of the police car. 'Excuse me. It's my sister, can I get through?' Somehow I manage to push my way in.

And there's Amy sitting on a wall, looking cheery. 'Lexi!' Amy turns to the policeman standing next to her. 'I told you she'd come.'

'What's been going on?' I demand, shaky with relief.

'I'm afraid this young lady's in trouble,' the policeman says. 'She's been exploiting tourists. A lot of angry people here.' He gestures at the crowd. 'Celebrity tours.' He hands me a leaflet. 'So-called.'

In disbelief I read the fluorescent yellow leaflet.

Undercover Celebrity Tour of London
Many Hollywood stars have settled in London. See them on this unique tour. Catch glimpses of:
—Madonna putting out her washing
—Gwyneth in her garden
—Elton John relaxing at home
Impress your friends with all the insider gossip!
£10 per person including souvenir A–Z
Important note: If you challenge the stars, they may deny their identities. Do not be fooled! This is part of their Undercover Secret!

I look up in a daze. 'Is this serious?'

The policeman nods. 'Your sister's been leading people round London, telling them they're seeing celebrities. People like her.' He gestures across the road, where a thin, blonde woman is standing on the steps of her big white stucco house, a little girl of about two on her hip.

'I'm not bloody Gwyneth Paltrow!' she's snapping irately at a pair of tourists in Burberry raincoats. 'And no, you can't have an autograph.'

Actually, she *does* look rather like Gwyneth Paltrow.

'Are you with her?' The Gwyneth lookalike suddenly spots me. 'I want to make an official complaint. I've had people taking pictures of my home all week—*For the last time, she's not called Apple!*' This woman is furious. And I don't blame her.

'I'm going to have to reprimand your sister officially.' The policeman turns to me. 'I can release her into your custody, but only when you've filled in these forms and arranged an appointment at the station.'

'Fine,' I say, and shoot a murderous look at Amy. 'Whatever.'

I fill in all the forms as quickly as I can, stamping a furious full stop after my signature. 'Can we go now?'

'All right. Try and keep tabs on her,' the policeman adds.

'Sure.' I give a tight smile. 'Come on, Amy.' I glance at my watch and feel a spasm of panic. It's already ten to twelve. 'We need to find a taxi.' I flag one down and bundle Amy into it. 'Victoria Palace Road, please. Quick as you can.' There's no way I'll make it for the start. But I can still get there and say my piece. I can still do it. I pull out my phone, dial Simon Johnson's office number, and wait for his PA to answer.

'Hi, Natasha,' I say, trying to sound calm and professional. 'It's Lexi. I'm having a slight holdup, but it's really vital that I speak at the meeting. Could you tell them to wait for me? I'm on my way in a taxi.'

'Sure,' says Natasha pleasantly. 'I'll tell them. See you later.'

I ring off and lean back in my seat, a tiny bit more relaxed.

'Sorry,' says Amy suddenly. 'Really, I am.'

I sigh. '*Why*, Amy?'

'To make money.' She shrugs. 'Why not?'

'Because you'll get in serious trouble! If you need money, can't you get a job? Or ask Mum?'

'Ask Mum?' she echoes scornfully. 'Mum doesn't have any money. Why d'you think the house is falling down?'

'But that's weird,' I say, puzzled. 'Didn't Dad leave her anything?'

'Dunno. Not much, anyway.'

'Well, whatever, you can't carry on like this. Seriously, you'll end up in jail or something.'

'Bring it on.' Amy tosses back her blue-streaked hair. 'Prison's cool.'

'Prison's not *cool!*' I stare at her. 'Where d'you get that idea? It's manky! You can't shave your legs or use cleanser.' I'm making all this up. 'There aren't any boys,' I add for good measure. 'And you're not allowed an iPod. You just have to march round a yard.' That bit I'm sure isn't true. But I'm on a roll now. 'With chains round your legs.'

'They don't have *leg chains* any more,' Amy says scornfully.

'They brought them back,' I lie. 'It was a new experimental government initiative. Jeez, Amy, don't you read the papers?'

Amy looks slightly freaked. Ha. That pays her back for Moo-mah.

'Well, it's in my genes.' She regains some of her defiance. 'To be on the wrong side of the law. Dad was in prison,' she declares triumphantly.

'*Dad?*' I stare at her. The idea's so preposterous I want to laugh.

'He was. I heard some men talking about it at the funeral. So it's like, my fate.' She shrugs, and takes out a packet of cigarettes.

'Stop it!' I grab the cigarettes. 'Dad didn't go to prison. You're not going to prison. And it's not cool.' I think for a moment. 'Look, come and be an intern at my office. It'll be fun. You can get some experience, and earn some money. And maybe I won't tell Mum about this. Deal?'

There's a long silence in the taxi. 'OK,' Amy shrugs at last.

The taxi pulls up at a red traffic light. It's twenty past. I just hope they started late. My gaze drifts to the yellow leaflet again and a reluctant grin creeps over my face. It was a pretty ingenious scheme.

'So, who were your other celebrities?' I can't help asking.

Amy's eyes light up. 'This woman in Kensington who looked just like Madonna, only fatter. I said that proved how much airbrushing they did. And I had a Sting, and a Judi Dench, and this really nice milkman in Highgate who looked the spit of Elton John.'

'Elton John? A milkman?' I can't help laughing.

'I said he was doing community service on the quiet.'

The taxi moves off again. We're nearing Victoria Palace Road now. I open my presentation folder and scan my notes.

'You know, they *did* say Dad had been in prison.' Amy's low voice takes me by surprise. 'I didn't make it up.'

It seems . . . impossible. 'Did you ask Mum about it?' I venture.

'No.' She shrugs.

'Deller Carpets, ladies.' The taxi has drawn up in front of the Deller building. I hadn't even noticed.

'Oh, right. Thanks.' I root in my bag for some money. 'Amy, I have to rush. I'm sorry, but this is really, really important.' I give her a brief hug, then skitter up the steps. I'm only half an hour late. I hurry to a waiting lift and wait the agonising seconds it takes to get to the eighth floor.

At last. I burst out, run towards the boardroom—and stop.

Simon Johnson is standing in the corridor outside the boardroom, talking cheerfully to three other guys in suits. A man in a blue suit is shrugging on his raincoat.

'What's going on?' I can barely speak.

All the faces turn towards me in surprise.

Simon shoots me a disapproving frown. 'We're having a break. We've finished the crucial part of the meeting and Angus has to leave.' He gestures at the guy in the raincoat.

I feel an almighty lurch of horror. 'Do you mean—'

'We've voted. In favour of the reorganisation.'

'But you can't!' I hurry towards him in panic. 'I've found a way to save the department! We just have to trim a few costs—'

'Lexi, we've made our decision.' Simon cuts me off firmly.

'But it's the *wrong* decision!' I cry desperately. 'There's value in the brand, I know there is! Please.' I appeal directly to Angus. 'Don't leave.'

'Lexi, you *cannot* behave like this at directors' meetings.' There's steel beneath Simon's pleasant voice; I can tell he's furious. 'I know things have been tricky for you since your accident so what I suggest is you take three months' paid leave. And when you return, we'll find you a more . . . suitable role within the company. All right?'

All the blood drains from my face. He's demoting me.

'If you'd recovered your memory then things would be different. But Byron's been filling me in. You're not up to a senior position right now.'

There's an absolute finality in his voice. 'Fine,' I manage at last.

'Now, you might want to go down to your department. Since you weren't here . . .' He pauses meaningfully. 'I gave Byron the task of breaking the unfortunate news to them.' With a final curt nod, Simon disappears into the boardroom. I run to the lift. I can't let Byron tell them the bad news. I have to do that myself at least. I punch Byron's direct line into my mobile phone and get voicemail. 'Byron! Don't tell the department about the redundancies yet, OK? I want to do it myself.' I pelt out of the lift, into my office and close the door. I'm shaking all over. I've never been so petrified in my life. How am I going to break the news?

And then a voice, outside the door. 'Is she in there?'

'Where's Lexi?' chimes in another voice. 'Is she *hiding*? Bitch.'

'I saw her! She's in there! Lexi! Come out here!' Someone bangs on the door. Gingerly I stretch out a hand and open the door.

They know. They're all standing there. All fifteen members of the

Flooring department, silent and reproachful. Fi is at the front, her eyes like stone.

'It . . . it wasn't me,' I stammer desperately. 'Please listen, everyone. It wasn't my decision. I tried to . . .' I trail off. I'm the boss. It was down to me to save the department. And I failed. 'I'm sorry,' I whisper, tears filling my eyes. 'I'm so, so sorry . . .'

There's silence. I think I might melt under the hatred of their gazes. Then they all turn and walk away. I back towards my desk and sink into my chair. How did Byron break it to everybody? What did he *say*?

Then I spot it in my in-box:

COLLEAGUES—SOME BAD NEWS.

To all colleagues in Flooring,

As you may have noticed, the performance of Flooring has been appalling of late. It has been decided by senior management to disband the department. You will all therefore be made redundant in June. In the meantime, Lexi and I would be grateful if you would work with improved efficiency and standards. Remember, we'll be giving your references, so no slacking or taking the piss.

Yours, Byron and Lexi.

OK. Now I want to shoot myself.

When I arrive home Eric is sitting on the terrace in the evening sun. 'Good day?' He looks up from the paper.

'To be honest . . . no,' I say, my voice quivering. 'It was a pretty terrible day. The entire department is being fired.' I dissolve into tears. 'They're all losing their jobs. And they all hate me. I don't blame them.'

'Darling. It's business. These things happen.'

'They don't just happen. These are my *friends*.' I shake my head vehemently. 'You stop them happening. You fight.'

'Sweetheart.' Eric appears amused. 'Do you still have your job?'

'Yes.'

'The company's not collapsing, is it?'

'No.'

'Well then. Have a gin and tonic.'

How can he respond like that? Isn't he human? 'Eric, don't you understand?' I almost shout. 'Don't you *get* how terrible this is?' All my rage towards Simon Johnson and the directors is channelling towards Eric. 'These people need their jobs! They're not all ultra-high-rich bloody billionaires!'

'You're overreacting,' Eric says shortly, and turns a page of his paper.

'Well, you're underreacting! I just don't *understand* you.' I want him to look up, to talk about it, but he doesn't. It's as if he didn't even hear me. My whole body is pulsating with frustration.

'Fine,' I say at last. 'Let's just pretend everything's OK and we agree, even though we don't . . .' I wheel round and draw a sharp breath. Jon is standing at the doors to the terrace.

'Hi. Gianna let me in. I'm not intruding?'

'No!' I turn away swiftly so he can't see my face. 'Of course not.'

Of all the people to pitch up. Just to make my day complete.

'Lexi's a little upset,' says Eric to Jon in a man-to-man undertone. 'A few people at her work are losing their jobs.'

'Not just a few people!' I can't help expostulating. 'A whole department! And I didn't do anything to save them. I fucked up.'

'Jon.' Eric isn't even listening to me. 'Let me get you a drink. I've got the Bayswater plans here, there's a lot to talk about.' He gets up and steps into the sitting room. 'Gianna! Gianna, are you there?'

'Lexi.' Jon comes across the terrace to where I'm standing, his voice low and urgent. He's trying it on again. I don't believe this.

'Leave me *alone*! Didn't you get the message? I'm not interested! And even if I *were*, it's not a good time. My whole department has just crumbled to nothing. So unless you have the answer to that, piss off.'

Jon takes off his shades and rubs his head as though perplexed. 'I don't understand. What happened to your big carpet deal?'

'What carpet deal?' I say aggressively.

'You're not serious. You don't *know* about it?'

'Know about *what*?' I exclaim, at the end of my tether.

'Jesus Christ.' Jon exhales. 'OK. Lexi, listen to me. You had this massive carpet deal all lined up in secret. You said it was going to change everything . . . So! You enjoy the view, huh?' He seamlessly switches track as Eric appears at the door, holding a gin and tonic.

Massive carpet deal? *Ignore him*, says a voice in my head. *This is all part of the game.* But what if it's not?

'Eric, darling, I'm sorry about earlier.' My words come out fluently. 'It's just been a difficult day. Could you possibly get me a glass of wine?'

'No problem, sweetheart.' Eric disappears inside again.

'Tell me what you're talking about,' I say in low tones. 'Quickly.'

'If I'd *realised* before that you didn't know . . . You'd been working on this thing for weeks. You had a big blue file. I don't know the exact details, but I know it was using retro carpet designs from some old pattern book. And I know it was going to be huge.'

'But why don't I *know* about it? Why doesn't anyone *know* about it?'

'You were keeping it quiet until the last moment. You said you didn't trust everyone at the office—' He breaks off suddenly as Eric reappears.

'Here you are, Lexi,' says Eric cheerfully, handing me a glass of wine. Then he heads to the table, sits down and gestures at Jon to join him. 'So the latest is, I spoke to the planning officer again . . .'

I'm standing perfectly still as they talk, my mind racing. It could be all bullshit. But how would he know about the old pattern book? What if it's true? If there's still a chance, even a *tiny* chance . . .

I take a deep swig of wine—then pull out my phone. With fumbling hands I find Jon's number and type a text: Can we meet? L

A moment later, without looking anywhere near me, Jon checks his phone and types back a return text. Eric doesn't even seem to notice.

I casually flip open my phone. Sure. J

We've agreed to meet in a cosy café called Fabian's in Holland Park. As I walk in and look around at the granite bar, the coffee machine, the battered sofa, I have the weirdest feeling, as if I've been here before. Maybe it's wishful thinking.

Jon is already sitting at a table in the corner. 'Hi.' I join him at the table, where he's drinking coffee. 'So. Let's talk about this deal. Is there anything more you can tell me?'

'Lexi, what *is* this? And what happened at the party?'

'I . . . I don't know what you mean.' I pick up the menu.

'Come on.' Jon pulls the menu down. 'What happened?'

'If you must know,' I say tightly, 'I spoke to Rosalie at the party, and she told me about your . . . predilections. I know you tried it on with her and Margo.' An edge of bitterness has crept into my voice. 'You just tell married women what they want to hear.'

Jon's expression doesn't flicker. 'I did try it on with Rosalie and Margo. But you and I agreed I should. That was our cover.'

Well, of *course* he'd bloody well say that. I glare at him in fury.

'We cooked up a story that would fool everyone, so if ever we were spotted together, that could be the explanation. Rosalie fell for it.'

'You *wanted* to be portrayed as a womaniser?' I retort.

'Of course not!' There's a sudden heat to his voice. 'This hasn't all been pretty.' He reaches a hand towards mine. 'But you have to trust me, Lexi. Please. You have to let me explain everything . . .'

'Stop it!' I whip my hands away. 'We're not here to talk about that, anyway.' A waitress approaches and I look up. 'A cappuccino, please. So, this deal,' I say briskly, as soon as the waitress moves away. 'It doesn't exist. I've looked everywhere, in the office and at home. The only thing I've found is this.' I reach into the briefcase and produce the piece of paper with the coded scribbles on it. 'It's my handwriting but I don't know what it means!' In frustration I throw the paper down. 'Why on earth didn't I keep my notes on the computer?'

'There's a guy at work, Byron? You thought he'd try and screw things up for you. So you were going to present the whole thing to the board when it was already done. I've been thinking back, and I do remember something. Your contact was Jeremy Northam. Northwick. Something like that.'

'Jeremy Northpool?' I can remember Clare thrusting a Post-it at me with his name on it. 'I think he called while I was in hospital.'

'Well.' Jon raises his eyebrows. 'Maybe you should call him back.'

'But I can't.' I drop my hands on the table in despair. 'I don't know enough! Where's all the information?'

'You must have moved the file. Hidden it somewhere.' Jon is stirring his cappuccino. 'I remember something else. You went down to Kent to your mother's house just before the accident. Maybe you took the file with you.'

'To my mum's house?' I say sceptically.

'It's worth a chance.' He shrugs. 'Call her up and ask her.'

I stir my coffee moodily. Ringing Mum is bad for my health.

'Come on, Lexi, you can do it.' Jon's mouth twitches with amusement at my expression. 'What are you, woman or walrus?'

I raise my head, stunned. For a moment I wonder whether I heard that right. 'That's what Fi says,' I say at last.

'I know. You told me about Fi.'

'What did I tell you about Fi?' I say suspiciously.

'You told me you met in Mrs Brady's class. You had your first and last cigarette with her. Losing her friendship has been really traumatic.' He nods at my phone. 'Which is why you should make the call.'

This is so *spooky*. What the hell else does he know? Sliding him wary glances, I take the phone out of my bag and key in Mum's number.

'Oh, Mum! It's me, Lexi. Listen, did I bring some papers down any time recently? Or like . . . a folder?'

'That big blue folder?'

I feel an almighty thrust of hope. 'That's right.' I try to stay calm. 'Do you have it? Is it still there?'

'It's in your room, exactly where you left it.' Mum sounds defensive. 'One corner may be *slightly* damp . . .'

I don't believe it. A dog's peed on it. 'But it's still legible?'

'Of course!'

'Great!' I clutch the phone tighter. 'Well, keep it safe and I'll come and get it today.' I flip my phone shut and turn to Jon. 'You were right! OK, I have to get to Victoria, there's bound to be a train . . .'

'Lexi, calm down.' Jon drains his coffee. 'I'll drive you, if you like. It'll have to be in your car though, I'm between cars at the moment.'

It's a sunny day, and as Jon reverses the car out of its parking space, he retracts the roof. Then he reaches in his pocket and hands me a black hair elastic. 'You'll need this. It's windy.'

I take the hair elastic in surprise. 'How come you have this?'

'I have them everywhere. I don't know what you do, *shed* them?'

Silently, I put my hair up into a ponytail. Jon turns onto the road. 'It's in Kent,' I say. 'You have to head out of London on the—'

'I know where it is.'

'You know where my mother's house is?' I say, a touch incredulously. 'I've been there.'

He's been to Mum's house. He knows about Fi. He has my hair elastic in his pocket. He was right about the blue folder. Either he's really, *really* done his research. Or . . . 'So, hypothetically, if we were lovers . . .'

'Hypothetically.' Jon nods without turning his head.

'What exactly happened? How did we . . .'

'Like I told you, we met at a launch party. We kept bumping into each other through the company. We'd chat, hang out on the terrace . . . It was innocuous.' He pauses, negotiating a tricky lane-change. 'Then Eric went away one weekend. And I came over. And after that . . . it wasn't so innocuous.'

I'm starting to believe. It's like a screen is going back. 'So what else happened?' I say. 'What did we say, what did we do? Just tell me stuff.'

Jon shakes his head, his eyes crinkled in amusement. 'That's what you always said to me in bed. "Tell me stuff." OK. Everywhere we've been together, we've ended up buying you socks. You rip off your shoes to be barefoot on the sand or the grass or whatever, and then you get cold and we need to find you socks.' He pulls up at a zebra crossing. 'What else? One weekend it rained. Eric was away playing golf and we watched every single episode of *Doctor Who*, back to back.' He glances at me. 'Should I keep going?'

Everything he's saying is resonating. My brain is tuning up. I don't remember what he's talking about, but I'm feeling stirrings of recognition. It feels like me. This feels like my life.

'Keep going.' I nod.

'OK.' He pulls away from the crossing. 'We play table tennis. It's pretty brutal. You're two games ahead but I think you're about to crack.'

'I am *so* not about to crack,' I retort automatically.

'Oh, you are.'

'Never!' I can't help grinning. 'Keep going.'

As we drive through the Kent countryside, Jon has exhausted all the details he can give me about our relationship. We're sitting in silence as the hop fields and oast-houses pass by. I'm watching the satnav screen in a trance. Suddenly it reminds me of my conversation with Loser Dave, and I heave a sigh.

'What's up?' asks Jon.

'I just still keep wondering what made me go after my career, get my teeth done, turn into this . . . *other* person?' I gesture at myself.

'Well,' says Jon, squinting up at a sign. 'I suppose it started with what happened at the funeral. The thing with your dad.'

'What about my dad?' I say, puzzled.

With a screech of brakes, Jon stops the Mercedes. 'Didn't your mother tell you about the funeral?'

'Of course she did!' I say. 'It happened. Dad was . . . cremated.'

'That's it?'

I rack my brain. Mum didn't say anything else about the funeral. She changed the subject when I brought it up, I suddenly recall. But that's normal for Mum. She changes every subject.

'Well, tell me! If it's so important.'

Jon shakes his head as the car moves off again. 'Your mum has to tell you this one.' He pulls into a gravel drive. 'We're here.'

So we are. I hadn't even noticed. The house is looking pretty much as I remember it: a red-brick house dating from the 1900s. The place hasn't changed since we moved in, it's just got more crumbly.

'So, you're saying Mum lied to me?'

'Not lied. Edited.' Jon opens the car door. 'Come on.'

'**O**phelia! Raphael!' I can just about hear Mum's voice over the scrabbling and yelping. 'Get down! Lexi, darling! You really did rush down here. What *is* all this?'

'Hi, Mum,' I say breathlessly, manhandling a dog off me. 'This is Jon. My . . . friend.' I gesture at Jon.

'Well!' Mum seems flustered. 'If I'd realised, I would have rustled up some lunch. *How* you expect me to cater at this late notice—'

'We don't expect you to cater. All I want is that folder. Is it still there?'

'Of course.' She sounds defensive. 'It's perfectly all right.'

I hurry up the stairs and into my bedroom. Amy's right, this place *stinks.* I can't tell if it's the dogs or the damp or the rot, but Mum should get it sorted. I spot the folder on top of a chest of drawers and grab it— then recoil. Now I know why Mum was defensive. This is so gross. It totally smells of dog pee. Wrinkling my nose, I gingerly extend two fingers and open the folder. I scan the first page, trying to glean as quickly as possible what I was planning. I turn the page, then another. And that's when I see the name. Oh. My. God. In an instant, I understand. That is *such* a good idea. I can already see the potential. It could be huge, it could change everything . . .

Filled with adrenaline, I grab the folder and rush out of the room.

'Got it?' Jon is waiting at the bottom of the stairs.

'Yes!' A smile licks across my face. 'It's brilliant! It's a brilliant idea!'

'It was your idea.'

'*Really?*' I feel a glow of pride which I try to quell.

'Now!' Mum is approaching bearing a tray of coffee cups. 'I can at least offer you a cup of coffee and a digestive.'

'Really, Mum, it's OK,' I say. 'I'm afraid we have to dash off.'

'I'd like a coffee,' says Jon pleasantly.

He *what*? Shooting him daggers, I follow him into the sitting room. Jon takes a seat as if he feels totally at home here. Maybe he does.

'So, Lexi was just talking about piecing her life together,' he says, crunching a digestive. 'And I thought, maybe knowing the events that happened at her dad's funeral would help.'

'Well, of course, losing a parent is always traumatic . . .'

'That's not what I'm talking about,' Jon says. 'I'm talking about the other events.'

Mum looks vague. 'Now, Raphael, that's naughty! Coffee, Lexi?'

The dogs are all over the biscuit plate, slobbering and grabbing. Are we supposed to eat those now?

'Lexi doesn't seem to have the fullest of pictures,' persists Jon.

'Smoky, it's *not* your turn . . .'

'*Stop talking to the dogs!*' Jon's voice makes me leap off my seat.

Mum looks almost too shocked to speak. Or even move.

'*This* is your child.' Jon gestures at me. 'Not that.' He jerks a thumb at a dog. 'Maybe you want to go through life in a state of denial. Maybe it helps you. But it doesn't help Lexi.'

'What are you talking about?' I say helplessly. 'Mum, what happened at the funeral?'

Mum's hands are fluttering. 'It was rather . . . unpleasant.'

'Life can be unpleasant,' says Jon bluntly. 'If you don't tell Lexi, I will. Because she told me, you see.'

'All right!' Mum's voice descends into a whisper. 'The bailiffs came!' Her cheeks are growing pink with distress. 'Right in the middle of the party.'

'Bailiffs? But—'

'They came with no warning. Five of them. They wanted to repossess the house. Take all the furniture, everything. It turned out your father hadn't been . . . totally honest with me. Or anybody.'

'Show her the second DVD,' says Jon.

There's a pause, then, without looking at either of us, Mum gets up, roots in a drawer and finds an unmarked, shiny disc. She puts it into the machine and the three of us sit back.

'Darlings.' Dad is on the screen again. 'If you're watching this, I've popped it. And there's something you should know. But this one's not for . . . public consumption. There's been a bit of a catastrophe on the old moolah front. Didn't mean to land you in it. You girls are clever, you'll find a way to sort it out.' He considers for a moment. 'But if you're stuck, ask old Dickie Hawford, he should be good for a bit. Cheers, m'dears.' He lifts his glass up—then the screen goes dark.

I wheel round to Mum. 'What did he mean, "catastrophe"?'

'He meant he'd remortgaged the entire house.'

'So what did we do?'

'We would have had to sell up. Amy would have been taken out of school . . .' Her hands are fluttering again. 'So my brother very kindly stepped in. And so did my sister, and . . . and so did you. You said you'd pay off the mortgage. As much as you could afford.'

'*Me?*' I sink back in the sofa, my mind reeling with shock. 'Is it an off-shore mortgage?' I say suddenly. 'A bank called Uni . . . something?'

'Most of Daddy's dealings were offshore.' She nods. 'Trying to avoid the tax man. I don't know *why* he couldn't just be honest—'

'Said the woman who kept her daughter in the dark!' expostulates Jon. 'How can you even *say* that?'

I can't help catching some of his exasperation.

'Mum, you didn't tell me *any* of this. Can't you see how it might have made things clearer for me? I had no idea where that money was going.'

'It's been very difficult!' Mum's eyes are swivelling from side to side.

'But—' I break off as something else even darker occurs to me. 'Mum, I have another question. Was Dad ever in . . . prison?'

Mum winces. 'Briefly, darling. Let's not dwell on that.'

'No!' In frustration I leap to my feet and stand right in front of her, trying to get her single-minded attention. 'Mum, listen! You can't just live in a bubble, pretending nothing's happened. Amy *heard* about Dad going to prison. She got the idea it's cool. No wonder she's been getting into so much trouble . . . Jesus!' Suddenly the pieces of my life are slotting together like a Tetris puzzle. '*That's* why I suddenly got ambitious. That funeral changed everything.'

'When the bailiffs arrived, she went to bits.' Jon glances scornfully at Mum. 'You had to make the decisions.'

'Stop looking at me as though it's all my fault!' Mum suddenly cries out, her voice shrill and quivering. 'Your father, that *man*—'

She breaks off and I catch my breath as her blue eyes meet mine. For the first time that I can remember, my mother sounds . . . true.

But already the moment's over. Mum's eyes are shifting sideways, avoiding me. 'It's nearly lunchtime, Agnes!' Her voice is bright and brittle.

'Mum, please. What were you going to say?'

'I was *simply* going to say that before you start blaming me for everything in your life, Lexi, that chap had a lot to answer for. That boyfriend of yours at the funeral. Dave? David?'

'Loser Dave?' I stare at her, thrown. 'But . . . Loser Dave wasn't at the funeral. He told me he offered to come but I turned him down. He said . . .' I peter out as I see Jon just shaking his head.

'What else did he tell you?'

'He said we broke up that morning, and that it was beautiful, and that he gave me a single rose . . .' Oh God. 'Excuse me.'

I march outside into the drive and direct-dial Loser Dave's office.

'Auto Repair Workshop,' comes his businesslike voice down the line.

'Loser Dave, it's me,' I say, my voice steely. 'Lexi. I need to hear about our breakup again. And this time I need to hear the truth.'

'Babe, I told you the truth.' He sounds supremely confident.

'Listen, you fuckhead,' I say in slow, furious tones. 'I'm at the neurological specialist's office right now, OK? They say someone has been giving me wrong information and it's messing up my neural memory pathways. And if it isn't corrected, I'll get permanent brain damage.'

'Jesus.' He sounds shaken. 'Straight up?'

He really is stupider than one of Mum's whippets.

'Yeah. So maybe you want to try again with the truth? Or maybe you'd like to speak to the doctor?'

'No! OK!' He sounds unnerved. 'I was trying to protect you.'

'Protect me from what? Did you come to the funeral?'

'Yeah, I came along,' he says. 'I was handing out canapés. Being helpful. Giving you support. Then I . . .' He clears his throat.

'*What?*'

'Shagged one of the waitresses. It was the stress!' he adds defensively.

'It makes us all do crazy things. I thought I'd locked the door—'

I caught Loser Dave two-timing me. Well of course I did. I'm not even that surprised.

'So how did I react? *Don't* say I gave you a rose and it was beautiful.'

'Well.' Loser Dave breathes out. 'To be honest, you went ballistic. You started yelling about your life. Your whole life had to change, it was all crap, you hated me, you hated everything . . . You stormed out.'

'Then what?'

'Then I didn't see you again. Next time I clapped eyes on you, you were on the telly, looking totally different.'

'Right.' I watch two birds circling in the sky. 'You know, you could have told me the truth, first time round.'

'I know. I'm sorry.' He sounds as genuine as I've ever heard him. 'And I'm sorry I shagged that girl. And I'm sorry for what she called you, that was well out of order.'

I sit up, suddenly alert. 'What did she call me?'

'Oh. I don't remember,' he says hastily. 'Er . . . I gotta go. Good luck with the doctor.' He rings off. I immediately redial his number, but it's engaged. Little sod.

I march into the house to find Jon still sitting on the sofa, reading a copy of *Whippet World*.

'What did the waitress call me at the funeral?'

Jon sighs. 'Lexi, it's a tiny detail. Why does it matter?'

'Look, Jon, you can't lecture my mum about denial and then not tell me something that happened in *my* own life, which I deserve to know. Tell me what that waitress called me. *Now*.' I glare at him.

'All right!' Jon lifts his hands as though in defeat. 'Dracula.'

Dracula? In spite of the fact that I *know* my teeth aren't snaggly any more, I can feel my cheeks staining with mortification.

'Lexi—' Jon's wincing.

'No.' I shake off Jon's hand. 'I'm fine.' My face still hot, I stand up and head over to the window, trying to put myself back in my own chewed-up, flat-heeled Lexi shoes. It's 2004. I didn't get a bonus. It's my dad's funeral. The bailiffs have just arrived to bankrupt us. I come across my boyfriend screwing a waitress . . . and she takes one look at me and calls me Dracula. Things are starting to make sense.

On the way back, I sit in silence for a long, long while. 'At least I *get* myself a bit more,' I say at last. I chew on my thumbnail. 'Did I ever talk to you about it? The funeral?'

'Once or twice.' Jon gives me a wry smile.

'Oh right.' I colour. 'All the time. I must have bored you to death.'

'Don't be stupid.' He takes a hand off the wheel and squeezes mine briefly. 'One day, really early on, when we were still just friends, it all came out. The whole story. How you took on your family's debt, booked a cosmetic dentistry appointment the next day, went on a crash diet, decided to change everything about yourself. Then you went on TV and everything became even more extreme. You rocketed up the career ladder, you met Eric, and he seemed like the answer. He was solid, rich, stable. A million miles away from—' He breaks off into silence.

'My dad,' I say eventually.

'I'm no psychologist. But I would guess.'

'You know, when I woke up, I thought I'd landed the dream life,' I say slowly. 'I thought I was Cinderella. I was *better* than Cinderella . . .' I trail off as Jon shakes his head.

'You were living your whole life under strain. You went too far too soon, you didn't know how to handle it, you made mistakes . . .' He hesitates. 'You alienated your friends. You found that the hardest of all.'

'I don't understand why I became a bitch,' I say helplessly.

'You didn't mean to. Lexi, give yourself a break. You were thrust into this boss position. You had a big department to run, you wanted to impress senior management, not be accused of favouritism . . . and you'd built up this tough persona. It was part of your success.'

'The *Cobra*,' I say, wincing. I still can't believe that nickname.

'You once said to me, if you could go back in time and do everything differently, you would. Yourself . . . your job . . . Eric . . . Everything looks different when the gloss is gone.'

'Look, I'm not some shallow gold-digger, OK?' I say hotly. 'I must have loved Eric, I wouldn't just marry a guy because of the gloss.'

'At first you thought Eric was the real deal,' Jon agrees. 'He's charming, he ticks the boxes . . . In fact, he's like one of the intelligent systems from our lofts. Put him on "Husband" setting and away he goes.'

'*Stop* it.' I'm trying not to laugh. 'Look. Maybe we did have an affair. But maybe I want to make my marriage *work* this time round.'

'You can't.' Jon doesn't miss a beat. 'Eric doesn't love you.'

Why does he have to be such a bloody *know-it-all*?

'Yes, he does.' I fold my arms. 'He said he fell in love with my beautiful mouth and my long legs. It was really romantic.'

'That's a crock of shit.' Jon doesn't even turn. 'So would he love you if you're legs *weren't* long?'

I'm momentarily stumped. 'I . . . don't know. That's not the point.' I jut out my chin. 'So what do *you* love about me?'

'I don't know. The essence of you. I can't turn it into a *list*,' he says.

There's a long pause. 'OK,' says Jon finally, as we draw to a halt in a queue of cars. 'I like the way you squeak in your sleep.'

'I squeak in my sleep?' I say disbelievingly.

'Like a chipmunk. Cobra by day.' He nods. 'Chipmunk by night.'

I'm trying to keep my mouth straight and firm, but a smile is edging out. As we crawl along the dual carriageway, my phone bleeps.

'It's Eric,' I say after reading the text. 'He's arrived safely in Manchester. He's scoping out some possible new sites for a few days.'

'Uh-huh. I know.' Jon swings round a roundabout. We're into the outskirts of the city now. 'You know, Eric could have paid off your dad's debt in his sleep,' he suddenly says, his voice matter-of-fact. 'But he left you to it. Never even mentioned it.'

I feel at a loss. I don't know what to think.

'It's his money,' I say at last. 'Why should he? And anyway, I don't *need* anyone's help.'

'I know. I offered. You wouldn't take anything. You're pretty stubborn.' He draws up behind a bus and turns to look at me. 'I don't know what you're planning for the rest of today if Eric's away.'

Deep within me, something starts stirring.

'Well.' I try to sound businesslike. 'I wasn't planning anything. Why?'

'It's just there's some stuff of yours at my flat you might want to pick up.'

'OK.' I shrug noncommittally.

Jon lives in the most beautiful flat I've ever seen. OK, it's in a daggy street in Hammersmith, but the house is big, with massive old arched windows, and it turns out the flat runs into the next-door building too, so it's a million times wider than it seems from the outside.

'This is *amazing*.' I'm looking around his workspace, almost speechless. The ceiling is high and the walls are white and there's a tall, sloped desk. In the corner is a drawing easel, and opposite is an entire wall covered in books, with an old-fashioned library ladder on wheels.

'This whole row of houses was built as artists' studios.' Jon's eyes are gleaming as he walks around, picking up about ten old coffee cups. 'Your stuff's through here.'

I walk where he's pointing, through an archway into a cosy sitting room. It's furnished with big, blue-cotton sofas. Behind the sofas are battered wooden shelves, haphazardly filled with books and magazines and plants and . . . 'That's my mug.' I stare at a hand-painted red pottery mug that Fi once gave me for my birthday.

'Yeah.' Jon nods. 'That's what I mean. You left stuff here.'

'And . . . my jumper!' There's an old ribbed polo neck draped over one of the sofas. I've had it for ever, since I was about sixteen. I look around in disbelief as more things spring into my vision. That furry fake-wolf throw that I always used to wrap around myself. Old college photos. My pink retro *toaster*?

'You used to come here and eat toast like you were starving.'

I'm suddenly seeing the other side of me. For the first time since I woke up in hospital I feel as if I'm at home. There're even my fairy lights draped around the pot plant in the corner.

All this time, all my stuff was here. Suddenly I have a memory of Eric's words, that first time I asked him about Jon. *You'd trust Jon with your life.* Maybe that's what I did. Trusted him with my life.

'Do you remember anything?' Jon sounds casual, but I can sense the hope underneath.

'No . . .' I break off as I notice a beaded frame I don't recognise. It's a photo of me. And Jon. We're sitting on a tree trunk and his arms are round me and my head is tossed back. I'm laughing as though I'm the happiest girl there ever was.

It was real. It was really real. All this time, he had proof.

'You could have shown me this,' I say, almost accusingly.

'Would you have wanted to believe me?' He sits on the arm of the sofa.

Maybe he's right. Maybe I would have explained it away, clung on to my dream life. I walk over to a table cluttered with old novels belonging to me and a bowl of seeds. I grab a handful. 'I love sunflower seeds.'

'I know you do.' Jon has the oddest expression on his face.

'What?' I look at him in surprise, seeds halfway to my mouth.

'It's nothing.' He shrugs. 'It was stupid. We just had this . . . tradition. The first time we had sex you'd been munching on sunflower seeds. You planted one in a yoghurt pot and I took it home. We started doing it every time. As a memento. We called them our children.'

'We planted sunflowers?' That rings a tiny bell.

'Uh-huh.' Jon nods. 'Let me get you a drink.'

'So where are they?' I say, as he pours out two glasses of wine.

Jon takes a sip of his wine. Then he turns on his heel and gestures for me to walk along a small corridor. We head through a sparsely decorated bedroom to a wide, decked balcony. And I catch my breath.

There's a wall of sunflowers all the way round. From huge yellow monsters reaching up to the sky, down to spindly green shoots in tiny pots, just starting to open. This was it. This was us. My throat is suddenly tight as I gaze around at the sea of green and yellow.

'So, how long ago . . . I mean . . .' I jerk my head at the tiniest seedling, in a tiny painted pot, propped up with sticks.

'Six weeks ago, the day before the crash.' Jon pauses, an unreadable expression on his face. 'I'm kind of looking after that one.'

I sit down and gulp at my wine, feeling totally overwhelmed.

'What about . . . the first time?' I say eventually. 'How did it all start?'

'It was that weekend Eric was away. I was over and we were chatting. We were out on the balcony, drinking wine. Kind of like we are now. And then halfway through the afternoon we fell silent. And we knew.'

He lifts his dark eyes to mine and I feel a lurch, deep inside.

Gently he removes the wineglass from my hand. 'Lexi . . .' He brings my hands up to his mouth, closing his eyes, gently kissing them. 'I knew . . .' His voice is muffled against my skin. 'You'd come back. I knew you'd come back to me.'

'Stop it!' I whip my hands away, my heart thudding in distress. 'You don't . . . you don't know anything!'

'What's wrong?' Jon looks shell-shocked, as though I'd hit him.

I almost don't know what's wrong myself. I want him so badly; my entire body's telling me to go for it. But I can't. 'What's wrong is . . . I'm freaked.' I gesture at the sunflowers. 'You're presenting me with this . . . this fully fledged relationship. But for me, it's just the beginning.'

'I'll go back to the beginning too,' he says quickly.

'You can't go back to the beginning!' I thrust my hands hopelessly through my hair. 'Jon, you're a guy who's attractive and witty and cool. And I really like you. But I don't love you. How could I?'

'I don't expect you to *love* me—'

'Yes, you do. You do! You expect me to be her.'

'You *are* her.' There's a sudden streak of anger in his voice.

'I don't *know* if I am, OK?' To my horror, tears are streaming down my cheeks. I want to be the girl laughing on the tree trunk. But I'm not.

At last I manage to get a grip on myself and turn round. Jon is standing in exactly the same place as he was before, a bleakness on his face that makes my heart constrict.

'I look around at these sunflowers.' I swallow hard. 'And the photo. And all my things here. And I can see that it happened. But it looks like a wonderful romance between two people I don't know.'

'It's you,' says Jon in a quiet voice. 'It's me. You know both of us.'

'I know it in my head. But I don't feel it. I don't *know* it.' I clench a fist on my chest, feeling the tears rising again. 'If I could just remember *one thing*. If there was one memory, one thread . . .' I tail off in silence.

'So, what are you saying?'

'I'm saying . . . I need time . . . I need . . .' I break off helplessly.

Spots of rain are starting to fall on the balcony.

At last Jon breaks the silence. 'A lift home?' His eyes meet mine—and there's no anger any more.

'Yes.' I wipe my eyes, and push my hair back. 'Please.'

It only takes fifteen minutes to reach home. Jon pulls the Mercedes into my parking space. Rain is thundering against the roof by now.

'You'll have to run straight in,' says Jon and I nod.

'How will you get back?'

'I'll be fine.' He hands me my keys, avoiding my eye. 'Good luck with that.' He nods at the blue folder. 'I mean it.'

I pelt through the rain to the entrance, nearly dropping the precious folder, then stand under the portico, gathering the papers together, feeling a fresh spasm of hope as I remember the details.

And all of a sudden I sag as the reality of my situation hits home. Whatever I have in this folder, Simon Johnson's never going to give me another chance, is he? I'm not the Cobra any more. I'm the memory-challenged embarrassment-to-the-firm. He won't even give me five minutes, let alone a full hearing. Never in a million years. Not unless . . .

No.

I *couldn't*. Could I?

I'm frozen in disbelieving excitement, thinking through the implications, Simon Johnson's voice running through my head like a soundtrack. *If you'd recovered your memory, Lexi, then things would be different.*

I pull out my mobile phone and direct dial. 'Fi,' I say as soon as it's answered. 'Don't say anything. Listen.'

Seven

THINK BITCH. Think boss. Think Cobra.

I survey myself in the mirror. My hair's scraped back and I'm wearing the most severe outfit I could find in my wardrobe. I spent two hours with Jeremy Northpool yesterday, at his office in Reading, and everything's in place. We both want this deal to work out. Now it's up to me.

'You don't look mean enough.' Fi, standing by my side in a navy trouser-suit, surveys me critically. 'You used to have this really chilling stare. Like, "You are an insignificant minion, get out of my way instantly."' She narrows her eyes and puts on a hard, dismissive voice. 'I'm the boss and I'll have things done *my* way.'

'That's really good!' I turn in admiration. 'You should do this.'

'Yeah, right.' She pushes my shoulder. 'Go on, do it again. Scowl.'

'Get out of my way, you minion,' I snarl in a Wicked Witch of the West voice. 'I'm the boss and I'll have things done *my* way.'

'Yes!' She applauds. 'That's better. And kind of flick your eyes past people, like you can't even waste time acknowledging they're there.'

I sigh. This bitchy behaviour is exhausting. Fi has been coaching me for the last twenty-four hours. She took a sickie yesterday and came over; she stayed all day, and night. And she's done the most brilliant job. I know *everything*. My head is so crammed full of facts it's ready to burst. And that's not even the most important bit. The most important bit is that I come across like the old, bitch-boss Lexi and fool everyone.

'Fi . . . thanks.' I turn and give her a hug. 'You're a star.'

'If you pull this off *you'll* be a star.' She hesitates, then adds, a little gruffly, 'Even if you don't pull it off. You didn't have to make all this effort, Lexi. I know they're offering you a big job.'

'Yeah, well.' I rub my nose. 'That's not the point. Come on, let's go.'

As we travel to the office in a cab, my stomach is clenched up with nerves. I'm crazy, doing this, but it's the only way I can think of.

'Jesus,' murmurs Fi, as we draw up. 'I don't know *how* I'm going to keep a straight face in front of Debs and Carolyn.' We haven't told the others what I'm up to. We reckon the fewer who know, the safer.

'Well, Fi, you'll just have to make an effort, OK?' I snap in my new-Lexi voice, and nearly giggle as her face jerks in shock.

'God, that's scary. You're *good*.'

We get out of the cab, and I hand the driver the fare.

'Lexi?' A voice comes from behind me. I look round.

'*Amy?* What the hell are you doing here?'

'I've been waiting for you. I'm here to be your intern.'

'Amy.' I put my hand to my head. 'Today isn't really a good day . . .'

'You said!' Her voice quivers. 'You said you'd sort it out. I've made a real effort to get here, I got up early and everything.'

'She might be a distraction,' says Fi. 'Can we trust her?'

'Trust me?' Amy's voice sharpens with interest. 'With what?'

'OK.' I make a snap decision. 'Listen, Amy.' I lower my voice. 'You can come in, but here's the thing. I'm telling everyone I've recovered my memory, to get a deal done. Even though I haven't. Got it?'

Amy doesn't bat an eyelid. There are some advantages to having a scam artist as a sister. 'So you're trying to make out you're the old Lexi.'

'Yes.'

'Then you should look meaner. Like you think everyone is just a worm.'

'That's what I said,' agrees Fi.

They both sound so sure, I feel a pang of hurt. 'Was I *ever* nice?' I say, a bit plaintively.

'Er . . . yes!' says Fi unconvincingly. 'Plenty of times. Come on.'

As I push open the glass doors to the building, I adopt my meanest scowl. 'Hi,' I snarl at Jenny on the reception desk. 'This is my temporary intern, Amy. Please make her out a pass. For your information, I'm fully recovered and if you've got any mail for me I want to know why it isn't upstairs already.'

'There's nothing for you, Lexi.' Jenny seems taken aback as she fills out a pass for Amy. 'So . . . you remember everything now, do you?'

'Everything. Come on, Fi. We're late enough already.'

I stride away, towards the lifts. A moment later I can hear Jenny behind me, saying in an excited undertone, 'Guess what? Lexi's got her memory back!' I glance over. Sure enough, she's already on the phone.

The lift pings, Fi, Amy and I walk in—and as soon the doors close, dissolve into giggles. 'High five!' Fi lifts her hand. 'That was great!'

We all get out at the eighth floor, and I head straight to Natasha's desk outside Simon Johnson's office, my head high and imperious.

'Natasha,' I say curtly. 'I assume you got my message about my memory returning? Obviously I'll need to see Simon as soon as possible.'

'I'm afraid Simon's quite booked up this morning—'

'Then juggle things around! Cancel someone else!'

'OK!' Natasha types hastily at her keyboard. 'I could do you a slot at ten thirty?'

'Fantast—' I stop as Fi nudges me. 'That'll be fine,' I amend, shooting Natasha my meanest scowl for good measure. 'Come on, Fi.'

'Where do we go now?' says Amy, as we get back in the lift.

'To the Flooring department.' I feel a stab of nerves. 'I'll have to keep this act up till ten thirty.'

I arrive at the main office door and stand there for a few moments, surveying the scene before me. Then I draw breath. 'So.' I summon a harsh, sarcastic voice. 'Reading *Hello!* is work, is it?'

Melanie, who had been flicking through the magazine, jumps as though she's been scalded and flames red. She hastily closes *Hello!*

'I'll be speaking to you all about attitude later.' I glare around the room. 'And that reminds me. Didn't I ask everyone to provide full written travel-expense breakdowns, two months ago? I want to see them.'

'We thought you'd forgotten,' says Carolyn, looking dumbstruck.

'Well, I've remembered.' I give her a sweet, scathing smile. 'I've remembered everything.' I sweep out, almost straight into Byron.

'Lexi!' He almost drops his cup of coffee. 'What the fuck—'

'Byron. I need to talk to you about Tony Dukes,' I say crisply. 'How did you handle the discrepancy in his calculations? Because we all know his reputation for pulling a fast one. Remember the trouble we had in October last year?'

Byron's mouth is hanging open stupidly.

'And where are the minutes of our last product meeting? You were doing them, as I remember.'

'I'll . . . get those to you.' He looks utterly gobsmacked.

Everything I'm saying is hitting right home. Fi is a total genius!

'So are you recovered?' Byron says as I open my office door.

'Oh, yes.' I usher Amy in and slam the door. I count to three, then I look out again. 'Fi, can you come in here?'

As Fi closes the door behind her, I collapse on the sofa, breathless.

'You should be on the stage!' Fi exclaims. 'That was so great!'

There's a knock on the door and we all freeze. The door opens and Clare appears. 'Um . . . Lexi,' she says. 'I don't want to interrupt, but Lucinda is here? With her baby?'

Lucinda. That means nothing to me.

Fi sits up. 'Lucinda who worked for us last year, do you mean?' she says quickly. 'I didn't know she was coming in today.'

'We're giving her a baby gift and we wondered if Lexi could present it to her?' Clare gestures out of the door and I see a small cluster around a blonde woman holding a baby-carrier. She looks up and waves.

Shit. There's no way out of this one. I can't refuse to look at a baby, it'll seem too weird. 'All right,' I say at last. 'Just for a moment.'

'Lucinda was with us about eight months,' Fi murmurs frantically as we head out of the office. 'Took care of European accounts, mainly. Sat by the window, likes peppermint tea . . .'

'Here we are.' Clare hands me a parcel. 'It's a baby-gym.'

'Hi, Lexi.' Lucinda looks up, glowing at all the attention.

'Hi there.' I nod curtly at the baby, which is dressed in a white Babygro. 'Congratulations, Lucinda. Anyway. On behalf of the department, I'd like to give you this.'

'Speech!' says Clare.

'Yes, speech!' calls someone else at the back. 'Speech!'

Oh God. I can't refuse. 'Of course,' I say, and clear my throat. 'We're all very pleased for Lucinda. But sad to say goodbye to such a valued member of our team.'

I notice Byron joining the cluster of people, surveying me closely.

'Lucinda was always . . .' I take a sip of coffee, playing for time. '. . . by the window. Sipping her peppermint tea. Managing her European accounts.' I glance up and see Fi at the back, frantically miming some kind of activity. 'We all remember Lucinda for her love of . . . biking,' I say uncertainly.

'Biking?' Lucinda looks puzzled. 'Do you mean riding?'

'Tell the story about Lucinda and the snooker table!' calls out someone at the back and there's a chorus of laughter.

'No,' I snap, rattled. 'So . . . here's to Lucinda.' I raise my coffee cup.

'Don't you remember the story, Lexi?' Byron's bland voice comes from the side. I glance at him—he's guessed.

'Of course I *remember* it.' I summon my most cutting tones. 'But it's not the time for silly, irrelevant stories. We should all be at work.'

'Wait! We forgot Lucinda's other present! The mother-and-baby spa voucher.' He brings a slip of paper up to me with an over-deferential air. 'It just needs Lucinda's name filled in, Lexi. You should do that, being head of department.'

'Right.' I take the pen.

'You need to put the surname, too,' he adds casually.

I look up and his eyes are gleaming. *Fuck*. He's got me.

'Of course,' I say briskly. 'Lucinda . . . remind me what name you're using these days.'

'The same as before,' she says. 'My maiden name.'

'Right.' As slowly as I can, I write 'Lucinda' on the dotted line.

'And the surname?' says Byron, like a torturer turning the screw. 'Lexi, face it, the pantomime's over. Do you *really* think you're kidding—'

'Hey!' Amy's high-pitched voice shoots across the office, drawing everyone's attention. 'Look! That's Jude Law! With no shirt on!'

'Jude *Law*? Where is he?'

Byron's voice is drowned out by an instant stampede to the window. Debs is pushing Carolyn out of the way, and even Lucinda is craning to see. I love my little sister.

'Right,' I say in a businesslike way. 'Well, I must get on. Clare, could you finish this up, please?' I thrust the voucher at her, swivel on my heel and walk rapidly out of the office.

The door of Simon Johnson's office is closed as Fi and I arrive upstairs, and Natasha gestures to us to take a seat. A moment later the phone rings and Natasha listens for a moment. 'All right, Simon,' she says. 'I'll tell her.' She puts down the receiver and looks at me. 'Lexi, Simon's in with Sir David and a few other directors.'

'Sir David Allbright?' I echo apprehensively. Sir David Allbright is chairman of the board. He's the total bigwig, even bigger and wiggier than Simon. And he's really fierce.

'That's right.' Natasha nods. 'Simon says you should just go in, join the meeting and see all of them. In about five minutes. OK?'

Panic is sending little shooters through my chest.

'Of course! Fine. Um . . . Fi, I need to powder my nose. Let's just continue our discussion in the Ladies.' I push my way into the empty loos and sit down on a stool, breathing hard. 'I can't do this. How am I going to impress Sir David Allbright? I'm no good at giving speeches—'

'Yes, you are!' retorts Fi. 'Lexi, you've given speeches to the whole company. You were excellent.'

'Really?' I'm silent for a few seconds, trying to picture it, *wanting* to believe it. But it doesn't chime in my brain. 'I don't know.' I rub my face. 'Maybe I'm just not cut out to be a boss.'

'No! You're totally meant to be a boss!'

'How can you *say* that?' My voice trembles. 'When I was promoted to director, I couldn't cope! I alienated all of you. I fucked it up.'

'Lexi, you didn't fuck it up.' Fi speaks in a rush, almost brusque with embarrassment. 'You were a good boss. We . . . weren't fair. Look, we were all pissed off at you, so we gave you a hard time.' She hesitates. 'Yes, you were too impatient some of the time. But you did some really great things. You are good at motivating people. Everyone felt alive and kicking. People wanted to impress you. They admired you.'

As I take in her words I can feel an underlying tension slowly slipping off me. 'But you made me sound like such a bitch. All of you.'

'You were a bitch some of the time.' Fi nods. 'But sometimes you needed to be. Carolyn was taking the piss with her expenses. She deserved a bit of a rocket. I didn't say that,' she adds quickly, with a grin. 'Thing is, Lex . . . We were jealous.' She looks at me frankly. 'One minute you were Snaggletooth. Next thing, you've got this amazing hair and perfect teeth, and you're in charge and telling us what to do.'

'I know.' I sigh. 'It's mad.'

'It's not mad.' Fi crouches down and takes both my shoulders in her hands. 'Lexi, remember when we were at primary school? Remember the sack race on sports day?'

'Don't remind me.' I roll my eyes. 'I fucked that up too.'

'That's not the point.' Fi shakes her head vigorously. 'The point is, you were winning. You were way out in front. And if you'd kept going, if you hadn't waited for the rest of us, you would have won.' She gazes almost fiercely at me, with the same green eyes I've known since I was six years old. 'Just keep going. Don't think about it, don't look back.'

The door opens and we both start. 'Lexi?' It's Natasha. 'Are you ready?'

I get to my feet and lift my chin high. 'Yes. Ready.'

'Lexi.' Simon beams. 'Good to see you. Come and take a seat. So, your memory is recovered! Tremendous news.'

'Yes. It's great!'

'We're just going through the implications of June 07.' He nods at the papers spread over the table. 'This is very good timing, because I knew you had some strong views about the amalgamation of departments.'

'Actually . . .' My hands are damp and I curl them round the folder. 'Actually, I wanted to speak to you. All of you. About something else.'

David Allbright looks up with a frown. 'What?'

'Flooring.'

'Lexi.' Simon's voice is tight. 'We're no longer dealing in Flooring.'

'But I've done a deal! That's what I want to talk about!' I take a deep breath. 'I've always felt the archive prints that Deller owns are one of its biggest assets. For several months I've been trying to find a way to harness these assets. Now I have a deal in place with a company that would like to use one of our old designs. It'll raise Deller's profile. It'll turn the department around!' I can't help sounding exhilarated. 'This can be the beginning of something big and exciting!' I stop breathlessly and survey the faces. I can see it at once. I have made precisely no impact whatsoever. Sir David has the same impatient frown on his face. Simon looks murderous. One guy is checking his BlackBerry.

'I thought the decision on Flooring had been made,' says Sir David Allbright testily to Simon. 'Why are we raising it again?'

'It has been decided, Sir David,' he says hurriedly. 'Lexi, I don't know *what* you're doing—'

'I'm doing business!' I retort with a clench of frustration.

'Young lady,' Sir David says. 'Business is forward-looking. Deller has to move with the times, not cling on to the old.'

'I'm not clinging!' I try not to yell. 'The old Deller prints are fabulous. It's a *crime* not to use them.'

'Is this to do with your husband?' Simon says, as though he suddenly understands. 'Lexi's husband is a property developer,' he explains to the others, then turns back to me. 'Lexi, with all due respect, you're not going to save your department by carpeting a couple of show flats.'

One of the men laughs and I feel a knife of fury. Carpeting a couple of show flats? Is that all they think I'm capable of? Once they hear what this deal is, they'll . . . they'll . . . I'm drawing myself up, ready to tell them; ready to blow them away. I can feel the bubbling of triumph, mixed with a bit of venom. Maybe Jon's right, maybe I am a bit of a cobra.

'If you *really* want to know . . .' I begin, eyes blazing. And then all of a sudden I change my mind. I can feel myself retreating, fangs going back in. 'So . . . you've really made your decision?'

'We made our decision a long time ago,' says Simon.

'Right. Well, if you're not interested, maybe I could buy the copyright of the designs? So I can licence them as a private venture.'

'Jesus Christ,' mutters Sir David.

'Lexi, please don't waste your time and money,' says Simon.

'I want to,' I say stubbornly. 'I really believe in Deller Carpets.'

I can see the directors exchanging glances.

'She had a bump to the head in a car crash,' Simon murmurs to a guy I don't recognise. 'She hasn't been right since.'

'Let's just sort it out.' Sir David Allbright waves an impatient hand.

'I agree.' Simon heads to his desk, lifts his phone and punches in a number. 'Ken? Simon Johnson here. One of our employees will be coming to see you about the copyright of some old Deller carpet design. Work out a nominal fee for the licence and the paperwork, could you? Thanks, Ken.'

He puts the phone down and scribbles a name and number on a piece of paper. 'Ken Allison. Our company lawyer. Call him to make an appointment. And Lexi, I know we talked about a three-month leave. But I think that your employment here should be terminated.'

'Fine.' I nod. 'I . . . understand. Goodbye. And thanks.'

Somehow I get out of the room without skipping.

Fi is waiting for me as I step out of the lift at the third floor. 'Well?'

'Didn't work,' I murmur as we head to the main Flooring office. 'But it's not all over.'

'There she is.' Byron heads out of his office as I pass by. 'The miracle recovery girl.'

I turn and regard him with a blank, perplexed gaze. 'Who's he?' I say at last to Fi, who snorts with laughter.

'Very funny,' snaps Byron. 'But if you think—'

'Oh, leave it out, Byron!' I say wearily. 'You can *have* my fucking job.'

I've arrived at the door to the main office. 'Hi,' I say, as everyone looks up. 'I just wanted to let you know, I haven't got my memory back, that was a lie. I tried to pull off a massive bluff, to try to save this department. I did everything I could, but . . .' I exhale sharply. 'Anyway. The other news is, I've been fired. So, Byron, over to you.' I register the jolt of shock on Byron's face and can't help a half-smile. 'And to all of you who thought I was a total hard-as-nails bitch, I'm sorry. I know I didn't get it right. But I did my best. Cheers, and good luck, everyone.'

'Thanks, Lexi,' says Melanie awkwardly. 'Thanks for trying, anyway.'

'Yeah, thanks,' chimes in Clare.

To my astonishment someone starts clapping. And suddenly the whole room is applauding. 'Stop it.' My eyes start stinging and I blink hard. 'You idiots. I didn't do anything. I *failed*.'

I glance at Fi and she's clapping hardest of all.

'Anyway.' I try to keep my composure. 'As I say, I've been fired, so I'll be going to the pub immediately to get pissed. I know it's only eleven o'clock . . . but anyone care to join me?'

By three o'clock, my bar bill is over three hundred quid. It was one of the best parties I've ever been to. Everyone had a great time; in fact the only one who didn't get totally pissed was me. I couldn't, because I have a meeting with Ken Allison at four thirty.

'So.' Fi lifts her drink. 'To us.' She clinks glasses with me, Debs and Carolyn. It's just the four of us sitting round a table now. Like the old days. Most of the Flooring employees have drifted back to the office.

'To being unemployed,' Debs says morosely.

I take a swig of wine, then lean forward. 'OK, you guys. I have something to tell you. But you can't let on to anyone. I've done a deal. That's what I was trying to tell Simon Johnson about. This company wants to use one of our old retro carpet designs. A special, high-profile limited edition. They'll use the Deller name, we'll get huge PR . . . it'll be amazing! The details are all sorted out, I just need to finalise the contract.'

'That's great, Lexi,' says Debs, looking uncertain. 'But how can you do it now you're fired?'

'The directors are letting me license the old designs as an independent operator. They're so *shortsighted*. This could be just the start! There's so much archive material. If it grows, we could expand, employ some more of the old team . . . turn ourselves into a company . . .'

'I can't believe they weren't interested.' Fi shakes her head.

'They've totally written off carpets and flooring. But that means they're going to let me license all the designs for practically nothing.

Then all the profits will come to me. And . . . whoever works with me.'

I look from face to face, waiting for the message to hit home.

'*Us?*' says Debs, her face glowing. 'You want us to work with you?'

'If you're interested,' I say, a little awkward.

'I'm in,' says Fi firmly. 'But Lexi, I still don't understand. Didn't they get excited when you told them who the deal was with?'

I shrug. 'They assumed it was one of Eric's projects. "You're not going to save your department by carpeting a couple of show flats!"'

'So, who *is* it?' asks Debs. 'Who's the company?'

I glance at Fi—and can't help a tiny smile as I say, 'Porsche.'

So that's it. I am the official licenser of Deller carpet designs. I had a meeting with the lawyer yesterday and another one this morning. Everything's signed. Tomorrow I meet with Jeremy Northpool, and we sign the contract for the Porsche deal.

As I arrive home I'm still powered up by adrenaline. I need to call all the girls, fill them in on developments.

There are voices coming from Eric's office as I walk into the flat. Eric must have arrived home from Manchester while I was with the lawyer. I peep round the open door to see a roomful of his senior staff grouped around the coffee table, with an empty cafetière at the centre.

'Hi!' I smile at Eric. 'Good trip?'

'Excellent.' He nods, then frowns. 'Shouldn't you be at work?'

'I'll explain later. Can I bring you all some more coffee?'

I head into the kitchen, humming as I make a fresh pot, sending quick texts to Fi, Carolyn and Debs to let them know all went well. We're going to make a good team, I know we are.

I head back to Eric's office with a full pot, and discreetly start pouring it out, while listening to the discussion. Penny, head of HR, is holding a list of names, with figures scribbled in pencil at the side. 'I'm afraid I don't think Sally Hedge deserves a pay rise *or* a bonus,' she's saying as I pour her a cup of coffee. 'She's very average.'

'I like Sally,' I say. 'You know her mum's been ill recently?'

'Really?' Penny makes a face as though to say 'So what?'

'Lexi made friends with all the junior staff when she came into the office.' Eric laughs. 'She's very good at that kind of thing.'

'It's not a "kind of thing"!' I retort, a little rankled by his tone.

'Anyway.' Penny turns quickly back to her paper. 'We're agreed, no bonus or pay rise this time, but perhaps a review after Christmas.'

I know this isn't my business. But I can't bear it. I can just imagine Sally waiting for the news of the bonuses. 'Excuse me! Can I just say something? The thing is . . . a bonus may not be much to the company but it's huge to Sally Hedge.' I look around at Eric's managers, all dressed in smart, grown-up clothes with their smart, grown-up accessories. 'Do *any* of you remember what it was like to be young and poor and struggling? Because I do.'

'Lexi, we know you're a tenderhearted soul,' says a guy called Steven whose role I've never been able to work out. 'But what are you saying, we should all be poor?'

'I'm not saying you have to be poor!' I try to control my impatience. 'I'm saying you have to remember what it's like, being at the bottom of the ladder. It feels like it was only six weeks ago that I *was* that girl. No money, hoping for a bonus, wondering if I'd ever get a break, standing in the pouring rain . . .' Suddenly I realise I'm getting a bit carried away. 'Anyway. I can tell you, if you give it to her, she really will appreciate it.'

There's a pause. Eric has a fixed, livid smile on his face.

Penny raises her eyebrows. 'Well . . . we'll come back to Sally Hedge.'

'Thanks. I didn't meant to interrupt. Carry on.' I pick up the coffee pot and try to creep out of the room silently.

I pick up the paper and am just flicking through to see if there's an 'Offices to Rent' section when Eric appears out of his office. 'Lexi. A word.' He walks me swiftly to my bedroom and closes the door, that horrible smile still on his face. 'Please don't interfere with my business.'

'Eric, I'm sorry,' I say quickly. 'But I was only expressing an opinion.'

'I don't need any opinions.'

'But isn't it *good* to talk about things?' I say in astonishment. 'Even if we disagree? I mean, that's what keeps relationships alive! Talking!'

'I don't agree.' He's still got that smile on, like a mask, as if he has to hide how angry he really is. And all of a sudden, it's like a filter falls off my eyes. I don't know this man. I don't love him. I don't know what I'm doing here.

'Eric, can I ask you a question? What do you really, genuinely think? About us? Our marriage? Everything?'

'I think we're making good progress.' Eric nods, his mood instantly better, as though we've moved on to a new subject on the agenda. 'We're becoming more intimate . . . you've started having flashbacks . . . I think it's all coming together. All good news.'

How can he believe that when he's not interested in what I think or any of my ideas or who I really am? 'Eric, I don't agree. I don't think we are becoming more intimate, not really. And . . . I have something to confess. I invented the flashback.'

Eric stares at me in shock. 'You invented it? Why?'

Because it was that or the whipped-cream mountain. 'I suppose I just . . . really wanted it to be true,' I improvise. 'But the truth is, I've remembered nothing.'

We lapse into silence. I pick up a black and white photograph of me and Eric at our wedding. Now I look more carefully, I can see the strain in my eyes. I wonder how long I was happy for. I wonder when it hit me I'd made a mistake.

'Eric, let's face it, it's not working out and I can't do it any more.'

Eric switches instantly into concerned-husband-of-deranged-invalid mode. 'Maybe you've been pushing yourself too hard. Take a rest.'

'I don't need a rest! I need to be *myself*! Eric, I'm not the girl you think you married. I don't know who I've been these last three years, but it hasn't been me. I like colour. I like mess. I like . . . pasta! All this time, I wasn't hungry for success, I was *hungry*.'

Eric looks totally bemused. 'Darling,' he says carefully. 'If it means that much to you, we can buy some pasta. I'll tell Gianna to—'

'It's not about the pasta!' I cry out. 'I've been acting for the last few weeks. And I can't do it any more. I'm not into all this high-tech stuff. I don't feel relaxed. To be honest, I'd rather live in a house.'

'A *house*?' Eric looks as horrified as if I've said I want to live with a pack of wolves and have their babies.

I suddenly feel bad for slagging off his creation. 'This place is stunning and I really admire it. But it's not me. I'm just not made for . . . loft-style living.' Aargh. I can't believe it. I actually did the sweeping, parallel-hands gesture.

'I'm . . . shocked, Lexi.' Eric looks truly poleaxed.

'But the most important thing is, you don't love me. Not *me*.'

'I do love you! You're talented and you're beautiful . . .'

'You don't think I'm beautiful. You think my collagen job is beautiful,' I correct him gently. 'And my tooth veneers and my hair dye.' Eric is silenced. I can see him eyeing me up incredulously. I probably told him it was all natural. 'I think I should move out.'

'I guess we rushed things,' Eric says at last. 'Maybe a break *would* be a good idea. After a week or two you'll see things differently.'

'Yeah.' I nod. 'Maybe.'

I'm stuffing the absolute minimum into a suitcase—some underwear, jeans, a few pairs of shoes. I don't feel I have any right to all the beige designer suits. Nor, to be honest, do I want them. As I'm finishing, I sense a presence in the room and look up to see Eric in the doorway.

'I have to go out,' he says stiffly. 'Will you be all right?'

'Yes, I'll be fine.' I reply. 'I'll take a cab to Fi's house. She's coming home early from work.' I zip up the suitcase.

'I care for you deeply. You must know that.' There's genuine pain in Eric's eyes, and I feel a stab of guilt. But you can't stay with people because of guilt. Or because they can drive a speedboat. I stand up and survey the massive, immaculate room. I'm sure I'll never live in such a luxurious place again in my life. I must be crazy.

As my gaze sweeps over the bed, something crosses my mind. 'Eric, do I squeak in my sleep?' I ask casually.

'Yes, you do.' He nods. 'We went to a doctor about it. He suggested you douche your nasal passages with salt water before retiring, and pre-scribed a nose clip.' He heads to a drawer and produces a gross-looking plastic contraption. 'Do you want to take it with you?'

'No,' I manage after a pause. 'Thanks.' I'm making the right decision.

Eric hesitates—then comes over and gives me an awkward hug.

'Bye, Eric,' I say against his expensive, scented shirt. 'I'll see you.'

Ridiculously, I feel near tears. Not because of Eric . . . but because it's over. My whole, amazing, perfect dream life.

At last, he pulls away. 'Bye, Lexi.'

An hour later, I really have finished packing. In the end, I couldn't resist stuffing another suitcase full of La Perla and Chanel make-up and body products. And a third full of coats. I mean, who else will want them? There's still a few minutes till the taxi's due. I feel as if I'm check-ing out of a posh, boutique-style hotel. It's been a great place to stay, and the facilities were amazing. But it was never home. Even so, I can't help a massive pang as I step out onto the huge terrace for the very last time. I can remember arriving here and thinking I'd landed in heaven. I guess I didn't have the perfect life handed to me on a plate, after all.

Which probably means I was never Gandhi.

As I'm locking the terrace door it occurs to me I should say goodbye to my pet. I flick on the screen and click on to 'Pet Corner'. I summon up my kitten. 'Bye, Arthur,' I say. Maybe I should say goodbye to Titan, too, just to be fair. I click on 'Titan' and at once a six-foot spider appears on the screen, rearing up at me like some kind of monster.

'Jesus!' In horror I recoil backwards and, the next moment, hear a loud crash. I wheel round to see a mess of glass, earth and greenery on the floor. Oh *great*. I've knocked over one of those bloody posh plant things. As I'm staring at the wreckage in dismay, a message flashes up on the screen, bright blue on green, over and over.

Disruption. Disruption.

This place is really trying to tell me something. Maybe it is pretty intelligent, after all.

I fetch a broom from the kitchen, sweep up all the mess and dump it in the bin. Then I find a piece of paper and write Eric a note.

Dear Eric,
I broke the orchid. I'm sorry.
Also, I ripped the sofa. Please send me an invoice.
Yours, Lexi.

The doorbell rings. 'Hi,' I say into the entryphone. 'Can you possibly come up to the top floor?' I might need some help with my cases.

'Hello!' I begin as the doors start opening. 'I'm sorry, I've got quite a lot of—' And then my heart stops dead.

It's not the taxi driver standing in front of me. It's Jon. He's wearing jeans and a T-shirt. His dark hair is sticking up unevenly and his face looks crumpled. He's the opposite of Eric's Armani-model groomedness.

'I called you at work,' he says. 'But they said you were at home. I need to say something to you, Lexi.' He takes a deep breath and every muscle in my body tightens in apprehension. 'I need . . . to apologise. I shouldn't have pestered you, it was unfair.'

I feel a jolt of shock. That's not what I was expecting.

'I've thought about it a lot,' Jon continues rapidly. 'I realise this has been an impossible time for you. I haven't helped. And . . . you're right. I'm not your lover. I'm a guy you just met. What I want to say is, don't beat yourself up. You're doing your best. That's all you can do.'

'Yeah. Well . . . I'm trying.' Oh God, I'm going to cry.

Jon seems to realise this, and moves away as though to give me space. 'How'd it go at work with the deal?'

'Good.' I nod.

'Great. I'm really pleased for you.'

'I'm leaving Eric.' I blurt it out like a release. 'I'm leaving right now.'

I don't mean to look for Jon's reaction, but I can't help it. And I see it. The hope rushing into his face like sunshine. Then out again.

'I'm . . . glad,' he says at last, carefully measured. 'You probably need some time to think everything over. This is all still pretty new for you.'

Through the glass behind Jon, I suddenly see a black taxi down below, turning into the entrance. Jon follows my gaze. 'I'll help you down.'

When the bags are all packed into the taxi, he touches my hand briefly. 'Look after yourself.'

'You . . .' I swallow. 'You too.' With slightly stumbling legs I get into the cab and pull the door to. 'Jon.' I look up to where he's still standing. 'Were we . . . really good together?'

'We were good.' His voice is so low and dry it's barely audible, his face full of mingled love and sadness as he nods. 'Really, really good.'

And now tears are spilling down my cheeks; my stomach is wrenched with pain. I'm almost weakening. I could fling open the door; say I've changed my mind . . . But I can't. I can't just run straight from one guy I don't remember into the arms of another.

I pull the heavy door shut. And slowly, the taxi pulls away.

Eight

THE WORLD HAS GONE MAD. This is the proof. As I walk into Langridge's and unwind my bright-pink scarf, I have to rub my eyes. It's only October 16, and already there's a Christmas tree covered in baubles.

'Special-offer festive Calvin Klein pack?' drones a bored-looking girl in white, and I dodge her before I can get sprayed. Although on second thoughts, Debs quite likes that perfume. Maybe I'll get it for her.

'Yes, please,' I say, and the girl nearly falls over in surprise.

As she ties up the parcel, I survey myself in the mirror behind her. My hair's still long and glossy, though not quite as bright a shade as before. I'm wearing jeans and a green cardigan and my feet are comfortable in suede sneakers. My face is bare of make-up; my left hand is bare of a ring. I like what I see. I like my life.

I'm not a millonairess living in penthouse glory, but Balham's pretty cool. What's even cooler is, my office is on the floor above my flat, so I have the world's shortest commute. Which is maybe why I don't fit into the skinniest of my jeans any more. That, and the three slices of toast I have for breakfast every morning.

Four months on, the business has all worked out well. The Porsche contract is all happening. We've done another deal supplying carpet to a restaurant chain, and just today, Fi sold my favourite Deller design— an orange circle print—to a trendy spa. That's why I'm here, shopping. I reckon everyone in the team deserves a present.

I walk on through the store. As I pass a rack of teetering high heels

I'm reminded of Rosalie, and can't help smiling. As soon as she heard Eric and I were splitting up, Rosalie announced that she wasn't going to take sides and she was going to be my rock, my absolute *rock*.

She's come to visit once.

Still, she's done better than Mum, who's managed to cancel each planned visit with some dog ailment or other. But Amy's kept me posted. Apparently, the day after I visited, Mum got a man in to sort out the dry rot. I know it doesn't sound very much. But in Mum's world, that's huge strides.

And on the completely positive and fantastic front, Amy is doing spectacularly at school! She's wangled a place on Business Studies A level, and her teacher is bowled over by her progress.

As for Eric . . . He still thinks we're on a temporary separation, even though I've contacted his lawyer about a divorce. About a week after I moved out, he sent me a typed document entitled *Lexi and Eric: Separation Manual*. I can't bring myself to look at his section entitled '*Separation Sex: Infidelity, Solo, Reconciliation, Other.*' *Other*? What on earth—

No. Don't even think about it. The thing is, there's no point dwelling on the past. It's like Fi said, you have to keep looking forward.

I pause in the Accessories department and buy a purple patent bag for Fi. Then I head upstairs and find a cool T-shirt for Carolyn.

'Festive mulled wine?' A guy in a Santa hat offers a tray full of tiny glasses, and I take one. As I wander on, I realise I seem to have strayed into Menswear. I'm just looking for somewhere to put my empty glass down when a bright voice greets me. 'Hello again!'

It's coming from a woman with a blonde bob who's folding pastel-coloured jumpers in the Ralph Lauren men's department.

'Er . . . hello,' I say uncertainly. 'Do I know you?'

'Oh no.' She smiles. 'I just remember you from last year. You were in here, buying a shirt for your . . . chap.' She glances at my hand. 'For Christmas. We had quite a long conversation as I gift-wrapped it. I've always remembered it.'

I stare back at her, trying to imagine it. 'I'm sorry,' I say at length. 'I've got a terrible memory. What did I say?'

'Don't worry!' She laughs gaily. 'Why should you remember? I just remembered it, because you were so . . . you seemed so *in love*.'

'Right.' I nod. 'Right.' I tell myself to walk away. It's no big deal. Come on, smile and go.

But all sorts of buried feelings are emerging; thrusting their way up like steam. I can't keep the past in its place any more.

'This might seem . . . odd, but did I say what his name was?'

'No.' The woman eyes me curiously. 'You just said he brought you alive. You hadn't been alive before. You were bubbling over with it, with the happiness of it. Don't you *remember*?'

'No.' Something is clenching at my throat. It was Jon. Jon, whom I've tried not to think about every single day since I walked away.

'What did I buy him?'

'It was this shirt, as I recall.' She hands me a pale green shirt.

I hold the shirt, trying to conjure up the happiness. Maybe it's the wine; maybe it's just the end of a long day. But I can't seem to let go of this shirt. 'Could I buy it, please?' I say. 'Don't bother wrapping it.'

I don't know what's wrong with me. As I walk out of Langridge's and hail a taxi I've still got the green shirt, clasped to my face like a comfort blanket. My whole head is buzzing.

A taxi draws up and I get in, on autopilot. 'Where to?' asks the driver but I barely hear him. I can't stop thinking about Jon. I'm humming . . .

I'm humming a tune I don't know. And all I know is this tune is Jon. It means Jon. It's a tune I know from him.

I close my eyes desperately, chasing it, trying to flag it down . . . And then, like a flash of light, it's in my head. It's a memory.

I have a memory. Of him. Me. The two of us together. The smell of salt in the air, his chin scratchy, a grey jumper . . . and the tune. That's it. A fleeting moment, nothing else. But I have it. I *have* it.

'Love, where to?' The driver has opened the partition.

I stare at him as though he's talking a foreign language. I can't let anything else into my mind; I have to keep hold of this memory.

'For Chrissake.' He rolls his eyes. 'Where-do-you-want-to-go?'

'To . . . to . . . Hammersmith.'

He turns round, puts the taxi in gear and we roar off.

As the taxi moves through London, I sit bolt upright. I feel as though my head contains a precious liquid and if it's jolted it'll be spilled. I have to keep this memory intact. I have to tell him.

As we arrive in Jon's road I thrust some money at the driver. I ring the bell. The next minute the front door swings open at the top of the steps and there he is, in a polo neck and jeans, old Converse sneakers on his feet.

'I remembered something,' I blurt out before he can say anything. 'I remembered a tune. I don't know it, but I know I heard it with you, at the beach. We must have been there, one time. Listen!' I start humming the tune, avid with hope. 'Do you remember?'

'Lexi . . .' He pushes his hands through his hair. 'What are you talk-ing about? Why are you carrying a shirt?' He focuses on it. 'Is that mine?'

I'm babbling but I can't help it. 'I can remember the salty air and your chin was scratchy and it went like this . . .' I start humming again, but I'm getting more inaccurate, scrabbling for the right notes. At last I give up and stop expectantly. Jon's face is screwed up, perplexed.

'I don't remember,' he says.

'*You* don't remember?' I stare at him in outraged disbelief. 'Come on! Think! It was cold and you hadn't shaved, you had a grey jumper on . . .'

Suddenly his face changes. 'Oh God. The time we went to Whitstable.' He's nodding. 'To the beach. It was freezing, so we wrapped up and we had a radio with us . . . hum the tune again?'

OK, I should never have mentioned the tune. I'm such a crap singer.

'Wait. Is it that song that was everywhere? "Bad Day".' He starts hum-ming and it's like a dream coming to life.

'Yes!' I say eagerly. 'That's it! That's the tune!'

Jon looks bemused. 'So that's all you remember? A tune.'

When he says it like that it makes me feel utterly stupid for dashing across London. Cold reality is crashing into my bubble. He's not inter-ested any more. He's probably got a girlfriend by now.

'Yes.' I clear my throat. 'That's all. I just thought I'd let you know that I'd remembered something. So . . . um . . . anyway. Nice to see you. Bye.' My cheeks are flaming miserably as I turn to leave. This is so embarrassing. I don't know what I was *thinking*—

'Is it enough?' Jon's voice takes me by surprise. I swivel, to see he's come halfway down the steps, his face taut with hope. 'You said you needed a memory. A thread linking us.' He takes another step down towards me. 'Now you have one.'

'If I do, it's the thinnest thread in the world. One tune.' I make a sound that was supposed to be a laugh. 'It's like . . . cobweb. Gossamer thin.'

'Well then, hold on to it.' He's coming down the rest of the steps. 'Hold on, Lexi. Don't let it snap.' He reaches me and wraps me tightly in his arms.

'I won't,' I whisper and grab on to him. I don't ever want to let him go again. When at last I resurface, three children are staring at me from the next-door steps.

'Ooh,' says one. 'Sex-eee.'

I can't help laughing, even though my eyes are shiny with tears. 'Hey, Jon. Guess what? I suddenly remember something else.'

'What?' His face lights up. 'What do you remember?'

'I remember going into your house . . . taking the phones off the hooks . . . and having the best sex of my life for twenty-four hours solid,' I say seriously. 'I even remember the exact date.'

'Really?' Jon smiles, but looks a bit puzzled. 'When?'

'October the 16th, 2007. At about . . .' I consult my watch, '4.57 p.m.'

'*Aaah.*' Jon smiles in comprehension. 'Of course. Yes, I remember that too. It was a pretty awesome time, wasn't it? Come on.' He leads me up the steps to the cheers and jeers of the children.

'By the way,' I say as he kicks the door shut behind us. 'I haven't had good sex since 2004. Just so you know.'

Jon laughs. He peels off his polo neck in one movement and I feel a bolt of instant lust. My body remembers this, even if I don't.

'I'll accept that challenge.' He comes over, takes my face in his two hands and just surveys me for a moment, silent and purposeful.

I can't hold out any more. I have to pull his face down to me for a kiss. And this one I'll never forget; this one I'll keep for ever.

Sophie Kinsella

Can you tell me a little about yourself?

I was born in London. I studied music at New College, Oxford, but, after a year, switched to Politics, Philosophy and Economics and gained a first after only two years of studying. I then worked as a teacher and as a financial journalist.

When was your first book published?

When I was twenty-four. It was called *The Tennis Party* and was published under my real name, Madeleine Wickham.

After writing seven books as Madeleine Wickham, why did you change your pen name to Sophie Kinsella when you started to write your *Shopaholic* novels?

When I had the idea for *Shopaholic*, it was as though a light switched on. I realised I actually wanted to write comedy. No apologies, no trying to be serious, just full-on entertainment. The minute I went with that, and threw myself into it, I thought, 'Yes, this is what I want!' It felt just like writing my first book again—it was really liberating. I chose to publish the first *Shopaholic* book under a pseudonym because I wanted it to be judged on its own merits. I knew that if I tried to pitch the idea to my publishers they might be dubious, because it was very different to what I'd written before. So I thought I'd just present them with the finished novel under a different name. They could either like it or not like it.

How long does it take you to write a novel?

Usually about nine months in total. I have two stages: the first is the coffee-shop stage, where I sit down, order a coffee, make notes and plan it all. I do that for weeks before I actually start to write. The second is sitting upstairs, alone, writing intensely and listening to very loud music. It's like soundproofing, because it blocks out the rest of the world and allows me to focus.

Where did the idea for *Remember Me?* come from?

Just me thinking, What if you woke up and everything in your life was perfect? It's never going to happen to most of us but . . . Also, I've always been fascinated by memory, so having a heroine with amnesia was the obvious way to tell the story.

Would you like a house with 'home screen system' technology?

I'm not at all technology-minded, although we have just invested in a big screen for our basement sitting room. I did joke that we should have some virtual pets on it!

Lexi has a whole room devoted to shoes in the novel. Do you have a shoe room?

I don't, sadly! Although I aspire to one. What I do have, though, is a gorgeous shoe cupboard. It's painted pink inside and has all my shoes in rows. The only trouble is my shoes now spill out of the cupboard! My husband tried to instigate a rule: 'Only as many shoes as fit into the shoe cupboard' but that didn't really work.

I know that you are involved in the film of your *Shopaholic* novels, which is due to be released in the autumn. What's that like?

The film options were bought seven years ago and now, at last, it's actually happening. Disney are making the movie, which is called *Confessions of a Shopaholic*. It's being re-set in the States and Isla Fisher is playing Becky Bloomwood and Hugh Dancy is Luke. During the last few weeks, I've been with the film crew in New York. The sets are fantastic and I love Becky's room. And *her* shoe collection is amazing!

Do you love New York or hate it?

I love New York, so I was thrilled that the film would be shot here. We've been shooting in a fabulous boutique the last couple of days, so I've even managed to do some shopping between takes!

Have you written the screenplay?

No, but I would have loved to.

How old are your sons now?

Freddy is eleven, Hugo's nine and Oscar is two.

How do you cope with being a successful writer and mother to three young sons?

I'm very lucky. I have a really supportive husband in Henry and there's my mum too. I couldn't have a career and manage the kids' routines and household things single-handedly. I'd just go crazy. I know what my strengths are: making up and writing stories. I'm not so good at remembering to send back the school letters with boxes ticked and signed. Luckily, Henry is brilliant at that.

So while you are in New York, is it web cam or just long phone calls home?

I've really missed the boys while I've been out here and I have thought that a web cam would be good. For the moment, it's just phone calls—and next week it's half term and they're all coming out to visit the set! I can't wait.

Jane Eastgate

Kristin Hannah
Firefly

At fourteen, Tully and Kate vow to be
'Best friends for ever'—a promise they
keep for over thirty years.
But what is it that makes a best friend?
For both women, it's the one person who
knows you better than you know yourself, who can drive you crazy, make you
cry and break your heart, but who, in the
end, when the chips are down, is there,
sharing your memories and making you
laugh—even in your darkest hours.

Prologue

THEY USED TO BE called the Firefly Lane girls. That was a long time ago—more than three decades to be exact—but just now, as she lay in bed, listening to a winter storm raging outside, it seemed like yesterday.

In the past week (unquestionably the worst seven days of her life), she'd lost the ability to distance herself from the memories. Too often lately in her dreams it was 1974; she was a teenager again, riding her bike at midnight with her best friend in a darkness so complete it was like being invisible. The place was relevant only as a reference point, but she remembered it in vivid detail: a meandering ribbon of asphalt bordered on either side by a deep gully of murky water and hillsides of shaggy grass. Before they met, that road seemed to go nowhere at all; it was just a country lane named after an insect no one had ever seen in this rugged blue and green corner of the world.

Then they saw it through each other's eyes. When they stood together on the rise of the hill, instead of towering trees and muddy potholes, they saw all the places they would someday go. At night, they sneaked out of their houses and met on that road. On the banks of the Pilchuck River they smoked stolen cigarettes, cried to the lyrics of 'Billy, Don't Be a Hero', and told each other everything, stitching their lives together until by summer's end no one knew where one girl ended and the other began. They became to everyone who knew them simply TullyandKate, and for more than thirty years that friendship was the bulkhead of their lives: strong, durable, solid. The music might have changed with the decades but the promises made on Firefly Lane remained.

Best friends for ever.

They'd believed it would last, that promise, that someday they'd be old women, sitting in their rocking chairs on a creaking deck, talking about the times of their lives, and laughing.

Now she knew better, of course. For more than a year she'd been telling herself it was OK, that she could go on without a best friend. Sometimes she even believed it.

Then she would hear the music. Their music. 'Goodbye Yellow Brick Road', 'Dancing Queen', 'Bohemian Rhapsody', 'Yesterday'.

She eased back the covers and got out of bed, being careful not to wake the man sleeping beside her. For a moment she stood there, staring down at him in the shadowy darkness. Even in sleep, he wore a troubled expression.

She took the phone off its hook and left the bedroom, walking down the quiet hallway towards the deck. There, she stared out at the storm and gathered her courage. As she punched in the familiar numbers, she wondered what she would say to her once-best friend after all these silent months, how she would start. *I've had a bad week . . . My life is falling apart . . .* Or simply: *I need you.*

Part One: THE SEVENTIES
Dancing Queen
young and sweet, only seventeen

FOR MOST of the country, 1970 was a year of upheaval and change, but in the house on Magnolia Drive, everything was orderly and quiet. Inside, ten-year-old Tully Hart sat on a cold wooden floor, playing with her dolls.

Her grandma sat in her rocking chair by the fireplace, doing needlepoint. She made hundreds of samplers, most of which quoted the Bible.

And Grandpa . . . well, he couldn't help being quiet. Ever since his stroke, he just stayed in bed.

Tully reached for her yellow-haired doll. Humming very quietly, she made her dance to 'Daydream Believer'. Halfway through the song, there was a knock at the door. It was such an unexpected sound that Tully paused in her playing and looked up. No one ever came to visit.

Gran put her needlework in the bag by her chair and got up. When she opened the door, there was a long silence; then she said, 'Oh my.'

Tully heard something weird in her gran's voice. Peering sideways, she saw a tall woman with long messy hair and a smile that wouldn't stay in place. She was one of the prettiest women Tully had ever seen.

'Thass not much of a greeting for your long-lost daughter.' The lady pushed past Grandma and walked straight to Tully, then bent down. 'Is this my little Tallulah Rose?'

Daughter? That meant—

'Mommy?' she whispered in awe, afraid to believe it. She'd waited so long for this, dreamt of it: her mommy coming back.

'Did you miss me?'

'Oh, *yes*,' Tully said. She was so happy. She'd prayed for this.

Gran closed the door. 'Why don't you come into the kitchen for a cup of coffee?'

'I didn't come back for coffee. I came for my daughter.'

'Tully needs—'

'I think I can figure out what my daughter needs.' Her mother seemed to be trying to stand straight, but it wasn't working. She was kind of wobbly and her eyes looked funny.

Gran moved towards them. 'Raising a child is a big responsibility, Dorothy. Maybe if you moved in here for a while and got to know Tully you'd be ready . . .' She paused, then said quietly, 'You're drunk.'

Mommy giggled and winked at Tully.

'Iss my birthday, Mother, or have you forgotten?'

'Your birthday?' Tully shot to her feet. 'Wait here,' she said, then ran to her room. Her heart was racing as she dug through her vanity drawer, looking for the macaroni and bead necklace she'd made her mom at Bible school last year. Gran had frowned when she saw it, told her not to get her hopes up, but Tully hadn't been able to do that. Her hopes had been up for years. Shoving it in her pocket, she rushed back out, just in time to hear her mommy say,

'I'm not drunk, Mother dear. I'm with my kid again for the first time in three years. Love is the ultimate high.'

'Six years. She was four the last time you dropped her off here.'

'That long ago?' Mommy said, looking confused.

'Move back home, Dorothy. I can help you.'

'No, thanks. Come on, Tallulah.' Her mom was already lurching towards the door.

Tully frowned. This wasn't right. This wasn't how it was supposed to happen. Her mommy hadn't hugged her or kissed her or asked how she was. And everyone knew you were supposed to pack a suitcase to leave. She pointed at her bedroom door. 'My stuff—'

'You don't need that materialistic shit, Tallulah.'

Gran moved towards Tully, pulled her into a hug that smelt sweetly familiar, of talcum powder and hairspray. These were the only arms that had ever hugged Tully, this was the only person who'd ever made her feel safe, and suddenly she was afraid. 'Gran?' she said. 'What's happening?'

'You're coming with me,' Mommy said, reaching out to the door frame to steady herself.

Her grandmother let go of Tully and stepped back. 'You know our phone number. You call us if something goes wrong.' She was crying.

Mommy swooped over and grabbed her by the shoulder. 'Come on.' She took Tully's hand and pulled her towards the door.

Tully stumbled along behind her mother, out of the house, down the steps and across the street to a rusted VW bus that had plastic flowers all over it and a giant yellow peace symbol painted on the side.

The door opened; thick grey smoke rolled out. Through the haze she saw three people in the van. A black man with a huge Afro and a red headband was in the driver's seat. In the back was a woman in a fringed waistcoat and striped trousers; beside her sat a man in bell-bottoms and a dirty T-shirt. Brown shag carpeting covered the van floor; a few pipes lay scattered about, mixed up with empty beer bottles, food wrappers and eight-track tapes.

'This is my kid, Tallulah,' Mom said.

Tully didn't say anything, but she hated to be called Tallulah. She'd tell her mommy that later, when they were alone.

'She looks just like you, Dot. It blows my mind.'

'Get in,' the driver said gruffly. 'We're gonna be late.'

The man in the dirty T-shirt reached for Tully, put his arm round her waist and swung her into the van, where she positioned herself carefully on her knees.

Mom climbed inside and slammed the door shut. Tully edged closer to the metal side to make room beside her, but Mom sat next to the lady. They immediately started talking about pigs and marches. None of it made sense to Tully and the smoke was making her dizzy. When the man beside her lit up his pipe, she couldn't help the sigh of disappointment that leaked from her mouth.

The man heard it and turned to her. Exhaling a cloud of grey smoke, he smiled. 'Jus' go with the flow, li'l' girl.'

Mommy looked at Tully then for the first time, really *looked* at her. 'You remember that, kiddo. Life isn't about cookin' and cleanin' and havin' babies. It's about bein' free. Doin' your own thing. You can be the president of the United States if you want.'

The woman patted Mom's thigh. 'Thass tellin' it like it is. Pass me that bong, Tom.' She giggled. 'Hey, that's almost a rhyme.'

Tully frowned. She didn't want to be the president. She wanted to be a ballerina. Mostly, though, she wanted her mommy to love her. She edged sideways until she was actually close enough to her mother to touch her. 'Happy birthday,' she said quietly, reaching into her pocket. She pulled out the necklace she'd worked so hard on. 'I made this for you.'

Mom snagged the necklace and closed her fingers round it. Tully waited for her mom to say thank you and put the necklace on, but she didn't; she just sat there, swaying to the music, talking to her friends.

Tully finally closed her eyes. The smoke was making her sleepy. For most of her life she'd missed her mommy. She'd promised herself that if her mommy ever came back, she'd be good. Whatever she'd done or said that was so wrong, she'd fix or change. More than anything she wanted to make her mommy proud.

But now she didn't know what to do. In her dreams, they'd always gone off together alone, just the two of them, holding hands.

'Tallulah. Wake up.'

Tully came awake with a jolt. Her head was pounding and her throat hurt. When she tried to say, *Where are we?* all that came out was a croak.

Everyone laughed at that as they bundled out of the van.

On this busy downtown Seattle street, there were people everywhere, chanting and yelling and holding up signs that read: MAKE LOVE, NOT WAR, and HELL NO, WE WON'T GO. Tully had never seen so many people in one place.

Mommy took hold of her hand, pulled her close.

The rest of the day was a blur of people chanting slogans and singing songs. By the time it got dark, Tully was tired and hungry and her head ached, but they just kept walking, up one street and down another. The crowd was different now; they'd put away their signs and started drinking. People swelled round them, dancing and laughing. From somewhere, music spilt into the street.

And then, suddenly, she was holding on to nothing.

'Mommy!' she screamed.

No one answered or turned to her, even though there were people everywhere. She screamed for her mommy until her voice failed her.

She'll be back.

Tears stung her eyes and leaked down her face as she sat at the kerb, waiting, trying to be brave.

But her mommy never came back.

A policeman took her back to the house on Queen Anne Hill, where her grandma held her tightly and told her it wasn't her fault.

But Tully knew better. Somehow today she'd done something wrong, been bad. Next time her mommy came back, she'd try harder.

Tully got a chart of the presidents of the United States and memorised every name in order. She told anyone who asked that she would be the first woman president; she even quit taking ballet classes. On her eleventh birthday, while Grandma lit the candles on her cake and sang 'Happy Birthday', Tully glanced repeatedly at the door, thinking, *This is it*, but no one ever knocked and the phone didn't ring. Later, with the opened boxes of her gifts around her, she tried to keep smiling. In front of her, on the coffee table, was an empty scrapbook.

'She didn't even call,' Tully said, looking up.

Gran sighed tiredly. 'Your mom has . . . problems, Tully. She's weak and confused. I've told you that a hundred times. You've got to quit pretending things are different. What matters is that you're strong.'

She'd heard this advice a bazillion times. 'I know, Gran.'

Gran sat down on the worn, floral sofa beside Tully and pulled her onto her lap. Tully loved it when Gran held her. She snuggled in close, rested her cheek on Gran's soft chest.

'I wish things were different with your mama, Tully, and that's the God's honest truth, but she's a lost soul. Has been for a long time.'

'Is that why she doesn't love me?'

Gran looked down at her. 'She loves you, in her way. That's why she keeps coming back.' Gran tightened her hold on Tully. 'Someday she'll be sorry she missed these years with you. I'm certain of that.'

'I could show her my scrapbook.'

'That would be nice.' After a long silence, Gran said, 'Happy birthday, Tully,' and kissed her forehead. 'Now I'd best go sit with your grandfather. He's feeling poorly today.'

After her grandmother left the room, Tully sat there, staring down at the blank first page of her new scrapbook. It would be the perfect thing to give her mother one day, to show her what she'd missed.

She picked up a pen and very carefully wrote the date in the upper right-hand corner; then she frowned. What else? *Dear Mommy. Today was my eleventh birthday* . . .

For some years after, whenever she had a good day, she hurried home and wrote about it. Somewhere along the way she started adding little embellishments to make her look better. Anything that would make her mom someday say she was proud of her. She filled that scrapbook and then another and another. On every birthday, she received a brand-new book, until she moved into the teen years.

Something happened to her then. She wasn't sure what it was, maybe the breasts that grew faster than anyone else's, or maybe it was just that she got tired of putting her life down on pieces of paper no one ever asked to see. All she knew was that by fourteen, she was done. She put all her little-girl books in a big cardboard box and shoved them to the back of her closet, and she asked Gran not to buy her any more.

She didn't care about her mother any more and tried never to think about her. She quit buying her clothes in the little girls' departments and spent her time in the juniors' area. She bought midriff-bearing tight shirts that showed off her new boobs and low-rise bell-bottoms that made her butt look good.

She learned that if she dressed a certain way and acted a certain way, the cool kids wanted to hang out with her. By eighth grade, she was the most popular girl in junior high, and it helped, having all those friends. When she was busy enough, she didn't think about the woman who didn't want her.

On rare days she still felt—not lonely—but something. Adrift, maybe.

Today was one of those days. Sighing, she sat quietly in her regular seat on the school bus, hearing the buzz of gossip go on around her. Everyone seemed to be talking about family things; she had nothing to add to the conversations. She knew nothing about fighting with your little brother or being grounded for talking back to your parents. Thankfully, when the bus pulled up to her stop, she hurried off, repositioned her backpack over her shoulder and started the long walk home. She had just turned the corner when she saw it.

There, parked across the street, in front of Gran's house, was a beat-up rusted VW bus. The flowers were still on the side.

Her mother was back.

It was still dark when Kate Mularkey's alarm clock rang. She groaned and lay there. The thought of going to school made her sick.

In sixth grade she'd had two best friends; they'd done everything together—showed their horses, gone to youth group and ridden their bikes from one house to the next. The summer they turned twelve, all that ended. Her friends turned wild; there was no other way to put it. They smoked pot before school and skipped classes and never missed a party. When she wouldn't join in, they cut her loose. Period. And the 'good' kids wouldn't come near her because she'd been part of the stoners' club. So now books were her only friends. She'd read *Lord of the Rings* so often she could recite whole scenes by memory.

It was not the kind of skill that aided one in becoming popular.

With a sigh, she got out of bed, took a quick shower and braided her straight blonde hair, then put on her horn-rimmed glasses. They were hopelessly out of date now—round and rimless were what the cool kids wore—but her dad said they couldn't afford new glasses yet.

Downstairs, she went to the back door, folded her belled trouser leg round each calf, and stepped into the huge black rubber boots they kept on the concrete steps. Moving like Neil Armstrong, she made her way through the deep mud to the shed out back. Their old mare limped up to the fence, whinnied a greeting. 'Heya, Sweetpea,' Kate said, throwing hay onto the ground, and then scratching the horse's velvety ear.

She clomped back up the dark, muddy driveway and left her dirty boots on the porch.

When she opened the back door, she stepped into pandemonium. Mom was inside the small kitchen, making breakfast and yelling an answer to some unknown question. As always, she stood at the stove, dressed in her faded floral housedress and fuzzy pink slippers, smoking a menthol cigarette and pouring batter into an electric frying pan. 'Set the table, Katie,' she said without glancing up. 'Sean! Breakfast.'

Kate did as she was told. Almost before she was finished, eight-year-old Sean came running down the stairs and rushed towards the beige speckled Formica table.

Kate was just about to sit down at her regular place when she happened to glance across the kitchen and into the living room. Through the large window above the sofa, she saw something that surprised her: a removal van turning into the driveway across the street.

From their position on the hill, this house looked out over their three acres and down on the neighbour's place. It had been vacant for as long as anyone could remember.

'Someone's moving in across the street,' Kate said.

'Maybe they'll have a girl your age. It would be nice to have a friend.'

Kate bit back an irritated retort. Only mothers thought it was easy to make friends in junior high. 'Whatever.'

Mom's sigh was so quiet it could hardly be heard. 'Why are we always bickering lately?'

'You're the one who starts it.'

'By saying hello and asking how you're doing? Yeah, I'm a real witch.'

'You said it, not me.'

'It's not my fault, you know.'

'What isn't?'

'That you don't have any friends. If you'd—'

Kate walked away. Honest to St Jude, one more *if you'd only try harder* speech and she might puke.

Thankfully Mom didn't follow her. Instead, she said, 'Hurry up, Sean. The Mularkey school bus leaves in ten minutes.'

Her brother giggled. Kate rolled her eyes. It was so lame. How could her brother laugh at the same stupid joke every day?

The answer came as quickly as the question had: because he had friends. Life with friends made everything easier.

She hid in her bedroom until she heard the old Ford station wagon start up. The last thing she wanted was to get driven to school by her mom. Everyone knew it was social suicide to be driven to school by your parents. When she heard tyres crunching slowly across gravel, she went back downstairs, washed the dishes, gathered her stuff and left the house. Outside, the sun was shining, but last night's rain had studded the driveway with inner-tube-sized mud holes. Mud sucked at the soles of her fake Earth shoes, making her progress slow. So intent was she on saving her only rainbow socks that she was at the bottom of the driveway before she noticed the girl standing across the street.

She was gorgeous. Tall and big-boobed, she had long, curly auburn hair, pale skin, full lips and long lashes. And her *clothes*. She wore the coolest low-rise, three-button jeans with huge, tie-dyed wedges of fabric in the seams to make elephant bells. Her cork-bottomed platform shoes had four-inch heels, and the angel-sleeved pink peasant blouse she wore revealed at least two inches of her stomach.

Kate clutched her books against her chest, wishing that her jeans weren't Sears's Rough Riders. 'H-hi,' she said, stopping on her side of the road. 'The bus stops on this side.'

Chocolate-brown eyes, rimmed heavily with black mascara and shiny blue eye shadow, stared at her, revealing nothing.

Just then, the school bus arrived. Wheezing and squeaking, it came to a shuddering stop on the road. Kate boarded the bus, collapsing into her usual front-row seat—by herself—waiting for the new girl to walk past her, but no one else got on. When the doors thumped shut and the bus lurched forwards, she dared to look back at the road.

The coolest-looking girl in the world wasn't there.

Already Tully didn't fit in. It had taken her two hours to choose her clothes this morning—an outfit right out of the pages of *Seventeen* magazine—and every bit of it was wrong.

When the school bus drove up, she made a split-second decision. She wasn't going to go to school in this hick backwater.

She marched down the gravel driveway and shoved the front door open so hard it cracked against the wall. She hated it when she felt like this, all puffed up with anger.

In the master bedroom, her mom was sitting on the floor, cutting pictures out of *Cosmo*. As usual, her long hair was a wavy, fuzzy nightmare held in check by a grossly out-of-date beaded leather headband.

'I'm *not* going to this backwater school. They're a bunch of hicks.'

'Oh.' Mom flipped to the next page. 'OK.'

'OK? *OK*? I'm fourteen years old.'

'My job is to love and support you, baby, not to get in your face.'

Tully counted to ten and said, 'I don't have any friends here.'

'Make new ones. I heard you were Miss Popular at your old school.'

'Come on, Mom, I—'

'Cloud.'

'I'm not calling you Cloud.'

'Fine, Tallulah.'

'I don't belong here.'

'You know better than that, Tully. You're a child of the earth and sky; you belong everywhere. The Bhagavad-Gita says . . .'

Tully walked away while her mother was still talking.

For the next week, Kate watched the new girl from a distance.

Tully Hart was boldly, coolly different. She had no curfew and didn't care if she got caught smoking in the woods behind the school. Everyone talked about it. For a group of kids who'd grown up in the dairy farms and paper mill workers' homes of the Snohomish Valley, Tully Hart was exotic. Everyone wanted to be friends with her.

Her neighbour's instant popularity made Kate's alienation more unbearable. She wasn't sure why it wounded her so much. All she knew was that every morning, as they stood at the bus-stop beside each other and yet worlds apart, Kate was desperate to be acknowledged by Tully.

Not that it would ever happen.

'Kate? Katie?'

Kate lifted her head from the table. She'd fallen asleep on her open social studies textbook at the kitchen table. 'Huh? What did you say?' she asked, pushing her glasses back up into place.

'I made a casserole for our new neighbours. I want you to take it across the street.'

'But . . .' Kate tried to think of an excuse, anything that would get her out of this. 'They've been here a week.'

'So I'm late. Things have been crazy lately.'

'I've got too much homework. Send Sean.'

'Sean's not likely to make friends over there, now, is he?'

'Neither am I,' Kate said miserably.

Staring at Kate, Mom crossed the room and sat down at the table. 'Can I say something without you jumping all over me?'

'Probably not.'

'Life is hard sometimes. Especially at fourteen.'

Kate rolled her eyes. Her mother knew nothing about how hard life could be for a teenager. 'No shit.'

'I'm going to pretend I didn't hear that word from you. Right?'

Kate couldn't help wishing she was like Tully. *She'd* never back down so easily.

Mom dug through the baggy pocket of her skirt and found her cigarettes. Lighting up, she studied Kate. 'You know I love you and I support you and I would never let anyone hurt you. But, Katie, I have to ask you: what is it you're waiting for?'

'What do you mean?'

'You spend all your time reading and doing homework. How are people supposed to get to know you when you act like that?'

'They don't want to know me.'

Mom touched her hand gently. 'It's never good to sit around and wait for someone or something to change your life. That's why women like Gloria Steinem are burning their bras and marching on Washington.'

'So that I can make friends?'

'So that you can be whatever you want to be. But you have to take a risk sometimes. Reach out. One thing I can tell you for sure is this: we only regret what we don't do in life.'

Kate heard an odd sound in her mom's voice, a sadness that tinted the word *regret*. But what could her mother possibly know about the battlefield of junior-high popularity? 'Yeah, right.'

'It's true, Kathleen. Someday you'll see how smart I am.' Her mom smiled and patted her hand. 'If you're like the rest of us, it'll happen at about the same time you want me to baby-sit for the first time.'

'What are you talking about?'

Mom laughed at some joke Kate didn't even get. 'I'm glad we had this talk. Now, go. Make friends with your new neighbour.'

Yeah. That would happen.

'Wear oven mitts. It's still hot,' Mom said.

Perfect. The mitts.

The house across the street was long and low to the ground, a rambler-style in an L-shape that faced away from the road. Moss furred the shingled roof. The ivory sides were in need of paint, and the gutters were overflowing with leaves and sticks. To the casual observer, it would look as if it were still abandoned.

At the front door Kate paused, drawing in a deep breath.

Balancing the casserole in one hand, she pulled off one oven mitt and knocked. *Please let no one be home.*

Almost instantly, she heard footsteps from inside.

The door swung open to reveal a tall woman dressed in a billowy caftan. An Indian-beaded headband circled her forehead. There was a strange dullness in her eyes as if she needed glasses and didn't have them, but even so, she was pretty in a sharp, brittle kind of way. 'Yeah?'

Weird, pulsing music seemed to come from several places at once; though the lights were turned off, several lava lamps burped and bubbled in eerie green and red canisters.

'H-hello,' Kate stammered. 'My mom made you guys this casserole.'

'Right on,' the lady said, stumbling back, almost falling.

And suddenly Tully was coming through the doorway, sweeping through, actually, moving with a grace and confidence that was more movie star than teenager. Without saying anything, she grabbed Kate's arm, pulled her through the living room, and into a kitchen, in which everything was shocking pink: walls, cabinets, curtains, tile counters, table. When Tully looked at her, Kate thought she saw a flash of something that looked like embarrassment in those dark eyes.

'Was that your mom?' Kate asked, uncertain of what to say.

'She has cancer.'

'Oh.' Kate didn't know what to say except, 'I'm sorry.' Quiet pressed into the room. Instead of making eye contact with Tully, Kate studied the table. Never in her life had she seen so much junk food in one place. 'Wow. I wish my mom would let me eat all this stuff.' Kate immediately wished she'd kept her mouth shut. Now she sounded hopelessly uncool. She put the casserole on the counter.

Tully lit up a cigarette and leaned against the pink wall, eyeing her.

Kate glanced back to the living room. 'She doesn't care if you smoke?'

'She's too sick to care.'

'Oh.'

'You want a drag?'

'Uh . . . no. Thanks.'

'Yeah. That's what I thought. Well, you probably have to get home.'

'Oh,' Kate said again, sounding even more nerdy than she had before. 'Right.'

Tully led the way back through the living room, where her mother was now sprawled on the sofa. 'Bye, girl from across the street with the cool neighbour attitude.'

Tully yanked open the door. 'Thanks for the food,' she said. 'I don't know how to cook, and Cloud is cooked, if you know what I mean.'

'Cloud?'

'That's my mom's current name.'

'Oh. Well . . . bye.' Kate stepped past her and into the night.

She was halfway to the road when Tully called out to her, 'Wait up.'

Kate slowly turned round.

'What's your name?'

She felt a flash of hope. 'Kate. Kate Mularkey.'

Tully laughed. 'Mularkey? Like bullshit?'

It was hardly funny any more, that joke about her last name. She sighed and turned back round.

'I didn't mean to laugh,' Tully said, but she didn't stop.

'Yeah. Whatever.'

'Fine. Be a bitch, why don't you?'

Kate kept walking.

A few nights later, after a dinner of Pop-Tarts and Alpha-Bits cereal, Tully took a long, hot shower, shaved her legs and underarms carefully, and dried her hair until it fell straight from her centre parting without a single crease or curl. Then she went to her closet and stood there, trying to figure out what to wear. This was her first high-school party. She needed to look just right. None of the other girls from the junior high had been invited. But Pat Richmond, the best-looking guy on the football team, had chosen Tully for his date.

She still couldn't believe it. They could fall in love; she knew it. And then, with him holding her hand, she'd stop feeling so alone.

She finally made her clothes choice. Low-rise, three-button, bell-bottomed jeans, a pink scoop-necked knit top that showed off her cleavage, and her favourite cork platforms.

In the living room, Mom looked up blearily from her magazine. 'Hey, iss almos' ten o'clock. Where are you going?'

'This guy invited me to a party.'

'Oh. Cool. Don't wake me up when you get home.'

'I won't.'

Outside, it was dark and cold. Tully waited by her mailbox on the main road, moving from foot to foot to keep warm. Across the street and up the hill, the pretty little farmhouse glowed against the darkness. They were probably all at home, clustered around a big table, playing Risk.

She heard Pat's car before she saw the headlights. At the roar of the engine, she forgot all about the family across the street and stepped into the road, waving.

His green Dodge Charger came to a stop beside her. She slid into the passenger seat. The music was so loud she knew he couldn't hear what she said. Grinning at her, Pat hit the gas and they were off like a rocket, blasting down the quiet country lane.

As they turned onto a gravel road, she could see the party going on below. Dozens of cars were parked in a huge circle in a pasture, with their headlights on. Bachman-Turner Overdrive's 'Taking Care of Business' blared from the car radios. Pat parked over in the strand of trees along the fence line.

There were kids everywhere, gathered round the flames of the bonfire, standing beside the keg of beer set up in the grass. Down by the barn, a group of guys were playing touch football.

Pat held her hand tightly, leading her through the crowd of couples towards the keg, where he poured two glasses full.

Taking hers, she let him lead her down to a quiet spot just beyond the perimeter of cars. There, he spread his letterman's jacket down on the ground and let her sit on it.

'I couldn't believe it when I first saw you,' Pat said, sitting close to her, sipping his beer. 'You're the prettiest girl ever to live in this town. All the guys want you.'

'But you got me,' she said, smiling at him.

He took a big drink of his beer, practically finishing it, then he set it down and kissed her.

Other guys had kissed her before; mostly they were fumbling, nervous attempts during a slow dance. This was different. Pat's mouth was like magic. She sighed happily. When he drew back, he was staring at her with pure, sunshiny love in his eyes. 'I'm glad you're here.'

'Me, too.'

He finished off his beer and got up. 'I need more brew.'

They were at the keg again when he said, 'You aren't drinking.'

'I am.' She smiled nervously. She'd never really drunk before, but he wouldn't want her if she acted like a nerd. 'Bottoms up,' she said, tilting the plastic tumbler to her lips and drinking it all in record time.

'Far out,' he said, nodding, pouring two more beers.

The second one wasn't so bad and by the third beer, Tully had completely lost her sense of taste. For almost an hour, they sat on his jacket, tucked close together, drinking and talking. She didn't know any of the people he talked about, but that didn't matter. What mattered was the way he looked at her, the way he held her hand and didn't let go.

'Come on,' he whispered, 'let's dance.'

She felt woozy and kind of cottony when she stood up. Her balance was off and she kept stumbling during their dance. Finally, Pat took her hand and led her to a dark, romantic spot in the trees. Giggling, she hobbled awkwardly behind him, gasping when he took her in his arms and kissed her.

It felt so good; made her blood feel tingly and hot. She pressed up against him like a cat, loving the way he was making her feel. Any minute he was going to draw back and look down at her and say, 'I love you,' just like Ryan O'Neal in *Love Story*.

His tongue slipped into her mouth, pressing hard, sweeping around. The feel of it, pushing and poking, scared her. Suddenly it didn't feel so good any more, didn't feel right. She tried to say *stop*, but her voice had no sound; he was sucking up all her air.

His hands were everywhere: up her back, round her side, plucking at her bra, trying to undo it. She felt it come free with a sickening little pop. And then he was touching her boob.

'No . . .' she whimpered, trying to push his hands away. This wasn't what she wanted. She wanted love, romance, magic. Someone to love her. Not . . . this. 'No, Pat, don't—'

'Come on, Tully. Don't be a prick tease.' He pushed her back and she stumbled, fell to the ground hard, hitting her head. For a second, her vision blurred. When it cleared, he was on his knees, between her legs. He held both her hands in one of his, pinning her to the ground.

Shoving her top up, he stared down at her naked chest. 'Oh, yeah . . .' He cupped one breast, tweaked her nipple hard. His other hand slipped into her jeans, beneath her underwear.

'Stop. Please . . .' Tully tried desperately to get free. 'Don't—' She was crying so hard she could taste her own tears, but he didn't seem to care. She squeezed her eyes shut as pain ripped between her legs, scraped her insides.

Then it was over. He rolled off her, lay beside her, holding her close, kissing her cheek as if what he'd just done to her had been love.

'Hey, you're crying.' He gently smoothed the hair away from her face. 'What's the matter? I thought you wanted it.'

'Wanted *that*?' She rolled onto her side. 'Go away.'

'You acted like you wanted it, damn it. You can't lead a guy on and then just go cold. Grow up, little girl. This is your fault.'

She closed her eyes and ignored him, thankful when he finally left her. For once she was glad to be alone.

She lay there, feeling broken and hurt and, worst of all, stupid. After an hour or so, she heard the party break up, heard the car engines start and the tyres peeling through loose gravel as they drove away.

And still she lay there, unable to make herself move. This was all her fault; he was right about that. All she'd wanted was someone to love her.

'Stupid,' she hissed, finally sitting up.

Moving slowly, she dressed and tried to stand. At the movement, she felt sick to her stomach and immediately puked all over her favourite shoes. When it was over, she bent down for her bag, clutched it to her chest, and made her long, painful way back up to the road.

As she walked home she relived what had happened. The more she replayed it in her mind, the lonelier she felt.

If only she had someone she trusted to talk to. Maybe that would ease a little of this pain. But, of course, there was no one.

As she neared her driveway, the thought of being so alone in a place that should be a refuge for her, with a woman who was supposed to love her, was suddenly unbearable.

The neighbours' old horse trotted up to the fence and nickered at her.

Tully crossed the street and walked up the hill. At the fence, she yanked up a handful of grass and held it out to him. 'Hey there, boy.'

The horse sniffed the handful of grass, snorted and trotted away.

'She likes carrots.'

Tully looked up sharply and saw her neighbour sitting on the top rail of the fence. Long minutes passed in silence between them; the only noise was the horse's quiet nickering.

'I love it out here at night,' the neighbour girl said. 'The stars are so bright. Sometimes if you stare up at the sky long enough, you'll swear tiny white dots are falling all around you, like fireflies. I figure that's how this street got its name. You probably think I'm a nerd for saying that.'

Tully wanted to answer but couldn't. Deep, deep inside she'd started to shake and it took all her concentration just to stand still.

The girl—Kate, Tully remembered—slipped down from her perch. She was wearing an oversized T-shirt and as she moved forward her boots made a sucking noise in the mud. 'Hey, you don't look so good.'

'I'm fine,' she said, stiffening as Kate drew close.

'Are you OK? Really?'

To Tully's complete horror, she started to cry.

Kate stood there a moment, staring at her from behind those dork glasses. Then, without saying anything, she hugged Tully.

Tully flinched at the contact; it was foreign and unexpected. She started to pull away, but found that she couldn't move. She couldn't remember the last time someone had held her like this, and suddenly she was clinging to this weirdo girl, afraid to let go, afraid that without Kate, she'd float away.

'I'm sure she'll get better,' Kate said when Tully's tears subsided. 'Do you want to talk about it?'

Tully drew back, frowning. It took her a second to understand. The cancer. Kate thought she was worried about her mom.

'Come on,' Kate said, and led her up the hill to the slanted front porch of the farmhouse. There, she sat down, pulling her threadbare T-shirt over her bent knees. 'My aunt Georgia had cancer,' she said. 'Lost all her hair. But she's fine now.'

Tully sat down beside her, put her bag on the ground. The smell of vomit was strong. She pulled out a cigarette and lit up to cover the stench. Before she knew it, she'd said, 'I went to a party down by the river tonight.'

'A high-school party?' Kate sounded impressed.

'Pat Richmond asked me out.'

'The quarterback? Wow. My mom wouldn't let me stand in the same check-out line as a high-school senior. She thinks eighteen-year-old boys are dangerous. She calls them penises with hands and feet. She's so lame.'

Tully took a deep, steadying breath. She couldn't believe she was going to tell this girl what happened tonight, but the truth was a fire inside her. If she didn't get rid of it, she'd burn up. 'She's not lame. He raped me.'

Kate turned to her. Tully felt her green eyes boring into her profile, but she didn't move, didn't turn. Her shame was so overwhelming that she couldn't stand to see it reflected in Kate's eyes. She waited for Kate to say something, to call her an idiot, but the silence just went on and on. Finally, she couldn't stand it any more. She looked sideways.

'Are you OK?' Kate asked quietly.

Tully relived it all in those few words. Tears blurred her vision.

Once again, Kate hugged her. Tully let herself be comforted for the first time since she was little. When she finally drew back, she tried to smile. 'I'm drowning you.'

'We should tell someone.'

'No way. They'd say it was my fault. This is our secret, OK?'

'OK.' Kate frowned as she said it.

Tully wiped her eyes and took another drag on her cigarette. 'Why are you being so nice to me?'

'You looked lonely. Believe me, I know how that feels.'

'You do? But you have a family.'

'They *have* to like me.' Kate sighed. 'The kids at school treat me like

I've got an infectious disease. I used to have friends, but . . . You probably don't know what in the heck I'm talking about. You're so popular.'

'Popular just means lots of people think they know you.'

'I'd take that.'

Silence fell between them. Tully finished her cigarette and put it out. They were so different, she and Kate, as full of contrasts as this dark field bathed in moonlight, but it felt so completely easy to talk to her. Tully found herself almost smiling, and on this, the worst night of her life. That was something.

For the next hour, they sat there, talking now and then and sometimes just sitting in silence.

Finally, Kate yawned and Tully stood up. 'Well, I'd better go.'

She wanted to hug Kate and tell her how much she had been helped through the night by her, but she didn't dare. She'd learned a thing or two about vulnerability from her mother, and she felt too fragile now to risk humiliation. Turning, she headed down to her house. Once inside, she went straight to the shower. There, with the hot water beating down on her, she thought about what had happened to her tonight—what she'd let happen because she wanted to be cool—and she cried. When she was done and the tears had turned into a hard little knot in her throat, she took the memory of this night and boxed it up. She shelved it alongside memories of the times Cloud had abandoned her and immediately began working on forgetting it was there.

Kate lay awake long after Tully had left. Finally, she threw back the covers and got out of bed.

Downstairs, she found what she needed: a small statue of the Virgin Mary, a votive candle in a red glass holder, matches and her grandmother's old rosary beads. Taking everything back up to her room, she created an altar on top of her dresser, and lit the candle.

'Heavenly Father,' she prayed, head bowed and hands clasped, 'please watch out for Tully Hart and help her through this hard time. Also, please heal her mother's cancer. I know You can help them. Amen.' She said a few Hail Marys, and then went back to bed.

But all night Kate tossed and turned, dreaming about the encounter with Tully, wondering what would happen in the morning. Should she talk to Tully today at school, smile at her? Or was she expected to pretend it had never happened?

Kate was so nervous she arrived at the bus-stop early. Every minute that passed seemed to last an eternity, but there was still no sign of Tully when the bus drove up and came to a shuddering stop.

Kate dropped her chin and took a seat in the first row.

All through morning classes, she looked for Tully, but didn't see her. At lunch she hurried past the crowd of popular kids, and sat down at one of the long tables at the very end of the cafeteria. On the other side of the room, kids were laughing and talking and shoving each other; these tables in social Siberia were sadly quiet, though.

So intent was she on her lunch that when someone came up to her and said, 'Hey,' she practically jumped out of her seat.

Tully.

'Have you told anyone about last night?'

'No. Of course not.'

'I knew I could trust you. So, we're friends, right?'

Kate didn't know which surprised her more: the question or the vulnerable look in Tully's eyes when she asked it. 'We're friends.'

'Excellent.' Tully sat down beside Kate. 'Now let's talk about a makeover. You totally need one, and I'm not being a bitch. Really. I just know about fashion. It's a gift. Can I drink your milk? Good. Thanks. Are you gonna eat that banana? I could come to your house after school . . .'

Kate stood outside the drugstore looking up and down the street for someone who might know her mom. 'Are you sure about this?'

'Don't you trust me?'

There it was, the big question. She had to trust her new friend. 'Of course I do. It's just that I'm not allowed to wear make-up.'

'Believe me, I'm such an expert your mom will never know. Come on.'

Tully walked boldly through the drugstore, choosing colours that were 'right' for Kate, and then—amazingly—she paid for everything. When Kate said something, Tully said airily, 'We're friends, aren't we?'

On the way out of the store, Tully bumped her, shoulder to shoulder.

Kate giggled and bumped her back. They made their way through town and followed the river towards home. All the while, they talked, about clothes and music and school. Finally, they turned off the old road and went down Tully's driveway.

'My gran would freak if she saw this place,' Tully said, looking embarrassed. 'She owns this house, you know.'

'Does she visit you?'

'Nah. It's easier to wait.'

'For what?'

'My mom to forget about me again.' Tully opened the door. Inside, the smoke in the room was thick. Her mom was in the living room, lying on the sofa, with her eyes half opened.

'H-hello, Mrs Hart,' Kate said. 'I'm Kate from next door.'

Mrs Hart tried to sit up, but obviously she was too weak to manage it. 'Hello, girl from nex' door.'

Tully grabbed Kate's hand and pulled her through the living room and into her bedroom, then slammed the door shut. She immediately went to her stack of records, pulled out 'Goodbye Yellow Brick Road' and put it on the turntable. When the music started up, she dragged a chair over to the dressing table. 'You ready?'

Kate's nervousness came swooping back. She knew she'd get in trouble for this, but how would she ever make friends or become popular if she didn't take a few risks? 'I'm ready.'

'Good. Sit down. We'll do your hair first. It needs some highlights.'

'Is there any chance I'm going to end up bald?'

'Hardly any. Now be quiet. I'm reading the instructions.'

Tully separated Kate's hair into strips and began spraying Sun-In onto the pieces.

'What's it like, being popular?' Kate hadn't meant to ask the question; it just slipped out.

'You'll see. But you'll stay my friend, won't you?'

Kate laughed at that. 'Very funny. Hey, that sort of burns.'

'Really? That can't be good. And some of your hair is falling out.'

Kate managed not to make a face. If going bald was the price of being Tully's friend, she'd pay it.

'I got my period,' Tully said. 'So at least assface didn't knock me up.'

Kate heard the bravado in her friend's voice and saw it in her eyes. 'I prayed for that.'

'You did? Wow. Thanks,' Tully said. 'OK. Take a shower and rinse it out.'

Kate did as she was told. A few minutes later, she got out of the shower, dried off and got dressed again.

Tully immediately grabbed her hand and led her back to the chair. 'Is your hair falling out?'

'Some is,' she admitted.

'If you're bald, I'll shave my head. Promise.' Tully combed and dried Kate's hair.

Kate couldn't look. She closed her eyes and let Tully's voice meld into the whine of the dryer.

'Open your eyes.'

Kate looked up slowly. At this distance, she didn't need her glasses. The girl in the mirror had straight streaked blonde hair, parted with precision and dried perfectly. For once it looked soft and pretty instead of thin and lank. The white highlights showed off her leaf-green eyes and the hint of pink on her lips. She looked almost pretty. 'Wow,' she said, too choked up with gratitude to say more.

'Wait till you see what mascara and blush can do,' Tully said.

'I'll always be your friend,' Kate said, thinking she'd whispered the promise, but when Tully grinned, she knew she'd been heard.

Kate didn't even bother to hide her face when she came into the house. That was how confident she felt. For the first time ever, she knew she was beautiful.

Her dad was in the living room, sitting in his La-Z-Boy. At Kate's entrance, he looked up. 'Good Lord,' he said, clanking his drink down on the French provincial end table. 'Margie!'

Mom came out of the kitchen, wiping her hands on her apron. She wore her school-day uniform: striped rust and olive polyester blouse, brown corduroy bell-bottoms and a wrinkled apron. When she saw Kate, she stopped. Slowly, she untied her apron and tossed it on the table.

'Did you give her permission to do that to her hair, Margie?' Dad said.

'I'll handle this, Bud. The girl across the street do this to you?'

Kate nodded, trying to hold on to the memory of feeling pretty.

'Do you like it?'

'Yes.'

'Me, too. I remember when your aunt Georgia dyed my hair red. Grandma was livid.' She smiled. 'But you should have asked. You're still young, Kathleen. Now, what have you done to your eyebrows?'

'Tully shaved them. Just to give them shape.'

Mom made a face, as if she were trying not to smile. 'I see. Well, plucking is really the way to go. I should have taught you how already but I thought you were too young.' She sighed. 'After dinner, I'll show you how. And I suppose a little lip gloss and mascara would be all right for school. I'll show you how to make it look natural.'

Kate hugged her mom. 'I love you.'

'I love you, too. Now get started on the cornbread. And, Katie, I'm glad you made a friend, but no more breaking the rules, OK? That's how young girls get into trouble.'

Kate couldn't help thinking of the high-school party Tully had gone to. 'OK, Mom.'

Within a week, Kate became cool by association. Kids raved over her new look and didn't turn away from her in the corridors. Being a friend of Tully Hart's meant she was OK.

Even her parents noticed the difference. At dinner, Kate wasn't her usual quiet self. Instead, she couldn't shut up. Story after story spilt out of her. Who was dating whom, who got detention for wearing a MAKE LOVE, NOT WAR T-shirt to school, and what movie was playing at the drive-in this weekend. She was still talking about Tully after dinner, while she and Mom did the dishes.

'I can't wait for you to meet her. She's totally cool. Everyone likes her.'

Mom took the glass meat-loaf pan from her and dried it. 'I've . . . asked around about this girl, Katie. She tries to buy cigarettes from Alma at the drugstore.'

'She's probably buying them for her mom.'

'Just do me a favour, Katie. You think for yourself around Tully Hart. I wouldn't want you to follow her into trouble.'

Kate threw the crocheted dishrag in the soapy water. 'I can't *believe* you. What about all your take-a-risk speeches? For years you tell me to make friends, and the second I find someone, you call her a slut.'

'I hardly called her a—'

Kate stormed out of the kitchen. With each step she expected her mother to call her back and ground her, but only silence followed her dramatic exit. By the time she reached her bedroom she felt positively victorious. She'd never walked away from her mother before.

She sat down on her bed and waited. But Mom didn't show, and by ten o'clock, Kate was starting to feel bad. Had she hurt her mom's feelings? She got up, paced the small room.

At 10.05, there was a knock at the door.

She raced over to the bed and climbed in. 'Yeah?'

The door opened slowly. Mom stood there. 'May I come in?'

'Like I could stop you.'

'You could,' Mom said quietly. 'May I come in?'

Kate shrugged, but scooted to the left to make room for her mom.

'You know, Katie, life is—'

Kate couldn't help groaning. Not another *life is* speech.

Mom surprised her by laughing. 'OK, no more speeches. Maybe you're too old for that.' She paused at the altar on the dresser. 'You haven't made one of these since Georgia was in chemo. Who needs our prayers?'

'Tully's mom has cancer and she was ra—' She snapped her mouth shut, horrified by what she'd nearly revealed. For most of her life she'd told her mother everything; now she had a best friend, though, so she'd need to be careful.

'I hadn't heard that.' Mom sat down on the bed beside Kate, just as they did after every fight and smoothed the hair off Kate's forehead in a touch that was as familiar as breathing. Kate always felt five years old when she did that. 'I'm sorry you thought I was judging your friend. And you're sorry for being so mean to me, right?'

Kate couldn't help smiling. 'Yeah.'

'Why don't you invite Tully over for dinner Friday night?'

'You'll love her. I know you will.'

'I'm sure I will,' Mom said, kissing her forehead. ''Night.'

''Night, Mom.'

Long after her mother had left and the house had gone quiet for the night, Kate lay there, too wound up to sleep. She couldn't wait to invite Tully for dinner. Afterwards, they could—

Tap.

—talk about boys and kissing and—

Tap.

Kate sat up. That wasn't a bird on the roof or a mouse in the walls.

Tap.

It was a rock, hitting the glass!

She threw the covers back and hurried to the window, shoving it open. Tully was in her back yard, holding a bike beside her. 'Come on down,' she said, much too loudly, making a hurry gesture with her hand.

'You want me to sneak out?'

'Uh. Duh.'

Kate had never done anything like this, but she couldn't act like a nerd now. Cool kids broke the rules and sneaked out of the house. Everyone knew that. Everyone knew, too, that trouble could follow. And this was exactly what her mom had been talking about.

You think for yourself around Tully Hart.

Kate didn't care about that. What mattered was Tully.

'I'm on my way.' Closing the window, she dressed quickly, then crept down the hall. As she passed her parents' bedroom, her heart was pounding so fast she felt light-headed. The stairs creaked with every footfall, but finally, she made it.

Tully was waiting. Beside her was the most amazing bike Kate had ever seen. It had curly handlebars and a tiny kidney-shaped seat on a platform, and a bunch of cables and wires. 'Wow,' she said.

'It's a ten-speed,' Tully said. 'My grandma gave it to me last Christmas. You want to ride it?'

'No way.' In the carport she found her old pink bicycle with a white wicker basket. It was hopelessly uncool, a little girl's bike.

Tully didn't even seem to notice. They mounted up and rode down the wet, bumpy driveway to the asphalted road. There, they veered left and kept going. At Summer Hill, Tully said, 'Watch this. Do what I do.'

They crested the hill as if they were flying. Kate's hair whipped back from her head; tears stung her eyes. All around them black trees whispered in the breeze. Stars glittered in the velvet black sky.

Tully leaned back and put her arms out. Laughing, she glanced at Kate. 'Try it.'

'I can't. We're going too fast.'

'That's the point. Come on. Let go.' Then, she added, 'Trust me.'

Now Kate had no choice. Trust was part of being friends.

Taking a deep breath, she said a prayer, and eased her arms out.

She was flying, sailing through the night sky, down the hill. She heard Tully laughing beside her, but before she could even smile, something went wrong. Her front tyre hit a rock; the bike bucked like a Brahman bull and twisted sideways, catching Tully's tyre in its arc.

She screamed, reached for the handlebars, but it was too late. She was in the air, really flying this time. The pavement rushed up, smacked her hard, and she skidded across it, landing in a heap in the muddy ditch.

Tully rolled across the asphalt and slammed into her. The bikes clattered to the ground.

Dazed, Kate stared up at the night sky. Every part of her hurt. She could feel where the road had ripped off her skin in patches.

'That was *incredible*,' Tully said, laughing.

'Are you kidding? We could have been killed.'

'Exactly. Wait till we tell the kids about this.'

The kids at school. This would be a *story*, and Kate would be one of the stars in it. People would listen raptly, ooh and aah, say things like *You sneaked out? Summer Hill without hands? It's gotta be a lie . . .*

And suddenly Kate was laughing, too.

They helped each other to their feet and retrieved their bikes. By the time they were across the road, Kate barely noticed where she was hurt. She felt like a different girl suddenly—bolder, braver, willing to try anything. So what if trouble followed a night like this? For the past two years she'd followed all the rules and sat at home by herself. No more.

They left their bikes by the side of the road and limped towards the river. Tully sat down by an old, moss-covered log in a place where the grass was thick. Kate sat down beside her. They were so close their knees were almost touching. Together they stared up at the star-spangled sky.

'I wonder who named our street,' Tully said. 'I haven't seen a single firefly.'

Kate shrugged. 'I've never seen one either. Over by the old bridge is Missouri Street. Maybe some pioneer was homesick.'

'Or maybe it's *magic*. This could be a magical street.' Tully turned towards her. 'That could mean we were meant to be friends.'

Kate shivered at the power of that. 'Before you moved here, I thought it was just a road that went nowhere.'

'Now it's our road.'

'We can go all kinds of places when we grow up.'

'Places don't matter,' Tully said.

Kate heard something in her friend's voice, a sadness she didn't understand. She turned sideways. Tully was staring up at the sky.

'Are you thinking about your mom?' Kate asked tentatively.

'I try not to think about her.' There was a long pause; then she dug into her pocket for a Virginia Slims cigarette and lit up. 'If my mom were normal—not sick, I mean—I could have told her about what happened to me at the party.'

'Do you think about it a lot?'

'I have nightmares about it.'

Kate wished she knew what to say. 'What about your dad? Can you talk to him?'

'I don't think she knows who he is. Or he heard about me and ran.'

'That's harsh.'

'Life is harsh. Besides, I don't need them. I've got you, Katie. You're the one that helped me through it.'

Kate smiled. The sharp tang of smoke filled the air between them, stung her eyes, but she didn't care. What mattered was being here, with her new best friend. 'That's what friends are for.'

That next night Tully was reading *The Outsiders* when she heard her mother yelling through the house. 'Tully! Answer the damn door.'

She slammed the book down and went out into the living room, where her mother lay sprawled on the sofa, smoking a joint.

'You're right by the door.'

Her mother shrugged. 'So?'

'Hide your bong.'

Sighing dramatically, Cloud leaned over and put her bong beneath the end table beside the couch. Only a blind person would miss it, but that was as good as Cloud was likely to do.

Tully smoothed her hair away from her face and opened the door.

A small, dark-haired woman stood there, holding a foil-covered casserole dish. Electric-blue eye shadow accentuated her brown eyes, and rose-hued blush—applied with too heavy a hand—created the illusion of sharp cheekbones in her round face. 'You must be Tully,' the woman said. 'I'm Kate's mom. I brought you and your mom a tuna casserole for dinner. I imagine she doesn't feel much like cooking. My sister had cancer a few years ago so I know the drill.' She smiled and stood there. Finally, her smile faded. 'Are you going to invite me in?'

Tully froze. *This was going to be bad.* 'Um . . . sure.'

'Thank you.' Mrs Mularkey moved past her and went into the house.

Cloud lay on the sofa, still sort of spread-eagled; she had a pile of marijuana on her stomach. Smiling blearily, she tried to sit up and failed.

Mrs Mularkey came to a stop. Confusion pleated her forehead. 'I'm Margie from across the street,' she said.

'I'm Cloud,' her mother said. 'It's cool to meet you.'

'And you.'

For a terrible, awkward moment, they just stared at each other. Tully had no doubt at all that Mrs Mularkey's sharp eyes saw everything—the bong under the end table, and the marijuana. 'Also, I wanted to let you know that I'm home most days, and I'd be happy to drive you to the doctor's office or run errands. I know how chemo can make you feel.'

Cloud frowned blearily. 'Who's got cancer?'

Mrs Mularkey turned to look at Tully, who wanted to curl up and die.

'Tully, show our cool neighbour with the food where the kitchen is.'

Tully practically ran for the kitchen. In that pink hell, junk-food wrappers covered the table, dirty dishes clogged the sink and over-flowing ashtrays were everywhere.

Mrs Mularkey walked past her, bent over the oven, put the casserole onto the rack, then shut the door with her hip and turned to face Tully. 'My Katie is a good girl,' she said at last.

Here it comes. 'Yes, ma'am.'

'She's been praying for your mother to recover from her cancer. She even has a little altar set up in her room.'

Tully looked at the floor, too ashamed to answer. How could she explain why she'd lied? No answer would be good enough, not for a mother like Mrs Mularkey, who loved her kids.

'Do you think lying to your friends is OK?'

'No, ma'am.' So intently was she staring at the floor that she was startled by a gentle touch on her chin that forced her to look up.

'Are you going to be a good friend to Kate? Or the kind that leads her to trouble?'

'I'd never hurt Katie.' Tully wanted to say more, but she was so close to tears she didn't dare move or speak. She stared into Mrs Mularkey's dark eyes and saw something she never expected: understanding.

'You do it, don't you? Pay the bills, grocery-shop, clean the house. Who pays for everything?'

Tully swallowed hard. No one had ever seen through her life so clearly before. 'My grandmother sends a cheque every week.'

Mrs Mularkey nodded. 'My dad was a fall-down drunk and the whole town knew it,' she said in a soft voice that matched the look in her eyes. 'He was mean, too. Friday and Saturday nights, my sister, Georgia, would have to go to the tavern and drag him home. All the way out of the bar he'd be smacking her and calling her names. Then she got married and moved out, leaving me alone with him. By the end of my senior year I knew why she ran with the fast crowd and drank too much.' She smoothed the hair from Tully's face in a touch that was pure *mom*. All her life she'd longed for that kind of touch.

'She didn't want people to look at her like she was pitiful.'

Mrs Mularkey nodded. 'She hated that look. What matters, though, isn't other people. That's what I learned. Who your mom is and how she lives her life isn't a reflection of *you*. You can make your own choices. And there's nothing for you to be ashamed of. But you'll have to dream big, and you'll need to be strong, Tully Hart. And to trust your friends.'

'I do trust Kate.'

'So you'll tell her the truth?'

'Do I have to? What if I just promise—'

'One of us is going to tell her, Tully. It should be you.'

Tully took a deep breath and released it. 'OK.'

'Good. So I'll see you for dinner tomorrow night. Five o'clock. It'll be your chance to start over.'

The next night, Kate's mom opened the door to Tully. Smiling, she said, 'I warn you, it's loud and crazy in here.'

'I love loud and crazy,' Tully said.

'Then you'll fit right in.' Mrs Mularkey put an arm round Tully's shoulder and led her towards the beige-walled living room with its moss-green shag carpeting, bright-red sofa and black recliner.

'Bud?' Mrs Mularkey said to the beefy, dark-haired man sitting in the recliner. 'This is Tully Hart from across the street.'

Mr Mularkey smiled at her and put down his drink. 'So you're the one we've been hearin' about. It's nice to have you here, Tully.'

'It's nice to be here.'

Mrs Mularkey patted her shoulder. 'Dinner's not till six. Katie's upstairs in her room. It's the one at the very top of the stairs. I'm sure you girls have plenty to talk about.'

Tully got the message and nodded. Now that she was here, in this warm house that smelt of home-cooked meals, standing shoulder to shoulder with the world's most perfect mom, she couldn't imagine losing it all, becoming unwelcome. 'I'll never lie to her again,' she promised.

'Good. Now, go.' With a last smile, Mrs Mularkey left her and walked into the living room.

Mr Mularkey put an arm round his wife and drew her into the La-Z-Boy with him. Immediately they bent their heads together.

Tully felt a longing so sharp and unexpected she couldn't move. Everything would have been different for her if she'd had a family like this. She didn't want to turn away from it just yet. 'Are you watching the news?' she asked, moving into the room.

Mr Mularkey looked up. 'We never miss it.'

Tully looked at the TV. A woman reporter was speaking.

Mrs Mularkey smiled. 'That's Jean Enersen. A woman who gets to a place like that in her life knows how to go after what she wants.'

'I'm going to be a reporter,' Tully said suddenly.

'That's wonderful.'

'There you are,' Kate said suddenly, coming up beside her. 'Nice of everyone to tell me you were here,' she said loudly.

'I was just telling your mom and dad that I'm going to be a news reporter,' Tully said.

Mrs Mularkey beamed at her. In her smile, Tully saw everything that had been missing in her life. 'Isn't that a grand dream, Katie?'

Kate looked confused for a moment; then she hooked her arm through Tully's and pulled her away from the living room. Up in her small attic bedroom, she flipped through a stack of records. By the time she'd chosen one—Carole King's *Tapestry*—and put it on the record player, Tully was at the window, staring out at the lavender evening.

The surge of adrenaline she'd got from her announcement faded, leaving a quiet kind of sadness behind. She knew what she had to do now, but the thought of it made her sick.

'I got the new *Seventeen* and *Tiger Beat*,' Kate said, lying down on the blue shag carpeting. 'You want to read 'em?'

Tully lay down beside her. 'Sure.'

'Jan-Michael Vincent is so foxy,' Kate said, flipping to a picture of the actor.

'I heard he lied to his girlfriend,' Tully said, daring a sideways glance.

'I hate liars.' Kate turned the page. 'Are you really going to be a news reporter? You never told me that.'

'Yeah,' Tully said, really imagining it for the first time. Maybe she could be famous. Then everyone would admire her. 'You'll have to be one, too, though. 'Cause we do everything together. We'll be a team.'

'I don't know—'

Tully bumped her. 'Yes, you do. You're an excellent writer.'

Kate laughed. 'That's true. OK. I'll be a reporter, too.'

After that, they fell silent, flipping through the magazine. Tully tried twice to bring up the subject of her mother, but both times Kate interrupted her, and then someone was yelling, 'Dinner,' and her chance for coming clean had slipped away.

All through the best meal of her life, she felt the weight of her lie. By the time they'd cleared the table and washed and dried the dishes, she felt stretched to breaking point. Even dreaming about fame on television couldn't ease her nerves.

'Hey, Mom,' Kate said, putting away the last plate, 'Tully and me are going to ride our bikes down to the park, OK?'

'Tully and I,' her mother answered, reaching down into the magazine pouch of the La-Z-Boy's arm for the TV guide. 'And be back by eight.'

'Aww, Mom—'

'Eight,' her father said.

Kate looked at Tully. 'They treat me like I'm a baby.'

'You don't know how lucky you are. Come on, let's get our bikes.'

As always, they rode at a breakneck speed down the bumpy county road. At Summer Hill, Tully flung her arms out and Kate followed.

When they got to the river park, they ditched their bikes in the trees and lay on the grass, side by side, staring up at the sky, listening to the river gurgling against the rocks.

'I have something to tell you,' Tully said.

'What?'

Tully took a deep breath. 'My mom doesn't have cancer. She's a pothead. She's always high.'

Kate turned to her. 'You *lied* to me?'

Tully could barely maintain eye contact she was so ashamed. 'I didn't mean to.'

'People don't lie accidentally.'

'You don't know how it feels to be embarrassed by your mom.'

'Are you kidding? You should have seen what my mom wore out to dinner last—'

'No,' Tully said. 'You don't know.'

Kate twisted round to look at her. In the darkness her eyes were unreadable. 'Tell me.'

Tully knew what Kate was asking of her; she wanted the truth that had spawned the lie, but Tully didn't know if she could do it. If she told Kate the reality and then lost her as a friend, it would be unbearable. Then again, if she didn't tell the truth, she'd lose the friendship for sure.

'I was two years old,' she finally said, 'when my mom first dumped me at my grandparents' house. She went to town for milk and came back when I was four. When I was ten, she showed up again and I was so excited. I thought it meant she loved me. That time she let go of me in a crowd. The next time I saw her I was fourteen. My gran's letting us live in this house and sending us money every week. That'll last until my mom bales again—which she will do.'

'I don't understand.'

'Of course you don't. My mom isn't like yours. In my whole life I've lived with her for, like, a month. She just forgets me and moves on.'

'How can a mother do that?'

Tully shrugged. 'I think there's something wrong with me.'

'There's nothing wrong with you. She's the loser. But I still don't get why you lied to me.'

Tully finally looked at her. 'I wanted you to like me.'

'*You* were worried about *me*?' Kate burst out laughing. Tully was just about to ask her what was so funny when Kate sobered and said, 'No more lies, right?'

'Absolutely.'

'We'll be best friends for ever,' Kate said earnestly. 'OK?'

That was when Tully learned that one person could change your life. 'You mean you'll always be there for me?'

'Always,' Kate answered. 'No matter what.'

Tully felt an emotion open up inside her like some exotic flower. She could practically smell its honeyed scent in the air. For the first time in her life, she felt totally safe with someone. 'For ever,' she promised. 'No matter what.'

Kate would always remember the summer after eighth grade as one of the best times of her life. She and Tully rode their bikes all over the valley and spent hours inner-tubing down the Pilchuck River. In the late afternoons, they stretched out on tiny towels, wearing neon-coloured crocheted bikinis, their skin slick with a mixture of baby oil and iodine, listening to Top 40 music on the transistor radio they never left behind, and talking. They talked about everything: fashion, music, boys, what it would be like to be a reporting duo, movies. Nothing was off limits. Now, it was late August and they were in Kate's bedroom, packing make-up for their trip to the fair. As usual, Kate had to change clothes and put on make-up after she left the house. If she wanted to look cool, anyway. Her mom still thought she was too young for every-thing. 'You got your tube top?' Tully asked.

'Got it.'

Grinning at their own brilliant plan, they headed downstairs, where Dad was sitting on the sofa, watching television.

'We're going to the fair now,' Kate said, thankful that her mother wasn't here. Mom would notice the bag that was too big for the fair.

'Be careful, you two,' he said without looking up.

They headed down the driveway, swinging their bags.

'Do you think Kenny Markson will be at the fair?' Kate asked.

'You worry too much about boys.'

Kate bumped her friend, hip to hip. 'He has a crush on you.'

Suddenly Tully stopped. 'Oh, shit,' she whispered.

'What's the matter?'

Then she noticed the police car parked in Tully's driveway.

Tully grabbed Kate's hand and kept walking. They made their way across the street, and to the front door, which stood open.

A policeman was waiting for them in the living room.

'Hello, girls. I'm Officer Dan Myers.'

'What did she do this time?' Tully asked.

'There was a spotted owl protest up by Lake Quinault that got out of hand yesterday. Your mother and several others staged a sit-in that cost Weyerhaeuser a full day's work. Worse, someone dropped a cigarette in the woods.' He paused. 'They just got the fire under control.'

'Let me guess: she's going to jail.'

'Her lawyer is seeking voluntary treatment for drug addiction. If she's lucky, she'll be in the hospital for a while. If not . . .' He let the sentence trail off.

'Has someone called my grandmother?'

The officer nodded. 'She's waiting for you. Do you need help packing?'

Kate didn't understand what was happening. She turned to her friend. 'Tully?'

There was a terrible blankness in Tully's eyes, and Kate knew suddenly that this was big, whatever it was. 'I have to go back to my grandma's,' Tully said, then she walked past Kate and went into her bedroom.

Kate ran after her. 'You *can't* go!'

Tully pulled a suitcase out of the closet and flipped it open. 'I don't have any choice.'

'I'll *make* your mother come back. I'll tell her—'

Tully paused in her packing and looked at Kate. She was crying now.

'You can't fix this,' she said softly, sounding like a grown-up, tired and broken. For the first time, Kate really understood all the stories about Tully's loser mom. They'd laughed about Cloud, made jokes about her drug use and her fashion sense and her various stories, but it wasn't funny. And Tully had known this would happen.

'Promise me,' Tully finally said, her voice cracking, 'that we'll always be best friends.'

'Always,' was all Kate could say.

For the next three years, they wrote letters faithfully back and forth. It became more than a tradition and something of a lifeline. When her grandfather died, it was Kate to whom Tully had turned. She hadn't cried for him until she got the phone call from her best friend that began with, 'Oh, Tul, I'm so sorry.'

Now, it was the summer of 1977. In a few short months they'd be seniors, ruling their separate schools.

And today Tully was finally going to actually step onto the road Mrs Mularkey had shown her all those years ago.

The next Jean Enersen.

The words had become her mantra, a secret code that housed the enormity of her dream and made it sound possible. She hadn't realised how much she needed a dream, but it had transformed her, changed her from poor motherless and abandoned Tully to a girl poised to take on the world. The goal made her life story unimportant, gave her something to reach for, to hang on to.

Tully had got a job at the *Queen Anne Bee*, her neighbourhood weekly newspaper. Her duties pretty much matched the measly per-hour wage they paid her, but she didn't care. She was in the business. She spent almost every waking hour of the summer of 1977 in the small, cramped offices, soaking up every bit of knowledge she could. When she wasn't bird-dogging the reporters or making copies or delivering coffee, she was at home, playing gin rummy with Gran. Every Sunday night, like clockwork, she wrote to Kate and shared the minute details of her week.

Now, she sat at her little-girl's desk in her bedroom and reread this week's eight-page letter, then signed it *Best friends for ever, Tully* ♥, and carefully folded it into thirds.

On her desk was the most recent postcard from Kate, who was away on the Mularkey family's yearly camping trip. Kate called it Hell Week with Bugs, but Tully was jealous of each perfect-sounding moment.

She addressed the letter, then went to check on Gran, who was already asleep.

Alone, Tully watched her favourite Sunday-night television pro-grammes—*All in the Family*, *Alice* and *Kojak*—and then closed up the house and went to bed. Her last thought as she drifted lazily towards sleep was to wonder what the Mularkeys were doing.

The next morning she woke at her usual time, six o'clock, and dressed for work. She hurried down the hall and tapped on the last door. Though she hated to wake her grandmother, it was the house rule. No leaving without a goodbye. 'Gran?'

She tapped again and pushed the door open slowly, calling out, 'Gran . . . I'm leaving for work.'

Gran lay in bed. Even from here, Tully could see the shape of her, her white hair, the ruffle of her nightdress . . . and the stillness of her chest.

'Gran?'

She inched forward, touched her grandmother's velvet, wrinkled cheek. The skin was cold as ice. No breath came from her slack lips.

Tully's whole world seemed to slide off its foundation. It took all her strength to stand there, staring down at her grandmother's lifeless face.

Memories came at her like a kaleidoscope through her tears: Gran braiding her hair for her seventh birthday party, telling her that her mommy might show up if she prayed hard enough, and then years later, admitting that sometimes God didn't answer a little girl's prayers, or a grown woman's either; or playing cards last week, laughing as she swept up the discard pile—again—saying, 'Tully, you don't have to have every card, all the time . . .'; or kissing her good night so gently.

She had no idea how long she stood there, but by the time she leaned over and kissed Gran's papery cheek, sunlight eased through the sheer curtains, lighting the room.

There were things she was supposed to do now; she knew that. She and Gran had talked about this, done things to prepare Tully. She knew, though, that no words could have really prepared her for this.

Tully stood outside the church, watching the crowd of elderly people stream past her. A few of Gran's friends recognised her and came over to offer their condolences.

I'm so sorry, dear . . .

. . . She's in a better place . . .

. . . wouldn't want you to cry.

She took as much of it as she could because she knew Gran would have wanted that, but by eleven o'clock, she was ready to scream.

If only Katie and the Mularkeys were here, but she had no idea how to reach them in Canada, and since they wouldn't be home for four days, she had to go through this alone. With them beside her, a pretend family, maybe she would have made it through the service.

Without them, she simply couldn't do it. Instead of sitting through the terrible, heart-wrenching memories of Gran, she got up in the middle of the funeral and walked out.

Outside, in the hot August sunlight, she could breathe again, even though the tears were always near to the surface, as was the pointless query, *How could you leave me like this?*

Nearby, a twig snapped and Tully looked up. At first all she saw were the haphazardly parked cars.

Then she saw her.

Cloud stood in the shade, smoking a long slim cigarette. Dressed in tattered corduroy bell-bottoms and a dirty peasant blouse, she looked rail-thin. The lawyer must have got a hold of her . . .

Tully couldn't help the leap of joy her heart took. She wasn't alone. Cloud had come back. Tully ran to her, smiling. She would forgive her mother for all the missing years, all the abandonments. What mattered was that she was here now, when Tully needed her most. 'Thank God you're here,' she said, coming to a breathless stop. 'I need you so much.'

Her mother lurched towards her, laughing when she almost fell. 'You're a beautiful spirit, Tully. All you need is air and to be free.'

Tully's stomach seemed to drop. 'Not again,' she said, pleading for help with her eyes. 'I'm your flesh and blood and I need you now. Otherwise I'll be alone.'

Cloud took a stumbling step forward. The sadness in her eyes was unmistakable, but Tully didn't care. 'Look at me, Tully.'

'I'm looking.'

'No. *Look*. I'm ruined. I can't help you.'

'But I need you.'

'That's the tragedy of it,' her mother said.

'Why?' Tully asked. She was going to add, *Don't you love me?* but before she could form the pain into words, the doors of the church opened and black-clad people swarmed into the parking lot. Tully glanced sideways, just long enough to dry her tears. When she turned back, her mother was gone.

The woman from social services tried to say the right things, but Tully noticed that she kept glancing at her watch as she stood in the doorway.

'I still don't see why I need to pack my stuff,' Tully said as she packed her case. 'I'm almost eighteen. Gran has no mortgage on this house—I know 'cause I paid the bills this year. I'm old enough to live alone.'

'The lawyer is expecting us,' was the woman's only answer.

She placed the stack of Kate's letters in her suitcase, closed the lid and snapped it shut. Then she took one last, lingering look around.

Gran had decorated this room for the little girl who'd been dumped here all those years ago. Every item had been chosen with care, but now they'd all be boxed up and stored in the dark, along with the memories they elicited. Tully wondered how long it would be before she could think of Gran without crying.

She closed the door behind her and followed the woman through the now-quiet house, down the steps outside, to the street, where a battered yellow Ford Pinto was parked.

'Put your suitcase in the back.'

Tully did as she was told and got into the passenger seat. After a short drive they parked in front of a well-kept Victorian home in downtown Ballard. A hand-painted sign out front read: BAKER AND MONTGOMERY, ATTORNEYS AT LAW.

'You don't need to bring your suitcase,' the woman said.

'I'd like to, thanks.' If there was one thing Tully understood, it was the importance of a packed bag.

The woman nodded and led the way up the concrete walkway to the white front door. Inside the overly quaint space, a pudgy man with a balding head and horn-rimmed glasses came to meet them.

'Hello, Tallulah. I'm Elmer Baker, your grandmother Hart's attorney.'

Tully followed him to a small, upstairs room with two overstuffed chairs and an antique mahogany desk littered with yellow legal pads.

'Now, Tallulah—'

'Tully,' she said quietly.

'Quite right. I recall Ima saying you preferred Tully.' He put his elbows on the desk and leaned forward. 'As you know, your mother has refused to take custody of you.'

It took all her strength to nod.

'I'm sorry,' he said in a gentle voice, and Tully actually flinched at the words. She'd come to truly loathe the stupid, useless sentiment.

'Yeah,' she said, fisting her hands at her sides.

'Ms Gulligan here has found a lovely family for you. You'll be one of several displaced teens in their care and you'll be able to continue in your current school placement. I'm sure that makes you happy.'

'Ecstatic.'

Mr Baker looked momentarily nonplussed by her response. 'Of course. Now. As to your inheritance. Ima left all her assets—both homes, the car, the bank accounts and stocks—to you. She has left instructions for you to continue with the monthly payments to her daughter, Dorothy. Your grandmother believed it was the best and only way to keep track of her. Dorothy has proven to be very reliable at keeping in touch when there's money coming.' He cleared his throat. 'Now . . . if we sell both homes, you won't have to worry about finances for quite some time. We can take care—'

'But then I won't have a home at all.'

'I'm sorry about that, but Ima was very specific in her request. She wanted you to be able to go to any college.' He looked up. 'You're going to win the Pulitzer someday. Or that's what she told me.'

Tully couldn't believe she was going to cry again, and in front of these people. She popped to her feet. 'I need to go to the restroom.'

'Oh. Certainly. Downstairs. First door to the left of the front door.'

Tully got up from her chair, grabbed her suitcase and made her halting way to the door. Once in the hallway, she shut the door behind her and leaned against the wall, trying not to cry.

Foster care could not be her future.

She glanced down at her wristwatch. It was August 20.

The Mularkeys would be home in two days.

For almost four hours Tully stood at the corner of her house, watching the Mularkeys unload the car. She'd thought about running up the hill a dozen times, just showing up, but she wasn't ready for the boisterousness of the whole family just yet. She wanted to be alone with Kate, somewhere quiet where they could talk.

And so she waited until the lights went out and then crossed the street. It took four stones before Kate stuck her head out of the window. 'Tully!' She ducked back into her room and slammed the window shut. It took less than a minute for her to appear at the side of the house. Wearing a Bionic Woman nightshirt and her old black-rimmed glasses, Kate ran for Tully, arms outstretched.

Tully felt Kate's arms wrap around her and for the first time in days, she felt safe.

'I missed you so much,' Kate said, tightening her hold.

Tully couldn't answer. It was all she could do not to cry. She wondered if Kate knew, really knew, how important their friendship was to her. 'I got our bikes,' she said, stepping back, looking away so Kate wouldn't see her moist eyes.

'Cool.'

Within minutes they were on their way, flying down Summer Hill, their hands outstretched to catch the wind. At the bottom of the hill, they ditched their bikes in the trees and walked down the long and winding road to the river.

Kate flopped down in their old spot, her back rested against a mossy log, her feet stretched out in the grass. Tully lay down beside Kate, scooting close enough that their shoulders were touching. After the last few days, she needed to know that her best friend was finally beside her.

'Hell Week with Bugs was even worse than usual,' Kate said. 'I did talk Sean into eating a slug, though. It was worth the week's allowance I lost.' She giggled. 'You should have seen his face when I started laughing. Aunt Georgia tried to talk to me about birth control. Can you believe it? She even said I should—'

'Do you even know how lucky you are?' The words were out before Tully could stop them, spilling like jellybeans from a machine.

Kate shifted her weight and turned, until she was lying sideways in the grass, looking at Tully. 'You usually want to hear everything about the camping trip.'

'Yeah, well. I've had a bad week.'

'Did you get fired?'

'That's your idea of a bad week? I want your perfect life, just for a day.'

That hurt Kate, Tully could tell. Her friend drew back, frowning. 'You sound pissed at me.'

'Not at you.' Tully sighed, tried to smile. 'You're my best friend.'

'So, who are you mad at?'

'Cloud. Gran. God. Take your pick.' She took a deep breath and said, 'Gran died while you were gone.'

'Oh, Tully.'

And there it was, what Tully had been waiting for all week. Someone who loved her and was truly sorry for her. Tears stung her eyes; before she knew it, she was sobbing. Big, gulping sobs that wracked her body and made it impossible to breathe, and all the while, Kate held her, letting her cry, saying nothing.

When there were no tears left inside, Tully lay back against the log and stared up at the night sky.

Kate waited a moment, then said, 'So what will happen?'

'I have to go into foster care. It's only for a while, though. When I'm eighteen I can live alone.'

'You're not going to live with strangers,' Kate said fiercely. 'I'll find Cloud and make her do the right thing.'

Tully didn't bother answering. She loved her friend for saying it, but they lived in two different worlds. In Tully's world, moms weren't there to help you out. What mattered was making your own way.

What mattered was not caring.

And the best way not to care was to surround yourself with noise and people. She'd learned that lesson a long time ago. She didn't have long here in Snohomish. In no time at all, the authorities would find her and drag her back to her lovely new family, full of displaced teens and the people paid to house them. 'We should go to that party. The one you wrote about in your last letter.'

'At Karen's house? The summer's-end bash-o-rama?'

'Exactly.'

Kate frowned. 'My folks would have a fit if they found out.'

'We'll tell them you're staying at my house across the street. Your mom will believe Cloud is back for a day.'

'If I get caught—'

'You won't.' Tully saw how worried her friend was, and she knew she should stop this right now. It was reckless, maybe even dangerous. But she couldn't stop the train. If she didn't do something drastic, she'd think about the mother who'd repeatedly abandoned her, and the strangers with whom she'd soon live, and the grandmother who was gone. 'We won't get caught. I promise.' She turned to Kate. 'You trust me, don't you?'

'**K**ids! Breakfast is ready.'

Kate was the first one at the table. Mom had just put a plate of pancakes down when there was a knock at the door.

Kate jumped up. 'I'll get it.' She ran for the door and yanked it open. 'Mom, look. It's Tully. Gosh, I haven't seen you in *for ever*.' Linking arms, they walked into the kitchen.

Mom stood near the table, wearing her zip-up, floor-length, red velours robe and pink fuzzy slippers. 'Hey, Tully, it's good to see you.'

Tully lurched forward, practically falling in her haste to be close to Kate's mom.

'What is it?' her mother said, touching Tully's chin, forcing her to look up. When Tully didn't answer, her mother said, 'What's going on?'

'My gran died,' Tully said softly.

'Oh, honey . . .' Mom pulled Tully into a fierce hug. Finally, she drew back, put an arm round Tully and led her to the sofa in the living room.

'Turn off the griddle, Katie,' Mom said without even looking back.

Frowning, Kate turned off the griddle and then followed them to the living room. She hung back, standing in the archway that separated the two rooms. Neither of them seemed to care that she was there.

'Did we miss the funeral?' Mom asked gently, holding Tully's hand.

Tully nodded. 'Everyone said they were sorry.'

'People don't know what to say, that's all.'

'My favourite part was the ever-popular "she's in a better place". As if dead is better than being with me.'

'And your mom?'

'Let's just say she doesn't call herself Cloud for nothing. She came and went.' Tully glanced at Kate and added quickly, 'But she's here for now. We're staying across the street.'

'Of course she is,' Mom said. 'She knows you need her.'

'Can I spend the night there tonight, Mom?' Kate asked; her heart was beating so hard and fast she was sure her mom could hear it.

Mom didn't even look at Kate. 'Of course. You girls need to be together. And you remember this, Tully Hart: you're the next Jessica Savitch. You will survive this. I promise.'

'You really think so?' Tully asked.

'I know so. You have a rare gift, Tully. And you can be certain that your gran is in Heaven watching out for you.'

'I'll make you proud, Mrs M. I promise I will.'

Tully went out to the garage and opened the doors and then slid into the cracked black driver's seat of her grandmother's Queen Victoria.

'You have her car?' Kate said, opening the passenger door.

'Technically it's my car now.'

Kate slid onto the seat and closed the door.

Tully popped a Kiss tape into the eight-track player and cranked up the volume. Then she put the car in reverse and eased her foot onto the gas. They sang at the top of their lungs all the way to Karen Abner's house, where at least five cars were already parked.

Inside, the sweet smell of pot and incense was almost overpowering. The music was so loud it hurt their ears. Tully grabbed Kate's hand and led her down the stairs to the room in the basement.

'Tully!'

Before she could respond, her old friends had surrounded her, pulled her away from Kate. She let one of the boys give her a plastic cup full of foamy gold Rainier beer. She stared down at it, jolted by the memory that came with it: *Pat, pushing her to the ground* . . .

She looked around for Kate, but couldn't see her friend in the crowd.

Then everyone began chanting her name. 'Tu-lly. Tu-lly.'

No one was going to hurt her. Not here; tomorrow maybe, when the authorities caught up with her, but not now. She chugged the beer and held the cup out for another, yelling out Kate's name as she did.

Kate appeared instantly, as if she'd been just out of view, waiting to be called for. Tully shoved the beer towards her. 'Here.'

Kate shook her head. It was a slight there-and-gone motion, but Tully saw it and felt ashamed that she'd offered the beer, and then angry that her friend was so innocent. Tully had never been innocent; not that she could remember anyway.

'Ka-tie, Ka-tie,' Tully yelled, getting the crowd to chant with her. 'Come on, Katie,' she said quietly. 'We're best friends, aren't we?'

Kate took the beer and chugged it. More than half of it spilt down her chin and onto her halter top, making the shimmery fabric cling to her breasts, but she didn't seem to notice.

Then the music changed. As 'Dancing Queen' blared through the speakers. *You can dance, you can j-ive . . .*

'I love this song,' Kate said.

Tully grabbed Kate's hand and dragged her over to where kids were dancing. There, Tully let loose of everything and fell into the music and the movement. By the time the music changed and slowed down, she was breathing hard and laughing easily.

But it was Kate who was the more changed. Maybe it was the one beer, or the pulsing beat of the music; Tully wasn't sure. All she knew, as they danced and drank, was that Kate looked gorgeous, with her blonde hair shining in the light from an overhead fixture and her pale, delicate face flushed with exertion.

Then, from behind them, someone yelled, 'Cops!'

In an instant, they were making their desperate way out of the house. By the time they got to the car Kate's head was swimming and her stomach was in open revolt. 'I'm gonna puke.'

'No, you aren't.' Tully yanked open the passenger door and shoved Kate inside. 'We are *not* gonna get busted.'

Tully ran round the front of the car and opened her door. Sliding into the seat, she stabbed the key into the ignition, yanked the gearshift into reverse and stomped on the gas. They rocketed backwards and slammed into something so hard they both went flying forwards. Kate's forehead hit the glove box and she screamed in pain. When she finally opened her eyes, she felt blood dripping down her nose. She wiped her eyes, tried to focus.

Tully was beside her, rolling down the driver's-side window.

There, in the darkness, was good old Officer Dan, the man who'd driven Tully away from Snohomish three years ago. 'I knew you Firefly Lane girls would be a pain in my ass.'

'Fuck,' Tully said.

'Nice language, Tallulah. Now, will you please step out of the car?' He bent down, looked at Kate. 'You, too, Kate Mularkey. The party's over.'

The first thing they did at the police station was separate the girls.

'Someone will come talk to you,' Officer Dan said, guiding Tully into a room at the end of the hall.

A gunmetal-grey desk and two chairs sat forlornly beneath a bright hanging light bulb. The walls were a gross green colour and the floor was plain, bumpy cement. The entire left wall was a mirror. All it took was one episode of *Starsky and Hutch* to know that it was really a window.

She wondered if the social worker was out there yet, shaking her head in disappointment, saying, 'That fine family won't want her now,' or the lawyer, who wouldn't know what to say.

Or the Mularkeys.

At that, she made a little sound of horror. How could she have been so stupid? The Mularkeys had liked her until tonight, and now she'd gone and thrown that all away, and for what? Because she'd been depressed by her mom's rejection? By now she ought to be used to that. When had it ever been any other way?

'How could I be so stupid?'

Across the room, the door opened and Mrs Mularkey walked into the room. She looked tired and poorly put together, as if she'd been woken in the middle of the night and dressed in whatever she could find in the dark. Which, of course, was exactly what had happened.

Mrs Mularkey reached into her dress pocket for her cigarettes. Finding one, she lit up. Through the swirling smoke, she studied Tully. Disappointment emanated from her, as real and visible as the smoke.

Shame overwhelmed Tully. Here was one of the very few people who had ever believed in her, and she'd let Mrs M down. 'How's Kate?'

Mrs Mularkey exhaled smoke. 'Bud took her home. I don't expect she'll leave the house again for a good long while.'

'Oh.' Tully squirmed uncomfortably. 'I know I let you down.'

'Yes, you did.' Mrs Mularkey pulled a chair away from the table and sat down in front of Tully. 'They want to send you to juvenile hall.'

Tully looked down at her hands, unable to stand the disappointment she saw on Mrs M's face. 'The foster family won't want me now.'

'I understand your mother refused to take custody of you.'

'Big surprise there.' Tully heard the way her voice cracked on that. She knew it revealed how hurt she'd been, but there was no way to hide it. Not from Mrs M.

Mrs Mularkey leaned back in her chair and said quietly, 'Katie wants you to live with us.'

Just hearing it was like a blow to the heart. She knew she'd spend a long time trying to forget it. 'Yeah, right.'

It was a moment before Mrs Mularkey said, 'A girl who lived in our house would have to do chores and follow the rules. Mr Mularkey and I wouldn't stand for any funny business.'

Tully felt tears sting her eyes. 'Are you saying I can live with you?'

Mrs M leaned forward and touched Tully's jaw. 'I know how hard your life has been up to now, and I can't stand for you to go back to that. Welcome to our family, Tully,' Mrs M said, pulling Tully into her arms.

Through all the decades of Tully's life, she would remember that moment as the beginning of something new for her; the becoming of someone new. While she lived with the loud, crazy, loving Mularkey family, she found a whole new person inside her. She didn't keep secrets or tell lies or pretend that she was someone else, and never once did they act as if she were unwanted or not good enough. No matter where she went in her later years, or what she did or whom she was with, she would always remember this moment and those words: *Welcome to our family, Tully*. Always and for ever, she would think of that senior year of high school, when she was inseparable from Kate and a part of the family, as the single best year of her life.

Part Two: THE EIGHTIES
Love Is a Battlefield
heartache to heartache, we stand

THE UNIVERSITY OF WASHINGTON was everything Tully had hoped it would be and more. Spread out over several miles and comprised of hundreds of Gothic buildings, it was a world unto itself. The size daunted Kate, but not Tully; she figured if she could triumph here, she could triumph anywhere. From the moment they moved into their sorority, she began the inexorable journey that would prepare her to get a reporting job at the networks. In addition to taking the core classes in communications, she made time to read at least four newspapers a day and watch as many newscasts as possible. When her big break came, she was going to be ready.

'Where are you headed?' Kate asked as they crossed the campus.

'Drama/TV.'

'That's right! Your first broadcast-journalism class—and with that famous guy you've been stalking since we got here.'

'Chad Wiley.'

'How many letters did you have to write to get in?'

'About a thousand.'

'You need me to walk you over?'

Tully loved her friend for that. Somehow Kate knew that despite all her show of courage, she was nervous about this. 'How can I make my big entrance with someone else?'

She watched Kate walk away from her. Standing there, alone among the crowd of students moving between the buildings, Tully took a deep, relaxing breath. She needed to appear calm. Then she strolled confidently into the Drama/TV building and hurried down the hallway. In the auditorium, she walked boldly to the first row and took a seat.

In the front of the room, the professor sat slumped in a metal chair. 'I'm Chad Wiley,' he said in a sexy, whisky-rough voice. 'Those of you who recognise my name get an A in the class.'

There was a smattering of laughter around the room. Tully's was the loudest. She knew more than his name. She knew his whole life story. He'd come out of college as a kind of Wunderkind in broadcasting, getting his first anchor position in a top-fifteen market before he was twenty-five years old. He'd moved up the ranks fast, becoming a network anchor before he was thirty. Then, quite simply, he'd lost it. A car crash that broke both of his legs and injured a child, and his star had fallen. There'd been a couple of years when there had been no mention of him at all, until, finally, he'd surfaced at the university, teaching.

Wiley stood. He was unkempt, with long dark hair and at least three days' growth of beard, but the intelligence in his eyes was undiminished. The stamp of greatness was still on him. No wonder he'd made it.

He handed her a syllabus and started to move on.

'Your coverage of the Karen Silkwood case was inspired,' she said.

He paused, looked down at her. There was something unsettling about the way he stared—intensely, but only for a second, like a laser beam switched on and off—and then he kept walking past her and on to the next student.

He thought she was just another front-row suck-up who wanted to curry favour. She'd need to be more careful in the future. Nothing mattered more to her right now than getting Chad Wiley to notice her. She intended to learn everything she could from him.

By the end of her sophomore year, there was no doubt in Tully's mind that Chad Wiley knew who she was. She'd taken two of his classes: Broadcast Journalism I and II. Whatever he taught, she took; whatever he asked of her, she did.

The problem was this: he didn't seem to recognise her talent. They'd spent all of last week reading the news from a Teleprompter. Each time she finished, she immediately looked at him, but he barely glanced up from his notes. Rather, he spooled off a criticism, then called out, 'Next.'

But that was about to change; Tully was sure this time. Last week she'd finally racked enough credits to sign up for a summer internship position at KTVS, the local public programming station that was housed on campus. When she'd been given the audition piece, she'd gone home and practised it endlessly, trying it at least a dozen different ways until she found the tone of voice that perfectly matched the tone of the story. Yesterday she'd nailed the audition. She was certain of it. Now, finally, it was time to find out how she'd got on.

'How do I look?'

Kate didn't look up from *The Thorn Birds*, a book she had already read at least once before. 'Awesome.'

Tully felt a flash of irritation that was more and more familiar these days. Sometimes she just looked at Kate and felt her blood pressure skyrocket. It was all she could do not to yell.

The problem was love. Kate went to one fraternity dance after another, and though she never fell in love with any of the doofuses she dated—and definitely didn't have sex with them—she talked about them constantly. Even worse, she hardly seemed to care about their broadcasting plan. Whenever one of their sorority sisters got engaged, Kate rushed to be a part of the crowd that swooned over the ring.

'You aren't looking.'

'I don't have to.'

'You don't know how important this is to me.'

Kate finally looked up. 'Believe me, I know how psyched you are. I also know you'll get the job.'

Tully grinned. 'I will, won't I?'

'Of course. You'll be the first junior to actually be on air.'

'Professor Wiley will have to admit it this time.' Tully snagged her sunglasses off the dresser and headed out.

The campus was bathed in cool sunlight on this mid-May day. Every plant was in bloom and the grass was so thick and lush it looked like patches of green velvet tucked neatly between strips of cement. Tully strode confidently through campus to the building that housed KTVS.

There, she paused just long enough to smooth her sprayed hair, then went into the quiet, utilitarian-looking hallway.

Room 214 was shut. No slice of light ran along the floor beneath the door. Beside it, a piece of paper was tacked to the bulletin board.

SUMMER INTERNSHIP POSITIONS/DEPARTMENT

News/Anchor...Steve Landis
Weather..Jane Turner
Marketing & Community Relations............Gretchen Lauber
Sports..Dan Bluto
Afternoon Planning.....................................Eileen Hutton
Research Desk/Fact-checking...........................Tully Hart

Tully yanked open the door and slipped into the dark auditorium where no one could see her. 'Chad Wiley, you loser. You wouldn't know talent if it grabbed your tiny pecker and squeezed—'

'I imagine you're talking about me.'

She jumped at the sound of his voice.

He was not twenty feet away from her, standing in the shadows.

'Ask me why you aren't an evening news intern and I'll tell you.'

'I couldn't care less why.'

'Really.' He looked at her, unsmiling, then walked away from her, down the aisle and up onto the stage.

She could either keep her pride or risk her future. By the time she made her decision and hurried after him, he was backstage.

'OK . . .' The word seemed to catch in her throat. 'Why?'

He stepped towards her. For the first time she noticed the lines on his face, the creases in his cheeks. 'Whenever you come to class, I can tell you've chosen your clothes carefully and spent a lot of time on your hair and make-up.'

He was looking at her now, *seeing* her. And she could see him, too. Past the shaggy unkemptness to the sharp bone structure that had once made him so handsome. But it was his eyes that grabbed her; liquid brown and sad, they spoke to the empty places inside of her. 'Yeah. So?'

'You know you're beautiful,' he said.

'I'm talented, too.'

'Maybe someday.'

The way he said it pissed her off. She was gathering her wits for a scathing comeback when he closed the distance between them. All she had time for was a bewildered 'What are—' before he kissed her.

At the touch of his lips, gentle yet firm, she felt something exquisite and tender blossom inside her; for no reason at all, she started to cry.

He must have tasted her tears, because he drew back, frowned at her. 'Are you a woman, Tully Hart, or a girl?'

She knew what he was asking. As hard as she'd tried to conceal her innocence, he'd sensed it, tasted it. 'Woman,' she lied, with only the barest wobble. She knew now, after just one kiss, that whatever there was to know about sex, her pathetic rape in the woods had taught her none of it. Although she wasn't a virgin, she was something worse somehow, a reservoir of bad and painful memories, and yet, now, with him, for the first time she knew how it felt to want more.

He kissed her again, murmuring, 'Good.' This time the kiss went on and on, deepening into something that made her ache with need.

He swept her into his arms and carried her to a broken-down sofa tucked against the shadowy back wall. There, he laid her down onto the bumpy, scratchy cushions and slowly, gently began to undress her.

When they were both naked, he lowered himself to the sofa and took her in his arms. The springs sagged beneath their weight, pinged in protest. 'No one has taken time with you, have they, Tully?'

She saw her own desire reflected in his eyes, and for the first time she wasn't afraid in a man's arms. 'Is that what you're going to do—take your time?'

He brushed the damp hair away from her face. 'I'm going to teach you things, Tully. Isn't that what you wanted from me?'

It took Tully two hours to find Kate, sunbathing all by herself, in a skimpy white bikini on the roof terrace, reading a paperback novel.

Tully climbed through the window beneath and out onto the ledge. 'Hey,' she said. 'Let me guess: you're reading a romance novel.'

Kate cocked her head and squinted into the sun, smiling. '*The Promise* by Danielle Steel. It's really sad.'

'You want to hear about real romance?'

'Like you would know anything about it. You haven't gone on a date since we got here.'

'You don't have to go on a date to have sex.'

'No *way*,' Kate said. 'You did not get laid.'

Trying not to smile, Tully stared up at the blue sky and said, 'Three times, to be exact.'

'But you were going to find out about the summer internship . . .' Kate gasped and sat up. 'You *didn't*.'

'You're going to say we're not supposed to have sex with our professors. I think it's really more of a recommendation. A guideline. Still, you can't tell anyone.'

'You had sex with Chad Wiley.'

Tully sighed dreamily at the way that sounded. 'It was totally cool, Katie.'

'Wow. Were you scared?'

'I was scared,' Tully said quietly. 'At first all I could think about was . . . you know . . . the night with Pat. I thought I was going to get sick, or maybe run, but then he kissed me.'

'And?'

'And . . . I just sort of melted. He had my clothes off before I was even paying attention.'

'Did it hurt?'

'Yeah, but not like before.' It surprised Tully how easy it was suddenly to mention the night she was raped. Chad's gentleness had shown her that sex could be beautiful. 'After a while it felt amazingly good. Now I know what all those *Cosmo* articles are about.'

'Did he say he loved you?'

Tully laughed, but deep inside, it wasn't as funny as she wished it were. 'No.'

'I need to meet him,' Kate said firmly.

'It's not like we can double-date.'

'Then I guess I'll be the third wheel. Hey, he can probably get the senior rate if we go out to dinner.'

Tully laughed. 'Bitch.'

'Maybe, but I'm a bitch who wants more details. I want to know *everything*. Should I take notes?'

Tully sat at a table way in the back, tucked in a shadowy corner. When she saw Kate, she stood up and waved.

That was when Kate saw Chad Wiley.

He wasn't at all what she'd expected. He sat lazily in a chair, with one leg stretched out. Even in the smoke and shadows, she could see how handsome he was. He didn't *look* old. Tired, maybe, but in a world-weary kind of way. The smile he gave her started slowly, and in his eyes, she saw a knowledge that surprised her, made her miss a step.

He knew why she was here: a best friend coming to save a girl making a mistake by dating the wrong man.

'You must be Chad,' she said.

'And you must be Katie. You're even prettier than Tully said.'

She flinched at the unexpected use of her nickname. It was a forcible reminder that Chad knew Tully, too.

'Sit down,' Tully said. 'I'll go get a waitress.' She was on her feet and gone before Kate could stop her.

Kate looked at Chad; he eyed her back, smiling as if at some secret. 'They'd fire you—the university—if they found out about you and Tully, wouldn't they?'

He drew his leg back, sat up straighter. 'So that's how you want to play it. Good. I like direct. Yes. I'd lose this career, too.'

'Have you slept with your students before?'

He laughed. 'Hardly.'

'So, why?'

He glanced sideways, at Tully, who was at the crowded coffee bar. 'You, of all people, shouldn't have to ask that. Why is she your best friend?'

His answer pulled the air out of her. 'She's special.'

'Indeed.'

'But what about her career? She'd be ruined if word got out that she was with you. They'd say she slept her way to a degree.'

'Good for you, Katie. You should be looking out for her. She needs that. She's . . . fragile, our Tully.'

Kate didn't know which upset her more—his description of Tully as fragile or the way he said *our Tully*. 'She's a steamroller. I don't call her Tropical Storm Tully for nothing.'

'That's on the outside. For show.'

Kate sat back, surprised. 'You care about her.'

'More's the pity, I imagine. What will you tell her?'

'About what?'

'You came here to find a way to convince her not to see me any more, didn't you? You can certainly say I'm too old. Or the prof angle is always a winner. Just so you know, I drink too much, too.'

'You want me to tell her those things?'

He looked at her. 'No. I don't want you to tell her those things.'

He was studying her intently. She knew how much it meant to him, this conversation, and how much Tully meant to him. Now, sitting here, she was worried that Tully would ruin this man, who frankly looked as if he didn't have the stamina to take another hit like that. Before she could answer the question he'd posed, Tully was back, dragging a purple-haired waitress with her.

'So,' she said, frowning and a little breathless, 'are you friends yet?'

Chad was the first to look up. 'We're friends,' was all he said.

'Excellent,' Tully said, sitting on his lap. 'Now, who wants apple pie?'

Chad dropped them off two blocks from the sorority house.

'Well?' Tully demanded, turning to Kate. 'Did you like him?'

'Of course I liked him. He's got a great sense of humour.'

'But?'

Kate bit her lip, stalling for time. She didn't want to hurt Tully's feelings, but what kind of friend would she be if she lied? The truth was, she *had* liked Chad and she believed he truly cared about Tully; it was also true that she had a bad feeling about their relationship and meeting him had only made it worse.

'Come on, Katie, you're scaring me.'

'I wasn't going to say anything, Tully, but since you're forcing me . . . I don't think you should be going out with him.' Once her opinion broke through the dam, she couldn't stop. 'I mean, he's thirty-one years old. You can't be seen publicly with him or he'll get fired. What kind of relationship is that? You're missing your college years.'

Tully took a step back. 'Missing my college years? You mean going to dances in Tahitian costumes and shotgunning beer? Or dating guys like the nerds you seem to choose.'

'Maybe we should just agree to disagree . . .'

'You think I'm with him for my career, don't you? To what—get better grades or a spot at the station?'

'Aren't you? Just a little bit?' Kate knew instantly she shouldn't have said it. 'I'm sorry,' she said, reaching for her friend. 'I didn't mean it.'

Tully wrenched free. 'Of course you meant it. Miss Perfect with the best family and the flawless grades. I don't even know why you hang around with me: I'm such a slut career hound.'

'Wait!' Kate called out, but Tully was already gone.

Chad answered the door almost instantly, dressed in a pair of old grey sweats and a Rolling Stones T-shirt. She could tell by the way he smiled at her that he had expected her. 'Hey, Tully.'

'Take me to bed,' she whispered throatily, pushing her hands up underneath his shirt.

They made their fumbling, kissing way through the house and to the small bedroom in the back. She lost herself and her pain in the pleasure of him, and when it was over, and they lay there, entwined, she tried not to think of anything except how good he made her feel.

'Do you want to talk about it?'

She lay back in the pillows, staring up at the plain, high-pitched ceiling. 'What do you mean?'

He touched her face in a gentle caress. 'You and Kate fought about me, and I know how much her opinion means to you.'

The words surprised her, though they shouldn't have. In the month they'd been sleeping together, she'd somehow begun to reveal pieces of herself to him. It had begun accidentally, a comment here or there after sex or while they were drinking, and somehow grown from there. She felt safe in his bed, free from judgment or censure. They were lovers who didn't love each other, and that made talking easier. Still, she saw now that he'd listened to all of her babble and let the words form a picture. The knowledge of that made her feel less lonely all of a sudden, and even though it scared her, she couldn't help being comforted by it.

'She thinks it's wrong.'

'It is wrong, Tully. We both know that.'

'I don't care,' she said fiercely, wiping her eyes. 'She's my best friend. She's supposed to support me no matter what.' Her voice broke on the last words, the promise they'd made to each all those years ago.

'I'm falling in love with you, Tully, and I wish I weren't.' He smiled sadly. 'Don't look so scared. I know you don't believe in it.'

The truth of that settled heavily on her, made her feel old suddenly. 'Maybe someday I will.' She wanted to believe that, at least.

'I hope so.' He kissed her gently on the lips. 'And now, what are you going to do about Kate?'

'She won't talk to me, Mom.' Kate leaned back against the cushioned wall of the tiny cubby known as the phone room. She'd had to wait almost an hour for her turn on this Sunday afternoon.

'I know. I just hung up with her.'

Of course Tully would call first. Kate didn't know why that irritated her. 'What did she tell you?'

'That you don't like her boyfriend.'

'That's all?' Kate had to be careful. If Mom found out Chad's age, she'd blow a gasket and Tully would *really* be pissed if she thought Kate had turned Mom against her.

'Is there more?'

'No,' she said quickly. 'He's all wrong for her, Mom.'

'Your vast experience with men tells you this?'

'She didn't go to the last dance because he didn't want to. She's missing out on college life.'

'Did you really think Tully would be your average sorority girl? Come on, Katie. She's . . . dramatic. Big. Her dreams drive her hard. It wouldn't hurt you to have a little of that fire, by the way.'

Kate rolled her eyes. Always there was the subtle—and not so subtle—pressure to be like Tully. 'So what do I do? She is avoiding me completely. I was trying to be a good friend.'

'Sometimes being a good friend means saying nothing.'

'I'm just supposed to watch her make a mistake?'

'Sometimes, yes. And then you stand by to pick up the pieces.'

'So what do I do?'

'Only you can answer that. I do know, however, that she's going to be in the editing room at KTVS at one o'clock.'

'Thanks, Mom. I love you.'

'Love you, too.'

Kate made her way across campus in record time. At the door to KTVS, she paused, steeling herself as if for battle, and then went inside.

She found Tully exactly where Mom had predicted: in an editing bay, hunched over a strand of tape. At Kate's entrance, she looked up.

'Well, well,' she said, straightening up. 'If it isn't the head of the Moral Majority.'

'I'm sorry,' Kate said.

Tully's face crumpled at that, as if she'd been holding her breath in and suddenly let it go. 'You were a real bitch.'

'A total Cruella. I shouldn't have said all that. It's just . . . we've never held back from each other.'

'So that was our mistake.' Tully swallowed, tried to smile. Failed.

'I wouldn't hurt you for the world. You're my best friend. I'm sorry.'

'Swear it won't happen again. No guy will ever come between us.'

'Never.' Kate meant it with every fibre of her being. Their friendship was more important than any relationship. Guys would come and go; girlfriends were for ever. They knew that.

By fall semester of her senior year, Tully was growing impatient with the rarefied world of college. Out in the real world, things were happening. John Lennon had been shot and killed outside his New York apartment; a guy named Hinckley had shot President Reagan in a pathetic attempt to impress Jodie Foster; yellow ribbons hung on trees in quiet neighbourhoods to remind people of the hostages that were still being held in Iran; and Diana Spencer had married Prince Charles in a ceremony so fairy-tale perfect that every girl in America had believed in love and happy endings for the entire summer.

And all of it was headline news, made during Tully's life, and yet because she was in school, it was before her time. Oh, sure, she wrote the articles for the school paper and sometimes even got to read a few sentences here and there on air, but it was all make-believe, warm-up exercises for a game she wasn't yet allowed to play.

She'd done everything the university had to offer, taken every broadcast and print-journalism class that mattered, and learned what she could from a year's worth of interning at the public affairs station. It was time now to jump into the dog-eat-dog world of TV news. She wanted to surge into the crowd of reporters and elbow her way to the front.

'You're not ready, Tully,' Chad said, sighing. 'A reporter needs to exhibit a perfect mix of objectivity and compassion. You're too objective, too cold.'

This was the one criticism that bugged her, and he knew it. She'd spent years *not* feeling things. Now she was suddenly supposed to be both compassionate and objective at the same time. Empathetic but professional. She didn't quite pull it off and she and Chad both knew it. 'I'm not talking about the networks yet. It's just one interview for a part-time job until graduation.' She walked over to the bed. In her black suit and white blouse, she was the picture of conservative chic. Sitting on the edge of the mattress, she pushed a long lock of hair away from his eyes.

'Admit it: I'm ready for this.' She intended to sound sexy and grown-up, but the vulnerable tremble in her voice betrayed her. She needed his approval like she needed air or sunlight.

'Ah, Tully,' he said finally. 'You were born ready.'

Smiling triumphantly, she kissed him—hard—then got up and grabbed her vinyl briefcase.

All the way through the University District and over the Lake Union Bridge, Tully thought about what she knew of the man she was going to meet. At twenty-six, he was already a well-respected former on-air reporter who'd won some big reporting award during a Central American conflict. Something—none of the articles said what—had brought him home, where he'd changed career tracks. Now he was a producer for the smaller office of one of the local stations. She had practised endlessly what she would say.

It's nice to meet you, too, Mr Ryan.

Yes, I have had an impressive amount of experience for my age.

The small concrete building with curtainless windows sat in the middle of the block with a parking lot beside it. Inside, she consulted the tenant board and found what she was looking for: KCPO—Suite 201.

She perfected her posture, smiled professionally and went up to Suite 201. There, she opened the door and almost walked right into someone.

For a moment Tully was actually taken aback. The man standing in front of her was gorgeous—unruly black hair, electric-blue eyes, shadowy stubble of a beard. Not what she'd imagined at all.

'Are you Tallulah Hart?'

She extended her hand. 'I am. Are you Mr Ryan?'

'I am.' He shook her hand. 'Come in.' He led her through a small front room cluttered with papers and cameras and stacks of newspapers everywhere. Another guy stood in the corner, smoking a cigarette. He was huge, at least six foot five, with shaggy blond hair and clothes that looked as if he'd slept in them. At their entrance, he looked up.

'This is Tallulah Hart,' Mr Ryan said by way of introduction.

The big guy grunted. 'She the one with the letters?'

'That's her.' Mr Ryan smiled at Tully. 'He's Mutt. Our cameraman.'

'Nice to meet you, Mr Mutt.'

That made them both laugh and the sound of their laughter only cemented her anxiety that she was too young for this.

He led her into a corner office and pointed to a metal chair in front of a metal desk. 'Have a seat,' he said, closing the door behind him.

He took a seat behind the desk and looked at her.

'So, you're the one who has been clogging my mail with tapes and résumés. I'm sure, with all your ambition, you've researched us. We're the Seattle team for KCPO in Tacoma. We don't have an internship programme here.'

'Did you read my articles and watch my tapes?'

'Actually, that's why you're here. When I realised you weren't going to stop sending me audition tapes, I figured I might as well watch one.'

'And?'

'And you'll be good one day. But you're a long way from ready.'

'That's why I want this internship.'

'The non-existent one, you mean.'

'I'll work twenty to thirty hours a week for free, and I don't care if I get college credit or not. I'll write copy, fact-check, do research. Anything. How can you go wrong?'

'Anything?' He was looking at her intently now. 'Will you make coffee and vacuum and clean the bathroom?'

'Who does all that now?'

'Mutt and me. And Carol, when she's not following a story.'

'Then absolutely I will.'

He sat back, studying her closely. 'You understand you'd be a grunt, and an unpaid one at that.'

'I understand. I could work Mondays, Wednesdays and Fridays.'

Finally he said, 'OK, Tallulah Hart.' He stood up. 'Show me what you can do.'

'I will.' She smiled. 'And it's Tully.'

He walked her back through the office. 'Hey, Mutt, this is our new intern, Tully Hart.'

'Cool,' Mutt said, not looking up from the camera in his lap.

At the door, Mr Ryan paused and looked at her. 'I hope you intend to take this job seriously, Ms Hart.'

'You can count on me, Mr Ryan.'

'Call me Johnny. I'll see you Friday. Say eight a.m.?'

'I'll be here.'

A month before graduation, Tully took Kate to see the KCPO offices.

'That's Mutt.' She pointed to a huge, long-haired, hunched-over guy standing by the open window, blowing his cigarette smoke outside.

'Hey,' he said, barely lifting a single finger in greeting.

'Carol Mansour—she's the reporter—is at a city council meeting,' Tully said, leading Kate towards a closed door.

As if Kate hadn't been hearing Carol Mansour stories for ever.

Tully stopped at the door and knocked. When a male voice answered, Tully opened the door and pulled Kate inside. 'Johnny? This is my friend, Katie.'

A man looked up from behind his desk. 'You're Kate Mularkey, huh?'

He was, hands down, the best-looking man Kate had ever seen. He was older than they were, but not by much; maybe five or six years. His long black hair was thick and feathered back, with the barest hint of curl at the ends. When he smiled at her, she drew in a sharp breath, feeling a jolt of pure physical attraction that was unlike anything she'd ever experienced before.

'I'll leave you two alone,' Tully said, skipping out of the office, closing the door behind her.

'Please. Have a seat,' he said, indicating a chair across from his desk.

She sat down, perching nervously on the edge of the chair.

'Tully tells me you're a genius.'

'Well, she is my best friend.'

'You're lucky. She's a special girl.'

'Yes, sir, she is.'

He laughed at that; it was a rich, contagious sound that made her smile, too. 'Please, don't call me sir. It makes me think some old guy is behind me.' He leaned forward. 'So, Kate, what do you think?'

'About what?'

'The job.'

'What job?'

He glanced at the door, said, 'Hmmm, that's interesting,' then looked at her again. 'We have an opening for an office person. Carol used to do all of the phones and filing, but she's going to have a baby, so the cheap-ass station manager has finally kicked in for a little help.'

'But Tully—'

'She wants to stay an intern. Says that thanks to her grandmother she doesn't need the money.'

This was all coming at Kate too fast. Lately she'd started having second thoughts about a career in television journalism. That was Tully's dream. 'What's the pay?' she asked, stalling.

'Minimum wage, of course. Come on, Katie,' he said, smiling. 'How can you turn me down? You can be a receptionist in an ugly office for next to no money. Isn't it every college grad's dream?'

She laughed. 'When you put it that way, how could I refuse?'

'It's a start in the glamorous world of TV news, right?'

His smile scrambled her thoughts, and the way he said her name, Katie, made her melt. 'Is it? Glamorous, I mean?'

He looked surprised by the question, and for the first time he really looked at her. His fake smile faded, and the look in his blue eyes turned hard, cynical. 'Not in this office.'

Behind her, the door opened. Tully came through, practically bouncing. 'Well, did you say yes?'

It was crazy to take a job because you were hot for the boss. Then again, he was offering her a start in television.

She didn't look at Tully. If she did, Kate knew she'd feel as if she were selling out, following again, and for all the wrong reasons.

But how could she say no? Maybe in a real job she'd find that passion and brilliance she needed. The more she thought about it, the more possible it seemed. School wasn't the real world. That was why the news business hadn't seized hold of her. Here, the stories would matter.

'Sure,' she said at last. 'I'll try it, Mr Ryan.'

'Call me Johnny.' The smile he gave her was so unsettling she actually had to look away. She was sure somehow that he could see inside her or hear how fast he made her heart beat. 'OK, Johnny.'

'All *right*,' Tully said, clapping her hands together.

Kate couldn't help noticing how her friend instantly seized Johnny's full attention. He was sitting at his desk now, staring at Tully.

That was when Kate knew she'd made a mistake.

The summer after graduation was pure heaven for Tully. She and Kate found a cheap Sixties-style apartment in a great location—above the Pike Place Market. They brought in furniture from Gran's house and filled the kitchen with forty-year-old Revereware pots and Spode china.

As working single girls, they fell into an easy routine. Each morning they went out for breakfast, sat at ironwork tables on the sidewalk, and read the various papers that they collected. The *New York Times*, the *Wall Street Journal*, the *Seattle Times* and *Post-Intelligencer* became their bibles. When they were done, they drove to the office, where every day they learned something new about the business of TV news, and after work, they changed into glittery, big shoulder-padded tunics and peg-legged pants and went to one of the many downtown clubs.

And since Tully didn't have to hide Chad's existence any more, he often took both Katie and her out, and they had a blast.

It was everything she and Kate had dreamt of, all those years ago on the banks of the Pilchuck River, and Tully loved every minute of it.

Now they were pulling up to the office. All the way out of Tully's new car and into the building, they talked.

But the minute Tully opened the door, she knew something was up. Mutt was near the window, hurriedly packing up his camera gear. Johnny was in his office, yelling at someone on the phone.

'What's going on?' Tully asked.

Mutt looked up. 'There's a protest going on. It's our story.'

'Where's Carol?'

'In the hospital. Labour.'

This was Tully's chance. She went straight into Johnny's office, without even bothering to knock. 'Let me go on air. I know you think I'm not ready, but I am. And who else is there?'

He hung up the phone and looked at her. 'I already told the station you'd do the report. That's what all the yelling was about.' He came round the desk and moved towards her. 'Don't let me down, Tully.'

Tully knew it was unprofessional, but she couldn't help herself: she hugged him. 'You're the best. I'll make you proud. You'll see.'

Without Mutt and Tully, the office was quiet. It was the first time all summer that Kate had been alone with Johnny. A little unnerved by the silence—and the sight of his open door and the knowledge that he was just on the other side of it—she tended to answer the phone too quickly and even sounded a little breathless when she did it.

It was pathetic.

She'd assumed her infatuation wouldn't last. At the very least, she thought she'd develop an immunity to his smile.

No such luck. Everything he said and did just tightened the noose round her heart. Beneath his cynical veneer, she'd glimpsed an idealist, and even more: a wounded one. Something had broken Johnny, left him here, on the fringes of the big story, and the mystery of it tantalised her.

She went over to the corner, where a stack of tapes lay in a heap, waiting to be put away. She'd just picked up an armful when Johnny appeared in the doorway of his office. 'Hey,' he said. 'Are you busy?'

She dropped the stack of tapes. *Idiot.* 'No,' she said. 'Not really.'

'Let's grab lunch.'

'Uh . . . sure.' She concentrated on the tasks in front of her: switching on the answering machine, picking up her bag.

She walked alongside him across the street. Now and then his body brushed against hers, and she was acutely aware of every contact.

When they finally got to the restaurant, he led her over to a table in the corner that overlooked Elliott Bay and the shops at Pier 70. A waitress showed up almost instantly to take their orders.

'Are you old enough to drink, Mularkey?' he asked with a smile.

'Very funny. But I don't drink, on the job.' At the words, which couldn't have sounded more prim, she winced and thought, *Idiot*, again.

'You're a very responsible girl,' he said when the waitress left; he was obviously trying not to smile.

'Woman,' she said firmly, hoping she didn't blush.

He smiled at that. 'I was trying to compliment you.'

'And you chose *responsible*?'

'What would you prefer?'

'Sexy. Brilliant. Beautiful.' She laughed nervously, sounding more like a girl than she would have wished. 'You know: the words every woman wants to hear.' She smiled. This was her chance to make an impression on him, get his attention as he'd got hers. She didn't want to blow it.

He leaned back in his chair. 'You've been at the station, what—two months now?'

'Almost three.'

'How do you like it?'

'Fine.'

'Fine? That's an odd answer. This is a love-it-or-hate-it business.' He leaned forward. 'Do you have a passion for it?'

'Y-yes.'

He studied her, then smiled knowingly. She wondered how deeply into her soul that blue gaze had seen. 'Tully certainly does.'

'Yes.'

He tried to sound casual as he asked, 'Is she seeing anyone?'

Kate considered it a personal triumph that she didn't flinch or frown. Now, at least, she knew why he'd asked her out for lunch. She should have known. She wanted to say, *Yes; she's been with the same man for years*, but she didn't dare. Tully might not hide Chad any more, but she didn't flaunt him, either. 'What do you think?'

'I think she sees a lot of men.'

Thankfully, the waitress returned with their orders and she was able to pretend to be fascinated by her plate. 'What about you? I get the feeling you're not exactly passionate about your job.'

He looked up sharply. 'What makes you say that?'

She shrugged and kept eating, but she was watching him now.

'Maybe not,' he said quietly.

She felt herself go still; her fork stayed in midair. For the first time they weren't making idle chitchat. He'd just revealed something important; she was somehow certain of that. 'Tully told me you used to be a war correspondent. Tell me about El Salvador.'

'You know what went on down there? The massacre? It was a blood bath. Things have been getting worse lately, too. The death squads are killing civilians, priests, nuns.'

Kate hadn't known all that, or any of it, really, but she nodded anyway, watching the play of emotions cross his face. She'd never seen him so animated, so passionate. Again there was an unreadable emotion in his eyes, too. 'You sound as if you loved it. Why did you leave?'

'I don't talk about this.' He finished his beer and stood up. 'We'd better get back to work.'

She looked down at their barely eaten lunches. Obviously she'd gone too far, probed too much. 'I got too personal, I'm sorry—'

'Don't be. It's ancient history. Let's go.'

All the way back to the office, he said nothing. They walked briskly upstairs and into the quiet office.

There, she couldn't help herself, she touched his arm. 'I really am sorry. I didn't mean to upset you.'

'Like I said, it's old news.'

'It isn't, though, is it?' she said quietly, knowing instantly that she'd overstepped again.

'Get back to work,' he said brusquely, and went into his office, slamming the door shut behind him.

When Tully and Mutt came back, the team clicked into high gear. The four of them crammed into the editing room and turned twenty-six minutes of tape into a sharp, impartial thirty-second story.

When they finished working, Johnny picked up the phone and called the Tacoma station manager. He talked for a few moments, then hung up and looked at Tully. 'They'll air it tonight at ten unless something comes up.'

Tully jumped up and clapped her hands. 'We did it!'

Kate couldn't help feeling a stab of envy. Just once, she wanted Johnny to look at her the way he looked at Tully.

If only she were like her friend—confident and sexy and willing to make a grab at whatever—and whomever—she wanted. Then she might have a chance, but the thought of Johnny's rejection kept her standing in the shadows.

Tully's shadow, to be precise.

From the moment Tully did her first on-air broadcast, everything changed. They became the fearsome foursome; Kate and Tully and Mutt and Johnny. They were together constantly, huddled in the office, working on stories, going from place to place like Gypsies. The second story that Tully covered was about a snowy owl who'd taken up residence on a streetlamp in Capitol Hill. Next, she followed Booth Gardner's campaign to be elected as governor, and though she was one of dozens of reporters on the case, it seemed that Gardner often answered her questions first. Everyone at KCPO knew that Tully wouldn't last on the local channel for long.

They all knew it, but perhaps Johnny most of all. So, though the three of them didn't talk about the future, they felt its shadowy presence constantly, and somehow that made their time together sweeter and more intense. On the rare night when they weren't working on a story, Johnny, Tully and Kate met at Goldies to play pool and drink beer. By the end of their second year together, they knew all there was to know about each other; at least, all that each was willing to share.

Except the stuff that truly mattered. Kate often thought it ironic that three people who searched through the rubble of life to find pebbles of truth could be so stubbornly blind about their own lives.

Tully had no idea that Johnny wanted her, and he was completely unaware that Kate wanted him. So their silent triangle went on, until a cold November day in 1984, when Johnny called her into his office.

They were alone again, that day. Tully and Mutt were tracking down a Sasquatch sighting in the Olympic rain forest.

Kate smoothed her angora sweater and schooled her face into an impersonal smile as she went into his office and found him standing at the dirty window. 'What is it, Johnny?'

He looked terrible. 'Remember I told you about El Salvador?'

'Sure.'

'Well, I still have friends down there. One of them, Father Ramón, is missing. His sister thinks they've taken him somewhere for torture, or killed him. She wants me to come down and see if I can help.'

'But it's dangerous—'

He smiled, but it was like a reflection on water, distorted and unreal. 'Danger is my middle name.'

'This isn't something to joke about. You could be killed. Or disappear like that journalist in Chile during the coup.'

'Believe me,' he said, 'I'm not joking. I've been there, remember? I know what it's like to be blindfolded and shot at.' He turned his head. His eyes took on a vague, unfocused look, and she wondered what he was remembering. 'I can't turn my back on the people who protected me. Could you turn away from Tully if she begged you for help?'

'I would never turn my back on her. Although, I don't expect to see her in a war zone, unless you count the sale at Nordstrom.'

'I knew you were my girl. So you'll keep this place running while I'm gone?'

'Me?'

'Like I once once, you're a responsible girl.'

She couldn't help herself; she moved towards him, looked up. He was leaving, could be hurt down there, or worse. 'Woman,' she said.

He stared down at her, unsmiling. She felt the mere inches between them. It would take nothing, barely a movement to touch.

'Woman,' he said.

Then he left her there, standing alone.

When Johnny was gone, Kate learned how elastic time was, how it could stretch out until minutes felt like hours. Every time the phone rang, she tensed up.

'You look terrible,' Tully said, dropping a stack of tapes on Kate's desk. 'What in the hell is wrong with you? You've been moping around for more than a week.'

Kate couldn't help glancing at Johnny's door and then up at her friend. Longing welled up inside her, sharp and strong; if only she could tell Tully the truth: that she'd accidentally fallen in love with Johnny and now she was worried about him. In ten years, this was the first thing she'd ever hidden from Tully and it physically hurt to conceal it.

But her feelings for Johnny were so fragile; she knew that Tropical Storm Tully would rain all over them, ruin them.

'I'm just tired,' she said. 'This producing is hard work. That's all.'

'But you love it, don't you?'

'Sure. It's great. Now go on, meet Chad. I'll close up.'

She went home by herself. The bus dropped her off at the corner of Pike and Pine. Amid the colourful crowd of tourists and weirdoes and hippies, she picked up some food for dinner. Back in her apartment, she curled up on the couch, ate her dinner out of white cardboard containers, and watched the nightly news.

Halfway through, the doorbell rang.

Frowning, she went to the door. 'Who is it?'

'Johnny Ryan.'

The jolt Kate felt almost knocked her off her feet. Relief. Joy. Fear. She experienced all three emotions in a heartbeat of time.

She glanced in the mirror hanging on the wall beside her and gasped. She looked like a fashion magazine 'before' photo—limp hair, no make-up, eyebrows untrimmed.

He pounded on the door again.

She opened it.

He stood there, leaning heavily against the door frame, wearing dirty Levi's and a torn BORN IN THE USA tour T-shirt. His hair was long and uncombed, and though he was tanned, his face looked worn, older. She could smell alcohol, too.

'Hey,' he said, opening his fingers from along the door frame in greeting. At the movement he lost his balance and almost fell.

Kate moved towards him. Holding him up, she guided him into the apartment, kicked the door shut, and led him to the sofa, where he half stumbled to a sit.

'I've been sitting in the Athenian,' he said, 'trying to get up the nerve to come over here.' He glanced blearily around the place. 'Where's Tully?'

'She's not here,' Kate said, feeling a clutch in her heart.

'Oh.'

She sat down beside him. 'How did it go in El Salvador?'

When he turned to her, the look in his eyes was so devastating that she reached out, put her arm round him and drew him close.

'He was dead,' he said after a long silence. 'Before I even got there, he was dead. But I had to find him . . .' He pulled a flask out of his back pocket and took a long drink. 'Y' want some?'

She took a sip, felt it burn all the way down her throat and settle like a hot coal in the pit of her stomach.

'It's damned heartbreaking what's going on. And not enough is getting on air. No one cares.' He took another drink.

'Maybe you should slow down a little.' She tried to take the flask from him. Instead, he grabbed her wrist and pulled her onto his lap. He touched her face with his other hand, caressing her cheek as if he were blind and trying to come up with an image of what she looked like.

'You're beautiful,' he whispered.

'You're drunk.'

'You're still beautiful.' He slid one hand up her arm and the other down her neck until he was holding her in his arms. She knew he was going to kiss her, felt the knowledge in every nerve ending in her body, just as she knew she should stop him.

He pulled her towards him and all her good intentions disappeared. The kiss was like nothing she'd ever experienced before: tender and sweet at first, then searching, demanding.

She gave herself in to it all, surrendering to him as she'd so often dreamt of doing. She became greedy for him, desperate. Without thinking, she shoved her hands up under his T-shirt, feeling his warm skin, needing to be closer . . .

Her hands were at his collarbone, pushing the soft, warm cotton upwards, when she realised he'd gone still. Breathing hard, aching with this new need, she drew back enough to look at him.

He lay back against the sofa, his eyes at half mast. He lifted his hand slowly, jerkily, almost as if he weren't quite controlling his own movements, and touched her lips, tracing their contour with his fingertip. 'Tully,' he whispered. 'I knew you'd taste good.'

And with that blow to the heart, he fell asleep.

Kate wasn't sure how long she sat on his lap, staring down at his sleeping face. Once again, time seemed elastic between them. It felt as if she were bleeding—but it wasn't blood that leaked out of her, not something that could be so easily transfused. Instead, she was losing her dreams. The fantasy of love she'd constructed and tended so carefully.

She climbed off him and settled him onto the sofa, taking off his shoes and covering him with a blanket.

In her own bed, with a door closed between them, she lay awake for a long time, trying not to replay it over and over in her mind, but it was impossible. She kept tasting his lips, and hearing him whisper, *Tully*.

When she finally fell asleep, it was well past midnight and dawn came much too quickly. She slammed the silencer on her alarm, brushed her teeth and hair, put on a robe and hurried into the living room.

Johnny was sitting at the kitchen table, drinking coffee. At her entrance, he got to his feet. 'Hey,' he said, shoving his fingers through his hair.

'Hey.'

He glanced at Tully's door.

'She's not here,' Kate said.

'So you put me to bed on the couch and covered me.'

'Yep.'

He moved towards her. 'I was pretty baked last night.'

'Yes, you were.'

'Did . . . anything happen? I mean, I'd hate to think—'

'Between us? How could it?' she said before he could finish saying how much he would regret a liaison between them. 'Don't worry. Nothing happened.'

The smile he gave her was so relieved she wanted to cry. 'Then I guess I'll see you at work today, huh? And thanks for taking care of me.'

'Sure.' She crossed her arms. 'What are friends for?'

Late in 1985, Tully got her big break. Assigned to do a live broadcast, she was surprised by the flurry of nerves that made her fingers tremble and her voice break, but when it was over, she felt invincible. She'd been good. Maybe even amazing.

Afterwards, it had taken for ever to load up all the gear and get back on the road, but she didn't care. The longer this night lasted, the better. She hadn't even taken off her earpiece or walkie-talkie. They were her badges of honour.

'Pull over at that 7-Eleven,' Johnny said from the back of the van. 'I'm thirsty.'

Mutt drove into the parking lot. 'It's Tully's turn. I went last time.'

When they parked, Tully collected their money, then got out of the van and headed for the brightly lit mini-mart.

'None of that new Coke for me,' Johnny said into her earpiece.

She pulled the walkie-talkie off her belt, switched it on and said, 'You say that to me every time. I'm not an idiot.'

Inside the store, she looked around for the cooler case, found it, and just as she was reaching for the handle, she noticed a shadow move across the glass. Turning, she saw a man in a grey ski mask point a gun at the cashier.

'Oh my God.'

'Are you talking about me?' Johnny said. 'Because it's about time—'

She fumbled for the volume on the walkie-talkie and switched it off before the robber heard something. She clipped it to her belt and pulled her jacket over it.

At the register, the robber swung to face her.

'You! Get on the floor.' The masked man pointed his gun at the ceiling and pulled the trigger to make his point.

'Tully? What the *hell* is going on?' came Johnny's voice through the earpiece.

'Someone's robbing the store,' she whispered as loudly as she dared.

In her earpiece, she heard Johnny say, 'Mutt, call 911. Tully, keep calm and get the hell to the floor. I'm getting hold of the station. Stan, are you receiving this?'

The news director's voice cut in. 'I've got it. I'm putting this through to Mike. He's on air with the ten o'clock news. Your audio is going on live.'

The masked man swung towards her again, pointing his gun at her. 'I told you to get down, damn it.'

She just had time to process 'I've had enough o' this shit' when he pulled the trigger.

She saw a flash of light, a puff of something that might have been smoke, and then pain knocked her off her feet.

She crashed into the aisle beside her, was vaguely aware of coloured boxes falling around her. Her head hit the linoleum floor hard.

For a moment, she lay there, gasping, staring up at a wiggling snake of fluorescent lighting.

'Tully?'

It was Johnny's voice, in her ear. She eased slowly—slowly—onto her side. Her shoulder throbbed with pain, but she gritted her teeth and kept moving. Keeping low, she crawled to the end of the aisle, ripped open a box of Kotex and shoved a pad over her wound. The pressure hurt like hell and made her dizzy.

'Tully?'

She lifted the walkie-talkie to her mouth. 'I'm here. I just put . . . a dressing on my wound. I think I'm fine.'

'Hey, Tallulah. Mike here, at the news desk. You're audio is coming to us live. Can you describe the scene?'

She got to a crouch, wincing at the pain, and moved forward slowly, trying to gauge when she could actually look up. 'Moments ago, a masked man came into this mini-mart on Beacon Hill, wielding a hand-gun and demanding money from the clerk. He fired once into the air to make his point and once into me.'

She heard a noise; it sounded like crying. Keeping low, she came round the corner and found a little boy.

'Hey,' she said, holding out her hand. He took it greedily, squeezing so tightly she couldn't pull away. 'Who are you?'

'Gabe. I'm with my grandpa. Did you see that guy shoot his gun?'

'I did. I'm going to go find your grandpa to make sure he's OK. You stay here. What's your last name, Gabe, and how old are you?'

'Linklater. I'm gonna be seven in July.'

'OK, Gabe Linklater. You stay low and keep quiet. No more crying, OK? Be a big boy.'

'I'll try.'

'Tallulah,' Mike said into her earpiece. 'Can you hear me?'

She brought the walkie-talkie to her mouth. 'I just found six-year-old Gabe Linklater in the candy aisle. He came in with his grandfather, who I'm looking for now. I can hear the gunman over at the register, threatening the cashier. Tell the police there's only one robber.'

She turned the corner. There she found an old man, sitting cross-legged on the floor. 'Are you Gabe's grandfather?' she whispered.

'Is he OK?'

'A little scared, but fine. He's in the candy aisle. What did you see?'

'The robber drove up in a blue car. I saw him through the window.' He looked at her shoulder. 'Maybe you should—'

'I'm fine. I'm going to move in closer.' She compressed the pad against her wound again, winced at the pain, and waited for the nausea to pass. This time, her hand came away bloody. Ignoring it, she reported in again, whispering into the walkie-talkie. 'Apparently, Mike, the lone gunman arrived in a blue car, which should be parked outside in front of one of the windows. I'm happy to say that Gabe's grandfather is also alive and unharmed. Now I'm working my way towards the register. I can hear the gunman yelling that there has to be more money and the cashier saying that he can't open the safe. I can see the flash of lights outside. So the police have arrived. They're shining the lights into the store, telling him to come out with his hands up. Tell the police he's taken off his mask, Mike. He's blond-haired, with a snake tattoo that wraps round his neck. The gunman is extremely agitated. He's screaming obscenities and waving his gun around. I think—'

Another gunshot rang out. Glass shattered. Seconds later a SWAT team stormed through the glass doors.

Tully stood up slowly. 'Seattle SWAT has just shot the glass out of the window and come in. They have the robber on the ground. I'll see if I can get close enough to ask them some questions.'

Then she passed out.

The drive to the hospital seemed to last for ever. All the way there, through the stop-and-go city traffic, Kate sat in the back seat of the smelly cab and prayed that Tully would be OK.

Johnny and Mutt were already there, slumped in uncomfortable plastic chairs, looking haggard. At her entrance, Johnny stood.

She ran to him. 'I saw the broadcast. What happened?'

'She walked into a robbery, wearing her earpiece and carrying her walkie-talkie. A man shot her in the shoulder and she kept on broadcasting. You should have seen her, Mularkey she was brilliant. Fearless.'

Kate heard the admiration in his voice, saw it in his eyes. Any other time it might have wounded her, that obvious pride; now it pissed her off. 'That's why you're so in love with her, isn't it? Because she has the guts you don't. So you put her in harm's way and get her shot and you're proud of her *passion*.' Her shaking voice drew the last word out like poison. 'Screw the heroics. I wasn't talking about the news. I was asking about her life. Have you even asked how she is?'

He looked startled by her outburst. 'She's in surgery. She—'

'Katie!'

She heard Chad call out her name and she turned, seeing him run into the lobby. They came together as naturally as wind and rain, clinging to each other. His arms coiled round her, held her close, giving her a safe place in which to finally cry.

'How is she?' he whispered, his voice as fragile as she felt.

'In surgery. But she'll be fine. Bullets can't stop a storm.'

'She's not as tough as she pretends to be. We both know that, don't we, Kate?'

She swallowed, nodded. In an awkward silence they stood there, still close together, bound by the invisible threads of their mutual concern. She saw it in his eyes, as clear as day; he *did* love Tully, and he was scared. 'I'd better go call my mom and dad. They'll want to be here.'

With a tired smile, she walked away. As she passed Johnny, she couldn't help but say, 'That's how real people help each other through hard times.'

At the bank of payphones, she put in four quarters and dialled home. When her dad answered—thank God it wasn't her mother; Kate would have lost it then—she gave him the news and hung up.

She turned round and Johnny was there, waiting for her. 'I'm sorry.'

'You should be.'

'One of the things about this business, Katie, is that you learn to put the story first. It's a hazard of the trade.'

'It's always about the story with people like you and Tully.' She left him standing there and went to the sofa, where she sat down.

After a moment she felt him sit down beside her. 'When did you get to know me so well?'

'It's a small office.'

'That's not it.' He sighed and leaned back. 'I did put her in danger.'

'She wouldn't have it any other way,' she conceded.

'I know, but . . .'

When he let his sentence trail off, she looked at him. 'Do you love her?'

He didn't respond, just sat there, leaning back, with his eyes closed.

She couldn't stand it. Now that she'd finally dared to ask the question she wanted it answered. 'Johnny?'

He reached over for her, put an arm round her shoulder, and drew her to him. She sank into the comfort he offered. It felt as natural as breathing being beside him like this, though she knew how dangerous that feeling was.

There, saying nothing more, they sat together through the long, empty hours of the night. Waiting.

Tully came awake slowly, taking stock of her surroundings: white acoustic-tile ceiling, bars of fluorescent lighting, silver rails on her bed and a tray beside her.

Memories trickled into her consciousness: Beacon Hill. The minimart. She remembered the gun being pointed at her and the puff of smoke. And the pain.

'You'll do anything to get attention, won't you?' Kate stood by the door, wearing a pair of baggy UW sweat pants and an old T-shirt. As she approached the bed, tears filled her eyes. She wiped them away impatiently. 'Damn. I swore I wouldn't cry.'

'Thank God you're here.' Tully hit the button on her bed control until she was sitting up.

'Of course I'm here, you idiot. Everyone is here. Chad, Mutt, Mom, Dad. Johnny. He and my dad have been playing cards for hours and talking about the news. We've been so worried.'

'Was I good?'

Kate laughed at that even as tears spilled down her cheeks. 'That would be your first question. Johnny said you kicked ass.'

'I wonder if *60 Minutes* will want to interview me.'

Kate closed the distance between them. 'Don't scare me like that again, OK?'

'I'll try not to.'

Before Kate could say anything, the door opened and Chad stood in the doorway, holding a pair of Styrofoam coffee cups. 'She's awake,' he said quietly, putting the cups down on the table beside him.

'She just opened her eyes. Of course, she's more interested in her chances of winning an Emmy than in her recovery.' Kate looked down at her friend. 'I'll leave you two alone for a minute.'

As soon as Kate was gone, Chad moved closer. As he stared down at her, his beautiful eyes were bright. 'I thought I'd lost you.'

'I'm fine,' she said impatiently. 'Did you see the broadcast? What do you think?'

'I think you're not fine, Tully,' he said softly. 'You're farther from fine than anyone I know, but I love you. And all night I've been thinking about what my life would be without you and I don't like what I see.'

'Why would you lose me? I'm right here.'

'Marry me, Tully.'

She almost laughed, thinking it was a joke; then she saw the fear in his eyes. 'You mean it,' she said, frowning.

'I got offered a job at Vanderbilt in Tennessee. I want you to come with me. You love me, Tully, even if you don't know it. And you need me.'

'Of course I need you. Is Tennessee a top-forty market?'

His rough face crumpled at that; his smile faded. 'I love you,' he said again, softly this time.

The door behind him opened. Mrs Mularkey stood there, arms akimbo, wearing a cheap denim skirt and a plaid blouse. 'The nurse said five more minutes with visitors and then they're throwing us all out.'

Chad bent down and kissed her. It was a beautiful, almost haunting kiss that somehow managed both to bring them together and highlight how far apart they could be. 'I loved you, Tully,' he whispered.

Loved? Had he said *loved*? As in past tense? 'Chad—'

He turned away from the bed. 'She's all yours, Margie.'

'Sorry to kick you out,' Mrs Mularkey said.

'Don't worry about it. I think my time was up. Goodbye, Tully.' He left the room, letting the door bang shut behind him.

'Hey, little girl,' Mrs Mularkey said.

Tully surprised herself by bursting into tears.

Mrs Mularkey just stroked her hair and let her cry.

'I guess I was really scared.'

'Shhh,' Mrs Mularkey said soothingly, drying her tears with a Kleenex. 'Of course you were, but we're here now. You're not alone.'

Tully cried until the pressure in her chest eased and the tears dried up. Finally, feeling better, she wiped her eyes and tried to smile. 'OK. I'm ready for my lecture now.'

Mrs Mularkey gave her The Look. 'Your professor, Tallulah?'

'Ex-professor.'

'Do you love him?'

'How would I know?'

'You'd know.'

Overnight, Tully became a media sensation in Seattle. Newspaperman Emmett Watson wrote a column about courage under fire and how proud we should be of Tallulah Hart's commitment to news. Radio station KJR dedicated a whole day of rock'n'roll songs to the 'news chick who used a microphone to stop a robbery', and even *Almost Live*, the local comedy show, aired a segment that made fun of the bumbling robber and showed Tully in a Wonder Woman outfit.

Flowers and balloons poured into her room, many signed by people who normally made the news themselves.

'So, you're the genius here. What do I do?' She sat up in bed, going through the pile of pink While You Were Out messages that Kate had brought with her from the office. It was an impressive list of names, but she was having trouble concentrating. Her arm hurt and the sling made even little tasks difficult. Worst of all, she couldn't stop thinking about Chad's out-of-left-field proposal. 'I mean: Tennessee. How can I get to the top in a place like that? Or maybe that's exactly where I could get to the top fast and get noticed by the networks.'

Kate sat at the other end of the bed, her legs stretched out alongside Tully's. 'Look. Maybe I'm not the best person to ask, but it seems to me that at some point you've got to at least mention love.'

'Your mom said I'd know if I loved him.' She looked down at her bare left hand, trying to imagine a diamond ring.

The bedside phone rang. Still staring at her hand, she picked it up quickly, hoping it was Chad. 'Hello?'

'Tallulah Hart?'

She sighed, disappointed. 'This is she.'

'I'm Jim Rorbach from KLUE-TV. We're probably not the first station to call you, but we feel certain we'll make the best offer.'

He had her full attention now. 'Oh, really?'

'We want to do whatever it takes to make you part of the KLUE news family. When can you come in to talk to me about this?'

'I'm being discharged right now. How about tomorrow? Ten a.m.'

'We'll see you then.'

Tully hung up the phone and shrieked. 'That was KLUE-TV. They want to hire me!'

'Oh my gosh,' Kate said, jumping up and down. 'You're going to be a star. I knew it. I can't wait to—' She stopped in the middle of her sentence; her smile fell.

'What?'

'Chad.'

Tully felt something twist deep inside her. She wanted to pretend there was something to think about, a decision to be made, but she knew the truth, and so did Kate.

'You're going to be a huge star,' Kate said firmly. 'He'll understand.'

Ever since Kate had picked her up from the interview, Tully hadn't stopped spinning out the old little-girl dreams. *We're on our way, Kate. As soon as I get an anchor spot, I'll make sure they hire you to replace me.*

Kate knew she should put the brakes on this dual future of theirs. She was tired of following Tully, and she didn't want to quit her job.

Johnny.

How pathetic was that? He didn't love her, but she couldn't help thinking that maybe now, with Tully gone, she'd have a chance.

It was ridiculous, and embarrassing, but her dreams centred more on him and less on broadcasting. Not that she could admit that to anyone. Twenty-five-year-old college-educated women were expected to dream of more money and higher positions on the corporate ladder and running the very companies that had refused to hire their mothers.

'Hey, you missed the turn.'

'Oh. Sorry.' Kate turned at the next block and circled back, pulling up in front of Chad's house. 'I'll wait here.'

Tully didn't open her door. 'He'll understand why I can't marry him yet. He knows how much this means to me. Wish me luck.'

'Don't I always?'

Tully got out and walked up to the front door.

Kate opened her paperback and started to read. It wasn't until much later that she looked up, noticing it had begun to rain. Tully should have come back by now, told her to drive on home, that she'd be spending the night with Chad.

Kate closed the book and got out of the car. As she walked up the cement path, she got a bad feeling that something was wrong.

She knocked twice, then opened the door.

Tully was in a totally empty living room, kneeling in front of the fireplace, crying. She handed Kate a piece of paper that was splotched with tears. 'Read it.'

Kate looked down at the bold black handwriting.

Dear Tully,

I was the one who recommended you to KLUE, so I know all about the job you've come to tell me about, and I'm proud of you, baby. I knew you could do it.

When I took the job at Vanderbilt I knew what it meant for us. I hoped . . . but I knew.

You want a lot from this world, Tully. Me, I just want you.

Here's what matters: I'll always love you.

Light the world on fire.

It was signed simply C.

'I thought he loved me,' Tully said.

'It sounds like he does.'

'Then why would he leave me?'

Kate looked at her friend, hearing the echo of all the times Tully had been abandoned by her mother. 'Did you ever tell him you loved him?'

'I couldn't.'

'Maybe you don't love him, then.'

'Or maybe I do,' Tully said, sighing. 'It's just so hard to believe in.'

That was the fundamental difference between them. Kate believed in love with all her heart; unfortunately, she'd fallen in love with a man who didn't know she existed. 'I think if you really loved Chad, you'd know it. At least, if I loved someone, I'd know it.'

'Everything is always black and white with you. I don't see the world like that. How do you always know what you want?'

'You know what you want, Tully. You always have.'

'So I don't get to fall in love? That's my price for fame and success? Always being alone?'

From the moment Tully took the new job, Kate found herself watching her friend's life from a distance. Months passed with them living separate lives, connected only by place. Their tiny apartment, once the container of their lives, had become something of a way station. Tully spent twelve hours a day, seven days a week, working. When she wasn't technically at work, she was following stories, trying like hell to do something—anything—that would put her in front of the camera.

Without Tully, Kate's life lost its shape, and like some overwashed sweater, no amount of positioning or folding could make it right again. Her mother told her repeatedly to snap out of her funk and start dating, have some fun, but how could she date when she had no interest in the guys who had interest in her?

Tully did not suffer from the same malaise. While she still cried about Chad when they were drinking late at night, she had no problem meeting guys and bringing them home. Kate had yet to see the same guy come out of Tully's bedroom twice. According to Tully, that was the plan. She had no intention of ever falling in love. In retrospect, of course, Tully came to believe that she'd loved Chad desperately, so much so that no other man could measure up. But not enough, as Kate repeatedly pointed out, to call him or move to Tennessee.

To be honest, Kate was growing tired of her friend's drunken reminiscences about the epic love she'd had for Chad. Kate knew what love was, how it could turn you inside out and dry up your heart.

After that long night spent with Johnny in the hospital waiting room, Kate had thought there might actually be some hope. She'd felt that a door had opened between them. But whatever inroads had been made in the bright light of the waiting room had faded with the dawn. She'd never forget the look on his face when he learned that Tully would be fine. It was more than relief.

That was when he'd pulled away from her.

Now, all these months later, she knew it was time for her to pull away from him. Time to leave her little-girl fantasies in the sandbox along with other forgotten toys and move on. He didn't love her. Any dreams to the contrary were simply that.

Now, sitting at the kitchen table, with her half-eaten dinner still in cartons around her, she opened the *Seattle Times* and turned to the classified section. There, she saw several interesting choices. Reaching for a pen, she was about to circle one when the door behind her opened.

She turned round and saw Tully in the doorway; her friend wore her dating clothes—an artfully torn sweatshirt that exposed one bare shoulder, jeans tucked into slouchy ankle boots.

Of course she had a guy with her; she was draped all over him.

'Hey, Katie,' she said in a slurred, I've-already-had-three-margaritas voice. 'Look who I ran into.'

The guy stepped out from behind the door.

Johnny. The sight of him with Tully was a kick in the chest.

'Hey, Mularkey,' he said, smiling. 'Tully wants you to come dancing with us.'

She closed the newspaper with exaggerated care. 'No, thanks.'

Tully let go of Johnny's hand and stumbled towards her. 'Please,' she said. 'I had a bad day today. I need you.'

'Come on, Mularkey,' Johnny said, moving in her direction. 'It'll be fun. Like old times.'

The way he smiled made it impossible to say no, even though she knew it was a bad idea to join them.

'OK,' she said. 'I'll get dressed.'

She went into her bedroom and put on a sparkly blue dress with shoulder pads and a cinch belt. By the time she came back out of her room, Johnny had Tully pressed up against the wall, with her hands over her head and his hands covering hers, and was kissing her.

'I'm ready,' she said dully.

Tully wiggled out from underneath Johnny and grinned at her. 'Excellent. Let's rock'n'roll.'

Three abreast, their arms linked, they walked out of the apartment and down the empty cobblestone street. At Kells Irish Pub, they found a small empty table close to the dance floor.

The minute Johnny left to get them drinks, Kate looked across the table. 'What are you doing with him?'

Tully laughed. 'What can I say? We ran into each other after work and had a few drinks. One thing led to another, and . . .' She looked sharply at Kate. 'Do you *care* if I sleep with him?'

There it was. The question that mattered. Kate had no doubt that if she bared her soul and told the truth, this horrible night would be over. Tully would shut Johnny down faster than a storm door in a tornado, and she wouldn't tell Johnny why.

But what good would come of that? Kate knew how Johnny felt about Tully, how he'd always felt. He wanted a woman with passion and fire; losing Tully wouldn't make him turn to Kate. And maybe it was time for drastic measures, finally. Kate's hope had endured so much, but this—him sleeping with Tully—would be the end of it.

She lifted her gaze, praying her eyes were dry. 'Come on, Tully, you know better than that. But he cares about you. You could break his heart.'

Tully laughed. 'You Catholic girls worry about everyone, don't you?'

Before Kate could answer, Johnny returned to the table with two margaritas and a bottle of beer. Setting them down, he took Tully's hand and dragged her onto the floor. There, they melted into the crowd, where he took her into his arms and kissed her.

Kate reached for her drink. She had no idea what that kiss meant to Tully, but she knew what it meant to Johnny, and the knowledge seeped through her like some kind of poison.

Much later, when she lay in her lonely bedroom, listening to the sound of lovemaking coming from another room, she finally cried.

In the two months since their night at Kells Pub, Kate was not the only one to notice the change in Johnny. He seemed lately to be simply rolling out of bed and coming to work. His hair was too long and beginning to curl in all kinds of weird ways. He hadn't shaved in days, and his clothes didn't match.

Kate knew what the problem was.

Tully.

Just that morning, as they'd been having breakfast, Tully had said, 'Johnny keeps calling me. Should I go out with him again?'

Fortunately for Kate, it had turned out to be a rhetorical question.

'No way. I want a relationship like I want a lethal injection. I thought he knew that.'

Now, Kate sat at her desk, supposedly filing their new insurance information. She and Johnny were alone in the office for the first time in days. Carol and Mutt were out on assignment.

She got up slowly, walked to his closed office door. It made no sense for her to go to him, but he was hurting, and she couldn't stand that. After a long minute, she knocked.

'Come in.'

She opened the door.

He was at his desk, hunched over, writing furiously on a yellow legal pad. Hair fell across his profile; he impatiently tucked it behind his ear and looked up at her. 'Yeah, Mularkey?'

She went to the fridge in the corner of his office and got two Henry Weinhard's beers. Opening them, she handed one to him, then sat down on the edge of his cluttered desk. 'You look like a man who is drowning,' she said simply.

He took the beer. 'It shows, huh?'

'It shows.'

He glanced at the door. 'Are we alone?'

'Mutt and Carol left about ten minutes ago.'

Johnny took a long drink of his beer and leaned back in his chair. 'She won't return my phone calls.'

'I know.'

'I don't get it. That night—our night together, I mean—I thought . . .'

'Do you want the truth?'

'I know the truth.'

They sat there in silence for a long time, each sipping beer.

'It's fucking awful to want someone you can't have.'

And with those few words, Kate knew; she had never had a chance with him. 'Yeah, it is.' She paused, looking down at him. 'I'm sorry, Johnny,' she finally said, getting up from the edge of his desk.

'What are you sorry about?'

She wished she had the nerve to answer him, to tell him how she felt, but some things were better left unspoken.

'**W**ell, Ms Mularkey, you have an impressive résumé for someone your age. May I ask why you're considering a career change to advertising?'

Kate tried to look relaxed. She'd dressed carefully for today in a plain black wool gaberdine suit, with a white blouse. She hoped it was a look that said professional through and through. 'In my years in TV news I've learned a few things about myself and a few things about the world. The news, as you know, is go-go-go. We're always moving at top speed, just getting the facts and then moving on. I often find myself more interested in what comes after the story than the story itself. I'm better, I believe, at long-range thinking and planning. Details, rather than broad strokes. And I'm a good writer.'

'You've given this a lot of thought.'

'I have.'

The woman across the desk leaned back, studying Kate. She seemed to like what she saw. 'OK, Ms Mularkey. I'll discuss this with my partners and we'll get back to you. When could you start work?'

'I'd need to give two weeks' notice and then I'd be ready to go.'

'Excellent.' The woman stood.

Kate shook the woman's hand firmly and left.

Kate walked briskly along First Avenue, buttoning up her old college coat as she went. She caught the uptown bus and got off at the stop in front of the office at exactly 3.57.

Surprisingly, the main office was empty. Kate hung up her coat and tossed her bag and briefcase under her desk, then went round the corner to Johnny's office. 'I'm back.'

He was on the phone, but he motioned for her to come in. '. . . Come on,' he was saying in an exasperated voice, 'how am I supposed to help you with that?' He was silent for a moment, frowning, then, 'Fine. But you owe me one.' He hung up the phone and smiled at Kate, but it wasn't the old smile, the one that had taken her breath away. She hadn't seen that one since the night with Tully.

'You're wearing a suit,' he said. 'Around here, that means only two things, and since I know you aren't anchoring the news . . .'

'Mogelgaard and Associates.'

'The ad agency? What position did you apply for?'

'Account executive.'

'You'd be good at that.'

'Thanks, but I don't have the job yet.'

'You will.'

She waited for him to say more, but he just stared at her, as if something troubled him. 'Well, I'd better get back to work.'

'Wait. I'm working on this story for Mike. I could use some help.'

'Sure.'

For the next few hours, they sat huddled together at his desk, working and reworking the problematic script. Kate tried to keep her distance from him and told herself never to make eye contact. Both resolutions failed. By the time they finished work, night had fallen.

He looked at her. 'How will I get along without you?'

When there was still hope, she would have blushed at a moment like this. 'I'll help you hire someone.'

'You think replacing you will be easy?'

She had no answer for that. 'I'm going now—'

'I owe you dinner. Please.'

'OK.'

They went downstairs and got into his car. In minutes, they were pulling up to a beautiful, cedar-shingled houseboat on Lake Union.

'Where are we?' Kate asked.

'My house. Don't worry, I'm not going to make you dinner. I just want to change my clothes. You're all dressed up.'

Kate followed him down the dock and into a house that was surprisingly spacious. Johnny immediately went to the fireplace and hit the button; a fake fire roared to life. Then he turned to her. 'Would you like a drink?'

'Rum and Coke?'

'Perfect.' He went to the kitchen, poured two drinks, and returned. 'Here you go. I'll be right back.'

She stood there a moment, uncertain of what to do. She glanced around the living room, noticing how few photographs he had. On the television cabinet there was a single picture of a middle-aged couple, dressed in brightly coloured clothing, squatting together in a jungle-looking setting with children clustered around them.

'My parents,' Johnny said, coming up behind her.

She spun round, feeling as if she'd been caught snooping. 'Where do they live?' she said, going to the couch, sitting down. She needed distance between them.

'They were missionaries. They were killed in Uganda by Amin's death squads.'

'Where were you?'

'I was sixteen, at school in New York.'

'So they were idealists, too.'

'What do you mean, too?'

She saw no reason to put it into words, this knowledge she'd gleaned over the years. 'It doesn't matter. You were lucky to be raised by people who believed in something. Is that why you became a war correspondent? To fight in your own way?'

He sighed and shook his head, then walked over to the sofa and sat down beside her. The way he looked at her, as if she were somehow out of focus, made her heartbeat speed up. 'How do you do that?'

'What?'

'Know me?'

She smiled, hoping it didn't look as brittle as it felt. 'We've worked together a long time.'

It was a moment before he said, 'Why are you quitting, Mularkey?'

She leaned back a little. 'Remember when you said it was awful to want something you can't have? I'm never going to be a kick-ass reporter or a first-rate producer. I don't live and breathe the news. I'm tired of not being good enough.'

'I said, it was awful to want some*one* you couldn't have.'

'Well . . . it's all the same.'

'Is it?' He put his drink on the coffee table.

She shifted her weight to face him, pulled her legs up underneath her. 'I know about wanting someone.'

He looked sceptical. 'Who?'

She knew she should lie, gloss over the question, but just now, with him so close, she felt a wave of longing that overwhelmed her. 'You.'

He drew back; it was obvious that he'd never imagined this. 'You never . . .'

'How could I? I know how you feel about Tully.'

She waited for him to say something, but he just looked at her.

For years, she'd expended effort to keep her longing for him concealed, but now that he was so close, there was no holding back. This was her last chance. 'Kiss me, Johnny. Show me I'm wrong to want you.'

'I wouldn't want to hurt you. You're a nice girl, and—'

'What if not kissing you hurts me?'

'Katie . . .'

She loved the way he said her name. For once, she wasn't Mularkey. She leaned closer. 'Now who's afraid? Kiss me, Johnny.'

Just before her lips touched his, she thought she heard him say, 'This is a bad idea,' but before she could reassure him, he was kissing her back.

It wasn't the first time Kate had been kissed; it wasn't even the first time she'd been kissed by a man she cared about, and yet, absurdly, she started to cry.

He tried to pull away when he noticed her tears, but she wouldn't let him. One moment they were on the sofa, making out like teenagers; the next thing she knew, she was on the floor in front of the fire, naked.

He knelt beside her, still clothed. 'Are you sure?'

'That would have been a good question *before* my clothes came off.' Smiling, she angled up and began unbuttoning his shirt.

He made a sound that was part desperation, part surrender, and let her undress him. Then he took her in his arms again.

His kisses were different now, harsher, deeper, more erotic. She felt her body responding in a way it never had before; it was as if she became nothing and everything, just a ragged collection of nerve endings. His touch was her torture, her salvation.

Sensations became everything, all that she was, all that she cared about: pain, pleasure, frustration. She felt her body arching up, as if the whole of her were reaching for something, needing it with a desperation that made her ache, but she didn't even know what it was.

And then he was inside her, hurting her. She gasped at the suddenness of the pain but made no sound. Instead, she clung to him, kissing him and moving with him until the pain dissolved and there was none of her left; there was only this, the feelings of them where they came together, the sharp, aching need for something more . . .

I love you, she thought, holding him, rising to meet him.

'Katie,' he cried out, thrusting deep inside her.

Her body exploded, like some star in space, breaking apart, floating away. Time stopped for a moment, then settled slowly back in place.

'Wow,' she said, flopping back onto the warm carpet.

He stretched out beside her, his sweat-dampened body tucked in close to hers. Keeping one arm round her, he stared up at the ceiling.

'You were a virgin,' he said, sounding frighteningly far away.

'Yes,' was all she could say. She rolled onto her side, slid her naked leg over him. 'Is it always like that?'

When he turned to her, she saw something in his blue eyes that confused her: fear.

'No, Katie,' he said after a long time. 'It's not.'

Katie woke in Johnny's arms. They both lay on their backs, with the sheets puddled round their hips. She stared up at the ceiling, feeling the heavy, unfamiliar weight of his hand between her naked breasts.

She didn't know what she was supposed to do now, how she was supposed to act. From their first kiss, this had been a magical and unexpected gift. They'd made love three times during the night, the last time only a few hours ago. They'd kissed, they'd made omelettes and eaten in front of the fire, they'd talked about their families and their jobs and their dreams.

What they hadn't talked about was tomorrow, and it was here now, as much a presence between them as the soft sheets and the sound of their breathing.

When she felt him stir beside her, she tensed up.

'Morning,' he said in a gravelly voice.

She didn't know how to play coy or act indifferent. She'd loved him too long to pretend otherwise. What mattered now was that they didn't just get up and go their separate ways. 'Why did you quit reporting?'

'You always go right for deep water, don't you?' He sighed. 'I think you've figured it out anyway. I went down there like some kind of white knight, ready to shine my light on what was happening. And then I saw what was happening . . .'

She said nothing, just kissed the curl of his shoulder.

'I thought I was prepared, but you can't be. It's blood and death and body parts being blown off. It's dead kids in the street and boys with machine guns. I got captured . . .' His voice faded away; he cleared his throat. 'I don't know why they let me live, but they did. Lucky me. I tucked my tail between my legs and ran home.'

'You didn't do anything to be ashamed of.'

'I ran like a coward. And I failed. So now you know it all.'

'Do you think it changes how I feel about you?'

It was a moment before he said, 'We need to take this slow, Katie.'

'I know.' She rolled over, so that she was pressed against him.

'I don't want to hurt you.'

It only made her love him more. She wanted to say simply, *Then don't,* but this wasn't a time for simple answers or pretence. It was a time for honesty. 'I'll take the risk of getting hurt if you will,' she said evenly.

A hint of a smile played at the edges of his mouth. 'I knew you'd be dangerous.'

'Me? You must be joking. No one has ever thought I was dangerous.'

'I do.'

'Why?'

'Because you're the kind of girl a guy could fall in love with.'

He didn't sound particularly happy as he said it.

Outside her front door, Kate paused. Only moments before she'd been flying high, revelling in the night spent in Johnny's arms, but now she was back in the real world, where she'd just slept with a man her best friend had slept with first.

What would Tully say?

She opened the door and went inside. She tossed her bag on the kitchen table and made herself a cup of tea.

'Where the hell have you been?'

She turned, flinched.

Tully stood there, her hair dripping wet, wearing nothing but a towel. 'I almost called the cops last night. Where—You're wearing the suit from yesterday.' A slow, knowing smile crept across her face. 'Did you spend the night with someone? Oh my God, you did. You're blushing.' Tully laughed. 'And I thought you were going to die a virgin.' She grabbed Kate's arm and dragged her over to the sofa. 'Talk.'

Kate stared at her best friend. Tully could ruin it all with a word, a look. *He's mine*, her friend could say and what would Kate do?

Kate took a deep breath. 'I'm in love.'

'Whoa there, Penelope Pitstop. Love? After one night?'

It was now or never. 'No,' she said. 'I've loved him for years.'

'Who?'

'Johnny.'

'*Our* Johnny?'

Kate refused to let the pronoun wound her. 'Yes. Last night—'

'He slept with me, what, two months ago? Then wouldn't stop calling. He's on the rebound, Katie. He can't be in love with you.'

Kate tried not to let the word *rebound* find purchase, but it did. 'I knew you'd make it about you.'

'But . . . he's your boss, for God's sake.'

'I quit. I'm starting a job in advertising in two weeks.'

'Oh, great. Now you're giving up your career for a guy.'

'We both know I'm not good enough to make it at the networks. That's your dream, Tully. It always was.' She could see that her friend wanted to argue the point; she saw, too, that any argument would be a lie. 'I'm in love with him, Tully,' she said finally. 'I have been for years.'

'You have a funny way of showing it. Why didn't you tell me?'

'I was scared.'

'Of what?'

Katie couldn't answer.

Tully stared at her. In those dark eyes, she saw everything: fear, worry and jealousy. 'This has disaster written all over it.'

'Can you be happy for me?'

Tully stared at her, and though she finally smiled, it wasn't the real thing and both of them knew it. 'I'll try.'

Rebound. The word, like the image it represented, kept springing into Kate's mind.

He slept with me, what, two months ago?

. . . can't be in love with you . . .

As soon as Tully left the apartment, Kate called in sick to work and crawled into bed. She hadn't been there more than twenty minutes when a knock at the front door startled her out of her thoughts. 'Damn it, Tully,' she muttered, pulling on her pink velours robe and slipping into her bunny slippers. 'Can't you ever remember your key?' She opened the door.

Johnny stood there. 'You don't look sick.'

'Liar. I look terrible.'

He reached forward, untied the belt and pushed the robe off her shoulders. It fell around her feet in a poofy pink puddle. 'A flannel nightgown. How sexy.' He closed the door behind them.

She tried not to think about her conversation with Tully—

rebound

can't love you

—but the words chased one another across her mind, tripping every now and then over his: . . . *don't want to hurt you.*

She saw now, suddenly, the danger she'd accepted so naively. He could shatter her heart and there was no way to protect herself.

'I thought you'd be happy to see me,' he said.

'I told Tully about us.'

'Oh. And there was a problem?'

'She thinks I'm a rebound girl.'

'She does, does she?'

Kate swallowed hard. 'Do you love her?'

'That's what this is about?' He swept her up into his arms, carrying her towards her bedroom as if she weighed nothing at all. Once in bed, he began unbuttoning her nightgown, planting kisses along the way. 'It doesn't matter,' he said finally. 'She didn't love me.' He peeled back the soft flannel to reveal her breast and the nipple that was already hard.

She closed her eyes and let him rock her world again, but when it was over and she was curled against him, the uncertainty returned. She might not be the most experienced girl in the world, but neither was she the most naive, and there was one thing of which she was sure: it mattered whether Johnny had loved Tully.

It mattered very much.

Falling in love was everything Kate had dreamt it would be. For the last few months, she and Johnny had been an honest-to-God couple; they spent most of their weekends together and as many weeknights as possible. She'd finally brought him home to meet the parents and they'd been ecstatic. A nice Irish Catholic boy with a great career and a good sense of humour who liked to play board games and cards. Dad called him a 'good egg' and Mom declared him to be perfect. 'Definitely worth waiting for,' she'd whispered at the end of the first meeting.

For his part, Johnny had fitted into the Mularkey clan as if he'd been born into it. He'd never admitted it, but Kate was certain that he liked being part of a family again after so many lonely years. Although they didn't talk about the future, they enjoyed every minute of the present.

But that was all about to change.

She was in bed, staring up at the ceiling. Beside her, Johnny lay sleeping. It was just past four o'clock in the morning and already she'd thrown up twice. There was no point in putting off the inevitable any longer.

She peeled back the covers gently, careful not to wake him, and got out of bed. Barefooted, she crossed the thick pad of carpet and went into his bathroom, closing the door behind her.

Opening her bag, she dug through the clutter and withdrew the package she'd purchased yesterday. Then she opened it and followed the directions.

Less than two hours later, she had an answer: pink for pregnant.

She stared down at it. Her first ridiculous thought was that for a girl who'd dreamt of becoming a mother, she was damned close to crying.

Johnny wouldn't be happy about this. He was nowhere near ready for fatherhood. He hadn't even said he loved her yet.

She hid the package and indicator back in her bag—the extraordinary thing mixed in the ordinary debris of her life—and took a long hot shower. By the time she was dressed and ready for work, the alarm was going off. She went to the bed and sat beside him, stroking his hair as he woke up.

He smiled up at her, said, 'Hey,' sleepily.

She wanted to say simply *I'm pregnant*, but the admission wouldn't come. Instead, she said, 'I've got to go in early today.'

He looped a hand round the back of her neck and pulled her down for a kiss. When it was over, she meant to ease away. 'I love you,' she whispered.

'And that makes me the luckiest guy in the world.'

For most of the day, she moved forward on autopilot, but somewhere around four o'clock, her will failed her. Picking up the phone, she dialled the familiar number and waited impatiently.

'Hello?' Tully said.

'It's me. Kate. I'm having a crisis.'

'I'll be there in twenty,' Tully said without hesitation.

For the first time all day, Kate smiled. Just being with Tully would help; it always had. Fifteen minutes later, she left her office.

Outside, Kate buttoned up her coat just as Tully pulled up in her brand-new metallic-blue Corvette convertible.

As always, the car made Kate both shake her head and smile. It was so damned . . . phallic, and yet somehow Tully fitted it perfectly. Her wool trousers and silk blouse were even the same colour blue as the car.

Kate hurried round to the passenger side and got in.

'Where do you want to go?'

'Surprise me,' Kate answered.

'You got it.'

In no time at all, they'd snaked through the downtown traffic, rocketed over the West Seattle Bridge, and arrived at a restaurant on Alki Beach. On this faded spring day the place was empty, and they were seated instantly at a table overlooking the steely Sound.

'Thank God you called,' Tully said. 'This was the week from hell. They've had me travelling to every armpit town in the state. Last week I interviewed a guy in Cheney who's built a truck that runs on wood. I kid you not. I could barely see the damn truck through the black smoke it belched out, and he wanted me to report that he'd discovered the future. Oh, and last week . . .'

Kate leaned back and let Tully's monologue wash over her.

'So, what was your crisis about?'

Kate swallowed. There was no way to do this except to plunge in. 'I'm pregnant.'

'Holy shit . . .' Tully leaned back in her seat, looking stunned. 'Pregnant. Wow. What did Johnny say?'

'I haven't told him yet.'

'What are you going to do?' The question was heavy, weighed down as it was by the unspoken option.

'I don't know.' Kate looked up, met Tully's gaze. 'But I know what I'm not going to do.'

Tully stared at her, saying nothing. In those amazingly expressive eyes, Kate saw again a parade of emotions—disbelief, fear, sadness, worry and, finally, love. 'You'll be a great mother, Katie.'

She felt the start of tears. It was what she wanted; now, here, for the first time she dared to admit it to herself. That was what a best friend did: hold up a mirror and show you your heart. 'He's never said he loved me, Tully.'

'Oh. Well . . . you know Johnny.'

With that, Kate felt the past rear up between them. She knew Tully was feeling it, too, this thing they tried so hard to forget: their shared knowledge of Johnny Ryan. 'You're like him,' she finally said. 'How will he feel when he finds out?'

'Trapped.'

It was exactly what Kate had told herself. 'So what do I do?'

'You're asking me? A woman who can't keep a goldfish alive for more than a week?' Tully laughed; it sounded only the tiniest bit bitter. 'You go home and tell the man you love that he's going to be a dad.'

'You make it sound so easy.'

Tully reached across the table, taking her hand. 'Trust him, Katie.'

She knew it was the best advice she could get. 'Thanks.'

'Now, let's talk about the important shit, like names. You don't have to name her after me. Tallulah sort of sucks—no wonder dopehead picked it—but my middle name is Rose. That's not so bad . . .'

The rest of the afternoon passed in quiet conversation. They avoided talk of the baby and focused on inconsequential things. By the time they'd left the restaurant, and driven back to town, Kate's desperation had eased. It wasn't gone, but having a plan of action helped.

When Tully parked behind the houseboat, Kate gave her friend a fierce hug and said goodbye.

Alone in Johnny's house, she changed into a pair of sweats and an old T-shirt, then went into the living room to wait for him.

As she sat there, knees pressed together (too late for that), her hands clasped, she listened to the ordinary sounds of this life she'd grown accustomed to—the slap of the waves on the pilings around them, the squawking of seagulls, the ever-present chug of a motorboat going past.

Across the room, the lock clicked and the door opened. Johnny smiled when he saw her. 'Hey there. I called you before I left the office. Where were you?'

'I played hooky with Tully.'

'Happy hour, huh?' He pulled her up into his arms and kissed her.

She let herself melt against him. When she put her arms round him, she found that she couldn't let go.

She held on so tightly he actually had to pull her away. 'Katie?' he said, stepping back enough to look down at her. 'What's wrong?'

In the last hour she'd imagined a dozen different ways to tell him, but now, standing in front of him, she saw what a waste all those plans were.

'I'm pregnant,' she said in as firm a voice as she could manage.

He stared at her for an eternity, uncomprehending. 'You're what? How did that happen?'

'The normal way, I'm pretty sure.'

He let out a long, slow breath and sank to the sofa. 'A baby.'

'I didn't mean for it to happen.' She sat down beside him. 'I don't want you to feel trapped.'

The smile he gave her was a stranger's, not the one she loved, which crinkled up his eyes and made her smile back. 'All this time I thought I could just pick up and leave when I was ready. Follow a big story and redeem myself. That's been in my head for so long . . . ever since I screwed up in El Salvador.'

She swallowed hard, nodded. Her eyes stung, but she refused to draw attention to her tears by wiping them away. 'I know.'

He reached out, touched her flat stomach. 'But I couldn't just leave any more, could I?'

'Why not?'

'Because I love you,' he said simply.

Now there was no way to hold back her tears. 'I love you, too, but I don't want to—'

He slid off the couch, positioned himself on one knee, and she drew in a sharp breath.

'Kathleen Scarlett Mularkey, will you marry me?'

She wanted to say yes, but she didn't dare. Fear was still too much a part of how she felt. So, she had to say instead, 'Are you sure, Johnny?'

And then, finally, she saw his smile. 'I'm sure.'

Kate had taken Tully's advice—of course—and gone for timeless elegance. Her wedding dress was an ivory silk gown with a heavily beaded bodice and an off-the-shoulder neckline. Her hair had been drawn back from her face and coiled into a Grace Kelly twist. The veil, when she put it on, would float over her face and fall down to her shoulders like a sparkling cloud. For the first time in her life she felt movie-star beautiful.

Standing in front of a full-length mirror that captured her fairy-tale reflection, she glanced over at Tully, who'd been uncharacteristically quiet. Dressed in the pale pink strapless taffeta bridesmaid's gown, she looked vaguely out of place and fidgety.

'You look like you're gearing up for a funeral instead of a wedding.'

Tully looked at her, trying to make a smile look real, but they'd been friends too long to pass each other such counterfeit emotions. 'Are you sure about getting married? I mean really sure? There's no—'

'I'm sure.'

'Good,' she said, nodding stiffly. ''Cause it's for *ever*.'

'You know what else is for ever?'

'Dirty diapers.'

Kate reached out for Tully's hand, noticing how cold her friend's skin was. How could she convince Tully that this was the Y in their lives, the inevitable separation, but not an abandonment? 'Us,' she said pointedly.

'We'll be friends through jobs and kids and marriages.' She grinned. 'I'm sure I'll outlast several of your husbands.'

'Oh, that's nice,' Tully laughed, bumping her shoulder into Kate's. 'You think I won't be able to stay married.'

Kate leaned against her friend. 'I think you'll do whatever you want, Tully. You're such a bright light. Me, I just want Johnny. I love him so much it hurts sometimes.'

'How can you say you only want Johnny? You have a great career. Someday you're going to be running that agency. This pregnancy won't throw you off course. These days women can have it all.'

Kate smiled. 'That's you, Tully. And I'm so proud of you. But I need you to be proud of me, too. No matter what I do. Or don't do.'

'I'm always there for you. You know that.'

'I know.'

They stared at each other, and in that moment, with both of them dressed up like princesses and standing in front of a mirror, they were fourteen years old again, planning the whole of their lives.

Tully finally smiled. This time it was the real thing. 'When are you going to tell your mom about the baby?'

'After I'm married.' Kate laughed. 'I'll confess to God, but I'm not telling my mom till I'm Mrs Ryan.'

For a single, glorious moment, time simply stopped. They were TullyandKate again, girls sharing secrets.

Then the door opened.

'It's time,' Dad said. 'The church is full. Tully, you're up.'

Tully gave Kate a big hug, then hurried out of the dressing room.

Kate stared at her dad in his rented tux, with his newly cut hair, and felt a rolling wave of love for him. Through the doors, they heard the music start up.

'You look beautiful,' he said after a moment. His voice was uneven, not his usual sound at all. He touched her chin, tilted her face up. That was when she saw the tears in his eyes. 'You'll always be my little girl, Katie Scarlett. Don't you forget that.'

'I could never forget it.'

Inside, the music changed to 'Here Comes the Bride'. They linked arms and walked towards the church's double doors. One halting step after another, they made their way down the aisle.

Johnny stood at the altar, waiting for her. When he took her hand in his and smiled down at her, she felt that swelling in her chest again, the sweet aching knowing that this was the man for her. No matter what else would happen to her in this life, she knew that she was marrying her true love, and that made her one of the lucky ones.

From then on, the night took on the hazy, insubstantial edges of a dream. They stood at the end of the receiving line, kissing friends and relatives and collecting their well-wishes.

When the music started—Madonna's 'Crazy for You'—Johnny found her in the crowd and reached for her hand.

'Hey, Mrs Ryan.' She moved into the circle of his arms, loving the feel of him against her.

All around them, people stepped back, making room for the newly-weds to dance. She could feel them watching, smiling, saying how romantic the song was and how beautiful the bride looked.

It was the Cinderella-at-the-ball moment that Kate had dreamt of all her life. 'I love you,' she said.

'You'd better,' he whispered, kissing her gently.

It wasn't until the tail end of the most magical of nights that Kate's smile first left her. She was at the bar, getting another glass of champagne and talking to her aunt Georgia when it happened.

Later, over the years that followed, especially in troubled times, she'd wonder why she looked up at precisely that instant, or why, with all the people in the room, dancing and laughing, she'd had to look up at just that moment to see Johnny, standing all by himself, sipping a beer.

And looking at Tully.

Part Three: THE NINETIES
I'm Every Woman
it's all in me

'JUST KNOCK ME OUT. I mean it. If they won't give me drugs, get a base-ball bat and hit me. Aagh!' Kate felt the pain twist through her insides and tear her apart.

Beside her, Johnny was saying, 'Come on . . . ha ha ha . . . You can do it. Breathe ha . . . ha . . . like this. Remember our class? Focus. Visualise.'

She grabbed him by the collar and yanked him close. 'So help me God, if you mention breathing again I'm going to seriously take you down. I want drugs—'

For the first six hours she'd been pretty good. She'd focused and breathed and kissed her husband when he pressed a cool, wet cloth to her forehead. In the second six hours she lost her natural sense of optimism. The relentless, gnawing pain was like some horrible creature biting away at her, leaving less and less.

Kate tried to concentrate on her breathing, but it didn't help. The pain was rising again, cresting. She clung to the bedrails with sweaty hands and yelled at Johnny to go and get her mom.

A few minutes later, the door to her private room banged open. 'I hear someone is being a total bitch-o-rama in here.'

Kate tried to smile. 'I don't . . . want . . . to . . . do this any more.'

'Changed your mind? Good timing.' Tully moved to the bed.

The pain hit again.

'Scream,' Tully said, stroking her forehead.

'I'm . . . supposed to . . . breathe through it.'

'Fuck that. Scream.'

She did scream then, and it felt good. When the pain subsided again, she laughed weakly. 'I take it you're against Lamaze.'

'I wouldn't call myself a natural childbirth kind of gal.' She looked at Kate's swollen belly and pale, sweaty face. 'Of course, this is the best birth-control commercial I've ever seen. From now on I'm using three condoms every time.' Tully smiled, but her eyes were worried. 'Are you OK, really? Should I get the doctor?'

Kate shook her head weakly. 'Just talk to me. Distract me.'

'I met a guy. We spent most of last weekend in bed. It was totally rockin' sex.'

Another contraction hit. Kate arched up and screamed again. As if from a distance she could hear Tully's voice, feel her stroking her forehead, but the pain was so overwhelming she couldn't do anything except gasp. 'Shit,' she said when it was over. 'The next time Johnny comes near me I'm going to smack him.'

'You were the one who wanted a baby.'

'I'm getting a new best friend. I need someone with a shorter memory.'

'I have a short memory. Did I tell you I got lucky this weekend?'

'Is that why you didn't answer when Mom called?'

'We were in the middle of it, but as soon as we finished, I started packing.'

'I'm glad to see you have—oh, shit—priorities.' Kate was in the middle of another contraction when the door to her room opened again. The nurse was first, followed by her mother and Johnny. Tully stood back, let everyone get in closer. At some point the nurse checked Kate's cervix and called the doctor in. He bustled into the room, smiling, and put on some gloves. Then the stirrups came out and it was time.

'Push,' the doctor said in an entirely reasonable, pain-free voice that made Kate want to scratch his eyes out.

She screamed and pushed and cried until as quickly as it had begun, the agony was over.

'A little girl,' the doctor said. 'Dad, do you want to cut the cord?'

Kate tried to lift herself up but she was too weak. A few moments later, Johnny was beside her, offering her a tiny, pink-wrapped bundle. She took her new daughter in her arms and stared down into her heart-shaped face. She had a wild shock of damp black curls and her mother's pale, pale skin, and the most perfect little lips and mouth Kate had ever seen. The love that burst open inside her was too big to describe. 'Hey, Marah Rose,' she whispered, taking hold of her daughter's grape-sized fist. 'Welcome home, baby girl.'

When she looked up at Johnny, he was crying. Leaning down, he kissed her with a butterfly softness. 'I love you, Katie.'

Never in her life had everything been so right in her world, and she knew that, whatever happened, she would always remember this single, shining moment as her touch of heaven.

Tully had moved to New York to work for NBC and now, just two weeks after she got home from helping Kate with the new baby, a storm dumped snow on Manhattan. For a few hours, the ever-present traffic vanished as pristine white snow blanketed the streets and sidewalks and turned Central Park into a winter wonderland.

Still Tully made it to work at 4 a.m. Inside the lobby, she stamped the snow off her boots, signed in, and went upstairs. Instantly she could tell that much of the staff had called in sick.

At her desk, she immediately went to work on the story she'd been assigned yesterday. She was doing research on the spotted owl controversy in the Northwest. Determined to put a local's 'spin' on the story, she was busily reading everything she could find—Senate subcommittee reports, environmental findings, economic statistics on logging, the fecundity of old growth forests.

'You're working hard.'

Tully looked up sharply. She'd been so lost in her reading that she hadn't heard anyone approach her desk.

And this wasn't just anyone.

Edna Guber, dressed in her usual black gaberdine trouser suit, stood there, one hip pushed slightly out, smoking a cigarette. Edna was famous in the news business, one of those women who'd clawed her way to the top in a time when others of her sex hadn't been able to come in the front door unless they had secretarial skills. Edna—only the single name was ever used or needed—reportedly had a Rolodex filled with the home numbers of everyone from Fidel Castro to Clint Eastwood. Supposedly there was no interview she couldn't get and nowhere on earth she wouldn't go to find what she wanted.

'Cat got your tongue?' she said, exhaling smoke.

Tully jumped to her feet. 'I'm sorry, Edna. Ms Guber. Ma'am.'

'I hate it when people call me ma'am. It makes me feel old. Do you think I'm old?'

'No, m—'

'Good. How did you get here? The cabs and buses are for shit today.'

'I walked.'

'Name?'

'Tully Hart. Tallulah.'

Edna's gaze narrowed. She looked Tully up and down steadily. 'Do you have a pen and paper?'

'I do.'

'I don't need an answer, just do as I ask and do it quickly. First off, I want a detailed report on the upcoming election in Nicaragua. You do know what's going on there?'

'Certainly,' Tully lied, sitting back down.

'I want to know everything about the Sandinistas, Bush's Nicaraguan policy, the blockade, the people who live there. And you've got twelve days to get it done.'

'Yes—' She stopped herself from saying ma'am just in time.

'We'll be leaving on the 16th. Before we go—'

'We?'

'Why the hell do you think I'm talking to you? Do you have a problem with this?'

'No. No problem. Thank you. I really—'

'We'll need immunisations; get a doctor here to take care of us and the crew. Then you can start setting up advance interview meetings. Brief me on Friday morning at, say, five a.m.?'

'I'll get started right now. And thank you, Edna.'

'Don't thank me, Hart. Just do your job—and do it better than anyone else could.'

'I'm on it.' Tully picked up the phone. Before she'd even finished punching in the number, Edna was gone.

'Hello?' Kate said groggily.

Tully looked at the clock. It was nine. That meant it was six in Seattle. 'Oops. I did it again. Sorry.'

'Your goddaughter doesn't sleep. She's a freak of nature. Can I call you back in a few hours?'

'Actually, I'm calling to talk to Johnny.'

'Johnny?' In the silence that preceded the question, Tully heard a baby start to cry.

'Edna Guber is sending me to Nicaragua. I want to ask him some background questions.'

'Just a second.' Kate handed the phone over; there was a flurry of whispers, then Johnny came on the line.

'Hey, Tully, good for you. Edna's a legend.'

'This is my big break, Johnny, and I don't want to screw up. I thought I'd start by picking your brain.'

'I haven't slept in weeks, so I don't know how much is left up there, but I'll do what I can.' He paused. 'Let's start with the relevant history. In 1960 or 1961, the Sandinista National Liberation Front, or FSLN, was founded . . .' Tully wrote as fast as she could.

For just under two weeks Tully worked her ass off. Twenty hours a day she was reading, writing, making phone calls, setting up meetings.

When they finally left, Tully was nervous. For the endless hours of their flights, through Dallas and Mexico City and finally onto a small plane in Managua, Edna fired questions at Tully.

The plane landed in what looked to Tully like a back yard. Men— boys, really—in camouflaged clothing stood on the perimeter, holding rifles. Children came out of the jungle to play in the air kicked up by the propellers. The dichotomy of the image was something Tully knew she'd always remember, but from the moment she got out of the plane until she reboarded the flight for home five days later, she had precious little time to think about imagery.

Edna was a mover. They hiked through guerrilla-infested jungles, lis- tening to the shrieking of howler monkeys, swatting mosquitoes, and floated up alligator-lined rivers. Sometimes they were blindfolded, sometimes they could see. Deep in the jungle, while Edna taped her interview with *el jefe*, the general in charge, Tully talked to the troops.

The trip opened her eyes to a world she'd never seen before; more than that, it showed her who she was. The fear, the adrenaline rush, the story; it turned her on like nothing ever had before.

Later, when the story was done, and she and Edna were back in their hotel in Mexico City, having straight shots of tequila, Tully said, 'I can't thank you enough, Edna.'

Edna leaned back in her chair. 'You did well, kid.'

'Thank you. I learned more from you in the past few weeks than I learned in four years of college.'

'So, maybe you want to go on my next assignment.'

'Anywhere, anytime.'

'I'm interviewing Nelson Mandela.'

'Count me in.'

Edna turned to her. She looked tired, maybe even a little drunk. 'Have you got a boyfriend?'

'With my work schedule?' Tully laughed and poured herself another shot. 'Hardly.'

'Yeah,' Edna said. 'The story of my life.'

'Do you regret it?' Tully asked. If they hadn't been drinking she never would have asked such a personal question.

'There's a price, that's for sure. For my generation, at least, you couldn't do this job and be married. You could get married—I did; three times—but you couldn't stay married. And forget about kids. When a story broke, I needed to be there, period. It could have been my kid's wedding day and I'd have left. So I've lived alone.' She looked at Tully. 'And I've loved it. Every damn second. If I end up dying in a nursing home alone, who gives a shit? I was where I wanted to be every second of my life, and I did something that mattered.'

Tully felt as if she were being baptised into the religion she'd always believed in. 'Amen to that.'

The first twelve months of motherhood was a rip tide of cold dark water that all too often sucked Kate under. It was embarrassing how ill-equipped she turned out to be for this blessed event that had been her secret girlhood dream. So embarrassing, in fact, that she told no one how overwhelmed she sometimes felt.

The truth was that her gorgeous, pale-skinned, dark-haired, brown-eyed daughter was more than a handful. From the moment she came home Marah was sick. Ear infections, colic. Kate had lost count of the times she'd found herself in the living room in the middle of the night, holding her red-faced, shrieking daughter and quietly crying herself.

She carried her daughter back to bed and gently tucked her in beneath the expensive pink-and-white cashmere blanket that had been a gift from Tully. Luxuriously soft, it had become the thing Marah chose to sleep with. 'Try to sleep till seven o'clock. Mommy could use it.'

Yawning, Kate went back to bed and snuggled up to her husband.

He kissed her cheek. 'You're so beautiful.'

She opened her eyes, staring blearily at him. 'OK, who is she? Guilt is the only reason you'd say I was beautiful at this godforsaken hour.'

'Are you kidding? With your mood swings lately it's like having three wives. The last thing I want is another woman.'

'But sex would be nice.'

'Sex would be nice. It's funny you brought that up.'

'Funny ha-ha or funny I-can't-remember-the-last-time-we-made-love?'

'Funny that you're getting lucky this weekend.'

'Yeah, how's that?'

'I've already talked to your mom. She's taking Marah, and you and I are going to have a romantic night in downtown Seattle.'

'What if I can't fit into any of my nice clothes?'

'Believe me, I have no problem with nudity. We can order room service instead of going out.'

'No wonder I love you so much.'

'I'm a god. There's no doubt about it.'

When the weekend arrived, Kate wasn't sure that she could leave Marah. 'I don't know, Mom.'

Her mother touched her hand gently. 'Your father and I raised two kids, Katie. We can watch our granddaughter for a night. Go have some fun with your husband. Marah will be safe with us.'

'You have a lifetime to be afraid,' Dad said. 'That's what parenting is. Might as well embrace it, kiddo.'

Kate tried gamely to smile. 'This is how you guys felt all the time.'

'How we still feel,' Dad said.

'Let's go gather Marah's things. Johnny's going to be back in a couple of hours to pick you up,' said Mom.

Kate packed Marah's clothes, making sure she had her pink blankety, her pacifiers, her formula and her beloved Pooh bear.

When she held Marah one last time and kissed her soft cheek, Kate had to hold back tears. She stood on the porch of her new Bainbridge Island house, with her hand tented across her eyes until long after the car had disappeared down the driveway.

Then, back inside, she wandered aimlessly for a few moments, not quite certain of how to be alone any more.

She tried calling Tully, but had to leave a message.

Finally she found herself in her closet, staring at her pre-pregnancy clothes, trying to figure out what she had that was sexy and would fit her. She'd just finished packing when she heard the door downstairs open and close, heard her husband's footsteps on the hardwood floor.

She went down to meet him. 'Where are we going, Mr Ryan?'

'You'll see.' He took her hand and got her overnight bag and closed up the house. Out in his car, the radio was on. Loud, like the old days. Bruce Springsteen was singing, *Hey, little girl, is your daddy home . . .*

Kate laughed, feeling young again. They drove down to the ferry terminal and onto the waiting boat. It was five o'clock in the evening and the sky and Sound were a Monet of lavender and pink. In the distance, Seattle sparkled with a million lights.

Once they were off the boat, Johnny manoeuvred through the downtown traffic and pulled up in front of the Inn at the Market, where a liveried doorman opened her door and collected her bag.

Johnny came round for her and took her hand. 'We're already checked in.' To the bellman, he said, 'Room 416.'

They strolled through the quiet brick courtyard and into the intimate, European-style lobby. Their room was a corner suite that had a sweeping view of the Sound. On a table by the window a bottle of champagne stood tilted in a silver ice bucket.

Kate smiled. 'I see someone wants to get laid in the worst way.'

'What you see is a man who loves his wife.' He swept her into his arms and kissed her.

They fell into bed together and made love as if they hadn't done it in months instead of weeks, with every part of their minds and bodies.

Afterwards they lay entwined, the expensive hotel sheets tangled round their bare legs.

'You know how much I love you, don't you?' he said quietly. They were words he'd said hundreds of times, so often that she knew how they were supposed to sound.

She rolled onto her side, instantly worried. 'What is it?'

'What do you mean?' He eased away from her and went to the table, where he poured two glasses of champagne.

'Look at me, Johnny.'

Slowly—too slowly—he turned, but he wouldn't meet her gaze.

'You're scaring me.'

'Let's not do this now, Katie. We have all night and all day tomorrow to talk. For now, let's—'

'Tell me.'

Finally, he let his gaze meet hers, and in his blue eyes she saw the kind of sadness that made her breath catch. He went to the bed and squatted down beside it so that he was looking up at her. 'You know what's going on in the Middle East.'

His words were so unexpected that she just stared at him. 'What?'

'There's going to be a war, Katie.'

War.

'I have to go.'

'You said you lost your nerve.'

'There's the irony; you gave it back to me. I'm tired of feeling like I failed, Katie. I need to prove to myself that I can do it this time.' He came up on his knees, took her face in his hands and held her steady. 'They need me. I've got experience.'

'I need you. Marah needs you, but that doesn't matter, does it?'

'It matters. If you say no, I won't go.'

'OK, no. You can't go. I love you, Johnny. You could die over there.'

He stared at her. 'Is that your answer?'

The tears fell, streaked down her cheeks. Angrily, she wiped them away. She wanted to say, *Yes. Yes. That's my answer.*

But how could she deny him this? Not only was it what he wanted, but down even deeper, there was something else: that tattered, ugly remnant of fear, which floated to the surface sometimes, reminded her that he'd loved Tully first. It made Kate afraid to deny him anything. She wiped her eyes again. 'Promise me you won't die, Johnny.'

He climbed into bed and took her in his arms and while she held him as tightly as she could, already it felt as if he were dissolving in her embrace, disappearing bit by bit. 'I promise I won't die.'

Katie sat in her living room, watching the war coverage on television. The last six weeks had been the longest, hardest days of her life. She was waiting, always waiting, for a phone call that said he was coming home, for a special report that heralded the end of the war. Now they were saying that the final allied assault should begin any day. A ground assault. That scared her as much or more than anything else because she knew her Johnny. Somehow, he'd end up on a tank, directing a story that no one else could tell.

Today she'd begun several chores and left all of them unfinished. Instead, she sat on the couch, watching television. She'd been here for more than two hours.

Marah stood by the coffee table, clutching its wooden edge in her pink, pudgy hands, swaying like a breakdancer and babbling in baby talk. Finally, she plopped down on her diaper-padded butt and immediately began to crawl away from the couch.

Kate bent down and picked up her daughter, who looked up at her through huge, bright brown eyes and started to babble. She couldn't help smiling at how earnestly Marah was trying to communicate, and as always, her daughter's obvious joy lifted her spirits. She turned off the TV—enough was enough—and turned on the radio instead. The Eagles were singing 'Desperado'.

Holding her daughter close, she danced in the living room, singing along. Marah giggled and bounced in her arms, which made Kate laugh for the first time in days.

They were having so much fun Kate didn't register instantly that the phone was ringing. When she did hear it, she ran for the radio, turned it down, and answered.

'Mrs John Ryan?' The connection was scratchy. Sounded long-distance.

She froze, tightened her hold on Marah. 'This is she.'

'This is Lenny Golliher. I'm a friend of your husband's. I'm over here in Baghdad with him. I'm sorry to have to tell you this, Mrs Ryan, there was a bombing yesterday . . .'

The maître d' showed Edna to her regular table, and Tully followed along behind, trying not to gape at all the power brokers and celebrities who were here today for lunch. Clearly 21 was one of the places to be seen in Manhattan. Edna stopped at nearly every table to say hi to someone and she introduced them all to Tully, saying, 'Here's a girl you should keep your eye on.'

By the time they arrived at their table, Tully felt as if she were floating. She knew the value of what had just happened. Edna had given her the gift of recognition. 'Why me?' she asked, once the waiter had left.

Edna lit up her cigarette and leaned back. 'You remind me of me. That surprises you, I see.'

'Flatters me.'

'Ms Guber?' It was the maître d' again, carrying a phone. 'There's an urgent call for you.'

She took the phone, said, 'Talk.' Then she listened for a long time. 'What're their names? How? Bomb?' She began taking notes. 'Reporter killed, producer wounded.'

Tully didn't hear anything after *producer.* Edna's voice turned into white noise. She leaned forward. 'Who is it?'

Edna pressed the phone to her chest. 'Two guys from the affiliate in Seattle were injured in a bombing. Actually, the reporter was killed. The producer, John Ryan, is in a critical condition.' She went back to her call.

Tully's whole body seemed to go cold. She started to shake. All she could think was, *Johnny.* 'Oh my God,' she said.

Edna looked up at her, mouthed, 'What is it?'

'Johnny Ryan is my best friend's husband.'

'Really?' Edna looked at her, then said into the phone, 'Put Tully on the story. She has an in. I'll call you back,' and hung up.

'I need to help Katie,' Tully muttered.

'It's a big story,' Edna said.

Tully waved that off impatiently. 'I don't care about that. She's my best friend.'

'Don't care?' Edna said sharply. 'Oh, you care. Everyone wants this assignment, but you have an in. Do you know what that means?'

Tully frowned. It seemed vaguely wrong, to make this about her career. 'I don't know.'

'Then you're not the woman I thought you were. Why can't you get an exclusive *and* comfort your friend?'

Tully thought about that. 'When you put it that way . . .'

'What other way is there? You can get an interview that no one else will have. A thing like this will put you on the map. Could get you the news nook.'

Tully couldn't help but be seduced by that. The news nook was a desk on set from which the day's biggest news stories were covered. The recognition factor for anyone assigned there was high. Daily national exposure. Several people had made the jump from news nook to host. 'And I can protect Kate from everything while I'm there.'

'Exactly.' Edna picked up the phone and dialled the number. 'Hart can get us an exclusive, Maury. It's as good as done. I'll vouch for her.' When she hung up, Edna's look was steely. 'Don't let me down.'

All the way from the restaurant and back to the office, Tully convinced herself that she'd done the right thing. At her desk, she threw her coat onto the back of her chair and called Kate. The phone rang and rang. Finally the answering machine picked up.

At the beep, Tully said, 'Hey, Katie, it's me. I just heard—'

Kate picked up the phone and disabled the answering machine. 'Hey,' she said, sounding lost. 'So you got my message? Sorry about the machine. Those bloodsucking reporters won't leave me alone.'

'Katie, how—'

'He's in a hospital in Germany. I'm catching a military flight in two hours. I'll call you when I land.'

'Hardly. I'll meet you at the hospital.'

'In Germany?'

'Of course. I'm not going to let you go through this alone. Your mom has Marah, right?'

'Right. You mean it, Tully?' Kate's voice took on an edge of hope.

'Best friends for ever, isn't it?'

'No matter what.' On that, Kate's voice broke. 'Thanks, Tully.'

Tully wanted to say, *That's what friends are for*, but the words stuck in her throat. All she could think of was the exclusive she'd promised Edna.

For sixteen hours, Kate rode an emotional pendulum that swung between hope and despair. As she approached the hospital entrance, she saw reporters dotted out front. Someone in the crowd must have recognised her, because they turned in unison, like some suddenly roused beast, and pushed forward.

'Mrs Ryan, what word do you have on his condition?'

'Is it a head injury?'

'No comment.' She pushed through the crowd and entered the hospital. They'd clearly been alerted to her arrival because a woman in a white nurse's uniform strode towards her, smiling sympathetically.

'You must be Mrs Ryan,' she said in heavily accented English.

'I am.'

'I will take you to your husband's room. The doctor will arrive shortly to speak with you.'

Thankfully, the nurse didn't make small talk as they walked to his room.

Johnny looked frail and broken, like a child in his parents' bed. His head was sheathed in white bandages. The entire left side of his face was swollen and discoloured; both his eyes were bandaged. Machines and lines and IVs were clustered around him.

The nurse patted her shoulder. 'He is alive,' she said. 'He needs you to be strong.'

They were the words Kate needed to hear. She had a job here; the time for falling apart would come later when she was alone. 'Thank you,' she said to the nurse, and walked towards the bed.

Behind her, the door shut quietly, and she knew they were alone now, she and this man who was and wasn't her Johnny.

'This was not our deal,' she said. 'I distinctly remember that you promised to be OK. So, I'm going to assume you'll honour that.' She wiped her eyes and leaned down to kiss his swollen cheek. 'Mom and Dad send their prayers. Marah is with them right now. And Tully is flying over to be with us. You might as well wake up now before she badgers you to death.' She tripped over the last word, winced. 'I didn't mean that,' she whispered, gripping the bedrail tightly. 'Can you hear me, Johnny Ryan? Let me know you're in there.' She reached down, took his hand in hers. 'Squeeze my hand, baby. You can do it.'

'Mrs Ryan?'

Kate hadn't even heard the door open. When she turned, there was a man standing not more than ten feet away from her.

'I'm Dr Carl Schmidt. I am in charge of your husband's care.'

The polite thing to do would have been to cross the room and shake Dr Schmidt's hand, but she couldn't move, couldn't pretend to be OK.

'He has suffered a serious head injury. He is heavily sedated right now, so we cannot do a comprehensive testing of his brain function. The doctors in Baghdad removed a section of his skull to allow the brain to swell. Do not worry. This is most routine in such an injury.'

'Why are his eyes bandaged?'

'We don't know yet if—'

The door behind him banged open, cracked against the wall. Tully burst into the room. 'Sorry it took me so long, Katie. No one would tell me where the hell you were.'

'I am sorry,' the doctor said. 'It is family only in here.'

'She is family,' Kate said, reaching for Tully's hand.

The doctor said, 'We do not know yet if he will be blind. These are things we will know if he wakes up.'

'When he wakes up,' Tully said, but her voice was unsteady.

'The next forty-eight hours will tell us much news,' the doctor said seamlessly, as if he hadn't been interrupted.

Forty-eight hours. It sounded like a lifetime.

'Keep talking to him,' the doctor said. 'This couldn't hurt, yes?'

Kate nodded, stepping aside as the doctor moved to the bed and checked Johnny. He made a few notes on the chart and then left.

The minute he was gone, Tully took Kate by the shoulders, gave her a little shake. 'We are not going to believe any bad stuff. Herr Doctor doesn't know Johnny Ryan. We do. He promised to come home to you and Marah and he's a man who keeps his promises.'

Tully's mere presence buoyed Kate, kept her afloat. 'You'd better listen to her, Johnny. You know what a bitch she can be when she's wrong.'

For the next six hours they stayed there, beside his bed. Somewhere in the middle of the night—Kate had no conception of what time it was—they went down to the empty cafeteria and bought food from vending machines.

'What are you going to do about the press?'

Kate looked up. 'What do you mean?'

Tully shrugged and sipped her coffee. 'You saw the reporters out front. He's a big story, Katie.'

'You think he wants the world to know that he might be blind or brain-damaged? No way. This story stays contained until I know how he is.'

'It's news, Kate,' Tully said softly. 'If you gave me an exclusive, I could protect you.'

'If it weren't for the damn news, he wouldn't be fighting for his life right now.'

'I'm not the only one who believes in it.'

It was a direct reminder of the thing Johnny and Tully shared, that bond which had always excluded Kate.

Tully covered Kate's hand with her own. 'Let me handle the media for you. Just me. That way you don't even have to think about it.'

Kate smiled for the first time in probably twenty-four hours. 'What would I do without you, Tully?'

Kate sat in Dr Schmidt's office, listening. 'So the swelling isn't going down,' she said, trying not to twist her sweaty hands together. She was so tired on this, her fourth day since the phone call that changed her life that it was a struggle simply to keep her eyes open.

'Not as quickly as we would wish. If soon there is not some improvement, I am thinking we will go to surgery again.'

She nodded.

Dr Schmidt stood. 'I must see a patient now.'

Kate headed back to Johnny's room. She turned the corner and saw a tall, long-haired man in a puffy blue jacket and ragged jeans standing at the door. A black video camera rested on his shoulder. He was filming; she could tell by the red light on the camera.

She ran down the hall, grabbed the man's puffy sleeve, and spun him round. 'What in the hell are you doing?'

That was when she saw Tully. Her best friend stood at the end of Johnny's bed, dressed in a red V-neck sweater and black trousers, her hair and make-up camera-ready, holding a microphone.

'Oh my God,' Kate whispered.

'It's not what you think.'

'You're not reporting on Johnny's condition?'

'I am, you know I am, but I was going to talk to you about it. This is just establishing stuff. I came up to talk to you—'

'With a cameraman,' Kate said, stepping back.

Tully ran over to her, pleading. 'My boss called. They're going to fire me if I don't get this story. I knew you'd understand if I just told you the truth. You know the news and how much this means to me, but I would never do anything to hurt you or Johnny.'

'How dare you! You're supposed to be my friend.'

'I am your friend.' Tully's voice took on an edge of panic. 'I shouldn't have started filming, but I didn't think you'd mind. Johnny sure as hell wouldn't. He's a newsman, like me. He knows that the story—'

Kate slapped Tully across the face as hard as she could. 'He's not your story. He's my husband.' On that last word, Kate's voice broke. 'Get out. Get away.' When Tully didn't move, Kate screamed, 'Now. Get the hell out of this room. It's family only.'

Beside Johnny's bed, an alarm blared. White-clad nurses streamed into the room, pushed Kate and Tully aside. They transferred him to a gurney and wheeled him out of the room.

'Katie—'

'Get out,' she said dully.

Tully grabbed her sleeve. 'Come on, Katie. We're best friends for ever. No matter what. Remember? You need me now.'

'You are hardly the kind of friend I need.' She wrenched free and ran out of the room. It wasn't until she was in the women's room, staring at the green metal door of the stall, that she cried.

Hours later, Kate sat alone in the family waiting room. Never, in any of the days spent in this hospital, had time crawled so slowly. Without Tully here to buoy her, she felt herself sinking into despair.

'Mrs Ryan?'

Kate got quickly to her feet. 'Hello, Doctor. How did the surgery go?'

'He is most well. There was extensive bleeding in his brain, which we think accounts for the continued swelling. We have now stopped it. Perhaps this will give us reason for new hope, yes? Shall I walk you back to his room?'

It was enough that he was still alive.

'Thank you.'

She went inside and sat down. In a quiet, halting voice, she closed her eyes and talked to Johnny. About what, she couldn't have said. All she knew was that a voice could offer light in a dark place, and light could lead you out.

The next thing she knew, it was morning. Sunlight glowed through the exterior window. 'Hey, handsome,' she murmured, leaning down to kiss his cheek. The bandages on his eyes had been removed. 'No more bleeding in the brain allowed, OK? When you need attention, just try the old-fashioned ways, like getting mad or kissing me.'

She kept talking until she ran out of things to say. Finally she turned on the television that hung in the corner. 'The TV is on. You're big news.' Idly she flipped through the channels till she found something in English. She took his dry, slack fingers in hers just as Tully's face filled the screen.

She was standing in front of the hospital with her microphone held in front of her mouth. Captions along the bottom of the screen translated her words: 'For nearly five days the world has wondered and worried about John Patrick Ryan, the TV news producer who was seriously injured when a bomb exploded near the Al-Rashid Hotel. Although funeral services were held yesterday for the reporter, Arthur Gulder, who was with him, the Ryan family and the German hospital remained unavailable to journalists. And how can we blame them? This is a time of deep personal tragedy for the Ryan family. John— Johnny to his friends, which was pretty much everyone he knew or worked with—suffered a serious head trauma in the explosion. A complicated medical procedure was performed on him at a hospital in Baghdad.'

The picture on the screen changed. Now, Tully was standing beside Johnny's bed. He lay motionless on the white sheets, his head and eyes bandaged. Though the camera lingered on Johnny for only an instant before returning to Tully's face, the image of him was hard to forget.

'Mr Ryan's prognosis is uncertain. The specialists with whom I spoke said it is a waiting game to see if the swelling in his brain recedes. If it does, he has an excellent chance of survival. If not . . .' Her voice trailed off as she moved round to the end of the bed. There, she looked directly into the camera. 'Everything about this case is uncertain right now, except this: this is a story of heroes, both in the war zone and at home. John Ryan wanted to bring this story to the American people, and I know him well enough to say that he knew the risks he was taking. And while he was covering the news in Iraq, his wife, Kathleen, was at home with their one-year-old daughter, believing that what her husband was doing was important. Like any soldier's wife, it was her sacrifice as much as his that made it possible for John Ryan to do his job.' The picture cut back to Tully on the hospital steps. 'This is Tallulah Hart, reporting from Germany. And may I say that our prayers are certainly with the Ryan family today.'

Kate stared at the television long after the segment had ended. 'She made us look like heroes,' she said to the room. 'Even me.'

She felt a flutter-soft movement against her palm. It was so gentle that at first she almost didn't notice. Frowning, she glanced down.

Johnny slowly opened his eyes.

Kate gasped. 'Johnny?' she whispered. 'Can you see me? Close your eyes once if you can see me.'

Slowly, he closed his eyes.

She kissed his cheek, his forehead, his cracked, dry lips. 'Do you know where you are?' she finally asked, hitting the nurses' button.

She could see the confusion in his eyes and it scared her. 'How about me? Do you know who I am?'

He stared up at her, swallowed hard. Slowly, he said, 'My . . . Katie.'

'Yes,' she said, bursting into tears. 'I'm your Katie.'

The next seventy-two hours were a whirlwind of meetings, procedures, tests and medication adjustments. Kate accompanied Johnny to consultations with ophthalmologists, psychiatrists, physical therapists, speech and occupational therapists, and, of course, Dr Schmidt.

'He is lucky to have you,' Dr Schmidt said at the end of their meeting.

Kate smiled. 'I'm lucky to have him.'

'Yes. Now, I suggest you go to the cafeteria and have some lunch. I will return your husband to his room when the tests are finished.'

Kate rose. 'Thank you, Dr Schmidt. For everything.'

He made an it's-nothing gesture with his hand. 'This is my job.'

The cafeteria was mostly empty on this late Thursday afternoon. Kate made her way through the tables to the window. Even with the distortion of the glass, she could see how tired she looked, how spent.

It was odd, but somehow it was harder to be alone with her relief than with her despair. Then, she'd wanted mostly to sit quietly and blank out her mind and try to imagine the best. Now she wanted to laugh with someone, to smile and raise a glass in celebration and say she'd known all along it would end like this.

No. Not someone.

Tully.

For all Kate's life, Tully had been the first line of celebration, the party just waiting to happen. Turning from the window, she sat down.

'You look like you could use a drink.'

Kate looked up. Tully stood there, dressed in crisp black jeans and a white boat-necked angora sweater. Although her hair and make-up were perfect, she looked tired. And nervous.

'You're still here?'

'You thought I'd leave you?' Tully tried to smile, but it wasn't the real thing. 'I brought you a cup of tea.'

Kate stared at the Styrofoam cup in Tully's hand. It was the only apology Tully knew how to make for what she'd done. If Kate accepted it, she knew that the episode would have to be forgotten—the betrayal and the slap would have to dissolve into nothing so they could step back onto the track that had connected their lives. No regrets, no grudges. They'd be TullyandKate again, or as close to that as grown women could be.

'The story was good,' she said evenly.

Tully's eyes pleaded for forgiveness and understanding, but what she said was, 'I'm getting the news nook for next week. It's a replacement gig, but it's a start.'

Kate thought, *So that's what you sold me out for*, but knew she couldn't say it. Instead, she said, 'Congratulations.'

Tully held out the cup of tea. 'Take it, Katie. Please.'

Kate looked at her friend for a long time. Finally, she reached for the cup, saying, 'Thanks.'

Tully grinned and sat down beside her. Before she'd even scooted up to the table, she was talking.

Soon, Tully had Kate laughing. That was the thing about best friends. Like sisters and mothers, they could piss you off and make you cry and break your heart, but in the end, when the chips were down, they were there, making you laugh even in your darkest hours.

Part Four: THE NEW MILLENNIUM
A Moment Like This
some people wait a lifetime

TULLY'S ALARM CLOCK went off, as it did every weekday morning, at half past three.

As she left her building, her uniformed driver handed her a double-shot latte. 'Good morning, Ms Hart.'

She took the coffee gratefully. 'Thanks, Hans,' she said, getting into the black limousine. Settling back, she stared out of the tinted window.

The dark streets of Manhattan glistened with early-morning rain. This time of day was as close as the city came to sleeping. Only the hardiest of souls were out—garbage collectors, bakers, newspaper deliverymen.

For more years than she wanted to count, Tully had lived this routine. Almost from her first day in New York, she'd been waking up at 3.30 a.m. for work. Success had only made her long days even longer. Since CBS had lured her over to host their morning show, she'd had to include afternoon meetings in addition to her morning broadcasts. Fame and celebrity and money should have allowed her to slow down and enjoy her career, but the opposite had occurred. The more she got, the more she wanted, and the harder she worked. Every job that came her way, she took—narrating a documentary on breast cancer, guest-hosting a super new game show, even being a judge for the Miss Universe contest. And then there were her guest appearances on Leno, Letterman, Rosie, etc. She made sure no one could forget her.

In her early thirties, it had been easy to keep up the schedule. Back then, she was able to work long hours, sleep all afternoon, party all night, and wake up looking and feeling great. But she was approaching forty now, and she was beginning to feel tired, a little old to be running from one job to the next, and in heels, no less. More and more often when she came home from work, she curled up on her sofa and called Kate or Mrs M or Edna. Being seen—and photographed—at the It new club or at some red-carpet premiere had lost its appeal. Rather, she found herself longing to be with people who really knew her, really cared.

Edna repeatedly told her that this was the deal she'd made, the life she got in exchange for success. But what good was success, she'd asked over drinks last week, if there was no one to share it with you?

Edna had simply shaken her head and said, 'That's why they call it sacrifice. You can't have it all.'

But what if that was exactly what you wanted: everything?

Kate rarely paused in the whirlwind chaos of her everyday life to wonder where the years had gone. Contemplation and reflection, like relaxation, were thoughts from another era, ideas from another life. A woman with three children—Marah was now twelve and the twins, Lucas and William, were five—didn't have time to think about herself.

Her days were consumed by details. The chores stacked up, until she found herself running from sunrise to well past sunset. The crappy part was that she never seemed to accomplish anything substantial.

Now, Kate sat in the driver's seat of her car, parked in the car-pool lane, as the kids poured out of the middle school.

Marah usually came out of the brick building in a clot of girls. Like orc whales, pre-teen girls travelled in pods. But today, she was alone, walking fast, with her head down and her arms crossed tightly. She set off through the crowd, looked at no one, and reached the car.

Kate knew something was wrong. The question was, how bad was it? Everything was big drama these days. 'Hey,' Kate said tentatively, knowing one wrong word could cause a fight.

'Hey.' Marah climbed into the front passenger seat and reached for her seat belt, clicking it into place. 'Where are the brats?'

'Evan's birthday party. Daddy's picking them up on his way home.'

'Oh.'

All the way home Kate tried to begin a conversation, but at best Marah offered a one-word answer, at worst an eye roll or dramatic sigh. When they pulled into the garage, Kate gave it one more try. 'I'm making cookies for Thanksgiving. You want to help me?'

Marah finally looked at her. 'Those pumpkin-shaped ones with the orange frosting and green sprinkles?'

For a split second, her daughter looked like a little girl again, her dark eyes wide with hope, her lips curving into a hesitant smile. Years' worth of parties were between them now, a net of shared memories.

'Of course,' Kate said.

'I love those cookies.'

'So, you want to help me?'

'Sure.'

For the next hour they worked side by side in the big country-style kitchen. They talked about little things, this and that; nothing important. Kate was gauging the scene like a hunter. Instinctively, she knew when the time was right. They'd just frosted the last of the cookies and were stacking the dirty dishes by the sink when Kate said, 'You want to make another batch? We could take them over to Ashley's house.'

Marah went still. 'No,' she said in a voice almost too quiet to be heard.

'But Ash loves them. Remember when—'

'She hates me,' Marah said, and just like that the floodgates opened. Tears gathered in her eyes.

'Did you two have a fight?'

'I don't know.' Marah burst into tears and turned away.

Kate lunged for her daughter, grabbed her sleeve and pulled her into a fierce hug. 'I'm right here, Marah,' she whispered.

Marah hugged her tightly. 'I don't know what I did wrong,' she wailed, sobbing.

'Sshh,' Kate murmured, stroking her daughter's hair as if she were still little. When Marah's crying finally subsided, Kate drew back just enough to look down at her. 'Sometimes life is—'

Behind them the door banged open. The twins burst into the house, yelling at each other, making their toy dinosaurs fight. Johnny came in after them, chasing them down.

Marah wrenched free from her mother, slammed the door shut behind her and ran upstairs.

The next morning, Kate pulled into the school drive-through lane just three minutes before the lunch bell rang. Parking illegally, she hurried into the office, signed Marah out for the day, and then walked down to her classroom. Last night, after the moment of conversation and connection between them, Marah had shut Kate out again. No amount of prompting could restart the engine, and so Kate had had to formulate plan B. A surprise attack.

Peering through the rectangular glass window, she knocked once, saw the teacher wave at her, and went inside.

Most of the kids smiled at her and said hello. Marah seemed to be trying to melt into her desk. Her face wore the what-are-you-doing-at-school-embarrassing-me grimace. Kate was more than familiar with it.

The bell rang and the kids ran from the room, talking loudly.

When they were alone, Kate went to Marah.

'What are you doing here?'

'You'll see. Get your things. We're leaving.'

Marah stared up at her, obviously assessing the situation from every possible social angle. 'OK. I'll meet you at the car, OK?'

Ordinarily Kate would make a comment about that and force Marah to walk out with her, but her daughter was emotionally fragile right now. That was why Kate was here. 'OK.'

The easy victory surprised Marah. Kate smiled at her, touched her shoulder. 'See you in a minute.'

Actually, it took a bit longer than that, but not much. In no time, Marah was in the passenger seat, buckling up. 'Where are we going?'

'Well, first we're going out to lunch.'

'You got me out of school to have lunch?'

'And something else. A little surprise.' Kate drove to the diner-style restaurant that was next door to the brand-new multiplex on the island.

'I'm going to have a cheeseburger, fries and a strawberry milkshake,' Kate said when they were seated.

'Me, too.'

After the waitress took their orders and left, Kate looked at her daughter. Slouched down in the blue vinyl seat, she looked thin and angular, her brown eyes revealing every nuance of emotion she felt.

The waitress delivered their shakes. Kate took a sip. 'Ashley still being mean to you?' she finally said.

'She hates me. I don't even know what I did to her.'

'When I was twelve, I had two best friends,' Kate told her daughter. 'We did everything together—showed our horses at the fair, had slumber parties, hung out at the lake in the summer. And then one day, they stopped liking me. I still don't know why. They started hanging around with boys and went to parties and they never called me again. Every day I went to school and sat on the bus by myself and ate lunch by myself, and every night I cried before I went to sleep.'

'Really?'

Kate nodded. 'I can still remember how much it hurt my feelings.'

'What happened?'

'Well, when I was at my very most miserable—and I mean miserable—I met Aunt Tully waiting at the bus-stop. She was the coolest-looking girl I'd ever seen. I figured she'd never want to be friends with me. But you know what I found out?'

'What?'

'Inside, where it counts, she was as scared and lonely as I was. We became best friends that summer. Real friends. The kind that don't purposely hurt your feelings or stop liking you for no reason.'

'How do you make friends like that?'

'That's the hard part, Marah. To make real friends you have to put yourself out there. Sometimes people will let you down—girls can be really mean to each other—but you can't let that stop you. If you get hurt, you just pick yourself up, dust off your feelings, and try again. Somewhere in your class is the girl who will be friends with you all through high school. I promise. You just have to find her.'

Marah frowned at that, thinking.

The waitress delivered their meals, left the bill and walked away.

Before she took a bit of her cheeseburger, Marah said, 'Emily's nice.'

Kate had hoped Marah would remember that. She and Emily had been inseparable in grade school but had drifted apart in recent years. 'Yes, she is.'

Kate saw her daughter finally smile, and it lit Kate up inside, that tiny change. They talked about little things through lunch, mostly fashions, about which Marah already obsessed and Kate knew next to nothing. When she'd paid the bill and they were ready to leave, Kate said, 'There's one more thing.' She reached into her handbag and pulled out a small, wrapped package. 'This is for you.'

Marah tore off the shimmery paper, revealing the paperback book that had been beneath it.

'*The Hobbit*,' Marah said, looking up.

'In that year when I had no friends, I wasn't completely alone. I had books to keep me company, and that is the start of one of my favourite stories of all time. I must have read *The Lord of the Rings* ten times in my life. You may not be ready for *The Hobbit* yet, but someday something might happen to hurt your feelings again. Maybe you'll feel alone with your sadness, not ready to share it with me or Daddy, and if that happens, you'll remember this book in your nightstand. You can read it then, let it take you away. It sounds silly, but it really helped me.'

'I love you, Mommy,' Marah said.

To the world at large, perhaps this was an ordinary moment in an ordinary day, but to Kate it was extraordinary. This was the reason she'd chosen to stay home instead of work. She judged the meaning of her life in nanoseconds, perhaps, but she wouldn't trade this instant for anything. 'I love you, too. That's why we're playing hooky for the rest of the day.'

Tully remembered the years by the stories she covered. She'd witnessed the escalating issues with Iraq and the beginning of the war; she'd seen first hand the devastation of Hurricane Isabel, and watched in disbelief as the Terminator was sworn into office in California.

Although no one who saw her on television would notice it, Tully was quietly coming undone. She wanted a real life; not this perfect, glittery cotton candy one she'd created for herself.

But she had no real idea how to go about starting over at her age. She loved her job too much to give it up; besides, she'd been famous and rich for so long that she couldn't imagine being ordinary again.

If there was one thing Tully had always done well, it was to ignore unpleasantness. For most of her life she'd been able to box up bad memories or disappointments and store them deep in the back of her mind, in a place so dark they couldn't be seen.

But now, for the first time in many years, she found herself thinking about Cloud, really thinking. She focused on the times her mother came back for her instead of the times she left. Had she missed the meaning of Cloud's many returns?

The thought of that, the hope of it, wouldn't remain in the dark.

Finally, she had taken two weeks off work, called it a vacation, packed a suitcase, and boarded a plane heading west.

A little less than eight hours after she left Manhattan, she was pulling up to the Ryan house in a sleek black limousine.

On this beautiful, sunny afternoon, the old-fashioned farmhouse looked like something out of a photo album of the Good Life. A fresh coat of stain made the shingles look like caramel and the white, glossy trim caught the sunlight and kept it. Toys and bikes lay scattered about, reminding her sharply of the old days, back when they'd been the Firefly Lane girls. Their bikes had been magic carpets to another world.

Come on, Katie. Let go.

Tully smiled. She hadn't thought about that summer in years—1974—the beginning of it all. Meeting Kate had changed her life, and all because they'd dared to reach out for each other, dared to say, *I want to be your friend.*

Tully rang the doorbell. Normally she'd just walk in, but normally, she'd be expected. This trip had been so spur-of-the-moment that she hadn't called ahead. To be honest, she hadn't really expected to make it. She'd thought she'd chicken out along the way. But here she was.

The door opened and Marah stood there. 'Aunt Tully!' she shrieked, launching herself forward.

Tully caught her goddaughter and held her tightly. When they drew apart, she stared at the girl in front of her, a little nonplussed. It had been only seven or eight months since she'd seen Marah—and yet the girl in front of her was a stranger. A near woman, Marah was taller than Tully, with pale skin, penetrating brown eyes, lush black hair that fell in a waterfall down her back, and cheekbones to die for. 'Marah Rose,' she said. 'You're all grown up. And *gorgeous*. Have you tried modelling?'

Marah's smile made her even more breathtakingly beautiful. 'Really? My mom thinks I'm a baby.'

Tully laughed. 'You, my dear, are no baby.' Before she could say more, Johnny came down the stairs, holding a squirming boy in each arm. Halfway down, he saw her and stopped. Then he smiled. 'You shouldn't have let her in, Marah. She's got a suitcase.'

Tully laughed and closed the door behind her.

'Katie,' Johnny yelled up the stairs. 'You won't believe who has come to visit.' He put the boys down on the floor at the base of the steps and went to Tully, folding her into his arms. She couldn't help thinking how good it felt simply to be held. It had been a long time.

'Tully!' Kate's voice rose above the other sounds in the room as she hurried down the stairs and pulled Tully into a hug. When Kate drew back, she was smiling.

'What in the hell are you doing here? Don't you know I need *notice* for one of your trips? Now you'll give me crap about the haircut I need.'

'Don't forget the make-up you don't have on. But I could give you a make-over. I'm good at that. It's a gift.'

The past enveloped them, made them laugh.

'Are you kidding me? I'm lucky to have eyebrows at all.' Kate linked arms with Tully and led her to the sofa. There, they spent at least an hour catching up on each other's lives. At around three o'clock they moved their little party to the back yard, where the boys and Marah competed with Kate for Tully's attention. When darkness began to fall, Johnny fired up the barbecue, and on a picnic table in the grass, beneath a dome of stars and beside the placid Sound, Tully had her first home-cooked meal in months. While Kate and Johnny were upstairs, putting the twins to bed, Tully sat outside with Marah.

'What's it like to be famous?'

Tully hadn't really thought about that in years; she'd simply taken it for granted. 'It's pretty great, actually. You always get the best tables, get into all the best places; people give you free stuff all the time.'

'Parties?'

Tully smiled. 'It's been a while since I cared about parties, but yeah, I get invited to a lot of them. And don't forget the clothes. Designers send me dresses all the time. All I have to do is wear them.'

'Wow,' Marah said. 'That is so totally cool.'

Behind them, music started. Jimmy Buffet, 'Margaritaville'.

'You know what that means,' Kate said, appearing beside them with two margaritas.

Marah immediately whined, 'I'm old enough to stay up.'

'Bedtime, little one,' Kate said, bending down to offer Tully a drink.

Marah looked at Tully as if to say, *See? I told you she thinks I'm a baby.*

Tully couldn't help laughing. 'Your mom and I were once in a hurry to grow up, too. We used to sneak out of the house and—'

'Tully,' Kate said sharply. 'The old stories won't interest her.'

'My mom sneaked out of the house? What did Grandma do?'

'She put her on restriction for life. And made her wear clothes from the sale rack at Fred Meyer,' Tully answered.

Marah shuddered at the thought.

'Polyester,' Kate added.

'You two are lying to me,' Marah said, crossing her arms.

'Us? Lie? Never,' Tully said, taking a sip of her drink.

Marah got out of her chair, gave a long-suffering sigh, and headed into the house. As soon as the door banged shut, Tully and Kate laughed.

'Tell me we weren't like that,' Tully said.

Still laughing, Kate sat down in the Adirondack chair beside her.

Tully hadn't realised how tense she'd been until she began to relax. As always, Kate was her safety net, her security blanket.

The door opened behind them and Johnny walked out, holding a beer. Dragging another chair over to where they were, he sat down. The three of them formed a ragged semicircle that faced the dark Sound. 'Has she told you yet?'

'She's just about to get to it,' Kate said, putting her hand on her husband's arm. 'Come on, Tully. What's the matter?'

She looked at both of them, sitting so close together, a husband and wife who still laughed together and touched each other after more than fourteen years of marriage, and her chest felt tight with longing. 'I'm tired of being alone,' she finally said. 'I need my family.'

Kate frowned, drew back. 'You mean Cloud?'

'She's my mother.'

'Biologically speaking. A reptile is a better parent, and they bury their eggs and leave.'

'I know you're only trying to protect me, Kate, but it's easy for you to discount her. You *have* a family.'

'She hurts you every time you see her.'

'But she kept coming back. Maybe that meant something.'

'She kept leaving, too,' Kate said. 'And each time it broke your heart.'

'I'm stronger now.'

'What are you two actually *saying*? It's like you're speaking in code,' Johnny said.

'I want to go find her. I've got her last-known address—I send money every month. Have done ever since my gran died. I thought maybe if I could get her into a treatment programme we'd have a chance.'

'She's been in treatment a lot,' Kate pointed out.

'I know, but never with support. Maybe that's all she needed.'

'I'm hearing a lot of maybes,' Kate said.

'I know it's crazy and it probably won't work and no doubt I'll end up sobbing or drinking or both, but I'm tired of being so damned alone and I don't have a lover or kids to count on. What I do have is a mother, as flawed as she is. And, Katie, I want you to come help me find her.'

Kate looked completely taken aback by that. 'What?'

'I want to find her. I can't do it alone.'

'But . . . I can't just leave, Tully. I've got commitments. I . . .' She cast her mind over her schedule. 'Maybe I could go with you for a few days at the end of next week.'

'If I wait I won't go,' Tully said, trying to gather the courage to do it alone. 'I guess I can go by myself. I was just worried—'

'You should go with a crew,' Johnny said.

Tully looked at him. 'What do you mean?'

'You know, film it. You're a big star with a poor-little-rich-girl story. I don't mean to sound insensitive, but your viewers would love to go on this journey with you.'

Tully turned the unexpected idea round in her head. It was danger-ous for her, certainly; she could be humiliated by her mother. Then again, she could be triumphant, too. A mother-daughter reunion would be TV gold. It surprised her, frankly, that she hadn't thought of it her-self. Was it worth the risk?

What she needed was a producer who cared about her.

She looked at Johnny. 'Come with me,' she said, angling towards him. 'Be my producer.'

Kate sat up straighter. 'What?'

'Please, Johnny,' Tully pleaded. 'I need *you* if this is going to happen. I wouldn't trust anyone else. It'll give you national exposure. I'll call your boss. Fred and I are friends from way back.'

Johnny looked at his wife. 'Katie?'

Tully held her breath, waiting for her friend's answer.

'It's up to you, Johnny,' Kate said at last, though she didn't look happy about it.

Johnny sat back. 'I'll talk to Fred. Assuming he's on board, we'll get started tomorrow. I'll call Bob Davies to run the camera.' He grinned. 'It'll be nice to get out of the station for a few days, anyway.'

Tully laughed out loud. 'That's *great.*'

The screen door banged open; Marah rushed out into the yard. 'Can I go with you, Daddy? There's no school tomorrow, and you said you wanted me to see you work sometime.'

Tully took Marah's hand, pulled her goddaughter down into her lap. 'That's a fantastic idea.'

Beside her, Kate groaned.

Johnny stood up and flipped his cellphone open. Punching in numbers, he walked into the house.

'Kate?' Tully said, leaning close. 'Tell me it's OK.'

Her best friend's smile was slow in coming. 'Sure, Tully. Take my whole family if you want.'

Their first stop was at a mobile-home park in Fall City. Cloud's last known address. But her mother wasn't there, and hadn't been at the location for a few months. After that, the trip became a scavenger hunt.

For the next six hours they drove from place to place, following leads—Tully, Johnny, Marah and a cameraman who called himself Fat Bob for good reason.

At every stop, they filmed a segment of Tully talking to people at the various campgrounds and communes. Several people knew who Cloud was, but no one seemed to know where to find her.

They were finishing dinner at a diner in North Bend when Johnny's boss, Fred, called with a report that Cloud's last cheque had been cashed at a bank on Vashon Island. Fat Bob was in the van and Marah had just left for the ladies' room.

'You think we'll find her?' Tully asked, pouring sugar into her coffee.

It was the first time they'd been alone all day. She'd been waiting for the opportunity to ask him this question.

'I think we can't make people love us.'

'What's it like, Johnny, being loved?'

'That's not the question you want to ask. You want to know what it's like to love someone.' He gave her a grin that made him look like a kid again. 'Besides yourself, I mean.'

She leaned back. 'I need new friends.'

'I won't pull back, you know. You'd better be OK with that. The camera will be there, seeing all of it. If you want to pull out, this is the time.'

'You can protect me.'

'That's what I'm telling you, Tully. I won't. I'll follow the story. Like you did in Germany.'

She understood what he was saying. Friendship ended when the story rolled; it was an axiom of journalism. 'Just try to shoot me from the left. It's my good side.'

Johnny smiled and paid the bill. 'Go get Marah. If we hurry, we might be able to catch the last ferry.'

In fact, they missed the last ferry and ended up sleeping in three rooms in a run-down hotel near the waterfront.

By nine the next morning they were on the ferry, headed to a berry-growing commune on Vashon Island.

It wasn't until almost ten o'clock when they pulled up to the SUNSHINE FARMS sign. The commune was like the others she'd seen: long, rolling acres covered in crops, shaggy-looking people dressed in the modern-day equivalent of sackcloth and ashes. The main difference was the housing. Here, people lived in domed tents, called yurts.

Johnny pulled into a parking place and got out of the van. Fat Bob followed suit, sliding the van door open.

Marah said worriedly, 'Are you OK, Aunt Tully?'

Tully knew they were waiting for her; still she sat there. People waited for her all the time; it was one of the perks of celebrity.

'You can do this,' she said to the scared-looking woman in the rearview mirror. She'd spent a lifetime creating a hard casing round her heart, and now she was purposely peeling it away, exposing her vulnerability. But what choice did she have? If she and her mother were ever going to have a chance, someone had to make the first move.

Cautiously, she stepped down into the muddy street. Fat Bob and his camera were right there.

Tully took a deep breath and smiled. 'We're at the Sunshine Farms commune. We've been told that my mother has lived here for almost a month, although she hasn't yet sent in this address to my attorney.'

She walked up to the long row of tables, covered by cedar lean-tos, where tired-looking women sold their wares. Berries, jams, syrups, berry butters and handicrafts.

No one seemed to care that a camera was approaching. Or a celebrity. 'I'm Tallulah Hart. I'm looking for this woman.' She held out an old, creased picture of her mother—the only photo she had of her.

'Cloud,' the woman said without smiling.

Tully's heart skipped a beat. 'Yes.'

'She's not at Sunshine any more. Too much work for her. Last I heard she was out at the old Mulberry place. What has she done?'

'Nothing. She's my mother.'

'She said she didn't have any kids.'

Tully knew the camera saw her reaction to that, her flinch of pain. 'That's hardly surprising. How do we get to the Mulberry place?'

As the woman gave Johnny directions, Tully turned to the camera. She didn't bother to wipe the tears from her eyes. 'I guess I still want her to love me,' she revealed quietly. 'Let's go.'

They climbed back into the van and drove out to the highway. On Mill Road they turned left and drove down a bumpy, rutted gravel road until an old beige mobile home came into view. It sat on blocks in a grassy field, surrounded by rusted, broken-down cars. Three ragged-looking pit bulls were chained to the fence. They went crazy when the van pulled into the yard, barking and snarling and jumping forward.

'It's *Deliverance*,' Tully said, giving a weak smile as she reached for the door handle.

They all got out at once, moving forward in formation: Tully in the lead, advancing with false confidence; Fat Bob beside or in front of her, filming; and Johnny behind them, holding Marah's hand.

Tully went up to the front door and knocked.

No one answered.

She knocked again, and was just about to give in to relief and say, *No luck!* when the door swung open to reveal a huge, straggly-haired man in boxer shorts. 'Yeah?' he said, scratching his underarm.

'I'm here to see Cloud.'

He cocked his head to the right and stepped out of the trailer, moving past her, going towards his dogs.

Tully's eyes watered at the smell that came from the mobile home. Inside, she found piles of junk and old food containers. But mostly what she saw were empty booze bottles and a bong. A huge pile of pot lay on the kitchen table.

Fat Bob mirrored every step, filmed her journey through this mobile-home hell.

She went to the closed door behind the kitchen, knocked and then turned the knob. The bedroom was small, made smaller by the piles of clothes everywhere.

Her mother lay curled in the foetus position on the unmade bed, with a ragged blue blanket wrapped around her body.

Tully bent close, noticing now how greyed and wrinkled her mother's skin had become. 'Cloud?' She said the name three or four times, and got no response at all. Finally she reached out, touched her mother's shoulder, gently at first and then not so gently. 'Cloud?'

Fat Bob got into position, pointed the camera at the woman in bed.

Slowly, her mother opened her eyes. It took her a long time to focus; she had a vague, vacant look. 'Tallulah?'

'Hey, Cloud.'

'Tully,' she said as if just remembering the nickname her daughter preferred. 'How did you find me?'

'Are you trying to be lost?'

Cloud sat up slowly, reaching into her dirty pocket for a cigarette. When she lit up, Tully noticed how palsied her mother's hand was. 'I thought you were in New York, getting rich and famous.'

'I'm both,' Tully said, unable to squelch the pride in her voice. She hated it that still, after all the disappointments, she craved this woman's admiration. 'How long have you been living here?'

'What do you care? You live in some fancy place while I'm rotting away.'

Tully looked at her mother. The wild, unkempt hair was now threaded with grey. And her face. Lined, dirty, and greyed from cigarettes and alcohol and a life poorly lived. Cloud was barely sixty and she looked fifteen years older. 'You can't want this, Cloud. Even you . . .'

'Even me, huh? Why did you come looking for me, Tully?'

'You're my mother.'

'We both know better than that.' Cloud cleared her throat and looked away. 'I need to get away from here. Maybe I could stay with you for a few days. Take a bath. Eat something.'

Tully had waited a lifetime for her mother to want to come home with her, but she knew how dangerous a moment like this could be. 'OK.'

'Really?' The disbelief on Cloud's face was the saddest thing Tully had ever seen. It showed clearly how little faith they had in each other.

'Really.' And for an instant, Tully forgot the camera was even there. She dared to imagine the impossible: that they could become mother and daughter instead of strangers. 'Let me help you to the car.'

The camera caught it all: Tully's hope and fear and need. On the long drive home, while Cloud slept slumped in the corner, Tully spilled her heart to the lens. She answered Johnny's questions with honesty, revealing at last how wounded she'd been by her distant mother.

Now, though, Tully added a new word: *addicted*.

For as long as she'd known her mother, Cloud had been hooked on drugs or booze or both. The more Tully thought about that, the more it seemed like the cause of their problems.

If she could get her mom into rehab and help her through the programme, maybe they could make a new start.

'Are you sure that's a good idea?' Johnny asked.

They were in the sitting room of the luxurious Cascade Suite at the Fairmont Olympic Hotel in Seattle. Marah lay curled catlike in an overstuffed chair, reading her book.

'She needs me,' Tully said simply. She stood up, stretching. 'I think I'll hit the sack.'

'Can I sleep with Aunt Tully?' Marah said.

'It's OK with me,' Johnny said, 'if Tully doesn't mind.'

'Are you kidding? A slumber party with my favourite goddaughter is a perfect end to the day.'

After Johnny went to his own room, Tully played mommy to Marah—telling her to brush her teeth and get into her jammies.

'I'm too old for jammies,' Marah informed her smartly, but when she climbed into bed, she snuggled up to Tully like the little girl she'd been only a few short years ago.

'This was so awesome, Aunt Tully,' she said sleepily. 'I'm going to be a TV star when I grow up. If my mom lets me, which she probably won't.'

'What do you mean?'

'My mom won't let me do anything.'

'You do know that your mom is my best friend, right?'

'Yeah,' she answered grudgingly.

'Why do you think that is?'

Marah twisted round and looked at her. 'Why?'

'Because your mom rocks.'

Marah made a face. 'My mom? She never does anything cool.'

Tully shook her head. 'Marah, your mother loves you and she's proud of you. Believe me, princess, that's the coolest thing in the world.'

The next morning Tully got up early and went to the bedroom door across the hall. There, she paused, gathering her nerve, and knocked. When no one answered, she quietly opened it.

Her mother was still asleep.

Smiling, she left the suite and closed the door quietly behind her. At Johnny's door, she paused and knocked.

He answered quickly, dressed in one of the hotel's robes, his hair dripping wet. 'I thought we were starting at eight.'

'We are. I'm just going to get Cloud some clothes to take to rehab and some breakfast for all of us. Marah's still asleep.'

'You're moving awfully fast, Tully. The stores aren't open yet.'

'I've always been fast. And everything is open for Tallulah Hart. It's one of the perks of my life. You have a key to my room?'

'Yeah. I'll go over there now. You be careful.'

Ignoring his concern, she went to the market and stocked up on croissants and cinnamon rolls. Then she went to La Dolce, where she bought her other too much: jeans, tops, shoes, underwear and bras, and the thickest jacket she could find. She was back at the hotel by nine.

'I'm home,' she called out, kicking the door shut behind her. 'And wait till you see what I've got.'

Fat Bob was in the corner, filming her entrance.

She gave him her best smile. 'My mother needs to put on a few pounds. This should do it. I got practically every coffee Starbucks sells. I don't know what she likes.'

Johnny sat on the sofa, looking sad and tired.

'It's like a morgue in here.' Tully went to her mother's door and knocked. 'Cloud?'

There was no answer.

She knocked again. 'Cloud? Are you in the shower? I'm coming in.'

She opened the door.

The first thing she noticed was the smell of cigarettes and the open window. The bed was empty.

'Cloud?' She went to the bathroom, which was still damp and cloudy with steam. Thick Egyptian cotton towels lay in a heap on the floor.

Tully knew instantly what had happened. She backed out of the steamy bathroom and faced Johnny and the camera. 'She left?'

'A half-hour ago,' he said. 'I tried to stop her.'

Tully was stunned by how betrayed she felt, like that ten-year-old girl, abandoned on the Seattle street. Worthless and unwanted.

Johnny came over to her, took her in his arms and held her. She wanted to ask him *why*, ask what was wrong with her that no one ever stayed, but the question caught in her throat. She clung to him for too long, taking the comfort he offered. He stroked her head, whispered, *Shhh*, in her ear as if she were a child.

In time, though, she remembered the camera and pulled back, wiping her eyes, and forced a smile for the camera. 'Well, there it is. The end of the documentary. I'm done, Bob.'

The documentary aired two weeks later, and even Kate, who was used to Tully's amazing successes, was caught off guard by the public's reaction. It caused a media frenzy. For years Tully had been seen on camera as the cool, witty professional, following stories and reporting on them with her journalist's detachment. Now, the public saw beyond the journalist to the woman within, and they couldn't stop talking about her. The phrase heard most often was *just like me*. The documentary—and segments from it—were played and replayed on entertainment news shows. America, it seemed, couldn't get enough of Tully Hart.

But while everyone was watching Tully and the sad encounter with her estranged mother, Kate saw something else entirely on that tape, and she watched it just as obsessively.

She couldn't help noticing the way Johnny looked at Tully at the end, when Cloud's disappearance was revealed, the way he'd gone to her and taken her in his arms.

She studied their body language like a primatologist, but in the end she had only what she'd had in the beginning: two old friends working together on an emotional documentary and a wife who'd worried for a long time about them.

That should have been the end of it. If nothing else had happened, Kate would have boxed up her old jealousies and put them away again, just as she'd done dozens of times over the years.

But something *had* happened.

Syndiworld, the second-largest syndication company in the world, had seen the documentary and offered Tully her own one-hour show, of which she would be a majority-interest owner.

The idea had rocked Tully's world, offered her a way to be herself on camera, to show the world who she really was and how she really felt. The minute she heard the idea, she said it was exactly what she needed, but even so, she'd put down two conditions: first, they had to shoot in Seattle; second, John Ryan had to be her producer. Neither of these had she bothered to clear with her friends.

From the moment it aired, *The Girlfriend Hour* was a runaway success. Suddenly Tully was more than a journalist or a morning news anchor; she was a bona fide star. Everything about the show had been designed to play to her strengths and highlight her talent. What she did well—what she'd always done well—was talk to people.

The summer before Marah started high school was hands down the worst summer of Kate's life.

'You are not going to wear jeans that show the crack of your butt to school,' Kate said, striving to keep her voice even.

'Everyone is wearing these jeans at the high school.'

'Everyone except you, then.' Kate pressed a pair of fingertips to her throbbing temples. She was vaguely aware of the boys running through the store like banshees, but she let that go for now. If she was lucky, maybe security would come and lock her up for failing to control her children. Right now, a little solitary confinement sounded heavenly.

Marah threw the jeans on the floor and stomped off.

'Do you even know how to walk away any more?' Kate muttered, following her daughter.

By the time they were finished, Kate felt like Russell Crowe in *Gladiator*: beaten, bloodied, but alive. No one was happy. The boys were whining over the *Lord of the Rings* action figures she'd denied them, Marah was fuming over the jeans she hadn't got and the practically see-through blouse that had also got away, and Kate was angry that school shopping could so drain her energy.

On the drive home from Silverdale, the car was divided into two discernible halves: the back seat was noisy, boisterous and full of fighting; the front seat was frigid and silent.

When they turned down the gravel driveway and parked, the boys unhooked their seat belts and climbed over each other in their haste to get out. Kate knew that whoever got to the living room first controlled the remote.

Once indoors, Kate said to Marah, 'You got some lovely things today.'

Marah shrugged. 'Yeah.'

'You know, Marah, life is full of—' Kate stopped herself mid-sentence. She'd been about to offer one of her mother's *life is* speeches.

'What?'

'Compromises. You can go around seeing what you did get, or you can focus on what you didn't. The choice you make will ultimately determine what kind of woman you become.'

'I just want to fit in,' Marah said in a voice that was unexpectedly small. It reminded Kate how young her daughter really was.

Kate reached out, gently tucked some hair behind Marah's ear. 'Believe me, I remember the feeling. I had to wear secondhand clothes to school when I was your age. The kids used to make fun of me.'

'So you know what I mean.'

'I know what you mean, but you can't get everything you want.'

'It's a pair of jeans, Mom. Not world peace.'

Kate looked at her daughter. For once, she wasn't scowling or turning away. 'I'm sorry we fight so much.'

'Yeah.'

'Maybe we could sign you up for that modelling class. The one in Seattle.'

Marah jumped on that scrap like a hungry dog. 'The next session starts Tuesday. I checked. Tully said she'd pick me up from the ferry.' Marah smiled sheepishly. 'We've been talking about it.'

'Oh, you have, have you?'

'Daddy said it would be OK if I kept my grades up.'

'He knows, too? And no one talks to me? Who am I, Hannibal Lector?'

'You get mad pretty easily these days.'

'And whose fault is that?'

'Can I go?'

Kate had no choice, really. 'OK. But if your grades—'

Marah launched herself into Kate's arms. She held her daughter tightly, revelling in the moment.

That was the sly, ruinous thing about motherhood, the thing that twisted your insides with guilt and made you change your mind and lower your standards: giving in was so damned easy.

When the phone rang, Kate didn't even bother answering. In these last few weeks of summer, she'd learned one true thing: teenage girls lived on the phone.

'Mom! It's Grandma for you,' Marah said. 'But don't take too long. Gabe is gonna call me.'

She picked up the phone and heard the exhalation of smoke on the other end. Smiling, she plopped onto the couch. 'Hey, Mom.'

'You sound terrible.'

'You can tell that from my breathing?'

'You have a teenage daughter, don't you?'

'Believe me, I was never this bad.'

Mom laughed; it was a hoarse, hacking sound. 'I guess you don't remember all the times you told me to butt out of your life and then slammed the door in my face.'

The memory was vague but not impossible to recall. 'I'm sorry, Mom.'

There was a pause. Then Mom said, 'Thirty years.'

'Thirty years what?'

'That's how long before you'll get an apology, too, but you know what's great?'

Kate groaned. 'That I might not live that long?'

'No. That you'll know she's sorry long before she does.' Mom laughed. 'And when she needs you to babysit, she'll *really* love you.'

Tully stood at the window of her enormous office, staring out. She'd hoped that moving back to Seattle and starting her own show would somehow fill that empty place inside of her, but she was still dissatisfied. As always when she was unhappy, she turned to her career for the fix.

'You're insane,' Johnny said. 'Our ratings are second only to *Oprah*, and last year you were nominated for an Emmy. Companies can't line up fast enough to provide giveaways and promos to our audience. These are indicators of success.'

'I know,' she said. 'But I need to shake things up a bit. Mix it around.'

'Why?'

That was the $64,000 question.

'You're going to have to trust me on this, Johnny.'

'It could turn all *Jerry Springer* in an instant, and our credibility would be shot to hell.' He moved in towards her, frowning slightly. 'Talk to me, Tul.'

'I need to make a mark.'

'Twenty million viewers watch you every day; what's that, nothing?'

'You have Katie and the kids.'

She saw when understanding dawned. He gave the poor-Tully look; no matter how far she ran or high she climbed, that look seemed somehow to follow her. 'Oh.'

'I need to try this, Johnny. Will you help me?'

'When have I ever let you down? One try, Tully. Then we assess. Fair enough?'

'Fair enough.'

Now, finally, the moment of truth had arrived, and she was worried. What if Johnny was right and her idea degenerated into melodrama?

She checked herself in the mirror one last time, pulled the white make-up protector away from her collar and headed backstage, waiting for her cue. When the red lights lit up, she walked onstage.

As always, she stood there a moment, smiling, letting the strangers' applause wash through her, fill her to overflowing.

'Today we have a very special show for you. My guest, Dr Wesley Tillman, is a noted psychiatrist who specialises in addiction recovery and family counselling . . .'

Behind her, a huge screen played a film clip showing an overweight man with thinning hair. He was trying not to cry, and losing the battle. 'My wife is a good woman, Tallulah. We've been married for twenty years and we have two beautiful children. The problem is . . .' He paused, wiping his eyes. 'Booze. It used to be just cocktail hour with friends, but lately . . .'

The clip showed the painful disintegration of a family.

When it ended, Tully turned back to the audience. She could see how moved they were by the piece. 'Mr McAdams is like too many of us, living lives of quiet desperation because of a loved one's addiction. He swears that he's tried everything to convince his wife to go into treatment and quit drinking. Today, with Dr Tillman's help, we're going to try something radical. Mrs McAdams is backstage, alone, right now. She believes she's won a trip to the Bahamas and is here to collect it. In fact, though, her family—with Dr Tillman's professional help—is going to confront her about her alcoholism. Our hope is that we can force her to see the truth and seek treatment.'

There was a moment of silence in the audience.

Tully held her breath.

Then applause.

It was all Tully could do not to laugh. She glanced over at Johnny, who was standing in the shadows by Camera 1, giving her a thumbs up.

This would help her, fill her up. She would genuinely help this family and America would love her for it.

Lately, it seemed that Kate was always exhausted, and yet, when she went to bed she rarely slept well.

She flicked off the light in Johnny's office, and went downstairs. Johnny looked up from the *New York Times*. 'eBay suck you in again?'

She laughed. 'Of course. Were the boys good?'

He leaned forward, tousled their hair. 'As long as I sing along with "Poor Unfortunate Souls", they're happy as clams.'

She couldn't help smiling at that. *The Little Mermaid* was this week's favourite movie. That meant they watched it every day if they could.

The front door banged open and Marah was home, looking excited. 'You'll never guess what happened to me today.'

Johnny put down his paper. 'What?'

'Christopher, Jenny, Josh and I are going to the Tacoma Dome to see Nine Inch Nails. Can you believe it? Josh asked *me*.'

Kate took a deep breath. She'd learned to react slowly with Marah.

'A concert?' Johnny said. 'Who are these kids? How old are they?'

'Josh and Chris are juniors.'

'When is the concert?' he asked.

'Tuesday.'

'On a school night? You think you're going on a date, with a junior, to a concert, on a school night.' Kate looked at Johnny. 'That's wrong on so many levels.'

'When does it start?' Johnny asked.

'Nine. We should be home by two o'clock.'

Kate couldn't help herself: she laughed. She had no idea how her husband could stay so reasonable. '*Should* be home by two o'clock? You must be joking, Marah. You're fourteen years old.'

'Jenny's fourteen and she gets to go. Daddy?' Marah turned to Johnny. 'You have to let me go.'

'You're too young,' he said. 'Sorry.'

'I'm not too young. Everyone gets to do stuff like this except me.'

Kate's heart went out to Marah. She remembered being in a hurry to grow up, knew how sharp that need could be in a girl. 'I know you think we're too strict, Marah, but sometimes life—'

'Oh, please. Not another lame *life is* speech.' With a snort, she ran upstairs and slammed her bedroom door shut.

Kate felt a wave of exhaustion so profound she almost sat down. Instead, she looked at her husband. 'I'm so glad I came downstairs.'

Johnny smiled. It came easily, too. How was it that he could do the same battles with Marah that Kate did, but manage to come out unscathed? And loved? 'Your timing with her is always impeccable.' He stood up, kissed her. 'I love you,' he said simply.

She knew it was meant to be a Band-Aid, those words, and she appreciated it. 'I'll go make dinner and then try talking to her. Give her some time to cool down.'

She went into the kitchen and for almost an hour, lost herself in slicing and dicing for stir-fry, and making Marah's favourite teriyaki marinade. At six o'clock, she tossed the salad, put the biscuits in the oven, and set the table.

'OK,' she said, coming back into the living room, where Johnny was sprawled on the floor with his boys, building something out of Lego. 'I'm going in.'

Johnny looked up. 'The Kevlar vest is in the coat closet.'

In the comforting wake of his laughter, Kate went upstairs. At the closed door to her daughter's room, she steeled herself, then knocked.

There was no answer.

'Marah?' she said. 'I know you're upset, but we need to talk.'

She waited, knocked again, and opened the door.

In the jumble of clothes and books and movies, it took Kate a moment to process what she was seeing.

An empty room.

With an open window.

Just to be sure, she searched the entire upstairs, her heart pounding so fast she felt light-headed. At the top of the stairs, she held on to the banister for support. 'She's gone,' she said, hearing the crack in her voice.

Johnny looked up. 'Huh?'

'She's gone. I think she climbed out her window.'

He was on his feet in a second and ran outside. Kate followed.

They stood beneath her bedroom window, seeing where her weight had broken the white wooden trellis and ripped through the ivy. 'We need to start calling everyone she knows,' Johnny said.

Even on a cold night like this, Tully loved being on the deck of her condo. It was a big, stone-tiled space that had been designed to replicate an Italian villa's terrace. Big, leafy trees grew from terracotta planters, their branches strung with tiny white lights.

She went to the railing and stared out. What were the Ryans doing tonight? she wondered. Maybe they were playing board games round that big old-fashioned trestle table of theirs. Or perhaps Marah and Kate were curled up on the couch together, talking about boys. Or maybe she and Johnny had stolen a moment together to kiss—

The phone rang in her apartment. It was just as well. Thinking about Kate's family only made Tully feel more lonely.

She went through the open doors and closed them behind her, then answered the phone. 'Hello?'

'Tully?' It was Johnny. His voice was tight, unfamiliar.

She was immediately worried. 'What is it?'

'Marah ran away. We don't know when exactly, probably about an hour and fifteen minutes ago. Have you heard from her?'

'No. I haven't. Why did she run away?' Before Johnny could answer, Tully's doorman buzzed her. 'Just a second, Johnny. Hold on.' She ran to the intercom, pressed it. 'What is it, Edmond?'

'There's a Marah Ryan here to see you.'

'Send her up.' Tully released the button. 'She's here, Johnny.'

'Thank God,' he said. 'She's there, honey. She's fine. We'll be right over, Tully. Don't let her leave.'

'Don't worry.' Tully hung up the phone and went to the door. As the penthouse unit, hers was the only door on this side of the building, so she opened it and stood there, trying to look surprised when Marah stepped out of the elevator.

'Hey, Aunt Tully, I'm sorry to come here so late.'

'This isn't late. Come on in.' She stood back, let Marah enter the condo first. 'What happened?'

Marah flopped onto the couch and sighed dramatically. 'I got invited to a concert at the Tacoma Dome.'

'Uh-huh.'

'On a school night.' Marah gave her a sideways glance. 'The boy who asked me is a junior.'

'That's, what, sixteen, seventeen?'

'Seventeen.'

Tully nodded. 'I went to see Wings in the Kingdome when I was about your age. What's the trauma?'

'My parents think I'm too young.'

'They said no?'

'How lame is that? Everyone gets to do stuff like this except me. My mom won't even let me drive with boys who have their licence. She still picks me up from school every day.'

'Well, sixteen-year-old boys are notoriously bad drivers, and sometimes it's not . . . safe to be alone with them.' She thought about that night in the woods, all those years ago. 'Your mom is just protecting you.'

'But we'll be in a group.'

'A group. That's different. As long as you all stay together.'

'I know. It's not like I'll be alone with him. Nothing can go wrong. She's just worried about their driving.'

'Oh. Well, I could take you guys in a limo.'

'You'd do that?'

'Sure. Solves all the problems. Chaperone. Driver. We'll have a blast. I'll make sure no one gets hurt.'

Marah sighed. 'It won't work.'

'Why not?'

'Because my mom is a bitch and I hate her.'

That caught Tully off guard, shocked her so much that she couldn't think of what to say. 'Marah—'

'I mean it. She treats me as if I'm a child. She doesn't respect my privacy. She tries to tell me what I can do. No make-up, no thongs, no belly ring, no staying out after eleven, no tattoos. I can't wait to get away from her. Believe me, once I graduate, it's sayonara, Mom. I'm going straight to Hollywood to be a star like you.'

That last bit flattered Tully so much she almost forgot what had preceded it. She had to force herself back on track. 'You're not being fair to your mom. Girls your age are more vulnerable than you think. A long time ago, when I was your age and thought I was invincible, I—'

'You'd let me go to the concert if you were my mom.'

'Yes, but—'

'I wish you were my mom.'

Tully was surprised by how deeply she felt those words. They found a soft spot inside her. 'You two will get past this, Marah. You'll see.'

'No, we won't.'

For the next hour Tully tried to crack through Marah's anger, but it was a durable shell, impossible to breach. She was stunned by how easily Marah claimed to hate Katie, afraid that these two would never repair their damaged relationship. If there was one thing Tully knew, it was how ruined you could be without a mother's love.

Finally, the intercom buzzed and Edmond's voice came through: 'The Ryans, Ms Hart.'

'They know I'm here?' Marah said, popping to her feet.

'It couldn't have been hard to figure out,' Tully said, going to the intercom. 'Let them up, Edmond. Thanks.'

'They're going to kill me,' Marah said, pacing, wringing her hands, and all at once she was a child again, gangly and tall and gorgeous, but still a child, afraid that she was going to be in trouble.

Johnny was the first to walk through the open door. 'Damn it, Marah,' he said, 'you scared the hell out of us—' He broke his sentence off, as if he were afraid to say more.

Kate came up behind him.

Tully was stunned at the sight of her friend. She looked tired and sick and smaller somehow, as if she'd just taken a beating.

'Katie?' Tully said, worried.

'Thanks, Tully,' she answered, giving her a wan smile.

'Aunt Tully said she'd take us to the concert in her limo,' Marah said. 'And chaperone us.'

'Your aunt is a moron,' Johnny snapped. 'Her wacko mother dropped her on her head. Now, get your stuff. We're going home.'

'But—'

'No buts, Marah,' Kate said. 'Get your things.'

Marah put on a real show—sighing, stomping, uttering, whining. Then she gave Tully a fierce hug, whispered, 'Thanks for trying,' and left the condo with Johnny.

Tully waited for Kate to say something.

'Sometimes when she looks at me, I see hate in her eyes. I can't tell you how much that hurts.'

'She'll grow out of it.'

'That's what everyone says, but I don't believe it. If there was just some way that I could force her to talk to me, and to listen.'

Like magic, Tully knew exactly how to help. 'Why don't you come on my show? You and Marah. We'll do a mother-daughter segment. Live would be best so she knows there's no editing. She'll see how much you love her and how lucky she is.'

Hope took ten years off Kate's face. 'You think it would work?'

'You know how badly Marah wants to be on TV. She'd never let herself look bad in front of the camera. She'd have to listen to you then.'

That tired desperation finally left Kate's eyes. In its stead was a bright anticipation. 'What would I do without you, Tully?'

'We'll never have to find out.'

Kate still couldn't quite believe today was going to happen. She'd waited so long, and prayed so hard, for a change in her relationship with Marah that she'd almost given up hope. Tully, and this programme, had given it back to her.

She went downstairs, made breakfast for everyone, and set it out on the table. The boys were down the stairs in record time, clambering over each other in their quest for the perfect chair.

When Marah came downstairs, clearly excited for the taping, Kate felt a new surge of hope.

'Stop grinning, Mom. You're creeping me out,' Marah said, pouring milk into her oatmeal bowl and carrying it to the table.

'Leave your mom alone,' Johnny said, walking past her. He paused behind Kate, squeezed her shoulders, and kissed the back of her neck. 'You look gorgeous.'

She turned and put her arms round him, gazing into his eyes. 'I'm glad you're going to be my husband today and not Tully's producer. I need you in the audience.'

'Don't thank me. Tully pushed me completely on the outside. No one on-set is allowed to tell me anything or show me a script. Tully wants me to be surprised.'

From that moment on the day flew forward like the *Millennium Falcon* in hyperspace. It wasn't until they were on the ferry, crossing the bay, that Kate started to get nervous.

In the studio, there were people everywhere, running to and fro, yelling at one another.

'Kate!'

She heard her name ring through the busy hallway and looked up. Tully, looking gorgeous, was coming at her with open arms.

Tully pulled her into a fierce embrace, and Kate felt herself relax.

This wasn't just a TV show; it was Tully's show. Her best friend would make sure Kate did well.

'I'm a little nervous,' Kate confided.

Tully looped her arm through Kate's. 'There's nothing to worry about. You're going to be great. Everyone is excited to have you and Marah on the show.' She led them to the make-up room and left them there.

'This is exciting,' Kate said.

Marah was too busy staring at her own reflection to answer. In the mirror, a stranger emerged: the woman Marah would someday become.

The make-up artist had accentuated Marah's pale skin, highlighted her sharp cheekbones with a shimmering pink hue, and added just enough mascara to make her eyes look full of dark mysteries.

Kate saw the future then, recognised a truth that had until now been hidden from her beneath the pretty gauze of childhood. In no time Marah would be dating, and then driving, and then going off to college.

'I love you, Munchkin,' she said, purposely using the nickname that had gone out of fashion with Winnie-the-Pooh lunch boxes. 'Remember when we used to dance to those old Linda Ronstadt songs?'

Marah looked at her. For a second—just that—they were Mommy and Munchkin again, and though it didn't last, couldn't last in the hurricane of the teen years, it filled Kate with hope that someday they'd come together again, be as inseparable as they'd once been.

'Yeah.' Marah looked poised to say something, then smiled instead.

'Kathleen and Marah Ryan? We're ready for you,' said a young, pretty woman with a clipboard.

Kate reached out for Marah, who was excited enough to take her hand. They followed the young woman up to the green room.

'There's water in that fridge, and feel free to eat anything in that basket,' the woman said. Then she handed Kate a lapel microphone and the corresponding pack that attached to her waistband. 'Tallulah said you'd know how to work this?'

'It's been a while but I think I can manage. I'll show Marah. Thanks.'

'Great. I'll come and get you when it's time. As you know, we're live today, but don't let that worry you. Just be yourself.'

And then she was gone.

This was really happening. It meant so much to her, this chance to reconnect with her daughter.

A few moments later there was a knock on the door.

'We're ready for you, Kathleen,' the woman with the clipboard said. 'Marah, stay here. We'll come for you in a minute.'

Kate rushed forward in a flurry of nerves.

'Mom!' Marah said urgently, as if she'd just remembered something important. 'I need to tell you something.'

Kate smiled. 'Don't worry, honey. We'll be great.' She followed the woman down the busy corridor. Through the walls she could hear applause, even a smattering of laughter.

At the edge of the stage, the young woman paused. 'When you hear your name, you'll walk out.'

Breathe.

She heard Tully say, 'And now, I'd like you all to meet my good friend Kathleen Ryan . . .'

Kate stumbled round the corner and found herself in the bright glare of the stage lights. It was so disorientating that it took her a second to process her surroundings.

There was Tully, standing centre stage, smiling at her. Behind her was Dr Tillman, the psychiatrist who specialised in family counselling.

Tully swept over to her side, took her arm.

Kate glanced over at the screen behind them. There was a huge image of two women shouting at each other. Then she looked at the audience. Johnny and her parents were in the front row.

Tully faced them. 'Today we're talking about overprotective mothers and the teenage daughters who hate them. Our goal is to get a dialogue going, to break up the log jam of communication that comes with adolescence and get these two talking again.'

Kate actually felt the blood drain from her face. 'What?'

Behind her, Dr Tillman moved from his place in the shadows to a chair onstage. 'Some mothers, especially the controlling, domineering type, actually damage their children's fragile psyches without ever really seeing what they're doing. Children can be like flowers, trying to blossom in too small a space. They need to break out, make their own mistakes. We don't help them by wrapping them in rules and rigid expectations and pretending that we can keep them safe.'

The full impact of what was happening hit Kate.

They were calling her a bad mother, on national television, with her family right here.

She wrenched her arm away from Tully. 'What are you doing?'

'You need help,' Tully said, sounding reasonable and just a little sad. 'You and Marah both do. You two are ruining your happy family. Marah wants to confront you about it, but she's afraid.'

Marah walked onstage, smiling brightly at the audience.

Kate felt the start of tears, and that sign of vulnerability only fuelled her anger. 'I can't believe you'd do this to me.'

Dr Tillman came forward. 'Come on, Kathleen, Tully is being your friend here. Your parenting style—'

'*You're* going to help me be a better mother?' she said to Tully. 'You?' Then she turned to the audience. 'You're taking advice from a woman who doesn't know the first thing about love or family or the hard choices women have to make. The only person Tully Hart ever loved is herself.'

'Katie,' Tully said in a low, warning voice. 'We're live.'

'That's all you care about, isn't it? Your ratings. Well, I hope they keep you warm when you're old, because you won't have anything or anyone else. What the hell do you know about motherhood or love? Your own mother didn't love you.'

Kate wrenched off her microphone and power pack and threw them on the floor. As she stormed offstage, she snagged Marah's arm and pulled her along.

Backstage, Johnny rushed at her, took her in his arms, and held her tightly, but even his body heat couldn't reach her. Her parents and the boys ran up behind him, creating a circle round Kate and her daughter. 'I'm sorry, honey,' he said. 'I didn't know . . .'

'I can't believe Tully did that,' Kate's mom said. 'She must've thought—'

'Don't,' Kate said sharply, wiping her eyes. 'I don't care what she thought or wanted or believed. Not any more.'

Tully ran out into the hallway, but Kate was gone.

She stood there too long, then turned and went back onstage, where she stared at a sea of unfamiliar faces. She tried to smile, she really did, but for once her will failed her. She heard the quiet murmuring of the crowd; it was the sound of sympathy. Behind her, Dr Tillman was talking, filling the void with words she could neither follow nor understand. She realised that he was keeping the show going since they were live.

'I just wanted to help her,' she said to the audience, interrupting him. She sat down on the edge of the stage. 'I didn't do anything wrong, did I?'

Their applause was loud and went on and on, their approval unconditional. It should have filled up the empty places in her, that had always been their role, but now, the applause didn't help.

Somehow she made it through the rest of the broadcast.

Finally, though, she was as alone onstage as she felt. The audience had filed out and her employees had all left. None had had the courage to even speak to her on the way out. She knew they were angry at her for ambushing Johnny, too.

As if from a great distance, she heard footsteps. Someone was coming towards her. Dully, she looked up.

Johnny stood there. 'How could you do that to her? She trusted you. *We* trusted you.'

'I was just trying to help her. Dr Tillman told me that drastic situations call for drastic measures. He said suicide was—'

'I quit,' he said.

'But . . . tell her to call me. I'll explain.'

'I wouldn't count on hearing from her.'

'What do you mean? We've been friends for thirty years.'

Johnny gave her a look so cold she began to shake. 'I think that ended today.'

Kate sat in bed, with a book open in her lap. As she stared at the pages, the type blurred and danced like black dots on the creamy paper. Yesterday's fiasco kept playing in her mind, over and over. The title: Overprotective mothers and the teenage daughters who hate them.

Hate them.

She still felt shell-shocked, numb. Beneath the numbness, though, was a raw and terrible anger that was unlike anything she'd felt before. She had so little experience with genuine anger that it scared her. She actually worried that if she started screaming, she'd never stop. So she kept the lid on her emotions and sat quietly.

She kept glancing at the phone, expecting Tully to call.

'I'll hang up,' she said. And she would. She was actually looking forward to it. For all the years of their friendship, it had fallen to Kate to apologise, whether it was her fault or not. Tully never said she was sorry; she just waited for Kate to smooth things over.

Not this time.

This time Kate was so hurt and angry she didn't care if they stayed friends or not. If they were to get back together, Tully was going to have to work for it.

She sighed, wishing the thought made her feel better, but it didn't. She felt . . . broken by yesterday.

There was a knock at her door. It could be any member of her family. Last night they'd circled the wagons round her, protecting her. Mom and Dad had spent the night; Kate thought her mom was on suicide watch, that was how overbearing she was. Dad kept patting her shoulder, and the boys, who didn't know exactly what was wrong but sensed that it was big, hung on her constantly. Only Marah stood back from the drama, watching it all from a distance.

'Come in,' Kate said, sitting up taller, trying to look more durable than she felt.

Marah walked into the room. Dressed for school in low-rise jeans, pink fake Ugg boots and a grey hoodie sweatshirt, she tried to smile, but it was a failure. 'Grandma said I had to talk to you.'

Kate was relieved beyond measure by her daughter's presence. She moved to the middle of her bed and patted the empty place beside her.

Marah sat down opposite her instead, leaning back against the silk-upholstered footboard, with her legs drawn up.

Kate couldn't help longing for the time when she could have scooped her daughter into her arms and held her. She needed that now. 'You knew about the show, didn't you?'

'Tully and I talked about it.'

'And?'

Marah shrugged. 'I just wanted to go to the concert.'

The concert. It hurt Kate deeply, that simple, selfish answer. She'd forgotten about the concert and Marah's running away.

'Say something,' Marah said.

But Kate didn't quite know what to say. She wanted Marah to understand how selfish she'd been and how deeply that selfishness had hurt Kate, but she didn't want to load guilt on her. The weight of this debacle fell on Tully. 'Did it occur to you when you and Tully were hatching this plan that I might be hurt and embarrassed by it?'

'Did you think that I'd be hurt or embarrassed by not getting to go to the concert? Or rockin' midnight bowling? Or to—'

Kate held up a hand. 'So it's still about you,' she said tiredly. 'If this is all you have to say, you can leave. I don't have the strength to fight with you now. You were selfish and you hurt my feelings, and if you can't see that and take responsibility for it, I feel sorry for you. Get out. Go.'

'Whatever.' Marah got off the bed, but she moved slowly. At the door, she paused and turned round. 'When Tully comes over—'

'Tully won't be coming over.'

'What do you mean?'

'Your idol owes me an apology. That's not something she's good at. I'd say it's something else you two have in common.'

By the following autumn, Kate had stopped waiting for Tully to call. In the nine long months of their estrangement, she'd settled—albeit uncomfortably—into a rarefied and contained world, a kind of snow globe of her own creation. At first, of course, she'd cried about their lost friendship, ached for what had been, but in time, she accepted that there would be no apology from Tully, that if one were to be offered it would have to—as always—come from her.

The story of their lives.

Kate's ego, usually such a fluid and convenient thing, became solid on this point. For once, she would not yield.

But it exhausted her, drained her. Lately, it took all her effort to get up in the morning and take a shower. For the last week, washing her hair had been such a daunting prospect that she'd avoided it altogether. Cooking dinner and doing the dishes sapped so much energy that halfway through she had to sit down.

'I don't know why you're making such a big deal out of it,' she'd said to her husband that night when he asked her about it. He'd taken a job at his old station, which gave him too much time to notice Kate's flaws.

'You're depressed,' he'd said, pulling her against him on the sofa. 'And frankly, Kate, you don't look good.'

That had hurt, although, to be honest, not as much as it should have. 'So make me an appointment with a plastic surgeon. I hardly need a physical exam. I see my doctors regularly. You know that.'

'Better safe than sorry,' was his answer, and so now, two weeks later, she was on the ferry, going in to the city. The truth was—although she wouldn't have admitted it to her husband—she was glad to be going in. She was tired of being depressed, tired of feeling worn out. Maybe a prescription of some kind would help, a pill to forget a thirty-year friendship that had ended badly.

After she'd read every article in *Parents* magazine, she was led to an examination room, where a nurse took all the usual information.

Then Dr Marcia Silver stepped into the room. 'Hey there, Kate. It's good to see you again.' Sitting down on her wheeled stool, she glided forward, reading Kate's chart. 'So, is there anything you want to tell me?'

'My husband thinks I'm depressed.'

'Are you?'

Kate shrugged. 'A little blue maybe.'

Marcia made a note in the chart. 'OK, Kate, we'll start with the pap smear. Slide on down to the end here . . .' For the next few minutes Kate gave herself over to the little indignities that came with female health care. All the while she and Dr Silver made impersonal conversation.

It wasn't until nearly thirty minutes later, when the exam had moved to her breasts, that Marcia actually stopped making chitchat. 'How long have you had this discoloration on your breast?'

Kate glanced down at the quarter-sized red patch beneath her right nipple. The skin was slightly puckered like an orange peel. 'Nine months or so. Maybe a year, come to think of it. It started as a bug bite. My family doctor thought it was an infection and put me on antibiotics.

It went away for a while and then came back. Sometimes it feels hot—that's how I know it's an infection.'

Marcia stared down at Kate's breast, frowning. Long enough for Kate to start to be afraid. 'I had my mammogram. Everything was clean.'

'I see that.' Marcia went to the wall phone, punched in a number and said, 'I want to get Kate in for a breast ultrasound. Now. Tell them to fit her in. Thanks.' She hung up and turned round.

Kate sat up. 'You're scaring me, Marcia.'

'I hope it's nothing, Kate, but I want to be sure, OK?'

Kate's mind was a whirl. Before she knew it, she was dressed again and being shepherded down the hall. There, after an interminable wait, she endured another breast exam, more frowning and an ultrasound.

'I always do my self-exams,' she said. 'I haven't felt a lump.'

When the ultrasound was over, she was again shuffled out of the exam room and deposited back in the waiting room. Like all the other women in the small, interior waiting room, she read magazines, trying to concentrate on anything except the results of the ultrasound.

It'll be fine, she told herself whenever the worry crept through. *Nothing to worry about*. Cancer wasn't something that crept up on you, certainly not breast cancer. There were warning signs and she watched for them religiously.

Finally, a plump, doe-eyed nurse came for her. 'Kathleen Ryan?'

She stood up. 'Yes?'

'I'm going to take you across the hall. Dr Krantz is waiting to do a biopsy on you.'

'Biopsy?'

'Just to be sure. Come on.'

Clutching her bag, Kate followed the nurse. She wished Johnny were here, holding her hand, telling her everything was going to be fine.

Or Tully.

Tully was woken by the phone ringing. She came awake hard, looked around. It was 2.01 in the morning. She reached over and answered. 'Hello?'

'Is this Tallulah Hart?'

She rubbed her eyes. 'Yes. Who is this?'

'My name is Lori Witherspoon. I'm a nurse at Harborview Hospital. We have your mother here, Dorothy Hart.'

'What happened?'

'We're not sure. It looks like a drug overdose, but she was pretty badly beaten up, too. The police are waiting to question her.'

'Did she ask for me?'

'She's unconscious. We found your name and number in her things.'

'I'll be right there.'

Tully got dressed in record time and was on the road by 2.20. She pulled into the parking lot at the hospital and went to the desk.

'Hello. I'm here to see my mother, Cl— Uh, Dorothy Hart.'

'Sixth floor, Ms Hart. Go to the nurses' desk.'

'Thanks.' Tully went upstairs and was directed to her mother's room by a tiny woman in a pale-orange nurse's uniform.

Inside the shadowy room, she was surprised to find that she was frightened. For the whole of her life, she'd been wounded by her mother. She'd loved her as a child, inexplicably; hated her as a teenager; and ignored her as a woman. Cloud had broken her heart more times than she could count, and let her down on every possible occasion, and yet, even after all of that, Tully couldn't help feeling something for her.

Cloud was asleep. Bruises covered her face, blackened one eye; her lip was split open and seeped blood. She looked like a frail old woman who'd been beaten by more than someone's fists—by life itself.

'Hey, Cloud,' Tully said, surprised to find that her throat was tight.

She wished she knew what to say to this woman, with whom she had a history but no present. So, she just talked. She told her about the show and her life and how successful she'd become. When that started to sound hollow and desperate, she talked about Kate and their fight and how it had left her feeling so alone. As the words formed themselves and spilled out, Tully heard the truth in them. Losing the Ryans and Mularkeys had left her devastatingly alone. Cloud was all she had left. How pathetic was that?

'We're all alone in this world. Haven't you figured that out by now?'

Tully hadn't noticed her mother wake up, and yet she was conscious now, and looking at Tully through tired eyes.

'Hey,' she said, smiling, wiping her eyes. 'What happened to you?'

'I got beat up.'

'I wasn't asking what put you in the hospital. I was asking what happened to you.'

Cloud turned away. 'Oh. That.' She sighed. 'It doesn't matter now.'

'I think it does.'

'Go away, Tully.' Cloud turned her face into the pillow.

'Not until you tell me why.' Her voice trembled on that question; of course it did. 'Why didn't you ever love me?'

'Forget about me.'

'Honestly, I wish I could. But you're my mother.'

Cloud stared at her, and for a moment, no longer than it took to blink, Tully saw sadness in her mother's eyes. 'I wish . . .'

'What?'

'I could be what you need, but I can't. You need to let me go.'

'I don't know how to do that. After everything, you're my mother.'

'I was never your mother. We both know that.'

'I'll always keep coming back,' Tully said, realising just then that it was true. They might be damaged, she and her mother, but they were connected, too, in a strange way. This dance of theirs, as painful as it had always been, wasn't quite over. 'Someday you'll be ready for me.'

'How do you keep hold of a dream like that?'

'With both hands.' She would have added, *No matter what*, but the promise reminded her of Kate and hurt too much to utter aloud.

Her mother sighed and closed her eyes. 'Go away.'

Tully stood there a long time, her hands curled round the metal bedrail. She knew her mother was pretending sleep; she also knew when it became real. When intermittent snores filled the silence, she went to the small closet in the room, found a folded-up blanket, and grabbed it. That was when she noticed the small pile of clothes, folded neatly in the corner on the closet's bottom shelf. Beside it was a brown paper grocery bag, rolled closed at the top.

She covered her mother with the blanket and returned to the closet.

She wasn't sure why she went through her mother's things, what she was looking for. At first, it was the stuff she'd expected: dirty, worn clothes, shoes with holes along the sole, a makeshift toiletry set in a plastic bag, cigarettes and a lighter.

Then she saw it: coiled neatly at the bottom of the bag—a frayed piece of string, knotted into a circle, with two pieces of dried macaroni and a single blue bead strung on it.

The necklace Tully had made in her Bible study class and given to her mother on that day, all those years ago, when they'd left Gran's house in the VW bus. Her mother had kept it, all this time.

Tully turned to her mother, went to the bed. 'You kept it,' she said, feeling something brand-new open up inside her. A kind of hope. 'You know how to hold on to a dream, too, don't you, Cloud?'

She sat down on the moulded plastic chair by the bed. Sometime around four o'clock, she slumped in her chair and fell asleep.

The trilling of her cellphone woke her. She unfolded slowly, painfully, rubbing her neck. It took her a moment to realise where she was.

She stood up. Her mother's bed was empty. She wrenched open the closet doors. Empty. The bag was crumpled into a ball and left behind.

'Shit.'

Her cellphone rang again. She glanced at the incoming number. 'Hey, Edna,' she said, sinking back into the chair.

'You sound awful.'

'Bad night.' She tried not to think about the necklace. 'What time is it?'

'Six, your time. Do you still take off December?'

'So that my crew can enjoy the holidays with their families?' she said bitterly. 'I do.'

'I know you're usually busy with that friend of yours—'

'Not this year. Thanks for reminding me.'

'Good. Then maybe you'd like to come to the Antarctic with me. I'm doing a documentary on global warming. I think it's an important story, Tully. Someone of your stature would get it watched.'

It would be good to get away and you couldn't get much farther than Antarctica. 'How long?'

'Six weeks at the most.'

'Six weeks sounds perfect. When do we leave?'

Naked, Kate stood in front of the mirror in her bathroom, studying her body. All her life she'd been engaged in a guerrilla-type war with her reflection. Her thighs had always been too fleshy, no matter how much weight she lost, and her tummy pooched out after three kids. She did sit-ups at the gym, but still her middle sagged. She'd stopped wearing sleeveless shirts about three years ago—arm jiggle.

Now, though, when she looked at herself, she saw how little all of that mattered, what a waste of her time it had been.

She stepped closer, practising the words she'd chosen, rehearsing. If ever there was a moment in her life that required strength, this was it.

She reached for the pile of clothes on the counter and began dressing. She'd chosen a pretty pink cashmere V-neck sweater—a Christmas present from the kids last year—and a worn, soft-as-lambskin pair of Levis. Then she brushed her hair, pulled it away from her face and made a ponytail. She even put on some make-up. It was important that she look healthy for what was to come. When there was nothing else she could do, she left the bathroom and went into her bedroom.

Her husband, who'd been seated on the end of the bed, stood quickly and turned to her. She could see how hard he was trying to be strong. Already, his eyes were bright.

It should have made her cry, too, that shiny evidence of his love and fear, but somehow it made her stronger. 'I have cancer,' she said.

He already knew it, of course. Last night they'd waited together for the doctor's call, holding hands all the while, assuring each other it would be fine. But it hadn't been fine, not even close to fine.

I'm sorry, Kate . . . stage four . . . inflammatory breast cancer . . . aggressive . . . already spread . . .

At first Kate had been furious—she'd always done everything right, looked for lumps, got her mammograms—and then the fear set in.

Johnny took it even harder than she did, and she saw quickly that she needed to be strong for him.

She went to him. He curled his arms round her and held her as tightly as he could, and still it wasn't close enough.

'I have to tell them.'

'We have to.' He stepped back slightly, loosened his hold just enough to look down at her. 'Nothing will change. Remember that.'

'Are you kidding? They're going to take away my breasts.' Her voice caught on that. 'Then they'll poison and burn me. And all that is supposed to be the good news.'

He stared down at her, and the love in his eyes was the most beautiful, heart-wrenching thing she'd ever seen. 'Between us, nothing will change. It doesn't matter how you look or feel or act. I'll love you for ever, just like I do now.'

The emotions she'd worked so hard to submerge threatened to consume her. 'Let's go,' she said quietly. 'While I've still got the nerve.'

Hand in hand, they walked out of their bedroom and went downstairs, where the kids were supposed to be waiting for them.

The living room was empty.

Kate could hear the television in the family room. It blared out the *bleep-thump* of video games. She let go of her husband and went to the corner, by the hall. 'Boys, come on out here.'

'Aw, Mom,' Lucas whined, 'we're playing a game.'

She wanted to say, *Keep on playing; forget it*, so badly it actually hurt to say, 'Come on, please. Now.'

Behind her, she heard her husband go into the kitchen and pick up the phone.

'Downstairs, Marah. Now. No, I don't care who you're talking to.'

Kate went to the couch and sat down, perching stiffly on the cushion's edge. The boys rushed into the room together, fighting with plastic swords, laughing.

'Take that, Captain Hook,' Lucas said.

'I'm Peter Pan,' William complained, pretending to stab his brother.

At seven, they were just beginning to change. The little-boy freckles were fading; infant teeth were falling out. Every time she looked at them lately, some baby trait had been lost. What if she weren't here to see them grow up? What if—

No bad thoughts.

It had become her mantra in the past four days. Johnny came up beside her, sat down close, and took her hand in his. Immediately, his warmth affected her.

'I can't believe you picked up the phone,' Marah said, coming down the stairs. 'That is so totally an invasion of my privacy.'

Kate counted silently to ten, calmed herself enough to breathe.

Her children were in front of her, standing there, looking either bored (the boys) or irritated (Marah).

She swallowed hard. She could do this.

'Are you gonna say something?' Marah demanded. 'Because if you're just gonna stare at us, I'm going back upstairs.'

Johnny started to come out of his seat. 'Damn it, Marah.'

Kate put a hand on his thigh to stop him. 'Sit down, Marah,' she said, surprised to hear how ordinary she sounded. 'You, too, boys.'

The boys plopped onto the carpet like marionettes whose strings had been cut, landing in side-by-side heaps.

'I'll stand,' Marah said, flinging her hip out and crossing her arms.

'You remember when I went into the city on Friday?' Kate began, feeling the acceleration of her heartbeat and slight breathlessness that accompanied it. 'Well, I had a doctor's appointment. There's nothing for you to worry about, but I'm . . . sick.'

All three of them looked at her.

'Don't worry. They're going to operate on me tomorrow and then give me a bunch of medicine and I'll be fine. I might be tired for a few weeks, but that should be about it.'

'You promise you'll be OK?' Lucas said, his gaze steady and earnest and only a little afraid.

Kate wanted to say, *Yes*, but such a promise would be remembered.

William rolled his eyes and elbowed his brother. 'She just said she'd be fine. Will we get out of school to go to the hospital?'

'Yes,' Kate said, actually finding a smile.

Lucas rushed forward to hug her first. 'I love you, Mommy,' he whispered. She held on to him so long he had to wrench free. The same thing happened with William. Then, as one, they turned and went to the stairs.

'Aren't you going to finish your game?' Kate asked.

'Naw,' Lucas said. 'We're going upstairs.'

Kate glanced worriedly at her husband, who was already rising. 'How about a game of basketball, boys?'

They jumped on the idea and all went outside.

Finally, Kate looked at Marah.

'It's cancer, isn't it?' her daughter asked after a long silence.

'Yes.'

'Ms Murphy had cancer last year and she's fine.'

'Exactly.'

Marah's mouth trembled. For all her pseudo-sophistication, height and make-up, she looked suddenly like a little girl again, asking Kate to leave the nightlight on. Wringing her hands together, she moved towards the sofa. 'You'll be fine, right?'

Stage four. Already spread. Caught it late. She put a lid on those thoughts. They could do her no good. Now was a time for optimism.

'Right. The doctors say I'm young and healthy, so I should be fine.'

Marah lay down on the couch, snuggled close, and put her head in Kate's lap. 'I'll take care of you, Mommy.'

Kate stroked her daughter's hair. It seemed like only yesterday she'd been able to hold her in her arms and rock her to sleep. *Please God*, she prayed, *let me get old enough that someday we're friends . . .*

She swallowed hard. 'I know you will, honey.'

The Firefly Lane girls . . .

In Kate's dream, it is 1974, and she is a teenager again, riding her bike at midnight with her best friend beside her in a darkness so complete it is like being invisible. She remembers the place in vivid detail: a meandering ribbon of asphalt bordered on either side by a deep gully of murky water and hillsides of shaggy grass. Before they met, that road seemed to go nowhere at all; it was just a country lane named after an insect no one had ever seen in this rugged blue and green corner of the world. Then they saw it through each other's eyes . . .

Let go, Katie.

She woke with a start, feeling tears on her cheeks. She lay there in her bed, wide awake now, listening to a winter storm rage outside.

Best friends for ever.

That was the promise they'd made all those years ago, and they'd believed it would last, believed that someday they'd be old women together, sitting in their rocking chairs on a creaking deck, talking about the times of their lives, and laughing.

Now she knew better, of course. She'd learned that even their concrete friendship could be blown apart by a single act of betrayal.

For more than a year now she'd been telling herself that it was OK, that she could go on without her best friend. Then she'd hear the music.

292 | Kristin Hannah

Their music. Yesterday, while she'd been shopping, a bad Muzak version of 'You've Got a Friend' had made her cry, right there next to the radishes.

Enough was enough.

She eased back the covers and got out of bed, careful not to waken Johnny. For a moment she stood there, staring down at him in the shadowy darkness. Even in sleep, he wore a troubled expression. If only they could go back in time and undo the past week . . .

She took the phone off its hook and left the bedroom, then walked down the quiet hallway towards the deck. There, she stared out at the storm and gathered her courage. As she punched in the familiar numbers, she wondered what she would say to her once-best friend after all these silent months, how she would start. *I've had a bad week . . . My life is falling apart . . .* Or simply: *I need you.*

Across the black and turbulent Sound, the phone rang. And rang.

When the answering machine clicked on, she tried to marshal her need into something as small and ordinary as words. 'Hey, Tul. It's me. Kate. I can't believe you haven't called to apologise to me—'

She heard a click.

'Tully? Are you listening to this? Tully?'

There was no answer. Just another click.

Kate sighed and went on. 'I need you, Tully. Call me on my cell.'

She went to the window. Slowly, the storm lessened and the world lightened. Seattle looked shiny and new, huddled beneath the rays of the rising sun.

A few hours later, her family began to gather around her. The whole time they were together, having breakfast and packing their things into the car, she found herself glancing at the phone, expecting it to ring.

Six weeks later, when they'd taken both her breasts and poured poison into her blood and irradiated her flesh until it looked raw and burnt, she was still waiting for Tully to call.

On January 2, Tully came home to a cold, dark apartment.

'Story of my life,' she said bitterly, tipping the doorman, who carried her bulky, designer suitcases into the bedroom.

She tossed her bag on the sofa and glanced at the clock, noticing that the red numbers were flashing 5:55. The power must have gone out while she was gone.

She poured herself a glass of wine, got a piece of paper and a pen, then sat down at her desk. The numbers on the answering machine were flashing, too.

'Great.' Now she'd have no idea who had tried to call her after the outage. She hit the replay button and began the slow, arduous task of going through her messages.

She was barely paying attention when Kate's voice roused her.

'Hey, Tul. It's me. Kate.'

Tully sat up sharply. 'Finally.' She hit the rewind button, went back to the beginning and hit play again. Her heart was doing a crazy, breathless little dance in her chest.

'Hey, Tul. It's me. Kate. I can't believe you haven't called to apologise to me.'

Click. Then: 'Tully? Are you listening to this? Tully?' and another click. That was all there was. It was over. There were no more messages on the machine.

Tully felt a disappointment so sharp it made her flinch. She played and replayed the message until all she could hear was the accusation in Kate's voice. That wasn't the Kate she remembered, the girl who'd promised all those years ago to be friends for ever. That girl would never have called to taunt Tully like this, to berate her and then hang up.

'I can't believe you haven't called *me*,' she said to her empty apartment, trying not to notice how thick her voice sounded.

In 2006 *The Girlfriend Hour* rose even higher in the ratings. Week after week, month after month, Tully created magic with her selection of guests and her rapport with the audience. She had definitely reached the top of her game and seized control of the board. No longer did she let herself think about what she didn't have in her life. Just as she'd done at ten and fourteen, she boxed all that negative stuff up and put it in the shadowbox.

She went on. It was what she'd always done in her life when disappointment set in. She squared her shoulders, and set a new goal for herself. This year, she was starting a magazine. Next year, it would be a retreat for women. After that, who knew?

Now, as she sat in her newly decorated office, her intercom buzzed.

'Tallulah? There's a Kate Ryan on line one.'

Tully pushed the intercom button and said, 'Ask her if she's calling to apologise. Because if she's not, I'm not interested in talking to her.'

A moment later, her secretary was back on the line. 'Ms Ryan says she's past that and you should pick up the phone.'

'Tell her to go fuck herself.' Tully wished she could take back the words as soon as she'd said them, but she didn't know how to bend now. In the long months of their estrangement, she'd had to stay angry just to get by. Otherwise the loneliness would have been unbearable.

'Ms Ryan says, and I quote, "Tell that bitch to get her designer-clad ass out of her ridiculously expensive leather chair and come to the phone." She also says that if you ignore her on this of all days she's going public with pictures of you stuffing your bra.'

How could two sentences peel back so many years and blast through the sediment of so many bad choices?

She picked up the phone. 'You're the bitch, and I'm still pissed at you.'

'Of course you are, you narcissist, and I'm not apologising, but that doesn't matter any more.'

'It matters. You should have called long before—'

'I'm in the hospital, Tully. Sacred Heart. Fourth floor,' Kate said. Then she hung up.

Hurry up,' Tully said to her driver for at least the fifth time in as many blocks. When the car pulled up in front of the hospital, she got out and ran for the glass doors. The second she stepped inside, people recognised her and swarmed around her. Usually she factored what she called fan maintenance into her schedule—thirty minutes at every location to meet and greet—but now she didn't have time. She pushed through the crowd and went to the front desk. 'I'm here to see Kathleen Ryan.'

The receptionist stared up at her in awe. 'You're Tallulah Hart.'

'Yes, I am. Kathleen Ryan's room, please.'

The receptionist nodded. 'Oh. Right.' She glanced at her computer screen, entered a few keys, and said, 'Four-ten East.'

'Thanks.' Tully headed for the elevators.

She knew the moment she stepped into the small room that it was bad, this thing with Kate. Johnny sat there, in an ugly blue love seat, with Lucas curled up beside him. With one son's head in his lap, Johnny was reading to the other.

Marah was in the chair beside William, with her eyes closed, listening to an iPod through tiny headphones. She moved to the beat of music only she could hear. The boys were so big; it was a painful reminder of how long Tully had been apart from them.

Beside Marah, Mrs Mularkey sat, staring intently at her knitting. Sean was beside his mother, talking on his cellphone. Aunt Georgia and her husband, Ralph, were watching TV in the corner.

By the looks of it, they'd been here a long time.

It took a huge act of will to step forward. 'Hey, Johnny.'

At the sound of her voice, they looked up. For a moment, no one said anything and Tully remembered the last time they'd all been together.

'Kate called me,' she explained.

Johnny eased out from under his sleeping son and stood up. There was only a beat of awkwardness, a clumsy pause, before he took her in his arms. She could tell by the ferocity of his embrace that it was more to comfort himself than her. She clung to him, trying not to be afraid. 'Tell me,' she said, more harshly than she intended, when he let go of her and stepped back.

He sighed and nodded. 'We'll go into the family room.'

She looked down at Marah, who still had her eyes closed, swaying to the music, and then at the Mularkeys.

Mrs M stood up slowly.

Tully was struck by how much Mrs M had aged. The woman looked frail and a little hunched. She'd stopped dyeing her hair and it was snow-white. 'Katie called you?' Mrs M said.

'I came right away,' she said, as if speed mattered now, after all this time.

Then Mrs M did the most amazing thing: she hugged Tully, enveloped her once again in an embrace that smelt of Jean Naté perfume and menthol cigarettes, with just a hint of hairspray to give it spice.

'Come on,' Johnny said, breaking up the hug. He led both women to a small room.

Johnny and Mrs M sat down. Tully remained standing.

'Kate has cancer,' Johnny said. 'Inflammatory breast cancer.'

Tully had to concentrate on each breath to remain upright. 'She'll have a mastectomy and get radiation and chemotherapy, right?'

'She's already had all of that,' he said gently.

'What? When?'

'She called you several months ago,' he said, and this time his voice had an edge she'd never heard before. 'You didn't return her call.'

'When, exactly?'

'The 1st of December. Not a day we'll forget.'

Tully remembered the message. *I can't believe you haven't called to apologise to me. Tully? Are you listening to this? Tully?'* And the click.

'She didn't say anything about being sick,' Tully said.

'She *called*,' Mrs M said.

Tully felt tackled by guilt, overcome. Her legs threatened to give out. She should have sensed something was wrong. Why hadn't she just picked up the phone? Now all that time had been lost. 'Oh my God . . .'

'None of that matters now,' Mrs M said.

Johnny nodded and went on. 'The cancer has metastasised. Last night she had a minor stroke. They got her into the OR as quickly as possible, but there was nothing they could do.' His voice broke.

Mrs M laid her hand on his. 'The cancer is in her brain.'

Tully thought she had known fear before—like on that Seattle street when she was ten years old, or when Johnny had been hurt in Iraq—but nothing had ever turned her bones to liquid before and made her want to vomit. 'Are you saying . . .?'

'She's dying,' Mrs M said quietly.

'Can I . . . see her?' Tully was trembling so hard the words sounded choppy and broken.

A look passed between Johnny and Mrs M.

Johnny moved closer, said, 'She's fragile right now, Tul. Her faculties have been impacted by the cancer in her brain. She has good moments . . . and not-so-good moments.'

'What are you saying?' Tully asked.

'She might not know who you are.'

Tully tried to gather strength as she walked into Kate's room.

Closing the door, she reached for a smile, found one that was the best she could do under the circumstances, and went to the bed.

Kate lay there, angled up to a near-sit, looking like a broken doll against the stark white sheets and piled pillows. She had no hair or eyebrows left, and her bald head was a pale oval that nearly disappeared against the pillowcase.

'Kate?' Tully said quietly, moving forward.

Kate opened her eyes, and there was the woman Tully knew, the girl she'd sworn to be best friends with for ever.

Put your arms out, Katie. It's like flying.

How had it happened, after all their decades together, that they were estranged now? 'I'm sorry, Katie,' she whispered, hearing how small the words were; all her life she'd hoarded those few and simple words, kept them tucked inside her heart as if to let them out would harm her. Why, of all the lessons she should have learned from her mother, had she held on to this most hurtful one? And why hadn't she called when she heard Kate's voice on the answering machine?

'I'm so sorry,' she said again, feeling the burn of tears.

Kate didn't smile or give any indication of welcome or surprise. Even the apology—as little and late as it was—seemed to have no effect. 'Please say you remember me.'

Kate just stared up at her.

Tully reached down, let her knuckles graze Kate's warm cheek. 'It's Tully, the bitch who used to be your best friend. I'm so sorry for what I did to you, Katie. I should have told you that a long time ago.' She made a tiny, desperate sound. If Kate didn't remember her, remember them, she didn't think she could bear it. 'I remember when I first met you, Katie Mularkey-Ryan. You were the first person who ever really wanted to know me. Naturally I treated you like shit at first, but when I got raped you were there for me.' The memories overtook her. She wiped her eyes. 'You're thinking I'm only talking about me, right? Typical, you say. But I remember you, too, Katie, every second.' Tully shook her head, fighting to keep it together. Her whole life was in the room with them now. 'We were so damned young, Katie. But we're not so young any more. You remember that first time I left Snohomish, and we wrote about a million letters. We signed them *For ever friends . . .* or *Best friends for ever*. Which was it . . .?'

Tully spun out the story of their years. 'Oh, here's one you'll know. Remember when we went to *Pete's Dragon* because we thought it was an action movie, only it was a cartoon? We were the oldest kids in the theatre, and we came out singing "You and Me Against the World", and we said it would always be that way—'

'Stop.'

Tully drew in a sharp breath.

There were tears in her friend's eyes, and more streaking down her cheeks. 'Tully,' Kate said in a soft, swollen voice, 'did you really think I could forget you?'

Tully's relief was so huge she felt weak in the knees. 'Hey,' she said. 'You didn't have to go so far to get my attention, you know.' She touched her friend's bald head. 'You could have just called.'

'I did call.'

Tully flinched. 'I'm so sorry, Katie. I—'

'No looking back, OK?'

'That only leaves ahead,' Tully said, and the words were like bits of broken metal, sharp and cold.

'No,' Kate said. 'It leaves now.'

'I did a show on breast cancer a few months ago. There's a doctor in Ontario doing amazing things with some new drug. I'll call him.'

'I'm done with treatments. Do you think Johnny just gave up on me? You know my husband. He's just like you and we're almost as rich. For six months I saw every specialist on the planet. I did conventional and unconventional and naturopathic remedies. I even went to that faith healer in the rain forest. I have kids; I did everything I could to stay healthy for them. None of it worked.'

'So what do I do?'

Kate's smile was almost like the old days. 'That's my Tul. I'm dying of cancer and you ask about you.' She laughed.

'That's not funny.'

'I don't know how to do this.'

Tully wiped her eyes. The truth of what they were really talking about pressed in on Tully. 'We'll do it like we've done everything else, Kate. Side by side.'

Tully came out of Kate's room, shaken. She made a small sound, a kind of gasp, and covered her mouth with her hand.

'You can't hold it in,' Mrs M said, coming up to her.

'I can't let it out.'

'I know.' Her voice cracked, stumbled. 'Just love her. Be there for her. That's all there is. Believe me, I've cried and argued and bargained with God; I've begged the doctor for hope. All that's past now. She's most worried about the kids. Marah especially. They've had such a rough go of it—well, you know about that—and Marah seems to have shut down for all of this. No tears, no drama. All she does is listen to music.'

They walked back out to the waiting room, only to find everyone gone. Mrs M looked at her watch. 'They're in the cafeteria. You want to join us for dinner?'

'No, thanks. I think I need some fresh air.'

Mrs M nodded. 'It's good to have you back, Tully. I missed you.'

Tully went outside, surprised to find that it was light out here, warm and sunny. It seemed vaguely wrong that the sun was still shining while Kate lay up in that narrow bed, dying. She walked down the street, her breath coming in white puffs. Her body was stiff and cold; she hid her eyes behind huge, dark sunglasses so that no one would recognise her. The last thing she wanted now was to be stopped.

She passed a coffee shop, heard a bit of music waft through the door as someone came out. *Bye, bye, Miss American Pie.*

Her legs gave out on her, and she went down, hard, scraping her knees on the concrete sidewalk, but she scarcely cared she was crying so much. She didn't know how long she knelt there, her head bowed, sobbing, thinking of all their times together. It was a bad part of Capitol Hill, full of homeless people, so no one stopped to help her. Finally, feeling spent and shaky, she climbed back to a standing position and stood there, feeling as if she'd been beaten up.

'Oh, Katie . . .'

She walked dully up one street and down another until something in one of the display windows caught her eye.

There, in a store on the corner, she found what she hadn't even realised she'd been looking for. Spending an obscene amount of money, she had the gift wrapped and ran all the way back to Kate's room.

She was out of breath when she opened the door and went inside.

Kate smiled tiredly. 'Let me guess: you've got a film crew with you.'

'Very funny.' She eased round the curtain and stood by the bed. 'Your mom tells me you're still having trouble with Marah.'

'It's not your fault. She's scared of all this and she doesn't know how easy it is to say you're sorry.'

'I didn't.'

'You always were her role model.' Kate closed her eyes. 'I'm tired.'

'I have a present for you.'

Kate opened her eyes. 'What I need can't be bought.'

Tully tried not to react to that. Instead, she handed Kate the beautifully wrapped gift and helped her open it.

Inside was a hand-tooled, leather-bound journal. On the first page, Tully had written: *Katie's story*.

Kate stared down at the blank page for a long time, saying nothing.

'I always wanted to write,' she finally said.

Tully touched her friend's wrist, feeling how fragile and thin it was. 'For Marah,' she said quietly. 'And the boys. Someday they'll be old enough to read it. They'll want to know who you were.'

'How do I know what to write?'

Tully had no real answer for that. 'Just write what you remember.'

Kate closed her eyes, as if the thought alone were too much to bear. 'Thanks, Tully.'

'I won't leave you again, Katie.'

Kate didn't open her eyes, but she smiled just a little. 'I know.'

Kate didn't remember falling asleep. One minute she was talking to Tully and the next she was waking up in a dark room that smelt of fresh flowers and disinfectant.

She didn't want to be here. She wanted to be at home, in her own bed, in her husband's arms rather than looking at him from across the room, watching him sleep in the hospital bed beside her.

She sighed and rubbed her eyes. Leaning sideways, she turned on the bedside lamp. Johnny, who'd grown used to her weird sleeping schedule, rolled onto his side and murmured, 'You OK, baby?'

'I'm fine. Keep sleeping.'

Mumbling something, he rolled back over. In no time, she heard his quiet snore.

Kate reached over for the journal Tully had bought her. Holding it, she traced the leather etchings and the gold-edged sheets of paper.

It would hurt to do this, of that she had no doubt. To pick up a pen and write down her life, she'd have to remember it all, who she was, who she'd wanted to be. Those memories would be painful, both the good and the bad would wound her.

But her children would see through the illness to *her*, the woman they would always remember, but never truly have time to know. Tully was right. The only gift Kate could give them now was who she was.

She flipped the journal open. Because she had no clear idea of where to start, she simply began to write:

Panic always comes to me in the same way. First, I get a knot in the pit of my stomach that turns to nausea, then a fluttery breathlessness that no amount of deep breathing can cure. But what causes my fear is different every day; I never know what will set me off. It could be a kiss from my husband, or the lingering look of sadness in his eyes when he draws back. Sometimes I know he's already grieving for me, missing me even while I'm still here. Worse yet is Marah's quiet acceptance of everything I say. I would give anything for another of our old knock-down drag-out fights. That's one of the first things I'd say to you now, Marah: those fights were real life. You were struggling to break free of being my daughter but unsure of how to be yourself, while I was afraid to let you go. It's the circle of love. I only wish I'd recognised it then. Your grandmother told me I'd know you were sorry for those years before you did, and she was right. I know you regret some of the things you said to me, as I regret my own words. None of that matters, though. I want you to know that. I love you and I know you love me.

But these are just more words, aren't they? I want to go deeper than that. So, if you'll bear with me, I have a story to tell you. It's my story, and yours, too. It starts in 1960 in a small farming town up north, in a clapboard house on a hill above a horse pasture. When it gets good, though, is 1974, when the coolest girl in the world moved in to the house across the street . . .

Even with self-regulated pain meds, Kate found leaving the hospital a difficult endeavour. First of all, there was the crowd: her parents, her kids and husband, her aunt and uncle, her brother and Tully, who had cancelled *The Girlfriend Hour* indefinitely to be with Kate. Secondly, there was just so much movement—out of bed, into the wheelchair, out of the wheelchair, into the car, out of the car, into Johnny's arms.

He carried her through the comfortable, pretty island house that smelt of scented candles and last night's dinner, just as it always had. He'd made spaghetti last night; she could tell. That meant tomorrow night it would be tacos. His two recipes.

What will he cook for them when I'm gone?

The question made her draw in a sharp breath, which she forced herself to release slowly. Being home would hurt like this sometimes—so would being with her family. In a strange way, it would have been easier to spend her final days at the hospital, without all these reminders around her. But easier wasn't the point any more. Time with her family was what mattered.

Now, they were all in the house, scattering like soldiers to their different tasks. Marah had herded the boys into their room to watch television. Mom was busy making casseroles; Dad was probably mowing the lawn. That left Johnny, Tully and Kate, making their way towards the guest room, which had been adapted for her homecoming.

Johnny carried Kate to her bed and tucked her in. 'The bathroom down here is all set up for you. Everything has been installed—railings and a shower seat and all the stuff they recommended. A hospice nurse will be coming by . . .'

She wasn't sure when she closed her eyes. All she knew was that she was sleeping. Somewhere a radio was playing 'Sweet Dreams (Are Made of This)' and she could hear people talking in the distance.

She awoke with a start. The room around her was dark now; she'd slept through the remaining daylight hours, obviously. Beside her, a eucalyptus-scented candle burned. The darkness lulled her for a moment, made her think she was alone.

Across the room, a shadow moved. Someone breathed.

Kate hit the button on her bed and moved to a sit. 'Hey,' she said. 'Hey, Mom.'

She grew accustomed to the darkness and saw her daughter, sitting in a chair in the corner. Although Marah looked tired, she was so beautiful that Kate felt a cinching in her chest. When she looked at her teenage daughter, she glimpsed the whole arc of life—the child she'd been, the girl she was, the woman she'd become.

'Hey, baby girl.' She smiled and leaned sideways to turn on the bedside lamp. 'But you aren't my baby any more, are you?'

Marah stood up and moved forward, twisting her hands together. For all her grown-up beauty, the fear in her eyes made her look ten years old again.

Kate tried to figure out what she should say. From now on the words they said to each other would be weighted, remembered. That was a simple fact of life. Or of death.

'I've been mean to you,' Marah said.

Kate had waited years for this moment, actually dreamt of it in the days when she and Marah had been at war; now she saw it from a distance and knew that those battles were just ordinary life—a girl trying to grow up and a mother trying to hang on.

'I was a bitch to Grandma, too. That's what teen girls do: rag on their mothers. And your aunt Tully was a bitch to everyone.'

Marah made a sound that was half snort, half laughter and pure relief. 'I won't tell her you said that.'

'Believe me, honey, it will come as no surprise to her. And I want you to know something: I'm proud of your big personality and spirit. It will take you far in this life.' On those last words, she saw her daughter's eyes fill with tears. Kate opened her arms and Marah leaned down to her, pulling her into a fierce embrace.

Kate could have held on for ever, that was how good it felt. When Marah drew back she was crying. 'Remember when you used to dance with me?'

'When you were really little, I'd hold on and twirl you round until you giggled. Once I did it so long you threw up all over me.'

'We shouldn't have stopped,' Marah said. 'I shouldn't have, I mean.'

'None of that,' Kate said. 'Put down the bedrail and sit by me.'

Marah struggled with the rail, but finally got it down. She climbed into the bed and pulled her knees up.

'How's James?' Kate asked.

'I'm into Tyler now.'

'Did you apply for a summer job at the theatre?'

'I'm not gonna work this summer. I'll be home.'

'You can't put your life on hold, honey. That's not how this is going to work. You said a summer job would help you get into the University of Southern California.'

Marah shrugged. 'I decided to go to the UW, like you and Aunt Tully.'

'But the USC drama school is the best around,' said Kate.

'I don't want to talk about college,' Marah said, and Kate let it go.

For the next hour, they just talked. Not about It, the big thing on the horizon and how it would change them all. Instead they talked about boys and writing and the movies that were out.

'I got the lead in the summer play,' Marah said after a while. 'I wasn't going to try out because you were sick, but Daddy said I should.'

'I'm glad you did. I know you'll be amazing.'

Marah launched into a long monologue about the play, the costumes and her part. 'I can't wait for you to see it.'

The sentence hung in the air between them. Marah's eyes widened in realisation of what she'd said, the subject she'd unintentionally broached. She slid off the bed, looking almost desperate. 'I'm sorry.'

Kate reached up and touched her cheek. 'It's OK. I'll be there.'

Marah stared down at her. They both knew it could end up being a broken promise. 'Remember when I was in middle school and Ashley stopped being my friend and I didn't know why?'

'Of course.'

'You took me out to lunch and it was like we were friends.'

Kate swallowed hard, tasting the bitterness of tears in the back of her throat. 'We've always been friends, Marah. Even when we didn't know it.'

'I love you, Mom.'

'I love you, too.'

Marah wiped her eyes and bolted out of the room, closing the door quietly behind her.

It opened a moment later, so fast Kate barely had time to wipe her eyes before she heard Tully say, 'I've got a plan.'

Kate laughed, grateful to be reminded that life could still be funny and surprising, even now. 'You always do.'

'Will you trust me?'

'To my everlasting ruination, yes.'

Tully helped Kate into the wheelchair and wrapped her in blankets. 'Are we going to the North Pole?'

'We're going outside,' Tully answered, opening the French doors that led out to the deck. 'Are you warm enough?'

'I'm sweating. Grab that pouch off the nightstand, will you?' Tully dropped it in Kate's lap and then took control of the wheelchair.

The yard on this cool, early June night was stunningly, unexpectedly beautiful. Stars blanketed the sky and cast pinpricks of light onto the jet-black Sound. A full moon hung poised above the glittering distant city lights. The grassy lawn rolled down toward the water.

Tully manoeuvred her off the deck, down a wide wooden ramp that was a very new addition; then she paused. 'Close your eyes.'

'It's dark out, Tully. I hardly need—'

'Close your eyes and put your arms out, like an airplane's wings.'

Kate closed her eyes and extended her arms.

'We're kids again,' she whispered into Kate's ear. 'It's the Seventies and we've just sneaked out of your house and got our bikes.' She began to push the chair forward; it went slowly, bumping over the uneven grass, and still Tully talked. 'We're on Summer Hill, riding without our hands, laughing like crazy people, thinking we're invincible.'

Kate felt the breeze along her bare head, tugging at her ears, making her eyes water. She could smell the evergreen trees and rich, black earth. She put her head back and laughed. For a moment, just a heartbeat really, she was a kid again, on Firefly Lane with her best friend beside her, believing she could fly.

When the ride was over, and they were on the beach, she opened her eyes and looked up at Tully. In that moment, that one poignant smile, she remembered everything about them. The starlight looked like fireflies, falling down around them.

Tully helped her into one of the beach chairs, and then sat down beside her. They sat side by side, as they'd done so often in the past, talking about nothing that mattered, this and that.

Kate glanced back at the house, saw that no one was on the deck, and leaned towards Tully. 'Do you really want to feel like a kid again?'

'No, thanks. I wouldn't change places with Marah for the world. All that angst and drama.'

'Yeah, you're a real drama-free zone.' Grinning at her own wit, Kate dug into the purple pouch on her lap and pulled out a fat, white doobie. At Tully's awestruck expression, Kate laughed and lit up. 'I have a prescription.'

The sweet, strangely old-fashioned scent of marijuana mingled with the sea air. A cloud of smoke darted between them and disappeared.

They passed it back and forth and kept talking, giggling. They were so caught up in *then* that neither of them heard footsteps coming up behind them.

'I turn my back on you girls for ten minutes and you're smoking pot.' Mrs Mularkey stood there, dressed in faded jeans and a sweatshirt. 'You know that leads to worse things, don't you? Like crack or LSD.'

Tully tried not to laugh; she really did. 'Just say no to crack.'

'That's a lesson I tried to teach Marah in choosing her jeans,' Kate said, giggling. Mrs M pulled up another Adirondack chair and positioned it beside Kate. Then she sat down and angled towards her.

'Well?' Mrs M said. 'I taught you to share, didn't I?'

'Mom!'

Mrs M waved her hand. 'You girls from the Seventies think you're so cool. Let me tell you, I was around for the Sixties, and you've got nothing on me.' She took the joint and put it in her mouth, taking a long, deep drag, holding it, and blowing it out. 'Hell, Katie, how do you think I got through the teen years when my two girls were sneaking out of the house at night and riding their bikes in the dark?'

'You knew about that?' Tully said.

Kate laughed. 'I thought it was booze that got you through.'

'Oh,' Mrs M said. 'That, too.'

As the weeks passed, Kate felt herself weakening. Despite her best efforts and her purposely optimistic attitude, her body began to fail in a dozen little ways. A sentence she couldn't finish, a weakness in her fingers, a nausea that all too often became unbearable.

And then there was the pain. By late July, when the nights began to grow longer, she had nearly doubled her morphine dosage and no one cared. As her doctor said, 'Addiction isn't your problem now.'

Tully had taken over Kate's daytime routine as best she could, which left Kate time to work on her journal. Sometimes, lately, she worried that she wouldn't have time to finish it, and the thought scared her.

The funny thing was that dying didn't. Not so much any more. Oh, she still had panic attacks when she thought about The End, but even those were becoming less frequent. More and more often, she just thought, *Let me rest.* She couldn't say that, though. Even to Tully, who'd listen to her for hours and hours. Whenever Kate brought up the future, Tully flinched and made a smartass comment.

Dying was a lonely business.

'Mom?' Marah said quietly, pushing the door open.

Kate forced herself to smile. 'Hi, honey. I thought you were going over to Lytle Beach today with the gang.'

'I was going to.'

'What changed your mind?'

Marah stepped forward. 'I need to do something.'

'OK. What is it?'

Marah turned round, looked down the hall, then back to Kate. 'Could you come into the living room?'

'Of course.' Kate put on her robe, mittens and knitted cap. Fighting nausea and exhaustion, she got slowly out of bed.

Marah took her by the arm and steadied her, becoming for a moment the mother; she led her into the living room, where, despite the heat of the day, a fire burned in the fireplace. Lucas and William, still in their jammies, sat together on the couch.

'Hi, Mommy,' they said at once, flashing their gap-toothed grins.

Marah positioned Kate next to the boys, tucked her robe round her legs, and then sat down on the other side of her.

'A long time ago,' she said in an unsteady voice, 'you gave me a special book.'

A frown pulled at Kate's brow. 'I gave you lots of books.'

'You told me that someday I'd be sad and confused and I'd need it.'

Kate wanted to pull away suddenly, distance herself, but she was held in place by her children. 'Yes,' was all she could find to say.

'For the last few weeks, I've tried to read it and I couldn't.'

'It's OK—'

'And I figured out why. We all need it.' She reached over to the end table and picked up the paperback copy of *The Hobbit* Kate had given her. It felt like a lifetime ago now, and an instant.

'Yippee!' William said. 'Marah's gonna read to us.'

Lucas elbowed his brother. 'Shut up.'

Kate put an arm round her sons and stared at her daughter's earnest, beautiful face. 'OK.'

Marah settled in close to Kate and opened the book. Her voice was only a little wobbly at the start, but as the story took hold, she found her strength again. 'In a hole in the ground, there lived a hobbit . . .'

August ended too quickly and melted into a lazy September. Her journal was almost finished now. She'd written it all down, or as much as she could remember, and it had helped her as much as she'd hoped it would someday help her kids.

She opened to the page where she'd left off and began to write.

> *That's the funny thing about writing your life story. You try to remember dates and times and names. You think it's about facts, your life; that what you'll look back on and remember are the successes and failures, the time-line of your youth and middle age, but that isn't it at all.*
>
> *Love. Family. Laughter. That's what I remember when it's all said and done. I want my children to know how proud I am of them, and how proud I am of me. We were everything we needed—you and Daddy and me. I had everything I ever wanted.*
>
> *Love.*
>
> *That's what we remember.*

She closed the journal. There was nothing more to say.

Tully came home from the grocery store feeling triumphant. She put the bags on the counter, emptied them one by one, then opened a can of beer and went outside to join Kate.

'That grocery story is a jungle. I guess I went down the up lane, or in the out lane, I don't know. You'd have thought I was Public Enemy Number One. I never heard so much honking.'

'We at-home moms don't have long to shop.'

'I don't know how you did it. I'm exhausted by ten o'clock.'

Kate laughed. 'Sit.' She handed Tully her journal. 'You get this. First.'

Tully drew in a sharp breath. For all of the summer, she'd seen Kate writing on these pages, at first quickly and easily, and gradually, more slowly. In the last few weeks, everything had been slow going for her.

This was going to hurt.

She sat down—slumped, actually—unable to say anything past the lump in her throat. She knew it would make her cry, but it would make her soar, too. Reaching out, she held Kate's hand and then opened the journal to the first page.

A sentence jumped out at her.

The first time I saw Tully Hart, I thought, Wow! Look at those boobs.

Tully laughed and kept reading.

We're sneaking out?

Of course. Get your bike.

And: *I'll just shave your eyebrows to give them shape . . . Oops . . . Your hair is coming out . . . Maybe I should read the directions again . . .*

Laughing, Tully turned to her. These words, these memories had, for a glorious moment, made everything normal. 'How could you be friends with me?'

Kate smiled back. 'How could I not?'

Tully felt like an impostor as she slipped into Kate and Johnny's bed. She knew it made sense, her being in this room, but on this night it felt more wrong than usual. Reading the journal had reminded Tully of everything she had with Kate; everything they were losing.

Finally, sometime after three, she fell into a fitful sleep. She dreamt of Firefly Lane, of two girls riding their bikes down Summer Hill at night. The wind smelt of freshly cut hay and the stars were bright.

Look, Katie, no hands.

But Kate wasn't there. Her empty bike clattered down the road.

Tully sat up, breathing hard.

Downstairs, she made a cup of tea and went outside, where the cool, dark air allowed her to breathe again.

'Bad dreams?'

Johnny's voice startled her. He was in one of the Adirondack chairs, looking back at her. In his eyes she saw the same sadness that filled every pore of her skin and cell of her body.

'Hey,' she said, sitting in the chair beside him.

A cool breeze came off the Sound, whistling eerily above the familiar whooshing of the waves.

'I don't know how to do this,' he said quietly.

'That's the same thing Katie said to me,' she said, and just that made her realise how similar they were. 'It's quite a love story you two have.'

He turned to her, and in the pale moonlight, she saw the tense line of his jaw, the tightening round his eyes.

'You don't have to do it with me, you know,' she said quietly.

'Do what?'

'Be strong.'

The words seemed to release something in him. He crumpled forward, saying nothing; silently his shoulders shook.

She reached out and took his hand, held it tightly while he cried.

'For twenty years, every time I turn round, you two are together.'

Tully and Johnny both turned.

Kate stood in the open doorway behind them, bundled up in a huge terry-cloth robe. Bald and impossibly thin, she looked like a child playing dress-up in her mother's clothes. She'd said things like this to both of them before; they all knew it, but this time she was smiling. She looked somehow both sad and peaceful.

'Katie,' Johnny said, his voice raw, his eyes shining. 'Don't . . .'

'I love you both,' she said, not moving towards them. 'You'll comfort each other . . . take care of each other and the kids . . . after I'm gone—'

'Don't,' Tully said, starting to cry.

Johnny was on his feet. He gently picked his wife up and kissed her for a long, long time.

'Take her up to your bed, Johnny,' Tully said, trying to smile now. 'I'll sleep in the guest room.'

Johnny carried her upstairs with so much care. He put her on her side of the bed. 'Turn on the fire.'

'Are you cold?'

To the bone. She nodded and tried to gingerly sit up as he crossed the room and flicked the switch for the gas fireplace. With a *whoosh*, blue and orange flames shot up from the fake log, tinting the dark room with a soft golden light.

When he came back and settled in beside her, she reached up slowly, traced the outline of his lips with the tip of her finger. 'You first ravished me on the floor in front of a fire, remember?'

He smiled. 'If I remember correctly, you were doing the ravishing.'

'And what if I wanted to ravish you now?'

'Can we?'

Slowly, Kate took off her robe and peeled out of her nightgown, trying not to notice how white and stick-like her legs were. Even worse was the battlefield that had been her breasts.

Johnny stripped out of his clothes, kicked them aside, and climbed back into bed beside her, drawing the covers up to their hips.

Her heart was thumping hard as she looked at him.

'You're so beautiful,' he said, and leaned forward to kiss her scars.

Relief and love cracked her open inside. She kissed him, her breath coming hard and ragged already. In their twenty-some years of marriage they'd made love thousands of times, and it was always great, but this was different; they had to be so gentle. She knew he was terrified of breaking her bones. She hardly remembered later how it had all happened; all she knew was that she needed every part of him, and everything that she was, that she'd ever been, was irrevocably tied up with this man. When he finally entered her, slow and easy, filling her, she came to meet him, and in that glorious second, she was whole again. She bent down and kissed him, tasting his tears.

Finally, smiling, she snuggled up against him. He put an arm round her and pulled her close. They lay there a long time, half sitting against the mound of pillows, watching the firelight, saying nothing.

Then, quietly, Kate said what had been on her mind for a long time. 'I can't stand to think of you alone.'

'I won't ever be alone. We've got three kids.'

'You know what I mean. I'd understand if you and Tully—'

'Don't.' He looked at her. 'It was always you. Just you, Katie. Tully was a one-night stand, twenty years ago. I didn't love her then and I never have. You're my heart and soul. How can you not know that?'

She saw the truth in his face, heard it in the tremble in his voice, and she was ashamed of herself. She should have known this all along.

The day of Marah's performance dawned crisp and clear. They were so early when they arrived at the auditorium that no other cars were yet in the parking lot.

Inside, they took up most of the first row, saving places for the rest of the family; Kate's wheelchair was positioned on the end of the aisle.

'I'll be back in thirty minutes with your folks and the boys,' Johnny said to Kate.

When he was gone, she and Tully sat in the shadows of the empty auditorium. Kate shivered and tightened the blankets round her. Her head was pounding and she felt sick to her stomach. Leaning back in her seat, she said quietly, 'Do you still know the guy who runs the drama programme at USC?'

'I do.' Tully looked at her. 'Why?'

'Maybe you could call him. I know that Marah would love to go there.' With the words came the thought *I won't be there for her*. For any of it. Marah would go off to college without her . . .

'I thought you didn't want her to be in the arts.'

'It scares the hell out of me to think of my baby in Hollywood. But you're a TV star. Her dad's a news producer. The poor kid is surrounded by dreamers. What chance did she ever have?' She reached over, squeezed Tully's hand. 'You'll watch out for her and the boys, right?'

'Always.'

Kate felt the start of a smile; that one word released a little of her sadness. One thing about Tully: she kept her word. 'And maybe you'll look up Cloud again.'

'It's funny you mention that. I was planning on it. Someday.'

'Good,' Kate said softly but firmly. 'I was wrong about that. When you get . . . to the end, you see that love and family are all there is. Nothing else matters.'

'You're my family, Katie.'

'I know. You'll need more after—'

'Please don't say it.'

Kate looked at her friend. Bold, brassy, larger-than-life Tully, who'd barrelled through the years like a lion in a jungle, always the king. Now, she was quiet, afraid. The very idea of Kate's death had unravelled her, made her smaller. 'I'm going to die, Tully. Not saying it won't change it.'

'I know.'

'Here's what I want you to know: I loved my life. For so long I was waiting for it to start, waiting for *more*. It seemed like all I did was drive and shop and wait. But you know what? I didn't miss a thing with my family. Not a moment. I was there for all of it. That's what I'll remember, and they'll have each other.'

'Yes.'

'I'm worried about you, though,' Kate said.

'You would be.'

'You're afraid of love, but you've got so much of it to give.'

'I know I've spent a lot of years whining about being alone, and I've had a history of hooking up with inappropriate or unavailable men, but the truth is, my career has been my love, and mostly it's been enough. I've been happy. It's important to me that you know that.'

Kate gave her a tired smile. 'I'm proud of you, you know. Have I told you that often enough?'

'And I'm proud of you.' Tully looked at her best friend, and in that one look, thirty years crowded in between them, reminded them both of the girls they'd been and the dreams they'd shared, and of the women they'd become. 'We've done all right, haven't we?'

Before Kate could answer, the auditorium doors banged open and people streamed in.

Johnny, Mom, Dad and the boys took their seats just as the house lights flickered.

Then the stage lights came on, the heavy red velvet curtains parted slowly, revealing the poorly painted set of a small town.

Marah walked onstage, dressed in a high-school-drama version of a nineteenth-century gown.

When Marah began to speak, it was magic.

Kate felt Tully's hand close over hers, squeeze gently. When Marah walked offstage, to a standing ovation, Kate's heart swelled with pride. She leaned against Tully and whispered, 'Now I know why I gave her your middle name.'

Tully turned to her. 'Why?'

Kate tried to smile, but couldn't. It took almost a full minute before she could find enough voice to say, 'Because she's the best of both of us.'

The end came on a bleak and rainy October night. With everyone she loved standing round her bed, Kate said goodbye to them one by one, whispering one last special thing to each of them. Then, as rain hit the window and darkness fell, she closed her eyes for the last time.

Kate's last To Do list concerned her funeral and Tully followed it to the letter. The Catholic church on the island was filled with photographs and flowers and friends. Not surprisingly, Kate had chosen Tully's favourite flowers rather than her own.

For days Tully focused on nothing else. She handled the details and took care of everything while the Ryans and the Mularkeys sat together on the beach, holding hands and occasionally remembering to talk.

Tully prepared herself for the day, as well, reminding herself that she was a professional; she could smile her way through anything.

But when the time came, and they actually pulled up in front of the church, she panicked. 'I can't do this,' she said.

Johnny reached for her hand. She waited for comforting words, but he had none. While they sat there, in silence, with the kids in the back seat, all of them staring at the church, the Mularkeys pulled up beside them and parked.

It was time. Like a flock of black crows, they came together, hoping for strength in numbers. Holding hands, they walked past the throng of mourners and up the massive stone church steps.

'We're in the left front row,' Mrs M said, sidling close.

Tully looked down at Marah, who was crying quietly, and the sight broke her. She wanted to comfort her goddaughter, tell her it would be

OK, but they both knew better than that. 'She loved you so much,' she said, getting a strange and sudden glimpse of their future then. In time, Tully would give her the journal and they'd share the stories of who her mother had been, and those stories would bind them together and bring Kate back for a few precious moments.

'Come on,' Johnny said.

Tully couldn't move. 'You guys go up. I'm just going to stand here for a minute.'

Johnny squeezed her shoulder and then ushered the boys and Marah forward. Mr and Mrs M, Sean, Georgia, Ralph and the rest of the family followed; they all ducked into the front row and sat down.

Up front an organ began to play a slow, plodding version of 'You and Me Against the World'.

Tully didn't want to be here. She didn't want to listen to pathetic music that was designed to make you cry, or listen to the priest tell stories about the woman he'd known, who was only a shadow of the woman Tully knew. Before she could even think about it, she turned and walked out.

Sweet, fresh air filled her lungs. She gulped it greedily, trying to calm down. She closed her eyes, leaning back against the door.

'Ms Hart?'

Startled, she opened her eyes and saw the funeral director standing on the bottom step. 'Yes.'

'Mrs Ryan asked me to give you this.' He held out a big black box.

'I don't understand.'

'She entrusted me with this box and asked me to give it to you on the day of her funeral. She said you'd be standing out front when it started.'

Tully smiled at that, even though it hurt like hell. Of course Kate would know. 'Thanks.'

She took the box and walked down the steps and across the parking lot. Across the street, she sat down on an iron park bench.

There, she took a deep breath and opened the box. On top lay a letter. Kate's bold, left-slanted handwriting was unmistakable.

Dear Tully,

I know you won't be able to stand my funeral. There are so many things I should say to you, but in our lifetime we've said them all.

Take care of Johnny and the kids for me, OK? Teach the boys how to be gentlemen and Marah how to be strong. When they're ready, give them my journal and tell them about me when they ask. The truth, too. I want them to know it all.

It's going to be hard on you, now. That's one of the things I regret the most. So, here's what I have to say in my beyond-the-grave letter (very dramatic, don't you think?): I know you'll be thinking that I left you, but it's not true. All you have to do is remember Firefly Lane and you'll find me.

There will always be a TullyandKate.
Best friends for ever.
Kate

She pressed the letter to her chest.

Then she looked down in the box again. There were three things left.

A Virginia Slims cigarette with a yellow sticky note on it that read: *Smoke me*; an autographed picture of David Cassidy that said: *Kiss me*; and an iPod with headphones that said: *Play me and dance.*

Tully laughed through her tears and lit up the cigarette. The smell of smoke immediately made her think of their nights on the banks of the Pilchuck River, lying against fallen logs, staring up at the Milky Way.

She closed her eyes, put her head back, and tilted her face to the cool autumn sun. A breeze touched her face and tangled in her hair, and with it, she thought, *Katie.*

Suddenly she felt her friend beside her, above her, all around her, inside her. She heard Kate in the whispering of the wind overhead and the skudding of the golden leaves across the pavement.

She opened her eyes, gasping at the certainty that she wasn't alone.

'Hey, Katie,' she whispered, then put on the headphones and hit play.

'Dancing Queen' blared out at her, sweeping her back in time.

Young and sweet, only seventeen

She stood up, unsure of whether she was laughing or crying. All she really knew was that she wasn't alone, that Kate wasn't gone. They'd had three decades of good times and bad times and everything in between, and nothing could take that away. They had the music and the memories, and in those, they would always, always be together.

Best friends for ever.

There, standing in the middle of the street, all by herself, she started to dance.

Kristin Hannah

How long have you been writing?

I'm always a little bit surprised by my answer to this question: it's twenty-one years. Honestly, I don't know how that's possible, being as young as I am! That's certainly the upside of a career you love. Time flies.

How did you get started?

I was not one of those people who always wanted to be a writer. It all started when I was in my third year of law school. My mother had been diagnosed with breast cancer and was beginning to lose the fight. She was hospitalised in Seattle, so my daily routine became one of spending the day at school and the evening at her bedside. As anyone who's been through this sort of experience will know, there are many things you don't want to talk about. We spent a lot of time looking for happy thoughts. It just so happened that what my mom wanted to discuss were her beloved romance novels. 'You know,' she said to me at one point, 'you're going to be a writer.' Somehow, after that we decided to write a book together. It wasn't until much, much later that I realised the gift she'd given me: a dream.

A few years down the line, after she'd gone, I found myself in the middle of a difficult pregnancy. Bedridden for five months, I spent a lot of time reading and watching game shows. When I started to care who won *The Price Is Right*, I knew I was in trouble. That's when my wonderful hubby poked his head into my room and said, 'What about that novel you and Sharon started? This would be a great time to finish it.' There it was: the dream my mom had left me. I booted up a computer, pulled a keyboard onto my lap and started writing.

Did you find writing *Firefly Lane* a nostalgic trip down memory lane?

Oh, yes. This novel hits close to home on a lot of levels, so there are plenty of correlations to my own life. First and foremost—the clothes. Yes, I remember wearing them all: elephant-leg bell-bottoms, tie-dyed T-shirts, Earth shoes, shoulder pads, stirrup pants, leg warmers, and last but not least, polyester. And how about those hairstyles? Each one named after, and forever immortalised, by the celebrity who made it famous: Farrah Fawcett, Linda Evans and Rachel from *Friends*.

Your novels are very emotional. Do they make you cry when you're writing?

I get asked this question a lot. I think people imagine me sitting at my computer, sobbing—very much like Joan Wilder in *Romancing the Stone*. The truth is that I don't cry when I write. I'm too focused on the trees to see the forest, if you know what I mean. And I don't set out to write 'sad' usually. It just ends up that way.

Do you have a best friend, like Tully and Kate? Or do you have a number of close girlfriends?

I have a number of close girlfriends that have been 'in the circle' for years. I don't know how I'd get along without them. Especially during the raising teen years!

Mothers who have been through—or are currently going through—the teenage years will be caught up in the battles between Kate and her daughter, Marah. How did you cope with these years?

Like most mothers, I was consumed by them. Every moment, every battle, every disagreement seemed to pierce my heart. I was always so desperate to do the right thing, make the best decision, etc. I realise now, with the benefit of hindsight, that those battles were the stuff of life. I wish I had been able to see it all from a little more distance, to understand that it wouldn't last. That's the message I was able to bring to *Firefly Lane*. When all that craziness is going on, we think our children aren't listening to us, but they are. They hear everything, and once they get out into the world, they remember.

Do you think women still have to justify wanting to be stay-at-home mothers, as Kate does in the novel?

I don't know how it is for the women who are having children right now, but I know that when I was in my late twenties—with my law degree—I heard from a number of people that I was 'wasting my education' when I decided to be an at-home mom. There was a great deal of pressure on my generation to take over the world, become the CEO or whatever. I think a lot of people were surprised when many of us said, 'sure we can do anything, be anything . . . and what we want right now is to be great mothers.' I still believe that nothing I've done or will do is more important. Or more difficult.

If you had to pick one song from those you mention in the novel, which would it be?

Most evocative: 'Bohemian Rhapsody'. Most memorable: 'Goodbye Yellow Brick Road'. Favourite: anything by The Boss (Bruce Springsteen).

Visit Kristin Hannah's website and blog at www.kristinhannah.com

What would you do if you found out that your gorgeous fiancé was playing away from home with a shapely, long-legged, shiny-haired glamour girl?

Would you:

a) Start going to the gym every day?

b) Change your hairstyle?

c) Buy a whole new wardrobe?

d) Try playing him at his own game?

Chapter 1

MAKING A CAKE for Danny's school raffle was always going to be a messy business, given Stevie's predilection for taste-testing the gloopy, raw mixture at one-minute intervals. Not to mention her impatience in waiting for the blades to stop whisking before she lifted them, which resulted in her splattering herself and the kitchen with chocolate cream. Then, as usual, the bag of flour split and sent up a white cloud to descend over all surfaces. She must get a proper flour container, she said to herself for the six-hundredth time, knowing that she never would.

She put the cake to rise in the oven, and was in the process of licking out the bowl and the big spoon when the doorbell rang. No need to clean up, Stevie decided: it could only be her friend Catherine bringing Danny home after a post-school romp with her mob and the family mongrels. So she answered the door with enough flour and cocoa on her face to pass an audition for the part of main slapstick stooge in a panto.

The trouble was that it wasn't Catherine. It was a rough-looking man, approximately the size of Edinburgh Castle, with an auburn ponytail, a wild red beard, a scar on his left cheek and tattooed arms, which he used to push gently past Stevie in order to barge into her front room.

'Whurrrissseee?' came a broad Scottish burr.

'Excuse me, do you mind!' said Stevie, torn between calling the police and reaching for some wet wipes. Tough decision but the wet wipes won on embarrassment points.

'Whurrr's Finch?'

'Who the hell are you?'

'Adam MacLean, Joanna MacLean's man.'

So this was the mythical creature Stevie had heard so much about. This intruder was *him*. And there she was, thinking Jo had been exaggerating when describing the control freak she was married to. No wonder Matthew was so sympathetic to her at work. Well, Stevie wasn't going to be scared of him and cower in her own home waiting for him to stick his whisky-fuelled boot in, like Jo did.

In the same second, Adam MacLean had affirmed that this woman was the greedy, lazy, rarely sober, slob *thing* that Jo had reported her to be. That's why the kitchen resembled Beirut on a bad day and why she looked as if she had been hit by a chocolate bomb. On a binge, most likely. That's what these women who sat at home did all day—ate cakes, drank sherry and watched *Trisha*. And read all those Midnight Moon crappy romance books that seemed littered round the room, he noted. No wonder Jo had been so sympathetic to the poor bloke at work, about to be married to *that*.

Stevie pulled herself up to her full height of five foot two.

'Matthew is on business in Aberdeen.'

'I think you'll find,' said Adam, 'he's in Magalluf with Jo.'

'Don't be ridiculous!' said Stevie. Matthew had said that the Scot was a possessive, unhinged psycho with the part of his head empty that should have had a brain in it, but she hadn't realised to what degree.

'I thought you might say tha',' said Adam, reaching in his pocket to bring out a piece of paper, which he stuck under Stevie's nose. She unfolded it impatiently and looked at a confirmation letter of bookings, flight numbers, and today's date: *Sunshine Holidays, Hotel Flora, Magalluf, Mr Matthew Finch and Ms Joanna MacLean, April 25 for 7 days.* It had their address in the top corner: 15 Blossom Lane, Dodmoor. She would have slumped into a chair had the doorbell not rung again.

'Excuse me, it's my son,' said Stevie in a half-daze. She opened the door to find her best friend there, holding the hand of Stevie's small, bespectacled son. The half-daze expanded into a full daze as she noticed that Catherine's normally auburn hair was now bright pink.

Adam, seeing the guest on the doorstep, was unsurprised. He noticed the cheap hair. That she had friends who went out looking like that confirmed his low opinion of the woman in whose house he was standing. And the boy was too old to be Finch's if they had only been together a couple of years. Boy, she sure got around, didn't she?

Catherine looked at her friend's pale and chocolate-splodged face, then spotted the man beyond her. 'Are you all right?'

'No, not really,' said Stevie. 'Just got . . . something . . . to do.'

Catherine bobbed down to the fair-haired boy. 'Danny, let's go for a bun and some orange juice to the café round the corner. Mummy's just sorting something out.'

'Cool!' said Danny with a face-splitting grin.

Catherine then turned to Stevie. 'Go on, it's fine. I'll see you in a bit.'

'Thanks, Cath,' said Stevie, gulping back a big ball of emotion.

As Stevie came back into the room, Adam said with a subdued cough, 'I'm sorry, I never thought about your wee wan being here. I found tha' letter this morning when she'd gone. Tae a health farm in Wales, so she said. That explained the bikini but didnae explain why she'd taken her passporrrt.'

It was all too big to take in. A part of her brain was telling Stevie that Matthew wouldn't *ever* do *anything* like that. He'd known how hurt she was by what had happened to her in the past and had sworn that he would never put her through pain like that. Matthew was thoughtful and considerate. Matthew was the sort of man who befriended his work colleague, Jo MacLean, a woman desperately trying to muster the courage to leave her brute of a husband because he made her so unhappy—and you couldn't fake those sort of tears! Matthew wouldn't have brought her home if there had been anything going on—NO! There was no question but that she trusted both of them implicitly. Jo had become a friend in her own right now. Jo was sweet and uncompli-cated, and she was lovely to Danny. She had even been allowed to see *the* dress that was hanging in the spare room. She and Jo had talked for hours and Jo would be a wedding guest when Stevie put it on and mar-ried Matthew in thirty-nine days' time.

However, another part of her brain governed the eyes, and those were reading over and over again the brutal evidence.

'You could have made this up on a computer!' Stevie blurted out.

'Aye,' said Adam MacLean. 'Dae you know, I have so much spare time I often dae things like this. I really must stop it.'

OK, so she believed it wasn't a fake. Then again, she knew Jo and she knew Matthew and she didn't know this blaze-haired thug. Then again, Matthew had bought three pairs of shorts last week. For the honey-moon, he'd said. Then again, this was *Matthew*!

A light bulb went on in Stevie's head.

'I'll ring him!'

'You think he's going tae answer, dae you?' said the Scot with a mock-ing laugh. Stevie picked up the phone and rang Matthew's number. A muffled version of the song 'Goodbye-ee' started playing nearby. Stevie put the phone down, opened a drawer and retrieved the mobile tinkling out its mocking ringtone.

'Well, anyway,' Adam said, 'I thought you had the right tae know.'

'Thanks for telling me,' said Stevie numbly, which sounded a bit odd—but what did one say after being informed that one's fiancé was knocking off someone else's wife in the middle of Majorca?

Adam stroked his red beard like a small facial pet. 'Right, I'll go then.'

'Yes, I think you should rather,' said Stevie, and showed him out. Then she shut the door and stood behind it, fighting the urge to slither down it and become an emotional mess on the floor.

She went to the dresser, where they kept their passports, and opened the drawer—but she couldn't find Matthew's. Yet it was always there with her own, the pages of his around hers, as if they were spooning. *Maybe he moved it. Maybe he threw it away because it was out of date. Maybe he needed to take it with him as a form of ID.* Her head tried its best to rationalise the passport's absence, but it couldn't compete with the mighty guns of the information on the booking form.

And then smoke started billowing out of the kitchen and set off the alarm, and it felt like all hell had been let loose in her head.

Danny came home to find all the downstairs windows open in the hope of clearing the acrid smell of burnt baking, and his mum covered in even more flour, frenetically stirring up an anaemic and lumpy mixture in a bowl. Stevie forced herself into jolly mode as he ran in to greet her. She grabbed him and picked him up and kissed him. Catherine noticed how desperately she seemed to bury her head into his hair and how tightly she cuddled him.

'Is that my cake?' asked the little boy with a wrinkled nose as he looked over his mum's shoulder at the charcoal lumps in the cake-tin.

'No, of course not,' said Stevie. 'I'm making yours now.'

'Go upstairs, love, and get your pyjamas on,' said Catherine, sending him away. Then, when he was out of earshot, she said, 'Who was that?'

'Adam MacLean.'

'Ada . . . As in that Jo's husband? What did he want?'

'I'll never get this cake done. I've only got one egg left.'

'Sod the cake, Stevie,' said Catherine to her friend, who looked as grey as the horrible stuff in the bowl. 'Look, go and put the kettle on and I'll tuck Danny up and read him a quick story. Then we'll talk.'

'I haven't said good night to him.'

'One night won't kill either of you. He's bushed anyway. He's been bouncing about since he came back from school, and I bet he won't even notice. I'll be back in ten minutes max.' And with that, Catherine rushed upstairs, leaving Stevie feeling far more of a helpless child than her four-year-old currently slipping into his 'Incredibles' pyjamas.

She had not brewed the tea by the time Catherine returned. She was still stirring the limp liquid in the bowl. She had promised Danny a wonderful cake to take into class and she always kept her promises. Double always for her son.

'Is he OK?' asked Stevie.

''Course he is. Out like a light.'

'What happened to your hair?' said Stevie.

'Marilyn Monroe bleaching kit from abroad, don't ask. And don't ever let our Kate use you to test out her eBay buys. Anyway, never mind about me, what did Billy Connolly want?'

'Oh, just to tell me that Jo has run off with Matthew to Magalluf.'

'Oh, right. Stupid lout! Did you say you'd ring the police? What is he on? Run off with Jo? Ha! As if Matt . . .' Her words dried up as Stevie handed her the booking confirmation and her mouth moved like a goldfish wondering where the water in his bowl had gone. 'No! He wouldn't . . . he couldn't do that to you! Not Matthew!'

'It looks as if he has, Cath,' said Stevie in the sort of voice that Catherine's youngest used when she was trying to be brave. She continued to stir until Catherine extracted the bowl from her, gently, because it looked as if Stevie needed something to hold on to, and gripping the spoon seemed to be the only thing keeping her from falling over.

'This isn't going to make a cake, ever,' she said. 'Leave it. I'll get our Kate to knock one up tonight and I'll bring it over in the morning. It's the least she can do after this.' She pointed at her pink hair. Stevie said, 'Thank you.' Then Catherine tipped the mix down the sink.

'Danny wanted to start calling Matt Daddy,' said Stevie. 'It was a good job I told him to wait until after the wedding.'

'Look, Stevie, you need to talk to Matthew and find out what's going on. Will he ring you, to say he's arrived wherever he's supposed to be?'

'Aberdeen. Maybe. He hasn't been away before for any length of time so I don't know what the usual sequence of events would be.' Stevie shrugged. She didn't know if he would ring or not. She didn't know anything any more.

'Of course he'll ring,' said Catherine heartily. Every man was innocent until proven guilty. Except Mick, who should have been hung, drawn and quartered and his knackers cut off before he'd even got to trial. Although she shouldn't think ill of the dead.

'What if it's true? What do I do?' said Stevie, trying to keep the panic out of her voice. She'd panicked last time and it had made her lose her grip, sent her into such a downward spiral of emotional quicksand that she thought she was destined to drown in it. Until Matthew held out his hand and offered her the lifeline of his love.

And what about Danny? This was the only dad he'd ever known. He would lose two men in his life who had gone for the title and then bogged off before the crown was on their heads. What sort of damage would that do to his little heart? At that thought, Stevie caved into the huge pressure of tears and Catherine, her future chief bridesmaid, came over to give her a big hug.

'I don't know, love. Let's cross that bridge when we come to it. Pass me the phone. I'll ring Eddie and tell him I'm staying with you tonight.'

'No,' said Stevie. 'I need to think and I can do that better on my own. I'll just cry if you're here and I really don't want to do that. I'll be fine. You go—you've got three hundred kids and a zoo to sort out.'

'Come home with me,' said Catherine. 'You and Danny.'

'Honestly, I'd rather be alone.'

'Well, look,' said Catherine, when fully convinced, 'I'll go and sort out this cake for Danny and I'll be round first thing in the morning.'

After extracting fifty affirmations that Stevie would ring her if she changed her mind about coming over, Catherine went back to her huge brood to tackle an urgent hair repair and an emergency baking project. Making a cake for her godson was the least she could do after breaking the vow she had made to herself: never to let another dickhead break his mother's heart.

The phone rang about ten minutes after Catherine had gone; it showed 'number withheld' on the caller display. Knowing who it would be, Stevie's hand came out to pick it up. Then, realising she couldn't trust herself to act 'normal', she overrode the compulsion to speak to him, collapse into uncontrolled tears and beg him to come home. Instead, she let the answering machine handle it. It was, as she knew it would be, Matthew, her gorgeous, tall fiancé with the dark brown hair and the dark brown eyes and the smile that made her heart melt.

'Hi, Stevie, it's Matthew. Just to let you know I've arrived safely— motorway's a nightmare! Looks very busy, lots of people. All set for a good hard week so I don't know when I'll have the chance to speak to you again. Forgot my mobile didn't I, ha ha! Anyway, take care and hope everything's OK. Er . . . bye then.'

No *I love you*, no *Hope Danny's OK*, no *Miss you*. His voice sounded further away than Aberdeen. And she was probably imagining it, but every one of the million times she played that message back, she was sure she could hear the strains of 'Guantanamera' in the background.

In Catherine's big homely Waltonesque-style kitchen in the neighbour-ing village of Hoodley, black-haired, black-gowned, scarlet-lipped Kate Flanagan was expertly baking a cake. In her mother's frilly apron, she looked rather like a beautiful domestic vampire.

Her father gave her a big squashy squeeze as he passed her on his way to the teapot and said, 'Eeh, you'll make someone a lovely little housewife one day!' knowing it would greatly offend her feminist prin-ciples, and though Kate shoved him away, she was laughing a little too.

Catherine, towelled up, waiting for the auburn dye to restore her locks to their former fake glory, watched the interchange and it brought tears to her eyes; happy ones that she had such a loving family and sad ones because life seemed determined to short-change her dear friend on that score. What was it about Stevie that attracted plonkers? Stevie who was sweet and selfless and deserved so much better than the Micks and Matthews of this world, whereas she—Catherine Flanagan, out-spoken, brash and loud—had been blessed with a wonderful husband, six gorgeous (when they weren't fighting) kids and a big chaotic house full of love, laughter and daft pets.

'Here you are, love,' Eddie said, handing his wife a cup of tea. 'Matthew Finch! I'd have put my all on him not doing that to Stevie.'

'Tell me about it,' said Catherine, a quarter angry but three-quarters sad and disappointed. She had grown very fond of Matthew. She had never liked Mick and been proved right on that one, but Matthew was a good bloke—caring, considerate. Catherine had been instrumental in pushing Stevie and Matt together, following their initial meeting at a mutual friend's engagement party, because she knew they would be well matched. He was handsome, kind, big-hearted, and willing to take on a little boy who wasn't his, which spoke bucketloads.

After Mick had broken her best friend's heart, five years earlier, Catherine had screened every male who came within fifty miles of her. Matthew had put a tick in every box on her score-sheet of essentials.

'I'd be lying if I said a warning hadn't flagged up in my head when Stevie told me about this Jo woman he'd got friendly with at work,' said Catherine. 'Vulnerable women are never fully aware of the power they have to make a bloke feel like a hero, but admittedly it wasn't much of a warning. After all, this was Matthew we were talking about. Reliable, faithful old Matthew!' Catherine laughed hard.

'What's she look like, this Jo?'

'Tall, slim, long dark hair, big brown eyes. Very, very pretty.' Catherine suddenly realised that she wouldn't have liked a vulnerable Jo MacLean anywhere near Eddie, had the roles been reversed.

'It's a weird business,' said Eddie, having a long gulp of tea. 'I reckon he's having a midlife crisis and he'll be back.'

Catherine looked over at him and smiled. Brad Pitt he wasn't, but she loved the bones of her big, eighteen-stone husband with the Worzel Gummidge hairdo. Never once had she thought he would be unfaithful to her, but after the shocker of today, she wondered if anyone really knew their partners as well as they thought they did.

Eddie saw that look in her eye. 'Oy, you! Don't be tarring us all with the same brush,' he warned with a twinkle in his soft, hazel eyes.

'I don't know what you mean,' said Catherine unconvincingly.

'I wouldn't leave you, babe,' said Eddie, tilting her face up towards his and giving her a kiss on her lips that still made something deep within her tingle. He smelt of soap and Fahrenheit aftershave.

'Ugh, gross,' said the cake-baking Goth in the background.

'Mind your own business, Morticia,' commanded Eddie over his shoulder, before turning back to his wife.

'Well, all I can say is, that's men for you!' said seventeen-year-old Kate with a heavy sigh. She drifted from the room like a dramatic black plume of smoke, leaving Eddie and Catherine crippled from the effort of keeping in a bout of laughter that, at that moment, was so needed.

When Adam left Stevie's house he got into his car and studied the medium-sized detached house of his love rival. Boring, neat enough outside but nothing spectacular, how he'd always imagined Matthew Finch to be from the way Jo had described him. That was, until he'd seen a framed photo on the dresser (next to another ridiculous Midnight Moon book) of the frumpy (most likely bottle) blonde, lumpy girlfriend snuggling up to a clean-shaven Prince Charming type: dark hair, dark eyes, nice white-toothed smile. He presumed that must be *him*, and he was far too good-looking for *her*. Surely she must have realised that it was only a matter of time before Finch's chocolate-coloured eyes were drawn towards someone his physical equal, like his own doe-eyed Jo. *By Jings*, the very least that short, unspecial-looking untidy woman could have done was look after her house and brush her hair occasionally to keep her man interested. Anger-management classes might have been a good idea too. That way, her man might not have been desperate for love and attention. And he might not have pre-sented a tortured and vulnerable side to Adam's beautiful, sensitive lady of eighteen months—Joanna.

Funny though, he hadn't expected Finch's woman to look as stunned as she had by his revelation.

Adam sped out of the town, towards the estate of newly built 'Paradise' properties on the edge of an ex-pit village that had recently been given a make-over. There, he pulled onto the drive of the fortieth finished double-fronted detached house. He turned the key in the lock and then deactivated the alarm that protected their state-of-the-art entertainment equipment, although he was more of a deterrent to would-be burglars than any bell.

How could she leave all this? Her dream home. He looked around at the expensive curtains and carpets, the extensive CD and DVD collection, all the creature comforts anyone could desire. All for her. *He'd get her back; whatever it took, he'd get her back.*

He smoothed his hand over the freshly plastered wall where the dining room led out to their almost finished conservatory. Then with a huge primal roar, he pulled back his fist and drove it into the wall, leaving the deep, wide impression of his knuckles.

That night, Stevie didn't give way to the tears that threatened. Crying meant grieving, and grieving meant she had already lost him. Crying would have sapped the energy reserves that she badly needed to draw from. This wasn't a time for emotional output; she needed her head clear in order to think. *What was it about Jo that was better than her?* She began to write a list. It went on a bit longer than she had anticipated.

She remembered how, on the occasions when she'd moaned about her figure not being quite what she wanted, or that there seemed to be more laughter lines appearing at her eye-corners, Matthew had kissed her far from perfect nose and said she was just fine and dandy as she was. Obviously not fine and dandy enough if he'd buggered off to Majorca with someone with a flatter stomach, longer legs, smaller conk and all the other sickening -ers that she couldn't compete with.

Stevie turned to a new page in the pad. This time her head would lead on how to tackle this one, not her heart. She would work out a plan to get him back. She would let him slip back seamlessly into her life and pretend this had never happened. He would never suspect she knew of his unfaithful escapade. Whatever it took to make this happen, she would do. *Whatever.*

Next morning, Stevie found Danny downstairs in his dressing gown, staring at the empty cake-tin he had just found on the kitchen table.

'Mummy, where's the cake you promised me?' he asked.

'Wait and see. Breakfast first,' said Stevie. Danny had his usual orange juice and Coco Pops. Then he washed his face and brushed his teeth, before getting his blue and grey uniform on for school.

He was a bright little button, an added bonus because when he was born, Danny was so premature that there was a real chance he might have had some brain damage. Miraculously, her baby boy had pulled through and every year he got a birthday card from 'The Little Fighters' Club' at the Special Care Unit up at the hospital. Hard to imagine that the tiny, fragile scrap and the sturdy, clever little boy now in front of her were the same person.

Danny was always writing and making little books, like she used to do, although hopefully not for the same reasons. She would have liked him to follow in her footsteps and write for a living, but something a little loftier than Midnight Moon fiction, which was for ladies who liked to escape to a land where men were men and women sighed a lot and fainted but at least the endings were happy.

'Is my cake ready yet, Mummy?' he asked again.

Stevie straightened his tie, playing for time. 'Well . . . the thing is . . .'

The doorbell bing-bonged, a sound that translated as a hallelujah chorus in Stevie's head as she opened the door to Catherine, restored to auburn, wooden-acting worse than an extra in *Crossroads*.

'Hi, Stevie, here's the cake you baked last night. I'm sorry, I walked off with it instead of the empty tin, which I was borrowing off of you.'

Stevie mouthed, 'I will love you for ever,' to her friend and Danny's eyes rounded to dinner plates as the four-layer cake covered with crushed Maltesers, Buttons, Crunchie bits and melted down Mars Bar icing made its fanfare entrance into the Honeywell/Finch kitchen.

'Wow!' said Danny, which was his buzz word of the moment.

'Go get your shoes on,' said Stevie, spurring him on with, 'The sooner you do so, the sooner you'll get to show off your cake at school,' which sent him flying down to the cabinet in the hallway.

'Thank you, thank you, thank you,' said Stevie, hugging Catherine.

'Don't thank me, thank Kate. She did the cake, and after she'd put my hair right, I shoved all the bits on. Wasn't that long a job.'

Catherine had six children, a husband, four cats, a ferret, a Chihuahua called Chico and some huge mad-looking crossbreed called Boot. She had her hands full.

'I owe you both big time for this, Cath.'

'Don't be silly. Did you sleep? How are you feeling? Did he ring?'

'A little,' said Stevie, 'crap and yes. I let the answering machine pick it up. He said he was in Aberdeen.'

'Did you 1471 it?'

'Withheld.'

'Sod it. So what's your gut feeling?' Catherine cringed in advance.

'He's in Majorca, I reckon.'

'Holy shit! You're a lot calmer than I would be,' said Catherine.

'Yes, but I've a plan,' said Stevie, snapping off the conversation as Danny made a fully-shod appearance.

They both walked the proud boy to school; he was champing at the bit to show off the empress of all cakes to his friends and teacher. Lockelands was a nice school, only a ten-minute walk away from Stevie and Matthew's house in Blossom Lane. Well, it was Matthew's house really. Stevie had sold her little terraced home, a few streets away, and moved in with him on New Year's Day.

The two sides of Blossom Lane were very different. On one side were eight clones of 1980s box-like dwellings with a short path at the front and small square gardens at the back; on the other side was a row of four early-1800s large detached cottages, all individual, chocolate-box pretty. Ivy and honeysuckle rampaged over the stone and gave a delicious noseful of scent to passers-by in late summer. They had long gardens at the back all the way down to a little stream and the railway line, and high crumbly walls overgrown with foliage secured each cottage's privacy from its neighbours. The far end cottage, opposite Matthew's house, had been to let for a couple of months. It was the largest of the four. There had been no takers. It appeared character cottages went hand in hand with phenomenal rents.

'So fill me in on the plan then,' said Catherine, who never failed to peer into the empty cottage window in the hope of seeing some detail she had missed. It was her dream home: gnarled beams, big kitchen fireplace, exposed stonework. She sighed at its gorgeousness.

'Time for a coffee?'

'Quick one. Eddie's sorted the kids out this morning, he'll be on his third nervous breakdown by now.' They both knew that was a joke. There was only one creature more laid-back than Eddie and that was Boot, the dog.

Stevie made Catherine wait for the details until the kettle had boiled. Catherine humoured her strange hopefulness, despite having a heavy feeling about it all, but any positive plan that kept her friend from going down the path she had gone down last time had to be supported.

'Right!' said Stevie, stirring in the milk. 'Here's what I'm going to do. I've got six days left until Matthew comes back. So at lunchtime tomorrow I'm having my hair done.'

'Right,' Catherine nodded. 'Good girl. Make yourself feel better.'

'Then I'm going to join the gym to get some weight off.'

'Well, great,' said Catherine, smiling encouragingly. 'But . . .'

'But what?' Stevie's smile slipped a little.

Catherine sighed. With the best will in the world, Stevie wasn't going to get to size zero and look like a supermodel in six days. Even if she did, that wasn't going to bring Matthew back to her. There were darker forces at work here, forces for which a hairdo fairy was no match.

Then again, it wouldn't do Stevie any harm to go to a gym and see some nice males with bulging biceps and trim bums. That was better than sitting in and thinking about what those cheating scumbags were doing.

Catherine smiled. 'But nothing. In fact, I'll come with you for the first session, for moral support. They're always giving out free day passes, these gyms, trying to get you to join up. You can blag me one.'

'Oh, Catherine, that would be fab,' said Stevie, with gratitude.

'Which gym?'

'Well, Matthew goes to Gym Village, so the other—Well Life.'

'Ooh, posh and expensive—ring up and find out how you join before I go home.' Catherine slid the phone over the table.

So, Stevie started the three-point plan that would totally absorb her over the next six days and get her man back for her.

1) have great new-image hairdo
2) join gym and start to get thinner
3) practise pretending to have suspected nothing about his affair

Easy.

Listening to the shushing waves, savouring the scent of sun oil that smelt of coconuts, and lying next to a long, leggy woman with a supermodel-type body nearly covered by a white bikini with a sexy rhinestone clasp between the twin swells of her small but perfect breasts, Matthew waited for the guilt to kick in. A stray thought visited plump, ordinary little Stevie at home. She would be sitting at her computer, writing love stories for the lonely and rejected, unaware she was about to join them in five days' time. It made him feel guilty only for not feeling guilty.

He had been content with Stevie, sliding into the role of dad for Danny, until he had found Jo MacLean, one of the new designers, crying by his black Punto in the company car park the day after Valentine's Day. He had only seen her a couple of times before, but Jo MacLean, with her big brown eyes and her long, dark hair and her even longer legs, was someone once spotted, never forgotten. They had spoken once, after a meeting in late January. A few of them had hung around the buffet table drinking the last of the coffee. He'd found himself puffing up in front of her, trying to impress. Then, a fortnight later, there he was, offering her his handkerchief in the cold and the rain and asking if she wanted a coffee in the little café round the corner from work. There she had spilled out her life to him—a relative stranger—so desperate was she for consolation. She had told him how she had recently moved into a new house with the husband she so needed to get away from. She poured out stories of horrific abuse and Matthew had listened. Who could have predicted what she would be doing to the rest of his body, so soon after he'd offered his shoulder?

Despite being flattered by her attention, at first, he really had only wanted to help her escape Adam MacLean before the Scot went too far and killed her. He had told Stevie all about her at the beginning, when it had been innocent, and, horrified, she had offered herself as a friend to Jo too. Stevie couldn't bear to see anyone being unhappy, especially when she was so happy herself, planning her wedding.

It hadn't felt right to keep bringing Jo into his home when he knew he was falling in love with her, but Matt couldn't help himself—he just had to see her whenever he could. Then, when Jo admitted she felt the same about him, he had almost exploded with pleasure. Jo and Stevie got on so well, which made it harder and messier. But he couldn't give Jo up—it was not an option. Jo was a drug and he was hooked.

They hotfooted it to the sun to plan how he would leave Stevie and little Danny, and orchestrate how Jo could escape the Incredible McHulk. Matthew would have to make sure that he watched his back there. There was no telling what MacLean would do to Matthew, if he had no reservations about hitting a woman as fragile as Jo.

Looking at the vision on the sunbed next to his, Matthew knew it was all going to be worth it though. He couldn't feel guilt because there was no room for it in his heart, which was just too full of desire for this gorgeous being. She was *perfect*—well, except for the scar on the top of her leg where Adam's boot once went in. He had always hit her where the bruises didn't show, she said, although she looked pretty undamaged now, and in fantastic shape. And all the sex with that fantastic shape made him realise how much his feelings for Stevie paled in the face of this beautiful, long-limbed, washboard-stomached woman who needed his love and protection so much.

At first it crossed Matt's mind that Jo was so desperate to get away from Adam that she might be using him as a steppingstone, until she had suggested the two of them fly away abroad to plan the logistics of partner-leaving, wedding-cancelling and moving in together. Then she had gone down on him in a staff toilet to seal her intentions. By the time his breathing had got back to normal, he had booked the flights and the five-star hotel on his already overloaded Visa card.

Stevie would be OK. Heartbreak didn't kill you, and she had come through worse. She would have to move out (thank God the house was still in his name) so Jo could move in. Little Danny would forget him soon. It wasn't as if he had got used to calling him 'Daddy', and kids adjusted. He tried not to let the thoughts in about Danny's EuroDisney trip because that would make him feel bad. Especially as the savings for it were financing his Majorcan expenses. He would put the money back in the account, obviously. He wasn't a thief.

If asked, he would say he got the tan in the leisure facilities at the Aberdeen hotel, while Jo would say she had been under the sunbed at the Welsh health farm. At least Stevie would never know he'd jetted off with another woman to the sun. That detail really would be too cruel.

Lindsay flicked at Stevie's long, honey-coloured hair and together they studied the difference it made to her reflection. First she pulled it back, then she swooped it forwards. 'I think you should have it all lopped off. To here,' she said, making a chopping motion on her client's shoulders.

Stevie's eyes registered horror. 'A bob?' She wasn't convinced.

'Not quite,' said Lindsay, shaking her head. 'Something funkier, I think. Nice and choppy and really easy to do yourself at home.'

Stevie gulped. She was about to change her mind and ask for a trim when she heard Catherine's voice in her head nagging her: *What's the point of booking in with the top stylist and then not taking her advice?*

'And a few really pale highlights running through it as well,' Lindsay went on. 'I think it will make you look a hell of a lot younger.'

Younger. There. She had spoken the magic word. At thirty-six, Stevie was five years older than Jo, who had just recently had her thirty-first birthday. Stevie had bought her the (size ten) bikini they had both spotted on display in a shop window and wowed at. It was glistening white with a glittery rhinestone clasp at the front.

'OK, let's do it,' said Stevie, taking a deep breath.

Two hours later and she was staring at herself in the mirror, admiring the shorter, chopped style, brighter in colour at the front and the sides and infinitely lighter in weight. She was astounded how much thinner her face seemed. If only it could have done the same to her bum.

It cost a lot, but she didn't care. The plan had started to work. Now there was just the rest of her body to sort out.

Adam smoothed the plaster over the wall with the trowel. Apart from the colour, there was no evidence that his temper had given way and that he'd cannoned a fury-loaded fist into the wall. He knew that losing it was not the way forward, not this time. He had tried that one with Diane—and where had that got him? Shouting and screaming and breaking things and being totally out of control had done nothing but drive her right out of his life. And scare the neighbours. And lose his cat.

He thought back to that fateful day. The scene of devastation was burnt onto his brain: Diane screaming and running towards her car with a hastily packed suitcase and Humbug the striped tabby in his basket while Adam stood there holding a roaring chainsaw. The neighbours' curtains had twitched, but no one dared ring the police. Diane had given him that look he had seen in his mum's eyes too many times when his da' came in from the pub. Some folks turned jolly with spirit, not big Andy MacLean. The whisky went straight into his fists, and the fists went straight into his mammy and his sisters and little Adam.

Adam MacLean knew what he looked like with his archetypal boxer's nose, scarred cheek, powerful build and voice that could vibrate owls out of trees. He knew how Jo would suppose him to behave if she left him for another man. And, likewise, what Matty Boy would expect. So, as he did the plastering repair, Adam MacLean had been thinking it through. And now he had a plan.

Chapter 2

KITTED OUT IN HER new tracksuit, trainers and a strong bra that flattened her generously proportioned chest so she didn't give black eyes to herself or people on adjacent treadmills, Stevie presented herself at the gym for her induction hour with Hilary. She was horrified to find that Hilary was in fact a bloke. Not just an ordinary bloke either but a young, fit, tall, love-god with a killer smile and a backside that could crack open Brazil nuts. Then again, she of all people should have known that a name didn't always guarantee the sex. Midnight Moon had asked her to use a pseudonym, as 'Stevie' suggested she might be male, and Midnight Moon readers were very specific that only women writers were able to tap into their feminine needs. Their pen names needed to conjure up softness and romance and sweetness, which is why her fellow writers Paul Slack and Alec Sleaford became Paula Sheer and Alexis Tracey, and why she herself was published under Beatrice Pollen, her late granny's name. It was from Granny Bea that Stevie inherited her creative talents, her warm, considerate heart and her big, sky-blue eyes.

She paid for a year's subscription, because that way Stevie knew she was fully committing herself to her cause. Catherine was sitting in Reception when Hilary officially welcomed Stevie to the club, alas not with a big tonguey snog, but with a free seven-day pass for a friend of her choice, who at that moment was eagerly waiting for it, clad in some pretty impressive pink and grey gear. Stevie wolf-whistled as she approached her.

'It's our Kate's,' explained Catherine.

'Must be nice, to be able to fit into your seventeen-year-old daughter's clothes,' said Stevie.

'It is, until you see me naked and discover that most of my body is made up of stretch marks,' exaggerated Catherine. 'By the way, Steve, the hair is fab. It makes you look a hell of a lot younger. No bull.'

Stevie beamed. First stage of 'getting Matthew back' was mission accomplished, then.

The two gym-bunnies had a go on a few machines. Then they went for a coffee in the luxurious café after a slow walk past the spinning class to check out some very nice male bottoms.

Stevie's stomach suddenly made a noise like a mortally wounded hound as they waited in the queue.

'Have you eaten?' said Catherine.

'Not really,' Stevie said.

'What's that supposed to mean? You either have or you haven't.'

'Er . . . no, then.'

'You won't lose weight by not eating.'

'I'm not deliberately not eating. I just haven't felt hungry.'

'Right, well, you're having something now. You go and get those seats over there and I'll be with you in a minute.'

Stevie retired to the table by the window as instructed. She did feel a bit shaky, all that exercise and hairdo-ing with nothing in her stomach but cappuccinos and half a slice of unbuttered toast.

Catherine brought over big frothy coffees, toasted panini sandwiches, the length of Stevie's leg, filled with ham and Brie, and two enormous chocolate-covered slabs that smelt suspiciously of peanut butter.

'Do they sell this here?' said Stevie. She had been expecting two let-tuce leaves and a spring onion on something brown and inedible.

''Course they do. Some people just come in for lunch, not to exercise.' Catherine gave Stevie a sharp nudge. 'Braveheart alert at three o'clock,' she said through one side of her barely moving mouth.

Stevie twisted round to see the unmistakable figure of *him* in black tracksuit bottoms and a black T-shirt, with his luxuriant red hair flowing behind him. He looked like a muscular Duracell battery.

'Oh bloody hell,' said Stevie, as the big man's eyes locked onto hers and he started to come over. In slow motion—like the Terminator.

'Want a minute to yourselves?' said Catherine.

'Don't you dare leave me with that . . . that caber-tosser without an armed escort!' said Stevie.

'Don't be daft, Steve. He's not going to do anything to you here—the place is packed. Anyway, I really do need the loo and he looks as if he wants to talk to you.' Catherine got up, just as Adam MacLean reached the table. He nodded her a stiff hello as they crossed paths.

'I didnae know you were a member of ma gym,' he said, looking down at Stevie.

His gym? Crikey, he was possessive! 'Well, I am,' said Stevie, taking a diversionary sip of coffee, which burnt her lip, and then she accidentally bit it as well in an unfortunate reflex action.

'Can I sit doon for a wee minute, please?' he said. Civilised for him, thought Stevie, who glared at him but didn't say no, which he obviously took to mean yes, because he dropped his big, honed body into the chair that Catherine had vacated.

'Have ye heard anythin'?' he asked, his eyes compulsively drawn to her swelling split lip.

'No,' Stevie lied. 'Have you?'

'Naw. Jo left her mobile behind too, funnily enough. Probably so I couldnae ring her. The number she left for the health farm doesnae exist, of course. Nae doot she'll tell me she wrote it doon wrong.'

'Oh.' Stevie felt a little guilty about fibbing then after he had been so candid, but she didn't want to give him any details that might trigger him to go off and kill Matthew. She had one dead lover, she didn't want another, she thought with black amusement.

'I have a plan tae stop all this nonsense,' he said.

'So have I,' said Stevie stiffly. She suspected her plan of hairdos and gentle body toning might be slightly different from his, which would involve hijacking a plane and forcing Matthew to jump out of it.

'You see, by ma way of thinkin', it's tae dae with basic psychology—'

Stevie cut him off with a mirthless little laugh. *Like he would know!* The only thing he knew about heads was that they were meant to propel forwards at great speed into someone else's nose.

'Please don't take this wrongly, *Mr* MacLean, but I'll handle this in my own fashion,' she said bravely. Her lip throbbed and she was fighting back some annoying tears, and she didn't know if they were down to bodily pain or his frustrating, hateful presence and all he stood for.

Adam pulled out a card from his tracksuit pocket and slammed it on the table. 'Here's ma card. If you change yer mind and want tae hear whit I have tae say, gi' me a ring. We could smash this thing up before it gets too big and get back tae being happy. That is, if you seriously want tae get yerrr man back.' He looked accusingly at the feast on the table. Not exactly food for a seriously devoted body sculptor, he thought. Then he was off, just as Catherine returned.

'So?' she said, and then jumped back. 'Shit—your lip! He didn't hit you after all, did he?'

'No, I burnt my lip on the coffee. Then I bit it.'

'Ooh, look,' said Catherine, picking up his card. 'He's the General Manager here.'

'I hope you're flaming joking. I've just signed up for a whole year!' said Stevie, snatching back the card to see it there in black and white— *Adam MacLean, General Manager of Well Life Supergym, Dodmoor, Barnsley,* and the scribble of his mobile number. The information knocked Stevie for six because he looked more like the head of 'Thugs International' than something sensible, respectable and managerial.

A picture came into her head of him pushing past her into the house. If she hadn't opened the door, she would still have been in blissful ignorance. Jo and Matthew might have just had a quick fling and that could have been the end of it. Maybe that's all it was: a last-minute explosion of freedom before he finally settled down and got married. It happened. Stevie was thirty-six; she wasn't the naive baby she'd been nearly five years ago when she had found out about Mick, even if Mick and Matthew were very different animals. Mick wouldn't have felt the slightest bit of guilt, but she knew Matthew would most likely be pacing the Spanish hotel foyer vowing never to do anything like that again. But then *he* had to go and tell her just because *he* found out about it and got upset and wanted to upset everyone else too. No, she'd heard what McBigmouth had to say once; she wouldn't make that mistake again.

'He can go and stuff a live haggis up his backside,' said Stevie. Then she bit down and burnt the other side of her mouth on the panini.

PARIS SMILED THAT SPECIAL SMILE of hers as Brandon took her into his arms. 'I love you so much,' she said, her red lips parting slowly to alert him to the fact that she was ready for his kiss.

Brandon let her fall to the ground. 'I'm sorry, love, but I'm mad crazy bonkers over another woman. She's got everything you haven't, so no one can blame me really. So this is the big El Dumpo, I'm afraid. Have a nice life, pet.' And with that he mounted his black stallion and, a rose between his teeth, stuck his spurs into the side of his horse, who galloped him away to his new love La Joanna, which in Spanish means 'crafty two-faced cow'.

Stevie sighed, pushed back her chair and looked at the words that plopped out of her printer on the page. Yet another sheet to join the ream of bad writing destined for the recycling bin in the garage.

It was not often that writing felt like hard work, but today it did. Not that she usually wrote at the weekend, but seeing as she hadn't touched her keyboard since last Monday, she thought she might take advantage of the hour while Danny played Harry Potter on his GameCube. He seemed quite content, although Stevie felt guilty that she wasn't doing anything more exciting herself to entertain him.

She always tried to do something special at the weekends—take him for a walk to the park, or do some gardening together, or play board games. It was a kickback, she supposed, from her own childhood. She would get piles of games for Christmas and birthdays, but find there was no one to play them with. Her mum was always too busy to sit down and shake a dice, and even though their tiny home was like a new pin, Edna Honeywell was continuously scrubbing or Brasso-ing the ornaments. Much as she herself liked a nicely kept home, she vowed never to make such a god of the housework that she was too busy to play with her own children. Her dad worked long hours and so when he did get home, he could barely manage a 'hello', never mind a game of Cluedo. He needed to save his energies for the rabid arguments that Stevie listened to as she lay trembling in her bed.

So Stevie turned to herself for entertainment, drawing and scribbling, reading and writing, constructing little books and stories of love and happy families that became longer and more structured and crafted. Her diaries were detailed too. In them, she found an overflow pipe for her mixed-up emotions. Especially when her father ran off with the woman with a thick neck a few doors away, and her mother, in vengeance, took a slimy lover who stared too long at Stevie's budding breasts for her comfort.

It had been a relief to get away to university to study English, made possible because it was in the days when students were given grants.

'I'm bored,' said Danny, quitting Harry.

'Me too,' said Stevie. Paris and Brandon would have to wait. If only she could write her own destiny as easily as she could theirs. Then again, maybe that wasn't wise, with the self-destructive mood she was in at the moment. She would only have had herself trampled by Brandon's horse just to get some relief from the pain inside her.

It was a soggy day. The air was damp and the Yorkshire earth was dealing with the aftermath of heavy showers through the night.

'Danny, get your wellies on and your big coat,' she said impulsively.

'Cool. Where are we going?'

'Bluebelling,' said Stevie.

There was a lovely wood at Pogley Top that she had once discovered with Mick. The ground had been far too muddy to explore in his best shoes and her heels, which was a shame as Mick was all for having his wicked way with her, right there on the thick carpet of scented blue-bells. It was on that day he proposed.

Matthew had taken her there too one warm spring day when they had first started courting. He had made up a basket full of delicious food, only for most of it to get wasted when they spent all afternoon snogging on the gingham tablecloth under the trees, feeding each other the odd Twiglet to keep up the strength in their lip muscles.

There were nicer woods than Pogley Top, but none quite as magical. Maybe it was because the trees conspired overhead to give it a dark, mysterious feel. Maybe it was because it was sheltered on all sides and the air seemed extra still. She had come here so many times when things turned bad with Mick, hoping to rewind time to that perfect day.

They picked a way through the bluebells, collecting armfuls. Danny would definitely need throwing in the bath when they got home, clothes and all, but what the hell. The fresh air wasn't taking any of the pain away, but it was nice to get mucky with nature.

Back home in the kitchen, they stuck the flowers in vases, and when they ran out, in milk bottles and the cream jug. Once Danny was tucked up in bed, Stevie took up Paris's plight of unrequited love again, but still her head wouldn't play the game. There was no conviction in Brandon's proclamation of love. She wanted to warn Paris that he was bound to bugger off at some point, and the bluebell scent in the room only reminded her of kissing Matthew, or being besotted by Mick. Or even to take her further back, to memories of sunshine-filled picnics, when she was someone who still believed in fairies and magic and that princesses got their princes. And that there were such things as happy endings.

Two days later, when the bluebells had started to wither, Adam watched Stevie enter the gym. She had spotted him, he knew, but was trying to pretend she hadn't by whistling and looking everywhere but in his direction. Pathetic really. She had been here every morning since she joined; he had checked her records to find out when that was. The date alone had made it obvious why she was pounding away on the treadmills, although she wasn't going to lose a lot of weight building up a sweat and then going off and eating half the restaurant like he had caught her about to do on what he now realised was her first day.

Her friend's hair had looked better then, he had noticed, having got rid of the pink. *She* had had hers done too, but he *so* wanted to drum it into her obviously less than bright skull that it wouldn't do any good. She should have thought of making such improvements *before* she drove her man away. Did she seriously think she was going to lure him back by cutting off a few dead ends? Not when faced with the mighty attributes of his beloved Jo. She could not even hope to come near to Jo, who could knock any woman off the planet with her looks. She would be far better following *his* plan of action but she wasn't going to listen to him, she had made that perfectly clear. Well, he just hoped she didn't cock up his plans for reclaiming his woman. He was going crazy without her. He could hardly sleep for the nervous excitement that her home-coming tomorrow was giving him.

Stevie went into the gym with a heart that was stuffed full of blame and looking for a target, but Matthew was as protected and cloaked as the starship *Enterprise* during a Klingon attack. Her head just wouldn't let her attack him, because surely he was a victim in this—emotionally outmanoeuvred, a sitting duck. She had to grudgingly concede that even Joanna MacLean was a sort of victim too, and you didn't need to be a genius to point to the source of all this heartache: that Scottish animal, masquerading as something respectable behind that desk, the wild man who had come into Stevie's life and tried to wreck it.

That cocky look he was giving her made her want to storm over and tell him that if *he* hadn't been such a psycho, if *he* had treated his wife like a woman should be treated, if *he* hadn't brought her low with mental torture and physical violence, she would not have had that air of vulnerability which had been irresistible to her soft-hearted, gentle, uncritical Matthew. In comparison with *him*, Matthew had looked like a knight in shining armour, and no woman could resist that.

This mess was all Adam MacLean's fault. She despised him.

It seemed to her that the man was trying to pretend he hadn't seen her, which was good because she didn't want to talk to him either. What on earth could they possibly have to say to each other? Besides which, she was too busy with her preparations for tomorrow, and trying to cling on to her dwindling reserves of inner strength. The house was extra-sparkling clean, the fridge was stocked up with all Matthew's favourite things. The bills had all been paid, the banking was done; the joint-account status had been a bit of a shocker, but she would sort that one out with Matthew later. All that was left was to get on that treadmill and start running, in the hope that by some miracle she would have lost a stone by the time Matthew landed tomorrow, and also that she might burn off some of the hatred she felt for that red-haired gorilla.

Adam did a sweep of the place an hour later and saw that Stevie was still on the treadmill. He almost felt sorry for her, before remembering it was her fault they were in this position. He noticed she was glaring in his direction and so he glared back. Then she buckled, lost her footing, tripped over her own trainer and fell on the treadmill, which trans-ported her backwards, made her do a reverse roly-poly then deposited her with a thud on the floor. A couple of people started to come over to help, but Adam beat them to it.

His long legs thundered over to her. She was a customer, after all, and he had a responsibility to her. Even if she was the one who had wrecked his relationship with the most wonderful woman in the world.

'Are you awwwwrrright?' he asked, helping her up.

When she realised who it was, she shrugged him off. People were looking at her and she felt an idiot. It was her own fault, she knew, for not eating enough. In the past few days she had eaten little more than three bites of that ham and Brie panini, and was surviving mainly on the milky coffees she had been drinking on a half-hourly basis. It wasn't as if the caffeine would interfere with her sleep patterns, because she wasn't getting any sleep. As a result, she felt wired all the time, a condi-tion not helped by the adrenaline surging through her veins, generated by the anxiety of waiting for this week to be at an end.

Her nose felt clogged up and was swelling before everyone's eyes, and she wasn't going to be eight stone and beautiful by tomorrow. She would still be plump, but with blonder, shorter hair and a big, fat, swollen, split-open, red nose. There was no way she was going to cry in front of *him*, though, however defeated she felt. In fact, thinking about it, this was his fault as well. If she hadn't looked over and seen him star-ing at her, she would not have lost her rhythm. Bloody Scottish jinx. Was he making it his new mission to screw up her life totally?

'Let's get you tae the first-aid room,' Adam said.

'I'll fix it at homeb,' said Stevie, cringing with embarrassment as a big splodge of nose-blood landed on the floor. She hadn't a tissue or even a long sleeve, and was forced to accept the white hanky he offered her. His best one too, he thought. He wouldnae see that again.

'Dank you,' she said grudgingly.

'Come and sit doon fer a minute.'

'Doh. I just wand my bag and do go homeb,' said Stevie, sniffing and then wincing because it hurt. 'I'b bring dor hanky back dext timeb.'

She did look hellish pale, thought Adam, and a wee bit woozy.

'I really don't think you should drive for a wee while,' he said, attempting to take her arm again. 'Trust me, I'm firrrst-aid trained.'

'I'mb fine,' she insisted, pulling back as his hand made contact.

'Well, I cannae force you, of course,' he said, holding up his hands.

'Really? Ad there's be thinking dat's your sbeciality!' said Stevie, and turned on her heel and headed towards the changing rooms, leaving a stunned Adam thinking, Now whit the hell did the stupid woman mean by that?

Matthew packed the little red-hearted G-string into the side of Jo's case, sighing as he remembered the fun they'd had the previous night.

Jo came out of the bathroom. 'All set for tomorrow, darling?' she said.

'No, I want to stay here for ever,' he said, adjusting himself as his pants suddenly felt very tight. She noticed the impressive bulge and her eyes rounded.

'Well, it'll be like this from now on, won't it?'

'Exactly—only colder.'

'I'll think of lots of ways to warm you up,' she said smokily.

'Will you be OK, going to pick up your stuff from your house? Do you want me to come with you?' he asked Jo softly.

'I'll be fine,' she said. 'It's not as if Adam knows about us.'

'If he did, then he'd be pretty angry, right?' said Matthew with a gulp.

'He'd be waiting for us at the airport with a flamethrower if he did,' said Jo. She stroked his face soothingly. 'But he doesn't, so relax.'

'No, of course not—how can he know?' said Matthew, more to himself than to Jo.

'So, you're going to tell Stevie tomorrow to move out then?' said Jo.

'Well, I'll have to give her a bit of time to get packed up and find somewhere else. She has got Danny to think about.'

'Poor little Danny,' said Jo, sniffing sadly. 'This is going to be awful for him too. I can't bear to think about it. She'll probably—' Jo cut off.

'She'll probably what?' urged Matthew.

'Well, I think that you should be very careful how you handle Stevie,' said Jo. 'She may turn . . . feral.'

'She won't. She's not like that,' said Matthew. Jo gave him an 'I know better than you about women' look.

'Trust me, I'm not trying to be awful,' she said. 'God knows, this is going to be a living hell for the poor darling. It's just that . . . well, she herself told me how it was—last time.'

Matthew had to conclude that, actually, Jo might be right on that one. He rewound to some old conversations he'd had with Stevie about how she had reacted to Mick's infidelity. There had been lots of shouting, ripping things, throwing things, emotional blackmail, even a bit of stalking—totally out of character for the gentle person he knew and had loved. It was just as well that all he was going to tell Stevie was that he needed some space and it might be better if she moved out for a while. Once she was out of the way, he would pretend to get together with Jo, who would move in soon after, of course.

He could not wait to carry on at home where he and Jo would leave off in Majorca. It had been so good to wake up with her after a long night instead of skulking about, snatching moments when Stevie's back was turned. He didn't know at what point he was going to tell Stevie the wedding was off. He was sort of hoping she would draw that conclusion for herself and save him the hassle. It was a cliché all right, but all *was* fair in love and war. He had to keep thinking that or he would never be able to look at himself in a mirror again.

Obviously, Adam MacLean might not quite see it in those terms. Jo was going to tell him she wanted some space too, and then join Matt at the Queens Hotel in town, when she had packed a few essentials. She hadn't been quite so keen on his first suggestion of the B&B on Lunn Street, but what the hell—it wouldn't be for long, then any money worries would be over. No doubt Jo would go for a quickie divorce on the grounds of MacLean being violent, and the latter would have to pay her out once their house was sold. Matthew presumed she would buy half his house in Blossom Lane and then they could really start to enjoy themselves. Holidays in the sun, cosy romantic meals for two at home and cuddle-ups on the sofa, tiny Agent Provocateur G-strings to pull off with his teeth. His perfect life was just round the corner.

'So, what do you want to do on your last night?' he asked.

She sidled suggestively over to him, reaching behind her to unzip her dress. It fell to the floor and she stepped out of it, wearing nothing but some very small black see-through briefs.

'What do you think?' she said. 'I bet Stevie never wore anything like these for you, did she?'

Matthew groaned. *Stevie who?* was his last coherent thought of the day.

Stevie tucked Danny up and read him a story about a Useless Troll with a very grisly ending, which he listened to with rapture, sucking his pyjama collar, until she extricated it from his mouth. She kissed him good night and thought, The next time I see you will be the day I see Matthew. Then the phone went. It was Catherine.

'You all set for tomorrow? Are you going to let him know you know?'

'No. I'm going to be really nice. Calm and collected and cool.'

All of which was going to be difficult, since she had discovered that Matthew had taken out most of the money in their joint savings account; money that he hadn't put in. They had planned to take Danny to EuroDisney with it that summer. He had probably spent it on *her*.

'Don't let him get away with it entirely, he'll think you're a soft touch,' said Catherine, who was amazed at her friend's self-control. She had been witness to the crazy state she had been in when she found out that Mick was playing about.

'I take your point,' said Stevie, 'but if he carries on pretending he went to Aberdeen and that's the end of the matter, then I'm going to try to forget this ever happened.'

'And will you really be able to do that?' asked Catherine with a gasp.

'I'm going to have to,' said Stevie, with steely resolve.

Matthew's eyes darted around the airport as if Adam MacLean might swing down from a rope SAS style, carrying a machine gun. Jo, on the other hand, didn't seem half as perturbed as he expected her to be.

'Relax,' she said. 'If Adam is here, there are plenty of security men to overpower him and he will only end up in prison again.'

Which would be small comfort on the mortuary slab, thought Matthew, although he didn't want to admit being frightened after all the brownie points he had earned being Jo's Sir Lancelot. They picked up their luggage and then made their way to the long-stay car park.

They both looked very healthy and brown—too much so for it to be attributed to a sunbed—plus they were both far too blissed out to have been exercising on a Welsh treadmill or crammed up in an Aberdeen conference centre. Matthew was wondering if this really was going to be worth the fallout to come, when Jo's long fingers came out and squeezed his inner thigh.

'Drop me round the corner when we get there, usual place.'

'I thought that at this hour he wouldn't be at home?'

'He shouldn't be, but his shift pattern might have changed. Anyway, I have to see him some time, it's better that it's now.'

'I'm scared for you, sweetie.'

'Don't be,' she said. 'But . . . if you haven't heard from me by six o'clock, call the police, just to be on the safe side.'

'God, now you really are scaring me!'

'He threatened his first wife with a chainsaw.' Jo shook her head. 'He won't get the better of me, though. Not this time, I promise.'

She looked so determined that Matthew found himself smiling proudly. What a woman. She had come so far since they had first got together; back then, she was little better than a fragile shell with no confidence. He really had saved her, Matt thought with a proud glow. Jo MacLean was the most fantastic creature he had ever met. And after they had done the necessary this afternoon, nothing would ever part them.

When Matthew's car pulled up outside the house at thirteen minutes and twenty-eight seconds past two, Stevie was relieved to see that he was alone. She manufactured a smile, which trembled on her lips as she jumped across the room from the window to stage herself casually at the computer just before the door opened.

'Hey there!' she said, pulling her smile as wide as possible in a semblance of 'woman overjoyed to see missed fiancé' and sprang up to give him a welcoming hug. She noticed how stiffly he reciprocated it.

'Did you have a nice time?' she said breezily. 'Hey, I see you've been at the sunbeds there. Great leisure facilities, eh?'

'Yes, fantastic. Nice way to unwind—sitting in the . . . on the, er . . . sunbed. Especially after the long, hard, boring meetings.'

'Must have been tiring. Bet the journey back was hell,' she said as chirpily as a canary on Prozac.

'Yes,' he said, stretching and yawning with exhaustion at the imaginary long drive from Scotland.

'Cup of tea?' she said.

'No, I'm OK. Stopped off at some services at Scotch Corner.'

It was harder than she had thought, trying to be Mrs Nice Person while someone was lying to you, and what's more, you knew they were.

'Stevie.' He started scratching the back of his neck. Something he did when he was nervous, usually when opening a bank statement.

'Yes?' she said, still wearing that ridiculous smile.

'Stevie, when I was away, I did a lot of thinking. Alone. Lying under the sun . . . er . . . bed.'

Lying being the operative word. 'Oh, did you?' Smile, smile. *Thinking and shagging. And spending my son's holiday money!*

'I don't know how to say this so I'll just come straight out with it . . .'

Oh God, oh God . . . 'I'm listening,' she said, presenting her bravest and most understanding face.

'I think . . .'

Oh, please don't say it, Matthew, please don't!

'. . . I think we should take a bit of time out. Before the wedding.' Damn, I didn't mean to mention the wedding, Matt thought. Now I've made it look as if it's still on.

Which was what Stevie was thinking. *'Before the wedding'—it's still on! Thank You, God!* She tested him. 'You mean, like, split up?'

'No . . . yes . . . no . . .'

Damn! Her total reasonableness threw him. He had expected her to start crying and pleading and throwing things, then he would have had licence to storm off. This was so much harder, her being calm and nice.

'OK, if that's what you want,' she said, nodding. 'I understand.'

'Eh? Oh, right then.' Bloody hell! That was easy!

'So how do we do this?' said Ms Chirpy the drugged-up canary.

'Er, well, let's think.' He tapped his lip with his finger. 'Maybe if I move into a B and B for a few days, to give you a chance to get your stuff together,' he said, as if it had just come to him.

'My stuff?' echoed Stevie, a little breathlessly.

'Yes. I think it might be best if you . . . er . . . moved out for a bit.'

'Oh, yes, I see—of course "my stuff",' she said, stretching her smile that bit further. Her thoughts were screaming at her to focus on the fact that he hadn't asked her to cancel the wedding. This was all still salvageable if she stuck to being 'nice-accepting lady'. 'Right. OK then.'

'Just for a while,' he said, which again wasn't what he meant at all.

'I'll obviously need to take some money out of the EuroDisney trip account for a room or rent or whatever,' she said.

'Oh, er . . . I had to borrow some of it.' He looked sheepish.

'Did you? What was that for?' Plastic smile again.

'Petrol and stuff in Scotland. I'll pay it back. Obviously. Emergency.' He actually had the good grace to go red now.

'Oh, yes, OK. If you could, considering what it was for.'

'Absolutely, straight away.'

Stevie nodded, though she had heard that too often from him to believe it any more. 'Right, then,' she carried on, leashing her anger with desperate effort. She had to be in control. This, after all, was a much wider picture than a lost fifteen hundred quid and a couple of lust-driven lies.

'I'll go and get a few bits together then,' he said nervously.

'Yes, why not.' The smile weighed heavy and was getting painful.

Matthew backed off upstairs and she took some comfort from the fact that she had rattled him with her coolness and self-possession.

She could hear him padding about, opening drawers. He would pack that beautiful blue silk shirt, and the chinos that always made his bottom look nice, and his best suit so he could take Jo out for a posh meal somewhere. He liked to wine and dine, and he always looked so handsome in a suit, especially by candlelight.

She found she was not strong enough to hold all the tears back. They started to leak out of the corners of her eyes, faster than she could wipe them away, but wipe them away she did as soon as she heard footsteps coming down the stairs, faster than a child's on Christmas morning. Then he crossed to the drawer and got out his mobile phone.

'Look, I'll be in touch soon, promise,' he said, carrying a very large case and some suits in covers.

'Yes, well, you take care,' she said. She needed three big lads and some scaffolding now to hold up this smile.

'Goodbye, Stevie. Give my love to little Danny.'

'I will,' she said, thinking how final 'goodbye' sounded. Then he was gone, without one glance of recognition that she had had her hair done or was half a stone lighter.

She didn't wave his car off, she just sat on the sofa and let that infernal smile drop into a reverse of itself—a deep, downward arc. Then, when she could no longer hear the sound of his engine, she let her head fall into her hands and sobbed her heart out.

Chapter 3

MATTHEW HAD WORN a path into the carpet by the time he heard the footsteps outside the hotel room. He checked his watch for the millionth time—*six minutes and six seconds to six*—threw open the door before the soft knock had ended and fell upon a wide-eyed Jo.

'I was so worried!' he said, taking her in his arms. He had his mobile in his hand, ready to ring the police. It had been a close call.

'Sorry,' she said, sniffling. 'He was there. It was pretty gruelling.'

He pulled her away from him and studied her, looking for signs of violence but thankfully there was nothing, only pale lines on her face where tears had cut through her make-up.

'Are you OK? He didn't—?'

'No,' Jo said, snuggling further into him. 'Not really.'

'What do you mean, "not really", darling?' said Matthew.

'Well, at least I got away. Let's just say, he started getting a bit rough.'

She winced as his hands touched her shoulder and she let him gently unbutton the top of her shirt to find small, deep, fingernail-shaped crescents on her shoulder, and bruising already forming around them.

'The swine! I'm getting the police.'

Matthew pulled out his mobile, but Jo stilled his hand.

'No,' she said. 'It's over. I don't want any more police. Nothing ever comes of it anyway, except he gets more annoyed. Please, darling. Let's just get on with the rest of our lives now. I'm free of him.'

She looked at him with her heavily fringed dark treacle eyes glistening with tears and he relented.

'Oh, baby!' He squeezed her tight and then let go temporarily when someone else knocked on the door. Matthew opened it to find three porters standing there with six massive suitcases. 'Wow!' he said.

'It'll be a relief to get them over to your house,' Jo said, adding pointedly, 'sooner rather than later.'

'Stevie is going to move out as soon as she can,' said Matthew.

'How was she? Upset?'

'No, actually,' said Matthew, shaking his head, as if he didn't quite believe it himself. 'She was . . . er . . . very understanding indeed.'

Had he looked at Jo at that moment, he would have seen something cross her face like a cloud. A cloud that was full of the grey shades of confusion that said, 'Now *that is odd* . . .'

Eddie walked in from work and straight away asked his wife, 'So, how did Stevie get on with Buggerlugs today?'

'Don't ask,' said Catherine, giving him her customary peck. 'Apparently Matt came in, packed a bag and sodded straight off.'

'Never! Where's he gone?'

'To a B and B,' she said. 'He didn't give her the name of it. Told her he wanted a bit of space before the wedding.'

'The wedding? Still on then, is it?' Eddie shook his head. 'Blimey.'

'He's moved out for a few days. Until Stevie moves out.'

'Eh?'

'I couldn't have put it better myself, babe,' said Catherine, who was wondering when the Doppelgänger had taken over Matthew's soul, because this was so not the guy she knew. He was everything Mick wasn't, so why was he acting just as idiotically? Had it been anyone but Matthew, Catherine would have advised her friend to get out and draw a line under it all without so much as a backward glance, but Matt was a great bloke—steady and quiet, well, at least he had been.

'What's she going to do?' asked Eddie, stripping off his orange skip-deliverer's tunic. He was a plasterer by trade but he did a day here and there helping out an old friend in refuse and recycling.

'She hasn't a bloody clue,' said Catherine.

'Well, you'd better ring your auntie Madge and tell her that Stevie won't be going to Pam's wedding on Saturday.'

'Eddie, apart from the fact that Pam would kill her if she didn't go, I've told Steve that she needs to be seen enjoying herself and getting on with life, not moping about. That's not going to attract Matt back, is it?'

Pam was Catherine's formidable cousin. She was getting married to William, the guy who ran Gym Village, and they had all been invited. The tartan-ribboned invitation was on Catherine's pin-board in the kitchen, as it was in Stevie's; her own and Matthew's names on it bracketed together as a couple. The groom was a Scot and getting married in full tartan regalia, and it promised to be a jolly affair.

Eddie scratched his head. 'What if Matt goes and takes that Joanna? Have you thought about how that would make Stevie feel?'

'Don't be daft, he wouldn't dare! And even if he did think about bringing her, she wouldn't be that iron-faced as to come. Besides, I reminded Stevie how she'd promised Danny that he could stay at ours that night with Kate. She wouldn't dream of letting him down.'

Kate, who loved the little boy to bits and pieces, and was adored in return, had volunteered to baby-sit him, along with her other brothers and sisters. Volunteered after being offered a lump sum, that was. Danny was going to top and tail in little Gareth's pirate-ship bed and he'd had his Mr Incredibles bag packed for a fortnight waiting for it.

'That's below the belt,' said Eddie, wincing.

'I know.' Catherine grinned. 'But it worked. She's going. I'll ring Auntie Madge and get her to jiggle the seating arrangements a bit though.'

'Cath,' said Eddie kindly, 'are you sure it's the right thing for her?'

'Sure as eggs are eggs.' Catherine nodded. 'If Matt had known what he was doing, he would have cancelled the wedding. He'll come to his senses, I'm convinced of it. He'll be holed up in a grotty B and B wrestling with his conscience and having a last-minute commitment panic. Soon as he sees that Stevie is fine without him, he'll want her back.'

'And where's this Jo?' said Eddie. 'Has she gone back to her husband?'

'My guess is that she did. I tried to get Stevie to ring MacLean to find out, but she wouldn't. Do you think I should?'

'No, I bloody well don't,' said Eddie. Much as he loved his wife, it niggled him sometimes that she always thought she knew best.

Adam MacLean spotted Stevie on the weights. She had headphones on and was watching TV. Now which channel would she be tuned into? he mused. Sky News? Or *Morning Coffee* with Drusilla Durham and that smarmy Gerald Mandelton bloke talking about cakes?

He wondered how the day before last had gone at her end, when Matty Boy returned. Not too well, if her serious, pale face was anything to go by. If only the daft woman had listened to him, this stupid business might have been over and done with. No doubt she had shouted at Finch, pleaded, screamed, cried, and embarrassed him back to his Jo faster than if he was Sir Roger Bannister and his backside was on fire.

He could see that her teeth were gritted as she tackled far bigger weights than were on her programme. He should have gone over and told her she needed to do more reps on smaller weights, otherwise she would end up like a miniature Hulk Hogan, but he sent Hilary over because he would not have been able to resist asking how things were and she, no doubt, would have replied with some cocky remark that made him even more disgruntled than he was already.

The seven nights in bed without Jo's body beside him were hard enough, but the last two had hurt more than all of them put together, knowing all her wardrobes were empty and her jewellery and toiletries and make-up were gone from cupboards and drawers.

He knew he had played it like a master when she walked through the door looking tanned and glowing and telling him how wet Wales was. Like he had tried to say to Mrs Universe over there—*basic psychology*. Jo had been shaking when she left him, and even though she had gone out of his door with her suitcases, climbed in her car and driven off, he would have bet his own car that Round One had been to him.

'**M**ummy, is "happily" an adverb?'

'Yes, it is, love,' said Stevie, changing his wet pyjama top. 'As in "Danny Honeywell chews his pyjama collar *happily*".'

'Mummy? Where's Matthew?'

'Weeelll . . .' she began, then realised she hadn't a clue how she was going to answer, or even if she could because her voice felt as if it would be too wobbly to deliver the words. She wasn't quite sure where tears came from, but they seemed to be taking a fast train to her eyes these days, and the pressure of holding them back physically hurt.

'He's just living somewhere else for a while and we're going to live somewhere else for a while, too,' she said.

She knew this wouldn't be enough to satisfy his inquisitive little mind though and, sure enough, four seconds later he asked, 'Why?'

'Because grown-ups sometimes live apart to see if they miss each other. You see, when they get married, they want to make sure they live happily ever after.'

Stevie put him to bed after reading him *The Useless Troll* yet again. He knew what the ending was and still delighted in hearing the gruesome 'sting'. Stevie wished she knew what the ending to her story was.

She had not done a thing as regards finding somewhere else to live. The thought of leaving Matt's house was awful, but she knew she must—and soon. It would be far better, she supposed, to play the game and make all the necessary arrangements and then have to cancel them at the eleventh hour, when Matthew came to his senses, than to dither and risk Danny and her being thrown out forcibly.

It had been Matthew who had badgered her to move in with him, with the 'two could live as cheaply as one' philosophy, although she had ended up paying most of the bills and the mortgage since she'd been there. She had even cleared a few of his arrears, thanks to a nice profit from the sale of her house. She had also paid for her wedding dress, Matthew's wedding suit (which cost more than her whole outfit), Catherine's bridesmaid dress, Danny's pageboy outfit, the rings and the deposits on the reception, flowers and honeymoon.

Matthew's plans to contribute were bound up in procrastinations, not that she minded because life with someone was about sharing, wasn't it? After Mick, she had thought she would never trust anyone enough again to unlock the door to her heart and throw it open.

So Stevie settled down with the *Properties* section of the local paper. Buying somewhere wasn't an option, in case Matthew came to his senses and asked her to come back, so, as far as rental accommodation went, it had to be somewhere nearby for Danny's school, which ruled out most of the houses available. The cottage across the lane was featured, as always, but the bond alone was enough to have most people voicing the message to the landlord, 'Hope the sun shines for yer, mate!'

Stevie made a mental note to ring some estate agents very soon, but she knew she was stalling, waiting for a miracle to rescue her. The miracle that was, unbeknown to her then, just round the corner.

Jo was drying her hair after a dribbling shower. Matthew watched her fondly, the expression of a love-struck labrador pup on his face.

'What's the matter?' she said, catching his eye.

'Nothing, I'm just looking at you.'

'Well, stop it,' she said, and carried on wafting the hair dryer and trying to pretend that she wasn't being scrutinised quite so thoroughly.

Coming up behind her, he planted a kiss on her neck.

'Not now,' she said, wriggling away. 'I'm late for work.'

'*We're* late for work,' he said, 'but at least we can occupy a car-sharing parking space. They're always in plentiful supply.'

'Great,' said Jo sarcastically, which made his Tigger-bouncing heart deflate a little.

'You OK?' he said.

'Well, no, actually,' she said. 'I don't enjoy living out of a suitcase. I just want to move into your house as soon as possible.'

'I know it's hard, sweetie,' said Matthew sympathetically because he recognised that it was a lot easier for a bloke living in a hotel room than a girl with all her essential accoutrements. 'We'll be in there soon.'

'How soon is "soon"?'

'Well, I have to give Stevie a few days at least.'

'Of course,' said Jo, coming over for a snuggle. 'I'm sorry, I'm being selfish even asking. Forgive me, it's just that if I think too much about Stevie, I'll start to feel awful. I betrayed my friendship with her to get you, and the awful thing is that I would do it all over again if I had to.'

Matthew's arms closed round her. Building a relationship on the ruins of another wasn't what either of them had wanted. The whole Stevie thing had brought tears to Jo's eyes many times, because neither of them were the sort of sick people who went round hurting others for fun. It was just that when love like this called, you didn't hide and pretend you were out, you flung open the door, invited it right on in to sit in your most comfortable chair and fed it your best tin of biscuits.

Jo sighed. 'I'm so stressed out. I'm waiting for Adam's next move and I just want to be safe in your house with you rather than in some place where he could easily get to me if he wanted.'

'I understand,' he said, rubbing her shoulders and making her purr. 'I'll ring her later and push her along a bit.'

'Maybe she'll be at the wedding tomorrow—you can ask her then.'

'The wedding?'

'Yes. Will and Pam's wedding,' said Jo.

'You are joking. I can't go to that now!' said Matthew.

'Why ever not?'

'Well, they're more Stevie's and your ex's friends than mine and yours for a start.'

'Don't be silly,' said Jo. 'I'm sure you and I were invited on our own merits. You knew Will from the gym, before you even met Stevie. And I've met Pam and Will a couple of times and got on very well with them. Plus I've bought a new suit I have every intention of wearing.'

Matthew didn't look convinced so she came at him from another angle.

'Matthew, the sooner Stevie sees us as a couple, the sooner she'll realise it's over for you and her. She has to know.'

'Stevie won't go to the wedding after all that's happened.'

'So, what's the problem?'

'Well, I'm thinking about Adam.'

'Matthew,' began Jo. 'I have no intention of hiding away. *I'm* not the one that wrecked my relationship—I've nothing to be ashamed of.'

'We don't have to go. I'm sure we wouldn't be missed if we didn't turn up. You and I could do something special together instead.'

'People have to know sometime that we're an item, Matthew! Stevie will be less hurt thinking tomorrow is our starting point. We're both free agents now. No one can say it's wrong for us to be a couple.'

'Well . . . er . . .' started Matthew, who hadn't actually spelt it out to Stevie yet that he wasn't coming back, but Jo wasn't listening.

'It won't be very nice for Stevie at the beginning, but as soon as she knows you have found someone else, the healing process will kick in.'

Matthew was more worried about what MacLean would 'kick in' when he heard that someone was moving in on his wife.

'Trust me, Adam will be less upset,' said Jo, 'to see us getting together in front of him tomorrow than poking around to discover we've been having an affair behind his back for the past few months.'

'Look, let's talk about it on the way to work,' said Matthew, kissing the tip of her little pointy nose. He picked up her briefcase for her and they walked out into the corridor to find the lift out of order and the prospect for Jo of four flights of steps in very high stilettos.

'Bloody hotel,' she said. 'How much did you say you were paying?'

'Don't ask,' he sighed, following her fuming passage down the stairs. He was just at the top of the second flight when he realised what she had actually said: *How much did you say you were paying?*

The day of the wedding dawned. Danny woke up with a heart full of excitement. In the next bedroom, Stevie woke up with a heart full of dread. The day could take so many possible forms:

1)   Matthew doesn't turn up
2)   Matthew turns up and ignores her
3)   Matthew turns up with Joanna
4)   Matthew turns up with Joanna and announces his
        engagement
5)   Adam MacLean murders everyone

None of them was especially good.

Eddie bee-beeped outside at half past eleven and Danny moved as fast as if he had a nuclear rocket secreted down the back of his pants.

'Mummy, it's Uncle Eddie, it's Uncle Eddie!'

'Never!' said Stevie, smiling at his jubilation, which trebled when he saw Boot's massive and ugly profile in the back seat.

'Mummy, Boot's here! Come on,' he urged, dancing round like Michael Flatley with a bladder problem. Eddie wolf-whistled when Stevie came out to the car in her rainbow-striped dressing gown.

'Oh, get stuffed!' said Stevie, knowing she was hardly wolf-whistley-material.

'Stevie, what the bloody hell have you done to your conk?'

Stevie's hand shot up to her still-tender nose in horror. 'I fell at the gym. Oh God, can you see it? Is it really noticeable?'

'No, is it heck. Slap a bit of make-up on it, nobody'll notice.'

'I did that already.'

'Sorry,' said Eddie, twisting to the boy. 'Ready, sunshine?' Danny had clambered in the back and was fighting off a very licky Boot.

'Boot!' reprimanded Eddie. 'Get down!' Boot immediately lay down with his chin on Danny's lap and the little boy's face registered heaven as he stroked the big black head. It was part of a scenario Stevie had wished for him so many times: piling in a people carrier with a big sloppy dog and a big sloppy dad.

'Oy, you, cheer up,' said Eddie, seeing the shadow of sadness suddenly cross Stevie's features. He reached through the window, took her hand and squeezed it in his bear-like paw. 'We'll look after you today and we're going to have a great time, and no one will notice your conk because the rest of you will be so gorgeous.'

'See you at one outside the church, then,' said Stevie, clicking on a smile. She rapped on the window to Danny and said, 'You be good!'

'Ah, he's always good,' said Eddie. 'He's a cracker like his mam.'

'Well, this is as good as it gets,' she said to her reflection an hour later, which nodded back its approval. She had lost weight since she tried the red suit on in the shop; it fitted her not so snugly and the cut made her

354 | Milly Johnson

waist nip in nicely. Offset with slim black patent heels, a matching bag and a large-brimmed red and black hat, she looked OK, if she said so herself. An extra blob of foundation almost covered up the scab on the bridge of her nose and took some of the bluish hue of the bruise away. The taxi pipped outside and she quickly grabbed the wedding present and locked up the front door on her way out to get it.

It was a beautiful day for a wedding, sunny and no wind. The bells were pealing from the pretty little Maltstone village church where Catherine, resplendent in navy-blue and a gorgeous cloche hat, and Eddie in a dark grey suit and a tartan tie, were waiting for her outside.

'Lady in red, you look swanky,' said Eddie, giving her a kiss.

'So do you,' said Stevie, although even if Eddie had been wearing Armani he wouldn't have managed to lose that 'I hate suits' look.

'Stevie, you look lovely,' said Catherine, giving her a peck and a squeeze. Then her smile dropped. 'What happened to your nose?'

'Oh hell,' said Stevie, covering it up with her hand. 'I fell in the gym.'

'Ouch!' said Catherine. 'Look, the nose thing isn't really noticeable. It's only because I stared at you from point-blank range. Your hat throws it right into shadow . . .'

'Shut up about her beak,' said Eddie. 'Come on, let's get inside where it's dark and no one can see anyone's nose,' and he presented his arms to both ladies and led them down the church path.

They were so busy talking in the queue for hymn books that neither woman noticed him at first. It was only when it was Stevie's turn and the distinctive voice said, 'Brrride or Grrroom?' that she jumped and took a long sweep upwards from the big hairy legs appearing out of the bottom of a heavily sporraned kilt to the mashed but surprisingly clean-shaven face, and then further on to a very, very cropped hairdo.

As if he hadn't looked hard enough before. 'Pardon?'

'Brrride or Grrroom?'

He even managed to make that sound threatening. As if she was in a Belfast pub and he was asking 'Catholic or Protestant' and any answer would result in a kneecapping.

'Broom,' said Stevie, swallowing.

'She means "bride",' said Catherine, coming to her rescue.

'Right, tha' side there, then,' he said, pointing left, and handed over three hymn books and order of services.

'Thank you, so kind,' said Stevie.

Catherine and Eddie twittered on in the background as she filled Eddie in on who that was. They filed down to the middle of the church.

'What's he doing here?' Stevie asked finally.

'Haven't a clue. He must know William. Oy, Steve, did you see his legs?' asked Catherine in a whisper that seemed to echo. 'I thought he'd got furry oak trees under his kilt.'

'Where's his hair gone?' said Stevie.

'Will you two be quiet!' said Eddie, although even he had a good look when usher-time was at an end and Madman strutted down the aisle to take up his seat on the groom's side. He was obviously trying to get his physical house in order, thought Stevie.

The organist played 'Here Comes the Bride' and Pam swaggered down the aisle in a fishtail white velvet dress, her hair piled up on her head with white flowers in it and a light furry cape dressing her shoulders. She was a big lass but she looked gorgeous and sexy on her dad's arm. There were no bridesmaids. Pam didn't want anyone more glam than her stealing her thunder.

'Dearly beloved . . .' began the vicar. Stevie gulped. It was four weeks to her own wedding and she hadn't a clue if it was still on. Her head was clinging to the possibility that it was, but a voice within was telling her she needed to wake up and smell some espresso.

At last Pam and William sauntered back up the aisle as husband and wife, smiles bursting their faces open. In the absence of bridesmaids, the best man linked up with Pam's mum, William's doll-like mum linked up behind with Adam MacLean, and Pam's dad walked out with his own mother. MacLean flashed Stevie a look. She flashed one back as hard. They both transmitted 'what the hell are you doing here?' in international eye language. As if that wasn't enough to contend with, the first person she saw as she followed the others outside was Matthew. The plus point was that Jo wasn't with him. The minus point was that he had the suit on that he was supposed to be wearing for his wedding to her.

'Oh shit!' said Catherine. 'Have you seen who's over there?'

'Yes, I've just seen him,' said Stevie, feeling light-headed.

'No, not him.' Catherine did a discreet stabby point and Stevie followed it to see Jo there, in a black suit with red accessories, looking tall and slim and stunning. Stevie wanted to run across the graveyard and go home. No, she didn't, she wanted to charge at Jo with her head down like a bull and start clubbing her to death with an urn.

'Keep calm,' said Catherine. 'You're the one that hasn't done anything wrong. Let them be the ones to make fools of themselves.'

'She obviously hasn't gone back to MacLean then, so that answers that one,' said Stevie. 'Then again, why are she and Matthew ignoring each other?' She should have felt heartened by this but something was interfering with her ability to do that. Jo was, after all, a designer and this scene was looking distinctly designed.

'They're probably trying not to incur the wrath of the hairy-legged one,' said Catherine.

Stevie watched as Adam's eyes fell on Matthew and stayed there for a long, long second. His body locked like a Rottweiler's before an attack, then he snapped out of it quickly to be pulled into a smiling photographic tableau. Then, as a natural consequence of seeing Matthew, he looked around for Jo. He found her, he stared, he swallowed.

This must be as hard for him as it is for me, thought Stevie, recognising that blanched, brave look.

She let her eyes casually drift over to Matthew, who pretended that was the first he had seen of her and, how she managed it she didn't know, but she waved genially and smiled like the Queen, and then carried on perusing the crowd. Jo's red and blackness was harder to deal with. Stevie couldn't bring herself even to glance in that direction. Her suit seemed to keep creeping into Stevie's peripheral vision though, and she had to keep finding places for her eyes to rest away from Jo and Matthew and MacLean. It was exhausting.

'Last photo—group shot of friends!' announced the photographer, about three million years later.

Oh God, thought Stevie, as all the people in her worst nightmare seemed to converge onto the lawn. Jo was posing at the far end, Matthew was in the middle and Adam was nowhere to be seen, which meant he was probably somewhere behind her.

'That's one for the album—not,' said Catherine, giving her a nudge.

'Right, has everyone got lifts back tae the Ivy?' enquired big Adam MacLean in full duty mode. He didn't have to shout to be heard.

'We haven't,' replied Eddie, who had left the car at home so they could all have a drink. Adam organised them into a car with William's ancient Uncle Dennis. Stevie took a sly look over at Matthew, who appeared to be making a pretence of saying, 'Hi,' to Jo and asking her if she had a lift, if the extravagant hand gestures towards the church car park were anything to go by.

'I think I might skip the reception and go home,' said Stevie, who felt nauseous, something that couldn't be blamed on Uncle Dennis's wild driving. Tortoises and snails were overtaking them on both sides.

'No chance,' said Catherine. 'Think of "your plan".'

'Did he look at me at all?' asked Stevie.

'I don't know,' said Catherine. 'I was trying not to look at him.'

Behind her back, Catherine's fingers were crossed on the lie. She did not tell her friend that on the couple of occasions she had looked over, Matthew seemed to have eyes only for Jo.

Alas, the Ivy wasn't *the* Ivy, but a country hotel a mile away where trays of sherry were waiting. Stevie's hand was shaking so much that she managed to spill most of her sherry down her skirt.

Adam was laughing, circulating and being jolly Ginger Man. He looked totally different with all that hair off, thought Stevie. She wouldn't have said 'softer', because no one with that nose and scar could have looked remotely soft. 'Less hideous', was the assessment she preferred.

'Hi there!' Pam burst in and kissed them all. She had a champagne glass in one hand and a long menthol cigarette in the other.

'Congratulations,' said Stevie. 'You look fab.'

'So do you actually, Stevie. Have you lost weight?'

'A bit,' said Stevie.

'Sorry to hear about you, hon, hope it all works out for you.'

Pam then swanned off and left them standing in a quiet triangle.

'Sorry,' said Catherine apologetically, 'but I had to tell her about you and Matthew when I asked my auntie Madge to alter the seating plan.'

Stevie squeezed Catherine's hand gratefully. 'Thanks.'

'Laydeees and gelmen, would ye kindly make yer way tae the dinen arearrr,' came Adam MacLean's cannon of a voice.

They looked at the seating plan and Stevie found she was sandwiched between Eddie and a spaghetti-string of a teenage boy.

Matthew was further down the table on her side and out of spying sight and Jo was halfway down an adjacent table, between two middle-aged men in kilts. She didn't look very victimy, considering she was sitting five people away from her psychotic soon-to-be ex-husband, who was behaving with remarkable dignity in the circumstances, Stevie thought. He seemed very jocular. She didn't notice him glance over at Jo once, and by crikey, she was watching for it.

It was a full-blown Christmas dinner. Pam had wanted a Christmas wedding, hence the fur cape, but she didn't want to risk the weather, so she had the best of both worlds—sunshine and turkey.

There was Christmas pudding and mince pies to follow, then when coffee was served, the newlyweds cut the cake—a three-layered chocolate creation that apparently had more rum than butter in it, according to the best man's speech.

Stevie's wedding wasn't going to be as big or nearly as grand as this, but her dad was giving her away and she was having frothy pea soup, roast beef and Yorkshire puddings, and raspberry meringue roulade or fudge cake for afters at the White Swan, a lovely pub near Penistone out in the countryside. Matthew's brother was flying in from Canada to be best man and she had picked pink roses for her bouquet. Everything was in place and, so far, he hadn't called it off. '*So why is he wearing his suit now at someone else's wedding? And looking gorgeous in it for someone else, not you,*' said that annoying voice in her head again. She wished it would contract a serious and sudden case of laryngitis.

Her thoughts came back to the table as glasses were raised to 'the happy couple'. Stevie raised hers along with the others and tried to smile convincingly. Matthew was sleeping with someone else and she was in the process of moving out of his house. How feasible was it that they were going to be 'the happy couple' themselves in four weeks' time?

There was no ordinary disco for Pam's night entertainment, oh no. She had a ceilidh band and a dance demonstration team clad in Highland clobber, stripping the willow and reeling about.

Stevie watched as Matthew started to edge slowly towards Jo. It took him another four minutes before they engaged in conversation. Maybe they were pretending to 'get it together' at the wedding.

'I see contact has been made,' said Catherine, nodding over at the treacherous twosome.

'Yes, I noticed. I'll bet they're making a show in front of MacLean and me that this is their actual starting point.'

'The next dance is "The Birds and the Bees",' said the band leader. 'Come on, now, let's have you up herrre, laddies and lassies.'

'Where's the bonny bride?' shouted someone from the demo team and started chanting to get Pam up dancing.

'Right—well, if I'm going to make a twat of myself, then *everyone* is. Come up, get up,' slurred Pam. She stubbed out her fag and then came over to them and shovelled Eddie, Catherine and Stevie forwards. Everyone hit the dance floor because Pam had said so.

'Stevie, you can road-test Will for me,' said Pam, shoving her new husband in front of Stevie at the end of the formation. 'Adam, get your Scottish backside over here!' Pam dragged Adam opposite to her and he and Stevie glared at each other diagonally.

'We're a six, we need to be an eight,' said Eddie.

'Oy! We need another two over here!' shouted Pam.

A spare 'two' was pushed over from where it was clinging on to the next 'eight' hoping no one would notice it was superfluous.

'*Oh God,*' said every one of them, as Matthew and Jo took up their awkward positions next to Eddie and Catherine.

The demonstrators ran through the sequence. It looked simple in a twizzling-about way. In real life it proved to be slightly more difficult.

Pam cocked up and ended up going the wrong way, taking Will as her partner. This cast Stevie in the path of Adam MacLean, and Stevie was forced to link his arm and be spun round at G force.

'So, how's yer nose?' he asked, as they changed direction.

'Fine, thank you—and yours?' Stevie asked, not knowing quite why she had asked that. Then again, at that point she was trying to coordinate skipping backwards with not being sick.

'OK last time I looked,' he said humourlessly, tripping forward and catching her hand. He was surprisingly nifty on his feet for an Aberdeen Angus, Stevie thought.

'So, ready tae hear whit I have tae say yet? You don't look as if you're making much progress yer way.'

'And you are, I suppose?' said Stevie, quirking her eyebrow.

'Aye, I most certainly am!'

Stevie twirled round him with a little sarcastic, 'Ha!' and followed it with, 'No, thank you. I think I'll pass on this and every other occasion to discuss your "master plan".' Her arm brushed against Jo as she skipped down the back of the formation to meet Matthew. It was like being touched by an electric cattle prod. Stevie jerked to the side, bouncing into Will, and would have fallen over if Adam MacLean hadn't grabbed her elbow. By comparison, Jo's steps were perfect. She and Matthew looked like John Travolta and that Stephanie woman in *Saturday Night Fever* who were so spiritually and bodily synchronised.

Adam cast her off and she did a figure of eight round Pam and then bumped clumsily into Matthew, who stared straight ahead of him in a 'God, get me out of this quick' kind of way. Then Adam caught both of Stevie's hands at the top of the line and trotted down the middle of the other three partners with her. They were huge hands. Hands that smacked women. It made her feel ill to touch him and she tried to pull them away but MacLean hung on firmly.

'So you're no' goin' tae listen?' he grumbled.

'Not in this lifetime,' panted Stevie.

Adam sneered. 'Well, let's hope you're better at holdin' on tae yer man than y'are at dancin',' he said gruffly, as he let Stevie's hands go. As soon as the final chord had sounded, Adam, Jo and Matthew were gone from the dance floor, three people united in their desire to get away from the lumpy woman with her sherry-stained skirt and scabby nose.

Catherine watched her friend's eyes follow Jo to a quiet table for two in the far corner. Matthew joined her tentatively a few moments afterwards in a move choreographed as slickly as the sweetly named 'The Birds and the Bees' dance.

'I think I'll slip away home now,' said Stevie. 'I don't think my stiff upper lip can take any more.'

Catherine nodded and kissed her on the head.

'I'm proud of you. You've acted like a lady. Have a long lie-in and pick Danny up whenever. He won't thank you for being early.'

Stevie asked the lady on Reception to phone her a taxi. The taxi wasn't long in coming, but no sooner had she got to the glass exit doors than Matthew's voice came from behind.

'Stevie, Stevie, wait!'

She turned round, a hopeful flutter in her heart, but he wasn't making much eye contact, which wasn't exactly an encouraging sign.

'Sorry, bad timing. Your taxi's here, isn't it?'

'Yes, it is,' she said. Her heart was thumping like a tom-tom.

'Stevie, is it OK if I pop round tomorrow? About nine in the evening, when Danny's in bed.'

'Yes, yes, of course.'

Outside, the taxi driver gave an impatient jab on his horn.

'OK, see you tomorrow then,' said Matthew, then he waved weakly and disappeared quickly back inside to the party.

'Yes, see you tomorrow,' said Stevie to his cold slip-stream.

Chapter 4

A FORTNIGHT AGO, Adam had never even seen the bloody woman, and now it seemed that everywhere he went, she was there as well. If her hatred of him hadn't been so obvious, he would have thought she was stalking him. His gym, the wedding, and now the supermarket on a quiet Sunday morning. Was there no peace?

He had been fascinated to watch Matthew and Jo stage-manage their 'coming together', just before 'The Birds and the Bees' at the wedding last night. He had suppressed a wry smile at their guile, although seeing Jo flirt with another man in that way poked at something ancient and violent within him. She and Matty Boy had stayed together all evening after that, careful not to give away any clues to their already established

intimacy by making every move look casual, though this had been sab-
otaged somewhat as Jo kept having to sneak out her purse to pay for
the drinks that Matthew went up to the bar to get. She wouldn't have
liked that one bit, and might have just won him Round Two by default.

Not that he was watching them much. He was trying really hard to
look as if he was unbothered and jolly. It was all part of his master plan.

Dragging his thoughts back to the here and now, he watched *her*,
hovering around the salad vegetables. She was wearing jeans and a
green sweatshirt which complemented her ruffled blonde hair. She
looked quite neat now and had certainly scrubbed up *nae bad* in that
red suit and hat at the wedding, although she must have wanted to die
when Jo turned up in a reversal of the same colours. Jo looked so gorgeous that he would not have been able to stop himself kissing her and
carrying her home, if she had given him the slightest encouragement.

No little boy with *her* again—so who had she palmed him off onto
today? Adam wondered. He bet Mother of the Year awards were stacked
high on *her* mantelpiece. Mind you, the kid was better off away from a
mother with a temper like that. It must have been luck that he hadn't
been hurt in the crossfire when she threw pans in temper at Matthew.

She must have just come into the supermarket for she had only collected one item so far—*and what an item!* She hadn't seen him because
she was concentrating on trying to guide a trolley with a demonically
possessed front wheel, so the advantage was his. He couldn't resist
charging deliberately into her trolley with his own, full of many bottles
of spirits, mainly whisky. He gave her a look of mock surprise.

'Well, fancy meetin' yoooou here. Adjusting to single life verrry
quickly, I see,' he bellowed, pointing down to the very long cucumber
standing erect in her trolley. She blushed and threw the nearest thing to
hand in beside it to dilute the embarrassment. A tray of stir-fry.

'Oooh yum yum,' he said. 'Cucumber stir-fry, my favourite.'

'Was there something you wanted, Mr MacLean?' said Stevie haugh-
tily, trying not to blush any harder. 'Only I've far more important things
to do than stand here being insulted by you.'

'I wonder whit they could be?' He smiled like a barracuda, raised his
eyebrows and cast a look at the impressive cucumber.

'My fiancé is calling round later,' Stevie said, ignoring his pathetic
childish innuendos. He looked interested now and less piss-takey.

'Oh, really?' he said, folding his arms. 'Whit forrr?'

'I don't know, but he's coming when my son is in bed so he obviously
wants to talk. I'm quietly optimistic.'

'Well, good luck,' said Adam MacLean, 'but will you take some advice?'

'No,' said Stevie and started to wheel her trolley away, but he grabbed her handlebar forcefully and made sure she wasn't going anywhere.

'Well, I'm givin' it tae you anyway, so take it or leave it. *Basic psychology*. Play it exactly the opposite tae how he'd expect you tae behave. It's yer only weapon.'

Whether or not he meant to imply that her looks or her personality wouldn't do much in a head-to-head with Jo, that's the way she took it.

'Yes, well, thank you, Professor Platitude,' she huffed belligerently. 'I look forward to your next lecture with great eagerness. What will it be? I wonder. Jung's theory of the Absolutely Bloody Obvious?'

Not that he'd know who Jung was. Probably thought she meant the old DJ whose first name was Jimmy. And with that, Stevie and her enormous cucumber weaved off in the direction of the celery, while her trolley headed for Fresh Meats.

She turned up at Catherine's just after half past eleven to find the kitchen in chaos and Danny tucking into a full English breakfast.

'How the hell did you get him to eat that?' said Stevie, after she had given him a big 'hello' kiss. 'I can hardly get him to eat anything except for Coco Pops and chicken.'

'Ah, the wonderful mystery of children,' said Catherine. 'Violet doesn't eat eggs usually, she's only eating them because Danny is, and he's only eating them because Kate is. James obviously eats nothing because he never gets up.'

'Does Violet eat them when Kate eats them then?'

'No, it doesn't work like that—they're related,' said Catherine with a sniff, leading her pal off for a coffee in a quieter corner after swiping bits of uneaten bacon from the twins, Sarah and Robbie. 'Mmm, why is it that food stolen from kids always tastes so good?'

'Thanks for having Danny, Cath,' said Stevie. 'He looks so happy here.'

'Don't be daft, he's no trouble at all.'

'Matthew's coming round later when Danny goes to bed,' said Stevie, quietly. 'He caught me in the foyer, just before I got my taxi home.'

Catherine stopped mid-pour. 'Did he say what for?'

'No, he just made arrangements to come over and then disappeared. How were *they* after I'd gone?'

'Much the same,' said Catherine, plonking a packet of chocolate digestives in front of Stevie. 'They were just talking, nothing else.'

'Did they leave together?'

Catherine didn't answer, which answered the question anyway.

Stevie sighed heavily. 'Do you know, one minute I think he might be coming round to tell me he doesn't want me to move out, and then the next . . . I mean, if they left together, that means it's still on between them, doesn't it? He's not alone at that B and B, is he?'

'I don't know, Steve, but there's no point in driving yourself barmy speculating; you'll have to wait and see what he has to say. Have you eaten? You hardly had a thing yesterday.' She pushed the biscuits almost up Stevie's still-tender nose.

'I've not got much appetite. I went to the supermarket this morning to see if I could find anything to tempt it back, and only bumped straight into that flaming man MacLean again. His trolley was so full of booze the wheels were nearly flat. Typical piss-head Scot. Then he forced me to listen to his advice that I should play this exactly the opposite to what Matthew might expect of me.'

'That's what you're doing, isn't it?'

'Yes, but I'm a woman and he probably doesn't think I have the capacity for such logical thought. Chauvinistic butt-ugly thug.'

'Actually . . . Eddie thought he seemed a nice bloke,' said Catherine tentatively. 'Genuine.'

'Oh, come on, Cath, he's bound to have developed a super-charm gland, looking like that,' said Stevie. 'Otherwise he couldn't have pulled someone who looked like Joanna. Think about it.'

'I thought he was quite attractive close up,' said Catherine, 'especially with all that hair off. And he has fabulous legs. Bet his thighs are—'

'Stop, you're making me ill.'

'He was looking after all the old relatives.'

'I don't like him,' said Stevie. 'You won't convince me he's a really nice bloke.'

For once, Catherine didn't try. The last person she had said was a 'really nice bloke' was Matthew, and look how that seemed to have turned out.

Danny was tired out and asleep by half past seven, which left one and a half hours of nerve-jangling torture in which the hands of the clock seemed to stay still. The time went trebly slow from nine o'clock until five past, when Matthew's black Punto pulled up outside. For the millionth time, Stevie checked her precisely chosen casual clothes in the mirror and looked to see that there was no lipstick on her teeth. Matthew knocked on the door, which indicated a big marker of their estrangement, and Stevie was careful not to jump too quickly to open it. *Slowly, slowly*, she paced herself. She opened, smiled, invited him in and then went to sit in the big winged armchair.

Adam's words reverberated in her head. *Play it exactly the opposite tae how he'd expect*. Not that she was going to play it any other way, but he made her push it that notch further. Matthew would have expected her to be tarted up to the nines to seduce him back. He would have expected her to sit on the sofa in the hope that he would join her and not be able to resist snuggling up. He would have expected her to have the kettle on and offer him tea, so she did none of those things.

'What can I do for you?' said Stevie, with a small smile.

'Well, firstly I came to see if there was any post,' said Matthew.

'It's on the hall table waiting for you,' said Stevie.

'And secondly . . .' He raked his hand through his thick dark hair. 'Sorry, it's a bit awkward. I thought you should know, because I don't want there to be any lies between us'—which made Stevie gulp down the biggest sarcastic laugh her voice box could hope to create—'I . . . er . . . asked Joanna out last night.'

'Joanna? But she's married,' said Stevie, taking her place on the stage to receive her Oscar for 'best shocked actress'.

'She's . . . er . . . split up from Adam at last. As I found out last night. So . . . er . . . I'll need the house back as soon as I can.'

'What? You're moving her in already—after one night?'

'No, of course not.' Matthew's hand went nervously to his hair again, then he started rubbing his neck. He really wasn't very good at lying.

He must think I'm an idiot to believe all this, thought Stevie, suddenly filled with a boiling rage which took over her mouth, bypassing her brain. 'Well, actually, I was going to tell *you*, Matthew, that I've found somewhere and I'll be out by Wednesday. I can't make it any earlier than that, I'm afraid, so I hope that will be OK with you?'

'Oh, yes . . . great.'

Great? He actually said great. The rage temperature shot up a few more degrees. She was not even letting herself think of what she was saying; she just wanted to show him she was in control and OK and bigger than this. Even if inside she was vibrating with anger and fear and hurt, outside she would look as if she could cope.

Stevie stood up, surprised that her legs had been strong enough to support her. 'I'll pop my keys through the letterbox when I leave. Let's say, by Wednesday noon.'

'Five o'clock would do,' said Matthew.

'OK, five o'clock.'

'Right. Brilliant.'

'So let's get your post,' Stevie said, rising to her feet. 'Where are you staying?' She clung on to the amicable smile.

'Oh, just one of the hotels in town.'

Hotel. So it wasn't a grotty little B&B after all. She wanted to ask which one, and whether Jo was staying there too, and watch him squirm because, had she had any life savings left, Stevie would have put them on the perfidious pair being holed up together in a double room in this mysterious 'hotel in town'. But that's what he would be expecting her to do, cross-examine him, so she played outside his expectations. There was something she did need to ask, though.

'About our wedding,' she began, her voice croaking like a frog.

Matthew just looked at her with big, apologetic, brown eyes.

Stevie gritted her teeth and said, 'I thought so. Well, OK,' she managed. 'You tell your parents and your relatives, I'll do the rest.'

'Sorry,' he said, as if he had just accidentally stood on her toe.

'To be expected in the circumstances. Especially if you're asking other people out,' she said, her upper lip stiff.

'Bye, Stevie, you're such a lovely, understanding person,' he said, and he shocked her with a big grateful hug after he picked up his post. She extricated herself, battling the urge to stay there and fill herself with the smell and the feel of him and to beg him not to leave her.

'Bye, Matthew.'

She lasted five seconds after the door closed before breaking down. How could she have been so stupid as to think a nice hairdo and a few pounds off would make any difference? Hadn't she learned *anything* from last time?

When she first suspected Mick had been having an affair, she had post-mortemed herself to shreds. What was she? Too porky, too blonde, too unfit, too arty, too short, too straight-haired, too blue-eyed, too incredibly clumsy, too crap at cake baking? What was it that had caused Mick to turn his attentions to another woman? Then she had found out who he was having an affair with. A barmaid—Linda: hook nose, yellow teeth and proud owner of incredibly fat ankles.

'This hasn't happened because you've got a slightly bigger bum than you should have, girl,' said a kind part within her, eager to give some comfort. It hadn't stopped her from wanting to know just why it *had* happened though. Why was it so hard for blokes to understand that all an ex might need to go forward was a two-minute explanation? Even 'I ran off with Linda because I happen to have a thing about women who look like bulldogs' would have been better than the not knowing *why*.

Well, Stevie wasn't going to go mad this time. She wasn't going to hide Matthew's clothes, follow him in his lunch hour, or starve herself in a misguided, desperate attempt to get him back. All that would do was drive him further away, as she knew to her cost with Mick.

Stevie crunched herself up into a ball and sobbed quietly, so Danny wouldn't hear, though she wanted to keen and howl like a wolf at the moon and let out the pain. And what the buggery bollocks had made her say she had somewhere else to go? In three days' time too? *So what are you going to do now?* the sensible part of her brain shouted at the smartarse side. The smartarse side was not forthcoming with answers.

She couldn't stay at Catherine's, although she knew the Flanagans would shift and jiggle to accommodate her and Danny. There would be no space to work. Her mother lived too far away for Danny's school and anyway, Edna Honeywell only had a one-bedroomed flat, and a life in which there was even less room for them. As for her father—well, he wasn't even on the short list of people to ring with this one.

Five months ago, she had had her own house, a nice full bank account and a fabtastic boyfriend who loved her. So how had she got to this place—grossly depleted savings and three days away from being homeless? She hated to admit this, but there was only one person who just might be able to stop everything slipping away from her. Stevie went out to the recycle bin in the garage where all her scrap paper was kept awaiting collection, scavenged around until she found what she was looking for, and then rang the number on the retrieved business card.

'Hellooo,' said a voice full of nails and razor blades.

'Hello, Mr MacLean. It's Stevie Honeywell. I think I'm ready to talk.'

It was with a certain amount of cockiness that Adam MacLean swaggered up the path and rang the doorbell of 15 Blossom Lane next morning, at nine thirty, as arranged, and it was with a certain amount of humility that Stevie received him. He accepted her offer of a cup of coffee and followed her into the kitchen where a percolator was already chewing on some beautiful-smelling beans. The room looked different when it wasn't covered in flour, he thought. She had obviously tightened up her act a bit since Matty Boy left. It was gleaming actually, and so was the front room that they went into when the coffee was ready, give or take a bit of mess that made a home comfortable—Spiderman slippers, jotters and pens, a big tub of Lego and a very strange head made out of a sock, with grass for hair, sitting in a jam jar.

Adam sat down on a sofa that was meant to hold four people and took up nearly half of it. On the coffee table there was one of those infernal books that daft women read, called *The Carousel of Life* by

Beatrice Pollen. He picked it up, gave the back cover blurb a dismissive read and put it back down again in such a way that gave Stevie no doubt of his opinion of it.

'So?' he said, rather smugly. 'You changed yerrr mind.'

'It wasn't an easy decision.'

'I can bet.'

They even managed to make their coffee sipping look like a duel.

'What was it then that finally made you ring?'

'He—Matthew—came round last night.'

'Aye, you said he was comin' roond, when I saw you in the super-market. With the giant cucumber.'

Stevie bared her teeth a little but continued icily, 'He told me I have to leave this house as soon as possible and cancel my wedding. I told him I'd be out by Wednesday.'

'Oh.' It was a sympathetic 'oh' for him, who seemed to deduce from the speed at which she started slurping coffee, that she was upset.

'So where will you go?' he said.

'I don't have a clue. I'll have to start looking.' Her voice went funny.

'So you want tae know whit I think noo?' said Adam MacLean, who was wearing jeans and a cornflower-blue shirt that matched his eyes. 'I think you and I should pretend to start winchin'.'

Winchin'? What the hell did that mean? 'I'm sorry, you've lost me.'

'Winchin'. It means "go-in' out tae-geth-er".'

'You and me?' Stevie laughed, waiting for the punch line.

'It's nae a joke,' he said. 'This is part of my master plan.'

'Your *master plan*?'

'Is there an echo in here?' he grumbled. 'First of all, I didnae fight the decision for Jo tae leave me. I just let her go. I knew that would affect her far mair than if I acted like she might expect me tae.'

Stevie didn't ask how Jo would expect him to act. That seemed pretty obvious. It had to involve something dangerous that hurt a lot.

'And you want us to go out together?'

'Ma God, naw!' he protested. 'Just tae pretend.'

'You're barking mad.'

'Quite possibly, but have you any sane solutions?'

That shut Stevie up because she hadn't.

'Any chance of another coffee, please?' he asked.

'Yes, of course,' said Stevie, and went into the kitchen.

Adam picked up a Midnight Moon book from the table under the window. Another by Beatrice Pollen—*The Silent Stranger*—she must be *her* favourite. Obviously, this Pollen woman was some sad writer with a loveless life who lived her dreams through characters with names like Maddox Flockton and Devon Earnshaw. Jeez, who thought o' this crap?

> Devon flirtatiously pushed back her luxurious auburn hair, exposing her long creamy neck. Maddox grabbed her, ignoring her protests as he rained kisses onto that neck until she surrendered to him and groaned, 'Maddox, oh Maddox!'

Bollocks, oh bollocks, more like, he thought, closing the book and putting it back where he had found it by the window. Then his eye caught sight of the sign on the house opposite, just before Stevie returned to put a giant cup down on the coffee table for him.

'What's that hoos? Is it tae let?' He pointed to the cottage opposite.

'Yes,' said Stevie, roughly understanding what he was saying.

'Why don't you get that one?'

'You are joking!' said Stevie. 'I couldn't afford that in a month, sorry, year, sorry millennium of Sundays.'

'Will Housing Benefit no' cover it?'

'Housing Benefit?' said Stevie indignantly. 'What on earth makes you think I would get Housing Benefit?'

'I presumed, seeing as you're at the gym every day, you didnae work.'

'Well, I do work actually, thank you,' said Stevie.

'Whit do you dae?'

'None of your bloody business!' Like she was going to tell him that after he had tossed her book down as if it was worthless crap.

'Sorry I asked,' said Adam, holding his hands up in a gesture of peace. He took a sip of coffee. 'So, how expensive is it?'

Stevie sighed and got out the newspaper to show him some brief details. 'Too expensive for me, and my *salary*.'

'Christ almighty!' said Adam as the figure shot out at him from the page. 'Be cheaper tae move into a Hilton Penthoos.'

'Precisely.'

'Hmmm.' He rubbed his freshly shaven chin in thought. 'Although the Hilton doesnae have such a good view as that hoos has. And because you cannae afford it, that's even more reason for it to be the perfect place.' He was thinking aloud. *This was startin' to look verrry interestin'.* 'If you lived there, you would cause them mental hell. "How could she stand to live there opposite tae us? How could she afford it?" they'd ask. Then I turn up wi' floooers . . .'

Floooers? 'If you mean "floors", at a rough guess I think it might have them already, Mr MacLean. And possibly ceilings—'

'Fl-ow-errs. If I came with fl-ow-ers. Think aboot it. No' only have we no' reacted as rejected partners should naturally in accordance wi' the laws of heartbreak, but then we start oor own relationship—*pretend* relationship,' he emphasised for clarity. 'I think the wee green-eyed monster would be oot dain' . . . sorry, *out doing* his damage within a very short time. *Basic psychology.* No one wants tae be tha' replaceable, tha' quickly.'

OK, he had a point, Stevie thought, but at what cost to sanity?

'Like I tried tae say tae you before—*basic psychology*,' he said again. 'I expect Matthew thought you'd totally freak—as, I know, did ma Jo of me. But we didnae, we havenae given them whit they wanted. Trust me, their brains are trying tae process the strange wonderful creatures that we are and cannae. We are *haunting* them. They are expectin' more from us. They're waiting for us tae flip and revert tae type, but they're no' goin' tae get it and that will unsettle them more than anythin'. Tell me that Matty Boy isn't expectin' you tae kick up a fuss.'

Stevie thought of all she had told Matt about the breakup with Mick, how crazed she had acted in grief. 'Yes, he'll expect it.'

'Aye, well, there are reasons why Jo will expect the same.'

'Obviously,' said Stevie.

'Guid. Then, they'll no' anticipate this turn of events.'

Stevie hated to admit he might be right, but she was going to have to, because she was desperate. Crackers as the whole scheme was, it was worth a try. Well, it would have been if she'd had the money.

'I'll ring the landlord aboot the place—' MacLean started to say.

'Excuse me,' Stevie tried to interrupt. *Didn't he listen? Didn't he hear the bit about not being able to afford it?*

'If you'll agree tae consider movin' in there, we'll come to some arrangement about the money that disnae see you short,' Adam interrupted back. 'I might be able tae batter the landlaird doon on price.'

Yes, she could imagine he would be very effective at battering.

She nodded her head warily.

'So if you would be so kind as to give me yer telephone number . . .'

'OK, you're on,' Stevie said, with a heavy sigh of resignation.

She scribbled down her mobile number on a pad, then Adam left quickly—a man with a mission, locked on course.

He rang her an hour later: 'The landlaird willnae budge o' the price. But I'll cover whit you cannae afford. We'll sort oot the details later. I've signed the lease and I've got the key, which I'll drop roond to you this afternoon, so if you've anythin' heavy tae carry across, I'll do it fer you then, because you start movin' in tidae. Ring your man tomorrow and tell him the place is empty a day early. Now, go pack!' Then he put the phone down before Stevie could manage a single word of protest.

Adam arrived with the key as Stevie was disconnecting her computer. They walked across the road to inspect her new temporary home, whose address, according to the lease, was Humbleby Cottage. Humbleby was something of a misnomer, because there was nothing the least bit humble about it on the outside . . . nor on the inside either, as they were about to find out.

The cottage was chocolate-box pretty. The kitchen was roadside with a huge inglenook fireplace, an Aga and original wooden floors with thick rugs over them. Thankfully, the modern world had been allowed in too and there was central heating and double glazing, with security windows throughout. There was a good-sized study with hundreds of bookshelves, a lounge with an even grander fireplace, and a darling little sunroom round the back looking out onto a long private garden, which had been maintained by a gardener in the absence of a tenant. Upstairs was a huge spacious girlie bathroom and two massive, pretty bedrooms with exposed beams.

A domestic service had been going in to dust, so the cottage was ready to move into without Stevie having to clean it. It was immaculate and fully furnished with some very nice stuff.

'Whit dae you think?' said Adam.

'It's lovely,' said Stevie.

'Right—got anythin' heavy I can move for you?'

'I haven't got a lot of things,' she replied. 'I sold most of my furniture with my last house because it wouldn't fit in Matthew's.'

'You must have somethin', mon!'

'Just my computer for now.'

So off they went back to Matthew's house and he carried her computer over and set it up for her in the study. It would be a change to work in some generous space for a while, she thought, after being cramped in the corner of Matthew's tiny dining area.

'Work from home, dae you?' he asked, twiddling with leads.

'Yes,' she said, without furnishing him with further detail.

'On this?'

'Yes,' she replied. She had no intention of enlightening him.

'So, whit's next?' he said, when the computer was up and running.

'Well, I've got some books.'

'C'moan, then,' and he marched back over. She hadn't unpacked most of them from her last move so they were still in boxes. Matthew had been going to buy her some shelves for her birthday, but he had not had the spare money and the date had come and gone.

'They're a bit heav—'

'Nonsense,' Adam said, and lifted the first one up as if it was an empty crisp packet, then he came back for the other two and carried them as effortlessly. The bloke was an ox.

'What noo?' he asked, not even a bit out of breath.

'Nothing really. The rest will just be suitcases and black bags. I can manage those myself when I fill them.'

'Right, I'll be in touch,' he said, and then he dropped the cottage keys into her hand and went without further ado.

After he vroomed off, Stevie rang Catherine to tell her how the previous night had gone with Matthew.

'What will you do?' her friend said.

'Well, if you've a spare half an hour, I'll show you,' Stevie replied.

'Show?'

'Can you get your butt over here? You won't regret it.'

Five minutes later, Stevie led Catherine over the road.

Catherine gasped when she produced a key and slid it into the lock of her favourite house ever. 'You're not moving in here? You can't afford this, can you?' she said with breathless excitement.

'Yes, I am, and no, I can't,' said Stevie and proceeded to tell her the Adam MacLean part of the story.

'Well, even for a little while it'll be nice,' said Catherine, whose eyes couldn't move fast enough around the inside of the house.

Stevie nodded. It was beautiful, apart from the view from the kitchen—for the home she was leaving would sit there framed in the window like a taunting picture: *Ner ner ner ner ner, you don't live here, but guess who-o do-oes.*

'Well, for the record, I think it's a bloody good idea of Adam MacLean's,' said Catherine.

'Do you?' Stevie was surprised. Catherine wasn't usually one for wild schemes, or for siding with people who beat up women for a hobby.

'Yes, I think Jo and Matthew deserve a taste of their own medicine.'

'Will they get it, though?' said Stevie, who had made tea in her new temporary home and opened up a celebratory packet of chocolate shortbreads. Not that she had anything really to celebrate. Yet.

'Well, it's worth a try,' said Catherine and nudged her lasciviously. 'You and Adam MacLean, eh?'

'No, *not* me and Adam MacLean. There is no me and Adam MacLean. I want to hang on to my teeth and ribs a bit longer, thank you. Besides, the man is barely housetrained. Trust me, I wouldn't give the bloke so much as the time of day if I wasn't so desperate.'

'Well, he doesn't come across as the violent nutter *she* said he was.

Plus, can you really believe her word? Miss Butter-wouldn't-melt?'

'He's "acting" the nonviolent type for our benefit, that's the point. He can't risk losing his temper because he needs me as much as I need him. But I don't trust him as far as I could throw him.'

'Is there a house phone? You'll have to give me your new number.'

'I'll sort it out tomorrow—well, the day after tomorrow,' said Stevie.

'Why, what's happening tomorrow that's so important?'

'Tomorrow I'm going to cancel all the wedding stuff.'

Catherine came over to give her a hug. 'I can do all that for you.'

'No, no,' said Stevie. 'I have to do it myself. I have to face facts that this wedding is not going to happen.'

'Well, the offer will still be there in the morning,' said Catherine, stroking her friend's hair as if she were Boot, while thinking to herself, What an idiot you are, Matthew Finch. 'Right, come on now. Let's get ready to rumble.'

Stevie carried her clothes on hangers straight over the road. For herself, she picked the pretty bedroom at the back, which overlooked the garden. The front bedroom was larger but she did not want the first thing she saw when she drew the curtains every morning to be the house where her fiancé and his new lover lived. She took the soft white towels she had bought recently, leaving Matthew with his ancient ones that were more like wafer-thin loofahs. She would have left him a couple of hers, until she visualised Jo using them.

Shoes took up one of the suitcases she had bought for their honeymoon, and toiletries went into a box. Catherine carried the plastic-covered wedding dress over. Stevie was hoping to get some of her money back on that. She was stripping her bed when Catherine walked in from bagging up Danny's toys.

'What are you doing?' said her friend, her hands on her hips.

'Well, they won't want to sleep in my sheets. I was changing them.'

'Don't be so soft, Steve. Stick the sheets in the laundry basket and leave them to it. Let them make up their own bed.' Catherine had her 'do as I say or else' face on, so Stevie obeyed.

She took her Le Creuset pan-set from the kitchen and her new super-steamy iron and the ironing board that she had bought only a couple of weeks ago. Then it was time to pick up the children.

'I'll come round with Eddie at about seven o'clock,' began Catherine. 'I'll bring you a couple of spare duvets and some sheets and pillows to tide you over, and he'll carry the microwave over for you.'

'I can't take the microwave.'

'Who bought it?' Catherine said, being extra stern.

'I did,' Stevie relented grudgingly, 'but for both of us.'

'You can't split it so you take it. Besides, the cottage doesn't have one,' said Catherine, who was beginning to realise that Stevie's financial contribution to the arrangement had been a lot greater than was fair.

'Look, do you want *her* baking her spuds in it, while you and Danny do without?' urged Catherine, watching Stevie still deliberating.

'OK, I'll take it then.'

'Don't you dare try to lift it yourself. I know what you're like, Stevie Independent Honeywell, it'll weigh a ton! Promise?'

'Yes, Sergeant Major, sah, I promise!' said Stevie, saluting her. Then she went to pick up her son and tell him, with a softening ice cream bought en route, about their new domestic arrangements.

Danny's new bedroom was much bigger than the old one, plus he had a double bed in it, which was 'cool', and once he was arranging his toys in his new space and had put Mr Greengrass Head on the kitchen windowsill, he seemed happy with the changes.

Eddie and Catherine arrived and helped to move the boxes of Stevie's videos, DVDs and CDs. Eddie transported the microwave and Danny's portable TV. There was a huge television in the cottage and speakers all round the room. Eddie, a gadget maniac, fiddled and foddled and found out how to switch it to 'cinema surround'.

'Curtains closed, a big bag of popcorn and a Harry Potter on here, lad, and it'll be better than the pictures,' said Eddie, which had Danny's face lighting up. He was viewing all this as a great adventure.

Catherine made up Danny's bed, while Stevie got him pyjama-ed up, washed and toothpasted. He was tired, little lamb, after all the excitement of his busy day. In his Superman pyjamas under his Superman blanket and cuddling his Superman doll, he was asleep in minutes.

'So, are you sorted then?' said Eddie, who had been finishing off a thankyou bottle of lager from the Happy Shopper, while he relaxed on the reclining bit of the sofa that he had just discovered.

'I just need to clean over there tomorrow and that's that,' said Stevie.

'Clean?' screeched Catherine.

'I don't care what you say, I'm not having Jo slagging me off because there's a bit of dust where I've moved things,' returned Stevie. OK, this might be 'acting to type' but there was no way she was going to let anyone call her a mucky sod. 'There's not all that much to do but I'm doing it. Then I'll get on with the . . . other business.'

'What other business?' said Eddie.

'Cancelling the wedding,' said Stevie.

Catherine smiled kindly at her. 'You look worn out. You should get to bed yourself.'

'I don't think I'll sleep, to be honest.'

But Stevie did, and it was a sleep of far better quality than she'd had for quite a long time. As if it was a gift to rest her soul for the ordeals in store for her the following day.

Chapter 5

STEVIE'S EYES CAME into focus on soft tones of pale pink and old cream painted on uneven plaster walls rather than the familiar white wood-chip wallpaper.

She set about making breakfast and caught sight of her former home through the window, which was an odd, almost out-of-body experience moment. She tore herself away and concentrated on pouring out Coco Pops for two, deciding that she could not afford to let emotion get in the way of the task in hand and ruin everything.

As soon as she had dropped Danny off at school, she headed across the road with her cleaning kit. She gave the place a quick dust, a vacuum, and a double-extra going-over in the kitchen.

There was an empty feel to the house that was inexplicable because Matthew's stuff was still there. In fact, apart from being a lot cleaner and shinier, it looked just as it did the day she moved in at New Year. It was as if she had never been there and part of his house, part of his life.

Stevie wound the cord round her Dyson, ready to take it across the road. Matthew would just have to cope with his ancient cylinder in the under-stairs cupboard, which believed its primary function was to blow out more dust than it sucked in. Tough, but necessary because she *knew* that he would expect her to leave behind all this stuff, because that's what good-hearted old Stevie would do. Nice Stevie could not bear to see him surviving on sandpapery towels and incompetent electrical equipment. *Well, he had a little shock coming then!* Twisting the engagement ring off her finger, Stevie put it on the work surface. Then, remembering that she had paid for the flaming thing, she stuck it in her pocket. Not that she would ever wear it again, but she could visualise Matthew flogging it and then taking Jo out for dinner on the proceeds.

She took one last look at Matthew's house, which she had intended to share with him as Mrs Stevie Finch. Then she forced herself to leave it, locked the door and posted the key through the letterbox.

The first thing she did on entering Humbleby Cottage was to pick up her mobile. Taking a big breath, she rang Matthew's number. It clicked onto answering machine and she noticed how the recorded message was slightly different to his usual one. He sounded chirpier, cocky as a cat in a cream factory.

'Hi, it's Stevie,' she said. 'I've vacated the house now and posted the key through the letterbox, so it's all yours. Take care, bye.' Then she hung up and let all the air out of her lungs before taking up her notebook to make the first of the other dreaded calls.

'Hello, Kiss the Bride,' answered a jolly voice. 'Ros speaking.'

'It's Stevie Honeywell. I bought one of your wedding dresses. It was long, to the floor, white silk, crisscross breast panel.' She had brought the dress and accessories home so that she could show them to Jo.

'Ah, yes, I remember, we had to have it considerably shortened.'

'. . . And a pink bridesmaid dress, size ten, and a pageboy outfit. You've still got those in the shop.'

'Yes, I've just altered those too for you.'

'Er . . . yes. Well, the thing is, there isn't going to be a wedding any more, so I wondered if I could have a refund.'

'Oh dear,' said Ros. 'Is there no chance that maybe in the future . . .?'

Stevie didn't answer, merely shook her head, thinking, Even if there were, I couldn't wear that dress now with all its bad memories.

'Oh dear,' said Ros again in a not-too-encouraging way. 'Well, the thing is, we did have to have a lot taken off the hem.'

God, I'm five foot two, not Jimmy Krankie, thought Stevie. 'I haven't worn it at all. Isn't there anything you can do? The shoes haven't even been out of the box and the veil is still wrapped up.'

'Well, I said I would buy everything back for forty per cent if you wanted to sell it after the ceremony. That's the best I can do, I'm afraid.'

'The shoes and the veil haven't been altered,' said Stevie bravely.

'Yes, but they've still been sold to you. Oh dear, it is sad.'

Obviously not sad enough, though.

'I'd make him pay for it,' said Ros, still dreadfully sympathetic.

'Alas, that isn't an option,' said Stevie stiffly. Matthew hadn't contributed a penny towards the wedding and was swanning around in the seven hundred quid suit she had bought for him.

'I'm afraid that really is my best offer,' said Ros, as if embarrassed.

'OK,' said Stevie. 'May I bring the dress and other stuff in today?'

'Yes, of course,' said Ros.

Stevie threw the dress and all the accessories that Kiss the Bride supplied straight into the back of her car and headed into town.

Ros was dressing a dummy with a pageboy's outfit when she walked in. A little Scots boy with a kilt, wouldn't you just know it.

Satisfied that the dress hadn't been worn and that all the accessories were as perfect as Stevie had described, Ros wrote a cheque for exactly 40 per cent of the amount on the receipt. 'Well, if it's any consolation, you'll have all this excitement of picking another dress one day, I'm sure of it, dear,' said Ros with a big summery smile.

'Thank you, Ros,' said Stevie.

'I'm sorry I couldn't help more.'

'It's OK,' said Stevie, who found she was actually so relieved to have the stuff out of the house that, in the end, she would have taken less if pushed. Not that she would voice that to Ros. She would need all the money she could get to pay Adam MacLean for living in the cottage.

'Have you had to cancel everything, then?'

No, I thought I'd keep the cake and flowers for a laugh, she almost wanted to scream, but instead she answered calmly, 'Well, no. I've got that delightful task in front of me. You were first on my list.'

'Aw, I hope you have a friend there to help you. It's not something you'd want to do without support, is it?'

'No,' said Stevie with a loaded sigh, wondering how much support she would get from her mother, who was next on her list to ring.

'**G**ood job I haven't bought my outfit yet, then,' said Edna Honeywell with a big sniff. 'Anyway, I never liked him.'

'That's a lie, Mum—you said he was nice.'

'Too good-looking. You'd never have kept him.'

Thanks. 'He's not gone for good, Mum. We're just having a break.'

'So what's *she* like? I presume there is someone else.'

'There's no one else, Mum. We just want to be sure so we're putting the wedding off for a bit,' said Stevie, thrown out of kilter by her mother's powers of perception. She didn't want her parents knowing what the situation really was, because she knew this storm would blow over and she and Matthew *would* end up getting married.

'There will be another woman, mark my words,' said Edna. 'They don't leave unless they've sniffed another bitch. Have you told *him* yet?'

'I'm going to ring Dad next. Will you let Auntie Rita know?'

'Yes, I'll let our Rita know. I'll have to get off the phone soon, I was just on my way out.'

'Oh, going anywhere nice?' asked Stevie with a hopeful attempt at continuing the conversation for just a little longer.

'I've got a salsa class at half past.'

Her mother always had a class on the go. She had been doing great female poets during pregnancy and fallen in love with Stevie Smith's work, hence the choice of name for her daughter.

'OK, Mum, I won't keep you.'

'Well, anyway, I'm sorry for you, lass. It can't be easy.'

'It isn't easy. Danny's fine, by the way.'

'I was just going to ask!' snapped Edna. 'I don't know, you can cause an argument in an empty house, can't you?' she continued. 'No wonder your feller buggered off.'

Stevie ended the call before it degenerated into all the other conversations they had, where she ended up feeling surplus to requirements.

Stevie told her dad that she and Matthew had decided to take some time apart and think things through. She gave him her new address.

'Nay, lass, never,' said Jack Honeywell, strangely drawing the same conclusion as her mother. 'He wants shooting. Can't keep it in their trousers, some lads,' which was rich, considering he had kept *it* well out of his trousers when he'd left her mum for Thick Neck. Then he cheated on Thick Neck for Cyclops, who lost her left eye in a fight years ago after being biffed in it with a bingo dabber. Neither woman had felt the slightest obligation to welcome Stevie into the step-family fold.

'Are you all right? Are you coping?' he asked solicitously.

'I'm fine, Dad. I've moved out. Danny's fine, too, by the way.'

'Good, give him a big kiss from his granddad. I nearly called in last week. We were passing coming from Thelma's [Cyclops's] son's house. Good job we didn't, if you'd moved.'

'I only moved last night.'

'Oh.'

Stevie finished the conversation before it ended up like all the other calls to her dad, which made her feel insignificant and second-best to her step-family.

Next was the cake woman.

'I've already made the fruit-cake layers. I'll have to keep the deposit and just not charge you for the icing,' she said grumpily.

'Thank you,' said Stevie, who didn't feel up for a fight. The florist was next call. Thank God for gay male florists.

'Oh, you poor darling,' said Donny Badger before spitting, 'Bastard!' It was slightly disconcerting, the way everyone assumed she had been traded in for a better model. There seemed to be an awful lot of sceptics in the world. Maybe that's why her Midnight Moon books did so well, because her heroes and heroines were honourable and faithful and didn't hurt each other. True fantasy then. Stevie didn't want to turn into a hard-bitten cynic who didn't believe in love in real life any more. However, it was looking more and more as if any love that existed out there was never going to be for her.

'Look, love, what's your address again? I'll put you a full refund of your deposit in the post.'

Stevie started to give her old address, before correcting herself. She should have got a forwarding form from the post office, although her post going across the road would at least give her the excuse to have contact with Matthew again. In saying that, she wasn't 100 per cent sure she wanted to have that while her nerves were in this raw state.

The photographer hadn't taken a deposit and was grumbling that he had turned someone away on that date for her. The vicar offered counselling, which she refused, but he was sweet. The manageress of the White Swan promised to send the deposit back, if she didn't tell anyone, though any faith recovered was lost again with the printer, who had just completed the order of services and said he had put them and the invoice in the post, so she would have to stump up.

Stevie couldn't face making another call. She composed a letter on her computer to send out to the people on her side of the guest list:

Due to unforeseen circumstances, the wedding between Matthew and me has been called off. Please don't ring. I will be in touch. Sorry, folks. Hope you are all well. Love Stevie (Honeywell) x

She wondered how many of their guests would be of her mother's opinion and say, 'Well, I'm not surprised, he was far too good-looking for her.' It was one of many thoughts to torment her as she got on with the business of alternately addressing envelopes and wiping away the fat tears that were dropping from her eyes. Then, when she was done, she posted the letters as she went to pick up her son from school.

In the Queens Hotel, after a very nice evening meal, Jo had just finished packing. 'Thank goodness Stevie's left the house. I did wonder if she would start playing silly games.'

'Well, she's actually got out a day early for us,' reminded Matthew.

'It wouldn't do her any good at all psychologically, being in that house any more,' said Jo. 'I *so* cannot wait to get into a decent bed. I hope she hasn't left the place in a real mess for you.'

'I wouldn't have thought so, knowing Stevie,' said Matthew. 'Wonder where she's living?' It was a question that had been circling his head like a lost homing pigeon since he picked up the message that morning. Of course, he hadn't picked up the call because he was convinced she was ringing him to ask for extra time, or to cry and beg him to come back.

The porter started to load the cases into Matthew's and Jo's cars.

'You drop those off and come back for me,' said Jo. 'Just in case there are any nasty surprises waiting.'

'I shouldn't think—'

'I'll stay here and have some coffee, darling,' said Jo, brooking no argument. She gave him a long, warm kiss that reached all the way down to his toes before zooming back up to his groin, then she waved him off and headed back to Reception.

Matthew parked the car outside his house in Blossom Lane then entered it tentatively. Everything looked nice, tidy—as it should be—and there was lots more room now that Stevie's work corner had been freed up and her boxes of books had gone. The hotel was plush but he had missed the comfort of his house and he couldn't wait to climb into his lovely cosy bed with a lovely cosy Jo that evening.

He took the suitcases upstairs and found the undressed bed.

Oh hell, he thought, as it put paid to his plans to carry Jo over his threshold and then straight upstairs to tangle her up in the sheets. Then again, it was probably a bit much thinking Stevie would make up a bed in which she knew he might soon be making love to someone else.

He went back to the hotel, hoping that maybe Jo would have settled the bill. The holiday had cost him a fortune and he thought she might have stumped up for her share but no, she had merrily let him pay for the lot and thereby ruined his chances of borrowing a cash advance against his Visa for the mortgage. He couldn't hope that Stevie would pay it for him any more now.

It wasn't that Matthew didn't earn a good wage. It was just that he had managed to accumulate quite a lot of debts. Life was really too short not to have nice meals out and look the very best he could while he was young.

When Stevie moved in and offered to pay half the bills, he was determined to use the money he would save to finally become debt free, only to find that spending money on nice meals and flash clothes was even more fun with Jo. And he couldn't stop buying her presents, especially when he found out how she said thank you.

Stevie didn't earn a fortune but he'd rather taken advantage of her selfless generosity, and while she was paying all the bills, thinking she was helping him to clear off some of his debts, he was actually wining and dining Jo. He hadn't quite told either of them just how bad things were financially—a man has his pride, etc—but Stevie had been quite sweet about the little she knew anyway. She used to stuff his pocket with money if they went out with friends and he would produce it like a wizard and play the benevolent sybarite.

On the drive back to the hotel, he was thinking that he would need to approach the financial problem with Jo sooner rather than later because this holiday had just about wiped him out. His resolve doubled when she swanned regally out of the hotel to sit in her Golf, leaving him to settle the account there too. There was an embarrassing moment when his Barclaycard was declined and he had to hunt around for his emergency Goldfish. If the basic bill wasn't bad enough, he discovered all the ironing services she had charged to the room, and she had just wasted another fifteen quid on coffee and chocolate truffles while he had been taking the suitcases back to the house. Still, when she got her share from her divorce from MacLean, they would be laughing financially. Speculate to accumulate and all that.

He was like a kid who couldn't wait to unwrap his Christmas present when they both got back to Blossom Lane. He lifted her over the threshold and shoved the door to with his foot so as not to interrupt his smooth passage up the stairs, but, giggling, she broke away.

'Don't leave the suitcases in my car,' she said.

'Later,' he said sexily, moving back in for more kisses.

'No way, my jewellery is in them,' she said, pressing him back out.

'Oh, OK,' he said good-humouredly and went out to the Golf that she'd parked in his carport while his Punto stood behind it on the drive. There were lights on in the cottage across the road, he noticed. *Lord, some people have more money than sense!*

Jo was running her finger around the surfaces when he got back inside. 'Well,' she said, 'I'm surprised. Had it been my man moving another woman in, I'd have made sure it was an absolute tip.'

'Stevie's not like that.'

'Nice happy Stevie might not be like that but, as you know, unhappy scorned Stevie can be very nasty.'

'Hmmm,' said Matthew. 'Nasty' was not a word he could truly associate with his ex. Even when she told him how mad she had gone during the Mick business, she had not done anything that could truly be classed as 'nasty'. He had, however, thought she would be more upset about them splitting up than she was. Her acceptance of the situation had surprised him. And even though he knew it was unreasonable, it had slightly annoyed him too.

Jo followed him upstairs and sussed out the wardrobe space. 'So that's one suitcase worth, where do I put the others?'

'We'll figure it out,' he said. 'Personally I think you should throw all your clothes away and be naked for ever.'

She laughed, and slowly unbuttoned her shirt, and the sensations that started to missile his brain knocked all thoughts of Visas and Mastercards and bank loans and overdrafts into Kingdom Come.

Nothing could have prepared Stevie for the sight that met her eyes as she went to close the kitchen blinds. She could not possibly have ever found a big enough piece of padding to protect her heart against it, not even on the World Wide Web. She jumped back from the window as if it had just given her a belt of electricity and hid in the shadows, wanting to move away but unable to. With a gruesome compulsion, she watched the red Golf drive cosily into Matthew's carport then his black Punto pull up behind. Both drivers got out smiling, and then her ex-fiancé scooped up her treacherous ex-friend in his arms and carried her into her ex-home. They were giggling, probably singing a song from *Oklahoma* as well, because that's what it looked like—Hollywood happiness—the sort you dream of but only one person in a million ever gets, and it is never you. The door seemed to close slowly and magically behind them, and it felt as if someone had whipped away the top layer of Stevie's skin and everything that possibly could, hurt and throbbed. What the hell had possessed her to follow Adam MacLean's harebrained scheme and move into this cottage? It was going to kill her, day after day.

Mesmerised, she stayed there and was rewarded, if you could call it that, with the sight of Matthew speeding out again to get their suitcases, rushed and clumsy like some Ealing Comedy newlywed. Then she watched as the bedroom light went on upstairs, and then off.

Her imagination made a best friend and a powerful enemy. When dealing with the Parises and Brandons at work, it played a useful role, but here it tortured her with a horrible and vivid slideshow. They would have fallen onto the bed now. They would spend their lives bonking like beautiful body-perfect minks: Jo savouring Matt's toned, lightly muscular body while Matt marvelled at her velvet skin and cel-lulite-free arse. These were Stevie's thoughts as she stood in her *Technicolor Dreamcoat* dressing gown and Totes Toasties, and continued to sip from a mint Options, which had long since gone cold.

She did not know if she could go on. Her fiancé was a love rat, her friend was a love rattess, she couldn't face writing any more and she was in a house she couldn't afford. Not only that, but she had not yet sorted out terms and conditions with a bloke she owed money to, who had no qualms about bashing women he supposedly liked. So what would he do to women he couldn't stand the sight of? And what if McPsychopath demanded his oats instead of money—and she didn't mean the Scott's Porage variety? Then again, she had to go on, because she had a wee—a *little* boy sleeping upstairs who needed his mam to be strong and to provide for him and give him a home. Thank God she was only drinking cold hot chocolate and not up to her forehead in gin, because by now she would have had her Roy Orbison CD on and be upping the Kleenex shares by fifty quid each, and in a very dangerous state of mind.

She eventually dozed off in bed that night, but only in between many wakings that meant she bobbed in the shallow waters of sleep rather than surrendered to the deeper warm currents that rested the mind.

Stevie had read, and indeed written, about people who compartmentalised their pain, who put a jolly face on and confronted the world, even though their hearts were cracking inside them, only to sob into their pillows when they were safely alone, but she didn't really believe anyone could manage it successfully. She found, however, that next morning she scurried round the kitchen like Doris Day, for Danny's sake, *tra-la-la-ing* as she poured out Coco Pops and orange juice and made 'fresh cwoffee'. She kept the kitchen blinds open to a minimum, just enough to let some sunlight squeeze through, but at an angle that didn't allow her to see anything of the house opposite.

As soon as Danny was safely in school, her whole body seemed to sag, not helped by the fact that a day of trying to sort out Paris and Brandon's fates awaited her. She knew another morning of rubbish-quality writing would be the outcome, and that the only possible solution of working off some of the half-grief, half-murder feelings that were munching away inside her, lay up the road in Well Life.

She went home to get her kit and went up to the gym. It was the first time she had been there since doing her Norman Wisdom routine on the treadmill. Grabbing a towel, she put her bag in the locker and climbed carefully aboard the thing once more.

She tried to blank her mind and keep her rhythm to the music blasting out through the speakers, until she realised the track was 'Loneliness'. Her eyes started to leak and she tried to build a surreptitious eye-wipe into her routine, which nearly upset her balance. She had decided to rest the machine for a couple of minutes when she saw Adam MacLean heading towards her.

She acted out a scene of 'something in my eye . . . oooh good, it's gone now', while waiting for the inevitable.

'Sohowryougeinun?' he said, in the mistaken belief that volume would make her understand what he was saying. Seeing her look of utter confusion, he began again slowly. 'So how arrre you getting on?'

'Fine,' she replied. 'I've just got something in my eye.'

'Aye, the place is full of flyin' things.'

She suspected sarcasm, but he wasn't giving any clues.

'Any news aboot yer man?'

'He moved in last night with . . . er . . .' Her voice started to wobble.

'So it's time tae start a plan of action,' Adam said, after a big gulp.

'Right,' she replied warily. She rubbed her neck, which was straining because of the angle it had to achieve to talk to him up there.

He picked up on that and asked, 'Have ye time for a wee cup o' tea?'

'Um, yes,' said Stevie, following him to the coffee bar, where he grunted something about sitting down at a table (she thought) and then said something equally incomprehensible to the girl behind the counter who seemed to understand perfectly. It was obviously a prerequisite of his staff to be bilingual, she concluded. English and Caveman.

Stevie sat with her hands in the prayer position between her knees. She was trembling. It wasn't unlike waiting outside the headmaster's office for a roasting, which she had only had to do once.

Adam put down two cups of tea, a jug of milk and some sugar on the table and then sat opposite her, blocking out most of the light from the window behind him. He tipped the milk jug over hers first but she refused. Likewise the sugar. *Jeez, she disnae take sugar!* he thought.

Jesus, he's got manners! she thought.

Then she remembered he probably had a first-class degree from the University of Charm and quickly withdrew any thoughts of goodwill.

The tea was molten and burnt her mouth. Adam watched her gasp, gulp, fan her mouth in barely covered amazement, and asked, 'Are you sure you're no' a self-harmer?'

'It was extra hot!' she snapped. 'Where did it get brewed—hell?'

It wasn't outside the realms of possibility.

'So, have you any ideas whit you'd like tae dae next?' he said.

Stevie shrugged. She didn't want to do anything but pack up and escape to some place on the other side of the world. A thought that rocketed up freely, only to be brought down by the weight of practicalities.

'We have to sort out money,' she said tentatively.

'It's OK—if you don't pay, I'll throw you oot,' he said.

Her lungs inflated sharply.

''S'OK, only jokin',' he said, seeing the look of horror flash in her eyes. 'I'm no' worried aboot all tha', we'll sort tha' later, really. It'll give me an excuse to come roond to the cottage sometime soon and be seen. Talkin' of which, have they seen you yet?'

'No,' said Stevie, shaking her head.

'Guid—sorry—*good*. Noo, let me think.' He stroked the red stubble coming through even though he had shaved only a few hours earlier.

'We have tae leave them a tantalisin' trail of crumbs. They have tae realise that you're living there before they know there's anythin' going on between us two. No' tha' there is,' he added sharply. 'So, here's whit I think,' he went on. 'Did you get a forwardin' order for your post?'

'No, not yet. I—'

'Paarrrfect,' said Adam. 'Noo, here's what I want you tae dae . . .'

'**D**arling, where's the iron?' Jo called upstairs to Matthew, now alone in the bath that they had been sharing until five minutes ago.

'Under the stairs. Sorry, darling, didn't you hear me?'

'Yes, I know you said that, darling, but it isn't there.'

Matthew heaved himself out of the bath and into his robe. He padded downstairs to where Jo was waiting, then poked his head in the cupboard. 'But it's always there,' he said, scratching his damp head.

'Stevie will have taken it, won't she?' said Jo with some annoyance. 'Like she took your microwave and any towel that was half-decent.'

'Er . . . she might have. She only bought it a couple of weeks ago.'

'Great,' said Jo. 'So what do I use? Please tell me you've got a spare.'

'Look,' said Matthew, 'we'll pick up one tomorrow. You've got stacks of other clothes you can wear.' All of which had taken up her side of the wardrobe and half of his and they would still have to buy another at some point. If he managed to find credit on a Visa.

'OK, I'll find something else,' Jo sighed. 'I can't blame Stevie for taking a little revenge. I'm only glad it wasn't more.'

'Put anything on. We're only going out for something to eat at Giovanni's, not the Ritz,' he laughed.

'Matthew Finch, I shall always look my best even if we are eating fish and chips out of newspaper on a park bench.'

Matthew wished they were. He had just paid fifty quid off his credit card and he was going to be loading another hundred on. Did they need to celebrate their first day of living together by spending so much?

'We could stay in and eat each other,' he suggested.

'No, I want to see and be seen—with you, obviously,' she said, smiling a smile that would melt him into spending every last penny he didn't have. *Did life really get any better than this?* Then his mobile rang.

He was in such a dreamlike state that he never checked the caller ID and clicked straight onto answer. 'Hello, Matthew Finch.'

'Hello, Matthew, it's Stevie.'

Damn! 'Oh, hi, Stevie,' he said, tightening.

'Sorry to bother you, it's just a quick call. It's about my post.'

'Oh, of course, your post,' he said aloud for Jo's benefit.

'I have informed people of my new address, but just in case any stray letters slip through the net . . .'

''Course, I'll forward them to you,' he said, butting in, anxious to get her off the line. Jo was looking distinctly territorial. He grabbed a pen and notepad. 'OK, give me your new address and I'll post them on.'

'Er . . . well . . . there's no need,' said Stevie. 'You can just pop them through the letterbox. I'm in the cottage across the lane.'

'You're what?' Matthew drained white as he headed for the window to peer through the curtain. Sure enough, there at the other side of the road, was the figure of a person also on a mobile waving at him, although the voice was loud and clear in his ear.

'Hi! There you are!'

'W—' he said, but the word, whatever it was, refused to be formed.

'Anyway, that's all for now. So thanks, and er . . . good night.'

Matthew didn't say a word. He just clicked off his phone and answered Jo's flurry of questions with a flat, disbelieving voice.

'That was Stevie. She wants her post. She's moved into that cottage.'

'Which cottage, where?' said Jo, flicking back the curtain herself but seeing only a square of light from the big, pretty house opposite. 'There?' she said. 'No, not there—tell me not there!'

'Yes, there.'

'What's she playing at?'

'I don't know.'

'Well, it's obvious, isn't it? She's flipped!' said Jo. 'I knew this had gone too smoothly to be believed. Matt, you have to talk to her. She's nuts. Does she really think you'll go back to her if she stalks you? She's doing what she did with her husband all over again, isn't she?'

'I don't know,' said Matthew. It was going to be an expensive way to tail him. He should have seen this coming, because she did have history as a bit of a hanger-on when it was obvious the relationship was dead. 'Come on, let's just get ready and go out. We'll deal with this later, but for now, let's go and eat.'

'And drink,' said Jo, who threw down the useless, thin, bendy Ryvita of a towel that was wrapped around her hair but had absorbed nothing. Then she skipped upstairs to her extensive designer wardrobe, throwing behind her, 'I'll need champagne to drown out this little revelation!'

Matthew groaned.

Stevie breathed slowly in and out as she had done in labour to steady herself. She could barely press the disconnect button on the phone for trembling. When she felt able to cross to the window again, she snapped the blinds shut and leaned against the wall for some badly needed support. Then she stabbed in the text lettering mission accomplished on her mobile phone and sent it to Adam MacLean.

Chapter 6

A PACKAGE ARRIVED for Matthew just as he and Jo were setting off for work the following morning. He put it in the porch to deal with later, because he didn't have the time to open it then. He locked up the house and looked across at the old cottage before getting in the car, half expecting to see Stevie in the window. All he saw was a cottage with curtains drawn and blinds dropped, but knowing that Stevie was behind them still made him uncomfortable.

Jo had been right, scorned women were dangerous, irrational beings and she couldn't have moved in across the road for any other reason than to wreak havoc in his life. He should have realised she had trouble dealing with rejection. By her own admission, Mick's leaving had driven her half-mad. Certainly, her phone call had put a big dampener over their whole evening. All roads of conversation bent back to Stevie and her new living arrangements, however much they had tried to get on with enjoying the meal. They hadn't succeeded; it had not been ninety-two quid well spent.

Matthew had struggled to get an erection in bed because the thought of his ex-lover living directly across the lane had got in the way and stirred up feelings that had fingers in all sorts of emotional pies.

Jo was taking him shopping at lunchtime for an iron, a microwave, towels that didn't scratch her skin off, and some decent sheets. He pocketed the invitation to get a new Platinum Visa that arrived with that morning's post from one of the few banks with whom he didn't have one. His emergency Goldfish was starting to drown.

When Stevie rolled up at the garden centre, Catherine was already there. She had suggested lunch in the country, away from Blossom Lane and the gym, saying that the country air and carbs might do Stevie good. They hugged hello and plonked themselves at a nice table with a view of the stream, heavily populated by ducks and a gangsta goose.

'So how's it going, dare I ask? Got back into your writing yet?' asked Catherine, after they had sent the young waiter off with an order for caramel lattes and two pasta carbonaras. Stevie's shiny-eyed silence made any verbal answer unnecessary. Catherine reached over the table and gave her hand a comforting squeeze.

'Stevie, I've not really a doubt in my head that Matthew will come back to you after he's realised that Jo is a cold, calculating bitch who probably deserved to get clobbered by Highland Hairy Legs, but is he really the person you thought he was, to put you through this? Would you ever be able to trust him again?'

'I want him back, Catherine,' she said steadily. 'We'll sort it out between us afterwards, I'm sure of it.'

'It will happen,' said Catherine, who was totally convinced of it. 'Both Eddie and I think that Matthew's weak rather than wicked.'

There was a brief pause while the coffees arrived.

'I met Adam MacLean in the gym yesterday,' said Stevie. 'He told me to ring Matthew and ask him to drop any post off at the cottage.'

'So, Matt knows where you're living then. How did he take it?'

'He was too shocked to say anything then, but I had a peep through the blinds this morning and saw him glaring over at the house before he got into the car. He didn't look very pleased at all.'

'Good!' said Catherine, as their plates of pasta arrived.

'Not good really,' said Stevie, taking a mouthful of spaghetti. 'I don't want him to hate me. I want him to love me. It looks a bit obvious why I've moved there, doesn't it? He'll think I'm stalking him.'

'Not if you ignore him, he won't, and certainly not if you're seen on the arm of another bloke.'

'Don't remind me.' The prospect of that part of Adam MacLean's 'master plan' was making her feel ill. They would look the world's most ridiculous couple, and what would they talk about? His experiences when locked up in Barlinnie Prison? Jo had told her all about Adam's conviction for GBH. She despised people like him—bullies who used their size and looks to intimidate. The fact that she could join forces with someone who actually deserved to be deserted by his partner spoke volumes of her desperation to get Matthew back. Once she had, she hoped Jo and Adam MacLean would disappear back to hell.

Matthew went into the house, forgot the box was there and tripped right over it, which only added to his mood of annoyance. Not that opening it did anything to take those feelings away.

'What are those?' said Jo, looking over his shoulder as he unpeeled layers of tissue round some very pretty, beribboned stationery. It was funny to see his name there still together with Stevie's. It felt like years since they had chosen the paper and the lettering and the picture on the covers, when, in real time, it had been less than three months.

'Order of services and an invoice for . . . *how much?*'

Jo eased it out of his hand. 'You aren't going to like this, but hear me out,' she said calmly. 'This bill is in Stevie's name. You need to take it across the road now and let her deal with it.'

'I'd feel a bit rotten doing that,' said Matthew with a stab of guilt, not saying that it had been he who had picked such an expensive design.

'As I say, hear me out,' admonished Jo. 'The reason you need to do what I say is that if you are nice and offer to pay for these, Stevie will misread your actions and see hope where there is none. You have to be cruel to be kind here, Matt. Don't play her game, for all our sakes—especially Stevie's, darling. Just give her the box and come straight back. Don't let her use it as an excuse to engage you. You won't be doing her any favours in the long run. Trust me.'

'Yes, OK,' said Matthew. He hoisted the box up, marched across to the cottage and rapped loudly on the door.

When Stevie saw Matthew approach, she put two and two together to make a very accurate four. She straightened her back and opened the door. The straight-backed, unthreatening sight of her stole 100 knots of wind from his sails. She looked so *together*, and her stiff body language was not saying to him, 'How nice to see you, I'm glad you called.'

'These arrived for you,' he said, thrusting them forward.

'The order of services, I presume. Yes, the printer said they were on their way,' she replied, making no attempt to take them from him.

'Well, here you are.' He rattled the box at her, but her hands stayed by her sides.

'You could have saved yourself a trip and just put them in the bin,' she said flatly. 'I have as much use for them as you do, Matthew.'

'There's . . . er . . . an invoice.'

Despite her attempt at indifference, Stevie found herself unable to disguise the flare of contempt in her eyes, which hit him at point-blank range and stirred up something within him that didn't make him feel very good about himself. He deflected it back, attack being the best form of defence, etc, and found he didn't need to fake his annoyance.

'Why are you here, Stevie?'

'You wanted me out, quickly, and this house was available.'

'But why here? Why this road?'

'Matthew,' she began calmly, without surface emotion, even though she was bubbling inside with a cocktail of anger and frustration with base flavours of hurt and despair, 'this was the only house I could get that was near to Danny's school. You didn't exactly give me the luxury of time to shop around, did you? Besides, you have made it clear that you have another life now, and so have I—one that you're not part of. I am a free agent too now, remember? I can live where I like.'

She whipped the invoice from the top of the box.

'My wheelie bin's full so I'll deal with this and you deal with those. Please let's keep this civilised, Matthew. Thank you for bringing the bill.' And with that, Stevie slowly but firmly shut the door in his face.

Matthew felt as if he had been slapped, even though she hadn't been aggressive. There was no trying to win him back. She couldn't have forgotten him that quickly really, could she?

Stevie patted her heart and wondered how she could have spoken so coolly with the acrobatics it had been doing simultaneously in her chest. Her little victory did not stop her feeling inordinately sad, though. How could she and Matthew be such strangers to each other, when less than three weeks ago they had made love in the bed he now shared with another woman? She started to think about the details of that last time, how he had been mentally in another place while his body had been beside her, although he had put it down to being tired. With hindsight, she realised that it wasn't an act of love but a red-herring shag to put her off the scent that he was about to go on holiday with another woman.

She supposed she had better let Adam MacLean know; they had agreed to keep each other up to speed. She dialled his number.

'Hlloooadmcln,' he said.

'Hello, it's Stevie Honeywell,' she said.

'How can I help you?' he said brusquely.

'Just an update. Matthew came over with a box addressed to me and asked what I was doing in the cottage.'

'Dae tell me more,' Adam said, as if the drama was killing him. Not.

'Well, I told him that I had my life now and he had his. I think he was quite surprised.'

'Oh, right.'

'Mr MacLean, you asked me to keep you updated. That's what I'm doing. Sorry to have bothered you.' Then Stevie hit disconnect.

Adam MacLean had been about to say, 'Yes, I know you did and I appreciate it,' when she had a hissy fit and slammed the phone down on him. It was obviously *that week* every week with her. She should have been grateful he spoke to her at all; everyone else had had a grunt today, if they were lucky.

That morning the bed had seemed much emptier and colder than before and it hit him hard and low that Jo might just have gone for ever. Then he sprang out of that lonely bedroom and he knew that it wouldn't happen, because he wouldn't, *couldn't* let her go—and even if he had to marry that bloody Stevie woman to make Jo jealous enough to come back, then he would—although he hoped to heaven and back that it wouldn't come to that. Then Adam opened his birthday cards.

Catherine flopped on the sofa and stuck her feet up on the footstool.

'Here you go,' said Eddie, and placed a glass of white wine in her hand. 'All right if I go out with Large, White and Judd tomorrow for a couple of jars? I'll be back by eleven.'

'Yeah, 'course,' she said. 'You don't have to ask me, love.'

'I know,' he said and they settled into an easy relaxed silence.

'Funny though,' said Eddie eventually.

'What is?' said Catherine.

'Well, I've been thinking. If you did mind about me going out for a night, say if you were the possessive type, you wouldn't exactly let me go to a health spa for a week, would you? So how come the big Scottish bloke never let Jo out of his sight but he was OK about her going to that health spa? You know, the one she never actually went to.'

'Hmmm, I see what you mean, yes,' said Catherine.

'I was watching him at the wedding, you know, and he looked an OK bloke to me. I don't buy all that wife-beater stuff.'

Catherine nodded. Her thoughts had been running along the same lines. She lifted the phone to dial Stevie's number when it rang in her hand and she picked up to find the very person she wanted to speak to.

'Listen,' said Catherine. 'If Adam MacLean had Jo on such a tight leash, how come he was OK about her going to a health farm for a week?'

'I don't know,' said Stevie. 'It's a bit weird, I suppose. Maybe he suspected something but gave her space to smoke her out.' It wasn't information Stevie attached any great significance to, but, nevertheless, she filed it in her mind under 'B' for MacLean.

Across the road, all thoughts of cancelled weddings were now in the wheelie bin with the box of stationery. With an arm round his sleepy lover, Matthew flicked through Ceefax at the news, then the football results, then the numbers for the previous night's lottery draw. Not that he expected anything; he had only won about three tenners ever, or so it felt. At one point he had been buying Thunderballs, Euromillions, Hot Picks, Extras and then the Irish Lottery too until he realised he couldn't afford to carry on, and resigned himself to the occasional Lucky Dip and a regular line twice a week. He had just changed his numbers to his and Jo's birthdays and the date they first made love. Numbers that were now on the screen in front of him.

'That can't be right,' he said, dislodging Jo for a moment, in order to take his ticket out of the drawer.

'What's the matter?' Jo asked. She was just about asleep with the delicious combination of a very nice white wine, a very nice warm room and a very nice man stroking her arm.

'I've won the Wednesday lottery!' said Matthew, checking the screen numbers against his ticket numbers. Jo, now fully awake, snatched it out of his hand and double-checked it.

'Five, you've got five. My God, how much is that?' she shrieked.

'I don't know, I've only ever won tenners.'

Jo looked at the back of the lottery ticket. 'You have to ring Camelot! Quick, hand me the phone!'

Matthew handed her the phone. The line was engaged, so was his head. He could clear all his debts and start a clean slate. He would tear all his Visas up and live within his means. Then again, it was sensible to keep one or two to pay for purchases and holidays, for the extra insurance they gave. A holiday in Barbados for instance, Jo in that white bikini during the day, that little red G-string during the evening and nothing at all during the night.

'Matt, go and get some champagne. Let's toast our luck.'

Jo looked at him in that sultry big-lashed way of hers that was full of lust and promise of even more lust. Goddammit, she was gorgeous. He didn't need champagne to make his heart any more thrilled. He would have got the same effect from a carton of Um Bongo juice if it was shared with Jo. But she had other ideas.

'Please, darling. If ever there was a champagne moment, this is it.'

Twenty quid for some champagne, said the part of his head that governed his pant area. *You're going to have thousands in the bank in a couple of days, you can please the lady with a bottle, surely?*

'OK,' he relented, and she clapped her hands like a little girl.

'Bring back two,' she said. 'We'll get horribly drunk and ring in sick tomorrow and then spend all day in bed and plan what we're going to do with the money.'

Matthew already had his shoes on. 'Don't ring again until I get back,' he warned sexily. 'Or I'll have to smack your bottom.'

'Ooh, promises, promises,' she said.

'You're my good-luck charm, that's what you are,' he said, pulling her into his arms and kissing her lovely juicy lips.

'You'd better not be long,' she purred. 'Although I might have slipped into something more comfortable by the time you get back. My, it's so hot in here,' and she unbuttoned her shirt a couple more notches.

He shot out of the door to the car with a smile as big as his erection, although both reduced a little when he saw the light filtering through the blinds across the lane.

Then he drove to the off-licence.

There was a message waiting for Stevie after she had come back from an Adam MacLean-free hour on the weights at the gym.

'Bea darling, it's Crystal. Just ringing to see if everything's OK,' which was her boss Crystal Rock's way of saying, 'Where the hell is your manuscript? It's overdue and I never have to chase you—so what's wrong?'

Stevie bit the bullet and rang her back immediately.

'Darling! I was worried about you,' said Crystal.

'I was just ringing to say that my manuscript is nearly ready.'

'Nearly? Oh, darling, you've been neglecting me for your wedding plans, haven't you?' said Crystal, a threat tangled up in the banter.

'There isn't going to be a wedding,' said Stevie. 'Matthew has . . . has found someone else.'

'Oh, darling, the absolute . . .'

Stevie winced at the word she used, although even she had to admit it actually sounded quite classy being issued via Crystal's Swiss-finishing-school-educated voice box.

'Look, it's fine. When *can* you get it to me?' said Crystal, in a rare moment of leniency.

'I'll email it Tuesday first thing. It's nearly finished, I promise.'

'I'll expect it, darling. Oh, and start thinking about the next one.

We've had an absolute glut of Mediterranean heroes and yet our own Scots and Irish boys have been totally neglected.'

'I'll do an Irish.'

'No, I've given Paul the Irish. I want you to take the Scot. Call it *Highland Fling*—you know the format. But let's have some red hair and Gaelic testosterone and plenty of it.'

'Absolutely,' said Stevie, who suddenly felt herself being catapulted out of the frying pan into a very hot fire. *How the hell could she make a sex symbol out of a red-haired Scot when she would be imagining that . . . that man?* He would end up killing the heroine with a giant-handed slap in Chapter One—and how flaming romantic was that?

Matthew rose from bed feeling sick. The line to Camelot hadn't been engaged, it had been faulty, though they hadn't known that when they were ringing at five-minute intervals. After seven attempts, they cracked open the first bottle of champagne. After the second, to which they had added brandy and brown sugar to make cocktails, Matthew had carried Jo upstairs and attempted to make love to her, failing dismally—not that either of them cared. They were going to be rich— well, rich enough to have a bloody good spend and a fantastic holiday *au soleil*. More importantly, he could put off that looming money talk with Jo.

He was woken by Jo shaking his shoulder to say she had got through to Camelot to find he had won five hundred and fifteen quid.

'A record number of winners on that draw,' Camelot had said.

Four hundred and seventy five quid 'profit' then, if you took off the price of the champers. It wouldn't even make a dent in what he owed so there wasn't much point in chucking the money to a Visa company.

'Hello,' said Stevie, picking up the phone.

'Adam MacLean. Hreyooo?' boomed *his* voice. Why did he have to be so loud all the time?

Stevie felt her whole body stiffen. 'Fine, thank you. How are you?'

'OK. So, anythin' tae report?'

'Not really,' said Stevie, 'unless you want to know that his car is still outside. So they haven't gone to work today presumably, although that's a very trivial detail and I'm almost sorry to have mentioned it.'

She could sense his jaw muscle tighten and twitch with annoyance at the other end of the line and she got a little thrill out of that. Yes, writing about a Scot in her new book might be fun. She could have him jumping like a puppet to her call. She could have him trampled by a beautiful white horse, ridden by the gorgeous young strawberry-blonde heroine. She would call her Evie. Evie Sweetwell.

'I rang tae say I think we should initiate the next stage,' he said.

'Whatever you say, Mr MacLean.'

'Can you get a baby sitter tomorrow?'

'Er . . . not sure, why?' she asked, but knowing Catherine would help out in a crisis. Kate was saving up madly for whatever seventeen-year-olds save up for and would gladly welcome twenty quid, full access to a blackcurrant cheesecake and a sly couple of Bacardi Breezers.

'Because I think you should go oot, it being Saturday night an' all.'

'Me—out? Where?'

'Wi' me.'

Oh farts! 'With you?'

'Get yer best clobba on, lady,' said Adam MacLean. 'I'll pick you up at seven thirty. We're off to the picture hoos.'

'So, what are you going to wear?' said Catherine.

'Dunno, what you do think?'

'That green crossover top, definitely. That was Matthew's favourite so that's bound to strike a chord if he sees you.'

'*If?* How do I make that definite, so all this will be worth while? What if they don't happen to be looking out of the window watching us go off together? I mean, it's highly unlikely they will be, isn't it really?'

'If they don't see you, then you have to keep going at it until they do.'

'I was afraid you'd say that.'

'Well, it's all part of the plan!' Catherine laughed, although as every day passed, she was becoming less keen on the idea of a Stevie and Matthew reconciliation. Even though she wanted her friend to be happy, she also wished she would stuff it home to Matthew that there was life without him, and if it took Adam MacLean to help her do that, then so be it. She hoped Stevie wouldn't give in too easily when Matthew came crawling back to her, because he would, nothing surer. Catherine wanted Matthew to realise what he was missing in Stevie, though she was becoming increasingly confused as to what Stevie was missing in Matthew.

'I've to be ready for seven thirty.'

'Well, Kate will be over for seven. Nervous?'

'What have I to be nervous about? I'm only going out with a wife-beating psychopath.'

'I don't think he's anything of the sort,' said Catherine. 'I think the bloke has got some bad press. We believed everything Jo said—and look what a calculating cow she turned out to be. We only have her side of things.'

'Oh, Cath, come on. You only have to look at him to know he's not Mr Fluffy!' Stevie gave a disbelieving laugh. 'Have you seen that scar on his face? He didn't get *that* making daisy chains.'

'You really don't like him at all, do you?'

'No,' said Stevie, 'but we need each other, it seems. And at least being at the pictures means I don't have to talk to him.'

. . . **W**hich had been Adam MacLean's precise thought when he proposed the venue. Plus the cinema was central, popular and there was a good chance someone would spot them together and report their presence back to Jo. Even though she might not want him herself now, she wouldn't want anyone else to have him either. He knew what a jealous creature she could be, a fact that would work in his favour here.

Matthew was filling the kettle when he noticed Eddie's van at the other side of the lane dropping off his daughter. Kate had baby-sat for them, which was the only reason she ever came round. Stevie must be going out, he concluded. So where was she going?

He mentally slapped himself; it wasn't any of his business. He was with Jo now, so why should he even be interested? But still . . .

You look nice,' said Kate, trying not to fall over as Danny wrapped himself round her very long giraffe-y legs.

'Do I?' said Stevie.

'Green looks great on you,' said Kate. 'I wish I were blonde.'

'You are!' Stevie laughed. Kate was naturally the platinum blonde that people aspired to, but she persisted on dyeing her long, long hair Goth-black with various shades of wild colour shot through it.

'Going to help me demolish this then, Dans?' asked Kate, her big sapphire eyes rounding at the sandwich fest and cheesecake that Stevie had left out for her. 'Have you had your tea?'

'Yes,' said Danny. 'I had beans off toast.'

'Beans *off* toast?' Kate looked to Stevie for further explanation.

'He means beans minus toast,' Stevie sighed. 'My little boy has suddenly decided he doesn't like bread.'

'Bread's really good for you, Dans. Especially this brown stuff. I eat loads, it's *cool*,' said Kate, stuffing a sandwich in her mouth.

'Is it? Do you?' said Danny in amazement. 'Mummy, could I have one like Kate's got, please?'

As the second hand began its slow descent towards half past, Stevie was feeling more and more nauseous. The evening stretched long and hard in front of her and she had thrown the newspaper away so she didn't even know what was on at the 'picture hoos'. No doubt she'd have to sit through some all-action movie with a big macho hero who shot lots of people with huge guns, while a little girlie, accidentally caught up in the action, teetered behind him with stilt high heels and massive knockers.

'I think he's here,' said Kate, peeping out of the window.

'Shit!' said Stevie.

'Mummy!'

'Sorry, Danny,' said Stevie, slapping her hand over her mouth.

'Where are you going?'

'It's . . . er . . . a business meeting about Mummy's writing,' said Stevie. 'You go in there with Kate, darling,' and she ushered him towards the lounge before he could see MacLean and get nightmares.

'Come on then, Dans, let's go and watch a DVD with the cinema surround on full vol,' said Kate. 'Give Mums a kiss.'

'Bye, darling, be good for Kate,' said Stevie.

As soon as the lounge door closed, there was a battering-ram-type boom at the front door. Stevie grabbed her jacket and handbag and reached for the handle, noticing her hand was shaking. She opened it to find Adam MacLean colour-coordinated with her in a pale green shirt and stonewashed jeans.

'Both of us in mint—nice touch,' he said appreciatively. 'I took a slow walk from the car tae the door. Now we'll take a slow walk back to it.'

'OK,' said Stevie. He opened the car door for her (for show obviously), closed it behind her and then climbed in the driver's seat. The CD switched on with the ignition—Alvin Stardust. She had been expecting something a lot heavier: the Prodigy maybe, or some other group with a lead singer who bit the heads off live rodents.

They didn't speak at all. Stevie wished she'd brought a knife to cut the atmosphere between them, though actually, just bringing a knife would have been sensible. Adam drove steadily despite his car being such a long, fast, sleek number. She knew the myth about men and big cars, although she doubted very much that Jo was the sort of woman who would have entertained a man who was short in that area. Then she wondered why on earth she was thinking about Adam MacLean's willy and cut off those thoughts there and then.

They arrived at the car park round the corner from the cinema, crossed the road and joined the queue for the ticket booth.

'Whit dae you want tae go and see?' he asked.

There were two films showing. One was something like *The Strangulator*—no prizes for guessing that would be his choice, thought Stevie—or a psychological thriller with Denzel Washington, who, Stevie thought, was quite dishy and would certainly take her mind off the fact that she was on an obligatory evening out with *him*.

'Er . . . what do *you* want?' said Stevie diplomatically.

'It's up tae you.'

'Well, the thriller's got good press,' she suggested, hoping he would say he was off to see *The Strangulator* and would meet her in the foyer after the film was over, but he simply said, 'Aye, that'll dae, then.'

Stevie rummaged in her bag for her purse but he said, 'I'll get these. You awa' and get the popcorn.'

'OK,' said Stevie, thinking, Popcorn? This is looking too much like a real date! However, she then realised that he didn't want her to think she was getting away with not paying for anything.

He thinks I'm a freeloader, she said to herself. *Right, I'll show him!*

She was served, just as Adam appeared with the tickets. She was struggling with a 'small' popcorn the size of a mop bucket and a 'large' that was roughly a skip, and had cost as much. She had plumped for the special offer and got two drinks as well. Not having a clue what he wanted, she had chosen Diet Cokes seeing as a gallon of Bell's and Irn Bru wasn't an option. He had the nerve to look taken aback.

'I wes actually joking,' he said.

'Well, unfortunately I'm not yet fully acquainted with the nuances of your wit,' said Stevie.

'So which is mine?' he grunted.

'This big one!' said Stevie. *Is he joking or does he think I'm a hog?*

'Ba Christ, it'll take me all night tae eat this.'

'I didn't want you thinking I was mean,' said Stevie. 'Which brings me round to say I do very much want to get the financial side of our arrangement sorted soon. I don't want to be in for any nasty shocks.'

'Aye,' he said, and led the way into the darkened cinema.

'Here,' said Adam, picking one of the big cushioned seats with the row in front of them a distance away. 'I paid extra for the superior seats. Ma legs get all crunched up in the ordinary wans . . . ones.'

The lights dimmed and Stevie took a look round. The place was full of couples, silhouettes of their heads coming together as they passed a joke or a sweet nothing, so it felt odd to be part of them, and yet not part of them. How many others here were sitting with people they couldn't stand, and who they knew couldn't stand them either?

They munched and watched in entertained silence. Denzel was gorgeous and the plot was twisty and thrilling. At the end, the lights came up and Adam got up, stretched, and knocked all the stray knobs of popcorn off his shirt into his container.

'Tha' was quite guid—well picked,' he said.

'Yes, I enjoyed it,' said Stevie. 'The film, I meant,' she added. Just in case he thought she meant his scintillating company.

She really doesn't like me very much at all, he thought with faint amusement, although he couldn't for the life of him think why. Had he not treated her with anything but courtesy, that first meeting excepted? None of this situation was his fault.

He had gone over his relationship with Jo with a finer than fine-tooth comb, but he still couldn't work out where he'd gone wrong. It was torturing him, not knowing why she preferred a prick like Matthew Finch to someone who had treated her like a queen. It was Miss Stroppy Drawers here that hadn't made Matty Boy happy and he had strayed. It was *her* fault, not his. Slatternly, verbally abusive, prone to violent outbursts when she was drunk, and they were just at the beginning of the list. If she was adamant about flinging blame about, she should look nearer to home.

He led Stevie out and back to the car, where the cheesy Seventies CD blasted out 'Wig Wam Bam' and 'Do You Wanna Touch'. It seemed to her that his music taste was as dubious as everything else about him.

'Want me tae run your baby sitter hame . . . home?' he offered, as they turned into Blossom Lane.

'No, it's all right, thank you. I'll get her a taxi,' said Stevie quickly.

He was laughing now. The nicer he was to her, the more it seemed to annoy her. That made him want to be even nicer, because getting under her skin was the only bit of fun he was having at the moment.

They pulled up outside the cottage. The lights were on downstairs in Matthew's house and the curtains were still open.

'We'll sit here for a wee minute,' Adam MacLean said, 'and gi' them a chance tae see us. After all, tha's what lovers dae . . . do, isn't it? Sit in the car and talk and kiss and stuff.'

'There's no way I'm kissing you,' said Stevie, horrified.

'Dinnae worry yersel', lady,' said Adam. 'I'm just tryin' tae make this as realistic as possible. Without stooping to bodily contact. Agreed?'

'Agreed,' said Stevie.

He grunted.

'Would this be a good time to talk about money, then?' said Stevie.

'Look,' he said, sounding strained, 'I'll work out some figures. I cannae afford tae pay fer the entire cottage and my mortgage fer very long . . . If it bothers you that much, I'll make it ma priority, OK?'

'Yes, it does bother me, Mr MacLean,' said Stevie, 'so I'd appreciate it if you would, thank you.'

'Ma name's Adam, by the way. Might sound a wee bit odd if we're tryin' to convince people we're a couple when there's you callin' me by ma title and surname.'

'OK . . . Adam,' she said. It sounded rather intimate to call him by his Christian name, especially after she had got used to calling him 'MacLean' for so long. Well, that and a selection of fruitier alternatives.

'So, is Stevie short for Stephanie?'

'No, it's just Stevie. Like the poet.'

'Stevie Smith?'

Crikey—he's heard of her. 'Yes.'

She's surprised I've heard of Stevie Smith. She thinks I'm illiterate! Cheeky wee . . . Adam tried to contain his annoyance but it leaked out in the way he drummed his fingers on the steering wheel in an angry tattoo.

They waited a tad longer, but there was no activity from across the road. Matthew and Jo were probably on their way to bed. Both she and Adam started to say together that maybe they should go, and likewise, together, they thought, So this evening's been for nothing, after all.

'Maybe better luck next time, then,' said Adam.

Oh, God forbid a next time! Although that thought was quickly pushed out of the way by a more serious one as Adam got out of the car. *Where's he going? Oh, please don't tell me he wants to come in for coffee!*

However, he was only doing his gentlemanly duty in opening the door for her, then he got back in the car after a gruff and sarcastic, 'Good night and thanks for the popcorn!' and after doing a three-point turn in the lane, zoomed off with a frustration-laden squeal of tyres. Stevie flinched. She hated loud noises of any kind. They upset her, made her feel insecure, took her back to childhood days she would rather not think about.

Suddenly her heart was in her mouth, for out of the corner of her eye, she saw a figure at Matthew's window.

'Steady,' she told herself, and raised her hand, waving a fond farewell at the car that had already gone, not that whoever was at the window would know that. Then she slowly opened the cottage door and walked in, with another lingering stare up the lane for good measure.

After Kate's taxi had ferried her home, she made a quick call to Adam MacLean, who was more than surprised to hear from her. 'I think we were spotted,' she said excitedly. 'Well, enough to set the cat among the pigeons, although I could be getting it out of perspective. Your tyres made a bit of a noise as you sped off. You must have alerted them across the road, because there was someone watching through the window. I pretended to be waving goodbye to you.'

'Tha's guid news, said Adam. 'I just wish they'd seen me too and, you know, linked us together.'

Stevie caught sight of the invoice for the wedding stationery and a beautiful little plan hatched before her eyes. 'I think I know a way to do that, if you've got what I need,' she said, trying to fight off the strangest feeling that what she planned to do next felt dangerously akin to fun.

Chapter 7

STEVIE'S IDEA WAS as simple and delicious as a stuff-in-the-oven part-baked loaf, and was ready to be implemented three days later on the Tuesday, when she got a call from Adam to say that he was finally in possession of the required item. She met him briefly at the gym, where he handed it over, and after an accident-free half-hour on the treadmill, she went home to her new work brief until Matthew got home.

The realisation that this master plan of Adam's might actually work had brought such a light feeling to her heart that she had found herself able to sort out Paris and Brandon's final chapter at last. Their idyllic ending was created from a happy, hopeful bubble in her brain, and the manuscript was emailed to Midnight Moon HQ as promised.

It was a relief to be back on track writing. The pretty room she was using as an office made a major contribution to that. It was spacious but cosy and peaceful, with a bonny view of the long garden. Roses poked in through the windows, thrown open to let in some fresh air, along with the comforting rumble of the odd train in the near distance. It was the sort of room she could imagine sitting in and writing her blockbuster. Not that she wasn't grateful for her position at Midnight Moon. She and 'Alexis' and 'Paula' received a salary in advance of any royalties, and that gave them a steady income.

Stevie walked into town to get some fresh air and stretch her legs and do the final but hardest job—letting go of the wedding rings. She was going to sell them to the jeweller who was known for giving the fairest prices. The man offered her £120 for the two wedding bands, which would cover half the cost of the order-of-service booklets, and £105 for the engagement ring. Stevie took it without trying to barter him up to a better price. It wasn't as if she could ever have worn it, not with the memories it had collected. If—*when*—she and Matthew got back together, she would choose a new one.

When she got home, she chased away the dip in her spirits by scribbling some rough notes for *Highland Fling*. She decided to make her heroine small and feisty and the 'hero' mean and moody. Possibly give him a scar. The heroine would outwit him at every turn. *Ha!* Once she had pictures of 'Damme MacQueen' and 'Evie Sweetwell' in her mind, the ideas started to come through thick and fast.

In contrast, Matthew was finding it hard to concentrate at work. He had acted upon the letter asking him to apply for a Platinum Visa 'by ringing this number for an instant decision', only to be told that he had been instantly rejected.

'So why did you invite me to get one if you were going to tell me I couldn't?' said Matthew, taking their decision extremely personally.

'Sorry, sir,' said the operative, who went into automated spiel about how he could find out his credit rating. Matthew knew that the fact he had been refused their Visa would show up on his rating and influence future lenders. He hung up when she was in mid-flow and immediately felt guilty about being so rude and acting so out of character. Then again, he seemed to be doing quite a lot of things lately that were out of character and of which he didn't feel particularly proud.

One of his Visa bills had arrived that morning. The holiday cost had been added to the amount outstanding, which had taken him over the limit. Plus something was niggling him. He just happened to be about to close the curtains on Saturday night, when he saw Stevie standing on the doorstep of the cottage waving someone off. She had her best green top on and a big *dreamy* smile. Why that had affected him so much, he didn't know because it was none of his business. He had put it out of his mind numerous times, but it seemed to be on elastic and kept bouncing back.

The sunlight was streaming through the window when he got home that evening, highlighting how grubby the kitchen had become since Stevie had moved out. The work surface was full of crumbs and the floor badly needed a good scrub. He'd have to get a cleaner in. Jo wasn't the type to put on an apron and wear down her long, deliciously scratchy fingernails doing domestic chores; she wasn't a 'Stevie'.

Jo relaxed in the bath for half an hour while Matthew rustled up something tasty in the kitchen. While the pasta was boiling, he thought he might just tidy a few things away. Jo's detritus seemed to have taken over every surface like a virulent ivy, and how the hell could they roll around on the mat in front of the fire when it was dull with dust and mysterious house 'bits'. He went into the cupboard for the vacuum cleaner. Where on earth was the Dyson? *Oh, bloody hell!*

Stevie waited an hour after she had seen Matthew come in from work before going over the road. She had to be seen to be extra casual. Luck was on her side as Matthew's head seemed to be zipping across the window as if he was moving things from one place to another.

'I'm just popping across the road. I'll be ten seconds, poppet!' she called to Danny.

'OK, Mummy!'

Stevie lifted up the Amex bill that Adam had given her, and walked slowly and deliberately across the road.

He's seen me, she thought, noticing how Matthew jumped back from the window. That hurt a lot. Did he really have to insult her by pretending he wasn't in? That small act turned her jellied nerves to steel. She put the envelope through his letterbox and returned home, not looking behind her. Then she texted Adam to tell him she'd done it.

As soon as Matthew had jumped back from the window, he felt cross with himself. It was a puerile reaction and she must have seen him.

The letterbox clacked and the single envelope dropped on the doormat. He stole up to it, then tentatively lifted it to see it was just an Amex bill for Jo. He wondered if there was enough credit left on it to buy a vacuum cleaner. He stuck it on the mantelpiece to give to her later and thought no more about it.

Thought no more about it, that was, until half past midnight, when his cooling brain was resting on the pillow. When its attentions came to Jo's letter, it nudged him rudely awake. *Why did Stevie have Jo's post?*

Matthew went downstairs and got the envelope bearing Jo's old address, the one she shared with her husband. He couldn't work it out. The only way Stevie could have got this was if MacLean gave it to her. But why would he do that? How come they knew each other? What did it all mean? What was he up to? What was she up to? He didn't get it. His brain started to ache from trying to work it all out and he got no more sleep that night.

Next morning he handed over the envelope to Jo. She looked at it, then threw it down as if it was contaminated.

'How did you get this?' she asked. 'Did Adam bring it round? Shit, he knows where we live, doesn't he?'

'Well, there's the mystery. Stevie posted it.'

'Stevie? *Stevie?* How the hell did she get it?'

'I don't know.'

Jo ran to the window. 'What is she up to? Or should I say *they*?'

'They who?'

'My ex and your ex. They both have an axe to grind.'

Matthew laughed. 'You can't seriously be insinuating that Stevie and Adam have got together, can you?'

'Don't be ridiculous,' Jo jeered. 'Adam wouldn't look at someone like Stevie Honeywell.'

Matthew had been about to ask what was so wrong with Stevie, but the hard look in Jo's eyes told him that might be unwise.

'I'm going to go over there and ask her how she got this,' he said.

'Don't be silly!' snapped Jo. 'That's exactly what she wants you to do.'

'But I want to find out if he knows where I live!' Matthew gulped.

'I don't know how he could know that,' said Jo.

'He could have followed us. You said it yourself—he's nuts, isn't he?'

Jo nodded slowly. 'Yes, that's possible, I suppose. Then again, I think he would have done something a bit more drastic than this. Not exactly his style—grievous bodily letter delivering. And Adam wouldn't have got the wrong house.' *Which means he's up to something.*

'So what's going on then?' Matthew queried.

Jo thought of what had happened when she had returned home from Majorca and told Adam she was leaving him. She should have realised from his reaction that he had something more up his sleeve. *Hmmm.*

'Look, Matt, I'm sorry, but I am not playing psychological games with Stevie because that's what she wants me to do.'

'You seem very sure that's what she's doing.'

Jo nodded slowly. She felt suddenly empowered. *Adam still wants me.*

'I know how women think, Matt, because—surprise, surprise—I'm a woman myself.' She cocked an eyebrow. 'Wanna see some proof?'

'Yes, please.'

Once again, Jo and Matthew were late for work.

Adam MacLean rang Stevie at ten.

'What time does your wee boy go tae his bed?' he asked.

'About half past seven,' said Stevie. 'He's always asleep for eight.'

'I'll be round at nine,' said Adam. 'Feel free not to cook anything.'

And Stevie thought, Even when the guy's talking English, he makes no sense at all.

The anticipation of having Adam MacLean come to the house was worse than a real date because at least on one of those, you were going to be with a person who liked you. Was she supposed to cook or what? *Like she was going to give him the satisfaction of calling her inhospitable!* She wasn't the most fantastic cook but she could throw together a nice chilli. Stevie made a huge one and poured a big slug of red wine in it.

Once Danny was tucked up in bed, Stevie put on a light blue blouse and her jeans. On the off chance that Matthew happened to see them, she would look out to impress but with a foot in casual. Had posting Jo's letter done the trick? Had that one small stone caused ripples in their happy life? If so, they would be watching out for activity at her front door.

Knock knock. It was quite a soft knock for him. Considerate that Danny was in bed, maybe? *Yeah, right!* She wasn't ready to give him any benefits of any doubts yet; he had hardly earned the privilege. Stevie crossed to the door and opened it to a huge bouquet of flowers.

'Hi,' said a porridge-rich voice from behind a big pink rose.

'Oh, hello,' said Stevie. God, they were beautiful, expensive. If a lover had genuinely given these, she would have fainted. Then recovered to bonk him five seconds later.

'Can you see anythin' across the street?'

'No,' said Stevie. 'Their cars are there but there's no sign they're in.'

'Oh, the swine,' said the rose. 'Are you goin' tae invite me in?'

'Certainly, do come in,' said Stevie. Adam handed the flowers to her and she buckled under the weight of them. Once again, she and Adam had colour coordinated.

'Same blue claes,' he said, which she presumed meant 'clothes', in the absence of anything else they had coordinated in, apart from the number of eyeballs. Adam walked straight into the dining area to find it was neat and tidy, which saved him having to tell her to keep it so. The owners had been most specific about that. He had lied to them and said that his 'lady' was extremely houseproud. He then walked through to the kitchen, which was also scrubbed, he noted, as he did a slow warder-type walk round it—not a hint of flour or chocolate anywhere. There were lovely spicy beef waves coming from an enormous cauldron-like pot on the hob and his stomach keened in response to it.

'Well, at least they'll see the car, if they dinnae see me,' Adam said.

'Yes,' said Stevie, thinking, So what do we do for the next hour or so?
'So—money,' said Adam.

'Great!' *At last*. Now she'd find out just which percentage of the flesh nearest her heart she would need to cut out in order to pay him.

'May I?' He gestured towards the table.

'Yes, of course,' said Stevie, and he sat down at a chair there and got out a folded piece of paper from his pocket.

'Do you want something to drink?' she asked. 'Tea, coffee, wine?'

'Wine would be nice, thank you,' he said.

'White or red?'

'Red, please,' he answered, sure it would arrive at the table with the £1.89 label still on. She surprised him with a very rich little South African Pinotage, fragrant and heavy on the summer fruits and berries.

He nodded appreciatively. 'Nice,' he said.

'Yes, isn't it?' she drawled. I've surprised him, she thought.

'Look, here are ma calculations.' Adam smoothed out the paper. 'I've taken a three-month lease an' we'll assess the situation after tha', if it takes tha' long, but if you can pay me, say, four hundred pounds a month, I can cover the rest. Can you manage tha'?'

Stevie stared at him. She had been expecting so much more, a thousand a month at least. Four hundred was reasonable, too reasonable, but for all she couldn't stand the man, she wouldn't have cheated him.

'Mr MacLean . . .'

'The name's Adam.'

'Sorry . . . *Adam*. I can afford more.'

'Nae, I said I'd take four hundred—tha'll dae.'

Stevie shook her head. 'Sorry, I'm not a charity, Mr . . . Adam. Seven hundred. I know what this place is costing. That's what I can afford.'

'Four.'

'I can do eight at a push.'

'This is bartering in reverse!' said Adam. 'Are ye mad?'

'Obviously yes, to be here in the first place.' Four hundred was so low as to be suspicious. She would rather not be in his debt so much.

'Whit dae you dae for a livin' tha' you can afford tae throw your money aboot?' said Adam.

'None of your business,' said Stevie, 'and I'm hardly throwing it away. I'm living here and it's a lovely, big, expensive house. Eight hundred, Mr MacLean, that's my final offer.'

Adam MacLean sat back in the chair and slowly folded his arms. 'So if I say naw, wha' are you goin' tae dae? Refund me tae death?'

She stared him out until he broke eye contact and smiled resignedly.

'OK, if it makes you feel better, let's say seven hundred. That is *my* final offer. I can take a cheque.'

Stevie produced a cheque she had signed earlier, and now filled in the amount. Adam put it down on the table, shaking his head.

'Crazy lady,' was his only comment.

'Would you like to eat something?' said Stevie. 'I made a chilli. It'll help pass the time.'

'Food would be very nice. I am hungry,' said Adam. He excused himself and went upstairs to the loo. The front bedroom door was closed with a KEEP OUT SUPERHERO'S ROOM door hanger on the handle. Stevie's bedroom door was open and he poked his head inside to find it was tidy also, and subtly scented like a sweet summer garden. A Midnight Moon book by Alexis Tracey was on the bedside cabinet. The bed had a big puffy quilt like his granny Walker used to have. He and his sisters would creep in and bounce on it and his granny would turn a blind eye, because she knew they didn't have much else in life to make them smile.

'Want a hand?' he asked, appearing in the kitchen doorway once again and filling it more than the door would have done.

'You can stick that garlic bread in the oven if you want,' said Stevie, pointing to a tray with a herby loaf covered in cheese gratings and salsa.

Homemade garlic bread, Adam thought.

His eyes must have lingered on it a bit too long, for she said, 'What's wrong? Not to your taste, Mr MacLean?'

'No' at all,' said Adam, putting the bread in the oven. 'It's just the first time I saw you, you appeared no' tae have an affinity wi' cooking.'

'I was baking,' said Stevie. 'I can cook OK, I just can't bake. For some reason, if it involves flour, it just doesn't happen for me.'

'Oh, I see,' said Adam. He watched Stevie scurry about trying to locate the rice in one of the cupboards. 'Mind if I try oot the cinema surround?' he said, thumbing towards the lounge.

'It's your house,' Stevie sniffed.

'I'm tryin' tae be polite.' He smiled wearily.

'Go right ahead,' said Stevie in her best part nice-hostess and part bugger-off voice.

When the rice and bread were ready, she dished up and was about to carry it to the table when Adam came in to help her.

'This is nice,' he said, tucking right in. He sounded surprised.

'Why, thank you,' she said, with an ultra-sarcastic smile, but he seemed too absorbed in his food to notice.

He asked her again what she did for a living, and once again she told him she wasn't telling him. Then he asked her how her son had taken to the move and she answered that he had been remarkably 'cool'—in the warm sense—about it. She changed the subject because she didn't want Adam MacLean talking about her son; he was off limits. Adam MacLean, however, was nothing if not persistent.

'How old is he?' he asked.

'Four,' said Stevie.

'Hard work at tha' age, aren't they?'

'He's a good boy,' said Stevie.

'So Matthew's no' his daddy then?' he asked

'No,' said Stevie. 'I've only known Matthew for two years.'

Adam spooned a little more chilli his way. 'Wes he a local boy?'

'Matthew? Yes.'

'Naw, your wee boy's daddy.'

'Yes, he was a local boy too.'

'Wes?'

OK, she would end all the questions now.

'Yes, "wes". I'm a widow, Mr MacLean. My husband died when I was two months pregnant, if you must know. Danny never knew his father.'

Adam had the grace to look ashamed of himself for thinking her a loose piece. Jo had twisted that particular detail. She'd told him that Danny didn't know his father because Stevie wasn't sure who he was.

'I'm sorry.'

'Yes, well, that's life. Or rather it isn't,' said Stevie with a black laugh.

They chewed on some more and Stevie filled up their glasses. There was a ladleful of chilli left. Stevie offered it to Adam, but he refused.

'Tha' wes awful nice but I am so full,' he said. 'Thank you.' He stood and started clearing plates.

'Coffee?' she said, as he loaded the crockery into the dishwasher.

'Naw, you're OK,' he said, meekly for him. 'It's obvious there's goin' tae be nae joy tonight. I'll away.'

Stevie nodded. She was disappointed too.

'You'd better put those floooers in water,' he said. 'Are there vases in the hoos?'

Stevie had found two while the rice had been cooking. 'Yes, I'll do it soon. Thank you for reminding me,' she said tightly. She would make sure he knew she wasn't one for doing what *he* dictated.

'Naw bother,' he said. 'It would have been actually worth it if they'd seen them, though. Cost an absolute fortune.'

'Would you like me to pay half?'

'Naw, you're OK.'

'I'll wave them over if I see them arriving.'

They both smiled unwittingly at each other. Then they realised what they were doing and stopped it immediately.

'Here.' She handed him a flat packet of handkerchiefs. 'You lent me a hanky, remember? I couldn't get the blood out. So, there you go. They only sold them in threes.'

'You didnae have tae go and do tha'.'

'Yes, I did.'

Hmmm, thought Adam MacLean and walked to the door. She was trying awfully hard to prove she wasn't a freeloader. Too hard.

'Good night then, Mr . . . *Adam*,' said Stevie.

'Guid night, and thanks again fer the food.'

He got into his car. It was obvious that Matthew and Jo weren't in. He drove off, turning right at the end of the lane, not seeing the couple rounding the corner on the left. They had walked into town to see the Denzel Washington film and then broken the journey home by calling in at a bistro. The woman's eyes closed in on the number plate.

'God, that was Adam! What was *he* doing here?'

'It's OK,' said Matthew, putting his arm round her shoulders. He was the picture of heroic calm although inside his nerves were jangling.

Stevie saw Adam twice in the next week, but only in passing. He nodded to her from a distance when she was in the gym and she nodded in return. Then he nodded again a couple of days later when she was leaving, and once again, she nodded back. It was like the birth of another language, because there was something in each nod that told the other person that no, they had nothing to report.

The couple across the road continued to travel to work together each morning in perfect loved-up harmony, still holding hands as they walked from the front door to the car. Stevie's stomach heaved with jealousy and hurt.

On the seventh day since seeing Adam MacLean in the lane, the tension had started to leave Matthew's shoulders and he let himself believe that he was not suddenly going to be accosted by Jo's estranged husband, or his own ex-partner, although he still couldn't quite believe she had accepted the breakup with so little reaction. In fact, on one occasion he had actively encouraged her to make a move when, after seeing her buzzing near the kitchen window, he had darted straight out to deliver some post that had arrived for her. He knew she had seen him, and he *knew* that when he reached the letterbox she would open the front door as if by coincidence and force him to engage in conversation. However, he was wrong. Not a sausage.

The post had been occupying a lot of his mind recently. Every day seemed to bring a new bill and his mortgage payment had bounced. He was perpetually on the brink of asking Jo to contribute financially, but how did you broach a subject like that with a woman who spent every lunchtime in Harvey Nichols?

He decided to soften her up and went shopping in his lunch hour and bought fillet steaks, champagne and raspberries, white chocolate, cream and cognac. Expensive, but he hoped it would be a worthwhile investment. He ran Jo a bath after work and told her to stay in there until he called her. Then he brought her up a glass of chilled champagne and popped a truffle into her mouth and retired to the kitchen to work on a feast fit for the queen of his heart.

She came down in her robe to find the table lit by candlelight and a beautiful romantic supper waiting for her. He topped up her glass, chinked his own to it, and said, 'Cheers.'

'What's all this for?' she said, with surprised delight.

'Because I love you,' he said, pulling out the chair for her.

After the main course, he served her raspberries soaked in cognac resting in a cloud of cream whipped with the melted chocolate, with coffee to follow. Jo's eyes were full of heaven tasted. Matthew was a seductive cook. He just hoped he'd been seductive enough. He led her to the sofa, snuggled, and caressed her.

'Jo,' he said, 'I want you to divorce MacLean as soon as possible. I don't like the thought of you being married to him at all.'

She answered him by kissing him urgently. 'He's not in the way.'

He squeezed her to him. 'Serve MacLean his divorce papers, please.'

'There's no point. I'm not married to Adam. Surely you knew?'

'No,' he said, with a great puzzled inflection at the end of the word.

'MacLean is my maiden name, pure coincidence. We just lived together.' She snuggled into him once again. 'So, you see, he is out of my life totally; we have no bindings to each other.'

'Oh, I see.' She hadn't mentioned it. He would have remembered that one. And hadn't she always referred to MacLean as 'her husband'? 'But don't you have any financial commitment to him? The house, for instance?' he asked cautiously, in case she realised why he was asking.

'Alas no,' said Jo. 'I didn't have any money to put towards the house. Adam took everything I had—told me he was "looking after it for me" and that was the last I saw of it. That's why it's so great to go out at lunchtimes and spend, spend, spend, and to be with someone who doesn't take what I have.' And with that she kissed him with fervour.

'Oh . . . er . . . great!' Matthew said, when he was eventually forced up for air, although his head was screaming, 'Bugger bugger bugger . . .' He had been counting on Jo's share of the divorce money.

She raised her head and walked her long-nailed fingers saucily up his chest. 'Anyway, why did you really want me to divorce him? Because you want to marry me yourself, maybe?'

He took her lovely face in his hands. Well, it hadn't featured in his immediate plans but, seeing as she had come to mention it, yes, waking up to Jo MacLean for the rest of his life would be better than any Euromillions jackpot win.

'Jo, I would marry you tomorrow but I'm not asking you until I'm able to give you the wedding I know you'd want. Classic cars, morning suits, lobster for the wedding breakfast . . .'

Jo's head started to run with the theme: 'Mmm, seven bridesmaids and pageboys. Red roses filling the church . . .'

'No expense spared for you, my love,' he said. 'So we'll have to wait.'

'Your investments are due to mature soon though—so you said.'

'Ah, yes . . .' An insurance policy his mum had set up for him was due to mature on his thirty-fifth birthday at Christmas. It would yield about £5,000, but he had slightly exaggerated the figures to impress her. Well, more than slightly. Added two zeros at the end actually.

'We could honeymoon in the Med. Oh, Matt, it will be wonderful!'

'Jo, there's something . . . Ahhh!'

Her hand started to knead him *there*. He had to tell her the truth tonight. There had been too many lies and deceptions. But her fingers were delicious and then he heard the rasp of his zip.

'Stop, please, Jo . . . oh!'

She was out of his arms and kissing a molten trail down his shirt.

The children broke up for a lovely sunny May half-term at the end of that week and Stevie took time off from writing about other people's love lives to do nice things with Danny. Then, on the Friday, they went into town to try to find a present to take to Danny's friend Josh Parker's fifth birthday party the next day. She didn't really want to go but Catherine's little boy Gareth had been invited too and her friend was forcing her along. And Josh was, after all, one of Danny's special friends.

She settled on a badge-maker because it was a toy that Danny frequently played with. He had umpteen 'Superhero' badges, but his favourite alter ego was 'Dannyman'. He had designed a badge with a blue base, like Superman's, but instead of the 'S' there was a 'D'. Stevie had adapted a pair of pyjamas for him with the same design.

Her brain found a link to Danny's pyjamas and Matthew. One day,

Matt had stuck a paper M on his chest and he and Danny had chased each other round the house saving the world. She had laughed so much she had cried. Just like she was doing now, in Woolworths.

It was useless. Matt was slipping further away from her, and Adam's silly plan wasn't doing anything to stop it happening. *'Remember, he hasn't actually seen you together yet. Matt needs to see you and MacLean together . . .'* said the part of her brain that was still holding out hope.

Stevie fished her mobile out of her bag and rang Adam MacLean. 'We need to hammer this home once and for all,' she said, talking over his hello. 'They need to see us together next time. How do we do it?'

And Adam, who had been about to ring her, outlined his suggestion.

'Going to do *what*?' said Catherine incredulously down the phone.

'Follow them,' said Stevie. 'He's hiring a car on Sunday so we can follow them in secret and then surprise them by turning up where they do.'

'Bit hit and miss, surely?'

'Well, probably, but they seem to go out quite a lot and they will definitely go out on Sunday.' She knew that because Matthew hated Sunday evenings in the house. He had always dragged her out when they could get a baby sitter. 'Come on, let me treat you,' he would say. Although most of the time she had ended up paying. She wondered how many times he had done the 'empty wallet' trick on Jo. Probably never.

Catherine grimaced a bit. 'Are you sure it's worth it, love?'

'Yes. I want him back, more than ever. I miss him so much, Cath,' Stevie said, and it was true.

Chapter 8

STEVIE OPENED HER EYES to a Saturday morning full of a whole Junesworth of sunshine bursting through the curtains. It had all the promise of a gorgeous, warm, photographer's delight of a day. A gorgeous, warm, but awful day. Her wedding day.

She left the kitchen blinds closed and set the table in the sun lounge instead. The last sight she wanted this morning was the couple across the road sticking their tongues down each other's throats.

Across the road, Jo and Matthew had just finished having sex and were now relaxing in the glowing aftermath. She was nestled in the circle of his arms and talking about weddings. Theirs.

'I think I fancy a carriage drawn by white horses, and a chocolate wedding cake like Pam's only a lot bigger—three more tiers.'

Matthew just wanted to lie there and stroke her, and not talk about spending money. He had fallen asleep the previous night totting up how much exactly he owed, and it was a lot. At present rate of payback, the debt would be a millstone round his neck for fifteen years, not counting the extra to pay for the wedding that Jo was busy planning.

The clock said it was 9.15 on Saturday, June 3. If he had stopped at giving Jo MacLean his hanky in the car park that day instead of becoming involved, he would be getting married in a few hours. Contentedly so because nothing was actually wrong with Stevie: she was a good girl—generous, kind, warm, considerate, funny, sparky . . . and there would be less of a hole in his financial situation. He shuddered and pulled Jo into him.

'What's the matter?' she said.

'I should have been getting married today,' he said.

'What—and you're upset that you're not?' Jo pulled away from him.

'Don't be silly—hey, come back here!'

She let him drag her back but lay huffily in his arms.

'It's not very flattering being in bed with someone while he's thinking about marrying another woman,' she pouted.

'I'm not,' he protested. 'What can I do to make it up to you?'

'Well, there is something,' she said with that look in her eye. Then she lay back as his head disappeared under the duvet.

Josh Parker's party was in the function room in the annexe part of the Well Life gym. There was a bar there and Stevie was all too aware of how well used it would be by the dads who had been dragged along.

Catherine had arranged to meet her outside and her welcoming smile slid further off her face the closer Stevie got.

'Christ, you look like shit,' said Catherine.

'Thanks,' said Stevie. 'It's not the best I've felt.'

Catherine was overcome with guilt. Maybe it would have been better for Stevie to sit in the cottage and get drunk. She could have taken Danny to the party for her and let Stevie pretend the day wasn't happening. She'd been thinking about it the previous night then got sidetracked when the kids fell victim to some bug. Well, all of them except for Gareth, which was lucky, because he was excited about the party.

Catherine linked her arm and they walked in together, and immediately Stevie voiced the, 'Oh God,' that Catherine was thinking. The function room was not only full of balloons, but party poppers were piled up in small mountains on every table. The disco music was blaring out by the dance floor and the bar was thick with dad-customers. Josh's own father, Richard, waved them over with a balloon in his hand. He looked like it was *his* birthday when his eyes first locked on Stevie.

Stevie hated balloons, she hated party poppers and she hated Josh's noisy dad more than both those things put together. A legacy from her own mum and dad's shouting days, she suspected, when she had cried herself to sleep, waiting for her fragile world to be split apart.

Matthew had never come with her to any of the parties, so she had usually been on her own among a sea of couples, and what was it about some men that the title 'thirty-something single mum' was male-speak for 'easy prey'? At the first party they had ever been to, Richard Parker had leapt on Stevie's reaction to a popped balloon with a 'hilarious' tirade of many more. She had tried to laugh it off, but after two more hours of having her eardrums tormented, her nerves and her temper were in shreds. Ever since then, he had been there at every children's party, squeaking balloons near her, exploding party poppers behind her, until she wanted to scream at him to leave her alone. But how could she do anything but try to be a good sport? She didn't want to show Danny up or embarrass herself.

So Stevie suffered in silence and hoped he would get tired of the joke but he never did, and the more beers he had, the funnier he thought it was. Today he looked as if he had had quite a lot to drink already.

'Stand close to me,' said Catherine. 'I'll tell him to piss off, even if you don't.' With that, she squashed Stevie into a corner table out of the way and went to get the first round in. Josh, Gareth and Danny were dancing, but Stevie's smile at them was quickly knocked off by a big bang in her ear. She squealed and spun round.

'Gonna get you later big time!' said Richard Parker, staggering slightly behind her and waggling his finger. His rubbery lips moved over each other as if he was chewing a toffee but couldn't quite locate it.

'Excuse me!' said Catherine and barged him out of the way. She plonked herself down next to Stevie and handed her a drink.

Then Gareth threw up.

'Oh sod, I thought it was too good to be true,' said Catherine.

'I'll get your bag,' said Stevie, wishing, and feeling awful for doing so, that it had been Danny who had thrown up and given her the excuse to go home. But Danny was having a ball and it would have been unfair to take him home and upset his day too. And what would they do instead? She didn't want to go out or do anything but curl up into a ball and sleep the day away.

'Oh, Steve, I've cocked this up for you, haven't I?' said Catherine.

'It's not your fault, Cath,' said Stevie. 'Gareth's poorly and that's that.'

Catherine was reluctant to leave her friend, today of all days, but Eddie was working and Kate, not 100 per cent well herself, was looking after the other kids, so there really was no alternative.

'Mummeee!' cried Gareth.

'Go!' Stevie ordered. Catherine blew her an apologetic kiss and went.

Stevie endured the next hour, then stole off to the ladies. Her thoughts were so much on where she might go afterwards to keep herself occupied that she didn't see the figure hiding behind the corner when she emerged from the loo.

Bang.

Stevie screamed.

'Told you I'd get you!' said Richard Parker, eyes glazed and holding a clutch of balloons. He swaggered forward into her personal space, pointing to her chest. 'What I find amazing, though, is that you're scared of *these* balloons when all the time you've got *those* big balloons under your jumper.'

From nowhere, big Adam MacLean appeared with a not very friendly expression on his face and boomed loudly into the top of Richard Parker's bald patch, 'Hey, pal, are you botherin' this lady?'

Even Stevie blanched at the tone of his voice. She was witnessing the side of him now that she hadn't seen yet but had heard lots about. But despite it, boy, was she glad to see him.

'Er . . . oh . . . er . . . sorry, no offence!' *Mumble mumble.* Richard shrank and scuttled away back into the party room. Contrary to what Stevie might have expected of Adam, he didn't grab him and mince him between his fists or launch him through the nearest glass window. Then again, Adam was at work and a worm like Richard Parker throwing balloons about obviously wasn't worth risking his job and another assault charge for. Funny, that . . . she couldn't imagine how someone with a criminal record for GBH could be employed in such a posh place.

'Thank you,' she said, relief washing over her like a warm shower.

'I wid have done it fer anyone,' he said in his usual gruff, dismissive way. 'Whit were you doin' oot here alone wi' him anyway?'

Why is this my fault? thought Stevie. Her head suddenly flooded with voices: her mother saying '*No wonder he buggered off!*' and Mick's mother screaming at her, '*If you'd been more of a wife, he'd still be alive!*'

and pictures of the way Adam MacLean always looked at and spoke to her as if she was to blame for Jo leaving him. It was then that Stevie's last remaining nerve snapped, and it appeared that it was the one holding the lid down on her tear supply, because they moved at Exocet missile speed and there wasn't a damn thing she could do to stop them.

'I only went to the loo. Please, Adam,' she said, 'not today.' She wiped at her eyes with the flat of her hands. 'I don't care if you fight me for the rest of your life, but please, *please*, I beg you, not today.' Her throat failed on the last word and she turned away and melted back into the party room, grateful that it was so dark inside.

When at last the party was over, Stevie and Danny went to Blockbusters and got out the *Crocodile Dundee* trilogy and a big bag of popcorn. When they got home, they transformed the lounge of Humbleby Cottage into a cinema, closing the blinds and diverting the sound through the surround speakers. Then they snuggled up on the sofa with the popcorn and cola. It was a lovely day and a shame to be inside, but, today, Stevie didn't want to see the sunshine. She didn't want to know that she would have been outside the church bathed in it now, laughing and being beautiful and throwing her bouquet.

There was a knock on the door. *Oh no, no, no!* She didn't want to see anyone. Maybe she could pretend she wasn't in. *Boom boom boom.* There was only one person who knocked like that. And he was the last person she wanted to see.

BOOM BOOM BOOM! He'd break the damn door down if he carried on.

'Stay there, pet, I'll be back in a minute,' Stevie said, closing the lounge door behind her before opening the outside one.

Adam MacLean was standing there on the doorstep in his smart work clothes: a white shirt and a blue tie with a WL motif on it.

'Hellooo.' He sounded contrite. Jeez, she looks terrible, he thought.

'Hello.' The bloodshot shining eyes belied her air of composure.

'I . . . er . . . came tae say I'm sorry fer soundin' a wee bit aff.'

'Oh, right,' she said. He seemed a bit taken aback that she didn't seize on the opportunity to say that he'd never sounded anything other than 'aff' and not thought to apologise for it before.

There looked to be little fight left in her. It was over.

'Adam, this isn't working,' she started to say.

Then time stood still. The world stopped revolving for five seconds but it was enough to allow her to catch her breath and decide how to capitalise on this gift of a perfect moment. For there across the lane, Matthew was framed in the window. He was looking at her. And Adam's car. And Adam. On her doorstep. Smart in a shirt and tie.

Stevie arranged her tired features into a smile that twisted as sexily as she could at one side, then she reached forward for Adam's tie, reeling him slowly in, and down, and then kissed him gently on the mouth.

Adam didn't resist. There was only one reason she had just done that and it wasn't because apologetic butt-ugly Scotsmen turned her on.

'They're watchin', aren't they?' he whispered loudly.

'You don't think I'm doing this for fun, do you?' she confirmed through gritted teeth. He pushed her inside the house as if he was eager to get her alone and they slammed the door together and stood behind it, each of them wiping at their lips with the back of their hands.

'All this plannin' and the chance just falls into oor laps,' said Adam, fighting back the desire to whoop round the kitchen. For one horrible moment there, he had nearly been in danger of hugging her.

'I know,' said Stevie quietly, because her heart was pumping so fast it wasn't letting her breathe properly. Had she had more air in her lungs, she would have danced with him, leapt on him, hugged him, *yes him*. Then Danny appeared in the doorway, freeze-framed because there was a giant in the room who looked like a ginger Mr Incredible. Danny's only comment was, 'Hi.'

'Hi there,' said Adam, waving awkwardly.

'Who are you?'

'Oh God!' began Stevie, but Adam dropped to his haunches.

'I'm Well Life Man. See?' He showed off the letters on his tie. 'I just dropped by on a mission tae ask all people who work at hame tae come and be fit, but shhhh, you havenae seen me, OK? If anyone asks, I'm Adam MacLean. Like Superman is Clark Kent, understand?'

'Cool!' said Danny, nodding. Yes, he knew exactly what he meant.

'Danny, go and watch Dundee and let me and Mr . . . Well Life talk about . . . er . . . having a coffee.'

'OK,' said Danny, grinning. 'You're not going yet, are you?'

'No, I'll say goodbye before I go,' said Adam. Then, when Danny had gone, he crossed to the window to look across at Matthew's house.

'He's still there,' he said, smiling over at Stevie. 'Quick, come here.'

She came there as requested, but she didn't expect him to enclose her in a great big embrace and tip her back Hollywood snog-style.

'Right, you can get off me now,' said Stevie eventually.

'Bit longer, we're still bein' looked at. Put yer hands in ma hair.'

She started stroking his hair. They looked very *Gone with the Wind*.

'OK, he's moved away,' said Adam, letting her drop to the floor.

'Ow!'

'Oops, sorry.' He extended a hand and helped her up.

'There obviously isn't a word for chivalry in Gaelic, then.'

'Look, lady . . .' He nipped off what he was going to say because he didn't want to add any more grief to her day. She had probably had enough of a bad one and he hadn't helped.

He had been at work checking on the CCTV camera when the little boy had been sick, then recognised the woman rushing towards him—the one with the ex-candy-floss hair. Some time later, he had moved the camera around, looking for *her*. Eventually he'd found her, coming out of the ladies. He'd focused on her face and had seen how unhappy she looked. Then some dickhead holding a string of balloons had burst one close by her head, insensitive to her feelings. Adam had felt obliged to look into what was going on. When he'd found her, cornered outside the ladies, she'd looked so utterly defeated and helpless, and something had suddenly flagged up in his subconscious that today was the wedding day that never was.

He didn't know why he had been so hard on her outside the loo, when it obviously wasn't her fault. Her pale little face had haunted him all afternoon and he knew he wouldn't have slept, had he not driven over to see if she was OK.

'Is Well Life Man staying for tea?' said Danny, in the doorway.

The two grown-ups looked at each other. Stevie's thoughts had never been so perfectly at war. On the 'No' side was:

1) this was Adam MacLean
2) she didn't want Danny getting confused
3) she didn't want Danny getting eaten

But on the 'Yes' side was:

1) Adam needed to be there at least an hour for maximum effect
2) the damage had been done—he and Danny had met
3) Danny appeared to remain psychologically intact

'We're going to have fish and chips!' said Danny.

'Ooh, o' ma favourites!' said Adam, rubbing his hands together.

'Cool,' said Danny, stroking Adam's tie. 'I love Superheroes.'

'So, have yer got a name, fellow Superhero?'

'I'm Dannyman.'

'Glad tae meet you, Dannyman,' said Adam, holding out his hand. Danny's little mitt was swallowed up in it.

'When did you last save the universe then?' said Adam.

'Thursday,' said Danny, and off he trotted to watch the rest of *Crocodile Dundee*.

Matthew stood at the window and tried to process the information his eyes were sending to his brain. Stevie with a man. Not just any man. *Him*. How long had *that* been going on? This was supposed to be their wedding day and she was snogging MacLean!

So that's how Stevie got hold of Jo's Amex bill . . .

Was this why his leaving had seemed to cause such little interruption to her life, then? Had they embarked on their affair first? Is that why they were dancing together so clumsily at Pam and Will's wedding—double-bluffing to throw him off the scent? It couldn't be! They weren't a match. She was what—five foot two—and he was the bloody BFG! Well, a BVG—a Big Violent Giant!

Matthew was shocked, puzzled, confused, bewildered.

'**S**orry, it'll just be fish and chips,' said Stevie. 'I haven't been shopping.'

'It would be better if *you* went fer the fish and chips,' said Adam. 'It looks then as if I'm already established in the hoos.'

'OK,' said Stevie, seeing the sense in that. 'Danny, get your shoes on.'

'Aw, Mummy, can't I stay here with Well Life Man?'

'No, of course not,' said Stevie.

'He's OK,' said Adam. 'We can talk aboot hero stuff.'

'Cool!'

'I don't want my son used as a tactic, Mr . . . Adam,' said Stevie.

'He won't be. I'll look after him till you get back.'

'Absolutely no way. Impossible.' Stevie shook her head in such a way that it switched on a million-watt light bulb in Adam's head.

'You think I might hurt him, is that it?'

'Well, I don't know you that well, do I, to leave my child with you?'

'Surely you wouldnae think that your child isnae safe with me?'

No, she didn't think that, really. Ignoring the fact that he looked like a primitive heavyweight boxer-cum-maniac-savage, in her heart of hearts Stevie didn't think Adam MacLean would hurt her child.

'*Please*, Mummy!'

'Here, take this,' said Adam, stuffing a ten-pound note in her handbag while she was calming down her son.

'*Please, Mummmeee!*' whined Danny.

'No, Superheroes need . . . er . . . privacy to set the table. We'll only be five minutes. Come on, get your shoes on.'

'*Please, Mummy!*' With the non-negotiable obstinacy of a four-year-old, Danny was not going anywhere.

'C'moan, leave him, you'll only be five minutes,' said Adam.

Stevie knew when she was beaten. 'I'll be less than five minutes.'

Across the road, Matthew had just about shut his jaw when he saw Stevie come out of the house, on her own. That meant she had left Danny and MacLean alone together. *She would do that? After all she knew about him?* Then again, it hadn't stopped her snogging him. Or worse.

There was a queue at the fish-and-chip shop as a fresh batch of fish had only just gone in. The shop owner made a joke about it, and though Stevie smiled politely, she didn't find it in the least bit amusing.

I shouldn't have left him with MacLean, she thought, foot-tapping in the queue. She was on the verge of exiting empty-handed when the chip man said, 'Right, love, what can I get you?'

She ran back with the warm parcel in her hands, her head playing the most awful tricks on her. *Danny and MacLean alone together!* What sort of mother was she? To make it worse, she could hear sounds of distress that grew louder the nearer she got to the cottage. They weren't in her overactive imagination either—her boy really was screaming.

Stevie sprinted to the door and threw it open to find Danny squealing and MacLean attacking him. She threw down the parcel on the table and launched herself at MacLean, climbing on his back and trying to get a grip on his cropped hair. Failing, she clobbered him with her handbag.

'Get off my son, you animal!' she screeched.

'Mummy, what are you doing!' said Danny, in a most unharmed way. 'Adam was just showing me some Well Life Man Superhero moves.'

Stevie slid off the big Scotsman's back. 'Sorry,' she said. 'I thought . . .'

'It's OK,' said Adam, rubbing his head and wincing. 'It's just a bit of jujitsu. It means "the gentle art". Mebbe you should come tae a few classes. That's a heavy wee bag you've got there.'

Stevie didn't mean to burst into laughter, but then it was a very odd day. Adam's laugh joined hers, and then they both stopped abruptly.

Adam arranged the fish on plates, while Stevie shared the chips out.

'Nae chips for you, Dannyman?' said Adam.

'I don't like chips,' said Danny.

'Wannae try some of mine? Potatoes are really guid fer you, you know. They teach you that at Superhero School. Carbohydrates—give you energy. Isnae tha' right, Mammy?'

'Erm . . . yes,' agreed Stevie.

Danny's face registered total amazement. 'Really?'

There and then, the little boy rediscovered a fondness for the potato.

'She's been for fish and chips,' said Matthew. He had unconsciously gravitated back to the window and become so engrossed in what he was witnessing that he hardly realised he was thinking aloud. Stevie was running back to the house as if the devil was on her heels—*as if she couldn't keep away from him.* 'So he's eating there . . .'

'Who is eating where?' said Jo. Realisation dawned on her face and soured her smiling expression. 'Oh, I get it, you're spying on *her*.'

'I'm not,' said Matthew. Not wanting her to see MacLean's car, he shut the curtains. 'Shall we open a bottle of wine? I could do with a glass.'

'So, whit was goin' on at the party, then?' said Adam, helping Stevie to clear the table as Danny took an Alp of ice cream into the lounge.

'Oh, Richard Parker's one of the dads,' Stevie explained. 'He found out that I can't stand loud noises—party poppers, crackers, balloons. So he thinks it's hilarious to torment me with them every time he sees me.'

'Could you no' tell him to bugger aff?'

'I don't want to cause trouble,' said Stevie. 'I can live with it. It was just that today being today, well, it didn't help, I suppose.'

'Was it yer . . . er . . . today?' Adam coughed over the key words.

'Yes,' said Stevie, quickly changing the subject. 'Anyway, coffee?'

'Aye, please.'

She put a box of chocolates on the table. Crystal had sent it to her after reading the Paris and Brandon manuscript. She had loved it.

'Choccies! And expensive choccies tae!' said Adam with delight.

'Present from my boss,' said Stevie.

'So whit dae you dae again?'

'Not telling. Have as many chocs as you like. An extra sorry for trying to scalp you,' said Stevie, putting a cafetière on the table.

'Nae real damage done, so far as I can tell. I've a heid like a coconut,' he said with a twinkle and rapped on it with his knuckle. 'Tha' smells nice—whit sort of coffee's tha'?'

'Death by Chocolate. I've a spare packet if you want to take it home with you. I always go a bit mad in the shop and overbuy.'

'Thanks, tha' would be very nice,' said Adam, watching as Stevie crossed to the cupboard. Then he snatched his eyes away, suspecting he might have actually been on the verge of assessing her in a boy-girl way.

Stevie handed it over. 'It'll make your house smell like a cake shop.'

'I'm no' bothered aboot the hoos,' said Adam quietly. 'I don't wannae be in there withoot Jo really, and there are just tae many reminders of her aroond. If she doesnae come back, I'll sell it.'

They sat in contemplative silence for a moment, both realising that they might actually have to start making alternative plans for their lives soon, if Jo and Matthew didn't come back to them.

Adam took the initiative and poured the coffee. 'I dinnae think we need the hired-car adventure tomorrow now, dae you?' he said.

'No, I think today's probably done the trick,' said Stevie, and she giggled. Adam was halfway through his drink. The sound resonated like a bell. It was a sound that belonged to someone with a great capacity for joy, a merry heart. It jarred with the image he carried of her and made him feel uncomfortable. Putting down his mug and grabbing the coffee packet, he said stiffly, 'Think I'd better make a move.'

'Yes, of course,' Stevie responded.

'I'll ring you tae discuss whit we dae next.'

'You'll have to say goodbye to Danny. You promised,' said Stevie.

'I was goin' tae,' he snapped back. They glared at each other, enemies again, until she called Danny through.

'I'm off, pal,' said Adam, bending to him, and then gently jabbed his cheek with his enormous fist.

'Awww. Are you coming back soon?' said Danny.

'No doubt I will see you again,' said Adam, flashing a look at Stevie, but she wasn't looking at him. She was trying to work out what her son was making of it all, checking that he wasn't confused or upset by Adam's visit. Adam understood and respected that more than she could know.

'Shall we colour coordinate when I call again?' he asked her once he had stood again to his full height.

'I'll be in yellow and pink,' said Stevie.

'Well, maybe not,' said Adam with a cough. Then he left.

There was no one across the road watching Adam go. He could still feel where Stevie's handbag had hit his head, but he smiled as his hand came up to rub at the raised weal. You wouldn't have thought there was such a tigress in her tank to look at her. Therein lay the trouble. He had thought he had known her, before he had even laid eyes on her. Her reputation had preceded her and, respecting the source of the gossip, he had taken it as gospel. Really, tonight was the first time she had acted anything like Jo's reporting of her. *But wasn't that understandable, if she thought he was hurting her son?* So far, he had to admit, there hadn't been much evidence of her being a fraction of the lazy, unhinged, crockery-throwing harridan Jo had said she was, and the defence of her child wasn't the action of a mother who was borderline abusive.

He wished his mammy had been like Stevie in full flow, in the times when they got hurt. Especially the day when his da had been skelping wee Jinny with a heavy, drunken hand and Adam had stepped in. He wasn't a big boy then, but he was getting stronger by the day, and for the first time Andy MacLean had struggled to overpower him. So he had gone for the hot poker and burnt his son on the face. Branded him like an animal. Said that every time he looked in the mirror, he'd remember how he raised a hand to his daddy. And his ma had stood there like a scared ghost, watching it happen. She had not stepped in, like he'd seen Stevie do, mad for the safety of her son.

He was a hell of a big man now but that still hadn't stopped Stevie going for him. She had not given a single thought to what damage he could have done her.

'If you could give me a little more time, I get paid in a week,' said Matthew down the phone, believing he was whispering and not aware that his fellow office-workers could easily overhear him.

'I'm sorry, Mr Finch, but I can't stop the interest being charged, nor can I authorise to refund you the overdue fee. Plus, as you are paid monthly, you will have to find two months' mortgage from that single salary. Have you thought about that?'

'Of course I've sodding thought about it!' snarled Matthew.

'I'm sorry, but I won't be sworn at,' said the mortgage adviser, and she put the phone down on him.

'Bloody bitch!' said Matthew, a little too noisily.

'Personal calls, Mr Finch?' said a starchy voice behind him.

'Just the one urgent one, Colin,' said Matthew. It would have to be *him*—Colin Seed, head of personnel, doing his rounds. Creepy Colin, Seedy Colin, Colin the Cardigan. He couldn't have been more than ten years older than Matthew, but he looked near to retiring with his Shredded Wheat comb-over, ill-fitting brown suits that struggled to close over his paunch and a face to cure hiccups. He spoke to every man as if they were naughty schoolboys and he was their headmaster. Even Matthew, who was the thirty-four-year-old head of concessions.

'Of all people to be there when you're on the phone to someone not work-related,' said Matthew, telling Jo about it on the drive home. 'That bloke is always lurking about. He's got a real personality problem.'

'Who were you ringing?'

'Oh . . . er . . . just the bank, to see if a cheque had been paid in that I was expecting. Interest owed to me.' *Damn, what made him lie again?*

'Anyway, why do you think the man's got a problem?'

'Well, you only have to look at him,' said Matthew. 'He was born middle-aged, he's never had a girlfriend and he's never likely to get one.'

'Bitchy! I've always found him quite amiable in passing,' said Jo.

'Well, I think he'll be leaving soon, thank God. They've wanted him to go over and run the New York offices for ages, but he lived with his mum and that stopped him going. She died a couple of months ago and left him a stack.' Lucky bugger, thought Matthew.

'Poor man,' said Jo, with a heavy sigh.

'Poor man, nothing! He's a frustrated git who is jealous of anyone who looks as if they are getting a shag,' said Matthew, 'and the reason he is nice to you, darling, is because you are simply gorgeous and he probably wants to eat you all up, like I do.'

'Thank you,' said Jo, giving him her most beautiful smile. 'Talking of eating, shall we dine out tonight and celebrate how lovely I am, then?'

'Oh, what the hell, why not,' said Matthew, who did not want to be at home among the negative energy of a stack of unpaid bills, or drawn to the window to see what was going on at the cottage.

Adam MacLean rang her just as she was making a cup of Horlicks to take to bed. It was ten o'clock and Matthew and Jo had just arrived home. Stevie watched as Jo slammed the car door and fumbled angrily with the house lock, leaving Matthew in her wake and looking very sheepish. He flashed a look towards the cottage to see if anyone was witnessing his humiliation and for once Stevie didn't step back from the shadows. Why shouldn't she be at her window, closing her blinds?

'Hi there,' Stevie drawled into the mouthpiece, looking very dreamy as she was talking. *Let Matthew Finch observe that as well—ha!*

'It's me, Adam,' he said, thinking she couldn't have realised. She was talking like Emmanuelle.

'I know, I'm being watched.'

'They cannae hear you!'

'No, but the voice comes free with the expression.' Honestly, did he think she was trying to seduce him? 'It looks to me as if my neighbours across the street might just have had a row.'

'Guid. Have you got your invite fer Will and Pam's barbecue?'

'No.'

'Well, it's on its way. You know whit I'm goin' tae say, don't ye?'

'What? You and me to go together?'

'Absolutely.'

'Colour coordinated?'

'As long as it's blue. No yellow or pink.'

'When is it, though? It all depends if I can get a baby sitter.'

'Saturday. And the guid news is that you dinnae need tae find a baby sitter because the kids are invited tae. Pam's organised a bouncy castle and a magician and thousands of e-numbers-worth of sweets and pop.

Will asked me if I minded him invitin' Matthew and Jo and I said no' at all. In fact, I positively encouraged him to do so.'

'I don't know if I dare.'

'Oh, you dare,' said Adam with a sort of jolly threat. 'And whit's more, we'll take centre stage on this one, lady. Just you wait and see.'

Jo had never really forgiven Matthew for carrying no cash with him at Will's wedding. She had got sick of dipping into her purse to pay for all the drinks at the reception that night, but she swallowed it because she thought it was a one-off mistake on his part. But tonight was unforgivable! First she had to bear the embarrassment when his card was declined, then she had to stand by as he looked through a wallet he knew was empty. They were starting to attract attention for all the wrong reasons, and so she whipped out her Amex to reclaim some dignity, only to have to bear the indignity when that too was declined. Luckily, she had her chequebook. Funny how Matthew always had money on him when he went shopping for those poncey male moisturisers and face packs. Adam would not have been seen dead with a mudpack on. And he had paid her Amex bill every month. Foolishly, she had not considered that he might have cancelled his direct debit.

'Please, sweetie, I'm so sorry. Please, let me make it up to you,' Matthew pleaded in bed and started to smudge his mouth down her body, but she pushed him away and presented him with her back.

'Matthew, just go to sleep,' she said. Sex might have had a big place in Jo MacLean's life, but next to money, its importance was negligible.

Chapter 9

'HAVE YOU GOT YOUR INVITE?' said Catherine, with a just-dropped-the-kids-at-school Tuesday-morning phone call.

'Yes. And before you ask, I'm going with Adam MacLean. Is Matthew going?'

'They've both been invited. Apparently, Will asked Adam first if he minded and he said no, and Pam asked me to ask you if it was OK.'

'Yes, it's fine.'

'I said that. In fact, I insisted she invite them because I just know that you two have a plan up your sleeves, don't you?' laughed Catherine.

'We just want them to see us together.'

'About time too,' giggled Catherine. 'What are you going to wear?'

'I'm going shopping for something towards the end of the week.'

'Can I come?'

'Absolutely.'

They met for their shopping trip on Thursday, mainly because Stevie needed to get in a couple of days' hard writing on the story of Damme and Evie. Even with his (battle) scar, the big Scot was turning out to be an incredibly powerful character—against her will, it had to be said. He was evolving all on his own. Obviously, as a Midnight Moon hero, he had to be wonderful, but Damme MacQueen definitely had the McX factor. Evie presumed his roughness was not consigned to his exterior, and he thought her beauty was only skin-deep—it was sexual Semtex. They were far too good for Crystal's conveyor-belt fiction and Stevie wished she had saved him for the long romantic novel she so wanted to write. She was having a great deal of fun writing the lovers' verbal battle scenes, each one of them misjudging the other totally.

Was that what she and Adam were doing? she had thought more than once recently. She had seen the scar on Jo's leg, witnessed her tears and fears, but really it was all circumstantial evidence. Stevie had made herself a firm promise that she would butt out of the Honeywell/MacLean alliance at the first sign of violence, but there had been not even a hint of it so far. Could Jo have been telling lies?

Catherine picked out a very floaty blue summer dress from the rack.

'Wow, that's perfect,' Stevie said.

She came out of the changing rooms and gave her friend a twirl.

'That's the one,' said Catherine.

'Well, that's totally spoilt the morning then,' said Stevie.

'Nothing says you can't buy the first dress you see,' said Catherine. 'Anyway, now we'll have more time to accessorise and scoff buns.'

Stevie went off to pay lots of money. She had so much spare this month. Even with the big wodge of rent money out of her account, life was infinitely cheaper living without Matthew than with him.

Salvation came for Matthew in the form of a letter from Goldfish, which arrived on the same day as his invite to Pam and Will's barbecue. They had upped his Visa limit by two grand, so he immediately took out a cash advance and paid the mortgage arrears off before the interest crippled him any further. He called the bank and made an appointment to see his account manager, in the hope of getting a consolidating loan. Then he planned, once and for all, how he was going to tell Jo the truth: that he wasn't just in that house as a stopgap until his 'family' investments matured and allowed him to buy a nice pile in the country. That he couldn't afford a fancy wedding and the meals out every night would have to stop. She loved him, she would understand.

Jo still wasn't talking to him. They hadn't had sex since the weekend and nothing he did, or tried, had warmed up the frosty air between them. He saw her enter the office after her lunch break, waved over and smiled, but she sailed past him. He got out his Visa, then made a call to Interflora and ordered an extravagant bouquet to be sent to a Ms J. MacLean in Design. He did not notice that Colin Seed was in earshot.

Stevie had worked in the sunny garden all week, and a splash of freckles had appeared over her nose and cheeks as if flicked there by a paintbrush. Now it was Saturday, and the light tanning of her skin made her eyes seem as blue as the day's skies. She toasted a little further as she and Danny spent most of the day in the garden weeding out the potatoes that plagued the flowerbeds and digging out the dandelions, and the physical work took her mind nicely off the nervous anticipations of the evening to come. Danny fell asleep under the umbrella while she was mowing, and as it was going to be a late evening, she let him sleep until it was time to have his bath and then put his party shirt on. Catherine had arranged for Eddie to pick him up and take him to the Flanagans' house so Danny could go along with the rest of the children.

'That'll give you another two hours to make yourself beautiful,' she had said with a wink.

As soon as Danny ran joyfully down the lane to Eddie and Gareth in the car, Stevie jumped in a bath armed with exfoliators, hair treatments and her trusty razor—a woman with a mission.

She couldn't compete with Jo's salon perfection, but she had dropped over a stone and a half since all this business had started and the nipped-in waist of her new dress accentuated the curves below and above it. Teamed up with some strappy gold sandals, which would probably cripple her in an hour, and a blue flower holding back her hair at one side, she looked fresh and lovely.

She had met Adam briefly at the gym the previous day. He was zipping about busily but found her at the weight bench to say that he would pick her and Danny up at seven thirty. When Stevie told him that Danny was going on ahead, she thought he had looked disappointed. But then again, perhaps it was that Adam MacLean, 'Family Man', would have shoved Matthew's nose further out of joint.

At seven she heard a taxi beep and peeped through the upstairs window to see Matthew and Jo climbing into it. He was wearing a Hawaiian shirt that would have looked ridiculous on anyone else, but on him it looked fun and summery and his shoulders looked big and broad in it. *She* had on a white strappy sundress with incredibly high black sandals. The whole ensemble looked stunning, and Stevie's nerve took a bit of a nose dive. Then again, she knew there was nothing she could have done to look better than she did with what she had available.

She spent the last half-hour trying to keep her fingernails out of her mouth. She had manicured them herself and they looked nice, though they weren't talons like Jo's because she had to keep them short for typing. She was just doing the billionth check that there was no lipstick on her teeth, when she heard a car pull up outside.

Stevie opened the door. Adam was wearing the same colour shirt as her dress. He looked big and blue and a bit handsome, and she found that her breath got all snagged up in her throat and she gasped.

He, meanwhile, said quietly and as if surprised, 'You look nice.'

'Oh . . . er . . . thanks,' coughed Stevie. 'So do you, actually.'

'Aye, well, enough of the Mutual Appreciation Society annual day oot, let's get tae the party.' Stevie, who was more comfortable with Adam MacLean in hostile mode than being a pretend nice-person, took a deep breath and climbed into the passenger seat.

The journey to Will and Pam's house was too short. They had to park up at the end of the street as there were so many cars. Stevie's heart was boom-booming and she was trembling. When Adam turned off the ignition, he didn't look too keen to get out of the car himself.

'You OK?' he asked.

'No,' said Stevie.

'You . . . we'll be fine.' Sounds of laughter and music filtered into the ensuing silence. 'I'm a wee bit scared myself, fer the record.'

'Are you?'

'Aye.'

So it was Stevie who said, 'Well, come on, we know what we're doing. Let's get on with it.' And with that she opened the car door.

Adam rang Pam's doorbell. After a short wait, Pam answered, kissed and hugged them both and shoved them out into the back garden. There, they fell straight into the welcoming company of Catherine and

Eddie. Adam, with his advantage of height, did a quick sweep of the merrily drinking crowds, but there was no sign of the lovebirds. He shook his head and Stevie was a mix of relieved and disappointed.

'They're just round the corner to the left,' said Catherine in a low whisper. Then she started doing an odd eye-blinking thing to Stevie, as if trying to deliver a message in Morse code. Bizarre as it was, Stevie understood it. But then they had been friends for four thousand years.

'Oh . . . er . . . Adam, I know you've seen Catherine but you haven't really said a proper hello yet so, anyway . . . erm . . . meet Catherine and Eddie, my best friends. Cath, Eddie—this is Adam.' Hands were shaken and smiles exchanged. Adam had a nice smile, Stevie noticed.

'Can I get you a drink, mate?' said Eddie.

'Nae, thanks. I think we'll head off and get one ourselves in a minute,' said Adam, taking another look round and waving at someone.

'You look bloody lovely,' whispered Catherine to Stevie.

'Do I? I could be sick with nerves!'

'You look like a couple. You're both glowing. Interesting, that.'

'I just wish they'd see us and be done with it. Where's Danny?'

Catherine pointed over to the bouncy castle, where Danny was with Catherine's brood and having the time of his life.

'Come on,' said Adam, and he reached down and took up her hand. Stevie stared at it enclosed in his big square one and rounded her eyes at Catherine, who gave her a sly thumbs-up and a schoolgirl-giddy smile. Then, as if she was attached to a very energetic Doberman pinscher, Stevie lurched forward as Adam proceeded to move.

'There they are,' said Adam, tightening his grip. 'Stay calm.'

It was Catherine who recorded what happened next. As she was to tell it later to Stevie, Jo and Matthew were walking slowly back into the throng, engaged in conversation. As Jo's lovely head swung round, her eyes touched upon her ex, holding hands with Stevie, and her whole body seemed to stiffen. Matthew followed her eye-path and saw them too. Both of them watched as Adam moved towards the drinks table. Then he bent to Stevie to ask her what she wanted, and she placed a hand at the back of his neck as she was speaking into his ear.

Adam poured her a drink first and himself one, then they chinked their glasses and, after a respectable time, with a protective arm curled round her, Adam steered her back in the direction of her friends.

Matthew's mouth hung so wide open, it would have been easy to think the shock had dislocated his jaw. He could see Jo trying to act natural but she was a mess of nervous, annoyed gestures; the fingers on the hand not holding her glass were working at each other, her eyes were blinking and it was costing her a considerable effort to keep them away from her ex. Her smile was stiff. She looped her arm possessively through Matthew's and forced him back into the conversation, but his brain was scrambled egg and he wasn't contributing much other than a village idiot grin.

'You did guid,' said Adam, kneading the back of his neck.

'I feel shaky as hell,' said Stevie.

'We're OK. The worst is over and the good news is, it's workin'.'

Catherine butted in. 'Well, they definitely know now you're a couple, and they both looked far from happy about it.'

'Really?' Adam and Stevie said in unison.

'Everyone all right?' said Pam, making her usual big appearance. 'Stevie, I have to ask, when did you get to be so chuffing gorgeous?'

Stevie blushed as the others teased her. Adam found himself looking at her through man glasses and realised with a shock how lovely his companion appeared to everyone. Of course, he had given her a cursory once-over when he first saw her, but now he studied the detail of her—the tousled golden hair, the sky-blue eyes, the curves you could time eggs by. He wrenched his eyes quickly away, not wanting to look at her like that. That was not in his plan at all.

'I'm taking this one away for a bit. I'll bring her back safe and sound in a moment, promise,' Pam said, threading her arm through Stevie's and leading her off towards the conservatory.

'So how's married life?' asked Stevie.

'Fuck married life. Tell me about you and Adam MacLean. How long has that been going on?'

'Oh . . . er . . . not long,' bluffed Stevie.

'I don't know Adam as well as I know Matthew, but he strikes me as a really nice guy and I hope it works out for you both. Will thinks he is a great bloke and you look really good together. Bloody odd but good.' She clinked her glass against Stevie's. 'Shall I save you my wedding dress?' She roared with laughter.

'Let him get divorced first,' said Stevie.

'What are you on about, girl? He's a free agent—he is divorced.'

'Divorced from Jo? What, already?' Stevie was confused.

'No, divorced from his wife. He's not married to Jo. MacLean is her maiden name. One of those coincidences that probably started the conversational ball rolling between them,' Pam huffed.

'I never asked, I just presumed . . .' said Stevie.

'No, until a few years ago he was married to someone else, but she took up with her boss. A gold-digger, it seems, but very good-looking.

She took Adam for every penny she could, so Will said. Wouldn't surprise me if Jo MacLean was the same, so thank God they weren't married because I bet she would have tried to rip the financial arse out of him. Apparently she wanted a big, fancy wedding but Adam, understandably, was a bit scared.'

'Scared? Adam MacLean!' scoffed Stevie, then added a quick rebalancing, 'Er . . . I mean, my Adam scared?'

'Yes, scared. I suspect he wanted to make sure he had got it right this time, after losing everything he had to that Diane—I think that was his wife's name. I reckon that deep down he knew Jo wasn't right for him and that's why he was stalling.' She suddenly grabbed Stevie and hugged her. 'Awww! I'm keeping you from him. Come on, you get back to the wee laddie before he gets withdrawal symptoms.' Pam pushed her through the door. 'Enjoy yourself, Stevie. You deserve a bit of loving, and Adam MacLean looks like he needs a good woman.'

Cutting across the grass, Stevie turned her face bravely towards her nemesis. Jo was staring at her with narrowed eyes that wanted to slice her up into little pieces. Then, as Stevie shifted her gaze to Matthew, he suddenly broke from Jo's side as if he was coming over, only to be stopped by Jo's hand on his arm. Then she said something incredibly intense to him, but tried to disguise it as normal conversation. Matthew looked withered. Jo was actually telling him off.

'Welcome back,' said Catherine. 'We're going for something to eat.'

'She's quite a girl, Pam, isn't she?' said Adam as they started walking towards a huge barbecue where a group of blokes were grilling meat.

'Do you know her well?'

'Naw, we've just met a few times at parties. I know Will better. He was ma deputy at Gym Village before I deserted tae manage Well Life.'

'Pam seemed to be under the impression that you and Jo weren't married.'

'No,' said Adam, suddenly stiffening. 'No' yet.' He looked over at Jo, whose eyes flickered over to his and then locked with them, defiantly trying to outstare him. For a moment the rest of the crowd melted away. She was so beautiful, so tall and slim and lovely, and cruelly beautiful.

There was always a part of his mammy Adam had never had. Isa MacLean was tall, slim, lovely—and so, so cold. She worshipped Andy MacLean, who abused her, but never quite managed to love the son who adored her. And the more he loved her, the more apparent it became that she would never really let him into her heart. Maybe that's why he was drawn to beautiful women who were destined to hurt him—women like Diane and Jo.

The four of them got some hot dogs, then Adam went back for a steak, asking Stevie if she wanted anything too, like a proper date would.

'No, thanks. I'm just nipping off to the loo,' said Stevie, disappearing back to the house. As Adam helped himself to a steak, he spotted Danny coming off the bouncy castle and making his way over to the familiar face he had just seen. He kept his eye on the little boy as Danny tugged at Matthew's trousers and Matthew bent to hug him. Then Danny crossed to Jo and hugged her with gusto, as if he knew her too, but Jo subtly removed him and then, with smiling irritation, pushed him away, back into the crowd. Adam was suffused with anger, thinking of himself and his mammy, and he was glad Stevie hadn't been witness to it. She wouldn't have let anyone push her boy away.

Adam bounced towards the little boy who was now looking lost.

'Danny,' he boomed.

'Well Life Man!' screeched Danny with undisguised joy.

'Shhh! Whit did I tell you? It's Adam!'

'Sorry,' said Danny, clamping his hands over his mouth. Then he threw his arms round Adam's legs, as far as they would go anyway.

'Your mammy's just away to the washroom,' Adam said, bending right down until they were at eye level. 'Were you lookin' fer her?'

'No, I just wanted some pop.'

'C'moan, I'll get you some.' Danny slipped his hand inside the big man's paw and they trotted off to the drinks table.

'So, you havin' a guid time, wee man?' said Adam, twisting off the top of a bottle of cherryade and sticking a straw in it.

'Yes,' Danny said. 'I've had a big cheeseburger.'

'You want some of my steak? It'll give you special protein powers.'

'Ye-ah!' said Danny and Adam laughed as the boy took a huge bite.

'Mr Well Life, what do you think is morer important to a Superhero,' said Danny, when he had finished chewing his present mouthful. 'A cape, a good heart or tights?'

Adam threw back his head and laughed. 'I think tights are very important, and so is a cape, but I think a guid heart is the answer.'

'I think so too. Are you coming home with us?' said Danny.

'Oh, I don't know aboot that, fella,' said Adam, filling a pint glass with lemonade for himself.

'We used to live with Matthew but we don't any more,' said Danny, as if divulging a great secret. 'We've only got two bedrooms now.' He took a long slug of pop. 'But you could have my room. It would be cool. Anyway, see you,' and he trotted off back to the other kids, who were settling on the grass in front of the magician.

Stevie had taken a slow walk back to Adam. She had watched him find Danny in the crowd and take him to get a drink. It was instinctive, not the action of a man out to use a little boy to impress an ex. He had thrown back his head and laughed at something Danny had said and there had been real warmth there. Coupled with the conversation she had just had with Pam, it occurred to her then that maybe she didn't know the real Adam MacLean at all.

Pam bumped into Adam by the cheesecake. She was swaying.
'So how are you and Stevie getting on?' she asked.
'Great,' said Adam.
'Good girl, is Stevie. Be nice to think she was seeing someone who didn't break her heart for a change. That bastard Mick . . .' Pam shook her head in unmitigated disgust. 'I don't know how she held it all together really. Brilliant stuff she does. Have you read any yet? Then again, you're a bloke so probably not. But for Matthew to go and do the same as Mick—to Stevie, of all people! She wouldn't hurt a fly, Stevie. Never known a girl have as much bad luck with blokes!'
Adam pretended he knew what she was talking about and nodded.
'Stevie's an absolute diamond and I love her to bits. You look after her, Adam MacLean, or you'll have us to answer to.' She thumbed towards the crowd in the general direction of Matthew. 'His loss, your gain. I like Matt, but he is being such a knobhead at the moment. In fact, I'm going to speak to him, right now. I'm going to tell him—'
'Oh, no, you're not!' said Will, appearing and leading his wife off inside the house for some soft drinks and a cheese sarnie.
And as Adam's brain processed this new information, it occurred to him that maybe he didn't know the real Stevie Honeywell at all.

For the remainder of the party the pretend lovebirds managed to give the semblance of a truly together couple. They spent a fair bit of time apart with their friends, but the clues were there in the times they sought each other out—in the touches, the considerations which spoke far more than grandiose displays of snoggy-type affection. Then all too soon it was time to go home. Adam had been talking to Will and the gym guys when he looked over and caught Matthew staring at Stevie, who was chattering away to Catherine and Pam. It wasn't the look of someone who had lost all feeling for her, and Adam didn't know why, but it annoyed him. He made his way over to Stevie, put his arm possessively round her and squeezed her, then bent his head to her to say that they were being observed. She felt for his hand. Stevie had never been one for holding hands, so she knew that if Matthew was watching, it would strike a loud chord. Being swallowed up by Adam's meaty mitt, though, wasn't anything like the rare slim-fingered Matthew-hand experience. Adam was stroking her knuckles with his thumb absently while they were talking to Catherine. It felt as intimate as a kiss and for that reason, she felt herself pulling away, just before Danny came along, yawning. She gave Catherine and Eddie and her host and hostess a goodbye hug, then the three of them wended their way back to Adam's car.

Danny was asleep as soon as he was buckled into the back seat and Stevie wasn't far behind him. She felt exhilarated. She'd had a lovely time and it had been more successful on the Matthew/Jo front than she could have thought possible. Jo had spent most of the evening trying not to look cross and Matthew just looked weary. His disgruntled face and Jo's obviously snipey asides had added very much to the enjoyment of her evening, and if that made her a bitch, then so be it.

And Adam had been . . . well, lovely, actually. Even though he was faking the affection, it had been nice to imagine what it would be like to be wanted and touched and fussed over. Matthew had liked to be touched and fussed over, but he rarely gave back the affection he expected. Every day, Stevie was becoming more aware of how much she had given and how little she had received.

Adam carried Danny into the house, and deposited him gently on his bed. Stevie took off her son's shoes and threw his cover over him. Then she asked Adam if he wanted a coffee and he said he wouldn't mind. She put a half-packet of ground beans through the percolator, then they went into the lounge and flumped down. Stevie reclined on the sofa and kicked off her sandals. Surprisingly, she had only been aware of her feet hurting since she had walked in through the door.

When the coffee had brewed, they drank in a silence that was surprisingly companionable. For a while, she almost forgot she didn't like him. However, that wasn't to last.

'You seem tae like these books,' he said, picking up a Beatrice Pollen Midnight Moon from a stack at the side of his chair. 'I wouldnae have thought someone like you might be into crappy romances like these.'

'Yes, but you don't know me at all to judge me, do you?'

Adam couldn't believe she had snapped at him. He had actually meant what he said as a compliment! 'No,' he said, thinking back to his conversation with Pam, 'you're right, I don't. But I think I might get to know you quite a bit better soon.'

'Oh, do you really think so?' drawled Stevie, as all thoughts of goodwill towards him disappeared. The party was over, so was the pretence.

'Yes, I think we need tae capitalise on the impact we've made tonight.'

'Meaning?'

'Meaning, it's workin' so we have to give it our all.'

'So, Mr MacLean, how exactly do you propose to do that?'

'Easy, Miss Honeywell. Tomorrow I'm movin' in wi' you.'

'**W**ell, that was another great evening!' Jo grumbled, throwing her clutch purse down on the sofa and ripping off her shoes. 'I can't believe Adam would even *think* about going out with *her*. Obviously, he's doing it out of spite. What does he think he's bloody trying to prove? I mean, as if I'd be jealous of a fucking ugly fucking dwarf!'

'You think he's trying to actually do that? Make you jealous?' said Matthew, wincing at her foul expletives.

'What else? He can't actually like her, can he? He's obviously using her and the stupid bitch can't see it.'

'Don't be cruel,' said Matthew with a weary huff. 'Stevie hasn't done anything wrong. She's a good person.'

'She can't be that great if you left her at a minute's notice,' sneered Jo.

'I didn't leave her because she was horrible,' said Matthew.

'You're standing up for her?'

Matthew decided not to say that he was worried to death about Stevie and would have to step in soon to stop her from making the biggest mistake of her life.

'All I'm saying is, does anyone deserve to be a punchbag?'

'Oh, don't be stupid! Adam wouldn't—' Jo snapped off what she was going to say and flew into a different fury instead. 'How dare he? With her! How long has it been going on, that's what I'd like to know.'

'Does it matter?'

'Yes, of course it matters! No one is unfaithful to me. No one!'

She thought again how easily Stevie had let Matthew go. And how undramatic the scene had been when she had told Adam she was leaving. He had listened without saying a word and had even carried her cases downstairs for her and put them in the car. She saw heavy sadness in his eyes, but he had done nothing to stop her going. In the car, she had pressed her nails into her arm in frustration and anger, hardly feeling the pain. *How dare he let her go so easily?* She had despised him as weak at the time but now she was sure this was all part of some greater plan, and it excited her. No one had ever let Jo go without a fight.

'Jo, please explain why would you be cross that Stevie and Adam have got together? How can you be bothered, after all he put you through?'

Jo's mouth opened and then shut tight again. Then she started up the stairs, saying, 'I'm going to bed, Matthew. Come if you want.'

As he heard the bedroom door open, Matthew knew that her back would be waiting for him in bed and, for the first time, he didn't care.

In his cold, echoey four-bedroomed house that night, Adam packed a suitcase. It was Danny who had reminded him that there were only two bedrooms in Humbleby Cottage—something that Finch would probably know. If he moved in, Finch would presume the obvious— Danny in one bed, he and Stevie in the other. Their plan was working better than he could ever have expected it to. He had seen how many times Matthew's eyes had drifted over to Stevie at the barbecue. As for Jo, she was hurting. Adam was definitely getting to her. He could tell that by the way she sneered at him through the happy party crowd, as if she was enjoying the thought that he might be suffering. Like a wasp, Jo stung to kill when she was threatened. Then he had witnessed how she'd treated the boy. It had altered everything, seeing Danny try to cuddle her and Jo shove him off as if he was something abhorrent. Something about the events of that night had shifted all the pieces round in his heart.

Then he thought of how slowly Stevie's head had turned towards him when he had made the suggestion that he move in with her to Humbleby. He didn't think it was possible for anyone's eyes to open that wide without popping out and detaching from their optical nerves. It was all he could do not to burst out laughing, but he feared she would have whacked him with the nearest Midnight Moon rubbish.

'One last big push and I swear tae you tha' if they havenae broken up in seven days, I'll move oot again. But I promise you they will have.'

'Of course you're joking!' said Stevie breathlessly.

'No,' said Adam. 'I've never been more serious in ma whole life.'

It was obviously against her better judgment but she had soundlessly and slowly nodded her assent and continued to drink her coffee.

At 15 Blossom Lane, the next day was a very strained affair. Matthew made Jo an early breakfast in bed as a peace offering, although he wasn't quite sure what he was apologising for. He went out for a huge stack of Sunday newspapers and settled himself at the dining-room table as Jo went back to sleep. Was it his imagination or were there more debt articles than ever in the supplements?

He really could not afford to delay the money talk with Jo any longer, so he wished she would wake up. But she was still asleep when he called up to her at lunchtime, so he slunk back and reached for another newspaper, with only a bacon sandwich and some crisps for company.

He heard signs of her rising just after four, and waited while sounds of the bath taps filtered downstairs. An hour later, she came down. But his heart sank when he saw she was dressed to go out.

'Are we going out for something to eat?' were her first words to him.

Matthew took her hands and pulled her softly down on the sofa. 'I can't, Jo. I'm a bit broke at the moment. I'm sorry.'

'Broke?' She looked confused. 'What do you mean, "broke"?'

Matthew took the sort of breath one did before a bungee jump off the Grand Canyon. 'The thing is . . . it would help if you could give me something towards the household bills—the mortgage and . . . stuff.'

She stared at him as if he had just grown a pair of horns. Then she stood up abruptly. 'You are fucking joking, I take it. Now, like I say, are we going out or do I pack a bag and leave now?'

'We'll go out,' he said.

As Matthew was dreaming that night of a big Visa card with Colin Seed's cardigan on chasing him round the office, Adam's car was pulling up quietly outside Humbleby Cottage. Danny was asleep in the big bed that his mum would share with him for the next seven nights.

'Hi.' Stevie greeted Adam nervously.

'Hi,' said Adam, bringing in a suitcase and a sports bag.

'I've put you in my room,' said Stevie. He raised his eyebrows and she bristled. 'I will, of course, be sharing with Danny. I've told him you're having some decorators in and are just lodging here for a while.'

'I'd have taken the sofa. You didnae have tae move oot fer me.'

'I fell asleep on the sofa once after working late. Trust me, it's not at all comfortable even for someone my size, so . . .'

'You never said whit it is that you actually dae fer work?'

'Anyway, if you take your case up I'll put some coffee on,' said Stevie.

'I'll take tha' as an "I'm no' tellin' you, so bugger off".'

'That's it in a nutshell, Mr MacLean. You know where your room is.'

He laughed. 'Yes, ma'am,' he said, and saluted and obeyed.

The room smelt of something sweet like wild strawberries swirled in with the perfume she wore. He had noticed it on her at the barbecue— light and floral and violety—so unlike the heady, exotic, spicy scents that Jo preferred. Stevie had put fresh linen on the bed; lovely cool cotton sheets. She had left big white fluffy towels folded neatly on top of the duvet and she had cleared wardrobe and drawer space for him too. This was not a woman who lounged about all day watching TV through a layer of dust, he thought, and wondered again what it was that she did all day. He could have asked Will but he wanted to crack her secret himself. It amused him to puzzle on it.

He came down to the beautiful smell of coffee.

'Have you eaten?' she said.

'Don't worry yoursel'.'

'We had chicken. There's plenty left, if you want a sandwich.'

'Thanks, I might just do tha'—'

'I thought you might,' she said, putting down a substantial plate of sandwiches in front of him, garnished with crisps and salady bits. 'You don't look like the sort of bloke who says no to food.'

And then they watched a late-night murder mystery and munched chicken sandwiches and chocolate digestives until bedtime.

The first thing Matthew noticed as he opened the curtains the next morning was Adam MacLean's car outside Stevie's cottage, and it didn't take an idiot to work out he had been there all night. He presumed that was why Jo was extra-agitated and in a generally foul mood.

They journeyed to work in uncomfortable silence.

'Look, please, can't we be friends?' Matthew said, pulling into the work's car park. 'I'm sorry about mentioning the money and I don't care what's going on across the road. Let's get a sandwich at twelve and go and sit in the park and talk.'

'I'm going shopping,' said Jo, petulantly, through a very dry pout.

'I'll come with you,' he said, smiling at her. 'Would you like that?'

'No, Matthew, I wouldn't like that,' said Jo flatly. And she leapt out of the car and went into the building alone.

Matt waited for Jo in the foyer at the time when her lunch hour was due to end, hoping to catch her for a quick kiss-in-passing at least.

There was something different about her as she came in from town, then he realised it was that she didn't have any shopping bags.

'Why are you waiting for me?' she said, with the big scared eyes of a spooked deer. She didn't break stride, forcing him to trot alongside her.

'I thought we might snatch five minutes.'

'Not today, Matthew. I don't feel like I want your company today.'

'Please, darling.' He grabbed her arm to stop her. She ripped it away with disproportionate force and ran up the escalator. She looked like she did when she had first started speaking to him, when she had been scared of Adam. Matt couldn't get a handle on it at all.

However, coming through the revolving door into the building immediately behind her, Colin Seed knew he could.

Chapter 10

IT WAS CATHERINE'S YOUNGEST daughter Violet's birthday that same day.

The Flanagan matriarch picked Danny up from school to whisk him away for a party at Burger King, allowing Stevie time to get stuck into *Highland Fling*. It was turning out to be the best Midnight Moon she had ever written. There was a knock on her door just after six and she opened it to find Adam on the doorstep.

'I didnae like comin' straight in.'

'Well, it's going to look pretty weird if you start knocking, considering you're supposed to be living here.'

'Aye, I suppose so,' said Adam and he bent, placing his cheek near to hers to simulate a kiss, just in case they were being watched. She noticed that he smelt of work and clean sweat and woody aftershave. 'Where's the wee 'un?' he asked as Stevie closed the door.

'Scoffing a big burger. It's Catherine's daughter's birthday party.'

'Ah, I see. Have you eaten?'

'Er, no, I've only just stopped working.'

'C'moan, whit is it tha' you dae?'

'I'll put the kettle on,' she said.

He dropped his bag near the hall table where Stevie had put down her post—her unopened wage slip from Midnight Moon. The motif on a brown envelope caught his eye: a large moon with a clock face.

'You get post from Midnight Moon?' he said with an amused twist to his lip. 'Whit is this, then?' He pretended to open it.

'Give me that, please,' said Stevie, quickly abandoning the kettle. But Adam put it well out of her reach, high above his head.

'I'm serious, Adam, let me have it.' Stevie jumped up. She didn't want him to know what she did. He had made her feel sad enough, in the pathetic sense of the word, about her job. Adam danced around and Stevie leapt up like a Red Indian round a totem pole. It caused a very odd picture in the window, which Matthew, staring obsessively through *his* window, saw.

Matthew knew MacLean was using her, probably to tempt Jo back by driving her crazy with jealousy. He knew one day soon the charm would stop and the violence would begin. While this thought was on his mind, he saw MacLean and Stevie involved in some kind of tussle by the window.

Jo had just about been ready to forgive him and had come up for a snuggle when Matthew almost threw her out of the way and thrust open the outside door.

'**H**ey, look,' said Adam, dropping his arm, 'your man's on his way over here and he means business. Start laughin'. *Noo!*'

'Laughing? What do you mean, "laughing"?'

'As if we're havin' a good time.'

'I'm not that good an actress.'

'C'moan, *nooo!*'

Stevie shrugged. 'OK.' She managed a pathetically lame laugh.

'Och, try and dae better than tha'.'

'I can't just laugh like that.'

'Stevieareyouatiglsh?'

'Am I a wha . . . arrrgghh!' In a flash Stevie suddenly found herself being slammed onto the floor. Then for some bizarre reason Adam ripped his shirt open like the Hulk and sat astride her.

'What the hell . . .!'

'Sorry!' he said in advance as his hands made claws and descended.

Matthew didn't bother to knock before trying to open the cottage door, but it was locked and he banged hard on it. Stevie was screaming. Although the more he listened, the less sure he was that those were screams of pain. She was laughing maniacally and sounded more like she was being tickled than assaulted. In between various requests for him to stop whatever he was doing, she was shrieking out Adam's name and that made Matthew even angrier.

'Stevie, let me in!' He threw his shoulder into the door, but it was massive and oak and he couldn't have broken it down if he were Rambo.

Suddenly, Stevie arrived at the door looking very tousled. She was so red-faced, he could have been forgiven for thinking that she had just been mainlining beetroot. Her hair was mussed up, she was straightening her clothes and he got the distinct impression that she had just been rolling around on the floor. In the background, Adam MacLean appeared to be getting up from the same floor with his shirt ripped open and looking too fucking pleased with himself for Matthew's liking. Plus he was none-too-subtly adjusting his trousers.

'I heard you screaming, Stevie, are you OK?'

'I'm . . . er . . . fine,' Stevie said breathlessly.

'MacLean wasn't hurting you, then?'

'Er . . . no, quite the opposite, actually.'

'Oh, right—sorry to have bothered you,' Matthew said stiffly. He turned to go, but then, when he was at a safe distance, spun round with his finger projecting towards Adam like Harry Potter's wand.

'You hurt her, MacLean, and I'll . . . I'll kill you!' he spat.

Adam didn't react, other than with a surprised Roger Moore lift of his eyebrows. He stood there trying not to look amused.

Stevie was astounded. She had never seen Matthew act that passion-ately. Whatever she might think of MacLean, he certainly knew his *basic psychology*. That didn't stop her taking her hatred of him to new heights, though. *How dare he do that to her! Who did he think he was?*

'Wow,' said Adam when Stevie had shut the door. 'Sorry, by the way. I saw that trick once on a John Wayne film. It worked then as well.'

'You . . .' struggled Stevie, not able to find a word insulting enough.

'Tell me why Midnight Moon are writing tae you.'

'Go to hell,' said Stevie, snatching her letter and charging into the study where she sat and wondered if her heart would ever stop thumping.

Sheepishly, Matthew trudged back across the lane.

Jo was waiting for him with a slow handclap. 'How gallant. Shame you didn't do that for me when I needed rescuing from him.'

'She didn't need rescuing. I thought she was screaming because he was beating her up when actually they were about to have sex.'

'*Sex?*' Jo gasped.

'You know, that thing we used to have.'

'Fuck you!' Jo cried, and started to rain slaps on him.

'Jo, what's happening to us?' said Matthew, catching her hands. He needed to focus on his problems with her, but he was having difficulty getting the image of Stevie and MacLean having sex out of his mind. They must have been doing it on the kitchen floor. She'd never wanted sex like that when she'd been with him. Nor had he ever heard her make those sorts of noises before. He hadn't really associated her with that kind of passionate activity.

Jo pulled her hands away from him and paced the room like a caged tiger. 'We need to move. I don't want to watch Adam and that bitch living out their lives in front of us.'

'Why are you so horrible to her, Jo?'

But Jo wasn't listening; she was lost in a world filled only with her-self. '. . . Is that why he didn't try to stop me? He even carried my bloody suitcases to the car for me. Because he was carrying on behind my back with that short, fat cow.'

'Did Adam let you go that easily? I thought you said he—'

'How soon can you realise your investments, Matthew? Let's buy a house away from here, please. Leeds.'

'About my investments,' said Matthew quietly. Then he began.

Next morning, Adam woke to whispering outside his bedroom door.

'Can I go in and see him?' said a small boy's not-so-quiet voice.

'No, you'll see him later.'

'Please, Mummy!'

'No. Now, come on and don't make any noise or you'll wake him up.'

'But I *want* to wake him up, Mummy!'

'Superheroes really need their sleep, Danny, you should know that.'

'Aw, OK.'

Adam smiled. He reckoned they were counting down the days now until Dannyman, his fellow Superhero, would be back living across the road. A thought that made his smile fade surprisingly quickly.

Matthew woke feeling totally exhausted. He hadn't had as much sex as that in one night since the Freshers' Ball at university.

Jo had taken yesterday's news that he was not in fact a half-millionaire-in-the-making pretty well. He hadn't told her the *whole* truth, the story given being that his investments had taken a substantial crash and the only way he could recover the losses was to leave them where they were for at least five years. He told her he had a meeting with the bank to discuss the best plan of action as far as his 'investments' were concerned, and would sneak out of the office on the pretext of going to the dentist.

Jo had not shouted or screamed or thrown anything heavy in the direction of his cranium. She had just nodded her head resignedly and forced out a smile and said, 'Well, that's that, then.'

Then, when they had gone to a bed in which he expected not only the cold shoulder, but a cold everything else, she had surprised him by instigating sex. Quite energetic, almost brutal sex, actually. She had wanted him to bite her all over. At one point, he felt like going to the window and checking to see if the moon was full, because she was like an animal—insatiable and wild. Matthew wasn't really the type to mix pain with pleasure, though, and he fulfilled her requests halfheartedly. He had managed to give her a sucky love-bite on her chest, which he regretted next morning because she wore her blouses quite open, and it was showing there as an ugly, painful-looking bruise. Sex with Jo had been great and exciting in the beginning, but recently he had found himself missing the gentle intimacy and more considerate, warm love-making that he'd enjoyed with Stevie before he got greedy.

Adam had a day off, and as Stevie hadn't come back after dropping Danny at school, he presumed she had gone into town. He had just grilled up half a farmyard full of bacon and stuck it in between two half-loaves of bread when the phone rang.

'Hellooo,' he said.

'Hello,' said a cut-glass voice on the other end. 'Is Bea there?'

'Sorry, hen, wrang number.'

'I can't have, she's on short dial. Is Stevie there? Stevie Honeywell?'

'Stevie's oot . . . *out* at the moment. Can I help you at all?'

'And you are?' purred the voice.

'Adam MacLean.'

'Ah, *you're* Damme MacQueen.'

Poor old thing is deaf, thought Adam. 'No. A-dam Mac-Lean.'

'Yes, I heard you, darling.' The voice cut like glass too. 'I'm Crystal Rock, Stevie's publisher at Midnight Moon.'

Ah, thought Adam. Interesting.

'Sorry,' he bluffed. 'I apologise. She has told me so much aboot you.'

Crystal gave a tinkly laugh. She was half in love with Adam already.

'And I am getting to know all about *you*, Mr MacLean, or should I say Mr MacQueen. If the hero of *Highland Fling* is based on you, I think we can expect to have a bit of a best seller on our hands.'

What was that name she'd asked for at first? B something or other? Adam reached over and picked up a nearby Midnight Moon by Betty Proctor and said craftily, 'Do you think it will be better than *Forever in Dreams*?'

'Oh, good God, I hope so. Betty Proctor isn't a patch on Beatrice Pollen. She only lasted two books. Bea, sorry, Stevie, has a very great following. Can you ask her to give me a ring and tell her that I *love* Damme MacQueen, I *love* Evie Sweetwell and I want the rest of *Highland Fling* finished a.s.a.p. I'll die if he doesn't kiss her soon.'

'I will do tha' indeed.'

'And tell Miss Honeywell that she is a very dark horse and I expect a full update when she calls. She'll know what that means.' Crystal gave a very salacious giggle and finished with a '*ciao*' that was as rich as a tiramisu. Adam put the phone down slowly. Well, well, well! No wonder she wouldn't tell him what she did after all the scorn he had, inadvertently, poured on her stories. So that's why there were Beatrice Pollen books all over the place. He worked his way along the shelf until he came to a book written by Ms Pollen, then he got himself a coffee from the nice full percolator that belonged to Beatrice, aka Stevie, settled down with book and breakfast in the sunroom, and began to read.

'Flaming heck!' said Robert Gilroy, Matthew's bank account handler. He looked about twelve and made Matthew feel the same age. 'What a blooming mess! Is this the full picture or is there more? People tend to hide stuff and it's hardly wise if you want help.'

'That's it,' said Matthew. 'Honestly. Can you help?'

'Well, yep,' said Robert Gilroy. 'You'll be tied to this debt for at least five years but it will give you breathing space to have some quality of life. The debt will be cheaper if you secure it against your home, obviously. How solid is your job?'

'Rock solid,' said Matthew. He was good at his job so there were no worries about securing the loan against his house.

'Right, now get out your plastic,' said Robert Gilroy, handing him a pair of scissors.

'I've got a present to buy. For my girlfriend,' Matthew whimpered as the scissors scraped his emergency Goldfish.

'Give her a massage,' said Robert Gilroy. 'She'll only moan that you've made her fat if you buy chocolates.'

'I was thinking of a gold necklace.'

'She'll leave you anyway if you continue to wake up screaming and sweating in the middle of the night because you're so debt-ridden. If your heart doesn't give out first. Cut, please.'

Matthew sliced.

Stevie came home to find Adam MacLean in the sunroom, nearing the middle of a book. He had tidied around and vacuumed.

'Hello,' he greeted her.

'Hello,' she said. Then she realised he was reading *Winter of Content* by herself in disguise as Beatrice Pollen. It was one of her more passionate pieces, in which a Grand Duke of Russia falls for a servant girl. At least he didn't know she'd written it, for then, she suspected, her life wouldn't be worth living.

'I had a day off today. Didnae bring any books tae read wi' me so I thought I'd have a go at this,' he explained.

'Oh, right,' said Stevie. She acted uninterested.

'I can see noo why people buy them. There's actually quite a nice story goin' on here . . . Here, let me give you a hand,' he said and started to take things out of bags. 'Oh, and by the way, you had a call from someone called Crystal. She wanted you tae phone her back.'

'What did she say?' asked Stevie. Trying to sound as casual in return.

'Nothing really. Funny, she kept callin' me Damme MacQueen.'

Bugger!

'Oh, er, she's a bit old and doddery. Thanks for taking the message.'

He grinned behind her back. 'I thought I might take you and Danny oot for a pizza.'

'There's really no need.'

'I want to. I fancy a pizza and didnae want tae eat oot alone.'

'Thank you but I don't want my son getting too excited about you being here and becoming attached to you. He's already far keener to see you than I ever expected. I don't want him getting hurt.'

'OK, I understand,' said Adam, and he did, but he could not mask the note of disappointment in his voice. He liked the little boy. Danny reminded him of himself at that age, quiet and intense with a head full of stories about outsmarting life's baddies. Not that his mum had been anything like Stevie, and that, he considered, was a great shame.

As a courtesy to Stevie, Adam made himself scarce after saying a quick hello to Danny when he came in from school. He went for a run, making sure he wasn't back before Danny went to bed. He returned warm and sweaty to find Stevie outside deadheading a few of the roses that trailed up the front walls of the cottage.

'Hi,' he said, going into the cottage. 'Can I get you a cold drink?'

'I'm OK, thanks,' she said, and carried on snipping. He wondered if she was wishing each one was his head. He had gone a bit far the other day, chucking her on the floor and tickling her.

He heard Stevie yelp and the secateurs drop to the ground, and rushed out to see what the matter was.

'I think I've just been stung,' she said, trying to shake off her glove. Sure enough, in the crook of her arm was a still-throbbing sting.

'Here.' He pulled out her arm, then pincered out the sting, lowered his lips and started to suck.

'Ow!'

'Wheesht, woman, I'm trying tae help you.' He sucked and spat.

'**C**hrist, can't they get a fucking room,' said Jo, who had just gone to the sink for a glass of water and seen them in passing. She couldn't bear to stand and watch, but she couldn't move away from the window either. The sight of Adam with *her* was driving her mad. He was kissing her up the arm in full view of the road. They looked bloody ridiculous.

She tore herself away and jumped onto Matthew's lap on the sofa, knocking away the newspaper he was engrossed in. 'Make love to me now,' she said. *Take away the picture I have in my head.*

'Er . . . OK,' said Matthew, as Jo unleashed her breasts, but in the end, it was only her he satisfied. There was a picture in his own head that just kept getting in the way.

Stevie watched Adam's lips work on the soft skin on the inside of her arm and suddenly felt a greater sting inside her than the now-dead creature had given her. She gently pulled her arm away.

'I think that might have done it,' she said stiffly, to overcompensate for the swirly, heady feelings that were taking over her brain. Obviously the effects of insect poison. 'Thank you.' She retreated inside.

Jo had a headache next day and phoned in sick. Though she put it more dramatically than that, Matthew noticed as he eavesdropped over the upstairs balcony. She seemed to sob a little and say she couldn't get in and would explain later. Matthew volunteered to stay off and keep her company but she said she just wanted to sleep it off.

Later at work, Adam was catching up on some paperwork in his office but his head was all over the place. He thought of Danny's face lighting up every time he saw him. He thought of his own heart warming up every time he saw Danny. Then he thought of Danny's mother and he didn't know what the hell happened to him when he saw her. She was the most infuriating woman he had ever met, the antithesis to everything that had ever attracted him in a woman. She was nothing like Jo or Diane, or the others before them, in their tall, slender, cold, dark-haired moulds.

There was a confident knock on his door, and he yelled out his customary, 'C'moan on in.'

It wasn't a member of staff. It was a woman dressed in a powder-blue suit, looking tall and slender, cold and beautiful, with long, swishy dark hair and eyes the colour of molasses.

'Hello, Adam,' said the smiling red lips of the last person in the world he expected to see.

Stevie pulled into the gym car park next to a red Golf. Jo had a red Golf, although it was hardly likely to be her car, thank goodness.

She did a fifteen-minute run on the treadmill. She had grown to like coming to the gym. The physical exercise of running cleared her head. Having such a sedentary job, she needed to get her heart pumping a bit more, although it had been on an emotional treadmill that had made it pump quite enough recently. At least it would all be over soon. One way or another.

Matthew had always been smiling in the days when they had been together. Now every time Stevie saw him, he looked miserable. Crazy, when he had everything he set out to get. Jo didn't look much happier, either. She was always scowling, which was warped because Stevie had nothing she wanted. Jo had Matthew and his house and, with a snap of her fingers, she could have had Adam and his house back. She couldn't imagine that Jo was jealous of her figure and short legs, so if she wasn't happy with the lot she had created for herself, then she could rot in hell as far as Stevie was concerned.

She went back to her car to find that the red Golf had gone, and that someone had scraped their key viciously along her driver's side door.

When Matthew got home, Jo was still in bed. She looked really ill actually, pale and puffy-eyed, from a lot of crying.

'You need to take tomorrow off work too,' he said, soothing her brow.

'No, I need to go to work tomorrow more than anything,' she said, shrinking away from his hand. 'Please, Matthew, just leave me alone.'

'Guess what? Mum got stinged last night,' said Danny, flinging himself at Adam as he came in through the door.

'Yes, I know,' he said, attempting a smile, although he felt so tired and drained.

'Come on, Danny, let Adam get in through the door,' said Stevie.

'Honey is bees' poo. That's what Curtis Ryder says. And milk is cows' wee. Mrs Apple Crumble made him sit on the naughty chair today for trumping in storytime.'

'Mrs *Abercrombie* did the right thing then, didn't she?'

Adam let loose a lion's lung's-worth of laughter. It felt so good to laugh, and it felt even better to be home with a family, even though it wasn't his home or his family. Nevertheless, he was grateful for the welcoming presence of a child and the warm, no-nonsense of a woman.

'Well, tha' Curtis Ryder has things a little wrong there,' he said. '*Bees* make honey for food. They collect *pollen* as food fer their young.'

'Wow!' said Danny.

'Chicken nuggets!' Stevie alerted her son to the table. Was it her imagination, or had Adam MacLean given special emphasis to certain words just then? She had only seen the man for five minutes today and already she wanted to slap him.

'So, any mair news from Midnight Moon?' he casually asked later.

'No, why would there be?'

'I have no idea why there would *beee*.'

Stevie put down her sewing.

'You are lookin' at me as if you want me to *buzz* awf,' said Adam.

'You know, don't you?'

'Know whit?' He looked the picture of innocence.

'OK, I write trashy, crappy romance books for a living. Satisfied?'

He jumped back in mock surprise. 'No!'

'I presume Crystal said far more than you admitted.'

'Perhaps. I seem tae recall an extra minor detail or two.'

'Yes, I can imagine. Anyway, *you* may not like them, Mr MacLean, but thousands of other people do!'

Common sense told her to walk away. His mocking was attracting to him the anger that was swirling inside her for Jo; for her scratched car; for Matthew's pathetic, unhappy face; and most of all for Adam Bloody MacLean because she couldn't stop thinking about his lips on her arm. All afternoon her imagination had been taking those lips and putting them on other places on her body. This wasn't in 'the master plan'.

'In fact, I don't know why I didn't tell you before. There's a skill involved, unlike managing a place where people pay an obscene amount of money just to lift up heavy objects and sweat.'

Oh, she wants to fight, does she? he thought, crossing his arms. 'So, is tha' all I do, then? And there was me thinkin' I work quite hard.' He was enjoying the verbal parry. It was making him forget about the visitor who had weighed down his head for most of the day. 'Well, at least I don't sit on ma bum all day.'

'Me sitting on my bum all day has put money on the table to feed my child. Yes, I'm a Midnight Moon writer and I'm proud of it!' Stevie jutted out her chin.

'I'm sure sad people all over the world appreciate you.'

This, unfortunately, didn't come out quite as his gentle teasing had intended, adding a pint of petrol to her already blazing temper.

'Yes, sad people with a brain who can do joined-up lettering! You patronising Scottish git.'

She had a silly smattering of freckles on her nose. He had the sudden desire to kiss them. That would shut her up.

'I was tryin' to give you a compliment, actually.'

'I don't need compliments from a man like you, Mr MacLean.'

'And what sort of a man am I, *Ms Honeywell*? I see we're back on formal terms again.'

'The sort of man I can't wait to see the back of on Sunday! I'm going to work. Good night,' and off she went in the direction of the office, to write about Damme MacQueen being thrown off a cliff.

Adam smiled. The angrier she got, the funnier she was, but as soon as Stevie left him, his thoughts started to drift back to the afternoon and a life that felt a million light years away from this crazy set-up. A life he had the chance to go back to. A life with a beautiful house and a beautiful woman in it. The life he had fought to win back. The life he surprisingly found he had won back. So what was it that was stopping him?

Unless a miracle happened in the next twenty-four hours, Adam's prophecy that all would be settled by Sunday was not going to come true. Matthew and Jo were still together.

Adam had started gathering up his stuff and sorting out his laundry. His undies were drying on the line—they were white and Calvin Klein. Matthew was more of a briefs bloke—black and designer label also, but they paled into sexual second place as soon as Stevie saw those white boxers. Matthew's bum had been a bit skinny for her tastes; Adam's was quite chunky. Not that she'd looked at it much. *Well* . . .

They hadn't seen a lot of each other over the last few days. He hadn't been in the house much, and when he had been, Stevie had shut herself away in her office to work. Damme MacQueen was a good man—misjudged, kind and wonderful. He didn't beat up women and he was safe to love. Evie was going to be a lucky lady.

Adam had deliberately been coming home after Danny had gone to bed, for which Stevie was grateful. It was going to be bad enough having to uproot her son again to find yet another place to live, without finding out he'd got attached to 'Well Life Man' too.

'Can I help?' he asked, as she stomped round the kitchen, transferring crockery out of the dishwasher.

'No!' she said. Then softer, 'No, thanks.'

'Why the brass band?' he asked as pans crashed together.

'Because I want to.'

'Watch tha' bottom lip afore you trip o'er it!'

'Not listening, sorry.'

'I'll get you a teddy tha' you can throw oot your cot and make yersel' feel better.'

'Very funny. Ha ha!'

'Ah, so y'are listenin'! Maybe you need burpin'. Want me tae pat your back a wee bit?'

She would like to have screamed at him to bugger off, but Danny was in the garden so she couldn't. She was finding that the pressure of keeping her feelings in was making her blow steam out of her earholes, so she rough-handled the crockery instead and dropped one of the nice plates, which crashed to the floor, spattering pieces everywhere.

'Och, now you'll have tae pay for that oot your pocket money.'

She turned on him. 'Everything's a big joke to you, isn't it?'

'No, it isnae. But pretendin' you're at a Greek weddin' isnae goin' tae bring Matty Boy back tae you any quicker. And there's no use snappin' at me—this isnae ma fault.'

'Isn't it?' Stevie laughed, a hard unjolly sound. 'This situation is *all* because of you, Adam MacLean. *All!* I've lost my home and my man, and my little boy has lost his chance of a family. *You* might have thrown your relationship away, but I didn't. Make no mistake—this all happened *Because. Of. You!*' She barged past him to get the cutlery, not noticing that the teasing smile had dropped like a hot rock from Adam's lips and he moved quickly to block her way.

'Whoa! Whit was tha' bit aboot throwin' ma relationship away?'

'Nothing, I meant nothing.' She moved to skirt him and he moved with her and put his hands on her arms to pull her back in front of him. The startled little yelp she gave made him drop his hold immediately.

'Sorry, did I hurt you?'

'No,' she said, because he hadn't, but he saw in her eyes a flashing thought that he might. That fear. He knew that look so well. He had seen it in his mammy's and his sisters' eyes so many times.

'Whit's goin' on, Stevie? Whit am I supposed to have done in ma relationship that all this was ma fault? Please—whit dae ye mean? Whit dae ye know? Whit have you heard? You have tae tell me noo.'

'It's what Jo told us about you.'

'Jo?' He paled. 'You spoke tae Jo? When?'

'Lots of times.'

'Whit dae ye mean?'

Stevie sighed. 'Matthew and Jo got friendly at work,' she began.

'Aye, I know. You two weren't gettin' on.'

'What?'

'That's whit Jo told me. Tha' you two were going through a rough patch.' He didn't see the need to tell her that apparently she was also dirty and lazy and a terrible mother.

'Jo said what?' Stevie's mouth dropped open. 'We were fine. The reason he befriended her is because you . . . you made her unhappy.'

'In whit way?' Now it was Adam's turn to look shocked.

'She never stopped crying! I felt so sorry for her.'

'You met her?' He was breathless.

'She rang for Matthew one day, too scared to go home to you. I told her to come round to the house.'

'Scared—of *me*? Whit on earth for?'

'She was terrified. Shaking when she got here.'

'But she never said she met you.'

'Adam, we became friends, we went shopping together, she read to Danny. I even let her see my wedding dress. Jo was on our guest list.'

'Friends? She said Matthew loathed you.'

'She said you took all her money.'

'She said he'd called off the marriage but you were carryin' on wi' the arrangements regardless.'

'She said you put her through hell with the names you called her.'

'She said you used tae get drunk and throw things at Matthew.'

'She said you used to smack her around.'

The words hung in the air like a discordant bell. Of all the lies Adam MacLean was hearing, he found this one the most hard to stomach.

'Stevie, I've never laid a hand on a woman in ma life. The reason I got together wi' Jo was to rescue her from some crazy guy she was livin' with. He'd kicked her in the leg and she was limpin'. I found her cryin' outside the gym where I worked before this one.'

Stevie gulped. 'Top of her left thigh?'

'Aye,' he said.

'She said you did that.'

'Me!' He spun round, his voice booming, his bulk filling half the room, but he still didn't look in the least bit harmful. 'I cannae hit anyone. Look at the size o' me. I'd kill anyone I hit!'

'So you've not been in Barlinnie?'

'Barlinnie?' Adam laughed through the tears. 'Whit the hell for?'

'GBH.'

'Grievous bod . . .? Stevie, they wouldnae give me a job at Well Life sweeping flairs if I'd mair than three points on ma driving licence! I've never been in a jail in ma life.' He rubbed his head with his huge hands.

Stevie had the overwhelming desire to go to him and hold him. She knew he had been hurt by her revelations. Never had she seen even the slightest intimation that Adam was the man Jo had painted him to be, though she knew she had wanted to see him like that, because then she could blame him for what had happened and not her darling Matthew. They'd both been had. And Matthew was still being had. *Should she tell him?* What difference would it make? Hadn't Catherine tried to tell her what a bastard Mick was? And had she believed her? No.

'I'm sorry, Adam, I don't know what to believe any more.'

Adam looked cut down, felled like a big tree that wouldn't ever get up again. 'Well, if you think there is the slightest danger tae you and your child from me, maybe it would be better if I just got oot of your life totally tomorrow. We'll forget our plan and you get Matthew back your way. I don't think it will be long, fer the record.'

'OK,' said Stevie croakily. She didn't want him to go, but she needed to get away from thoughts of Adam MacLean's lips on her arm and the feel of her hand inside his. 'I think that might be best.'

Chapter 11

ADAM LAY on the treatment table and groaned. He had thought a Sunday-morning Kahuna session at the gym might ease the tension in his back and neck, if not take away the knot in his head. He never expected that the tiny South African masseuse could be capable of such brutality.

It was the sort of massage Stevie would have liked to perform on him, he thought. One that hurt. Thoughts of Stevie rubbing oil in his back ran ahead of him, her small hands kneading his muscles, her fingers tripping up and down his spine. He would reciprocate, dribble warm scented oil onto her body and smooth it over her soft curves, his thumbs circling her skin. A mutinous body part stirred and he groaned inwardly. *Och noo, tha' wasnae supposed tae happen at all!* Then he knew why he had said 'no' when Joanna MacLean had turned up at the gym and asked, then begged to come home.

As Stevie was preparing the last meal she would share with Adam MacLean in this beautiful house, she saw Matthew through the window, walking back home with an armful of Sunday newspapers. He looked like an old man with the cares of the world on his shoulders. Her heart lurched in his direction, in love or pity or both, she couldn't tell.

Danny was colouring at the table.

Stevie pulled his Dannyman collar out of his mouth. 'You'll suck all the dye out of your shirt and end up being blue like an alien.'

'Wow, yeah!' he said.

'I give up. Suck your collar then, Danny,' she said impatiently.

She turned her attention to the Yorkshire pudding mix. The flour rose in a cloud as the beaters hit it, blew it up her nose and made her sneeze. Adam, newly arrived in the doorway, hid the smile that came because he was catapulted back to the first time he had seen her. It surprised him, because he had thought it would be a long time until he smiled again. His back was in pain from the Kahuna, his head was in pain from thinking of Jo's treachery. But his heart pained him most of all.

'Have ye seen a big bunch of keys, Stevie?'

'Oh, I thought I saw them upstairs. Now, where was it?'

She put the bowl down and went upstairs to look for them. He followed her and she did a sideways walk up in case he was taking a critical look at her bum. Not that he'd be looking at her bum when he liked a Jo MacLean kind of bum, i.e. non-existent.

'Yes, here they are,' she said, spotting them. 'There on the windowsill.' She reached over, picked them up and then handed them to him. His fingers brushed against hers and it was unbearable for both of them.

'Thanks.' He looked into her blue eyes and was shamed that she had thought him the sort of man he despised. His master plan had been stupid. He would be left with a worse loss than when he started.

Stevie raised her head and saw him as he really was and how she had found him, not as Jo had led her to believe he was. You only had to look into his soft, gentle eyes to know he didn't have the capacity to hurt anything. And how had she missed how generous his mouth was? An unattainable mouth, because it still belonged to Jo MacLean.

Her thoughts stopped there because her senses were alerted to a noise that was hardly discernible to the ear, but that a mother's heart would pick up. It was coming from the kitchen and Stevie's feet flew downstairs in response to it.

Danny wasn't playing any more. He was on the floor, shaking as if in a fit and in great distress, and his lips were paling to blue.

'Adam!' she screamed. 'Adam, help me!'

Adam bounced down the stairs.

'He's hardly breathing!' said Stevie, bent over her son. She pulled her hand away to slap him on the back. Adam caught her arm.

'No, Stevie. Get an ambulance!'

'Yes,' she said. She rushed to the phone.

'Stevie, there's a button missin' on his collar—was there one here?'

'Yes, oh God, yes, there was. Hello . . . ambulance, please.' She sobbed as the phone connected with the emergency services and she hurriedly gave them her details.

Adam scooped his finger in Danny's mouth. 'I think he's swallowed his button and it's blockin' his airway. I cannae get to it.' He got to his feet and pulled the limp little boy up, wrapping his arms round the child from the back. He braced himself and thrust his fist under Danny's rib cage. And again. It looked so brutal, so abusive. Then something flew out of the little boy's mouth and Danny gasped and started making sicky, retching noises, and then he started crying. It was the most beautiful sound Stevie had ever heard.

Disorientated, Danny looked around for his mum, reached out for her, and Stevie pulled him into her arms and rocked him. They sat like that until the ambulance sirened up the lane and Adam met it at the door and explained to the paramedics what had happened.

'We'd better take you in, just as a precaution,' said one of the paramedics, giving Danny a quick once-over.

Adam lifted Danny away so Stevie could get up, and he cuddled up to the big Scot and wouldn't let him go. So Adam came too, in the back of the ambulance, to the hospital.

Stevie sat in a waiting room with Adam while Danny was in the consulting room with the doctor. She wasn't sobbing, but her eyes were piping out tears. Adam watched them rolling down her face. She looked so tiny and more fragile than he could ever have imagined.

'He was a premature baby,' she said at last. 'I didn't think he'd pull through—I was warned he might not. To have nearly lost your child once is terrible, to go through this twice . . .'

'Shhh,' said Adam. Even though he felt shaken himself, he couldn't imagine what Stevie must be feeling like.

'I told him if he didn't stop sucking his collar he'd turn blue and he did,' she wept. 'If you hadn't been there, he'd have died. If—'

'Stevie, if I hadnae been there, you'd have saved his life, don't ask me how, but I know tha' wi'oot a shadow of a doot. Noo, stop thinkin' aboot "if", there's nae point. Danny is safe. "If" didnae happen.'

'You saved his life, Adam, and I was useless. A totally crap mother.'

'You're a great mother, trust me on this,' said Adam. 'You put food on his table, clothes on his back and love in his heart.'

'You've been reading my books.'

'Awa', I wouldnae read that pap.' He nudged her and she laughed, although the tears didn't stop. Adam put his arm round her and squeezed her. She was all squashy and soft and warm and there was flour in her hair. He wanted to sink his face into her neck.

The door opened and a smiley nurse came in.

'Hi there, Danny's mum?' Then she threw an extra 'Heeeey' at Adam.

'Your little boy is fine,' she said. 'Scratched his throat a bit, that's all, but no lasting harm done. Do you want to come and get him?'

'Go on,' said Adam. 'I'll wait here fer you.'

Stevie smiled at him and followed the nurse.

'So you're Adam's lady, are you?' said the nurse.

'No, we're just'—*mortal enemies*—'neighbours.'

'Adam's one of our favourites.' She leaned in and winked. 'He raised over three thousand pounds for us when he cut all his hair off. He helps us a lot. And, of course, he's our Father Christmas. The kids love him!'

A Father Christmas with a scar? thought Stevie, and as if she had heard her, the nurse said, 'He tells the kids that he scraped his face on Rudolf's antler.'

Adam met them in the entrance hall. Danny reached out, gave him a big Superhero hug, and moved over into his arms. The wee boy smelt of his mother's perfume. He was so like her, with his honey-coloured hair and his big blue eyes, that Adam found himself gulping back something that made his eyes distinctly watery. His hold on the boy was tight and strong as they got a taxi home to Humbleby.

'I'll make you a cup of tea, huh?' Adam said, when they got inside the house. 'Then I'll get aff.'

'Will you go back home?' said Stevie.

'Aye,' he said, obviously not relishing the prospect.

'Stay,' said Stevie. 'Please.'

'Aye,' said Adam, and went to put the kettle on.

Matthew walked into work on Monday morning and had the weirdest feeling he was being watched. Eyes seemed to linger on him and he had the ridiculous notion that he was the subject of gossip.

Jo had driven her own car in very early that morning; his suggestion that he accompany her had been met with a weary sigh. It appeared that he couldn't win at the moment. If he paid her attention, he was crowding her, if he didn't he was ignoring her.

He settled himself at his desk, pondered over the dilemma of what to do for the best and then bit the bullet. He decided Jo would be less annoyed if he tried an active approach rather than a passive one, so he took a deep breath and dialled her extension.

'Jo MacLean,' she answered briskly.

'Hi, it's me. Fancy lunch?'

'Sorry, no,' she said, slamming the phone down on him. He stared at his handset in disbelief. What have I done wrong now? he thought.

Life had been so much less complicated with Stevie.

'Hiya, wee man!' said Adam, coming in from work, giving Danny a cuddle as the boy rushed at him. He was wearing new pyjamas with no buttons or collars to be seen and his Dannyman emblem was stitched on the front.

'Hey—nice jim-jams. Like the style!' said Adam, twirling him.

'He'll be in that style 'til he's forty-five, if I've anything to do with it,' said Stevie. 'Anyway, come on, bed, little man.' As Danny climbed the stairs, Stevie gave Adam a tentative smile. 'He wanted to stay up and say "hi". I hope that was OK?'

'Of course,' said Adam. 'Why wouldn't it be?'

'Because I've encouraged you to stay away from him, and then I'm throwing him at you. I didn't want to add to any confusion for you.'

He looked at her. What was that conversation he'd had with Danny once about the most important quality of a Superhero? He reckoned Danny's mum had just what it took to be one of the best.

'Nice smell,' he said, pulling his eyes away and to the kitchen.

'I made you a steak pie. As a thank you for . . . you know what . . .'

Words failing her, she followed Danny upstairs for their bedtime business. Then, after discreetly checking her make-up and squirting on an extra spray of perfume, she went back downstairs to find Adam looking across the lane at Matthew's house.

She went into the kitchen, opened the oven, and carried the pie to the table. It had been set just for one.

'You no' goin' tae join me?' he said.

'I'm not hungry, really. I have to get some work done. Can I get you a drink? Wine? Whisky?' She had bought a bottle of both.

'No, I'll just get a wee glass of water. Cannae stand whisky.'

'But you had a trolley full of it when I met you in the supermarket.'

'That was fer the hospital tombola. Did you think it was all fer me?'

'Well, yes . . . sorry. I got you so wrong on all fronts, didn't I?'

'Wasnae your fault,' he said, wisely not mentioning that he had believed Jo's stories that Stevie was a complete harpy, a car crash of a mother and a mega-slattern-fiancée.

She smiled bashfully and then doubled back quickly into the study, although she wanted to sit with him, wanted to be near him. But she couldn't. She wasn't slim or tall or pretty enough for him to cast *that* sort of glance in her direction.

Adam sighed deeply as the study door closed behind her, because he really wanted just to sit with her, wanted her to be near him. He shifted his attention to the thick-crusted pie she had set in front of him. She'd even made a pastry thistle on the top of it. He hadn't eaten properly since Jo had come to see him. Strangely enough though, his thoughts had not been for her tonight while he stood at the window and looked across at the house opposite. They had all been for Finch, who hadn't a clue yet that the hurricane that had swung into his life, would rip out his innards when it left—and that would be soon. He felt almost sorry for the man. His stomach gave a growl as the smell of the onion gravy drifted up his nostrils, but his heart gave a louder, hungrier growl for what that fool Finch had thrown away. Sadly, the thing that would have satisfied it was not on the menu.

Matthew went into work alone the next day, leaving Jo to pack for a two-day conference she had announced she was going on. They were barely talking at home, they hardly spoke at work, and he knew she was avoiding contact with him there. The only place they interchanged was in bed, and even that was tiresome. Her sexual demands were becoming rougher, the sulks greater when he denied her.

He had a lunch meeting at noon in the boardroom, which was, at least, something to look forward to. There would be a few big execs present and it promised to be a jolly affair. Matthew badly needed the lift of spirits such good company would give him.

At twelve, he walked into the boardroom and instantly felt the air temperature drop, as if someone had switched on a fan. There was nothing he could put his finger on. People spoke to him, but with a hint of coolness, a reservation. Maybe he was just worn down with all this business at home; maybe he needed to get some anti-paranoia pills. Or maybe he needed to be bitten by a werewolf and become one, because that's what Jo seemed to want in bed. He felt worse than ever when he came out of the meeting, which had only served to depress him more. If that wasn't enough, he got a call from Personnel at two thirty to ask if he could come down to see Colin Seed.

Colin Seed was slightly different from his usual dull, brown self when he let Matthew into his office. He was sporting a trendy tie with fish on it and his hair looked slightly darker, as if he had been experimenting with some 'Just for Men' but had got it ever so slightly wrong.

'Please sit down,' he said politely enough. Matthew sat and waited for Colin to begin, not able to imagine what this was about.

'It's come to my attention that you are making personal phone calls.'

'Colin, I've made a couple, and they were local and important.'

'. . . And you've been lying about your whereabouts.'

'My what? My where—'

'Even though you are a departmental manager, Matthew, this company has always prided itself on equal rights for all. If you had found out that one of your staff was at a personal meeting at the bank after filling in a request form for time off for a dental appointment, would you or would you not have taken action?'

'Well . . .' Matthew couldn't think of anything, except that the only person who knew about that was Jo.

'Quite frankly, Matthew, your work attitude stinks. I can't count the number of times you've been late in recently. And your blatant harassment of Miss MacLean will not be tolerated by this company.'

'My what?' He rose.

'Sit down!' barked Colin. 'I have witnessed your phone calls to her, obsessively keeping tabs on her, deluging her with unwanted gifts, seen first-hand the violence you've subjected her to—'

'Hang on, what's this got to do with work? We live together, Colin, we're lovers! You've got no right to interfere.'

'Miss MacLean has asked me for help. I think your inability to realise your relationship has ended has greatly affected your function in this company and made your position untenable. We are a big family here, we protect our people. We don't want men like you working here and threatening the safety of our females. So we shall have to let you go.'

Matthew laughed derisively. 'What do you mean, I can't accept my relationship's ended? It's still going strong!'

Colin shook his head. 'You'll be paid until the end of the month.'

Matthew felt sick. 'I'm being sacked? For living with my girlfriend?'

'No, Matthew, for gross misconduct,' said Colin Seed with disgust. 'At Miss MacLean's request, though frankly I think it's an overgenerous one, I will not record on your personnel file what a bully you are. The poor girl is a wreck. You're lucky she isn't pressing police charges.'

The first thing Matthew did when he got back to his office was ring Jo's mobile. It clicked straight onto voicemail. He stuffed things into his briefcase and left.

Jo MacLean heard the mobile ring and she clicked 'ignore'. It was Matthew. She felt no sympathy. What he had coming to him would serve him right, because if she had known the truth about his financial state, she would never have left Adam.

Of all the men she'd had, she had regretted letting Adam go the most. He'd been lovely—kind, generous and so gentle. She hadn't even minded that much about the revolting ponytail and beard he had been growing to shave off for charity. She wished now that she had stayed and married him—well, for a while anyway. He had been bitten hard before and was nervous about taking that step, but she would have won him over to the idea, had she not been distracted by Matthew and his hot-air talk about his so-called investments.

She had started to notice weeks ago that Colin Seed was a far more frequent visitor to the department than usual. Matthew had hit the nail on the head when he'd said he thought Jo was the attraction. It had been so easy to hook Colin: a few tears by his Bentley in the executive car park and he was putty in her hands.

Then she had seen Adam with Stevie and it had driven her half-crazy. She wanted him back immediately, and it never occurred to her that the space she had left in his life would not still be open to her. She had gone to see him at the gym, wearing one of the suits he had bought for her, her hair loose as he liked it best, but he had turned her down. He said he didn't love her any more.

Now Jo's suitcases were in her car ready to go to Colin's house— Colin's monstrously huge eight-bedroomed house in the most elegant part of Leeds suburbia—and even better, she had persuaded him to take the position in New York. Adoration, love-gifts, a new life in the Big Apple and pots of money to look forward to—this time Jo MacLean, the ultimate bird of passage, had really cracked it.

Matthew drove home carefully because his hands were shaking too much to speed. He pulled up noisily outside his house, got out of the car and slammed the door. He plunged the key into the front door lock then crashed through the rooms, calling out Jo's name in despair. She wasn't there, and nor were any of her things. His house looked shabby and dusty and full of ugly, unwanted bits. It wasn't unlike his life.

Stevie had all the same feelings as a seventeen-year-old on her first date as she waited for Adam to come home from work that night.

Danny was staying the night at Catherine's because there was a teachers' 'inset' day at school tomorrow, whatever that meant. Cath was always offering to baby-sit at the moment, for her own mischievous reasons, and tonight, well, Stevie was not prepared to look a gift-horse in the mouth.

She checked the coffee cake cooking in the oven. The vegetables were ready in their pans, the fillet steaks in the fridge waiting to be cooked, the wine breathing on the work surface. Why she was going to all this trouble was anyone's guess. Adam MacLean wouldn't look in her direction in a million years, she knew, but some romantic (and stupid) part of her wanted to run with the feeling that he might. Just until her head could get round the fact that soon they would go their separate ways and probably only see each other in passing in the gym. Then, one day she would see him roaring past in a sports car with a gorgeous, tall, slim woman next to him, her long, dark hair streaming behind. And Stevie would still be alone, still writing fictional lives full of the hope and love that she so wanted for herself.

She was just rolling the edges of the cake in battered-up Flake when he came in, dropped his bag by the door and smiled as the cocktail of nice domestic aromas hit him. He carried a couple of bottles of wine in his hand. He wanted to savour the last few days of being with her, for he knew that was all he had left. He should have told Stevie that Jo had gone, but he feared that would accelerate her journey back to *his* arms. He should leave now and not prolong the heartache, but he wanted to be with her a little longer, an hourglass-worth of time with someone who had the same capacity to love as he did. Someone warm and generous, imperfect, irritating, annoying, frustrating, bloody lovely.

'Hi,' she said. 'I got some steaks, if you want one. Nothing special.'

She had baked. This was special. Well, to him. No one, except his Granny Walker, had ever made him a cake before.

'I got some wine, if you fancy a glass.'

'Yes, I do, thanks. There's a bottle open already over there.'

'Ho'd on a wee minute until I get oot o' this clobba.'

He said he liked his steak well done, not still mooing and struggling on the end of his fork, as she had once thought he might. She slapped them in the pan and they sizzled in the hot olive oil.

He poured two glasses of the open red, when he at last came down in a T-shirt and jeans. She tried hard not to look at his muscular arms, the definition of his chest under the snow-white material, his fantastic chunk of a bum and big crushing thighs shaping the denim.

'Where's Danny?'

'He's at Catherine's. They're having a cinema night. *The Incredibles* again, I think, for the forty-billionth time.'

'Tha's a shame. I was goin' tae have a kickaboot wi' him out in the garden.'

Fond of him as Matthew had been, he had never once said 'that's a shame' when Danny wasn't around, Stevie realised.

'Can I help?' Adam asked.

'Yes, you can pass me the brandy and those peppercorns, unless you want your steak plain.'

'Plain for me, please. I want tae taste tha' meat, it looks braw . . . good.'

'I understand you now, you don't need to translate.'

He smiled. The wine swirled in his head already. He wanted to get horribly plastered and rip all her clothes off, but for now, he got on with slicing some tomatoes.

'Bea Pollen!' he chuckled, when they were sitting on the sofa, mellowing after a lovely meal and gentle banter. They had both suggested having a sobering raspberry-truffle-flavoured coffee afterwards. He, before he really did rip her clothes off, and she before she leapt on him and made a complete twat of herself. They had both kicked off their shoes and their feet were inches apart on the footstool. She couldn't imagine ever borrowing his socks. He had the biggest feet she had ever seen. She tried hard not to think what that might mean, scale-wise.

'Whitever possessed you tae call yersel' Bea Pollen?' he asked.

'It's *Beatrice* Pollen, actually. It was my granny's name. Crystal didn't like me to use the name Stevie, said it sounded too much like a man. Men don't sell well, you see. So . . .'

'Oh, I see. Is Honeywell your married name, then?'

'No. I went back to my maiden name after Mick was killed.'

'Whit happened? Only if you want tae talk aboot it,' said Adam, twisting sideways onto her, his arm dangerously close to her head.

'He was in a car crash. On the way to the airport.'

'Och, no. Business trip?'

'No, it was most definitely pleasure,' she said with a mirthless laugh.

Adam looked at her in a quizzical way that prodded her to go on.

'If you must know, he was running off with another woman. She was killed outright too. Apparently they didn't suffer, which I'm glad for.'

'Oh God, no! I'm sorry. Did you know aboot her?'

'I found out about a month before. I followed him to her house once, asked her . . . begged her to stop seeing him. I pleaded, I cried. Totally lost every bit of dignity I had. She just laughed and shut the door in my face, made me feel *this* big. I think I went a bit mad really.' Stevie cringed, but the wine had loosened her tongue and it felt easy to talk about it, even if she would probably recall this in the morning and want to die. 'I did everything to get him to come back, except leaving him alone to get it out of his system. I thought if I dogged him he'd give in, you see, but it got me absolutely nowhere. The only thing I had left to try was letting him get on with it and see if he came back, but I ran out of time for that one. On the day I got my pregnancy confirmed, I came home to find him packing. He said he was going to live in Tenerife with Linda. The car crashed on the way to the airport.'

'Oh my!' Adam's hand reached forward and brushed her fringe back from her eyes in an instinctive and sympathetic gesture. She let him do it without slapping his hand away, which amazed him.

'Mick had remortgaged the house to raise the money to go—got Linda to fake my signature, I presume. I was in big financial trouble when it all came to light. I was really sick, carrying Danny at the time, and found it hard to go out to work.' Stevie managed a little smile. 'Then Midnight Moon came up trumps for me and gave me a chance to find my feet.'

'Dae you think it would have made a difference if Mick had known aboot Danny?' Adam asked gently.

'He did know,' said Stevie, poking an escapee tear back inside. 'I showed him the test in case he thought I was trying to trick him. He told me to get shut and send him the bill. Six hours later, he was dead.'

Adam winced. 'Dae Mick's family ever see Danny?'

'I rang when I gave birth and left a message on their answering machine telling them how ill Danny was, and that if they wanted to see him, they ought to come straight away, just in case he didn't make it. I sent them some Polaroids, but they just sent everything back with a note to say they'd pray for him.'

'Some godly faith, turning yer back on a wee babe,' said Adam.

Stevie shrugged. 'They blamed me for not being a strong enough wife to keep Mick. If he hadn't been running away from me, you see, he wouldn't have had the accident, that was their reckoning.'

'Whit nonsense,' said Adam, shaking his head in outrage. 'How on earth could you have been to blame?'

'People need to have someone to focus their anger on, Adam. It's easier blaming outsiders than the ones you love.' Stevie's voice faded, realising what she was saying. She saw Adam shift uncomfortably too.

'Ye're no' close tae your own family?'

'Not really. That's why I feel such a failure. I wanted Danny to have the family life I never had. I thought we'd found it with Matthew.'

'So why Matthew? Why did you fall fer Matthew?' he asked quietly.

'My ex-husband Mick was wild, live-for-the-moment, intoxicating, a one-man charm offensive. Matthew was considerate, affectionate, faithful . . .' She gave a little laugh at that last quality. 'I think I fell for what Matthew wasn't, rather than what he was, if that makes any sense. Mick exhausted me, burnt me out, stamped all over my heart, then along came steady, nice Matthew. Chalk and cheese, or so I thought.'

'They weren't really all tha' different though, were they?' said Adam with his objective eye. 'From where I'm sitting, they were both takers.'

'Probably,' said Stevie, nodding. 'Anyway, I wasn't special enough for either of them in the end. I thought more of them than they did of me.'

Adam thought of Diane, and of Jo, and of his mother. He knew what it was like only too well to be on the begging end of love.

'So, come on, why Jo?' Stevie asked him. 'Why would you want someone as gorgeous and flawless as her?'

He laughed and flicked her hair, and she turned to him with her sweet, funny, smiling face and deep blue eyes. It wasn't the perfect, magazine-cover face of someone like Jo; there were fine lines around her eyes to show how much she had cried and laughed and loved and lived, but Stevie Honeywell was making his heart do flick-flacks in a way that no one else had ever made it do.

'Jo, eh? Because she promised me the sort of love I've been lookin' fer all my life. Some people just have the ability to mould themselves tae what you want. Jo was one of them.

'I was just recoverin' from a nasty divorce. My wife, Diane, had run off with her boss. You know the type: thirty years older than her, Satsuma tan, married, owned the company. If tha' wasnae enough, she then tried to get half of everything I had, too. I went a bit mad maself. I got a solicitor's letter sayin' she was entitled to half of everythin'. So rather than sell the stuff, I started to halve it wi' a chainsaw.'

He'd started to divide their furniture all right. He'd got as far as slicing two dining-room chairs down the middle, then realised he was scaring himself more than he was Diane.

'No!' said Stevie, horrified but sympathetic.

'Yes. I regret ma outburst noo. Because she ran off wi' ma cat. She took him and then she gave him away. She just didnae want me tae have him. Diane was so cold, and then along came Jo wi' her "vulnerability" and her soft words, just when I needed them most.'

'Crap at picking partners, aren't we?' said Stevie. 'I once went out with a policeman who was knocking off grannies behind my back.'

'I can beat tha'. My first proper girlfriend said she wouldnae sleep wi' me unless I covered ma hair up wi' a shower cap.'

'I can understand that, though.'

'Och, you cheeky wee . . .'

He leapt on her playfully and she shrieked with laughter, and suddenly the words and sounds dropped away because there was no more need for them, and his hands were cradling her face, and his lips started an achingly slow descent to hers as if he was scared she would push him away, but she didn't. Adam's lips brushed Stevie's teasingly and she thought she was going to explode if they didn't come into land.

Then someone knocked on the bloody door, and kept knocking.

'Matthew, whatever's the matter?' asked Stevie, forced to answer the door before he bashed it down. He looked terrible.

'Can I have a quiet word, Stevie?' He looked past Stevie to Adam, who melted into the background, leaving them to it.

'What is it?'

'Can you come across the road, please?'

Stevie looked at him in horror. 'Over there? No, I can't. Why?'

'Jo and I are finished.'

'What?' Stevie's head started swimming with shock.

She looked behind her. Adam wasn't there, but she knew he must have heard Matthew's words. She wanted to go and find him. Then again she didn't. *Jo was free.* It was obvious what it would mean to him.

'Please, Stevie!'

She couldn't say no. She couldn't have deserted anyone in that state. She slipped on her shoes, took another look behind her, and followed Matthew across the road.

'I don't want to go in there,' she said, as he opened up the door.

'Please. There's no way she'll be coming here again,' he said, and disappeared inside. Cautiously, she went in behind him, feeling a prickle at the back of her neck as if Adam was watching her.

It felt odd to be in the house. It was as if she had never lived there, but remembered it from old photos. It was untidy and there was a film of dust everywhere that gave the place a dull, dead appearance.

'Stevie, I'm sorry, I just don't have anywhere else to turn.' He was walking up and down in front of her, overdosed with nervous energy.

'Matthew, sit down, please. Start from the beginning.'

'I don't know where the beginning of this mess is. I've been sacked. Jo's left me. I don't know what to do.'

Stevie gulped. Jo had left him. Would she try to come back to Adam, then? Would she walk straight back into that soft, forgiving part of his heart that was for ever reserved for her? Stevie felt panicky and wanted to go back to the cottage. She stood up to go, but then Matthew started to make strange groaning noises and she knew she couldn't leave him.

'Why have you been sacked, Matthew?'

'For harassing Jo. I think she has been spreading stories at work that I've been hitting her.'

'*You* hitting her?' Anyone who knew Matthew wouldn't believe that. Then again, people judged on hearsay—wasn't she testament to that?

'It gets worse. I'm also, apparently, a sexual predator.'

'Why would she say things like that?'

'I think she got the idea that I had more money than I actually have.'

He looked shifty at that point. 'When she found out I was broke, things changed. She started . . . *Oh God! That's why!*' Matthew slapped his forehead as the realisation of what all that rough sex was about hit him like a bullet in the brain. *The bruises! That was why she wanted him to bite her.*

'What, Matthew?'

'She started asking me for rough sex. She wanted me to hurt her.'

Stevie shifted a little uncomfortably. It felt weird, listening to details of his intimacies with someone else. She couldn't tell if it hurt; her feelings were too mixed up to pick out any pure emotions.

'And did you?'

'No, of course not! Although . . . I gave her a love-bite, here'—he indicated the place on his own chest—'it looked pretty nasty. But it wasn't a real bite. And we both got a few bruises from banging into walls and falling off the bed and things. I'm not into that pain stuff, as you know.'

'But why tell all those lies? Why didn't she just leave you?'

'I don't know.'

Unless she had a new lover. Wasn't that what she had done to Adam? Invent cuts and bruises to get the new sucker onside? thought Stevie.

'Have you tried ringing her?'

'She's not answering. Please stay with me for a bit longer,' he said, as she looked eagerly across the road and saw a light switch off. 'Just ten minutes. Stevie, I've been so stupid. Will you let me make you a cup of coffee?'

'Just a quick one, then,' said Stevie, who didn't want one, but couldn't bear to see someone so lost. Matthew had a long sleepless lonely night in front of him; ten more minutes in his company wouldn't kill her.

'You can help me, Stevie. You are the only one who can.'

'In what way?' she asked cautiously.

'Please tell them at work that I'm not violent?' he snuffled. 'I'll never work again if they think I'm a sexual predator.'

And because Stevie had once been accused of apple scrumping at school and couldn't bear to see injustice, she said that she would.

When she went back to the cottage, Adam had gone to bed. She knocked gently on his door, but he didn't answer.

His plan had worked, after all. Jo was free. There was nothing stopping him going to her. Stevie didn't think she could bear it.

Adam was tracing the sounds of her footsteps up the stairs, her soft knock on his bedroom door, and he wanted so much to say, 'I'm here, come into my room. Come into my bed,' but he didn't answer. So it looked as if his plan had worked, after all. Matthew was free and with one click of *his* fingers, he had managed to get her over the road again. She had leapt out of Adam's arms to go to him. The sand in his hourglass had run out. Matthew was free. There was nothing stopping her going back to him. Adam didn't think he could bear it.

Chapter 12

ADAM HAD LEFT FOR THE DAY by the time she had got up the next morning. He must have crept out, Stevie reasoned, because she hadn't heard a thing. In a panic she tore into his bedroom and threw open his wardrobe, but his clothes were still there and she almost wanted to sob with relief. Then she rang Catherine and asked if Danny had been OK. Catherine told her that he had trotted off to school with the others as happy as Larry, and she was going to pick him up as well because Eddie had promised he could go over to the allotment with Boot and Chico, the dogs, and dig some veg. Stevie was to come for Danny after tea at six, and if she tried to take him away earlier she would be in big trouble. Then Stevie told her she was the best friend in the world, and Catherine said she knew and demanded chocolates every day of her life.

Stevie wrote a text to Adam, asking him if he was OK and could she ring him. Then she deleted it before sending. It was only fair to give him time to come to terms with Jo being available. Of course, Jo would hurt him again, but he loved her and she was his for the taking; Stevie knew that from all the jealous looks Jo had cast her at the barbecue.

She went over to Matthew's house at nine thirty as she had said she would. The sunlight didn't do him or the house any favours.

'Who do I need to ask for?' said Stevie, picking up the phone.

'Colin Seed. He's head of personnel. He's been giving me the evil eye.'

'What's he like?' said Stevie.

'Rich, forties, fat, 1982 trousers, jowly, drives a Bentley, lives in a big house. He'll be the next CEO in a year, if they don't ship him over to New York now that his mother's carked it,' said Matthew bitterly.

'And this evil eye—can I make a guess that it's happened quite recently?' said Stevie.

'Yes. Do you think that's relevant?'

'I think it may be,' said Stevie, and picked up the phone.

An hour and a half later, Stevie had just got out of Matthew's car and was walking across the forecourt to the entrance of Doyle International Foods. She booked herself in at Reception, under the name Ms B. Pollen, her business with the head of personnel being research for her latest book. She had told Colin's secretary on the phone that she only wanted five minutes of his time, and the secretary, who was an avid Midnight Moon fan, had squeezed her into a free eleven o'clock slot, on the proviso that she would autograph her copy of *Golden Bride*.

The secretary collected her from Reception and was twitteringly delighted to meet her in the flesh. After Stevie had autographed the book, she was shown through to Colin Seed's office. It was a very neat, modest office; the office of a man who obviously liked straight lines and things ordered and above-board. Minutes later, when Colin Seed walked in, Stevie caught an imaginary whiff of mothballs. It was a shame really, because he wasn't a bad-looking man at all. The love of a good, caring woman could transform him.

'Ms Pollen,' said Colin, with a strong handshake but a surprisingly warm smile too. He gestured to Stevie to sit down. 'How can I help you? I'm very intrigued.' He did not say that his recently deceased mum used to read Midnight Moon books, and that the last one she had read was by Beatrice Pollen.

'Mr Seed,' began Stevie. 'I confess, I'm here under false pretences. Yes, I *am* Beatrice Pollen, but I'm not here about any research. Please forgive my duplicity. I'm here about,' Stevie gulped, 'Matthew Finch.'

Stevie watched Colin Seed's welcoming smile elope with the warmth in his eyes. However, he said, 'Go on.'

'I'm Matthew's ex-partner. I understand he's been sacked for harassing an ex-friend of mine, Joanna MacLean.'

'Among other things, yes, that is correct.' Colin stiffened.

'I'm here on my own volition, after I heard the news. Matthew is not a sexual predator. Jo MacLean is an incredibly devious wom—'

'Thank you, Ms Pollen, but I really do not think this is a matter for discussion with an outside body.' Colin rose, preparing to show Stevie out, but Stevie stood her ground, or rather sat it, and continued to speak. She felt sure Colin Seed was personally involved with Jo MacLean.

'Please hear me out, Mr Seed. There is too much at stake for me to leave before I have said what I came here to say. I happen to know Jo MacLean's ex-partner very well, too, a lovely, respectable, gentle man—a Mr Adam MacLean—the Father Christmas for the local hospital. He first met her in a car park, crying that she was in a violent relationship . . .'

'Ms Pollen . . .'

'. . . and though not "rich" rich, he's comfortably well off. Then Matthew, head of concessions, high-flier here, caught her eye and she was led, I think, to believe that he was quite rich. Surprise, surprise, when did he first start talking to her? In the car park here, crying that she was in a violent relationship and needed to get away. Funnily enough, that relationship started to sour round about the time that she discovered he made church mice look like members of the Getty family. That, for your information, was very recently.'

Colin looked as if he was going to interrupt again, but stayed silent.

'Then, suddenly, Matthew is accused of being violent and predatory, and loses his job. Now, I was very hurt when he left me, but I can't stand back and watch someone's life be destroyed by malicious lies. Matthew Finch might be guilty of many things, but I'd stake my life on it that sexual violence wouldn't *ever* be one of them.'

Colin Seed was using his professionally trained brain to study body language and voice inflections, sifting for lies and truths.

'One more thing, Mr Seed,' said Stevie with an air of innocence. 'I'd deduce from Jo MacLean's modus operandi that she has probably found a new partner. A sitting target with a nice house and plenty of money. Someone who happens to meet a crying Jo MacLean in a car park with sob stories about her violent ex. She'll probably show them a supposed boot mark on her left thigh that Matthew did. In the same way that she showed it to Matthew and told him Adam did it, and in the same way she showed it to Adam and attributed it to the ex before that.'

Stevie had only guessed that Jo would have done that to Colin, but from his small cough, she knew she had guessed right.

'I understand you've had a recent loss,' said Stevie tentatively.

'Ms Poll . . . I don't see—'

'Sometimes when we're in pain, we'll snatch at anything that promises to stop it. Hope makes us see what we want to see.'

'I really must end—'

'All I'm saying is that if something appears too good to be true, it's probably because it is.'

Colin Seed gulped. That was one of his mother's sayings and, as such, it resonated loudly within him.

'I won't take up any more of your time, Mr Seed. Thank you for meeting me,' and with a gentle, caring smile, Stevie added, 'Good luck.'

There was a nerve ticking in Colin's neck, Stevie noticed. He nodded goodbye as if his throat was constricted and held his hand out to her.

Stevie shook that hand, warmly with both of hers, and then she left.

As she walked out of the building via the revolving door, Jo MacLean came in. They turned to stare at each other. For once, Jo's eyes had none of that victorious haughtiness in them. Stevie's presence in her workplace unsettled her. She hadn't bargained on Matthew finding a champion after her claims, because no one wanted to stick up for a sex beast. Least of all a disgruntled ex!

When Stevie got to Humbleby Cottage, Adam was gone, and so were his clothes. There was a note on the table that said *Dear Stevie, We both need some time to think. I will be in touch. Love to Danny, goodbye—Adam.*

Her eyes bloomed with tears.

Adam didn't need any time. He knew what he wanted but he had to get out of the way and not complicate things for Stevie. She had waited so patiently for Matthew to come back to her and now she had him. So how could he upset all that for her by declaring his feelings now?

He pushed open the door to his house. It was without heart, warmth, laughter or little boy's mess. It was big, bare and echoey, and the memories stored within its walls were cold and hollow. He would ring the estate agent that afternoon and put it on the market. Then he would award himself some time off work so he didn't bump into Stevie.

Stevie. Adam MacLean dropped on the cold leather sofa and thought of the softness of her face as he held it, remembered how she had gulped as he stared into her eyes and how his heart had trembled when her lips had touched his. He had never loved anyone in this way before, with a depth that made parodies of all the other times he thought he had been in love. Stevie deserved to be happy—with him or without him—and it looked as if it was going to be without him.

He didn't stop the tears when they came.

Jo sat in her bedroom in the Queens Hotel staring into her compact mirror as she applied a slick smear of lipstick. Was that a line appearing under her eye? she wondered. It was becoming more and more urgent to hook a rich fish who would be able to finance her fight against the ravages of time. Beauty was a talent on a timer.

Jo launched the compact across the room, smashing it against the wall. 'Damn you, Stevie Fucking Honeywell,' she snarled. Had it not been for that short, fat cow she would be in Colin's lovely oak-panelled house now, being fussed over, and not in the cheapest room in a glory-faded hotel paid for by pawned jewellery. Or, better still, she would be with Adam. He wasn't as rich as Colin, by far, and no one was more surprised than her to realise that it didn't seem to matter. Jo MacLean's mantra had always been, 'Happiness doesn't bring you money.'

There was a two-day Porsche business convention being held in the hotel, and a wealth of suits spilled into the large reception area, the wine garden, the bars and restaurant. Jo slipped on a plain black dress that emphasised her long, slim body, the cut of it adding the illusion of curves. She had never failed to 'pull' in that dress.

But before she explored the potential downstairs, there was one final thing she needed to do. She couldn't just leave it there with Adam and Stevie. If she couldn't have what she wanted, then why the fuck should they? Jo MacLean picked up her pen.

On the last day at work before his self-imposed break, Adam's hand stilled on the envelope in the middle of the pile of post in his office at Well Life. There was no stamp on it, so it had obviously been hand-delivered for maximum effect. He knew the beautiful, precise writing with the artistic loops well. He should have thrown it out, but curiosity got the better of him. It was Jo at her manipulative best.

Dearest Adam, whatever you think about receiving this from me, grant me one final kindness and read it to the end, I beg you. I'm so sorry I hurt you . . . I will always care for you . . .

He didn't want to read it, but the masochistic part of him couldn't rip his eyes away from the hypnotic soft swirls of ink. She put it oh so beautifully, how he could never be right for Stevie because he would never conform to her dull type . . . *and you deserve to find someone who will love you for the strong, selfless, unique, big personality that you are.* She said that playing happy families with Stevie and Danny was an illusion, because Stevie's own horrid experiences with step-parents would never allow him to be accepted unless he were perfect. She was saying this to be kind, of course. *Darling Adam, you were the best thing that ever happened to me and I shall always regret my mistake at falling for the lies of another. I still love you and if you ever change your mind, I will drop everything and come to you. Be happy, you wonderful man. Jo x.*

The words continued to sting him long after he had ripped it up and thrown it into the bin. Adam MacLean might have known his *basic psychology* well, but Jo MacLean was a past master.

Stevie found the letter on the mat. It had been hand-delivered and bore her name in extravagant script on the front. There was a friendly little smiling face drawn in the final 'e' to lend it affection. Stevie didn't want to open it, but its very presence there gave her no choice.

Dearest Stevie, I know you will never forgive me but please allow me this one act of genuine friendship and read this letter to the end . . . The words were exquisitely put, needles embedded in cotton wool. She knew this, but still she read on. *Adam is using you . . . he never stopped loving me . . . He invited me to the gym to talk about a reconciliation . . . He told me evil things you had said about me . . . I so regret believing him and scratching your car in temper . . .*

Stevie gasped. She remembered the day well. Why else would Jo have been at the gym, if not to talk to Adam?

Be careful of little Danny's heart . . . as you know only too well, dear friend, step-families are doomed to fail. Jo told her how Adam's 'type' would always be tall, beautiful, thin, dark-haired women, and how Stevie needed to find someone to love her for the *wonderful curvy sunshiny woman* that she was. *You deserve so much more than any of us. You were the best friend I ever had and I shall always think of you with a smile. Be happy, darling Stevie. Kindest regards and love—Jo x.*

Stevie ripped the letter up, but the words left a poison deep in her heart and there was no one on hand to suck it out for her.

A week had passed when the loud knock landed on Stevie's door and her heart started racing as she rushed to open it. It dropped like a stone though to find Matthew standing there; nevertheless, she formed a welcoming smile, which was roughly a quarter the size of his own.

'I've got some great news!' he said, angling for an invite.

And Stevie being Stevie, she said, 'Come in.'

'Is er . . .?'

'No,' said Stevie. 'Adam doesn't live here any more.'

Matthew's smile suddenly got a bit wider.

'Coffee?' said Stevie, because it would have been rude not to.

'Yes, please,' he said, because it would give him an excuse to stay a little longer. 'Lovely cottage,' he commented, looking around. Not only lovely but also shining and polished and clean, and there was that indefinable something in it that turned a house into a home. His house didn't have it any more. It hadn't had it since Stevie left.

'Yes, it is lovely,' she said quietly. She would be sorry to say goodbye to it too. So many times she had picked up the phone to ring Adam on the pretext of asking him when she needed to get out of the cottage, only to put it down again in case Jo picked it up. He would be a fool to have gone back to her, but Jo MacLean was like a flame to men and she attracted the sorts of hearts that could not stop themselves burning their fragile moth-wings many times against her. Adam must have taken her back; why else would he have left and not been in touch?

'Sorry I've not been across before, but it's been a mad week,' said Matthew.

'Oh,' said Stevie, barely realising how many days had passed. She had locked herself away in her office when Danny wasn't around, occupying all thought-space with Damme and Evie, because she did not want to think of her own empty life.

'I've been offered my old job back,' said Matthew. 'But . . .' He left a dramatic pause. 'I'm not taking it.'

'Why ever not?'

'Because I've decided to have a fresh start. I'm selling the house and clearing some of my debts with the equity, and then I'm moving to London. I've got interviews lined up and I've found a flat, sharing with some other people. It's cheap and cheerful but it will do until I get back on my feet. I've made too many mistakes here and I want to get away. I hear it was old Seedy who came through for me in the end, can you believe?'

'Yes, I can believe it,' said Stevie. He had looked a decent man. One who must be hurting terribly at the moment too.

'He's going to live in New York, apparently.'

'Good. A fresh start for him too. And . . . Jo?' asked Stevie.

'No one knows. She didn't turn up for work the day after you went into the office and hasn't been back since.'

Adam hadn't been seen either. He hadn't been working at the gym. They were obviously together. Maybe they had gone off on holiday. Not that it mattered really, for the words of Jo's letter had stung her hard. Even with no Jo MacLean on the scene, Adam's heart wasn't going to be fulfilled by a short, lumpy woman and someone else's kid.

'Apparently Colin looked rough for a couple of days after your meeting,' said Matthew. 'Someone said he was caught crying in his off—' A five-ton penny dropped. 'Hey, you don't think Jo and Colin . . . do you?'

'I'm almost sure of it, Matthew.' Stevie had been instrumental in that avenue of escape being closed to Jo, which would almost definitely have driven her back to Adam as a safe haven. 'So how come you know what happened at work?'

'People started ringing me again—once the truth filtered out that I wasn't a psycho-woman batterer. I got good-luck cards in the post and I'm meeting my department for a night out before I move.'

'I'm glad for you, Matthew, I really am. I hope you enjoy London.'

'Unless you . . . er . . .' Matthew stumbled. Stevie looked up into his eyes. They were soft, brown, warm and open, and he was looking nervously at her like the first time he had dared to ask her out.

'Unless of course you didn't want me to g-go and . . .' he stuttered on.

Stevie gulped. This was the moment she had been waiting for. Adam's plan had come through for her, too, it seemed. So why wasn't she hearing brass bands playing in her heart? There was nothing but the faint piercing sound of retreating bagpipes.

'No, I don't suppose . . . you would c-consider . . . you, me—again?'

'No, Matthew.' She answered him in a kind voice.

'I was a thick twat,' he said with frustration. 'My grass was lovely and green and I went looking for better.'

Matthew looked at her spun-gold hair, her lovely blue eyes, warmth and nice-person radiating from her, and could not believe he had let her go. Her strength in saying 'No' to him made him want her even more, but her eyes weren't registering that he was special any more. They looked at Adam MacLean quite differently, he had noticed.

'It's him, isn't it—Adam? You really fell for him, then?'

'Yes, Matthew, hook, line and sinker.'

'I thought you were just joking at first, you know. You'll laugh but I thought it was all a sort of plan to get us jealous.' He laughed at how stupid that seemed now. As if! 'So, what happened?'

'I don't know.' She shrugged. 'I presume Adam and Jo are planning a new start. I haven't seen or heard from him since . . . well . . .'

'Since I came round that night, by any chance?' Matthew said, his shoulders scrunching up with shame and embarrassment. Stevie didn't answer; she couldn't. There was a big lump in her throat.

'I'm sorry. I seem to have developed a habit of wrecking your life.'

For once she didn't say her customary kind 'Don't be silly' to let him off the hook. Matthew knew, by that, just how deeply he had hurt her.

'When the house is sold and I move to London, I'll give you some money from the proceeds to cover Danny's holiday and of course the wedding costs. I'm sorry, Stevie. I've been a total bastard. I don't want to be this Matthew. I want to get right away from him.'

'When do you leave?' she asked.

'Next week. Thanks, Stevie, you're a diamond and I owe you big time,' he continued, and threw his arms round her and hugged her. She wasn't as pliant as he remembered. She didn't melt against him and envelop him in her affection. But then, she wasn't his any more.

'Goodbye, Matthew, and good luck,' she said, and kissed his cheek, and though she smiled, the light seemed to have gone from her eyes. He wished, at least, he could put that back there for her.

That afternoon, Adam MacLean was watching something mindless on the television about doing up gardens, hosted by a woman with jolly features and wayward breasts, as he imagined Stevie's would be in that garb. He'd always gone for women with scraps of meat on their bones, like his mother, but Stevie had a bottom he wanted to bite lumps out of. She was so soft and curvy and warm, but Jo's words in the letter had haunted him. Stevie would want more for herself and her son than a 'unique' (i.e. ugly) man who made noise wherever he went.

He knew he would have to speak to her soon about the arrangements for the cottage, but he was scared he would turn the corner and see her back in Matthew's house, and find Humbleby Cottage lying as empty as his heart felt. He would have to face it, but not now. Just a few more days until he found the strength to look her in the eye, wish her all the luck and happiness in the world, let her go for ever.

He looked around at the cold, characterless room and decided that he really needed to clean up. The house hadn't been vacuumed in days, nor had the dishwasher been switched on. Then again, there had been no plates to wash because he hadn't been eating. He had managed to drag himself to the shower, but not over to the shaving mirror. He looked half-wild with his auburn stubble and flat, tired eyes.

He ignored the first 'bing bong' of the doorbell, as he wasn't in the mood for visitors. After the fifth bing bong, he thought he had better get rid of the irritation by telling them that, no, he didn't want to sponsor them, vote for them, buy their windows, look at their brochure or convert his energy supplies. He had no energy to convert.

When he opened the door, it was to a rather pale-looking Matthew.

'Hi,' his unexpected visitor said with a gulp. 'I realise you might want to murder me, but before you do, can I please tell you something?'

Stevie dropped Danny off at school then picked up some empty boxes from the Happy Shopper en route home. As she opened the cottage door, silence greeted her and the quiet was uncomfortably deafening in a way that Adam's noise could never be. She missed his big, booming voice more each day. She missed his cavernous sports bag by the door. She missed his boxers on the washing line. She missed the heavy tread of his large feet on the stairs, the way he crashed through doors . . . she missed everything about the man. And Danny's insistent questioning didn't help. *Where's Adam? When is he coming back? Will he be back tonight?* He hadn't asked half as many questions over Matthew and Mick combined. It seemed her little boy was hurting as much as she was.

She started to put books into one of the boxes until her eyes clouded over so much that she couldn't see what she was doing. She'd gone and fallen for Humbleby too, and having to leave it would half kill her. It sounded stupid, but the cottage felt 'sad' that she would be going soon, as if it had been lonely in its enforced long emptiness and had rather enjoyed having a funny little boy, an incurable romantic and a rather loud Gaelic giant enjoying its warmth and protection.

She was going mad, obviously, thinking about old houses having feelings. She needed to get out. Somewhere in the presence of other human beings doing something that would bat these ridiculous notions out of her head. She grabbed her car keys and headed out to Well Life.

Stevie looked at the calorie counter. Apparently, she had burnt up 350 of them in the last hour and she still wasn't tired, but then her body didn't feel connected to her head. Her legs were pounding but her brain wasn't giving out any messages for them to stop. It was too busy blotting everything out. It wasn't connected to her ears either so it didn't hear the track 'Loneliness' playing once again and it wasn't connected to her eyes so she didn't see the screens showing *Morning Coffee* on MTV. Nor did she see Adam MacLean walking up the side of the StairMasters either.

Not until she saw a big, hairy arm put a small jeweller's box on the water-bottle shelf and heard that big thunderous voice of his saying, 'I hear you've fallen fer me hook, line and sinker, woman,' was she even remotely aware of his presence. And in shock, she lost her footing, cracked her head on the control panel and did the sort of backwards flip that would have knocked the Romanian gymnasts off the Gold Medal spot in the Olympics.

'So once again I make a complete prat of myself in front of everyone because of you,' she said in his office, as he applied a bag of ice to the fast-growing egg-shaped lump. 'Ow, ow, ow!'

'Wheesht, woman.'

'And if vibrating me off the machine with your voice wasn't enough fun for you, you give me an empty box as well!'

''Course it's empty. I just wanted tae see whit yer reaction would be.'

'You are a sadist. I was right all along.'

'No' at all. Choosin' a ring is an important matter. I'd only have got something wi' too many diamonds in it.'

'Is there such a thing?'

He smiled a little and had a good look at the lump. 'I think this might hatch at any minute.'

'Anyway, what did you mean by you've heard that I've fallen for you "hook, line and sinker?" Which mentally deranged nutter could possibly have told you that?'

'Stop movin' yer head, woman! Matthew came tae see me earlier. Very brave in the circumstances. Said I was an idiot if I'd let you go.'

'Matthew?'

'Aye. He said you were the most wonderful woman he'd ever known.'

'Yes, well, I couldn't have been that wonderful if he dropped me.'

'He also said that he'd asked you tae go back tae him but you were in love wi' me. And you were under the impression I was back wi' Jo.'

'Did he now?' She cleared her throat in preparation for the next question. 'And are you?' It came out all shaky.

'Oh, aye, tha's why I'm givin' ring boxes tae you.'

'Empty ring boxes, though.'

'I explained the reason for tha'. You have tae wear the thing for ever, so it's no' fair fer me tae force ma tastes on you, is it, noo?'

'I suppose.' Stevie's heart was thumping so loudly she thought it might even deafen Adam. 'But you still haven't answered the question.'

'Stevie.' Adam looked her squarely in the eyes so she could read the truth in them. 'I don't know if I ever was in love wi' Jo. I was besotted, but I don't even know if there is a real Jo MacLean. I think she just borrows personalities off a peg. I certainly didnae know her—I realised tha' at Will's barbecue.' He didn't say he could trace that moment back to when she shoved Danny away and he saw the hurt in the boy's eyes. He knew then she wasn't the woman he had waited for all his life.

'So how come you left me a note saying we both needed space?'

'Because even though I wanted you more than anythin', I needed tae give you time tae find oot what you felt fer Matthew once he was free. I mean, I'm no' exactly yer archetypal romantic hero. You like handsome men who whisper and I'm a big, ugly, noisy bugger.'

'I don't want Matthew. I'm from Venus. I'm not like you Mars lot, who sod off into caves and play with elastic bands or whatever it is.'

'No, you're no' like anyone I've ever met, Stevie Pollen Bumblebee Nectar or whatever your name is.'

She blurted out a big pocket of laughter that pulled out a few bonus tears with it.

'Stop cryin', woman,' he said gruffly. 'OK, I admit it. I saw how quickly you jumped when Matty Boy called and I judged you on tha'. I thought you'd gone back tae him. After all, it's whit we planned fer.'

'He was suffering, Adam. Jo stuffed him too. I couldn't have walked away and see him branded a violent sex pest.'

'Aye, well, I know tha' noo.' He took the ice pack away and bowed his head. 'But, stupid tha' I am, I thought I'd lost you just when I was on the brink of gettin' you. And Danny, of course. I've missed the lad.'

'You stupid, stupid man,' said Stevie, for Danny and herself.

'Hang on a wee minute—you loved Matt, you didnae even like me!'

'Oh, Adam MacLean, you've got a nerve, considering how marvellous you thought I was in the beginning!'

Adam laughed, remembering the flour and the cocoa and that snotty 'I hate you' look on her face, and her friend with the mad pink hair. How very deceiving those first impressions had been. On both sides, too, for at the same time, Stevie was thinking of the wild, red man pushing a holiday reservation up her nose in Matthew's front room.

'And all the time I was thinking that now Jo was available, you'd be straight off back to her.'

'Naw.' He smiled. 'How could she compete wi' you?'

'Yeah, right,' said Stevie.

Adam looked at her sweet, disbelieving face and realised she would never know how lovely she was, which was a shame. He wanted to tell her how very deeply he had fallen for her, how she seemed to have flooded every chamber of his heart as only the right person could. But there was time, lots of it to come. For now, a kiss would suffice. He put down the ice pack, took her face in his great hands and carried on where he'd left off that night of the fillet steaks and her homemade cake and the raspberry-truffle coffees and the interrupting knock on the door. Her lips were sweeter than honey.

Epilogue

THEY MARRIED at the beginning of the next summer—a day full of balmy May sunshine. There were Scottish pipers and the bonny bride carried an armful of bluebells and heather instead of a formal rose bouquet. Adam took his vows in the tartan-trimmed church with a heart that was truly satisfied and content. There was no feeling that a part of him was pleading to an inaccessible part of his lady; he knew she was all his. For Stevie it was better than any ending she could have written. Like her alter ego Evie Sweetwell, she had found her Damme MacQueen. And he was even better in the flesh than he was on the page.

Matthew sent the happy couple a silver-plated bluebirds of happiness and a cheque for £3,000, made out to Mrs Stevie MacLean. It was the first time she had seen her new name in print and it made her insides as runny as the waters of the Clyde.

They had a ceilidh at the reception and a Scottish band, and wore kilts and danced jigs and reels such as 'Blue Bonnets' and 'The Birds and the Bees' well into the night. Things went awry as the champagne flowed, and some of the dancers ended up with different partners from the ones they started out with. But that seems to have turned out all right.

The newlyweds compromised on some of the Scottish traditions—the groom didn't drink whisky and he wore Calvin Klein boxers under his kilt. He did, however, eat a Sassenach alive for breakfast the next morning. And by all accounts, she enjoyed it too. They honeymooned for five days in a castle by a beautiful loch, then picked up Danny from Catherine's and whisked him to EuroDisney for a week.

Highland Fling became the best-selling Midnight Moon ever. The critics panned it as romantic claptrap, of course, but the readers loved it so much that a film was made with a gorgeously rough American actor who could actually manage quite a good Scots accent. Apparently, the top girls of Hollywood clawed each other to death for the part of Evie. The enormous cheque for the film rights arrived with Stevie exactly eighteen months after Adam MacLean first kissed her.

Adam discovered the turnon of women with soft curves, freckly noses and absolutely no ability whatsoever to control flour. Stevie was to wonder how she had ever lived without large crushing Highland thighs, red stubble and thunderous, unintelligible endearments.

Adam bought Humbleby Cottage for himself and his bride, his wee adopted laddie and their auburn-haired newborn daughter, Rìona, and they all still live happily there today with a huge sloppy dog, a mad ginger kitten and an enormous black rabbit called McBatman.

Life, for the MacLean clan, is *braw*.

All about Milly Johnson

Was there one event that triggered your first novel, *The Yorkshire Pudding Club*?

An ex-boss once called Barnsley 'a joke town'—the defining moment when I decided that when I did write a book, I would base it in Barnsley. I got pregnant at the same time as three of my friends and, one day, when we were all in my house showing off our newborns, I had a freeze-frame moment and knew that I was going to write about three long-term friends who go through their first pregnancies together.

It was a great success—did you find it easier or more difficult to write *The Birds & the Bees* after that?

I'd heard rumours of 'second book curse', but I was one of the lucky ones because I started book two straight after book one and I just loved writing it. I hope it shows.

Are there bits of yourself in the character of Stevie in *The Birds & the Bees*?

There's lots of myself in Stevie. We're both single mums worrying that we're doing the best for our families, both feisty and independent, both with awful taste in men, both worried about the size of our bottoms, both romantics and hard workers, both with great mates, both strong birds who've gone through some tough times without getting too hard-bitten and cynical. However, Stevie is much prettier than I am!

And do you have a soft spot for well-built Scotsmen with good legs?

Oh, yes—there's nothing more masculine than a pair of fine male legs emerging from the bottom of a swishy kilt.

Do you think lots of men fantasise about living with model-like women such as Jo, but would actually be much happier with loving homemakers like Stevie?

If appearances were everything, guys with gorgeous-looking wives wouldn't run after other women, would they? Of course, when you meet someone you like, your stomach flips, however homely or beautiful they are. It's all down to wonderful and inexplicable chemistry—beauty really is in the eye of the beholder!

Your sons, Terence and George, are still quite young, so do you tend to write in the evenings when they are tucked up in bed?

I now work when they are at school, splitting the day between writing jokes for the greetings card industry and my novels. When I'm 'on a roll' though, I'll get to work as soon as the boys have settled for the night, surrounded by lots of coffee and snoring cats.

Your books are full of fun. Does anything make you lose your sense of humour?

I can't abide rudeness and bad manners—especially the people who don't say 'thank you' when you open doors for them. And I hate meanness of spirit . . . grrrr!

A few of my favourite things . . .

A 'new night sheet' in bed; a good film; red wine; my breadmaking machine; thunderstorms when I'm cosy inside; red lipsticks, Italy, fairs.

Favourite thing about being a writer?
That every day brings something unexpected—in the nicest possible way.

Favourite book to read on a rainy day?
Anything by Agatha Christie

Favourite contemporary author?
Mo Hader and Marian Keyes—both very different but I can't choose.

Favourite heart-warming film?
The Corpse Bride and *Seabiscuit*—again, I can't choose.

Favourite items in your handbag?
Pen, lipstick, perfume, bag of Thorntons Alcohol Truffles.

Favourite items in your wardrobe?
My little black dress.

Favourite dish to cook for friends?
My Gruyère chicken and mushroom special.

Favourite guilty pleasure?
Lemon cheesecake.

Favourite word?
'Gorgeous'. There's something about this word that feels like the best compliment in the world, whether given or received.

Favourite moment in the last twelve months?
Being named joint winner of the Chicklit Club's Most Promising Author of 2007 title. It was the perfect endorsement that I was in the right job!

PICTURE CREDITS: COVER: © Reggie Casagrande/Riser. Sophie Kinsella's photograph and page 146 © Blake Little. Kristin Hannah's photograph and page 314 © charlesbush.com. Milly Johnson's photograph and page 478 © Chris Sedgewick. REMEMBER ME?: pages 6 & 7: Samantha Hedges@Velvet Tamarind. FIREFLY LANE: pages 148 & 149: Darren Walsh@Velvet Tamarind; images: Studio MPM. THE BIRDS & THE BEES: pages 316 & 317: Owen Rimington@advocate-art.com.

Printed and bound by GGP Media GmbH, Pössneck, Germany

601-045 UP0000-1